THE LAST CROWN

ALSO BY ELŻBIETA CHEREZIŃSKA

The Widow Queen

THE
LAST
CROWN

ELŻBIETA
CHEREZIŃSKA

Translated by Maya Zakrzewska-Pim

A TOM DOHERTY ASSOCIATES BOOK
New York

THE LAST CROWN

Copyright © 2016 by Elżbieta Cherezińska

English translation © 2022 by Tor

Translation by Maya Zakrzewska-Pim

All rights reserved.

Originally published as *Królowa* in 2016 by Zysk i S-ka Wydawnictwo s.j. in Poznań.

A Forge Book
Published by Tom Doherty Associates
120 Broadway
New York, NY 10271

www.tor-forge.com

Forge® is a registered trademark of Macmillan Publishing Group, LLC.

Library of Congress Cataloging-in-Publication Data

Names: Cherezińska, Elżbieta, author. | Zakrzewska-Pim, Maya, translator.
Title: The last crown / Elżbieta Cherezińska ; translated by Maya Zakrzewska-Pim.
Other titles: Królowa. English
Description: First edition. | New York : Forge/Tom Doherty
Associates, 2022. | Series: The bold ; 2 |
Identifiers: LCCN 2022011444 (print) | LCCN 2022011445 (ebook) |
ISBN 9781250775740 (hardcover) | ISBN 9781250775757 (ebook)
Subjects: LCSH: Princesses—Poland—Fiction. | LCGFT: Historical fiction. | Novels.
Classification: LCC PG7203.H474 K7613 2022 (print) |
LCC PG7203.H474 (ebook) | DDC 891.8/538—dc23/eng/20220308
LC record available at https://lccn.loc.gov/2022011444
LC ebook record available at https://lccn.loc.gov/2022011445

Our books may be purchased in bulk for promotional, educational, or business use.
Please contact your local bookseller or the Macmillan Corporate and
Premium Sales Department at 1-800-221-7945, extension 5442,
or by email at MacmillanSpecialMarkets@macmillan.com.

First Edition: 2022

Printed in the United States of America

0 9 8 7 6 5 4 3 2 1

To all the anonymous, forgotten princesses
The nuns, wives, mothers, and rulers about whom history is silent
The girls marked in biographies of dynasties with a sad "N.N."

The Aesti

Veliky Novgorod

The Livonians

NOVGORODIAN RUŚ

The Novgorod Slavs

The Lithuanians

Połock

The Yotvingians

The Krivichs

ns

ans

Drohiczyn

The Radimichs

OVIA

Brześć

ersk

OLAND

Lublin

KIEVAN RUŚ

Kiev

Wołyń

Sandomierz

THE CHERVEN CITIES (UNDER POLISH RULE UNTIL 981)

ków

Przemyśl

Sącz

The Volhynians

Halicz

NDS

UNGARY

POLAND
in the 10th century

THE BRITISH ISLES
in the 10th century

NORTH
SEA

ALBA

IRELAND

ISLE OF
MAN

Slane

NORTHUMBRIA

Bamburgh

York

GWYNEDD

Nottingham

POWYS

MERCIA

EAST
ANGLIA

DYFED

GWENT

ENGLAND

ESSEX

Ipswich

Oxford

Maldon

London

WESSEX

Andover

Winchester

Canterbury

KENT

Sandw

Folkest

HAMPSHIRE SUSSEX

Southampton

CORNWALL

Exeter

THE SOLENT

ISLE OF
WIGHT

ISLES OF
SCILLY

SCANDINAVIA
n the 10th century

FINNMARK

LAPLAND

LOFOTEN

HÅLOGALAND

NORWAY

SWEDEN

JAMTLAND

Lade

Agdaues

Nidaros
Trondheim

TRØNDELAG

SUNNMØRE

Hjorungavagr

SOGNEFJORD

SOGN   OPPLAND

HORDALAND   DALARNA

THE
ÅLAND
ISLANDS

The Finns

Fyrisvellir
Birka   Uppsala
Sigtuna

GULF OF FINLAND

ROGALAND   VIKEN

LAKE
MÁLAR

HAFRSFJORD

AGDER

The Aesti

Sola

SKAGERRAK

RANRIKE

HALLAND

GOTLAND

NORTH
SEA

Hobro

SWEDEN

Viborg

DENMARK

BLEKINGE

DENMARK
SKANIA

Jelling   Lejre
Roskilde

Lund

The Lithuanians

Ribe

DENMARK

BORNHOLM

Trelleborg
Arkona

Hedeby

RÜGEN

Gdańsk
Kołobrzeg   Truso

The Prussians

Lübeka
Hamburg

THE
CONFEDERACY
OF THE VELETI

Jomsborg
Wolin   POLAND

PART I

THE BATTLE OF THE THREE KINGS

997–1000

1

THE BALTIC SEA

The night from which the moon was stolen is cold and gloomy. It takes its vengeance with irregular gusts of wind and waves which treacherously flood the deck. Unpunished and confident in its invisibility, the night tangles the ropes, tugs at the sails, and whispers misleading directions. Its scrawny arms sink into the ocean's depths, searching for drowned men and drowsy fish. Running its fingers through the waters, it picks out that which cannot be revived and that which cannot rot in salty waters. A moonless night is not particular, but it's in a rush, chased by the dawn on its heels. It wants to surprise its pursuer with a deck decorated by its dead catches. It throws its treasure overboard with a hollow splash and disappears to escape the notice of dawn's scout, daybreak.

Astrid watched Tyra doze. The princess was snoring gently with her mouth open. *It's because of the poppyseed brew I gave her,* Astrid thought. *Or she has a cold. Even princesses get blocked noses, after all.*

Morcar Frog had provided every comfort, or at least that which was possible aboard a merchant ship. There was a small tent stretched out between the gunwales which offered protection from the wind, sun, and rain, as well as from the crew's curious stares. They were also given warm blankets and almost-warm meals. And wine, good red wine from the merchant's supplies. Astrid sipped it as she waited for Tyra to wake. She wasn't thinking about her, she was thinking about herself. About how life always seemed to place her near Olav but never quite in the right position. She'd thought that there could be nothing worse than bringing his son into the world, but fate had written another verse of this song and now she had aided Tyra's abduction so that this foreign girl could become Olav's wife.

If only it had been Świętosława. Her salty sister, so sharp and fierce. Astrid could have done it for Świętosława and been happy for her, but no, she was acting against her sister as much as against her own heart. *"My lady is in labor!"* She'd heard the servants' cries when she'd slipped unnoticed through the kitchens of Roskilde's manor. If she had gone to the queen's chambers instead of to Tyra's solitary rooms . . . If she had broken her word . . . No, she would never have done that. She had always been too mature for that. Mieszko would call her his "wise daughter Astrid." Yes, she was wise. And what good had that ever done her?

Tyra opened her eyes.

"Where am I?" she whispered.

"On a ship."

Tyra rose from her makeshift bed and leaned on one arm. Sleep had undone her three braids, and strands of hair, damp with sweat, spiraled in locks by her face. She rubbed her forehead and swollen eyelids.

"On a ship . . ." she repeated. "So, it worked, did it?"

"Yes. Do you want some wine?"

"Is it Friday today?"

"Yes."

"No, I can't today. I drink only water on Fridays."

"As you wish," Astrid replied as she took another gulp. "I find wine helps with the seasickness."

Tyra blinked. Astrid hated women who fluttered their eyelashes. She was always surprised that men fell for such a cheap trick.

"So, you're my savior," Tyra said. "I'm sorry, but in all the excitement I've forgotten your name."

"Astrid."

"Astrid . . ." Tyra seemed to regain her senses and reached for the pouch at her belt, rummaging in it until she pulled out a denar. "Duke Burizleif's sister?" She looked at Astrid's brother's name etched into the coin.

"Yes."

"I hadn't expected that Master Gretter's mission would bear fruit so soon. Your brother is an uncommonly proactive ruler, and I will be forever grateful to him for saving me from Sven's clutches. I'm very curious to meet my future husband."

What is this? Astrid wondered. *Does she always talk this way?*

"Tell me about my sister," she requested, swallowing more wine.

"Sister?" Tyra looked surprised. "Oh, forgive me, my lady! Where's my head! The queen is your and your brother's sister . . ."

What a dolt! Astrid thought, immediately blaming the insult on the wine she had consumed. Since her cup was empty, though, she poured herself some more.

"Yes, I met your sister in church and only then did I know her true nature. Because she is so regal in front of the people. Regal and beautiful. That monster Sven forced me to attend his feasts, where I would see the queen from afar. But she . . . forgive me, Astrid, but at the feasts your sister was just a queen to me, distant and foreign. She has two lynxes on a leash that walk with her, and before her walks a great, bald monster with a scarred face. There is also the boy who has a wolf's eyes and the horrible Jorun, Sven's comrade, and his axemen who chant your sister's name: "Sigrid Storråda!" My brother wants her to be known as Gunhild, but it hasn't stuck at court . . . Can I have some water?" Tyra paused and moistened her dry lips.

"Here." Astrid handed her a cup.

The princess swallowed a few mouthfuls, but when she noticed Astrid watching her, she slowed down.

"Are you hungry, my lady?" Astrid asked.

"Perhaps, but I told you that I fast on Fridays. What should I call you? If you're Duke Burizleif and Queen Sigrid's sister, shouldn't I be addressing you as a princess?"

"Call me Lady of Wolin, that will suffice. You were telling me of my sister."

"Oh, yes. What was I saying?"

"You told me her new name, that her husband wanted to call her Gunhild."

"An awful idea. The old Queen Gunhild, though it is embarrassing to say since she was my aunt, practiced . . . do you know?" Tyra fearfully made the sign of the cross and looked at Astrid meaningfully as she whispered: "Seidr. Do you understand?"

"She was a witch," Astrid said.

"Yes. And she died like a witch. They threw her into the swamp." Tyra shuddered at the thought. "No wonder the name didn't take. The people know that your sister is a Christian queen, but Sven's men, the ones who traveled with him to Sigtuna, decided they had brought back Sigrid Storråda, and that's what they prefer to call her. Astrid!" Tyra suddenly grabbed her hand. "Is the queen privy to our plans? Sven will suspect her, he knew that we had a good relationship, that we met for mass . . ."

"No, my lady. My sister knows nothing," Astrid replied, feeling nauseous.

She stood up and shakily walked out of the tent. She had to lean over the gunwale to vomit. The wine had done nothing for her seasickness or her guilt. Świętosława's bright face stubbornly kept appearing in her mind's eye. By the time she returned to Tyra, the girl had untangled her hair and was brushing it out.

"I should prepare to meet my husband," she said, a blush blooming on her cheeks.

As if on cue! Astrid thought with distaste.

"It will be another week or two before you reach him, but you can start preparing now if you wish," she told the princess.

"So long?" Tyra was surprised. "The sailors say the route to Nidaros is much shorter."

"You won't be sailing the whole way. Morcar will drop us off soon and we will proceed on horseback. We must lose our pursuers."

Tyra looked worried, as if she only now realized that the entire journey was dangerous, not just the escape.

"Tell me, Astrid, how did you get me out of the manor? How did I reach the ship? Forgive me, but I can't recall . . . I only remember the moment in which you entered my room and showed me the coin to prove that Duke Burizleif had sent you, and you said: 'You'll be safe when you wake up,' and then you gave me something to drink. I don't remember anything else . . ."

"I gave you a brew from poppyseeds," Astrid told her.

Because I suspected that courage was not your strong suit, she thought, but she kept it to herself.

"When you fell asleep, we hid you in a great chest in which Morcar's men had carried the weapons Sven had purchased earlier. We then carried you on board, right under your brother's nose."

"What?"

"Sven sat comfortably in a great chair as he examined Morcar's shiny merchandise and we walked right past him."

"That's incredible!" Tyra clapped her hands in joy.

Will Olav be happy with her? Astrid asked herself, feeling her stomach grow heavy again. *I'm vile; it is envy that speaks through me,* she thought, bringing herself down even further.

"What about the pursuers?" Tyra asked. "Do you think he sent any?"

"I'm certain he did, and I hope that his men were fooled by the group of riders who went west, toward Trelleborg. It was their job to draw Sven's attention away from the port."

"Is Morcar in danger?" Tyra asked in a whisper.

"Don't be naïve," Astrid retorted. "Everyone who played a part in this scheme faces Sven's wrath."

"Forgive me, Lady of Wolin. It's the poppyseed which has robbed me of my clarity of thought."

They spoke no more. Astrid lay down with her back to Tyra, pretending to be asleep. She wished she really was asleep so she could get away from her own intrusive thoughts. She had tricked Świętosława and undertaken the mission to bring Tyra out of Roskilde for the sole purpose of seeing Olav again. That was the truth, the embarrassing secret which weighed down her conscience. She had agreed to help in this endeavor only so she might look into his pale, translucent eyes once more, so she could smell the salt on his hair and hear his voice. She wanted to see him after all the years that had passed since Geira's death, after everything that had happened. *Damn it! What a fool I am!* she thought with disdain and pulled the blanket over her head. Before sleep took her, she had made up her mind.

The next morning, Morcar's ship sailed into a small bay by the estuary of Göta älv. Geivar, the chief of the house of scouts from Jom, was waiting for them.

"My Lady of Wolin," he greeted Astrid when she stepped onto dry land. "Is everything all right?"

"Yes, Geivar. Princess Tyra is with us. I think that she could use a day of rest before we move on."

"Whatever you think best, Astrid," Geivar replied.

"Is that your husband, the famous Jarl Sigvald, the Jomsviking leader?" Tyra asked.

"No. This is the chief of silence." Astrid chuckled. "You have the honor of meeting Geivar, who is the eye and ear of Jomsborg. He will be responsible for your journey from here. And if it makes any difference, he used to be a companion to Olav Tryggvason."

"I'm happy to meet you, Geivar." Tyra bowed her head in greeting and, unexpectedly, smiled. "It's extraordinary! Your husband abducted Sven during the war with Eric, while you, Astrid, have abducted me from Roskilde, and now we can both go to Olav under the care of his old friend. It is all so exciting . . ."

"Forgive me, my lady, but we must alter our plans," Astrid interrupted her sharply. "I won't accompany you any further. I will return to my husband."

POLAND

Bolesław stared gloomily at the silver coffin lid.

"You did the best you could," said Zarad, but his voice sounded hollow. "You paid for Adalbert's body with its weight in silver, you brought back his remains, you even managed to get back his head."

"This was Sobiesław's last brother. My uncle killed his entire family two years ago."

"My lord," Zarad argued, "he still has a half brother. The one who escaped the Prussians. Radim, or whatever his name was . . ."

"It's strange." Bolesław leaned over the coffin lid and saw his own distorted reflection in the polished silver. "The pagans killed only Adalbert, sparing his brother and vicar Bogusz. Do you have any idea why?"

"There are two reasons I can think of. First, Radim and the others fled like cowards and left Adalbert to face the Prussians alone. Second, the pagans, by killing only the bishop, wanted to send a message to communicate that while they are refusing the mission, they do not want a war."

"You're right," Bolesław agreed distractedly. He leaned over the coffin lid again. "It's ghastly." He showed Zarad his reflection in the lid. "And true."

"What do you mean, my lord?" Zarad sounded worried. "I'm only a simple soldier. If you want to read into some signs or something, perhaps I should call for Bishop Unger?"

"I'm the one responsible for the destruction of the entire Sławnikowic dynasty,"* Bolesław said. "I supported their ambitions, their rivalry with the Přemyslid dynasty. They were important to me—such strong allies, the dukes of Libice . . ."

"Do you blame yourself, brother?" a deep voice asked from the direction of the chapel wall.

At first, Zarad and Bolesław glanced at each other in terror.

"Ghost," Zarad whispered.

But it was Sobiesław who emerged from the shadows, clad in dark penitential robes.

"I didn't mean to eavesdrop," he said apologetically. "I was watching over the body and I fell asleep on the bench by the wall. I haven't left this place, even though I know it won't change anything. My headless brother will not rise again."

Bolesław felt uneasy knowing that his friend had overheard his words. He saw Sobiesław's dirty hair and untrimmed beard. The duke of Libice was suffering. It was only recently that his family had been rivalling the Přemyslids for influence in Bohemia. They had been powerful, wealthy, famous, and independent. Adalbert had twice abandoned the Praguian diocese; Sobiesław had fought at his side against the Veleti. In light of the swiftly deteriorating relations between the Přemyslids and the empire, their joint plan to overthrow the duke of Prague and replace him with Sobiesław seemed to be so close to fruition. His uncle Boleslav had cut it all short with the cruel murders, and now the death of the bishop of Prague when on a mission in Prussia concluded the destructive act.

Sobiesław came closer, throwing an arm around Bolesław and forcing them both to lean over the coffin. The smooth surface of the silver reflected both their faces.

"Do you see, brother?"

The duke could smell his stale breath.

"The fault is not yours alone, share it with me." Sobiesław let go of Bolesław and laughed like a madman. "But it doesn't matter, it's an illusion anyway. Anyone who leans over my brother's coffin would feel guilty. The living like to

---

* Also known as the Slavniks or Slavnikids, a dynasty in the Duchy of Bohemia in the tenth century.

see themselves in the deaths of others. Do you want to know who is responsible for all my family's misfortunes? Here he is!"

He retrieved a silver coin from his pouch and placed it on the coffin lid with a clang. Bolesław picked it up. There was an eagle taking flight on one side, and a hand holding a dagger on the other.

"And there's my name around the edge. By hammering 'Duke Sobiesław' onto the coin I condemned the dynasty of Libice myself. My own family!" Sobiesław's eyes flashed wildly. "The Přemyslid duke couldn't bear it and paid me back with his blade. If we were innocent, would God have allowed Adalbert to have died such a horrible death? No. God has pointed a finger at us. He wanted us to vanish from this world . . ."

"Sobiesław!" Bishop Unger interrupted him as he entered the chapel. "Be silent! You cannot judge vanity with vanity. It is not for you to deliver God's judgment; it is not your place to try to understand His perspective. Even amidst your suffering and grief for your loved ones, you must maintain some sense. Do you know why? To avoid questioning God's will. Control yourself, Duke!"

Sobiesław took a step back, while Unger issued orders to the servants who followed him:

"It's too dark. Light the torches and chase away the shadows which do not suit the Lord's light, because here I bring the word of God to those in need."

Bolesław took a careful look at Unger. His bishop was not a man to waste his words.

"Are you feeling all right, Unger?" he asked.

"Perfectly. My lord, Sobiesław, you have seen your own reflections in Adalbert's coffin as you searched for those responsible for his death. Look again, now that the chapel is brightened by light. What do you see?"

"The radiance reflected off the metal," Sobiesław muttered.

Only in the light did it become clear how deeply grief's claws had wounded him. The lines on the face of the duke of Libice were covered by a dirty beard, while the strands of unwashed hair made him look like a grubby old man, though he was only just older than Bolesław.

"Radiance," Unger repeated. "You're right. Today it is the metal that is radiant, but tomorrow it will be your brother's heavenly fame. Adalbert, in giving his life while on mission among the pagans, in the moment of his death became the Church's martyr. Its Holy son. Do you understand?"

It won't bring back his brother, but perhaps it might bring him some comfort, thought Bolesław.

"He knew the wealthiest men of this world," Unger continued. "He was friendly with Rome's leaders. Emperor Otto referred to him as his dear companion on his earthly path. A martyr who walked among us like Christ amidst the Apostles. Do you understand?" Unger asked hopefully, but he shook his head when he looked at them. "No, you don't."

Bolesław felt as if he was in the middle of a lesson, but thankfully Unger did not wait for an answer.

"In such times when the Church of Pope Sylvester searches for new saints, saints who can rise to the challenges with which the modern world faces them, we, in Gniezno, have the remains of a saint who gave his life for his faith, just as was done in the old days. We have a treasure!" Unger exclaimed, and Bolesław finally understood.

"How long will the canonization take?" he asked soberly.

"A martyr is canonized on the day of his death." Unger smiled. "Though we will, of course, send a delegation to Rome. I expect Emperor Otto will be supportive, since after all he was the one who sent Adalbert on his mission."

"No, Bishop," Bolesław announced firmly. "From now on this is not the emperor's mission, but mine. Otto sent him to the Veleti and we've all agreed that was unwise because of the war. I sent him to the Prussians, where he became God's martyr."

"I admire your wisdom, my lord." Unger bowed his head. "Your mission. What would you say to finding a middle ground? We could say it's a joint mission? Yours and the emperor's? That would help to spread Adalbert's cult."

"Yes, all right. But only because you have just taught us that vanity is a sin."

"By sharing fame with the emperor, you're giving evidence of . . ."

"Pity?"

"No."

"Caution?" the duke corrected himself.

"Prudence, my lord," Unger concluded.

2

NORWAY

Olav led Princess Tyra into the manor in Nidaros as his wife right after the wedding celebrations. Bishop Sivrit had pronounced them man and wife in the eyes of God. When Olav married Geira all those years ago, they had merely recited the words to one another. They'd both been lost souls then, wandering in the darkness, and the way in which their marriage ended testified to that. And now? How would it be now? He looked at the delicate beauty of the woman to whom he'd made his vows. Stunning dark red hair, a prominent forehead, a nose that was perhaps a little too long but which marred none of her loveliness. She was dressed modestly, since, as she had observed with some embarrassment, "I was abducted with only one dress."

"You'll receive new clothes from me, my lady," he'd promised, but she didn't want to accept any gifts from him until they made their vows.

Geivar, having escorted her, told him curtly that "She prayed at every stop." Olav was sorry to find that Astrid hadn't accompanied them as he'd wanted to see his old friend and to thank her for what she had done for him. "The Lady of Wolin was in a hurry to return to her husband," Tyra explained Astrid's absence.

Her husband. Jarl Sigvald. A strange man. From the four marriages orchestrated by Mieszko that time they'd all met in Poznań, only one had survived. Eric was dead, as were Bolesław's Hungarian wife, and his own, Geira. Only Astrid and Sigvald were still a couple, although it would have been difficult to fathom a worse-suited pair.

"King Olav and Queen Tyra!" the wedding guests greeted them in the great hall.

Once they'd taken their seats, Bishop Sivrit raised a toast.

"May God bless the Yngling dynasty."

"Amen," he and Tyra answered together and drank.

Was it a sign from God that Tyra had landed at the estuary of Göta älv, the exact place in which he had bidden his dreams of Świętosława goodbye? His dreams were haunted by the memory of the stone lovers and the axe hanging over their heads. He turned to his wife, placed a hand on hers, and decided that from this day forth, he would not indulge in memories.

"Has my brother inquired about me?" she asked quietly.

"No, my lady."

"He's probably still busy celebrating the birth of a second son," she said, smiling slightly. "Queen Sigrid wanted a daughter, but they say it's a son. It was on the day of my abduction," she explained.

"Why do you keep saying 'abduction'?" Olav asked. "It suggests that something was done against your will, but talk of marriage came from you, and what happened afterward would better be called 'freeing' you."

She blushed, embarrassed.

"You're right, my lord . . . husband," she corrected herself.

Vigi padded over to them and settled his white head on Olav's knee.

"A beautiful dog," she said. "What is he called?"

"Vigi."

Olav wanted to tell her the story of how he met Vigi, but he stopped himself. How could he describe the prophesied dog which had come to him by the lovers' rock and keep Świętosława's name out of his tale?

"I have heard much of your accomplishments, my lord." Tyra spoke again after a long pause. "Travelers who stopped at Roskilde spoke of how you christened your kingdom. I was touched to hear it."

So Świętosława has also heard about it, he thought.

"There is still much to do," he said quickly, trying to drown out his thoughts of the Bold One, thoughts so inappropriate to have on his wedding day when his wife was another woman.

"What do you mean?" Tyra asked with surprise. "Based on what was said in Denmark, almost all of your country has given itself to Christ."

"Travelers tend to exaggerate in more than stories of their own adventures." Olav laughed. "I must still address the headstrong north, Hålogaland—a world of northern lights, reindeer herds, and the most avid pagans. The Finnish nation is rife with all kinds of magicians; it used to be said that every Fin was one. That's undoubtedly an exaggeration, but it is true that I have some defiant jarls left in the north. I must set out to meet them soon, since I've just learned that Tore Hjort, that is, Tore Stag, the lord of Lofoten, appeared in his houses again, although he has previously succeeded in remaining entirely hidden from me."

"Is it a dangerous excursion?" Tyra asked, worried.

"No more than any other, my lady, but in taking the throne I made an oath."

"What kind of oath, if it is not secret?"

"That I will either christen the entire kingdom, or die trying," he replied honestly.

"Everyone must die someday," Tyra said, and their conversation faltered. They both sat stiffly, and Olav felt as if the feast dragged on into eternity.

Finally, when the guests had sated their first and second hunger, it was time for the consummation. Bishop Sivrit led the procession to Olav's alcove.

"Don't be afraid, my lady," he whispered into his wife's ear. "I have forbidden the pagan ritual of undressing the newlyweds."

She thanked him with a nod.

"I bless this bed so that God may allow the married couple to bring new life into the world." Sivrit sprinkled holy water over the bed and over them both, after which Olav and Tyra, holding hands, bowed to their people.

"Go and enjoy yourselves, drinking our health," Tryggvason called out.

Varin closed the door and they were left alone.

"Phew." He kissed Tyra's hand and let it go. "Too much in the life of royals is observed by everyone else."

"That's our fate." She smiled shyly. "Until my abduction . . . sorry, until I was freed, I always had my brother's men outside my door."

"Did Sven harm you, my lady?" Olav asked.

"Only once, but it was too great an insult for me to ever forgive him," she said, defiantly looking into his eyes. "He was my brother. I say 'was,' because from this day forth, you, my husband, have taken over caring for me."

Olav laughed.

"Do you hate him?"

"The good Bishop Oddinkarr said that hate is an unworthy emotion, and I'm trying to distance myself from anything that might separate me from God." She moved her head, and the firelight highlighted the bronze in her hair.

"Will you have mead? Or perhaps you prefer wine?" Olav realized that he was searching her features for similarities to Sven's.

"I prefer wine, but I don't drink it because my brother loves it so much. I'll have mead."

"Does your brother still have the supplies he took from England?" he asked as he handed her a goblet.

"No. He drank it quickly. He buys wine; he has plenty of silver," she said, and drank the goblet's contents in one go. "He lives like a rich man. He throws his money around." She choked out the words. "He likes adorned armor and jewels. He showers his queen with gifts, too. And his jarls. He never begrudges anyone anything, except when it's to build a church. The bastard didn't want to give anything for that until his wife said that every jarl promised her silver for the churches and Sven gave her the money she wanted because she'd made him so angry. That's what he's like. Everything is done in anger. Will you give me some more mead, my king?"

He refilled her goblet. The mead was clearly melting the icy walls she had built in the years she had been unable to speak out against her brother. She sat on the edge of the bench.

"The worst thing is that I was the only one he wouldn't spend money on. He was the only one that mattered. Only him! King Harald's son. And me?" She drank the second goblet and her voice took on the tone of a petulant child. "He was Queen Tove's child, I was a wealthy noblewoman's daughter, but still I was too lowborn to ever become anything more than a king's mistress. Do you know that nobody has ever even told me what my mother's name was, Olav? I lived feeling like I never belonged, abandoned and unwanted. If it weren't for Bishop Oddinkarr, it's likely that nobody would have taken an interest in my education and upbringing. Father only began to notice me when I got older. I'm no fool. Suddenly, I was useful, because I could be wed to suit him. But Mieszko turned down his offer and Harald lost interest in me again."

"Mieszko?" Olav asked.

"Yes. Harald wanted to wed me to Duke Burizleif. Pour me some more mead, please," she commanded.

Olav reached for the jug, fighting the impulse to correct her pronunciation. Like his sister, Bolesław had been given a name that made it impossible to forget his heritage, a name that made all foreigners stumble. Olav wondered whether the princess had turned to the duke for an entirely different reason than the one she'd given. Perhaps she had hoped Bolesław would marry her after all? Olav could get her drunk with this third goblet; he could see how every sip loosened her tongue. He hesitated, and then put it down.

"Wife," he said as he walked over to her. "Come to bed. We have a duty to fulfill."

Three days later, he bade Tyra goodbye as he boarded the *Short Snake* with Sivrit and Vigi. The crew was made up of sixty rowers and forty soldiers.

Sivrit grabbed his staff once they'd cast off. It was adorned with a carving that resembled two twisted ram horns. Praying for the success of their excursion, the bishop raised it high above his head and the sunlight danced on the polished wood, slipping through the carving to cast a golden pattern on the sail.

"The *Short Snake*'s maiden journey!" Varin called out as the oars began to beat a regular rhythm against the water.

Omold stood in the stern and began to recite:

The Snake *bites the waves with a hiss,*
Defiantly swallowing the wind . . .

"My king." Omold paused in his composing. "Did you name the ship *Short Snake* because you plan to build a *Long Snake*, too?"

"A philosopher as well as a bard," Varin praised him. "Just make sure that Bishop Sivrit doesn't steal you away and send you to a cathedral school."

"Do you think he might?" Omold asked seriously. "He never said a word about it to me. Maybe he hasn't had the chance to yet? No, Varin, you're making fun of me. We don't have a cathedral school!"

"But we will one day." Varin bared his painted fangs.

Hårek, a nobleman from Hålogaland, walked over to Olav. Tryggvason had recently christened him, repaying his loyalty with four districts in the northern part of the country. It was a steep price, but he needed a bridgehead in the lands that were mounting the strongest opposition against him. It was Hårek who had brought news of Tore Stag's return when he had come to attend Olav's wedding.

"We are sailing to hunt the Stag in its own den." Hårek laughed, and then sighed. "The weather is good, the wind favorable. Is this the first time you'll be seeing Lofoten, my king?"

"Yes."

"It's a heavenly land. Tore was lucky to see it every day. I'll be blunt, my lord. If we vanquish Tore Stag, will you grant me his lands in return for my help?"

"I'm sailing to defeat him, and I'm not going to consider any other outcomes," Olav said, surprised that Hårek was. "The jarl will be given a choice, just like every one of my subjects. And if he chooses life and baptism, I will let him stay where he is."

"I know Tore Stag, my lord. He will choose to fight."

"Look at my crew. The backs and shoulders of rowers tell their stories better than brags in a port tavern ever could. And my warriors? Look, not a single one of them is sitting idle. They are already cleaning their armor and sharpening their swords. Will the Stag send better men than these?"

Hårek pulled a face and shook his head.

"No, my king. He won't send men."

They were silent for a while. Hårek crossed his arms over his chest.

"My old friend Tore Hjort will test your men. But not their courage or strength; he will challenge their faith in Christ."

"And your faith, too, as fresh as it is?" Olav asked. Hårek had only been baptized recently.

"Mine? No, my lord. I knew the rules a long time before I accepted Christ at your bishop's hand. Did nobody tell you that my father had been Harald the Good's bard? I thought not. The memory of men is the strangest of puzzles.

Do you know what differentiates you from that king, Olav? He had faith in Christ, but merely asked the people to accept baptism, he never faced them with a choice as final as the one you place before them."

"The final choice will be made on Judgment Day," Olav replied and shrugged. "It is not for me to evaluate the actions of a past king. Each of us has a different task to fulfill. God has given me mine clearly: I am to give every man I meet a chance, so that's what I do."

"You're a tough man, King Olav. Let me just warn you that the north is also tough. For some reason, the old gods retain a strong grip there. Tore Stag will force your men to see the unexpected."

"Do you see that skerry, Hårek?" Olav pointed at a small rocky islet which was marked with a wooden cross. "It has been called the Magicians' Skerry for the past year."

"The white island?" Hårek shielded his eyes. "I hadn't paid attention to it. I heard about your slaughter of everyone who dabbles in magic. Was that where it happened?"

"Yes. Rafn God's Axe cut them all down. Healers, those who cast curses, those who imprison maidens at a distance. Anyone who admitted to practicing seidr. We threw their bodies into the water."

"I would have spared the healers," Hårek muttered.

When the *Short Snake* sailed close to the Magicians' Skerry, a colony of gulls launched themselves from the cross. In a split second, the white island turned into a gray rock. Rafn leaned over the gunwale and shouted:

"God's Axe sends his best to Magicians' Skerry! May hell consume you!"

"You allow such calls?" Hårek pulled a face. "What happened to God's mercy?"

"Mercy is only for those who believe in it. The magicians didn't want to accept the faith, not even in their final moments when they lay their heads on Rafn's tree stump. So what use is mercy to them?"

"Let's pray for them before we reach Lofoten," Hårek muttered. "We'll need it to avoid the whirlpools that surround the islands."

Olav took Hårek's words to heart. Despite its name, the *Short Snake* had a long, smooth hull. It was a warship, intended for swift, efficient transport of soldiers. It was a drakkar made to inspire fear with its lofty dragon bow, majestically large sails, and the way it seemed to slide effortlessly over the waves. The smaller snekkes made for the open seas were better suited to conquer these dangerous, hungry waters than Olav's long drakkar.

* * *

"We're getting close," Hårek said after a few days. His voice was colored by poorly controlled fear. "Look, my king, at the gray fog in front of us. It hides the biggest vortex I have ever heard of."

The temperature dropped within moments, and a strong gust of wind filled the *Snake*'s sails.

"Sivrit!" Olav called out. "Now!"

At the same time, he saw the enormous vortex emerge from the fog.

The bishop took his position at the ship's bow, staff in hand. The wind whipped his brown habit furiously, but Sivrit, as still as a statue and undeterred by the gusts, began to pray loudly. The crew of the *Short Snake* saw how far in front of the vessel the waves surged and rose. Some of the sailors crossed themselves fearfully. The warriors clutched their swords tightly. Varin held the helm, looking from the watery vortex toward which they sailed to the bishop and his raised staff.

"Don't hesitate!" Olav shouted to his helmsman. "Don't hesitate even for a moment. Go!"

A wave broke over the deck. Sivrit didn't even flinch.

"Praise the ancient Lord in the awe and beauty of creation!"

"For ever and ever, amen," the sailors chanted back in time with their oar strokes.

The sea began to settle and when the waves diminished, they saw green isles rise from the water on the horizon. Hårek ran over to Olav in a soaked caftan, slipping over the wet deck.

"If I hadn't already done so, I would take your faith now, my lord," he exclaimed, his eyes bright. "Lofoten is before you!"

With God's strength, the Short Snake *vanquished a vortex so terrible that the bones of the daring were seen glinting on the ocean bed . . .*

Omold choked on his own poem.

Sivrit, the priest who knows no fear, called on the Almighty when our vessel sailed toward the arms of inescapable death and the deck was drowned in waves . . .

The green stripes of land began to grow.

"My king," Ingvar, the brightest of his men, called out. "They are sailing out to meet us."

"How many ships are there?"

"Two."

"Archers!" commanded Olav. "Take your positions."

*The enemies sailed out to meet the conquerors of the seas and vanquishers of
vortexes. Two armed snekkes against the one* Short Snake. *Coming ever
closer . . .*

Omold notched an arrow to his bow and pulled back the bowstring.

"My king!" he called out. "Do you want me to compose poetry or to fight?
Because I'm not sure whether I should be searching for words or preparing
my arrows."

"Fight when the fight is upon us and leave the talking for when the mead is
poured," Olav replied, his eyes on the approaching vessels.

"Christ!" the bard groaned. "That was good! I need to remember it so I
can include it in my verses."

*Fight when the fight is upon us, and compose songs when the time arrives for the
golden mead and victorious feasts . . .*

"They're turning back!" yelled Ingvar.

"After them!" Olav commanded.

"They want to draw you onto land, my king," warned Hårek.

"The *Short Snake* should get to them before we reach land," Olav reassured
him, looking up at the sails stretched taut by the wind.

They were gaining fast. It wasn't long before they could make out individ-
uals on the decks of both retreating snekkes.

"Tore Stag is aboard the ship on the left. Do you see the tall man in a red
cloak?" Hårek pointed. "That's him."

"Archers!" Olav called, waiting until they had gained enough on the ships.
"Fire!"

Forty archers pulled back bowstrings in two shifts. They hit both helmsmen and chaos reigned briefly on both vessels.

"We batter them from the left," Tryggvason ordered. There were more
warriors aboard Tore's snekke.

"We're sailing into shallow waters," Varin warned.

"Hooks! Get the hooks ready!" Olav shouted as they slid along the gunwale
of Tore's ship. The *Short Snake* rocked from side to side. They heard the metallic clang of hooks being thrown over the gunwale.

"May God be with you!" Olav shouted, drawing his sword and leaping
onto the deck of the enemy vessel.

"After the king!" yelled Rafn God's Axe.

Olav slashed at a warrior dressed in hardened leather. He saw Tore Stag at the bow, his back to the battle, and Olav moved toward him, shouting, "Tore, surrender in the name of God!"

But the man just laughed as he turned and jumped overboard.

"He's escaping! He has a lifeboat!" someone shouted.

Olav ran to the ship's bow, cutting men down blindly as he went. The Stag was getting away. Tryggvason turned around. He grabbed a bow out of the hands of a dead man lying on the deck, but he couldn't see any arrows.

"On your left, behind you!" Varin called as he fought an axeman on the starboard side.

Olav glanced round. Yes, there was a corpse with an arrow in his chest. Tryggvason pulled it out of the body, notched it, and took aim. He felt cold. The lifeboat in which Tore had escaped was swaying beside a rock just off the shore, empty. Olav looked higher. There he was! He could see the red stain of the cloak. As Tore Stag deftly climbed, Olav released the arrow. It hit its mark between the man's shoulder blades. Tore Stag faltered and fell. Tryggvason sighed with relief, but at the same time heard Hårek's call:

"Christ save us! This is northern magic!"

Tore's red cloak floated into the air and arranged itself into the silhouette of a great stag with an arrow in its back. The animal shook its stunning antlers and made its way inland with a majestic step.

Olav heard the cries of surprise from his men as they faced the remaining men aboard the northern jarl's ship. They fought with a renewed and desperate vigor.

Tryggvason felt something warm rub against his legs. Vigi. The dog had come over from the *Short Snake*, only to run to the bow of Tore's ship and leap into the waves. Olav could hear his own heartbeat. Vigi emerged from the water and climbed the rock. The majestic stag with the arrow in its back had also spotted the dog. It took a few steps inland and turned its head to look behind it. Vigi shook the water from his fur and gave chase.

"A boat!" Olav shouted, returning to the *Snake*.

It was already being lowered. Varin, Rafn, Ingvar, and Hårek grabbed the oars.

"Me too!" the bard pleaded. "I need to see this!"

They took him aboard, but the boat was too slow. Olav jumped into the water and began to swim. *Vigi*, he thought, *you're chasing an illusion. It's not worth it!*

"My king! You'll drown!" Olav heard Hårek's terrified shout.

No, my friend. You've never wrestled me in the water. You don't know that I've learned to take off my armor underwater.

He didn't have to do so now, though. The shore was close. He could already feel stones under his feet. He ran onto the beach, looked around and, holding on to small trees, began to climb.

Vigi! he thought. *Don't let it be too late!*

"Vigi!" he shouted when he reached the top.

All he could see around him were green fields, here and there scattered with rocks. There was no sign of the white dog. Or the stag.

They searched until dusk, until finally, following tracks left by the stag's antlers, they found them.

"Vigi." Olav ran to his beloved animal. Blood soaked his white fur. "You're alive . . ."

The dog was panting heavily and whined when he saw Olav. He licked Olav's hand.

"You'll get through this, my friend," Olav promised, stroking him gently. He wrapped his cloak around the dog.

"My lord, look at this," Varin said hollowly, touching the stag's corpse with his foot.

At a distance, the stag had seemed an ordinary animal, but up close they saw that it was merely an empty skin. *How could that be?* Olav lifted it up with one hand. The skin was as light as moss. The arrow was still embedded in it.

"Burn it," he said, hurling it into the dirt.

When they finished, he picked up his dog and carried him to the boat.

The dusk lasted a long time. It was late summer. Hårek sailed the *Snake* along the shore and they entered the fjord. There was a large, comfortable port at the fjord's far edge. They moored the ship. Many of the settlements' inhabitants gathered on the shore.

"Your lord is dead!" Hårek announced. "King Olav has defeated him, and he will be your ruler from this day forth. Hear the survivors!"

They led out a handful of bound prisoners. There were no more than a score of them. Women who recognized their husbands threw themselves toward the men, crying. Those who couldn't see their loved ones among the lucky ones stood back in silence. Mothers embraced daughters. Not even the children made a sound.

"I promise freedom to those who accept my rule and faith," Olav said. He was tired. "I will give you time to consider, and I will return tomorrow to hear your decision."

3

Olav and his men celebrated atop a hill in Tore Stag's manor. It was a manor so big that neither his own home in Nidaros nor Świętosława's in Sigtuna could rival it. It was shaped like a massive boat with the keel facing upward. The walls were strengthened by ramparts made of turf, and the interior was decorated with ornate carvings that drew the eye of all who entered. Olav left a score of men with his ship, and though the remaining eighty sat with him now, the manor's grand hall was still half empty. His men only filled one long table and had pushed the rest by the walls.

Fight when the fight is upon us, and compose songs when the time arrives for the golden mead and victorious feasts . . .

Omold the bard was shouting and pouring mead into himself with no restraint, leaping along the empty benches.

"We're on foreign land, among defeated enemies. You should put up sentries," Varin told Olav.

"I wouldn't fear an attack from the rest of the Stag's army," said Hårek from his seat beside the king. "Without a leader, they have no reason to strike at you or your forces. It makes little difference to the common man who sits on the throne, so long as they aren't a tyrant."

"Who are you afraid of then?"

"You know what I mean, my lord." Hårek narrowed his eyes. "The north still has a few magicians who might seek vengeance. It is them that this excursion hurts the most."

"More light!" Olav called out to the few servants in the hall.

The fire burned in a long hearth which ran through the middle of the hall, and about a dozen torches flickered along the walls, but the hall remained dark even after the servants had brought in another dozen torches.

Vigi lay panting heavily at Olav's feet, wrapped tightly in one of the king's warm cloaks.

"God bless," Sivrit said, and looked around them. "Olav, we have brought the word of God to the north, to a place which has never heard it before. God has never reached so far. Perhaps one day you will be known as the Apostle of the North?"

Laughter reached their ears, coming from the direction of the door.

"What's that?" Varin asked, alert.

At first, they all thought that a bear cub had somersaulted into the hall. But when he landed opposite the king and straightened up with a graceful jump, they saw a man wearing a bear's fur. Varin instinctively reached for the hilt of the long dagger on his back, but Olav stopped him with a wave of his hand.

The man bowed low before the king and asked:

"Will the great jarl Tore known as the Stag accept the services of Bjarni, Son of the Jolly Bear? Your fame has drawn me here from far-off lands . . ."

"The jarl is dead," Olav replied coolly. "He fell in battle against the King of Norway, Olav Tryggvason."

The newcomer must have traveled far: his clothes were worn out, with bright yellows, greens, and reds barely distinguishable beneath the dirt, and he had bells hanging at his ankles.

"He fell . . ." the Son of the Jolly Bear repeated with concern and looked about him. "Have I walked in on his farewell feast?"

"No. It is a welcome feast for King Olav," Hårek replied. "And you have the honor of standing before the king."

Bjarni's wide, protruding eyes grew even larger. He now resembled a large, old, unshaven, and sad child. He bowed again and paused, bent over, looking at the wounded dog. He lifted his head and looked straight at Olav.

"Your dog suffers, my lord."

"And I with him," Olav responded. "His name is Vigi. He was the one to defeat the stag that had lived inside Tore."

"Would you like me to help him?"

"Can you?"

The newcomer straightened.

"I have seen many men ripped to shreds by magic. My mother used to heal . . . Sometimes she succeeded, sometimes she failed." He nodded sadly.

"If you heal my dog, I'll make you a free man," Olav told him.

"But I am free, my lord!"

They looked at each other for a moment. There was nothing but sincerity in Bjarni's gaze.

"Who are you really?" Olav inquired.

"Bjarni, Son of the Jolly Bear—that's what they call me." The guest smiled, though his eyes remained sad. "I know many songs and entertaining tricks that can liven up the long northern nights. I make bored children laugh, alongside weary wives and the men who miss the daylight and adventures. I travel from court to court, bringing joy, laughter, and sometimes even some musings."

"I will happily hear your songs, Bjarni, but it would mean more to me if you could help my dog, if you know how."

"I will do my best, my lord. I need to take him outside. It's too stuffy and loud in here, and he needs fresh air and grass under him. Will you allow it?"

Olav hesitated. He leaned over Vigi and placed a hand over his burning head.

"Will you allow it?" he asked the dog.

Vigi whined.

"Take him, Bjarni, and know that this dog is worth much to me. I paid for him with a bracelet of gold."

"That makes him the most valuable dog I know," Bjarni replied gravely.

"I'm telling you this so that you know I can repay you for healing him."

Varin himself picked up the dog and followed the newcomer outside the manor. He returned after a long moment and sat down beside Olav.

"The conjurer has found space at the back of the house. He lay the dog on the grass there, started a small fire, and ordered a cauldron be brought to him. He has many herbs in the pouches at his belt, which he's mixing and heating as we speak. I asked the women in the kitchens. They said they've heard of the Son of the Jolly Bear. Apparently, he's been here before, many years ago."

The feast continued and the men enjoyed themselves more with every horn of mead they drank.

"Here is the true beauty of the north." Hårek laughed. "We spend half the year feasting because the day never ends. We drink and drink because if there's no night, there is no dawn. And when the time of winter and darkness arrives, we drink, because it feels as if we are still at the same never-ending feast. To the king!"

"The king!"

"Stay, King Olav, until the fall," Hårek said between the toasts. "Wouldn't you want to see the lights dancing in the frosty sky? To hear the aurora sing to you?"

Olav and Sivrit exchanged a glance.

"Bishop?"

"My lord?"

"The Apostle of the North should see the northern lights," Olav observed without hesitating.

"And the queen?" Sivrit asked. "Have you sowed an Yngling heir in her womb?"

Olav didn't get the chance to respond because Bjarni reentered the hall.

The Son of the Jolly Bear leapt onto an empty bench against a wall and walked its length in a dancing step, somersaulting every few feet.

"Vigi?" Olav asked, but the racket his men made drowned out his question.

Bjarni jumped and began to pull colorful handkerchiefs from his sleeves much to the men's joy.

"What's happening with my dog?" Tryggvason called out.

"He's sleeping, my lord," Bjarni shouted back, pulling a live bird from his hood. "He needs sleep now, and the rest is up to the gods."

"Varin, check on Vigi," Olav snarled.

The conjurer never stopped his antics. He leapt into the air with the nimbleness of a squirrel, grabbing onto the beams which supported the ceiling and swinging from them. Olav's warriors laughed and they applauded him. Varin came back.

"He speaks the truth. The dog is asleep; his breath is regular."

"Didn't I tell you, my lord?" Bjarni laughed, hanging with his head down above Olav. "Everything is in the hands of the wild northern gods. The ones you scorn. The ones you seek to destroy . . ."

"Take him!" Olav commanded.

In the blink of an eye, Bjarni pulled himself up onto the beams and began to run along them. Olav's men finally seemed to process his order and threw themselves in pursuit. The conjurer, however, was impossible to catch; he slipped through their fingers with the agility of a wild animal. They threw a hook with a line attached, and it seemed that it might snare Bjarni's foot, but he pushed himself off a beam and flew, his arms spread wide. Varin leapt onto a table and pulled the flying man down by the corner of his cloak. Bjarni fell down with a crash.

"He's dead!" Ingvar shouted.

"He's alive," the conjurer corrected him. "And he is laughing at you and your dead god!"

Four men grabbed him roughly and pinned him to the ground.

"It's not Bjarni, look at him!" Varin exclaimed.

Olav leaned over their captive. The man was wearing the same dirty clothes in which the Son of the Jolly Bear had arrived, but he was certainly not the same man. A red-haired, red-bearded stranger looked back at them. Except that he wasn't a stranger.

"Sven?" Olav whispered, clutching the man's hair. "That's impossible. You cannot be Sven . . ."

"I can be whomever I wish," the man snarled, and yanked his head furiously.

Red hair remained in Olav's hand as the man they held down suddenly grew bald. *Like Eric Segersäll,* Olav thought with horror. *This is the devil who assumes the appearance of others.*

"Bishop!" the king shouted. "We have caught an unclean force."

The bald man changed into a handsome, dark-haired stranger in front of their eyes, someone Olav didn't recognize.

"Jarl Eric? My God, this isn't possible . . ." Hårek whispered. "You cannot be the young jarl, Haakon's son."

"I can be whomever I wish," the man exclaimed, banging his head against the floor. "Because I am the great Eyvind! Eyvind!"

"Not Eyvind," Hårek whispered. "My lord, if that's him . . ."

"Bring me fire," Olav commanded, knowing a demon must be defeated immediately, no matter who he was. "Fire!" he repeated, seeing that his people were stepping tentatively away, horrorstruck.

Omold handed him an iron basket with firebrands burning inside, though Olav had meant torches.

"Deny the devil, unclean spirit!" the bishop called. "Deny him!"

"No!" In a blink of an eye, the handsome young man changed into a gray-haired old man with a wizened beard. "I am Eyvind."

"It's really him," the frightened Hårek whispered. "The greatest magician of the north . . . Christ . . ."

"I don't want to kill you," Olav said firmly. "I'm giving you a chance. Deny the devil and accept the light of the one and only God."

"No," Eyvind snarled, and spat. "Never."

Olav grabbed the burning basket and placed it on the magician's stomach, making the man roar in pain.

"The fires of hell which will devour you will be a thousand times hotter than this. Deny Evil and I will save you from that fire in life as in death."

They could smell burning clothing. The magician stopped thrashing.

"Deny Evil and let me baptize you!"

"I can't," Eyvind replied with perfect composure. "Hear me, my lord, and you'll understand."

Olav had the basket removed. There was a black circle burned into the magician's caftan, and underneath it they could see red, blistering skin.

"Water! Pour it over him!" Olav commanded.

When Varin had thrown water from a basin over the injured man, the smell of burnt clothing and skin hit their nostrils.

"I cannot be baptized," Eyvind repeated, breathing heavily. "I want you to understand. My parents had a piece of land on the island known as Red Eye. They had riches, but they couldn't have an heir. They sailed to Fin, the famous magician. He took their money and called on the spirits who served him. What spirits? I cannot tell you their names, but I will tell you they came from the air, not the earth. One of them surrendered to Fin's power and let himself be enclosed in the dark, wet prison of a mother's womb. Yes, my mother gave me life, the spirit to whom Fin gave a human form. When I was born, I inherited my father's wealth and island. I lived on Red Eye, basking in people's appreciation for me. I helped them when they asked, because I still had the powers of the spirit even when in my human form. But when you ask if I will be baptized, I tell you I cannot, because even a great king such as yourself cannot baptize one who is not a man."

Eyvind finished speaking, panting. Suddenly, in a final burst of energy, he laughed and asked almost cheerfully:

"Am I wrong, my lord? Isn't old Eyvind right?"

Then he died. When he stopped breathing, he began to shrink, as if his skin were drying up and scattering right in front of them. Within but a moment, it was over, and all that was left was the smoldering clothing, worn shoes, and bells which the Son of the Jolly Bear had been wearing earlier.

"Bjarni?" Olav lifted his eyes from the clothes. "Vigi!"

He leapt up, followed by Varin and the others. They ran outside the manor. It was already light—or still light, since the northern day had no beginning and no end.

"There!" Varin pointed at a stream of smoke which rose from the fire at the back of the house.

Olav ran, tripping, with his heart hammering in his chest.

Vigi lay close to a naked man who had his arms around the dog; they were keeping each other warm.

"It's Bjarni . . ." Olav whispered. "Vigi?"

The dog lifted his white head and whined in greeting. He stood up, waking Bjarni. The man sat up and rubbed his eyes, looking dazed. He realized he was naked. He looked from the dog to Olav to the approaching men.

"Vigi . . . you're well again . . ." Olav stroked the dog's head and sides, where scars left by the stag's antlers marred his skin. He knelt and touched them. "The scars have healed, as if a month or more had passed since he was wounded," he whispered to his people. "Who are you, Bjarni?" he asked the sleepy naked man.

"I told you, my lord. I sing at courts, I tell stories, I do tricks that make children laugh . . ."

"Are you a magician?"

"No. I am a free man, my king."

"You have healed my dog."

"I only helped; he healed himself." Bjarni curled up, searching for something with which to cover himself.

Vigi licked Olav's face. Tryggvason took off his cloak and covered Bjarni. He fastened it on the man's shoulder with a great golden brooch and placed a bag of denars engraved with his name at Bjarni's feet.

"I told you I would give you your freedom if you healed my dog. Saying that, I thought I would give you the freedom which lies in having faith in the one true God. But I've changed my mind, Bjarni. I won't try to persuade you to convert. If you want to, you will come to me someday and say: 'Here I am,' and I will welcome you as a friend. There is no bad blood between us, healer. I'm grateful to you, and you are free."

Bjarni took the bag, wrapped the cloak closer around himself to hide his nakedness, and nodded as he got to his feet.

"Yes, I am free, my lord."

Vigi walked over to Bjarni and nudged him with his muzzle. Bjarni let go of the edges of the cloak to stroke him, and Olav saw a circle burned into the man's naked stomach.

4

DENMARK

Świętosława and Sven had the same reaction to Sigvald's news.

"What did you say?!"

The queen felt her head throb as anger surged through her. Sven must have felt the same, because he leapt from his chair toward the jarl of Jomsborg standing before them. Jorun stopped him, barring Sven's way and shouting:

"It's the jarl of Jomsborg! A messenger. The laws of hospitality protect him."

Sigvald stood still, unmoved by this outburst. Sven stopped, swore, and fell back heavily into his chair. Świętosława gripped her lynx's collar firmly and spoke only when she had regained control over her breathing.

"Forgive us, Jarl. You're not only a messenger and guest, but also my brother-in-law, the husband of my beloved sister Astrid. Forgive the king his outburst, but you must understand that this news pains us."

"If I wasn't aware of the gravity of the situation, I wouldn't have come myself," Sigvald replied stiffly. "Considering what has happened in the past between your late husband, your present king, and myself, I knew I might not be welcome here."

That was putting it mildly. Sigvald was risking his life; visiting Roskilde could cost him dearly. Everyone here remembered the Jomsvikings had been Eric's allies in the war against Sven. And Sigvald had imprisoned Sven in the fortress at Jom or, as he preferred to put it, been "forced to keep an expensive guest." Świętosława had no reason to distrust Sigvald's men. They sailed to her, to Roskilde, dressed as merchants from Wolin, and they conveyed messages between her and her brother Bolesław. They enabled her to be in regular contact with her family so the duke could rest easy knowing that she was in no danger in her marriage to the Redbeard.

"Can you tell us that again, please?" she requested. "Perhaps we misunderstood."

"I don't think you have, my queen." Sigvald shook his head. "But as you wish. Three belligerent young men came to Jom, asking to be admitted into our brotherhood. It is our custom to only accept those who have been brought to us by an existing Jomsviking. They knew nobody, but they claimed their heroic actions would speak for them. They told us that they participated in freeing Princess Tyra at the request of the Norwegian king. They boasted that they carried her out of court dressed as servants amid the confusion which reigned during your labor, my queen."

Sven cursed again. Świętosława hissed. Wrzask and Zgrzyt snarled furiously.

"They said that they had horses by the inn and rode with the princess to Trelleborg, where they boarded a ship, not suspected by anyone, and sailed to Nidaros where they handed Tyra over to Olav."

"Damn it!" This time it was Świętosława who swore. "To be tricked like this! Was Tyra abducted or had she played a part in planning this scheme?"

"Unfortunately, my lady, she was a willing participant. Tyra and Olav communicated in ways known only to them to arrange their marriage."

"I told you she's a treacherous bitch," Sven burst out at Świętosława. "But you defended her, as if the fact that she trotted to mass every day was enough to absolve her of any sin."

"How dare he," Świętosława hissed through clenched teeth. *How dare he marry Tyra?! He knew that I hadn't chosen Sven, that I did not marry him of my own free will! I had to do it, for Olof if nothing else! And it worked, I secured Sweden for my son. Taking Sven's sister for his wife is like a slap. He's mocking me! He's trampled everything that we had. Dishonored every moment. That night in the sailor's hut*... "How dare he!" she said aloud and cleared her throat. "He's insulted you, husband. Humiliated you by taking your sister without your consent."

"Damn him! Damn them both!" Sven howled and threw down the horn in his hand.

The force with which he threw it broke it in half, and it came apart like dry wood. The silver fitting fell off and rolled along the floor like a small empty crown.

"Forgive me," Sigvald said, his voice perfectly under control. "But that's not all."

"Wine!" Świętosława ordered, knowing that whatever they were about to find out, Sven was not going to be able to hear it sober. Neither would she.

The fair-haired Vali, nimble and thoughtful, sent away the servant who had appeared with glass goblets and had ordinary cups brought instead.

I'll thank her later, Świętosława thought.

"I told these men that in the eyes of the law, such a marriage is invalid," Sigvald continued as soon as Sven's cup reached his mouth. "A wife should bring with her a dowry, and a husband should repay her family. But they said that Tyra and Olav had taken care of everything. 'How,' I asked, 'if the entire scheme was secret?' And they said that apparently Olav had paid for Tyra's hand with an entire chest of denars. 'Plenty of silver,' they said. 'A royal gift, and so that no man would question it, he ensured every coin had been stamped with his name.' And Tyra, they said, had a chest with as many denars with her, stamped with your name. Every coin reads ZVEN REX DENER. She gave them to her husband on their wedding day."

Świętosława glanced at her husband, who had turned bright red.

"Where are these denars meant to be?" he hissed. "I've never seen them."

"They said they hid the chest under the floor when they came to take Princess Tyra," Sigvald replied.

"Jorun, take some men and tear apart my sister's room," Sven commanded coldly.

"Have some wine, Jarl," Świętosława offered. "In a moment we will discover the falseness of this tale, that it is nothing but a lie, and there are no denars to be found. Isn't that right, Sven?"

She glanced at her husband and knew immediately things were as bad as she'd feared. No, worse. The flaming red hair, fiery braids in his beard, and brightly flushed skin formed a uniform violet stain.

"Sven? Are you feeling all right?" she asked softly.

He didn't answer. She lifted her gaze and met Vali's terrified glance. The servant disappeared for a long time, during which the sound of axes chopping wood echoed from a distant part of the manor.

Jarl Sigvald took a sip of wine and, shaking out his long dark hair, said almost nonchalantly:

"Yes, my queen, it would be better if you were right. It would be better they had lied at least in the matter of the dowry. Because there is no reason to doubt that Olav gave his queen morgengeld as evidence of their consummation, since this was witnessed by his bishop and court. Yes, apparently, they showed in front of everyone that they had become man and wife that night. The only hope is, then, that the men lied about the dowry."

I don't care about her dowry, Świętosława thought, her hand going to her heart. *What pains me is her morgengeld!*

Sven stood up as the sound of the chopping axes ceased. A deaf silence reigned in the hall for a moment, broken only by the panting of the two wild cats. Świętosława clutched at the leash, winding it around her hands. Jorun appeared in the hall's entrance, carrying a chest.

"It was under the floor," he said hollowly, placing it on the table in front of Świętosława and Sven.

The king lifted the lid. There were denars inside, all bearing the name ONLAF REX NOR and a parchment covered in Latin words.

"Ion!" The queen summoned the monk. "Read."

"King Olav Tryggvason is leaving silver as a dowry for his wife, Princess Tyra," Ion read out.

"This still means nothing," Świętosława exclaimed desperately. "He may have paid, but did she . . ."

"Yes, my lady," Sigvald replied, and reached to the pouch at his belt. "The abductors received a coin from Olav which they had transported along with Tyra. I took it with me to show you."

Silver clinked on the table. ZVEN REX DENER.

"They say Tyra had a chest full of them," Sigvald concluded.

Ion picked up the coin, bit it, and smacked his lips.

"But where from?" Świętosława asked. "Where did she get them? Sven, say something!"

"Morcar Frog, the merchant from York," Sven said through clenched teeth. "I paid him that day with a jug full of silver svens. A jug of coins which carried my stamp and name."

"They robbed him," Sigvald said thoughtfully. "If they knew that the king gave the merchant his coins . . ."

"They could have caught him in the open sea," Jorun added. "Morcar sailed away that same day."

"Or they were all scheming together," Świętosława groaned.

"I doubt it, my lady. I am in Wolin often enough to know the merchants as well as if they were my own people." Jarl Sigvald laughed. "They cannot be bought. Just like the Jomsvikings. They prefer to stay out of royal affairs. And they do not start wars because, as Dalwin always says, 'War ruins business.'"

Świętosława's vision darkened. Vali hurried to the platform and handed Sven a cup filled with bloodred wine.

"Drink this, my lord, it will calm you," she beseeched.

Sven drank.

Autumn turned violently into winter. The days which followed Sigvald's visit seemed to blend into one another, storm after storm. Yes, she had gone to bed with Sven in anger. Their mutual rage bound them together. Their feeling of betrayal. Although each of them gave it a different color and sound, they made love fiercely, panting in anger, brimming with lust, shouting out in fury. They were like thunder and lightning. A hailstorm. A thunderstorm. Świętosława sank her nails into the skin on Sven's back. She pulled his beard with her teeth. She cried out when he took her from behind like a dog takes a bitch. They threw themselves at each other furiously, not knowing whether they wanted to come together or fight each other. Like soaring predators in mating season, they lost themselves and fell into sleep still clutching one another. And they woke up because the anger within them would not burn out. Sven brought a jug of wine to bed and they drank straight from it, spilling the bloodred liquid. He grabbed her shoulders, kneaded her breasts in his powerful hands and Sven, god of revenge, entered her again. Meanwhile, the goddess of anger awoke in her. Monstrous in the visions which filled her head she was bloodthirsty, desiring only destruction. Feeding on Sven's body like on dead meat, a carcass out of which she was sucking life. Until, finally, they had spent their anger on each other, and the lust evaporated.

When she woke up, all she felt was emptiness and pain. She left her husband's alcove and made her way to her own room.

"Dusza, draw me a bath," she said when she walked through the door.

When the servants had changed the swiftly cooling water three times, when she felt she had finally washed away those awful nights, she dressed, and asked Dusza to have Heidi Goat bring her sons to her.

Harald ran into the alcove shouting:

"Mama!"

And little Cnut reached his arms out to her. Goat passed him to Świętosława and she gathered both her boys close as she began to speak to them.

"Whatever happens, remember that I love you both."

"I know," little Harald said, winding a red curl around his finger. "Dusza told us . . ."

She held Harald close. Poor child, he had suffered during their days apart and he was confused. She didn't let her sons out of her arms until the evening. And when Heidi took them to put them to bed, Świętosława asked Dusza to bring her the cage with the second pair of Icelandic falcons.

"The ones Olav gave me."

Dusza returned with the cage.

"Now, leave me," Świętosława said.

5

DENMARK

Sven ordered Sigvald to leave Roskilde. He thanked him for the news, of course, and gave him the gifts and farewell which custom demanded. He didn't want the Jomsviking to see his fury, he didn't want Sigvald to revel in it. He wanted to stay alone with his rage to plan his vengeance on Olav and Tyra.

"Revenge is a dish best served cold, my lord, remember that, I beg you, in the name of all the years we have shared," Jorun pleaded with him. "Don't command us to board the *Wind Hunter* or ready the fleet. Winter is coming; it is a bad time for journeys. We'll go with you wherever you want to go, you know that. But don't let emotion cloud your judgment."

They spent all winter deciding on the best course of action. It occupied them in the long evenings and the short days which were barely marked by the lazy appearance of a weak sun. Sven found more energy when the time of Yule arrived—or, as his wife preferred to refer to it, Christmastime. She was the reason for his newfound liveliness: her belly had grown again.

"We conceived Cnut because of the knot on my handkerchief, while this child has been created in our anger," she observed sadly. "That's not a good omen for a new life."

"Why not?" he asked, affronted. "Maybe you'll give birth to an avenger."

"I don't want to wait that long for revenge, Sven," she told him. "The days we spend now in darkness are pure torment. We need to decide on something."

"I swear that we won't let this go without making them pay," he promised. "But now, accept this gift from me which I had intended to give to you long ago, but which slipped my mind in the aftermath of Tyra's disappearance."

He gave her the brooch he'd purchased from Morcar Frog. A golden fish clutched in the claws of two eagles. She looked lost in thought as she stroked the fish scales with her finger.

"It's a beautiful thing," she said, attaching the brooch to her dress. "Thank you."

She walked to her rooms, accompanied by Wilczan, Ion, and the axemen who had begun to serve her at some point in the past she couldn't determine, following Great Ulf's orders, guarding her door and never leaving her side. She walked away, taking Cnut, Harald, and the two lynxes with her.

Sven did not understand his wife or the violent mood swings which shifted from anger to sadness. He decided it must be her third pregnancy. He, as the king, had to make his plans with a level head so that his queen's wild need for vengeance could be sated.

He didn't tell her that he wasn't going to sail to Norway. He was afraid of her, in truth—of her anger, that she might not understand and brand him a coward. But he wasn't. If this was only about him, he'd gather a loyal crew, board the *Wind Hunter,* and be at Trondheimfiord within a week, shooting a burning arrow at Olav to declare war. But wars cannot be won with only one ship, and his chieftains were refusing him. They still had the bitter memories of the battle fought fifteen years earlier, the battle in Hjørung Bay which his father Harald Bluetooth had seen as an opportunity to discipline Norway and its then-leader Jarl Haakon. Harald had summoned the Jomsviking troops and many of his own men, few of whom returned, because Haakon defeated the united warriors on his waters and never paid tribute to Denmark again. The memory of that defeat was firmly lodged in the memories of his men and in Jomsborg's Jarl Sigvald, who had ordered his warriors retreat, sealing all their fates.

"My lord," Jorun said one night when they were discussing the best way to win the chieftains to their side. "The son of that victor, Jarl Haakon, is your daughter Gyda's husband. He comes from those lands and waters, so if there is any advantage to be found, he should know of it. Eric, though he was still young, fought at his father's side that day."

Sven summoned his son-in-law Eric to Roskilde.

"I won't tell you of that battle, my king, since you know what happened and I doubt you wish to hear of it again. Nobody really knows why things happened the way they did though. They said that my father Jarl Haakon sacrificed his youngest son, throwing him to his wild goddesses who sent hail to rain down on the united Danish and Jomsviking troops. A sky which was covered with black clouds. Those I saw, and I felt the hail, but I saw no divine beings. It's also true that my brother died, but whether he died as a sacrifice or drowned by accident, I don't know. I wasn't there, I was at the bow of my ship, fighting. I'll tell you something else, my king. There are men in Norway who still wish me well, and who travel around the country, watching, listening, and telling me what they learn. Olav Tryggvason may have disinclined many from supporting his cause by the brutal ways in which he is converting people to his faith, but he has proven to be a good king and leader. The law reigns supreme. It may be a hard law, but it is still the law. He has brought back the duty of burning fires on the islands, a duty my father neglected, which allows sailors to reach their ports safely, while the guards on the coast . . ."

"I understand," Sven interrupted. "They inform him of every approaching vessel."

"Yes, my lord," Eric confirmed. "There is no way for a fleet to reach Nidaros unnoticed. The trail of sea lanterns is so thick that the king will find out within a day that you are sailing to war even if he is far in the north. First, the nobles of the south will send their ships to face you. They are the weakest link and you will defeat them, but the time you lose in battle will be enough for Olav to gather his army. When you sail onward after defeating the lords of the south, the pirates of Sogn will attack you, since they serve the king. Tens of small, nimble boats will weaken your fleet, night after night. You won't be able to replenish your supplies on land because they will shoot your rowers and helmsmen from where they hide behind the rocks. It's a noose of fjords, bays, and islets, all of which look as beautiful as heaven on earth. A deadly noose. If you're lucky, you will sail through it and reach Gula, where you will be met with troops of the western lords. You won't reach any agreements with them since three of the most important ones are Olav's brothers-in-law. He gave them his sisters to wed when he baptized them. They will fight you. If by some miracle you make it past their ships, you'll face the king's main army. They will meet you either at the infamous Hjørung Bay, or at the entrance to Trondheimfiord. And I warn you now: the worst thing for an invader is not to see the defender's troops before entering."

"Why is that?" Sven asked.

"Because the fjord's waters are the best line of defense for those who occupy Lade and Nidaros. The king's defenders can win the war there without giving their archers a single order. All they need to do is wait for the wind which will awake the vortexes that lie dormant in the water and which will drown any invading ship. That's how the kings of old used to win the wars, the kings from the legends. The Danish ruled us not only because they defeated us in their own waters, but because they turned our own lords and rulers against each other. It's a sad secret, but you deserve a truthful answer."

Sven made his son-in-law comfortable and let his thoughts drift. Once the welcome feast was nearing an end and his men had fallen asleep with their heads on the tables and benches, his mind was clearer. He knew that he must kill Olav. He needed to do more than just to defeat his army; he needed to kill the king.

And he couldn't do it in secret. It couldn't be a silent, invisible assassin who took the life of the Norwegian king; it had to be he, the Danish king, and he must do it with the world watching them. Not in the deadly Norwegian fjords, but in his own waters.

"So, he must invade me, and not the other way around," Sven said, sweeping away empty cups the next morning. Olav would have to be drawn out of the fjords.

Jorun woke up at the sound of a jug clattering to the floor.

". . . other way around?" he repeated sleepily. "What reason will you give him to do that?"

"That's what I'm going to go find now," Sven said, and walked out toward the port.

Świętosława gave birth in summer.

"A daughter!" Heidi Goat howled happily. "We have a daughter!"

Fury's daughter, Świętosława thought. *My first daughter.*

"I need many of them, my lady." Sven kissed her forehead when he came to tell her of his joy at the news.

"Why?" she asked, trying to provoke him. "Are you planning alliances already? That's odd, I thought your mind was occupied with revenge."

"We'll talk once you've recovered from the trials of labor and you've come back to us." He leaned over her again and the smell of wine wafted off him. Świętosława felt nauseous and pushed him away.

"I haven't gone anywhere so I have no place from which I need to return," she said. "But you have been drinking, I can tell. You won't find the best route to Nidaros in your cup, you must ask the sailors. It's high time you sent for your sister and brought her back to Roskilde."

"What if Tyra has given Olav a son?" he asked with a smile.

"Then that's evidence that you've taken too long, my lord," she quipped.

He rarely entered her private chambers. He took the opportunity to have a careful look around now, which bothered her. She wanted to set her lynxes on him. The girl wriggled in her arms.

"What shall we name her?" she asked her husband.

"Gunhild, perhaps?" He grinned insolently and cocked his head.

"Haven't you had enough yet? Be serious," she snarled.

He stopped smiling.

"Astrid. Princess Astrid."

"Astrid?" she repeated thoughtfully. "A child conceived in anger is to bear the same name as my ever-serene sister?"

The child opened her swollen eyes.

"Astrid. It's a good name."

"My lady must rest and change," Melkorka said firmly, clearly made as uncomfortable by Sven's presence as Świętosława herself.

"You've named her. Leave us now."

The red-haired man moved toward the door, but he turned back. Leaning down, he rummaged between the floorboards and lifted his hand with something held between his fingers.

"A falcon's feather," he said thoughtfully, and glanced at Świętosława.

"I deplumed them," she replied with a shrug. "And I sent them back."

It was the most horrific thing she'd ever done. She could still feel the soreness in the tips of her fingers. She had been governed by rage, wounded pride, and the love she wanted to kill. *"If you want to see me, send a falcon."* Years ago, when she had sent one of them, Sven had arrived with his entire fleet. Had she called him? No. Had she desired him? No. Had he given her a choice? No. But Olav didn't have to marry Tyra. He did it anyway though, and that meant he deserved her anger. She sent him the deplumed falcons when they were still alive.

"To where?" Sven asked.

"Nowhere," she replied. "Go, I'm tired. I've given you a daughter."

"And a reason," Sven said as he walked out.

An excuse? She thought for a moment, but then Astrid began to cry and she had to be soothed. *How strange it is,* she thought as she gazed at her daughter, *that newborns can be distinguished from each other although they look so alike. Girls are so different from boys with their tiny little bodies.*

Dusza sat on the edge of the bed and did what she had done with all the previous children: she examined the baby's head. She lifted her pale eyes to meet Świętosława's, who knew immediately that something was wrong. Astrid had no mark on her skull. Świętosława held the girl tighter to her breast.

"It doesn't matter," she said defensively. "She's mine anyway."

But her milk ran dry after only three days, and Heidi took the baby. She hadn't been feeding Cnut for some time now, so she happily gave back the goldsmith's son and took Astrid instead.

"My first royal daughter," the Goat said with pride.

Świętosława was weak after she lost her milk. She didn't rise from bed or attend any of the feasts held by her husband. She ordered Arnora be brought to her so she wouldn't go mad in isolation.

"Tell me something, and Dusza will pour you wine," she welcomed the tribal queen.

"Maybe Dusza will speak while I drink the wine?" Arnora chuckled.

"Don't mock!" Świętosława reprimanded her. "I had a daughter."

"I know, I know. Your axemen made a lot of noise. 'A princess! A princess!' they shouted. Speaking of which, how did you take them away from Sven, eh?"

"You don't go to church, so you know nothing." Świętosława waved a hand. "I set them a good example and prayed with them, let's put it that way."

"I have nothing against the Church, my queen," Arnora replied. "But I hate those masqueraders. Your Ion drives me mad. I'm surprised to see that you keep such a cowardly odd thing at your side. Surely you know that cowards are the most dangerous men of all?"

"I know, Arnora. Cowards are unpredictable. But Ion is a harmless coward, I assure you. He's a poor monk, an unrivaled glutton, and probably an unsated lover, but he has been with me in my bloodiest moments and I have a soft spot for him. He saved my eldest son Olof's life. Leave him be."

"Whatever you say, my queen. Do you know who ordered my husband and sons beheaded?"

"Dusza, refill Arnora's goblet," she commanded, thinking that the tribal queen's cup could not be empty for such a story.

"The masquerader Oddinkarr," Arnora said accusingly after she took a sip of wine.

"The Bishop of Ribe?" Świętosława had thought it had been Sven who ordered Arnora's family to be murdered, in revenge for their old claims to the throne.

"Yes. He wanted to win your red-haired king's favor," Arnora said flatly. "His own hands were stained with treason, and a faithless man will always point at another traitor. They came to Lejre at night, like wolves. They surrounded our manor and dragged us from our beds. Oddinkarr stood in the yard and when his men wanted to kill us, he said: 'The old crone will bring the heads of her family with her.' So, they separated me from my husband and my sons, and took their heads."

"That's ghastly," Świętosława whispered.

"What was ghastly was the journey back. I sat in the cart and held their heads in my lap. Eyes wide open in horror, congealing blood . . ."

Dusza dropped the jug she'd been holding.

"And wine is spilled, is it, Dusza?" Arnora chuckled. "Tales of old had always been told in my family home. Before I was married, I knew all the gloomy stories of men and women, the hundreds of years of kinship forged by suffering, the tens of rivers of spilled blood. No, I was under no illusions, young queen, that my fate would be any brighter than that of the women who came before me. Do you know what befell Gudrun?"

"The song of Gudrun and Sivrit who killed the dragon and won its treasure? Yes, I've heard that one."

Arnora straightened her back and stretched her wrinkled neck.

"Her pain was nothing," she said. "He married her while he was in love with another, it happens. That's not suffering, that's just pain. Gudrun's suffering began when she was forced to marry the chieftain known as Atli."

"Jesus." Świętosława flinched with a bitter laugh. "When you talk like that,

I have chills all over. If my milk hadn't run dry days ago, it would undoubtedly have done so at your words."

"If you want to hear about the woman who was touched by death in all its guises, then listen . . ."

Arnora continued while Świętosława became lost in her own thoughts. *That wasn't suffering?* she repeated after the old woman. *That was just pain? He married one even though he loved another.* Why hadn't she realized before that Olav's decision was intended as a blow against Sven? Revenge for taking her, Świętosława, and forcing her to wed him. Since Jarl Sigvald had brought news of Olav and Tyra's marriage, she had thought only of herself and of Olav's betrayal. But none of them had decided for themselves before. They couldn't make decisions based on their own feelings. Could they? Could she not have acted differently just that one time, in Sigtuna, before Sven had arrived? She had been carried away by her pride and anger. She had refused him then, and she'd refused him now—refused him the right to be as angry as she'd been. She felt the pressure of every feather she'd pulled out of the falcons' bodies and a cold sweat broke over her brow. She had been in the wrong. She had been bold and wrong.

I need to confess, she thought feverishly. *I need to confess the sins which darken my soul, governed as it has been by anger and pride.*

". . . Gudrun knew that her brothers would meet their deaths at her husband's hand in his court. She wanted to warn them and sent them a ring with a wolf's hair twined around it, to communicate to them that if they accepted the invitation, they had a dangerous journey ahead . . ."

"Arnora," Świętosława interrupted her. "Forgive me, but I have just remembered something. Do you remember what you called me the first time we spoke?"

"Oh, youth! It always thinks that what is today is less important than what has already passed. But time is like a snake gnawing its own tail . . ."

"Arnora," she asked. "Please, tell me: Why did you call me Thorn Queen?"

The old woman looked at her with pale eyes that had lost none of their liveliness, as if time had made its mark on every part of her features but that. On her wrinkled skin, gray hair, stooping back, and dark spots on her hands. Her eyes carried a challenge and not a shred of pity.

"Because my eyesight is good up close," Arnora said. "The women of rulers are either wives or mistresses. Wives can be either child-bearers or queens. Both will decorate their heads and chests with jewels, but queens always carry thorns in their hearts."

"I understand," Świętosława said quietly. "Thank you for your stories. Dusza will help you back to your room."

Once Arnora and Dusza had left, she didn't hesitate for a moment longer. She ordered Ion be brought to her, and when he came, he sent all her servants away.

"Let nobody disturb me. The lynxes will guard the door."

They were left alone.

"My lady?" Ion asked. "What's happened?"

"Something that should have happened a long time ago. My monk, I need to confess."

"I . . ." Ion spread his chubby hands wide. "Well, you know . . . maybe I should call for Wulfric?"

"No," she forbade him. "Wulfric is Sven's man. I know you don't have the power to absolve me, but I need you to hear my confession. Only God can forgive me now."

6

NORWAY

Olav returned to Nidaros for winter, after his encounter with Bjarni. His queen seemed more beautiful to him than when he'd left her.

"Are you with child, my lady?" he asked, touching her braid.

"No, my king." She blushed. "They say two are needed for that to happen."

"Here I am!"

"Which is good, since we have had visitors from Roskilde while you were gone. They have brought the sound of Sven's anger with them."

Olav laughed. He could almost see the other king simmer and redden in anger. Tyra looked at him with surprise.

"That amuses you, my lord? They said that Sven and his queen have vowed to have their revenge."

"Are you saying this was not what you'd expected, my lady?" he asked coldly.

He wasn't afraid of Sven's anger, but he was stricken by Świętosława's fury. "Did they say anything else?"

"They brought with them two dead birds, but I had them thrown away. They'd started rotting."

"What birds?" he asked.

Supper was served at that exact moment, and Tyra, glancing at him meaningfully, shrugged.

"Let's not talk of such things over our meal."

"Whatever you wish, my lady."

He didn't come back to it. He knew that it must have been the falcons. He busied himself with things a king who had just returned from a voyage should occupy himself with. He passed his judgment on disagreements and took in peasants and sailors under his protection when they came to him, attracted by stories of his power. He gave away white baptismal robes. His home hearth did not keep him warm, or at least, not warm enough to keep his attention away from other matters. He had subdued Norway when he defeated Tore Stag, and he joined Lofoten to the rest of the kingdom, but now Iceland occupied his thoughts. A cross planted on the Isle of Ice would be the crowning achievement of his mission. But Iceland would have to wait until he won over the Orkney Islands.

He sailed there in spring to spread his faith and power. His first meeting with its inhabitants was not a happy one, since it involved the revolt of their leader, Sivrit, known as the Grandson of the Skull Cleaver.

"I'm tired," he told Varin, "of these people and their awful nicknames. Beside Skull Cleaver, Tore Stag sounds full of finesse. What will they call us when we die?"

"I will be Varin Painted Fangs. Unless they fall out and I end up a toothless old man. And you? They used to call you Silver Ole, but that was in the days that the danegeld you got from Ethelred was your greatest achievement."

"What do they call me behind my back?"

"The Beast with the Cross." Varin spat into the water. "It could be worse."

"It could be worse, my friend," Olav agreed. "Come on, let's baptize the Grandson of the Skull Cleaver."

They did baptize him, but only after Olav threatened to kill his son, also known as the Pup.

"The name you gave the boy will turn out to be prophetic," Olav warned the father. "Because he won't live long enough to become a man."

That was enough for them to denounce Evil. The bishop heard their confessions, baptized them, and Olav gave them his blessing.

"The Orkneys are yours!" Sivrit embraced him. "But you look tired, my lord."

"Let's sail to Lofoten. I want to see the northern lights," Olav replied.

Hårek, to whom Tryggvason had given Hålogaland when he left, lived at the great manor in Borg which they had taken from Tore Stag.

"I knew my king would return!" He spread his arms wide when he saw them at his door. "The household is yours, my lord. I am your servant, cup-bearer, and guide to the land of northern lights. Only don't make me sing."

"See, Hårek? Omold is with me; he's been thinking of what rhymes with 'lights' all the way here."

"Lights, sights, as our Lofoten bards say," Hårek suggested.

"Anyone can come up with that," Omold retorted.

"My lord, where is my head—there is a guest waiting for you!"

"Bjarni?" Olav asked hopefully.

"No. Were you expecting him?" Hårek narrowed his eyes. "If so, then the

Son of the Bear has disappointed you. Instead of a pagan, a man of God is waiting for you, Father Thangbrand. He's come from Iceland."

Olav had sent Thangbrand to Iceland two years earlier. Everything he'd heard of the Isle of Ice fascinated him, and he'd felt that baptizing it would be the ultimate evidence of his triumph.

"Many years ago, those who didn't like the rule of my ancestor Harald Fairhaired escaped from Norway to Iceland," he'd say. "When they accept the word of God from me and are baptized at my hand, it will be as if I'm returning them home."

Now returned, Thangbrand didn't look well. He'd lost weight and his skin looked gray.

"King," he called out when Olav entered the great hall. "My lord."

"What news do you bring, my friend?" Tryggvason asked in greeting.

"Not good news, I'm afraid." Thangbrand grimaced. "Icelanders are stubborn and have devilish natures."

"Maybe you didn't try hard enough to win them over?" Sivrit inquired.

"I baptized a few of them as soon as I landed. They volunteered. Gizur the White, Hall, and Hjati. Good men. But when I traveled inland, encouraged by my success, I was met only with sadness. The Althing, their great council, chased me away."

"I don't understand," Olav persisted. "Those three came to you of their own free will. Does that mean you didn't convert a single man there?"

"That's right," the priest admitted. "You understood correctly. Iceland is lost."

"You're wrong, Thangbrand," Olav replied. "You're lost to Iceland, not Iceland to God. Drink something while I think. Don't worry, I won't send you away in the middle of winter."

When the priest had left them, Olav turned to his bishop. "Thangbrand failed. I made a mistake sending him to a country I care for so much."

"True," Sivrit agreed. "But didn't we come here to relish God's spectacle? Do we have to constantly talk about our sins? Let's drink, my lord, not as a king and bishop, but as friends who are in the middle of a long and harrowing journey."

They drank until Hårek walked into the hall in the middle of the endless night and said, "Get your warmest furs. It has begun."

As they stood in the icy wilderness, it felt as if they stood on the edge of a world made entirely of snow. Above them, the sky pulsed with an unearthly light.

"The Fins say that any dead soul can be summoned through the lights. All you have to do is whistle and the one you call upon will come to us from beyond the grave," Hårek said as he stared up at the sky. "But that's just Finnish gossip . . . Pagans." He glanced nervously at the bishop.

Sivrit wasn't listening. He had spread his arms wide and was turning around in a circle, whispering all the while:

"The Lord's archangels are stepping down onto the earth." He dropped to his knees.

"My mother told me that this is the only chance, other than on your deathbed, to see the Valkyries. I think I see them . . ." Omold whispered. "Jesus, what beauty . . . I want to die . . ."

Vigi was running round in circles as if he were trying to determine where the lights began and ended. He never caught up with them or discovered their radiant source. He sat down, opened his muzzle and lifted his head upward as if he was going to howl, but he made no sound, only letting out a steamy breath. A white dog on white snow.

Olav absorbed the sight of the green light which seemed to be dancing circles around them. He thought he could hear the aurora's song. Yes, he could see all his men staring at the lights which commanded their attention, but he couldn't hear them. He was alone. It was just him and the aurora, the frozen breath of God. He spoke with the Almighty without using words, worshipping him in nature. *What if this is the path to eternal life?* he thought. *I'm ready, my Lord. Take me.*

The moment the thought crossed his mind, he heard a high-pitched whistle which transformed into a familiar voice. Świętosława? Yes, it was she! She was calling him melodically across the seas. *Be quiet,* he thought to her. *Don't say anything. I want to watch the lights with you.*

Hårek gathered them all together and led them back to the hall and the fire which burnt in the hearth.

"You'll freeze." He laughed. "The aurora will be here all winter, that's enough for now. Bard, I'm waiting to hear your poem. Where are your rhymes?"

Omold's face was red with cold and icicles adorned his beard. His gaze was absent.

"What do you want? What's going on?" he asked, staring at Hårek unseeingly.

"Rhymes! You were meant to write a poem about the lights."

"No way," the bard decided. "I'd be a fool to try to capture what I just saw in mere words. I will drink, not rhyme."

"The lights are God's work." Bishop Sivrit nodded with a blissful expression. "God's work."

Varin was whispering something, convulsively rubbing his eyes every now and then. Eventually he let out a long breath, grabbed a horn with mead from Hårek, drank it, and groaned.

"There was baptism by water and by fire. We have just been baptized by the aurora."

Olav was silent.

They sailed to Nidaros in spring.

Queen Tyra came out to meet them with an armful of flowers. Bishop Sivrit winked to Olav.

"I thought that Queen Tyra would greet us with your son in her arms. But children can be created at any moment, and who knows when we will sail to see the lights again."

"You're right, my friend," Olav replied just as quietly. "I hope that when we see them again, I'll feel what I did the first time."

"How would you describe it?" the bishop asked curiously.

Olav shook his head.

"I am no better than Omold, I don't have the words. I don't know if I saw nature in God, or God in nature."

"You're right, my friend," Varin muttered, moving to stand beside them. "But prepare yourself, for a queen approaches you and she is jealous of the northern lights."

DENMARK

Świętosława and Sven celebrated the Lord's Resurrection with their three children. Three-year-old Harald walked beside his father, two-year-old Cnut accompanied his mother while holding on to the lynxes' collars, and Sven carried Astrid in his arms.

The snakelike Thorgils of Jelling stood in the main crowd by the church with his son Ulf and was the first to cry out:

"Long live the royal family!"

"I invite everyone to the feast!" Sven announced. "Christ has risen again. Let us rejoice!"

Świętosława barely recognized him of late. Sven was acting different and no longer imposed himself upon her. Had he really decided he wanted to become a Christian king?

Joining them for the celebrations were Sven's eldest daughter, Gyda, and her new husband, Eric, the young jarl who had not long ago advised the king against sailing toward Norway. Gyda still looked very young, though Jarl Eric showed no sign of it bothering him. He treated her with the respect a wife deserved.

"They suit each other." Melkorka wiped away a tear, taking the children from Świętosława when they had grown bored of the festivities.

"Indeed," Świętosława said, knowing that young Eric had really married Sven, not Gyda. Only a strong father-in-law could help him return to power. And it was no secret at whose cost.

Since she had opened her heart to Ion, her fury had evaporated. She had no way of knowing whether God would forgive her, but she felt the relief that confession always brought with it. The months since Astrid's birth, as Sven's temper had cooled and he'd fallen silent and distant, no longer speaking of vengeance, had been a time of healing for her.

"Our lady grows more beautiful with every child." Haakon of Funen smiled at her so broadly that the scar under his eye seemed to lengthen.

"King Sven is a lucky man," the gray-haired Gunar of Limfiord called out. "Two sons and a daughter!"

"A second girl would be needed to balance the scales." The chubby Uddorm of Viborg contributed his wisdom.

"Maybe a third," Ragn of the Isles added.

Only Thorgils from Jelling spared her the empty words. She knew him to be far too cunning for it. She watched the jarl of Jelling discreetly. And he spent most of his time watching Eric when he thought no one was looking. Świętosława said nothing, drinking mead and watching the players.

"It's time to gather men for another journey to England." Jarl Stenkil of Hobro spoke up. "What do you say, King?"

Sven had never neglected England. He made sure that the English never forgot him, though he hadn't recently traveled there himself. In the past years he had named a different jarl each time to lead his men. This allowed his chiefs and soldiers to enrich themselves as well as him, and he did not have to show favor to any one in particular, keeping the power among the nobles balanced.

"Perhaps," Sven replied cryptically, taking a sip of wine. "But perhaps I will have different plans this year."

Świętosława noticed Thorgils's eyes narrow and Jarl Eric squirm in his seat.

"But it's my turn!" Stenkil's expression betrayed his dissatisfaction with the possibility of "different plans."

"What plans?" Ragn of the Isles asked with interest. He'd led the expedition to England the previous year.

"Royal plans." Sven chuckled.

She felt the blood drain from her face and, when Sven laid a hand on hers moments later, felt it freeze in her veins.

"My queen"—he raised her hand and kissed it in front of everyone—"expects an act of vengeance. I have promised my lady justice a long time ago, and only the birth of our sweet Astrid has delayed me. But we know this matter is urgent."

"My king," she said, smiling with pride, "overestimates my desire for revenge. It is the duty of queens to be merciful. If we are to speak of this ancient history, know, my lord, that I have forgiven the sinners."

He rose and walked to her while the smile never left his face. She knew that smile. It had nothing to do with joy. Wrzask slept on one side of her chair; Sven walked around the lynx and stood behind the throne, placing his hands on her shoulders, and brought his head close to hers. She could feel his breath on her hair.

"What could possibly have happened to have changed my lady's mind? Was it not in this very hall that our bold queen had shouted: *'How dare he! He's insulted you, husband. Humiliated you by taking your sister without your consent'?*"

The fingers of his right hand tightened on her shoulder while he stroked her hair with his left.

"Wife," he whispered to her. "Do you not remember when you told me to plan revenge instead of alliances?"

She felt like a bowstring strung too tight. She couldn't let herself be herself and answer his provoking questions. It took everything she had to make her laugh sound genuine.

"I will not deny my anger when Sigvald brought news of your sister's marriage, but anger evaporates with time. I had Astrid, our sons are growing up strong and healthy, and I, husband, am happy. I don't want to deny others the right to . . ."

"Love?" he suggested.

"And happiness," she added.

Their guests stared at them. She could see Great Ulf's wariness, Thorgils's narrowed eyes, Ion's nervous fidgeting. Jarl Eric leaned over to Gyda and whispered something to her. The girl shook her head, looking surprised.

Sven suddenly straightened and stopped stroking her hair, placing both of his hands on her shoulders again.

"Perhaps we should call you Good Lady instead of Bold Lady?"

"Whatever you wish. Everyone knows how much you like to give me names."

"Indeed. And how little you like to accept them." He laughed again. "For reasons known only to yourself."

What is he playing at? she wondered feverishly.

Wrzask growled in warning. Even without this, she knew that there was more to Sven's words than he was willing to share.

"It's too late," Sven called out melodically. "It's too late to change your mind. Even if the Bold One became Good, it's too late now."

Christ, save me! she implored inwardly, though her features remained unmoved.

"I have planned to invade Norway, thinking it would please my queen. But alas!" His fingers on her shoulders tightened even more.

Wrzask stood up and bared his fangs. Zgrzyt rose on the other side of her chair. Sven knew the lynxes' game. He kissed Świętosława's cheek and let go of her, returning to his seat. The cats watched him go before lazily lying back down.

It's a pity they didn't go for his throat, she thought, feeling a different spark of vengeance now.

"We will invade Olav Tryggvason, even if my lady has lost her heart . . . for vengeance," Sven announced firmly. "My feelings are more stable. Norway was ruled by Denmark in my father's times, before Jarl Haakon's revolt. Today, his dear son is our ally, and I will venture to assume his brother Jarl Sven is, too."

"I can confirm that, my king," the once-heir of Lade replied.

That's why he invited him for the celebrations, she thought. *He wants to defeat Olav using Eric's hands. The young jarl probably still has many friends in Norway, ones who will betray their king at a moment's notice. "A faithless man will always point at another traitor,"* like Arnora said.

"Is the drafting of men in Sweden going according to plan?" Sven asked.

"In Sweden?!" she exclaimed. "How dare you do anything in Sweden without my consent? That is my kingdom!"

"It was yours once," he replied. "Now it is your son's. Did you not insist that our wedding agreement name your son king of the Swedes?"

This is a despicable game, she thought.

"Yes. Olof King of Swedes, my firstborn son, is their only ruler. Why then are you drafting men from his lands?"

"Because my dear stepson is also my ally, my lady." He smiled coldly. "Your accusations are unfounded: I have no intention of threatening Olof's rule. Jarl Eric spoke to him on my behalf. Eric?"

"I did, my lady. I bring you your son's love. He asked me to send his warm-est wishes to his half siblings, too. He was happy to hear he had a sister."

"Olof agreed to give you his men to sail against"—she could barely force the words out—"King Olav?"

"And more besides. He thought it his duty and honor to do so. The young king follows your example and places honor above all else. He said that he never forgot how Tryggvason insulted you when he got angry."

This was unexpected. Świętosława's cheeks burned and she could do noth-ing to stop them.

"Ancient history." She laughed stiffly.

"But your son and husband remember it nevertheless," Sven declared.

She reached for her goblet. *Olof, my son*, she thought, *what have you gotten yourself into? And where was Wilkomir?*

"And so," the satisfied king continued, "we can be sure of Swedish support. Besides, we have all of the Danes who will not be sailing to England this year, and your army, son-in-law."

"It may not be big, my lord, but you know the men's worth," said Eric.

"It is not about how many men you lead into battle, but how many you lead out after it has been fought."

"I don't understand, my king." Eric looked confused.

You're too straitlaced to play against the Redbeard, she thought with horror. *You think of war as a fair fight, but he will have you convince Olav's men to refuse to follow him.*

She wasn't wrong. When Sven told Eric as much, the heir to Lade flushed. She held onto that, thinking that there may yet be hope in the young man. Perhaps he wouldn't agree?

"I don't know if that will be possible, my king. I'd have to go to Norway in secret and speak to the people," Eric admitted.

"Will you have time to drink with us to the success of your journey?" Sven asked cruelly. "Of course, sweet Gyda will stay in Roskilde under the care of her father and stepmother. Queen Sigrid can introduce her to the secrets of motherhood. Because you are expecting a child, isn't that right?"

"Not yet," whispered the embarrassed Gyda. "But I like children, and I'd love to help the queen with little Astrid . . ."

"Help her, my sweet." Sven was enjoying himself. "When your lord hus-band rises to the challenge I have given him, he will become Norway's viceroy before the year's end and he will return to his lands around Lade. An heir would please him, would he not, Eric?"

The young jarl nodded, no less embarrassed than Gyda.

Sven rose and spread his arms wide as he announced:

"My chieftains, lords and guests, let us rejoice and celebrate your king's resurrection!"

She went to his alcove that night.

"Sven? Are you asleep, my king?" she asked as she entered.

"No," he said from the shadows. "I've been waiting for you."

The darkness was her ally. She couldn't let him see her face.

"You knew I'd come," she purred affectionately.

"I knew," he replied.

"Are you ready?" She slipped under the soft covers and pressed herself against him.

"What for?" he asked, his voice sober and cold.

"For love." She stroked his chest.

"I have been ready for love since the day I took you as my wife."

She pressed herself even closer. Even if he had not been ready when she came into his bed, he was now, though Sven had made no move to bring her closer to him. He just lay there. She moved on top of him.

"Your sword in my scabbard," she groaned.

He still didn't move, though she did.

"Do you mean to conquer me, wife?" he asked.

"Yes," she said, grabbing his beard.

She pulled it gently. He moved his head out of her grasp, though usually he liked it. He still lay still, in complete control. Her hips were the ones moving skillfully.

"What are you fighting for?" he asked, and she could finally hear the quickened breath in his words.

"It's not a fight." She laughed throatily. "It's love! Ah . . ."

"For everything, then," he replied, and suddenly grabbed her hips.

He's breaking! she thought.

He pulled her off him and threw her onto the bed. He placed one hand on her back and entered her as he usually did. On his terms, brutally and hard, with no mercy. That's how her husband found his pleasure. Only this way could he reach bliss. She gave herself to him like a slave might, a captive of war, because she knew he liked the taste of that. She'd give herself to him like this as many times as he needed if she only knew that her surrender in bed would stop the war.

He cried out and rolled off her. They lay next to each other like wounded fighters.

"Who won?" she asked.

He didn't reply.

"Who is the victor?" she asked again in a whisper.

Her only answer was the sound of his loud breathing, shortly followed by a snore. She fell back onto the bed, powerless. Damn it! She had come here, subduing her fear and disgust, to win, but he only took what he wanted and fell asleep. Her fingers trembled when she put on her dress.

7

Astrid knew it was a bad idea, but her guilt would not let her refuse her sister. Świętosława's summons to Roskilde was not a queen's command, but a sister's heartfelt plea for help.

"How am I to do it?" she asked her husband. "Sven saw me when I was there as Morcar Frog's daughter, and he may remember my face . . ."

"I'd never forget you," Sigvald murmured into her ear.

"Stop it!" She jerked away from him. "Help me! We're in this mess together."

"Meet in Scania. Queen Sigrid ordered Jarl Gjotgar to oversee the building of a church in Lund on behalf of the king. It would provide a good excuse for her were she to journey there."

"No." Astrid dismissed the idea. "She said clearly that Sven is keeping a close eye on her, which is why we must meet in Roskilde."

Sigvald's long fingers wrapped around her waist. They were sitting in bed because this was the only place in which they could communicate.

"Which of Sven's men saw you near Morcar's ship?"

"The fair-haired one."

"Jorun. He was my guest in Jom alongside Sven." Sigvald stroked her belly button.

"And the axemen who protect him."

"They are harmless, they are now the queen's men."

"No one else."

"Then you can prepare for your journey, wife." He laid his head on her thigh. "Make sure you take stunning dresses, jewels, and such things with you. Those who saw you before will remember a modest merchant's daughter. Now, they'll see the rich and elegant Lady of Wolin. Believe me, people see what they want to see. You'll go with Geivar, because I wouldn't trust anyone other than that gloomy man with my wife's safety."

"And Sven? Do you think his eye can be tricked?" Astrid continued to worry.

"If you leave tomorrow, you should manage to avoid him. Geivar's scouts say that the king is headed to Funen to draft people to join his expedition to England. He's meant to go to Little Belt afterward for the same reason, to meet with the rich merchants of Hedeby."

"He won't be home? Are you sure?"

"Me? Geivar's men are sure. I'm only the bringer of good news, my lady."

"Stop!" Sigvald's games were driving her mad. Her husband clearly got some sort of unhealthy pleasure from the situation in which they found themselves. She snarled at him. "Don't forget that Świętosława knows nothing of our role in facilitating Olav and Tyra's marriage, and she can never find out."

"I'd be the last man who would want to tell her." Sigvald's hands were stroking Astrid's thighs. "Oh, if you only saw the fury with which she reacted at the news!" He chuckled as he kissed the inside of her thigh.

"That's enough." She pushed his head away. "I'm not amused by this. I'm angry for letting myself get involved in the first place."

THE BALTIC SEA

Astrid felt relief as they sailed out of Wolin. Sigvald was acting like a man devoid of any emotion. She knew him. Whenever he repeated his mantra, "the Jomsvikings don't meddle in kings' business," he was lying. He loved the business of kings. He played them as if he were playing hnefatafl.

Geivar was different; she enjoyed his silence. "The chief of the house of scouts doesn't speak because he knows how awful his fangs look," Sigvald would say when he was drunk. And every time he shared this pointless piece of wisdom, she wanted to tell him that a war hound did not need to bark. But she also preferred to keep her silence. Her power over Sigvald depended on her success at balancing discretion and pressure.

"When we reach the port, I'll send my men to court to notify the queen," Geivar told Astrid, laying out their plans as their destination neared. "We'll make sure that Sven is really gone and find out whether Jorun is with him. You, my lady, will have time to change and prepare for your meeting with the queen."

"With my sister," Astrid corrected him. "Believe me, Chief, after what has happened, I would much prefer to face Sigrid Storråda, the Bold One, than my sister."

"I understand," the Jomsviking replied. After a brief pause, he added, "I remember them both on the day she boarded the *Haughty Giantess* and left for Uppsala. I do not envy you, my lady."

That's reassuring, she thought.

DENMARK

Astrid's knees trembled when she strode into the manor in Roskilde, dressed up like a duchess and accompanied by Geivar's men who were presented as the Lady of Wolin's crew. Everywhere she looked reminded her of her last visit, when they had come in secret to steal a future queen, and she tried to push those thoughts away.

"Astrid!" Świętosława leapt up when she saw her. She held her daughter in her arms while her two boys played with the lynxes at her feet.

"My queen." Astrid bowed.

"Sister," Świętosława corrected her. "Come, we have been waiting for you."

She walked to meet Astrid and embraced her, still carrying her daughter.

"Meet my children! That red-haired ugly one is Harald, Sven's firstborn. The fair-haired beauty is Cnut . . ."

The queen's son, Astrid had heard people say on the day of his birth. She had been mere steps away from this very hall.

". . . while this sweet girl of yet undetermined charms is Astrid. Are you happy, sister? I never let your namesake out of my arms. You know the cats and they remember you . . ."

Most of all, on that day, Astrid had feared the cats. That she would see them, that they would greet her and lick her hands and face, alerting the servants to her identity.

". . . Wrzask, don't jump at Astrid! Chase him away or hit him, he won't harm you. You know, I am afraid that they might soon grow old and lazy . . . Ah, but where is my hospitality! You must be hungry and thirsty after your journey. Meet Vali. Yes, yes, this beauty is unmatched in the kitchen, ever since our dear Melkorka has agreed to look after our children. Melkorka, come here, I want my sister to meet you. And here is Astrid's wet nurse. Heidi, don't be embarrassed. Astrid, what would you call Heidi if you were giving people nicknames, as people often do?"

"Goat," Astrid replied without hesitation, interrupting the flow of words from her sister.

"Indeed. Heidi the Goat has the milkiest breasts in Roskilde. Do you want to hold Astrid?"

Before she had a chance to respond, Świętosława had handed her the baby.

"Do you recognize Great Ulf? He came to Poznań with me when I bid Father farewell. When I look at him, I think that some men never age."

That wasn't true. Even this giant wasn't immune to time; though his back was still straight and strong, and his years did not make their presence known in a big belly, the lines which marked his face were deeper than before.

"And Ion, our monk. Ion, bow to the Lady of Wolin."

She froze. The fat man in the habit. He had walked into her that day when she was running out of the manor. Tyra had been asleep in the chest, under the influence of poppyseeds, as she was carried out by Morcar's men who had to pretend the chest was light and empty. She had run ahead, as if she was in a hurry to get back to her father, and this fat man had walked into her in the manor's doorway. Did he remember her?

She bowed her head arrogantly and pretended she barely noticed him.

"Lady of Wolin," he said to her. "I heard that there is not a single temple of the Lord in the wealthiest port on the coast of the Baltic Sea. Is that true?"

"Not entirely, monk," she replied. "There is a Slavic temple, a place to worship Odin and Freya, a place where those faithful to the northern gods meet. Allah's followers meet in the Arabic merchant's home, and the Jews meet on the outskirts of town. Every one of them will call their god 'Lord,' so they are all temples of the Lord. But regardless of which god they pray to, the merchants all believe in one thing: profit. In this way, the wealthiest port on the Baltic coastline is one great temple to the god of profit."

Świętosława laughed so loudly that the lynxes began to growl.

"Forgive me, Ion," she said once she'd regained her breath. "I want to spend some time with my sister. I have you every day, but I see her rarely. Take whatever you want from the table; I know you like Vali's roasted ham."

"I would prefer her thighs," the monk muttered and picked out the finest bits while casting Astrid suspicious glances. "I will bid you both farewell. If I can be of any use, I won't be far."

"I know where to find you." Her sister laughed.

The monk snorted and walked out.

"Heidi, take Astrid. She looks hungry. Melkorka, my dear, bring us some mead. And you, sister, tell me news of Poznań," Świętosława ordered and, once the goat-like girl took the baby from her arms, added in a whisper: "Tell me anything. We will talk properly once we're in my rooms." Then, speaking at a normal volume again, she asked: "How is Bolesław? And Duchess Emnilda? Still milk and honey?"

"Nobody dares call his firstborn 'Bezprym the Black Hungarian' anymore, at least not within his earshot. He's grown up, he looks like a man, and Bolesław keeps him at his side, along with young Mieszko."

"How old are they?"

"Bezprym is almost fourteen, Mieszko is nine. Do you remember the girls?"

"Two angels wearing crowns of flowers."

"One of them will always wear a crown of something on her head, just not one made of flowers." Astrid sighed. "Bogumiła, the elder, has been sent to a nunnery."

"You're joking?"

"Bolesław decided that since he has been blessed with five children, he owes one to God."

"I wonder why he didn't choose a son for that honor." Her sister shrugged.

"He has only two, although if I know him at all, he won't leave Emnilda alone until he balances that out. Three daughters to three sons."

"Good." Her sister winked. "Then one of the boys can be given to the Church, too. We'll have a bishop in the dynasty!"

"He is planning to build a beautiful church in Gniezno. He has the remains of a saint there which have already attracted masses."

"Bishop Adalbert, yes, I heard. What about Unger?"

"I keep my distance," Astrid retorted.

"And nobody has managed to baptize you yet! You only got away with it because of Father's love for you. Although it really would be in the best interests of your soul . . ."

"Give it a rest." Astrid waved a hand. "Don't we have better things to talk about?"

Świętosława's eyes gleamed in a most feral-like manner.

When they were both in the alcove with no one but Dusza and the lynxes for company, Świętosława exploded.

"I beg you, sister, help me! I'm trapped. Please don't deny me, this is life and death!"

Astrid took a deep breath.

"Tell me."

"Sven is gathering his armies. This time, it is not to go to England, but to fight Olav. He has manipulated my son Olof, sending the jarl of Lade, Eric, to speak to him without my knowledge. Do you understand?"

Astrid understood more than her sister thought she did.

"The war of kings," she whispered, feeling her heart hammering in her chest as if it wanted to beat its way out of it.

"Yes, the war of kings. I did what I could to stop it, but it was impossible. I can change its outcome only by playing my last card. I need your help!"

"What do you mean?" She searched her sister's face.

"Treason." Świętosława sounded as if she were choking on a fish bone. "I have already committed it when I asked you to come here. I want you to warn Olav through your husband. And"—she looked directly into Astrid's eyes—"I want to pay the Jomsvikings to fight in this battle. For Tryggvason."

"Wait." Astrid chose her words carefully. "The Jomsvikings and Tryggvason? But your husband and son will be facing them."

"No." Her sister shook her head. "I sent a trusted man to Olof. He will convince my son to join the Norwegian king."

Damn it! Astrid thought.

"What do you think?" Świętosława whispered feverishly. "Who will my son listen to? His stepfather Sven or his mother? His mother, of course he'll listen to his mother. It's a chance for him. He can free himself of Sven and his increased influence in Swedish matters."

"Wait," Astrid requested. "Wait, I need to get my head around this . . . What about Sven?"

Świętosława clutched her hands. Her green eyes glittered as if she had a fever, and her expression was grave.

"They must defeat him," she said. "They must. My message to Olav is: Defeat my husband. I will give you my hand and Denmark's throne in return, which you can take when you come for the widow queen."

A loud sigh interrupted them—it sounded almost like a groan. They turned around as if someone had burned them.

"Dusza?" they both said.

A terrified Dusza covered her mouth with her hands. She made a sign to tell them to continue and ignore her.

"Sven, when he took me for his wife after Eric's death, indirectly took Sweden. My son is still king, but Sven's influence, as I have recently been made aware, is already too strong. Olav can do the same thing after Sven's death. It will work."

"If they defeat Sven," Astrid pointed out doubtfully. "But wait. The Jomsvikings really could change the battle's outcome."

"Yes, sister! I want my son to pretend to fight alongside Sven, to avoid rousing suspicion too early. I told him to change sides at the last minute. That will be one surprise. And the other will be the arrival of your Jomsvikings."

"They are not mine but Sigvald's, but I believe that Bolesław will support your plan. He has always sympathized with Olav. I think he will order the Jomsvikings to help."

He already promised as much the day Olav's marriage to Tyra was first discussed. Our brother predicted all this a long time ago, Astrid thought frantically.

"There is also the heir of Lade, Eric, and his brother Sven," Świętosława added quickly. "They will both stand against Olav. As you know, Eric is my husband's son-in-law. Olav must be told that Eric is searching for allies in Norway. Olav must know . . ."

"How much time do we have?"

"Not much. Sven didn't announce an exact time for the invasion, but he is now meeting with men in Hedeby. He is pretending to be drafting men to go to England because he doesn't want Olav to learn of his plans. Astrid, we have little time. I have to turn it all around. You understand that, don't you?" Her sister's eyes expressed more than her words could. "I admit that I was furious to learn of their wedding. Anger is a poor adviser. And anger combined with wounded pride is like a bow and arrow. I shot it, Astrid. I allowed anger to govern my words and actions . . . but then I confessed to Ion and I understood my mistake. But Sven could not be stopped. Oh, if only not for this marriage! But no, Sven would have found another excuse to move against Olav. He thrives on anger. He has gotten it into his head that he must compete with the 'second chieftain.'"

"Do you really think so?" Astrid hoped with her entire being that her sister was right.

"Yes. But it doesn't matter what I think now. What matters is that"—she inhaled deeply, and the words shot out of her—"I will tell Olav how I feel, just as I should have done all those years ago in Sigtuna. I made the wrong choice back then, and suddenly none of the choices were my own. Now, I will give him my hand and my throne. I want to save him from Sven. Will you go to Olav, sister?"

You have no idea what you ask of me, Astrid thought with anguish. *You know nothing, my salty sister. But to make up for the part I played in this . . .*

"I'll go." They heard a hoarse whisper, and froze.

8

⚛

DENMARK

Świętosława was sure she must be dreaming when she heard Dusza's voice.

"I'll go."

"You? . . . You . . . speak?" Her mouth felt dry.

Dusza nodded.

"Jesus! Astrid, pinch me." Świętosława grabbed her sister's hand because this had to be a dream.

"I can hear her, too," Astrid whispered. "Dusza? What's going on? How is this possible?"

"Duke Mieszko . . . he said it was a sign . . ." Dusza's voice was as toneless as a hollow, throaty whisper. It sounded like speaking caused her pain.

"Father knew?" Świętosława asked.

Dusza nodded.

"When I discovered that . . . I could repeat words . . . I went to tell him. And the duke . . ."

"Wait, have a drink." Świętosława leapt up to bring Dusza a goblet. "I get the feeling that every word hurts you."

Dusza shook her head and smiled apologetically.

"It's because my voice is never used."

"Since when have you been able to talk? When did you realize?" The two sisters talked over each other.

"My God! I remember the despair at court when you were discovered to be mute!"

Dusza looked embarrassed. Almost unconsciously, she began to explain using sign language, indicating her womb.

"When you started bleeding?" Astrid guessed.

Dusza nodded. Świętosława couldn't stop the tears, and she embraced Dusza tightly.

"Holy Mother, all these years together! And you never . . . not with a single word . . . why didn't you tell me? It would have been easier . . ."

Dusza shook her head and slipped out of Świętosława's arms.

"The lord duke wouldn't let me . . . he said there may come a day when only I can help you . . . because nobody would ever suspect a mute."

"Lord Father!" Świętosława and Astrid both groaned.

"He planned everything . . ."

". . . he arranged everything in a way that gave every person their place and purpose. Oh, Dusza, Dusza!"

"Oh, Mieszko, Mieszko!" Świętosława corrected. "It wouldn't surprise me to learn that he's looking down on us to make sure we are still following his orders. My God! I don't know what to say . . ."

"You've said enough. Don't say any more," Dusza whispered.

Astrid began to laugh hysterically.

"Calm down! You'll attract the curiosity of others and have them come here and hear Dusza speak! Oh! Now I understand what Harald said! I thought the child was muddled in his head, but you really did speak with him."

"No," Dusza denied firmly. "I spoke to no one. I only spoke to the children when they slept. I was their dream."

"Wait." Astrid's eyes gleamed. "If you learned to talk by listening to Świętosława, if you know her every thought, that means . . ."

"Yes," Dusza whispered, and turned to Świętosława, placing her hands on her shoulders. "I know what you know. I can speak every tongue you've learned. And I can use your words to express how you feel."

Tears streamed down Świętosława's cheeks.

"Only Dusza knows who I really am. I wish I didn't have to let you go out into the world on the very day I discover you can speak. Go to Olav. Warn him. And . . ."

"I know what you want to say." Dusza interrupted her.

Astrid looked around the room.

"I'm looking for mead. We need to drink to this."

"Let's finish planning first. Dusza, do you remember Arnora's story about Gudrun? She warned her brothers that they were going into a trap. Give this to Olav from me." She unfastened the brooch from her dress. "He'll understand."

The fish held in the clutches of two eagles.

"And you, Astrid?" Świętosława continued. "Will you convince Bolesław to stand with us? To send the Jomsvikings against Sven? And will your husband . . ."

"Leave him to me, as always. What are you staring at?" Her sister smiled bitterly. "Did you not handle Eric and Sven yourself when you wanted them to do something or other?"

You have no idea, Świętosława thought, and felt gratitude toward her sister. She hugged her like she used to do as a girl.

"That's enough, this is no time to get emotional." Astrid pulled away.

Dusza poured the mead and handed them goblets.

"Let's drink to the souls that speak!" Świętosława said.

Dusza smiled with tears in her eyes. Astrid nodded sadly, so sadly that for a moment Świętosława felt worse for her than she did for herself.

"If God is with us," she said when they had put down their goblets, "I will give birth to Sven's last child when he is already gone from this world." She placed a hand on her belly and looked at them both. "Yes, I'm with child again."

SWEDEN

Olof and Wilczan sailed a boat in Mälaren Bay. It was just the two of them. Wilkomir hadn't protested, though he made sure that Olof was never alone anywhere. He ordered guards to stand on the rocks along the bay and said: "Go. You haven't seen each other in five years."

"You only reached my shoulder when you sailed away from Sigtuna with my mother," Olof said, examining his friend. "Now you're almost as tall as I am."

"And you were as skinny as a bird. Now you have a chest that can bear the weight of chain mail without collapsing."

Olof laughed.

"It's all thanks to your father. He's been forcing me to train. Tell me about Roskilde though. But tell me the truth, none of those smooth lies that the messengers always spout."

"It's normal." Wilczan shrugged. "Almost the same as here. The king drinks with his men while the queen, your mother, rules so cleverly that barely anyone notices. But she forces Sven to go to church, and she never forced King Eric. She gives the king children and he rewards her. She's convinced him that a Christian king is more than a Viking. But they argue. They row so fiercely that sparks fly. Our lady doesn't mince her words."

Olof could almost see her. That's how he remembered his mother. Bold and regal, wearing crowns of golden hair wrapped around her head and holding her lynxes on a leash. Sometimes he would wake up from that dream, when his mother walked into the hall holding a sword dripping with blood; but sometimes what woke him was the emptiness. The coldness he could never chase away with any fires in the hearth or additional layers of blankets and furs. That's when he wished that Wrzask or Zgrzyt were there to jump into bed with him and lick his face.

"They argued recently when they couldn't agree on a wife for you," Wilczan said. "Sven thinks you should be married."

Olof turned his head away, pretending that he was watching something in the water; he didn't want his friend to notice his blush. Yes, it had happened, though he hadn't wanted it to. Well, he had, but he hadn't thought it would be like this. He'd recently found himself uncomfortable in the company of women. He kept staring at their breasts or backsides. He lost his concentration whenever he saw a pretty girl. He would tremble and flush, until one evening, when a servant came to add logs to the fire in his room . . . it happened. But she'd been too bold, she kissed him like mad and it was over before he'd even untied his trousers. He was embarrassed, horribly embarrassed, and had her sent away because he was afraid people would laugh if she told them. But it hadn't passed, and a week later there was another girl . . . he controlled himself better with the second one, but he could still only think of one thing. How could Sven possibly know?

"Marry? And?" he asked nonchalantly.

"The queen yelled at the king and told him to leave you alone, that you still had time. And that he won't force women on you just because he thinks they are the right choice, and other things like that. Sven dropped it after that."

They rowed in silence for a while, until Wilczan brought up the reason for which he had been sent to Sweden.

"So, what will it be, Olof?" he asked. "What will you do?"

Olof watched the water drip from the oar. He didn't answer.

"Come on, Olof, one doesn't refuse one's mother! Especially a mother like the Bold Lady, who . . ." Wilczan got carried away and hadn't noticed that the young king wasn't listening to him.

If it hadn't been for Sven and the presence of his men in Sigtuna, he may not have been king. The nobles had been increasingly daring since his mother had left for Denmark. When he imposed taxes for the army, they complained. They grumbled that a country is defended by men, not by silver. Sven's messenger Jarl Eric helped him; he knew how to speak to the nobles. And then there was the wealthy merchant from Birka, Rognvald, and his sons, Bjarne and Erling, the ones his father had sent to Denmark to collect taxes and whom Sven had sent back in ropes. Rognvald surrounded himself with anyone who might have a reason to oppose Olof. Birka was the source of rebellion: Olof had to be prepared at every assembly that there would be someone to speak out against him. He felt that he needed something to shut the rebels up once and for all. A victory after which they would see him as more than just his mother's son, the young king. When he heard people call him the "young king" he wanted to bite them. Because the use of the word *young* indicated disdain. He had once overheard someone say: "Olav Tryggvason commanded a ship which sailed out of Russia at his age. Olav had defeated the slave masters at his age." Why? Why was he being compared to Tryggvason behind his back? Yes, he'd heard the rumors. People said that Olav had been his mother's lover before he became king of Norway. But she'd refused him! He had been here, in Sigtuna, asking for her hand, and she'd said no. But what if it was true? What if she named him after her first love? Bullshit. He was named after his uncle, after his father's brother. "The king is your namesake, that's an obligation," she'd said. But whose obligation? He remembered Tryggvason's pale, searching eyes as the man stared at him like a snake before it strikes. And now his mother sent Wilczan to relay his orders. "Betray Sven. Prepare for war at his side but betray him. When the battle begins, stand by Olav Tryggvason." And she said: "You'll free yourself from Sven and his control, his meddling in your affairs." *Mother, if it wasn't for Sven and his meddling, your son would be too weak to keep his throne. They'd call me the "young king," spit at me, and that would be that. But you're right, my Danish stepfather is a burden. As is my queen mother.*

"Olof!" Wilczan nudged his elbow. "Are you rowing in your sleep?"

"No, friend, I'm awake."

"Good, because the queen told me to return as fast as possible."

"You have to ask?" Olof laughed. "One doesn't refuse a queen!"

NORWAY

Olav sat in the hall in Nidaros with his queen at his side, waiting for the Icelanders' arrival, Gizur the White and Hall and Hjati. He was certain that these men would do more to lead to the baptism of the Isle of Ice than the unfortunate Thangbrand, the holy man with no spirit. "Iceland is a land of sensible people. Let us therefore speak some sense into our people, my king," Gizur, who had been born there, had told him.

He was playing hnefatafl with Tyra. The queen had wanted the red pawns.

"I want to direct the hordes of the invaders," she said, blushing. "I want to know what it feels like."

"Very well, my lady. The white pawns will be mine, and I will defend the king."

"But you are the king!" She laughed. "I will attack you from four sides . . . isn't that exciting?"

No, he thought. *I am not excited by games in love. Tricks, ploys, strategies, wounded pride, stained honor . . . that's not love.*

"Do you know that the king's defenders win at hnefatafl most often?" Hallfred interrupted.

"I know, bard." Tyra jutted out her chin. "That's why I want to try to change fate."

Hallfred had come to them recently. Before he'd taken the faith, he had convinced Olav to be his godfather. Tryggvason was fond of him. Hallfred's broken nose, his playfulness, fierceness, and talent which by far exceeded Omold's all resulted in Olav welcoming him at court and honoring him with a patience far greater than the bard deserved.

"Hallfred, will you play with the queen?" Olav asked.

"I would like to, but I dare not, my lord. To play against you is a sin." His dark eyes gleamed teasingly.

"You've learned a new word and you use it when it is not called for. It would be a sin for you to sleep with the queen, not to play with her in a game."

"Olav!" Tyra blushed.

How does she do it? he wondered. *She always blushes when it is most appropriate for her to do so.*

"Beware, my lady," the bard hissed. "You're leaving a gap in your line of defense. Watch your pawns. All you need to do to defeat a warrior is to attack him from both sides."

"What do you need to defeat a king?" She glanced at Olav from under her eyelashes.

"You must surround me from three sides."

"My lord!" The bard moved from the queen's bench to his. "I would like to recite a poem in your honor."

"Go back to the queen." Olav smiled. "I don't want to play with you."

"This isn't a game," the bard assured him. "It's a poem. An artful one, I promise!"

"I don't want a poem right now. You can recite it at the feast."

"But why, my king? Poetry should not be kept waiting; it's like a hot, wet woman who must be taken while the flush is still in her cheeks and her nipples are hard . . ."

"Silence!" Tyra rose from the table, sending the board and pawns flying.

"Shh, my lady . . ." Olav caught her cold hand, but she yanked it back and moved away. "Hallfred had no intention of offending you."

He knows you're cold, Tyra. That your womb is beautiful and perfectly made, but it is dry. That your thighs are like marble columns which can be stroked, admired for their color and the masterly drawn lines of your veins, but they do not fan the fires of desire to make one want to kiss and knead them. That your noble, wonderful breasts cannot be squeezed or sucked. How could the bard know it? He can only guess as he watches you play.

Vigi barked. Omold walked into the hall and cast a cold glance at the bard.

"My king," he said. "Gizur and Hjati have arrived at port. The Icelanders will be in your manor soon."

"I'm waiting for them," Olav exclaimed. "Bring them to us as soon as they arrive. Vigi . . ." He stroked the white head. "You bark at good news!"

"My king," Hallfred persisted. "Let me recite my new poem for you."

Olav grabbed his sword.

"Here you go." He pointed the sword at the bard's chest. "Take this blade and leave."

Hallfred's breath quickened; he was frightened. Olav laughed.

"You're a troublesome bard, Hallfred. I like your rhymes, but you must understand that I don't always want to hear poetry."

"I don't understand that." The bard grinned. "But I'll take the blade. I'll pay for it with a rhyme when you're ready to hear it, my lord."

Hallfred grabbed the blade of the sword that Olav still held pointing at his chest and hissed. He let go and lifted his hand, his blood flowing freely.

"Rhymes created from blood," he said, narrowing his eyes. "A perfect melody for death."

Olav let go of the hilt and the bard caught the weapon again.

Tyra, who had been standing behind him, walked out, her skirts rustling as she moved.

"Oh!" The bard laughed. "The red pawns have walked off the board."

"Be quiet," the king said. "I told you—no songs. You've insulted the queen."

"I feel awful, my lord, so awful . . ." The bard lied with a smile.

Olav gritted his teeth. *I'm the one who feels awful as I defend a wife who waits for me in bed like an iceberg,* he thought.

Before he could reprimand Hallfred, his guests arrived.

"Hjati and Gizur, lords from Iceland!" Ingvar announced them as he led in the two men.

Vigi ran to them, wagging his tail. Olav stood up and exchanged a glance with Bishop Sivrit.

"Victory!" Gizur announced.

"The Isle of Ice has accepted your learning," Hjati added.

"How?" Olav asked.

"In a unanimous decision of the assembly, the Althing. Iceland waits for you to baptize her, my king."

"Tell me what happened, from the beginning." Olav forgot his wife and the cruel bard within moments of inviting his guests to sit with him.

"We presented our case to Thorgeir, proclaimer of the law."

"He's a devout pagan!" a surprised Hallfred interjected.

"Have you met my new bard?" Olav asked his guests. "I call him Troublesome because he speaks out of turn."

"You're very gracious, my lord," Gizur the White said. "Iceland remembers him as quarrelsome, a brawler and a murderer."

"I have confessed and done penance for that." Hallfred wagged a finger at Gizur. "I sit with the king and I don't sin, even though I play with the king."

"Don't try to draw my attention, Hallfred, Iceland is my concern right now, not you. Speak."

"We spoke with the proclaimer of the law before the assembly met. Gizur told him that you won't cease in your attempts to convert the island to Christianity. Thorgeir had heard the stories of those from Orkney, and heard about what had happened at Lofoten, and of course he knew what transpired before you reclaimed your throne. He's a sensible man and a born Icelander."

"What Hjati means to say is that Thorgeir loves Iceland as much as he loves freedom," Gizur added.

"He could easily imagine what would happen when the famous, warlike King Olav leads his fleet to the island's shores."

"You didn't frighten him?" Olav asked suspiciously.

"Us? No!" they both exclaimed.

"Besides, the proclaimer of the law isn't easy to scare. What distinguishes him from other people is that he listens."

Hjati gestured wildly as he spoke.

"Do you know, King, that most people assume from the outset that they are in the right, and when they listen to others, they hear only what suits their views? He, on the other hand, tried to understand everything. Including what we told him: 'The king does not force anyone to be baptized. One must choose baptism freely.' People usually understand this as an implicit form of blackmail, but Thorgeir, as a man of the law, understood the rule."

"Besides," Gizur added, "he doesn't restrict his view of the world because it wouldn't be in Iceland's best interest. Quite the opposite, he approached the entire issue with a clear head, and so understood that certain matters cannot be outrun."

"Yes, that's exactly how he put it. He said: 'The world has changed and even if we don't like the change, it doesn't mean we can evade it. Closing our eyes to the world doesn't change the world itself.'"

"Then we met with everyone else at the assembly. Our friend Hall spoke on behalf of the Christians. Thorgeir, as a pagan, didn't speak up about matters of the faith. He did, however, present your terms to the people. About half voted for and half against, and they asked him to help them decide."

"And he listened to all of those opposed to the new faith, he heard every argument, no matter how small it seemed. Then he ordered a day of rest in the deliberations and sought some solitude. He wrapped himself in a cloak and we all thought he'd fallen asleep."

Gizur and Hjati's eyes shone with excitement as they spoke. Bishop Sigurd was watching them carefully.

"After a day, the proclaimer stood by the Rock of the Law and said . . . Oh!" Hjati choked with emotion and nudged Gizur. "You tell them."

"Thorgeir explained to the people that Christianity is like spring which comes after winter, it cannot be stopped . . ."

"No, wait," Hjati interrupted him, spreading his arms. "He spoke about fire first, don't you remember? He said that in ancient times, people lived on raw meat because they didn't know about the existence of fire, but when they discovered the power of its flames they began to cook meat and warm themselves in its glow. And that was when the epoch of fire began. He said that many people were suspicious of cooked meat at first, and ate raw meat in secret, saying that that is how their ancestors used to eat."

A rather deceitful example, Olav thought, and glanced at Sigurd. The bishop's eyes gleamed in the half darkness as if he were a wild lynx.

"And . . ." Gizur the White began, "it went smoothly after that. The proclaimer of the law said that it is better to accept fire freely than insist that order in a country can only be maintained if one religion dominates all others, and that two religions cannot coexist."

"And now for the most important part, my king. Thorgeir suggested that Christianity be made the only official religion in Iceland . . ."

"But?" the king interrupted him. "There must be a 'but' in there."

"Indeed, my lord." Gizur nodded. "He wants permission to worship the old gods in private."

"Only in one's own home," Hjati clarified. "Never outside. He also wants to retain two traditions which he claims cannot be rooted out overnight: eating horsemeat and leaving crippled children out to die. But the proclaimer promises that the law will not allow horsemeat to be consumed publicly at feasts."

"And the children? Getting rid of that barbaric practice is one of the things I care about most!" Olav snorted with disappointment.

"My lord, if they accept baptism and begin to listen to Christ's teachings, then they will stop abandoning cripples of their own free will eventually. The proclaimer's suggestions for the new laws are sensible. Listen to him, don't be like those men who assume they are in the right from the outset and never listen to others."

"The Icelanders speak wisely," Bishop Sivrit observed. "You know the wonderful power of the word of God. He who hears it has a change of heart. Let them hear it."

Sivrit rose from his seat at the end of the table, where he had settled when the Icelanders arrived. He slowly walked over to where the fire burned in the hearth.

"They agree for Christianity to be the only official religion," he said. "They will have to attend mass every Sunday, and they will have to listen. Gizur is right. In a year, or two, or three, they will stop leaving the cripples on the rocks of their own volition. My king." The bishop's pale eyes shone with the same light that had convinced Olav to bend his knee before Christ all those years ago. "You know that what has happened in Iceland is a miracle, and we are its humble witnesses."

"I know," Olav agreed as he rose. "The world has never heard of a country that accepts the faith after one assembly. It is done."

"Amen!" the bishop exclaimed.

9

Astrid looked around for Duszan as soon as she reached Gniezno. Discovering Dusza's secret convinced her that Duszan must be hiding something, too. She was disappointed to find that Duszan had stayed in Poznań, where the lord duke had ordered him to look after his sons. The atmosphere in the yard of Gniezno's manor was tense.

"Where will I find my brother?" she asked his guards.

"On the building site, Lady of Wolin."

She drove her heels into her horse's sides and rode up the hill toward which they had pointed her.

"The duke?" The carpenter she asked seemed surprised at the question. "He was there just a moment ago." He pointed.

She tied her horse to a tree and began to walk, hiking up her skirts.

"No, my lady." The wagon driver shook his head. "The duke has already left, but I saw him in the middle of the square by the long platforms."

When she finally found her brother, she had to jog to keep up with him. Bolesław leapt over the trenches that had been dug on the hillside. The wagon drivers shouted at their horses, which were struggling to pull wagons filled with stones. Some servants were mixing lime in huge tubs, others carried baskets filled with sand, still others brought out buckets of water. Carpenters were erecting scaffolding on the platforms. The duke was building a great cathedral.

"This is where the main nave will be." He showed her when she reached him. "Can you see?"

"No. All I see are holes."

"These aren't holes! The long, narrow ones are the trenches in which the buttresses will go. The half-circular apsis will go there, do you see? And the tower will be here." He pointed at the sky.

"And this?" She pointed at a shed carelessly covered with wooden boards. "What's that?"

Bolesław gritted his teeth and grabbed her elbow. Too hard, as usual.

"That's the old martyrium. Old but new, Astrid; everything's changed. We built a small sanctuary with Unger to honor Adalbert's remains, and then, when I discovered he'd been made a saint, I began to build the church. I brought in masters from Saxony. Do you know how long it takes to build a temple? Ten, twenty years, and even that may not be enough!"

She cast a critical eye over the building site. Yes, it looked like something that would take twenty years to complete.

"I thought I would build it and we would move him to the church with full honors. Jesus Christ, Astrid! What a celebration that would be! But the emperor's messengers arrived last week and said that Otto wants to come to Gniezno to visit the saint's resting place before Easter. Where will he stay? In the middle of a building site?"

"Do you think that if you rush the men, they will build in two months what takes twenty years?" she asked with surprise.

"Don't provoke me," he snarled.

Bolesław never had any patience for bad news.

"You'll think of something," she said amicably. "You always come up with something."

"True," he agreed, and caught a stone which was rolling off the pile.

"Do you remember when you came up with the idea for Olav and Tyra to marry? A storm began around it . . ."

"No!" he yelled at a servant who was passing a stone to a worker. "Leave the gray ones for the apsis. Take them from here!"

"Are you listening to me?" she asked.

"Yes. You said that I always come up with something."

She grabbed his arm.

"Bolesław, I understand that you have to supervise the construction of a church and prepare for the emperor's visit, but you have to listen to me; this is a matter of life and death. Let's go somewhere quiet . . ."

"I understand!" he exclaimed, simultaneously throwing himself sideways and giving out more orders to the builders. "What were you saying?"

She didn't try to speak again. She pulled him away from the construction site and into the bushes which grew on the hillside. They startled a wagon driver who was trying to heed nature's call and pissed his trousers instead when he recognized the duke. Astrid forcibly sat her brother down on a stone, stood in front of him, and, not letting him turn away from her, said:

"You've made your bed, now you must sleep in it."

"Me?" He looked surprised.

"Yes, you. You pushed Tyra and Olav together, knowing it could lead to war. Now our sister is on one side of this war and is begging you for help."

"Begging?" He laughed. "Then it can't really be our sister! Someone is impersonating her."

"Stop mocking!" She lost her temper. "Świętosława, Queen of Sweden and Denmark, is begging her brother Duke Bolesław for help using my lips."

"What do I need to do?" He took her seriously now.

"Send an army."

"Absolutely not." He shook his head and his temper rose again. "I have the emperor coming to visit; do you know what that means? My border with Russia is the border over which two emperors are fighting. East and west. It's not just about the north, even if that's all that my sister can see right now. The emperor will come only with his personal guard, so I must ensure the safety of the country as well as His Majesty while he's here. Do you understand? If the Byzantine emperors, Constantine and Basil, decide they want to rid themselves of their western rival, then his visit in Gniezno is the perfect opportunity for them to strike.

"They could send their brother-in-law, Knyaz Vladimir, across the Bug. We will be busy here, in Gniezno, with the bones of the saint, attending mass after mass, while Vladimir's troops will gather outside the borough. Do you understand the situation I would find myself in if that were to happen? Yes! I am welcoming a great guest from the west, so I need to fortify my eastern borders and remember about the south. The devilish Přemyslids cannot forgive me that their Adalbert has become my Adalbert. Oh, wouldn't it suit them to organize a raid right under the emperor's nose! And you say that I should send an army to fight my sister's war?"

"Then send the Jomsvikings. You don't need them for the emperor's visit."

"No, I don't," he agreed.

"Pay them," Astrid insisted. "You promised."

"When?"

"When Sigvald first told you of Tyra's plea for help," she reminded him. "'You say, Jarl, that it would be a reason for war? Then I hope that none of the Jomsviking swords have rusted.' Those were your words."

"You must admit, I did not say a word about paying the Jomsvikings." He grinned.

"That's an ugly smile and a dirty move. It doesn't suit you, Duke." She jutted out her chin.

"You're wrong, Astrid. That is exactly what suits a duke." He rose from the stone on which he had been sitting. "But you're right, it doesn't sound good coming from a brother. I suggest we split it in half. I'll pay for them to fight and the Bold One can pay for them to win."

They heard Zarad's call from the direction of the building site.

"Duke! Where is the duke?"

"Here!" Bolesław shouted.

Dark-eyed Zarad slipped on the wet soil as he ran down the hill and rolled between them.

"Bloody hell," he cursed when he ground to a halt on a bare bush. "I've got mud all over my arse."

"So why are you running over bushes?" Bolesław reprimanded.

"They brought red sandstone from the mines. The stonemason wants to know what should be used for the columns and the sarcophagus, as apparently one of the blocks has a blemish."

"A blemish?" the duke roared at Zaraz as if his friend was solely responsible for the imperfect material. He turned back to her, trying to control his emotions. "You can see for yourself, Astrid, that I cannot leave." He shrugged helplessly. "Sort it out. Tell Sigvald what I have decided. He's to lead all his men to Olav's aid. See you, sister!" He embraced her and then paused for a moment. "I'll leave it to you to get him excited."

He let go and ran uphill, his strides long. Now it was Zarad who struggled to keep up with him.

"I'll take care of him, as I always do," she replied quietly to his retreating back. "As you command, my brother. My duke."

NORWAY

Olav was sure he must be dreaming when he saw Geivar walk into the great hall. Then he thought he might have had too much to drink. He put down his goblet.

"Is that really you, my old friend?!"

"It is I, my king!" Geivar replied as he kneeled.

"The chieftain of the house of scouts?" Varin called out cheerfully. "An iron boy of Jom? Ah! The other one with painted fangs!" He and Geivar embraced.

"I'd like to be happy to see you"—Olav also rose to greet his friend—"but the visit of a Jomsborg chieftain in Nidaros could mean trouble."

His features were, as always, impossible to read. This was the Geivar he had met on the Dnieper before he had survived his first storm aboard *Kanugård*. When they embraced, Geivar whispered to him:

"We must speak in private. I am not alone. A woman is with me."

Olav's fingers tightened on his friend's shoulder. *It's her*, he thought, but immediately dismissed the thought. The queen of Sweden and Denmark couldn't just visit Nidaros.

"Your lady knows her," Geivar added.

"I cannot ask the queen to leave," he replied quietly, glancing at Tyra, who was watching them curiously.

"Then make sure this conversation can continue once she retires. Not everything I have to say is meant for your lady's ears."

As Geivar said this, Olav saw a hooded woman walk into the hall. He knew who it was before she showed her face.

"That's Queen Sigrid's servant!" his wife exclaimed, as pale as if she'd seen a ghost.

"Yes, my lady," Geivar replied. "Dusza is the queen's messenger."

"Messenger?" Tyra looked surprised. "If I remember correctly, this woman is mute."

Geivar did not disagree, but he explained.

"She can still confirm everything that I'm about to tell you." Dusza nodded as Geivar continued. "Her presence here is meant to indicate the secrecy of this matter, and that it is known only to Denmark's queen, not its king."

"That's odd," Tyra observed, and Olav agreed with her.

"Speak, Geivar," he encouraged his visitor.

"Queen Sigrid Storråda wants to warn you that her husband is gathering forces to face your men, my lord."

It was bound to happen sooner or later, Olav thought.

"Who?"

"The Danes under King Sven's command. Jarl Eric and Jarl Sven, the heirs of Lade. And the young King Olof of Sweden."

"Christ save us," Tyra said.

"Perhaps you would like to retire, wife?" Olav asked, but before he'd finished speaking, he realized he'd done it too soon.

"How dare you?" She snorted angrily. "When our fate hangs in the balance, you would have me go to sleep?"

"Calm down, my lady. The fates of wars are decided in battle. For now, we are merely talking. Geivar, how many men do the jarls command?"

"Over a dozen of their own ships, but Sven has had them talking to men in Norway."

"Lies," Tyra interjected. "The Norwegians adore their king."

Dusza contradicted Tyra with a shake of her head.

"It's a trap. Beware, husband, for Queen Sigrid is clearly plotting with my brother. They want to draw you into a trap, and the mute is meant to help convince you. Don't trust them!"

"Be quiet or leave and stop insulting my guests." Olav was barely controlling himself.

"Olav, think! Why would Sigrid Storråda try to warn you?"

The queen's heart is as easily startled as a partridge,
her spirit is as fearful and timid
as her cheek is beautiful when covered in blushes.

Hallfred, the Troublesome Bard, appeared in the hall.

Tyra blushed.

"Will you let this brawler insult me again? For him to abuse your queen in front of your chieftains?" she demanded.

"Hallfred wasn't trying to insult you, my lady. He spoke the truth . . ."

Tyra rose, lifting her head proudly, and cast Olav a disdainful glare.

". . . about your cheeks being beautiful and frequently blushing. Everyone knows that. And that you're timid? Well, that is the prerogative of women . . ."

It worked. Tyra snorted and walked out without a word.

"Varin," Olav said quietly. "Have some guards stand by the queen's chambers. Discreetly. Hallfred!"

"Have I worked hard enough for you to hear my poem, King?" The bard's dark eyes gleamed. His broken nose cast an irregular, jagged shadow across half of his face, making the Icelander look demonic.

"You have. I will hear it soon, and if it is as good as you say, I will give you a ring. But now go. I need to stay with my guests and chieftains alone."

"At your service, my lord! Only don't make me play your queen tonight."

"Don't play with fire!"

"Oh, my lord! Playing with you is like playing with ice and fire. You are simultaneously fiery and cold, like an iceberg slipping into the flames . . ."

"Hallfred, leave," Olav concluded the bard's show-off coldly.

The only ones left in the hall were Sivrit, Varin, Omold, Ingvar, Thorolf, Rafn God's Axe, and the guests, Dusza and Geivar.

"Vigi, the cleverest of dogs, stand at the door and make sure nobody eavesdrops on us."

In the morning, once he had learned all Dusza's secrets, decided on the best plan of attack with Geivar, and sent his chieftains away to secretly start gathering the troops, he was left alone with Sivrit. He held the golden brooch that Świętosława had given him through Dusza's hands. He kept turning it over in his fingers.

"A fish torn apart by two eagles," Sivrit said thoughtfully. "An eloquent sign."

"Yes," Olav agreed. "What do you think about all this, Bishop?"

"We will all be judged by God one day."

"Iceland has accepted Christianity. I can die now!" Olav laughed hollowly.

"Would you not like to see the northern lights one more time, my friend?" The bishop smiled teasingly for a moment, but his features grew grave momentarily. "If Olof listens to his mother, it might be possible. With the Jomsvikings and the Swedes beside you, you will have enough men to match, or even surpass, the forces of Sven and the two jarls. I'm worried about something else. Queen Sigrid betrays her husband not to save you, but to win you. As if she's forgotten that in the eyes of God, you are married to Tyra. That woman is as generous as she is cruel."

"She is bold, as she has always been." Olav nodded.

"Sigrid is giving you a choice: 'life with me, or death.' But what choice is she giving your wife? She has pledged her love for you through Dusza's lips . . ."

"She has also confessed her sins. You must admit, this is unexpected. She was capable of sending me back dead, deplumed falcons to show me how furious she was, but now she has shown herself to be capable of change, you must see that!"

Sivrit was as collected as always, and his pale eyes reflected the embers of the hearth. He cocked his head and said, spitting out the words:

"I see her courage which borders on insolence. And I see the sin she has already committed. By betraying her husband's plans to us she is as good as killing him . . ."

"By not doing so she would be killing me." Olav kicked the bench in front of him. "Not necessarily using Sven's army which will come from the south. I believe that I could defeat Sven at sea even if Olof remained at his side. The devilish part of Sven's plan is how he uses the jarls of Lade. If they have already talked the lords of Trondelag into joining them, I could be assassinated right here. I underestimated Jarl Haakon's sons. I thought that they gave up on ever returning when they fled the country. I didn't appreciate the importance of Eric's marriage to Gyda. I was so focused on converting Norway that I committed the sin of abandonment."

"You were looking into the distance and you didn't see what was right under your nose." Sivrit sighed heavily. "I still think that Queen Sigrid's plan is risky. Although on the other hand . . . there is the genius of peace in her idea. She on the throne of Denmark, you rule Norway, and her son leads Sweden. The three kingdoms would be united for the first time, with no risk of aggression against each other . . . A vision so tempting I have chills . . . but this three-sided peace begins with treason, and it would have to end in treason, too, since you would be forced to send away Queen Tyra."

"*Forced* is the wrong word, Sivrit," Olav said slowly. "Hear the truth. I will happily send Tyra away and stand in front of God with Świętosława-Sigrid at my side. I have dreamed of her for fifteen years."

DENMARK

Świętosława did everything she could to hold the baby in. Sven promised that he'd be there for the child's birth, and she knew that Olav needed more time to gather enough men. It was the middle of summer. Wrzask and Zgrzyt found the manor stifling. They panted all the time. She heard their heavy breathing day and night. Oh, if only Astrid could have been at her side! Her wise sister, with her knowledge of herbs, would have thought of something! Melkorka only had one solution to all these problems: "I'll brew you some chamomile." Świętosława had had enough of chamomile. She couldn't eat or sleep, but that could only mean that her day was close, but she wanted to push it away as much as possible. To give him time.

Dusza's absence grated on her nerves all the time, though she never regretted Dusza's going to Olav. *She knows everything. She will convince him,* she kept telling herself. *Dusza is me.*

"Perhaps I should cook something for you, my lady?" the fair-haired Vali asked, appearing in the alcove's doorway.

Świętosława hadn't left her bed in a week—not because she couldn't walk, but because she was trying to delay her labor.

"Vali . . ." she groaned, pretending to be on the verge of death. "I can't eat in this heat. Do you want to help me, beautiful girl?"

"My queen knows I do." Vali blushed.

I know, she thought. *I know that Sven has been taking you to his bed since he decided to start this war. I know he finds solace in you, and I know that troubles you. But it doesn't worry me.*

"Is the king in Roskilde?" she asked.

"Yes." Vali looked embarrassed. "He sees to the building of the ships and gathers more men every day."

"Good. Come here, sit on my bed. Don't be afraid."

Vali sat down on the very edge of the great bed. Her hands trembled. Świętosława grabbed her fingers.

"Vali, I know . . ."

The girl tried to pull back her hand, but Świętosława held it tightly.

"Don't run away and stop being afraid. Do you love me?"

"Yes, my lady."

"Do you love the king?"

Vali froze.

"If you love the king, don't be afraid. Give him the love I cannot." She put a hand on her enormous belly. "Do you see? I will give him another heir any day now. I can't be with him as a wife. And a man needs love more than wine and mead before he sets out to war."

"Don't say that, my lady . . ." Vali sobbed.

"Oh, stop," she snorted. "What do you want me to do, send Melkorka to his bed?"

Vali laughed through her tears. Świętosława stroked her hand.

"Lie down beside me," she ordered.

Vali stiffly complied.

"Show me how you lie next to the king."

The girl turned on her side and whispered:

"My lord wants me this way. He doesn't look at my face, only . . ."

Świętosława struggled to sit up. She knelt on the bed, flipped the girl over onto her back, and sat down on top of her.

"Tonight, do this. He'll like it. And do it again tomorrow."

Vali looked up at her, her eyes wide.

"Don't be afraid." Świętosława pinched her cheek. "If you get pregnant, we'll take care of your child. The king chose you, and that's a great honor! Now go to him, please." She kissed Vali's cheek, which was wet with tears. "Go."

She lost control over her body in the early morning. Labor had started, and she had to call for Melkorka.

"I'll send for Vali," the housewife said.

"No! Leave her alone. We've managed with the three that came before, we will manage with the fourth one, too. Just you and me, all right?"

"As you command, my lady." Melkorka nodded.

The child was born before dawn.

"A healthy, red-haired girl," Melkorka announced. "I need to send for the king."

"Not yet," Świętosława groaned as tears streamed down her face.

He came in the morning. He picked up the girl and accepted her, raising her above his head.

"My second daughter," he said coldly. "Astrid was fury's daughter. What shall we call this one?"

"Whatever you want," Świętosława replied, hiding her face in her pillow.

"I sail tomorrow, so this is a daughter of war," he decided. "We will name her after you.

"You're silent," he observed after a moment. "That's odd for you. Wives should wish their husbands victory."

I wish you were dead, she thought, biting the pillow.

He put the baby down beside her and walked out.

When the guards sounded the horns to announce the king's departure, Świętosława sobbed.

10

⚮

THE NORTH SEA

Olav sailed aboard the most beautiful ship in the world. It was the *Long Snake*'s maiden voyage. The slender hull was decorated on the bow and stern with enormous, predatory dragon heads. Rig, the sculptor who had fashioned them, had a talent for making wood come to life. The dragon on the bow had eyes which burned with pieces of gold and scales encrusted with silver. Its arched neck was adorned with a band of garnet stones that glowed bloodred when the sunlight or moonlight danced across it. A second dragon proudly occupied the stern, no smaller than the one in the bow. The difference between them was in the expression of their jaws. The dragon at the back of the *Long Snake* spread fear with its golden fangs. Thirty-four benches and twice as many rowers. The gunwales were covered with sheets of metal like a steel-clad warrior. A golden weathervane fluttered on top of the mast.

The *Long Snake*'s older but smaller brother, the *Short Snake*, followed in its wake. Then came the cruel and beautiful *Crane* with a sculpture of the bird on its bow, under the command of Olav's half brother Torkil Nose. More floating predators followed behind. Seventy-one ships. A bitter lesson. Norway could have sent three times as many, but Dusza had been right; Trondelag had deserted its king. But the lords of the west stood beside him—his sisters' husbands. Lodin's men, his mother's husband's, were also there, and Hårek had sent ten ships from the distant Lofoten.

When the bows of his ships crossed into Skagerrak, he ordered a brief stop.

"We will heave to at Göta älv's estuary."

"That's the last place we can stop before entering Øresund." Varin wrinkled his nose. "Do you know what Øresund will be? A dragon's jaws so narrow that only one side will come out alive."

"I won't back down," Olav said.

"I know." Varin waved a hand. "You won't."

Olav walked down onto land. He wanted to see those rocks again and make sure that his memory wasn't failing him. Vigi led the way, finally stopping and barking. Olav hadn't realized the chieftains had followed him, but now he could hear their breathing behind him. His half brother, Torkil Nose, asked:

"Is that her?"

Olav replied with a question.

"Do you see what I see?"

"A pair of lovers."

"An axeman poised to strike above them."

Olav nodded. His mind hadn't tricked him. Omold the bard placed a hand on the rock and started to tear away the moss.

"Jesus . . ." he whispered. The rest of the chieftains joined him in trying to clear the stone.

They uncovered the rest of the etched image. Ships, tens of ships that sailed toward their destiny. But what would it be? The ships disappeared suddenly, and in their place there were only dots, nothing more.

He felt the almost-tangible fear that came over his men. He lay down with his face on the illustrated rock. He felt the coolness of the stone and the earthy scent of the moss. For a moment, he let himself believe that he could hear sounds of battle from within the rock: shouts of the wounded, the splash of oars against water, and the clang and crunch of steel on steel. He stood up and turned to his men.

"Chieftains! Surely you aren't afraid of an etching that was made years ago? The time of the True God has come, which means we should not fear. To the ships! The king will fight for his kingdom!"

"And his men for the king," Varin replied hoarsely. "Let's go, the throat of Øresund awaits us."

ØRESUND (A STRAIT BETWEEN DENMARK AND SWEDEN)

They entered the narrow waterway at dawn. An autumn fog floated above the water. It was quiet, so quiet that it felt like the world was refusing to wake. The *Ash Spear* overtook the *Long Snake*, Geivar's long and slender vessel. Olav's friend was meant to locate the Jomsvikings who were waiting in one of the surrounding bays and lead them to join Olav.

"Omold." Tryggvason tried to wake the bard. "Get up."

"You're wearing golden chain mail, my lord . . . Has it begun?" Omold rubbed his swollen eyelids.

"Yes," the king said.

The bard leapt up and looked around.

"No . . ." He shook his head. "Only silence and fog. Not even the shores are visible . . ."

"I assure you the shores are close. Øresund is narrow." Olav placed a hand on Omold's shoulder. "The last time I was here, there was a storm."

"I was with you then, King, I remember." The bard sniffed. "I could have gotten some more sleep, but you woke me before the battle has even begun . . ."

"Look!" Olav turned Omold's head to the right. "The *Ash Spear* is sailing into the bay."

"More like disappearing into the fog," the bard snorted.

"And it will come out of the fog with the strength of the Jomsvikings beside it."

"Why aren't we waiting for them?"

"The king of Norway won't wait to battle hiding behind the iron shields of the boys of Jom. They will sail behind us."

"Oh." Omold yawned.

"Perhaps I was mistaken to send Hallfred to Iceland, hmm?" Olav lost his temper. "Should I start regretting that I took you with me instead of the new bard?"

"Is that an island over there in the fog?" Omold woke up momentarily.

"No, that's a peninsula. There are two, one on each side. It's the narrowest part of the strait of Øresund. A comfortable place to drop anchor. Do you have mead?"

"I go nowhere without it. Half my talent is derived from mead." The bard passed Olav a skin.

Tryggvason took a sip, and the fog began to lift.

"On Freya's golden tits," the bard groaned, and immediately tried to correct himself. "Mary! . . . My God, Jesus forgive me, that's your mother . . . King . . ."

"Look and remember," Olav interrupted his mumbling. "I want you to include every moment in your rhymes. Forget nothing."

"What's the fleet on the right?"

"Those are the Danes. The Swedish forces should be on the left, behind the peninsula."

"The ones which are meant to come to our aid?" the bard asked nervously.

"Yes. I can't see the ships of the heirs of Lade anywhere yet."

"What will your tactic be, King? Will you attack from two sides?"

"No, bard. I will form a floating fortress. A wall of ships."

"But, my lord! If you have the ships tied together, there will be no turning back, and we won't be able to . . ."

"Exactly, Omold. I have no intentions of marring my honor by retreating."

"But then we won't be able to attack them!"

"I don't want to attack. I want to receive the battle. It is the Danish who want to invade my country. I will meet them here."

"Christ the Lord, I think I understand. You want to play hnefatafl with them on the water."

"Yes." Olav nodded and pulled a purple tunic over the chain mail. He glanced at the brooch which held the material together; a fish in the clutches of two eagles. He grabbed a helmet adorned with gold and shouted to the *Long Snake*'s crew: "Defenders of the king, prepare for battle!"

Sven held his forces back. At first, he had intended to sail aboard his recently renovated *Bloody Fox*, but after everything that had happened, he decided to use his newest ship, *Anger*.

He stood aboard the *Anger* and waited for the fog to lift. His scouts told him that today would be the day. They had sighted Olav's fleet the previous evening, when it stopped at Göta älv's estuary for the night, so it had to be today. He'd called a council of war and they'd drawn straws; Øresund was too narrow for them all to attack simultaneously. Yes, luck had been with him. He'd drawn the first attack.

"They're here!" Jorun shouted. "Their bows are coming out of the mist."

A groan of admiration rippled over *Anger*'s deck.

"They said that the *Long Snake* was the most beautiful ship to sail the seas, but the vessel emerging from the fog . . ."

"That's not the *Long Snake*, Jorun," a scout said. "That's only the *Crane*. The *Long Snake* is coming now."

Someone couldn't hold back an admiring whistle.

"I'll kill you," Sven snarled.

But even he had to admit that this was not what he'd been expecting. The vessel truly resembled an ocean dragon.

"Danes!" Sven called out. "We have pulled the lucky draw and we are attacking first!"

"*Anger* in front!" Jorun shouted, grabbing the helm.

"No." Sven stopped him. "My chieftains sail ahead, while the *Anger* protects her king and awaits the right moment. Sound the battle horns."

The deep, low signal bounced off the water. Ragn of the Isles, Haakon of Funen, Gunar of Limfiord, Stenkil of Hobro, and Thorgils of Jelling all responded, and the swift, agile warships sailed to meet the Norwegian vessels.

"Skuli!" Sven summoned the bard. "Can you see?"

"Yes, my lord. I see, remember, and write the song. It will begin like this:"

Sixty ships sailed like spears thrown by a steady hand,
Leaping into the depths of Øresund on King Sven's command!

The fog had lifted, and a bright autumn sun was rising, shining straight into the Norwegians' eyes. *Even the sunrise is against them,* Sven thought as he climbed into *Anger's* bow. He caught sight of Olav's royal tunic and the red glow on the neck of the dragon which decorated his ship.

"The *Long Snake* looks like its throat has been cut already," he said to himself, and breathed in the salty ocean air.

He heard the Norwegian horns and saw that Olav had tied his ships together.

He wants to stop us boarding, Sven thought. *He's bloody confident. He's let down his sails and is waiting for our move. Ragn of the Isles, I know it will be you! You like to sink your claws into the bows of pretty ships.*

"It's begun!" Jorun shouted, leaping to Sven's side.

They watched the cloud of arrows let loose by both sides. They saw the agile Danish ships try to surround Olav's motionless fleet of a fortress.

"I admire you, my king, for being able to stand still while all that is happening . . ."

"Do you remember the day when I first began to plan a war against Olav?" Sven asked Jorun, never taking his eyes off the battle.

"It seems to me now that you never thought of anything else since the moment we returned from England."

"Yes, but that night when I was consumed with rage, you told me: 'Revenge is a dish best served cold.' And you know what? I listened to you."

"It's sinking! One of Gunar's ships is sinking!" Jorun exclaimed. "And there's a fire on the other one. That's not good," he worried frantically.

Sven watched the men on the sinking ship try to reach the decks of nearby vessels; he saw the arrows shot from the *Crane* and the *Short Snake* find their marks in Danish soldiers.

"Can you hear that? Ragn is retreating!" Jorun called out in despair. "Sven, I don't recognize you. Are you just going to stand there and watch? Aren't you going to do anything?"

"They knocked out a few teeth, so what? Nothing. That was only the first attack, my friend. In a moment there will be a move that nobody could see coming."

Sigvald stood on the deck of the *Zealand Falcon* and watched the *Ash Spear* sail away with Geivar on board. He was under no illusions; he knew that although the chief of the house of scouts had given his vow to serve the Jomsvikings, he was still first and foremost loyal to Olav. He could give his men the order and they'd have time to shoot half of *Ash Spear*'s crew, but he knew he wouldn't do it. He wouldn't dishonor himself in such a way.

"Geivar is no longer a house chief! There is no place for him in Jom," he announced loudly enough to be heard by all his men. "The first law of Jom is to serve its jarl unquestioningly, and Geivar has broken that law. Jomsvikings, prepare your ships for battle. Thorkel the Tall, my brother, will lead you."

"Chief!" a fair-haired boy from the house of scouts called out. "We were meant to fight beside Tryggvason. At the Sacred Site they said they will attack the Danes alongside Norway!"

Sigvald laughed and grabbed on to the ropes.

"Jomsvikings don't listen to gossip at the Sacred Site. They follow their chieftain's orders. We are going to stab the Norwegians in the back. Ready? To the oars!"

"Jom! Jom! Jom!" the warriors of the house of sailors chanted, and the first of the fifty ships began to move. Thorkel, Sigvald's brother, sounded the horns of war from its deck.

Like a poisonous snake darting across the water toward its prey, the Jomsviking ships sailed from the bay to strike the *Long Snake*.

Sigvald stood with his sword at the ready at the bow. He saw Geivar's *Ash Spear* reach the line of Norwegian ships. *They should start to regroup any second,* he thought. *Any second now, Olav will find out that Sven offered to pay us more than Świętosława and her brother. Any second now, the Norwegian ships will be reigned by chaos, panic, and death. They will be caught in our pincers and there they will die.*

It wasn't true though. Sven hadn't offered them more money. Sigvald was attacking to soothe the pain inside him. He had once made Astrid a vow: *"For as long as you're loyal to me, Jomsborg and I will be loyal to you."* He valued silver, but he had enough of it that he could afford to hold in contempt whatever he was offered for this mission. Contempt, that was a good way of putting it. He could still taste the contempt that Astrid had fed him. Women were particularly venomous creatures. They could strike a deadly blow without leaving a single mark.

He had suspected for a while, but he'd drowned his suspicions with wine. When he heard her angrily question her brother's idea for Olav to marry Tyra, though, when he'd seen the truest of flushes on her cheeks, a flush she had never had when he was near, he felt as if he'd finally woken up.

And then, to hear Olav speaking sweetly about her, *"Women like your wife need to be taken care of,"* only convinced him further that there was something between Astrid and Tryggvason that should not be.

And the cold humiliation of losing three times when they wrestled underwater. Sigvald couldn't forgive him for that. From that moment, he'd known he had to watch closely to make sure he wasn't being used. In the name of Odin and Thor! He was the chieftain of Jomsborg, not a servant.

"Sigvald will carry out my order," they said, or, worse yet, *"Tell him."* As if he was a mere cabin boy rather than the jarl of the iron boys!

When Astrid had returned from Gniezno, from her brother the duke, they'd argued. His wife was like a stormcloud that tried to rush him. "Bolesław told you to stand with Olav, so hurry up, there's no time. Geivar has sailed to Nidaros from Roskilde along with Dusza. Sigvald, hurry!" She didn't notice that he said nothing. Then, she gave herself to him in bed, as she always did. She spread her legs for him and moaned, she writhed like a cat in heat. But when he entered her, he realized he'd been duped yet again. She was dry. There was not a drop of moisture in her. She moaned, feigning pleasure, but her body could not lie. He pretended not to notice. He took her hard, wanting to get back at her, until he heard real pain in her cries. Then he caressed and embraced her. He whispered to her that he would go. He would arm the ships, fifty vessels with the wolf's muzzle on their sails, fifty of Jom's famous ships.

"I will stand at Tryggvason's side," he'd said. "I'll protect his back and his flanks. He'll come out of it alive and well, our friend, our Norwegian king." He whispered first in her right ear, then her left, about how he had visited Olav in Nidaros. "Picture this: a white horse, a white dog, and a beautiful white king. When he walks among his people they kneel before him. I swam with him, did you know that? Our sailors in Jom have arms and backs sculpted by the work they do at the oars, but I tell you, Astrid, as Olav pulled his shirt over his head, I froze." Then his wife moaned again. As he'd whispered about Olav—Olav's strength, Olav undressing—Sigvald had slipped his fingers between her legs, and then there was nothing left to be said between them. Astrid's secret lay bare before him. This was the honesty of passion, that the body cannot hide. He kissed her and pretended to sleep. He didn't.

He listened to her steady breathing and tried to decide the best course of action. How best to take his vengeance. And he understood that this act of revenge would solve a lot of problems for him. He wouldn't have to be obedient to Bolesław anymore, an obedience that Mieszko had forced him into years ago in return for supporting his bid for the jarl of Jom. Times had changed, though, and now there was no threat to his position. He no longer had to bow down to the proud duke. And by killing Tryggvason, he would remove the stain of having called for retreat all those years ago. From Hjørung Bay when the Norwegians attacked. He would show that he, Sigvald, was not afraid of attacking a king.

They were approaching the back of Olav's fleet. He swore because that was where the smaller vessels were placed. To reach the *Long Snake*, he'd have to fight his way to the front.

"They have tied the ships together," a warrior at the bow of the *Zealand Falcon* announced.

"We will wait until they are occupied with the king's attack in front and aren't paying attention to us. Then we sail closer, shoot a hail of arrows at them, and pick off the first ship under the cover of shields and arrows. When we board it, we will use their floating fleet to go from deck to deck, killing all."

"Yes!"

Perfect, Sigvald thought. *All I had to do was get rid of any illusions I may have had about Astrid, and everything is simpler. Life has color once more!*

"Jarl!" A panting, red-faced boy ran over to him. "Your brother Thorkel sends a message: the *Salty Sister* is on the other side of Olav's fleet."

"What?!" Sigvald exclaimed. "Bitch!"

The *Salty Sister* was Astrid's ship.

"Thorkel is asking what we should do."

"Treat her as an enemy," Sigvald ordered coldly.

Olof stood at the bow of his first warship. He had called it the *Golden Shield*, and as he sailed out of Sigtuna, he'd told his people: "The *Golden Shield* will always protect my kingdom and its people!" He wanted to fight so badly that he could neither eat nor sleep. He was a man in bed by now—he could keep a girl with him until morning and give her pleasure without finishing too soon. Now, he wanted to become a man on the battlefield, too. A true king to his people. *"At his age Tryggvason had defeated . . ."* Yes. Olof was old enough to defeat the boy inside himself and to lead without Wilkomir at his elbow, watching his every step. "Lift your elbow higher. Cover yourself. Your shield is too low. Cover yourself or lose your teeth. Strike, now! Too slow. Too late. You're dead. Get up and practice. A man never gives up." He had had enough practicing on the training ground. Enough was enough. A real man proved his courage in battle.

"Go!" he shouted. "On my command, follow the *Golden Shield* . . . Now!"

He stood at the bow dressed in chain mail, clutching his sword which shone in the sun.

"Your father would be proud of you, my lord," a warrior the size of a bear praised him.

His father might be. But his mother? He shook it off.

To become a man, I must kill the mummy's boy inside me, he thought firmly.

"Toward Tryggvason's floating fleet, as fast as you can!" he called, and sixty ships ripped through the waves.

He had pulled the third straw.

He had shared his plans with his chieftains right after he had met with King Sven on an island in the strait of Øresund. "First Sven, then the Jomsvikings from the back, and then it's us coming in third. If anyone from Olav's fleet survives, Eric of Lade will take care of them, though I would prefer that they fall under our axes."

"So would we!" his chieftains agreed. Half of them had sailed with Eric.

When he had forced Wilkomir to stay in Sigtuna, saying: "I make you regent," there was no one left to accompany him who knew of his mother's desire for him to betray Sven. *"Betray Sven. Prepare for war at his side, but betray him before it starts. When the battle begins, stand by Olav Tryggvason."*

Never! I won't stain my honor with treachery in my very first battle, Mother, he imagined saying to her. *I can't, I won't do it. You and your pale-eyed, predatory Olav would make a boy of me again. But Sven understands that I'm a man. He promised me the three things I want: victory, fame, and a wife.* "Tryggvason will die, Olof, because he won't stand a chance. Our joined forces will crush him, so your first battle will be a victorious one. And you will always be known as one of the kings in this battle of the three kings. Skuli is writing songs about it already, rhyming Olof with Olav. And when we share the spoils of war, I will find you a princess worthy of your bed. A beautiful lady of a noble family who can be your queen. For now, accept a slave from me to show you the pleasures which await you. Her name is Edla, and she's a sweet Slavic girl." Sven hadn't lied; she was sweet. She was the one who had taught him how to last longer. And her tongue, the tongue of his mother, made her submission to him in bed doubly satisfying.

The *Golden Shield* was still sailing onward, aided by its oarsmen. Moving past the Danes, he lifted an arm to greet Sven. His mother's husband's red hair danced on the wind as if Sven's head had caught fire. Vestar from Uppsala was captain of the ship. Vestar's brother-in-law, Toki, was commanding the axemen in the stern.

He saw the *Long Snake* and thought how arrogant it was to build such a big ship. Sixty-eight rowers. A deck that could fit two hundred warriors.

He came to my mother modestly, with three ships. Each one had a stem, that is, a warship that had seen blood on its bow. If he had come on the Long Snake, *perhaps my Bold Lady mother would have accepted him. But he didn't respect her enough for that. He came like a beggar, asking her to aid him. He'd been wrong. Sigrid Storråda, queen of Sweden, wouldn't accept a man without a throne. Now that he was known in all the north, she'd changed her mind. It's too late, Mother. It's too late. Your husband loves you very much and he won't give you up without a fight. Your son will stand beside him and even if it were just us, we would still defeat your lover. But it so happens that it's four against one.*

"Archers . . . fire!" Vestar gave the order, and the sky turned black with flying arrows.

The shots fired back from the floating fortress were far sparser. A shield was enough to protect them. *"Higher, cover your whole head, hold it at an angle so the arrowhead slips away,"* he heard Wilkomir's voice in his head. For the first time in his life, Olof heard the sound of a real arrow bouncing off the smooth surface of his shield, not one fired in practice. What strength! He could almost feel it in the metal of his helmet. His ears were ringing. He moved his shield away hesitantly.

The helmsman had stopped the *Golden Shield.* "Roll up the sail!" he ordered.

Why? Olof thought. *Oh, to stop the wind from rocking the ship!* He felt furious with Wilkomir for not teaching him the rules of fighting on a ship. Only the training ground and the training ground again. Sword, shield, spear, bow, axe. But the training ground didn't shift under his feet when he needed to run to attack. Suddenly he felt bile rising in his throat. *I'm going to be sick.* He groaned. *I can't, they'll laugh at me!*

The helmsman violently turned the *Golden Shield* around. Tryggvason's ships, tied together, made it impossible to approach closer to board them. Olof lost his balance and was forced to kneel.

"What are you doing?" he called to the helmsman.

"Oars!" the man gave the command before answering him. "Let's take them from the side, my lord. From the first ship."

"I want to attack the *Long Snake!*"

"All in good time, my lord. We won't reach the bow of the royal ship, but we can reach the slender lady on the edge here. If Odin is with us, then we can jump from deck to deck to get to the king in the red tunic."

Only now did he see him. Yes, that was him! Although his face was hidden by a helmet, his pale hair, almost white, was visible on his shoulders. His height, his broad back—it could be no one else. The *Golden Shield* was already passing the *Long Snake's* gunwales; Olof, wanting to keep his eye on the king, would have to have run to the stern. At first, he was about to do that, but then he remembered where he was. He heard the arrows whistle above his head. *"Shield. Hold it at an angle."* He followed Wilkomir's order. An order from the training ground and from the safety of Sigtuna, far away. A real arrow, here and now. He knelt down under his shield and threw up. At the same moment, his men threw grappling hooks over the Norwegian ship's gunwales.

Olav slid his sword back in its sheath and grabbed a handful of spears. There were still no enemies on board, but the second row of ships had broken. The Jomsvikings had struck him from the back. He could almost see Sigvald cocking his head as he wrung water out of his hair and gave him a crooked smile after he'd lost their wrestling game. Now he was taking his revenge.

The warriors at the stern of the *Long Snake* protected the back now that the entire line had fallen apart. He focused on the Swedes. *Her son,* he thought coldly as he watched the ships turning sharply. *Her son has played me for a fool.*

He threw the spears, switching arms each time. He saw men boarding from the sides, but they were still two ships away. His archers' fingers bled as they shot arrow after arrow.

"My king," Varin called. "I have a message from the left. Do you see the green sail by the shore?"

"Yes!" Olav replied.

"That's the *Salty Sister*, the Lady of Wolin's ship. Astrid has come to fight the traitor Sigvald. She has brought twenty Slavic ships with her. She's asking where to position herself."

Astrid! He knew she wouldn't betray him. He knew that Sigvald had disregarded Bolesław's orders; Geivar, his friend, had reached them just before the Jomsvikings struck their treacherous blow. The *Ash Spear* had been right next to them, and when the *Zealand Falcon* had smashed it, twenty of Geivar's Jomsvikings had leapt aboard his ships.

"Tell them to stay in the bay and wait. I don't want Astrid to take part in the battle. They can take our wounded."

Our wounded and our dead. All of us—but he didn't say this out loud. He took aim at the third helmsman of a Swedish ship and killed him. *I had seventy ships. I've lost the second line so I have thirty left. Sven has lost ten, he has sixty left. Olof attacked with sixty. I have another ten or fifteen Jomsviking ships at the back. That's four to one. And then there's Eric; how many ships does he have? How many well-rested crews? God only knows.* He turned around and looked behind him. Shattered masts and gunwales. Flooding decks of sinking ships. The etching in the stone: ships, tens of vessels sailing to a fate that nobody could see, disappearing from the stone one by one with nothing but dots to mark their presence.

"You must know something, King," Sivrit had told him that night, once Geivar and Dusza left them. "Jesus, entering Jerusalem on the Sunday before he was crucified, waved to people who cheered at his presence, but he knew he was going to his death." *I am responding to Świętosława's call,* he had thought. *I won't turn back. It's as if she were watching me, even though she won't be there.* Sivrit stared at him piercingly as he continued: "Our Lord asked His Father to change His fate only once, when He prayed in the olive garden. But then He realized that His road led through death. God spared Abraham his son Isaac. He didn't test the ordinary man's faith. But He didn't hesitate to test His Son's. He ordered Him to walk through death because that was His will. That's what testing His faith required. Do you understand, my lord?" Olav had held the brooch in his fingers during that conversation. The fish torn apart by two eagles. Two kings. That was the moment he realized that Świętosława expected the other king, Olof, to betray him.

"There is no vanity in me to think that my journey is Christ's," he had told the bishop that night. "But if God wants me to be his tool then I won't step off this road. Will you take care of Tyra if I don't return?"

"Jesus Christ was first named king in the moment of his death," Sivrit said, and added: "Yes, I will take care of Queen Tyra."

"Olav!" Varin shouted. "The king of Swedes is nipping at our wings, but Jarl Eric is sailing to face us, and with him are the ships of the jarls of Trondelag. The ones who had sworn fealty to you . . ."

"The rooster has called," said Sivrit in Olav's head. The king leapt sideways for another handful of spears.

Sven stood at *Anger*'s gunwale and watched the battle unfold. Skuli was shouting out new verses of the poem he was writing, inspired by the smell of blood and mead.

> *Like hunting hounds catching a deer,*
> *The swords of the two kings have caught*
> *The third.*
> *He didn't hide but*
> *Stood proudly, accepting with courage each bite from the pack.*

"Skuli!" Sven roared. "I'm the one paying you!"
"It's just the beginning, my lord! Listen."

> *The Danish ships drew blood from their victim*
> *As the vessels of the iron brothers tore at its back.*
> *The young Swede attacked the sides*
> *And Eric, thirsty for revenge, sailed into the dragon's jaws.*

"Are you Eric's bard now?"

"Wait, my king. Poetry requires a warm-up. Listen!"

A pack of fierce wolves fights together
But it has only one leader.
The bloodred king with a beard braided into a fork
Like a river flowing down his face.
Sven, lord of the Danes, gave a command, and the stag fell to its knees.

Sven stood on the deck of his ship and watched his son-in-law sail at the *Long Snake* on his *Iron Beak*, armed with spikes. Olav had cut away the *Short Snake* and the *Crane* only moments earlier. The *Crane* was sailing away with a deck full of wounded men, heading toward the Slavic ship with the green sail. The *Anger* was so close that Sven could see what was happening on the ships. He could smell death and blood. He could hear Olav's orders. When Eric's *Iron Beak* headed toward the solitary *Long Snake* at full speed, he saw Olav hesitate. *Yes!* Finally, the second chieftain took off his helmet. A warrior only ever takes his helmet off when he knows he will not evade death. Olav shouted something and a woman ran toward him. Sven felt his heart skip a beat. He thought it was her. His wife. Sventoslava. But no. It was her servant, Dusza. Her hood had fallen back, and he could see her hair was flaxen, not golden. Olav whispered something to the mute and caught her face in both of his hands, leaving marks of blood on her cheeks. He kissed her lips.

The kiss of betrayal and the touch of death, Sven thought, and ordered Jorun, "Bring in the anchor! We're going in."

"Why?" Jorun asked. "Eric has only half of the *Long Snake* left to fight. The rest of the Norwegians are dead!"

"I want to stab him myself," Sven howled. "Go!"

When he felt the *Anger* shift under his feet in its newfound freedom, he started to play comparisons.

The white king is bleeding out!

The red king sails in with a sword!

The white king fought!

The red king waited! a cruel voice whispered to him.

The white king is loved by the queen, who betrayed the red king, she gave him children and betrayed him, betrayed!

Betrayed, betrayed—the voices in his head mocked him.

* * *

Olav was wounded. Blood seeped out from under his chain mail. He could hear Geivar's labored breathing at his back. His friend was fighting the wolf-men, Jom's iron boys.

"Sigvald! Come!" Geivar shouted, baring his painted fangs.

Varin was baring his at Olav's side, living up to his reputation as a ber-serker. He threw away his shield, helmet, and sword. He fought with his knife as if it were a claw. Świętosława's Dusza had fallen moments earlier with an arrow through her heart. She would never deliver his message to her mistress. A short message: "I love you." She died with it on her lips. Orm was draped over a gunwale, pierced by a spear. Rafn God's Axe was fighting on his knees with a knife in his back. Ingvar was fighting blind as blood poured into his eyes. Thorolf was still shooting arrows, though he had about a dozen in his chest. Omold the bard was shouting from afar, from aboard the *Crane* which was carrying away the wounded:

He joins the ranks of the immortals as blood colors his words . . .

Olav wiped blood from his face and saw the second chieftain across the water. Sven was sailing toward him. The Danish king's red hair twisted in the wind like the flame of a torch.

Bamburgh Castle. *"Shall we play?" "I won't swim with you,"* Sven had said. *"Won't you?"* Olav turned around and wiped away the blood that poured into his eyes.

The green sail of the *Salty Sister* appeared briefly in the rising eve-ning fog.

Thorolf fell, dropping his bow. Geivar bit into Sigvald's artery and was strangling him on the deck, clutching at him and spitting blood.

"Varin!" Olav called to his closest friend.

Varin, a berserker, a beast, was eating an enemy's heart raw.

"Vigi," Olav whispered, searching for his dog.

Once white, the dog's fur was now the royal red of blood. The dog ran to him and whined.

Anger rocked on the waves, bow to bow with the *Long Snake*. The red-haired second chieftain stood at the bow and drew his sword. The golden weather-vane sang as if it had just been moved by a gust of wind. Olav saw Sven's crew. He heard Varin's howl of death behind him.

"Vigi, we're jumping!" Olav commanded, and threw away his sword. "You won't take me! You won't defeat me!" he shouted at Sven, and, hiding behind his shield, he leapt into the waves.

"The battle of the three kings is ended!" someone shouted, but Olav wasn't sure who it was. He was already underwater. The cold ocean closed over his head.

"My king swims like a fish from the depths," Varin would have said if he'd still been alive.

PART II
THE CROWN OF THORNS

1000–1014

11

DENMARK

The moon hangs low over the empty world, like a great silver shield. Who is it trying to protect now that the noise of the battle has ended? The moors are abandoned, the woods are a dark smudge in the distance, and the black waves of the fjord scratch the cliff as if they were a jagged claw. The cold glow of the night's light follows the stag that forages for food, seeing the lurking predators that lie in wait. A silent wolf pack has caught scent of the blood which still pulses with life inside the creature's veins. The moon, the pale master of the night, will aid neither the prey nor the wolves. It rocks above the ground, perfectly indifferent to life and death alike.

Świętosława howled like a wolf in pain in Roskilde. Sven and his chieftains had not yet returned, as they had sailed to the estuary of Göta älv, to the place where the three kingdoms met, to share out the spoils of war. But they had sent word with the bard. Skuli's hands were stained with as much blood as the hands of every one of her husband's men.

"The Battle of the Three Kings," the bard said when she received him in Roskilde's great hall, "has concluded with our victory."

She dug her fingers into the throne's armrests. She didn't look at the bard, but at the intricate ornaments which ran along the hall's walls. Her eyes followed the carvings as she clenched her teeth. The wolf was catching the eagle in its claws as it pounced. The eagle was reaching its beak toward a horse's head. A wildcat was throwing itself at a weasel, jaws wide, its body part of the spiral patterns of the carvings. There was no beginning nor end in the mythical fight of the beasts. There was no winner. Each animal held on to the next with its claws, paws, or teeth. She could delude herself for a little while longer.

"My queen," the bard asked, "did you hear me?"

She struggled to find her voice.

"Tell me what happened, Skuli."

"King Sven has achieved a wonderful victory . . ."

I don't want to hear this, she thought.

". . . the united troops defeated Olav. They drew straws before the battle, and our king was the first to attack. The third attack was led by your son, Olof King of Swedes. Jarl Eric was the fourth . . ."

My God! Her heart almost stopped. *I wasn't wrong and Olof betrayed. He was the second eagle that sank its claws into the fish. They drew straws . . . like brutish soldiers for the Savior's cloak.*

"Olav Tryggvason had been counting on the Jomsvikings to help him, but Jarl Sigvald kept his troops on the side, and stabbed him in the back when he saw that Olav had no chance of winning. His fleet attacked from behind."

Oh God! Betrayed again by those he trusted . . .

"Tryggvason had ordered his ships tied together as soon as they reached the strait. That was his mistake. He had formed a floating fortress which stood still; he couldn't escape . . ."

He didn't want to escape, he wanted to win. He didn't know that two of his allies would betray him.

". . . but he defended himself bravely," Skuli continued. "We have to give him that. He cut off ship after ship filled with the dead and wounded . . ."

Corpse ships, she thought. *Like in the story about Ragnarök. Was this the battle at the end of time? Yes. Darkness will reign now, and the world that I know is gone.*

". . . until finally, when the last men aboard the *Long Snake* died, when King Sven struck the final blow, Olav, not wanting to give himself up to us, jumped into the water under the cover of his shield."

"He drowned?" she asked hoarsely.

"He never resurfaced. Many brave men found their way to the depths of the strait of Øresund that day."

The blood left her face.

"My lady! Rejoice and celebrate! The crown of Norway is yours! Do you know what they will call you from now on? The Lady of the Three Thrones. It's a great honor . . . Queen Sigrid, King Sven invites you . . ."

She felt a jerk. Wrzask and Zgrzyt were standing, and they had jerked their leash. She let them lead her out of the hall. They pulled her toward the moors of Roskilde. She ran, tripping over her dress. Only when she passed the last buildings did she drop to her knees and howl like a wounded animal. The lynxes ran around her. She lifted her face, disfigured with a spasm of pain. Gusts of wind tore at her hair. The wind came from the east, from Øresund. She breathed it in. It brought blood, salt, and death. This wasn't pain anymore; this was suffering. Zgrzyt and Wrzask lay down at her sides, panting heavily.

SWEDEN

Olof returned from the feast of the victors which Sven had thrown in the beautiful basin at the estuary of Göta älv. Edla greeted him in Sigtuna. Her embraces on the first three nights were sweet. He found solace and the taste of true triumph in his lover's arms. Every time he entered her, he felt the boards of the *Golden Shield*'s deck creak under his feet, he felt his ship smash against the floating fortress. Every time that Edla trembled, calling out "my king!" in his arms, he washed himself clean of the horrible smell of the cowardly vomit which he had not been able to stop. Edla's body and love cleansed him. Yes, he had stood on the side of the victors in the Battle of the Three Kings. Why didn't he feel like a hero? Why did he still remember how he knelt on the deck and covered himself with his shield? He'd seen the waves roaring onto the deck, and he'd been afraid.

"Edla, give me some wine."

"Not mead?" His lover stretched. "Since when does my king drink wine?"

"Since I received some from King Sven as a gift," he retorted angrily.

He sat on the bed. He could taste Edla's salty flavor on his lips, but the feeling of bliss had evaporated. He wiped his forehead. The girl threw on a cloak and walked out of the alcove to fetch some wine. When he was left alone, he slouched reflexively. For a moment he didn't have to be a king. He pulled his knees up to his chin. The door of the alcove opened, but he didn't lift his head, thinking that Edla had returned.

"Olof . . ." Wilkomir's voice emerged from the darkness.

Olof straightened immediately.

"Olof, I have just returned from Uppsala and I heard what happened at Øresund. What did you do?!"

"How dare you speak to me that way?" Olof demanded, covering his nakedness with a fox fur. "I am king, and you . . ."

"King?" Wilkomir walked over to him with the soft step of a predator. "What kind of king breaks his word?"

"She was the one who wanted me to break it!" Olof exclaimed, and he heard a boy's voice, not a man's, speaking the words. "She was the one who wanted me to act like a common traitor!"

"She has a name. She is your mother. The queen of Sweden and Denmark." Wilkomir's eyes gleamed in the dark.

"And now she is also queen of Norway, thanks to me," Olof retorted.

"Do you think she'll thank you for that throne?" Wilkomir was still circling the bed like one of his mother's lynxes. The skinny one, Wrzask. Olof felt afraid. "You betrayed her!" Wilkomir hissed. "You acted like a coward."

"Be silent! I am victorious, and my men . . ."

Wilkomir leaned over him and placed his hands on Olof's shoulders. He was so close that Olof could see every line on his face.

"Yes, you have won the battle, you brought back spoils, and your people will say it was a successful venture. But you will forever be the son who betrayed. The king who fought in a battle in which three were against one. And you know what? I'm sure that the bards, even those who are paid by all of you victors, will pay tribute to Olav in their verses about Øresund. The people love winners, that's true, but every verse will point out that it was three against one. Time will pass judgment on you all, my lord."

"Then you can keep yours to yourself, Wilkomir, teacher," he whispered.

"Either I have failed you as a teacher, or you as a student, Olof. What you did was dishonorable. I did not teach you that. I'm leaving." Wilkomir let go of his shoulders and stood tall.

"Go to hell! I don't want to see you again," Olof shouted, meaning every word. "Yes, you were a poor teacher. You didn't warn me that the deck rocks, that it's hard to keep your balance under the weight of armor and sword. You didn't teach me well, but I succeeded anyway . . ."

He fell silent because he realized that Wilkomir was no longer there. He had left without a word of farewell. Edla stood in the doorway with a jug of wine, startled by his shouts.

"What are you staring at?" he reprimanded her. "Pour me some!"

He lifted his goblet too violently and the wine streamed down his chin. He was growing his beard; it wasn't as thick as his father's, though, and rather resembled lichen. He wiped away the wine. Edla sat down beside him and put her arm around his shoulders.

"Don't be angry, my lord. You're a hero. And a hero needs an heir." She kissed his cheek. "I'm carrying your child, Olof."

"A son?" He almost choked.

She laughed and rested her head on his shoulder.

"I don't know . . ."

Now or later? he thought. *I'm strong enough to get this over with.*

"Edla, changes are coming. I must wed."

She wrapped her arms around him and placed a wet kiss on his cheek.

"I will be honored . . ."

"You won't be," he said quietly. "I won't marry you. Are you insane? You're only a mistress."

"The mother of your heir!" she muttered.

"Of my child," he corrected her. "And I swear that I won't deny either you or the child. But Princess Astrid will be my wife."

"She's still a child! And your mother's daughter, your sister . . ." she protested.

"No, not that Astrid, another. The daughter of an Obotrite duke. My stepfather Sven has chosen her for me. She will bring a great dowry with her . . ."

"Why do you want her dowry? You're rich, Olof . . ."

He grabbed her shoulders and pushed her away.

"Edla, control yourself! I can't marry you; you aren't noble enough. Even if you have had such dreams, get rid of them. The lives of kings are not their own, do you understand?"

"No," she sobbed.

"And that's why you can't be a king's wife. You don't understand. You're no good."

"Stop, please stop . . ." she whimpered. "You said that I can give you pleasure . . ."

"You can," he confirmed. "And that's why I won't send you away. You'll stay in Sigtuna and continue doing what you do best."

She lay on top of him a moment later to prove that she still could give him pleasure. He took it, and drank goblet after goblet of wine, until he could no longer picture Wilkomir turning his back to walk away from him.

DENMARK

Sven was returning to Roskilde aboard the *Anger*. He had waited in vain for Świętosława to join him at the estuary of Göta älv. He had sent the bard to her, but it seemed that Skuli hadn't succeeded in convincing his queen to join them for the victors' feast.

"She's put me in an awkward position again," he snarled to Jorun and spat overboard.

"Give it a rest, my king. That's what the Bold One is like." His friend tried to calm him. "We should celebrate our victory. I still can't believe that Tryggvason sailed into Øresund. He used to be far wiser when we were in England."

And would you have believed the real motives if you knew them? Sven wondered gloomily.

"Do you know what?" Jorun continued. "I keep wondering about that girl aboard the *Long Snake*. Did you see her?"

Sven turned his head away and the wind tore through his red hair, obscuring his face.

"I could have sworn that I knew her or had seen her before . . ."

"A girl is a girl," Sven muttered. "They all look alike. It's just evidence that Olav had someone on the side, someone other than my sister. What does it matter now that Tyra is dead, too? She was always a coward. She was too afraid to let iron take her life, so she starved herself to death instead when she learned of her husband's demise. Foolish Tyra. I would have forgiven her treason and I could have married her off as a widowed queen."

"You're right," Jorun agreed, and said nothing else about the girl.

They sailed into Roskildefiord, sounding the horns to announce the victorious king's arrival. He was still telling himself that Świętosława would behave as a wife should and that she would greet him at the port. But when they arrived, he saw that everyone had shown up except for her.

"The Bold Lady is probably in the manor, overseeing the preparations for the welcome feast . . ." Jorun said.

Nonsense. You don't believe what you're saying yourself, but you're still defending her, Sven thought, but he didn't reply.

She was waiting for him in the great hall with five-year-old Harald and three-year-old Cnut at her side. She wore an ash-gray dress, and the grayness gave Sven hope that they might make peace.

She wants to appear humble, he thought. *That's a good sign.*

But when he approached her, she stood up and both lynxes rose as if at her command, growling loudly. He frowned. The cats were straining against their leashes.

"My lady, we won't talk like this. Have them taken out."

She didn't reply. She summoned Wilczan with a nod and gave him the leash. The boy struggled to control the lynxes, but eventually managed to lead them out of the hall.

"Wife, I waited for you in the victors' camp. Did Skuli not convey my invitation?"

"He did," she replied.

"Why did you not come?"

"The winds weren't favorable, and our daughters were ailing," she replied. Her face showed no emotion.

He ruffled Harald's red hair and Cnut's blond fringe. The boys stood as stiffly as their mother.

"Are they well?" he asked, looking around for Melkorka and the Goat.

"They still have a cough. Heidi is with them."

He suddenly felt a growing hope that his wife wasn't lying.

"I want to see them," he said. "Now."

"As you wish, my king."

He turned to his guests and announced:

"Celebrate! Drink, eat, and make merry! The queen and I will join you soon."

The hall responded with laughter and grew noisy in a matter of seconds. He glanced at Świętosława and nodded to her. They walked to the alcove, where one of the Bold One's men was guarding the door.

"Go, celebrate." Sven clapped his shoulder.

The boy nodded but didn't leave his station. They walked inside. The Goat was sitting at his wife's bed, and both their daughters were asleep.

"Are they better?" he asked the wet nurse.

"Not yet, my lord," she replied. "They still have a fever."

He touched both their foreheads: they were burning up. He should have been worried, but instead he felt happy to find that Świętosława had spoken the truth.

"Heidi Goat, leave us alone," he said softly. "I want to speak to my wife. We'll call you if you're needed."

"Whatever the king wishes," she replied, and walked slowly toward the door. "But call for me if they start to cry. The Goat's breast is the best thing for a fever, that's what they say, and that's the truth."

He turned to his wife when she'd left.

"You didn't come because they were unwell," he said quietly. "You're a good mother."

She was silent.

"I bring victory, but you already know that. Norway belongs to us, my queen. I won't rule there in person, but I have made Eric of Lade my viceroy, and joined only Viken with Denmark. The eastern part of the country is your son's, and Jarl Sven, Eric's brother, will be his viceroy. It's a fair split."

She was still silent. He felt his blood begin to boil.

"Say something," he whispered. "Don't you understand? I'm trying to make peace, wife! You had me for a barbarian, but you were wrong. I'm generous. If you are humble and you apologize, I'm prepared to forgive your treason."

"Forgive?" she repeated tonelessly.

"Bloody hell, don't you understand?" he snarled. "I know about your treason. I know what you said to Olav and to your son. I know everything. I know that you were prepared to sacrifice me. Yes, you confessed to Ion, and Ion confessed to me. If I had told my men about this, they would have hacked you into pieces. But I kept Ion's words to myself. Even Jorun doesn't know what you've done. I protected you. And do you know what, my treacherous wife? I decided to give you another chance. Like a true Christian. But I expect deep remorse for your sins. Women love victors, and I'm laying this victory at your feet. Olav is dead. He jumped into the water like a coward. He's gone! You'll forget you ever loved him and . . ."

"Loved him?" she repeated hollowly. "You're wrong. I still love him."

He heard a high-pitched whistle fill his ears. He felt the blood rush to his face. He raised a hand and slapped her as hard as he could, but she didn't even flinch. She stood tall and lifted her head high. And in that moment, he knew he could kill her. He kicked the door open and stormed from the alcove.

As he pushed through the crowded hall, he could smell roasted meat, onions, beer, and mead, but he still couldn't hear anything. He could see his men's lips moving as they spoke, the smiling red faces and horns lifted in toasts, but he could hear nothing. He ran outside where the cold enveloped him. Cold—he realized. Revenge is a dish best served cold. He forced his heart rate to slow and waited. The whistling in his ears grew quieter and his hearing returned. He saw Wilczan's slender figure in the distance.

"Hey, wolf boy!" he called to him cheerfully. "Your mistress is looking for you."

"On my way, my lord," the boy called back.

"Leave the lynxes with me. I'll take a walk with them." Sven reached out for the leash, and though the cats growled, they walked over to him trustingly.

WOLIN, WOLIN ISLAND, POLAND

Astrid cared for the wounded from the battle at Øresund. Dalwin gave her one of the sailor's huts at the outskirts of Wolin, and some of his own servants to help her. Busla replaced her when she needed to leave. The first few weeks after the battle had been the worst. She was trying to come to terms with Sigvald's betrayal, but she couldn't make peace with what her husband had done.

The autumn night fell fast. She put on a cloak and headed to the port. There were still two large Frisian ships at the docks, with huge cargo holds and high gunwales; she had heard Dalwin say they would leave within a week. There were also a few ships from Truso, but not much else. The merchants were sailing away for the winter.

Leszko, her helmsman, was loitering around the *Salty Sister*.

"It's time to pull the ships onto the shore," he said to her. "It's getting bloody cold and the frost may come any day. What do you think, my lady? I can feel the coming chill in my bones."

"I need to sail to Rügen one more time," she replied, listening to the water splash against the gunwales.

"Well, I don't think we can."

Leszko often began his sentences by declaring something to be impossible.

"Then I'll get a different helmsman," she replied calmly. "Someone who isn't afraid of such a short journey before an autumn storm."

She tried not to look toward Jom. To avoid seeing it. Which wasn't that hard. Since Sigvald and Geivar had both fallen in battle, Jomsborg had no chieftains. The Jomsvikings had even stopped lighting the torches for sailors. There was nothing but darkness there now.

"I never said I was afraid," he said, insulted. "I said the cold approaches, and swiftly."

"Do you know where you can shove your nose?" She grimaced.

"Wherever you want me to, my lady."

"Be ready at dawn," she said, and turned back toward home.

She heard the horn sound from Jom's main gates. Without even thinking, she counted. Three times. *Visitors,* she thought. *I wonder who it is.* But she swiftly reprimanded herself. *It's not your business anymore, Astrid.*

She met Dalwin at the gate. Someone stood with him, a silhouette that she recognized but couldn't name in the darkness.

"Lady of Wolin," he said as he bowed.

She acknowledged him with a nod.

"Astrid, this is Bjornar," Dalwin reminded her, and she was sure she saw them exchange a meaningful glance.

"Bjornar," she repeated.

Dalwin sighed.

"I told you, my lord, that my Astrid isn't ready yet. Everything that's happened has left its mark on her. She was at Øresund. She saw everything that happened from her vantage point aboard the *Salty Sister*, she heard the cries of the dying, their screams for mercy . . ." Dalwin shook his head. "No, my girl cannot go to Poznań with you. She needs rest. Astrid"—he turned to her now— "Bjornar is a friend of your brother's. Red-haired as a squirrel, remember?"

"Yes, I remember," she said quietly. "I'm cold."

"Yes, let's go inside." Dalwin put an arm around her, giving her shoulder a squeeze. "A cold comes from the Dziwna strait in autumn. Come, Master Bjornar."

When they had sat down by the fire, the servants brought mulled beer with honey and butter.

She noticed Bjornar studying her.

"The duke has sent me," he said carefully. "He'd like to talk to you about what happened, and about what should happen next, but Dalwin tells me that you aren't well."

She nodded.

"Can you tell me what I should tell Duke Bolesław?"

"Sigvald betrayed us," she said hollowly. "Olof King of Swedes didn't join forces with Olav Tryggvason, but sided with Sven . . ."

"Yes, we know that," Bjornar interrupted her gently. "But we want to understand why Jarl Sigvald . . ."

Because of me. I didn't lie well enough. I didn't fake my love for him well enough. My brother won't understand. And my sister most certainly wouldn't, she thought, her fingers tightening around her cup.

"I don't know, Bjornar," she replied quietly. "I have no idea."

"Sigvald was a coward," Dalwin interjected angrily. "Duke Mieszko made a mistake when he married Astrid to a coward. Sigvald betrayed King Harald in the battle at Hjørung Bay, and he betrayed King Sven when he imprisoned him in Jom. Two betrayals will always choose a third for company. He waited until he was sure that young Olof wasn't going to join Tryggvason and he decided he preferred to be on the winning side. My Astrid has suffered enough because of that . . ."

"Leave it alone, Grandfather," she said gently. "He's dead, and I don't mourn him."

"And the wounded?" Bjornar asked carefully. "You brought the wounded back from the battle."

"They're in the hut." She nodded. "I didn't manage to save many, but there's a chance that Omold will recover his voice. His bard."

"And . . ." Bjornar was looking at her intently.

"He jumped."

"They didn't find a body?"

She shook her head, barely containing her tears.

"He was seriously wounded. He jumped wearing chain mail . . ." A sob choked her words.

"I understand, there's nothing more to be said. Please. Don't cry . . ."

"I saw Sigvald's death. Geivar . . . Geivar went berserk and bit through his artery, like a beast." She threw out the words as if she were throwing stones. "Rivers of blood flowed across the decks. Men's entrails hung over the gunwales. Bloody intestines and brown livers. I saw one of Olav's companions fighting on his knee when his leg had been chopped off . . . Ah!"

"Astrid, that's enough, don't cry." Bjornar reached out a hand, wanting to stroke her.

She pushed it away and shouted:

"Why? Because you feel uncomfortable in the face of a crying woman in pain? You start wars as if it was a game of hnefatafl, and then you say 'don't cry'? Tell my brother that he is as guilty as my cursed husband. He should never have made the match between Tyra and Olav. That was the source of all this evil, tell him that!"

That's a lie. Evil had its source much earlier, with Mieszko's decision, she thought grimly. *But he's dead and he can't change any of them. It is done.*

"You were right, Dalwin," Bjornar whispered. "Astrid isn't well enough to come to Poznań. Maybe later, maybe in spring. But there are two issues which worry the duke. The first is Świętosława—what's happening with her? And the second is Jomsborg, a fortress with no leader."

"Tell the duke," Dalwin said, his hand resting on Astrid's trembling one, "that the Jomsvikings are licking their wounds. They lost a third of their ships. More importantly, they lost their spirit. They have been left to themselves and there is no one to guard the four houses. They drink and argue since apparently Sven hasn't paid them. They curse Sigvald because they had expected to fight with Tryggvason. Anyone who saw the *Long Snake* with its sails billowing wanted to fight with it, not against it." Dalwin was overtaken by a coughing fit.

She looked at him carefully. He was coughing more and more frequently these days. He cleared his throat and continued.

"So, if Duke Bolesław has any plans for Jomsborg's future, he should put them into action sooner rather than later. He needs to find a good leader, one who will grab the reins and bring back the old, solid rules of the boys of Jom. Otherwise, they're finished." He spat and wiped his lips. "In a year or two they'll begin to plunder and that will be the end of the legend. Tell him that."

"What about Świętosława?"

"My poor sister . . ." Astrid sobbed. "My poor, poor sister . . ."

Bjornar blushed and answered his own question.

"The duke will send an official messenger to her."

"Bad idea," Dalwin criticized him. "An official messenger will imply that Bolesław knows that something in his sister's life has changed. He needs to send trusted men. I can give you some of my crews, like we used to do."

Bjornar glanced at Astrid and was already opening his lips to ask but changed his mind. She sighed.

"I cannot, Bjornar." She shrugged. "I can't look her in the eye after Sigvald's betrayal."

"I understand, and I do not dare ask you to. Perhaps in some time, when you recover, my lady. You look weak, very . . ."

"I'm going to retire," she replied, and stood up with difficulty.

Dalwin walked with her to the door and they both stepped outside. She kissed his cheek.

"I don't like your cough," she told him.

"I don't like your voyage," he replied, stroking her hair.

"I'll set out before dawn. If Bjornar asks about me tomorrow, tell him I'm unwell. Busla will confirm that and won't let him in, since the woman is hard as iron. I'll be back in a week."

"Be careful," he whispered.

"Be healthy," she replied, and set off at a run.

12

⚜

DENMARK

Świętosława's shouts echoed in the manor.

"Nooo! You wouldn't dare!"

She was terrified that her heart would stop. Sven stood in front of her, his head cocked, a smile on his face. Lynx fur was draped over his shoulders. Her lynxes. He threw the fur at her feet. She knelt and gathered it to her chest.

"Wrzask . . ." she whispered, stroking what was left of him. "Zgrzyt . . . Sven, you bloody barbarian!"

He laughed.

"I gave you the Christian opportunity of forgiving your sins. You refused it, just like you refused my love. You're the only one to blame. Did you think that I didn't realize you treated those cats as if they were Olav's children? Children you never had with him, and now you never will! I knew those lynxes came from him. You got what you deserve."

My God, she thought. *Even the lynxes die because of me.*

Her hands were shaking uncontrollably. She ran her fingers through the fur, but she couldn't stop the trembling. Sven was enjoying this. He was finally himself. The wolf had shed its lamb's skin.

"You have no idea how much you've helped me, wife. I've been struggling to come up with a way to get Olav out of the Norwegian fjords, how to lure him into our waters. And here we are, my own wife helped me better than anyone else might have done!" He laughed metallically, and it sounded more like a bark. "She was so in love that she planned a massive, horrific betrayal and sent a messenger to her lover. Geivar, I take it. But why did you send the mute? That's what I don't understand. Thank God for your devotion and that you confessed it all to Ion."

Ion, you disgusting traitor, she wanted to scream at him. *How could you? How could you break the seal of confession? You're a Judas!*

"I was heartbroken to learn of how much you hate me," Sven continued, shaking his head. "I could have killed you, or Geivar and Dusza, but Jorun once advised me to remember that revenge is a dish best served cold, so I waited. And that's when I realized that you'd given me exactly what I needed. Who better than a woman in love to lure her lover into a trap? Of course, he might have sailed to Øresund when he heard that I'm gathering an army, to attack me before I was ready, but if he'd have thought about it properly, he wouldn't have done it. He'd have known that his chances would have been better if he lured us into his waters. But a woman's plea? A promise of her son's armies and the Jomsvikings? One cannot turn down such offers lightly!"

She felt her temper cooling as she listened to him. It was almost as if her body, piece by piece, was turning to ice. She realized that Sven had used her, and that her love had dragged Olav into a deadly trap. She had killed him, just as she'd killed her beloved lynxes.

"What happened to Dusza?" she croaked, lifting her head.

"An arrow through the heart." He spread his arms wide. "Your Dusza rests at the bottom of Øresund."

"You're wrong," she hissed, looking at his contented face. "A human soul is immortal and mine, even if you took away what it loved, will not die."

"Wait, my lady, I'm not done yet." He glared at her.

She rose from where she'd fallen to her knees.

"Neither am I."

They looked at each other.

"You're a coward, Sven Haraldsson," she announced. "Yes, call me a traitor, I won't deny it. But I'll call you a coward and there is nothing you can say in your defense. You used me to lure him into a trap. You used my son's youth and naïvety to ensure he stood beside you. You bought the Jomsvikings so they'd betray . . ."

"You're wrong," he hissed. "Sigvald offered his services willingly! I didn't send for him, it was he who sought me out."

"You're lying!" she said, though she couldn't be sure. "Why would he do that?"

"He never said, though I suspect it was personal."

"Nonsense!" she exclaimed. "Sigvald was greedy!"

"Perhaps, my lady, but I didn't offer him any silver." Sven laughed. "Not a single piece. If you paid him an advance, then that's lost now. Sigvald is dead, and he's taken his secret to the depths. Perhaps one day he'll tell a fish. And by the way, I've noticed you aren't wearing the brooch I gave you, the one with the fish."

She wanted to slap him. The cold mockery was driving her into a frenzy. He hadn't even denied his cowardice!

"I despise you," she said.

"Finally, we reach the real issues in our marriage." He grinned. "You despise me while I hate you. We can't live with each other."

For a moment, they just looked at one another. She gritted her teeth, while

Sven was breathing heavily and his face grew redder. *He's furious,* she thought. *He'll explode.*

"Get out!" he shouted. "I don't want to see you again! I could kill you, but then I'd have your brother and the emperor to deal with. They say that since his visit in the Congress of Gniezno, Otto has raised your brother above any of the Reich lords. I'm no fool. I'll let you live, but I don't want to see you again. Get on a ship and get out of Roskilde. You can take Ion with you, two traitors like you are worth each other."

Her first impulse was to spit in his face, but she stopped herself and straightened her back.

"I'm taking my children, my men, the people who came with me from Sigtuna, and all of my treasures."

He laughed so hard that drops of spittle got caught on his forked red beard.

"My lady, the children stay here."

"No!" she exclaimed.

"Yes! The children do not belong to you, they belong to the dynasty. You've risked everything, and now you've lost it all."

Suddenly, she had moved back in time. She was standing in the hall in Poznań along with everyone else, listening to Bolesław as he spoke to Oda: *"You're mistaken, my lady. Sons belong to the dynasty."* She had turned around and left without swearing fealty to the new ruler, taking Lambert and Mieszko with her. But Bolesław hadn't needed those children, his half brothers. In fact, they were an annoyance, a hindrance on his way to becoming the sole ruler of Poland, so Oda's decision suited him. Harald and Cnut were Sven's only sons. His heirs. He would never let them go, she realized.

"Give me the girls, then," she said. "I'll give them back when they're old enough to marry. You'll wed them to whomever you please."

"No." He grinned again. "My children won't be dragged around the world with their exiled mother. My children will live surrounded by riches in the royal manor in Roskilde."

"They aren't your children, they're ours!" she snarled, but quickly altered her tone. "You know that I can raise them better in Poznań. They'll have better opportunities . . ."

"For what?" he interrupted her. "To grow feral, like their mother? Absolutely not. You're baring your claws for naught, my love. I won't let you have them. Heidi will feed them as she has all our children."

"Why do you want them?" she tried again. "Marry again, have new children who are humble and obedient . . ."

"I'll have as many as I want." He laughed at her. "But I don't need a wife. Where would I find another match like you?"

She threw herself at him. She scratched his face before he'd had a chance to grab her wrists. He pulled her toward him and held her like an animal. He breathed into her face. She could feel his lust. If she had had any hope that she might convince him to let her take even one child, she'd have overcome her revulsion and disgust. But she didn't trust him. She remembered their last night together, after her sacrilegious confession to Ion. He'd already known, and he'd tricked her. Now, he began to lower his lips to hers, but she spat on them.

"You'll have to force me. I hate you," she hissed.

He pushed her away so hard that she fell.

"I don't want you." He dusted his palms as if he wanted to get rid of any sign of her touch. "You plot right until the very end. You wanted to provoke me so that I'd take you to bed, to give you another child that you could steal from me and take away from Roskilde . . ."

"Your ideas are insane," she snarled, struggling to get up. She got tangled in her skirts. "I swear that if you hurt my children, I will come back and scratch out your eyes."

"To Roskilde?" He laughed. "Over my dead body! Don't forget the lynx furs, unless you want me to use them as cushioning on my throne."

She leaned down and gathered the furs to her chest.

"In case you wanted to know," Sven continued, running his fingers along the braids of his beard, "they died loudly. Wrzask and Zgrzyt. The names suited them."

She looked at him one last time. He pronounced the names of her cats deliberately and precisely, down to the last syllable. She'd underestimated him again. But it only made her despise him more.

POLAND

Bolesław seethed with anger.

"He did what?! Tell me again!"

Ostrowod was still dressed in the same clothes he'd worn on the journey, since the duke had summoned him as soon as he walked through Poznań's gates. He looked weary. He took a deep breath and, as calmly as he could, repeated what he'd already said:

"Your firstborn son Bezprym abandoned Emperor Otto's procession and made his way to the hermit monk Romuald. He announced that he won't be returning because God has called him. He has asked to tell you that he will become a recluse and begs for your permission and forgiveness."

"Never!" the duke exclaimed, leaping toward Ostrowod. He grabbed the messenger by the caftan and lifted him clear off the ground.

The messenger remained calm. Everyone knew that the duke did not receive bad news well. After a moment, Bolesław lowered him back down.

"Ostry," he snarled. "You were with my son to protect him and look over him, not to allow such madness. What on earth came over him? Has he gone mad?"

"Will my lord let me have a drink? I rode hard for a week, and although I changed horses, I have had no break."

"Don't brag." Bolesław's nose twitched. "I can tell by the way you smell that although you changed your horses, you didn't change your clothes. Sit down. Servants! Mead!"

The duke didn't sit down. He paced around the hall like a wildcat. His lungs could barely contain his fury, and his thoughts chased one another like mad, as if his head could barely contain them, too.

"Bloody hell, do something to make me understand!" He gritted his teeth.

"If I may ask"—Emnilda had appeared silently—"that you have a drink, husband." She placed a cup in his hand and poured him mead herself.

"The duchess is right." Ostrowod rubbed his mustache. "It's impossible to wrap your head around it sober. Do you remember Easter at Quedlinburg, my lord?"

How could he not, that had been barely a year ago! Before Easter Otto III had done something that none of the emperors who'd come before him had done: he'd crossed the border of his empire for a reason other than to wage war. He had come on a pilgrimage to Gniezno, to the martyr Bishop Adalbert's tomb. Bolesław had met him at the border and they had journeyed together. Little Otto had grown since he'd received the camel. He was a slender but tall twentysomething-year-old. A young man with the appearance of an angel, with perfect golden curls and a keen, if mystical, mind. When Otto had given him a royal gift in greeting, Saint Maurice's lance,* it became apparent that the meeting between them was about more than just saints.

"It is a replica of the spear," he'd said, "but the relic of the Holy Cross inside it is real. Only two exist in the world—yours and mine. This is a sign that I think of you as a brother." He hadn't revealed the price until later. "I want to create an empire so great that it will be like in the golden times, crossing the old borders. Imagining the four pillars of our world: Gaul, Italy, Germania, and Słowiańszczyzna. You're the ruler of the fourth pillar, Bolizlaus."

---

* Known as the Holy Lance, the Lance of Longinus, the Spear of Destiny, or the Holy Spear, which is believed to have been the lance that pierced the side of Jesus as he hung on the cross. There are three or four relics which are claimed to be the Holy Lance or parts of it, Saint Maurice's lance being one of them.

Bolesław understood what the emperor was really saying. *I'm to defend the entire eastern flank. My borders mark the boundary between the west and the east, between the Christian and Eastern Orthodox Churches.*

"All right," he'd told Otto. "But you must give me a royal crown because I can't be a ruler equal to the other three pillars without it. You have been crowned king of the Reich, king of Italy. I want a royal coronation."

"I have given you the spear. That's more than a crown. The kingdoms of warriors have been conquered by the sword and spear."

"I don't want a crown from you, Emperor," Bolesław had told him then. "I appreciate your gift. I want a crown from the pope." He was no fool. To receive a crown from the emperor would be to admit his inferiority to him, but Otto promised that they would be equals. If he was to be the ruler of the Slavonic people in Central Europe, people across Poland, Moravia,* Bohemia, and Kievan Rus,† only a crown from the pope would do.

"In that case, Bolizlaus, when I return to Rome, I will arrange matters with Pope Sylvester. In the meantime, please accept my diadem as a token of good faith." He'd taken it off his head and placed it on Bolesław's temples. That part of their discussion had gone well. But they'd disagreed when the topic of moving Adalbert's relics arose. Bolesław had prepared a wonderful martyrium of red sandstone into which the martyr's body was to be carried. But Otto had misunderstood his intentions, and he'd been under the impression that Bolesław would let him take the saint's body to Rome. Bolesław had no intention of parting ways with Adalbert, though, and it wasn't about the silver he'd paid for it. It was the cult of the martyr which mattered to him. The crowds of pilgrims. Old healers, having spent all their lives making sacrifices for the old gods, had visions at the saint's tomb and asked to be baptized. Thieves left their spoils. Peasants started to pray. He'd seen it himself. No bishop could accomplish as much as a single holy tomb did. It was out of the question; he'd been adamant that he wouldn't let the saint go. Otto had been almost in tears, saying that he had already funded two churches for the relics. Unger joined the negotiations, and Bolesław had finally agreed. He'd given the emperor Adalbert's entire right arm in return for three new dioceses in Kołobrzeg, Kraków, and Wrocław, and an archdiocese in Gniezno.

It was a greater success than his father's victory over Hodo and Wichman combined. His own ecclesiastical province, independent of the Reich archbish-

---

* Moravia included areas of today's eastern Czech Republic and Slovakia.

† Kievan Rus was a loose federation of East Slavic, Baltic, and Finnic peoples in Eastern and Northern Europe from the late ninth to the mid-thirteenth century. Today's Belarus, Russia, and Ukraine all claim Kievan Rus as their cultural ancestors and both Belarus and Russia derive their names from it.

ops. There was only one snag, and his name was Radim Gaudentius. He was made archbishop, and not Bolesław's Unger. Damn it! But Unger made his peace with the defeat, for the good of the kingdom. They'd then set off to Magdeburg with Otto; Bolesław had taken Bezprym since his son was fourteen now and almost a man. Bolesław wanted the Reich lords to meet his heir, for them to bow to his son just like they did to him, Bolesław. When they'd ridden into Magdeburg, two spears were carried in front of their procession: the emperor's and his own. And Giselher, Retar, Bernward, Idzi, Arnulf, Ramward, and the rest of the Saxon bishops and nobles had to acknowledge that he, Bolesław, was better than they were. He was the emperor's brother and ally. The expressions on their faces, their clenched jaws, ah! If he had paid Adalbert's weight in gold it would still have been worth it.

They'd spent Easter in Quedlinburg. After that, Otto had turned his steps toward Aachen; he'd wanted Bolesław to accompany him, but Bolesław chose to return home. Emnilda had just given him a son and he hadn't had a chance to celebrate his child's birth. He left Bezprym with the emperor, along with a royal procession and the order: "You will bow to Pope Sylvester and in my name ask him for a royal crown." Otto had replied: "I will take care of him as if he were my own son, Bolizlaus. God willing, I will complete my business in Italy and come to see you and the sacred Gniezno once more. Perhaps, along with Bezprym, I will bring you the crown from Rome myself." Bolesław hadn't dared refuse Otto, but he hoped that his son would bring him the crown sooner. The emperor's procession moved unbearably slowly; if he were forced to wait for them to return, he'd be gray before the coronation. Firstly, Bezprym would return faster alone, and secondly, Bolesław didn't want the emperor to crown him. That was when they'd parted ways.

"Do you remember, Duke, that your son was staying longer after mass even in Quedlinburg? He prayed as if there was no end to his prayers, as if he'd forgotten the cue for 'amen.' And it was even worse in Aachen."

"Ostry," Emnilda reprimanded him. "You can't say that. It's a good thing that the young prince is religious."

"It would be good if he were a little religious. But he's gone overboard."

"What can you do." The duchess sighed. "He's a Piast, after all."

Bolesław snorted.

"What happened in Aachen?"

"The emperor opened Charlemagne's tomb." Ostrowod rolled his eyes. "He really has a soft spot for tombs and corpses. He was shaking when Unger brought out Adalbert's body in Gniezno. It was the same in Aachen, except that the tomb was under the floor and Charles had been buried in a sitting position. Bezprym was with the emperor, and when he entered the tomb to tend the body . . ."

"Mary, mother of God," Emnilda whispered.

"Forgive me, my lady, I'm just an ordinary soldier," Ostrowod apologized. "I could tell it in a fancy way, that they bowed to the dead man and they took parts of him for relics, assuming he would be named a saint. That Otto sobbed emotionally, and Bezprym joined him, that they were amazed that the body seemed untouched, and more besides. But I know that my duke prefers that I tell him what my eyes had seen, and not try to compose verses like a bard. My duke is smart enough to write whatever rhymes he wants based on what I tell him."

"All right." The duchess waved a hand. "Just don't talk about tending bodies, please."

"Yes, my lady. Without any tending, they cut the dead man's fingernails, pulled out a tooth, cut off his beard, and took his cloak. And the throne."

Bolesław glanced at his wife. She was pale. He deeply regretted having left his son Bezprym in the emperor's care. It was no surprise that the boy had lost his wits after tending to a corpse with Otto. But what was it that drew Otto to famous corpses?

"The throne?" Emnilda asked weakly. "How could they have taken his throne? That's sacrilege! The throne from which Charlemagne ruled the world . . ."

"I don't know about that . . ." Ostrowod took a gulp of mead. "All I can say is that the emperor intended Charles's throne as a gift to Duke Bolesław."

"Did they place the dead man on another throne afterward?" Bolesław asked quickly.

"Yes!"

"Then it's not sacrilege, wife. It's just renovating the tomb. The old one was probably used up so they gave the dead man a new one."

"So why should you have the used one?" She frowned at him.

"I'll renovate it."

"Bolesław! Do what you want with it, just promise me that you won't share the emperor's strange passion."

"Have you brought it with you?" he asked Ostrowod. "You have."

"No, my lord. I told you that I have come alone from Ravenna in a week; how was I meant to bring it with me? It's a great throne because Charles . . . that is, his body . . . was also great. Almost as great as you, in terms of your height, my lord, though perhaps he was a little shorter. But he may have shrunk after death . . ."

"Stop talking about the corpse and tell me where my throne is."

"The throne is with our procession."

"And what the hell is our procession doing in Italy if my son has run away? I'll dismember you all!"

"Don't yell at Ostry, husband." This time it was Emnilda who reprimanded him. "Have a drink if you want to understand. Or ask Bishop Unger to accompany us. We'll be speaking of the spirit."

"Unger!" he called out thoughtlessly but stopped himself from continuing. "Go, ask the bishop to join us," he told a servant.

Unger's dark eyes gleamed when he walked into the hall and the earlier conversation was summarized for his benefit. The bishop's presence had a calming effect on him, just as his wife's did.

"After his stay in Aachen, particularly after visiting Charlemagne's tomb, Prince Bezprym began to demonstrate an even greater interest in all things spiritual . . ."

"Ostry," the duke interrupted. "Just because Unger is here doesn't mean you have to pretend to be better than you are. Just tell us what you saw and stop bullshitting."

"Thank you, my lord. If my lady and the bishop will forgive me . . ." He smiled at them. "It was like this. Whenever we stopped to rest, Bezprym, instead of going to take a piss, jumping around to get his blood flowing, drinking, eating, joking, he would go into the woods, spread out his arms, and pray, or at least I think that's what he was doing. Sometimes he'd kneel, but more often he'd just stand. Otto would usually attend two masses a day and additionally stop five times to pray. Our boy was with him the whole time. Both sang the psalms with vacant stares. When we neared Rome, I took the prince aside and said, 'Mass is mass, and this is all very pious, but if my lord would remember that he is traveling to bring back his father's crown.' And he told me, 'Earthly honors are nothing compared to the gifts of the Holy Spirit.' I wasn't sure I understood him, but then I thought, 'The Holy Spirit is probably the same as the Holy Father,' and I convinced myself that Bezprym hadn't forgotten the reason for our journey."

"I'll be happy to explain the difference between the pope and the gifts of the Holy Spirit, if you'd like," Unger offered. "At a more suitable time, of course."

Bolesław only realized Ostry had misinterpreted Bezprym's words because of Unger's reaction. He'd have done the same.

Ostrowod continued:

"The emperor flagellated himself . . ."

"What?" Bolesław interrupted.

"I'm not making it up." Ostry nodded sadly. "He whipped himself, and the leather had a little hook on it so it would hurt more. I discovered it by accident when I was searching for our prince on the last stop, and I saw Otto instead."

"Flagellation is a way for us to connect with the Savior's Suffering," Unger explained drily and added, noticing Bolesław's surprise: "It's not that strange."

"Aha, right," the duke agreed. "Wait, my son didn't do that, did he?!"

"No," Ostry reassured him. "He only wiped away the blood from Otto's back."

Bolesław gritted his teeth. He respected Unger's presence, however, and said nothing more about it.

"What happened then?"

"There was unrest in Rome. The nearby Tivoli announced they would no longer answer to Otto. We couldn't meet with the pope. The emperor had to lead his troops and he sent us to the abbey on Monte Casino where we were to wait until he summoned us. And in that abbey . . ."

"A sacred place," Unger said drily. "One of the most sacred. That's where Benedict of Norcia, enchanted by the mystical mountains and the closeness to God, built the abbey. He and his sister Scholastica ordered their bones be buried at Monte Casino."

"Hm." Ostry cleared his throat. "It was saintly. Fasting on water and bread with a drop of olive oil. The horses ate better than the people, since oats are the same everywhere. That's where we met the saintly Romuald. And so, it began. The old man has some sort of power; even I could feel it."

"A simple soldier felt the power of something other than his sword?" Emnilda asked suspiciously.

"Yes, my lady," a shamefaced Ostrowod admitted. "I felt it. When the old man appeared, I felt like he was looking right through me. When Romuald looks at you, it's like he sees the bones and muscles. Forgive me, Duke, I know I speak strangely, but that's what it felt like. I myself began to confess my sins when he was near! I confessed to his back once . . ."

"That's how God's will works." Unger nodded. His eyes looked like molten bronze or liquid lead.

"And Bezprym! What was the young prince supposed to do when the old man decided that he wanted to talk to no one else?"

"He chose him," the bishop observed as if it was the most obvious thing in the world.

"After a few days in the abbey at Monte Casino, Bezprym took off his royal clothes and donned a woolen habit. And when Otto came back in spring, Bezprym went to him and said, 'This is God's will. I will go with Father Romuald to the hermitage in Pereum.' The emperor went pale and, in his defense, spoke up in your name. He told the prince, 'You can't. You're the heir to the throne; your place is elsewhere.' But Bezprym looked just like you—no offense, my duke. His eyes flashed and he said firmly, 'God's will before man's.' The emperor fell silent and clearly had no idea how to change his mind."

"A hermitage, giving oneself to God in meditation," Unger explained. "No more tackling the issues of this world. The beginning of God's life on earth."

"But he's my son!" Bolesław interrupted.

"It's God's will, my lord. You can't take from God."

Bolesław disagreed. "If my firstborn has shown me the way, then it is my will to build a hermitage in Poland."

Poland. If Otto were with them, Bolesław would have had to give him his country's name to be recorded in the documents. Once, this land had been called Lechistan or Lechia, after Lestek. Then his father, with the stubbornness of an old man, insisted on it being called "Mieszko's land." But he saw that such a great kingdom couldn't keep changing its name to match its ruler's. When Otto had asked him, he'd said "Poland." He was inspired by the glades.* Those beautiful forest spots where riders found a place to rest after their journeys. And by the glades which were filled with growing trees that replaced the ones that had been cut down in his ancestors' times to build the boroughs, when hundreds of wagons of wood were transported. And by his memories, since he remembered his mother, sweet Dobrawa, calling his father the "prince of forest glades."

"A hermitage in Poland?" Unger repeated. "Missionaries would be more useful."

"You've just heard for yourself of the influence that hermits have on the people," Bolesław pointed out.

When Emnilda and Ostrowod had left, they looked at each other.

"Saint Adalbert's death has created a pious prince," the bishop observed.

"It's high time we control these miracles," Bolesław replied. "If Bezprym wants to be a hermit, he can be one on our land."

"Well said." Unger understood. "Although I'd advise you to word the message in a way that doesn't make it so personal."

"Of course." Bolesław smiled.

I won't tell him, while he's still in the arms of the Holy Spirit, that he will return to his rightful place on his father's throne the moment he falls back into mine.

---

* The word for "glade" in Polish is "polana."

13

⌘

SWEDEN

Olof King of Swedes was exasperated when he heard about his mother's exile. Why now, just when everything was beginning to fall into place? King Sven had kept his promise and had found him a wife. Olof married the pretty Astrid, the Obotrite princess, and she'd brought a dowry with her so large that it dazzled Sigtuna. He'd sent Edla away from the manor itself, to avoid any misunderstandings, but he still kept her nearby. Jarl Asgrim had taken his mistress under his roof. Everyone in Sigtuna knew who Edla was to him, and that she'd given the king a daughter. Asgrim looked after her, and Olof could visit her discreetly whenever he wanted. So far, his wife hadn't asked any uncomfortable questions; she was pregnant herself, and Olof expected a son.

"There'll be an heir," she promised him with pretty smiles.

But instead of a son, she gave birth to a daughter. They called her Ingegerd.

The days which followed found Olof brooding. Two daughters. One from a mistress, one from a queen. Was that a sign that there would be no sons?

"Two daughters, my lord," Jarl Asgrim reassured him, "mean two alliances when they grow up. You're young enough to have sons, too."

Young enough, he thought. He was sensitive about the word.

"So young and already so famous!" Asgrim corrected himself. "After your victory over Tryggvason everything is falling into place."

So it was. Until the day that the Danish merchants brought word that King Sven intended to exile his queen, Sigrid Storråda.

"Where is he sending her?" Olof asked, feeling his stomach clench.

"We don't know, King Olof, he didn't confide in the merchants. In port they said that the lady would have a ship and a team of warriors . . ."

His wife grabbed his shoulder.

"Your mother doesn't think she can come here, to us, does she?"

"My mother is still queen of Sweden and Denmark," Olof replied bitterly.

"And Norway," Asgrim added, "even if she doesn't rule there."

"But as your wife I am also queen!" Astrid protested. "How is that possible? Two queens?"

And then what he had feared most came to pass. He'd gone back in time. His chieftains from the battle of Øresund, the brothers-in-law Vestar and

Toki, and Torvald, his father's Icelandic bard, and everyone else in the great hall chanted:

"Queen Sigrid Storråda! Our Bold Lady!"

They raised a toast to her health and Torvald recited a poem that hadn't been heard in a long time.

Sigrid Proud, Sigrid Ruthless,
to whose bright home
suitors doggedly come,
from the rocky borders along a swampy path . . .

Those who come at a wrong time
Were reprimanded by our merciful lady.
The flames washed their soiled hands
The fire cleansed their . . .

Seeing his pretty wife's terrified expression, he whispered, "Now you know. Never say a word against my mother."

"But, Olof . . . I didn't say anything against her," she explained with a blush. "I only wanted to ask, how is it possible? Two queens?"

"Be quiet," he reprimanded her. "You hear yourself which one my men would choose. But don't think for a moment that I want Queen Sigrid to come to Sigtuna." He lowered his voice even further. "I want it even less than you do. My mother would take the power away from me. She'd steal my people's attention."

"What will we do?" his wife asked in a whisper.

He shrugged.

"Nothing. I can't deny her entry into the kingdom."

Jarl Asgrim approached then and asked of the king, "Why did Wilkomir and Helga leave Sigtuna?"

"They wanted to see their son," Olof lied. "I allowed it."

"I understand." He nodded.

"When do you think we can expect my mother's arrival, Jarl? I'd like to prepare the manor for her."

"It has already been a year since the battle of Øresund." Asgrim frowned. "Winter is coming, and that's not the right season for travel. If I were the queen's helmsman, I'd advise her a spring journey."

"There is still time, then," Olof observed drily.

"Queen Sigrid would undoubtedly have informed you if she intended to come here, my lord," Jarl Asgrim continued. "Her presence in Sigtuna would affect the balance of power . . ."

That's one way to put it. Olof sighed to himself.

". . . because if she's parting with King Sven in anger, which is a safe assumption to make since he speaks of her exile, then it means that by returning to Sweden she could place us in an awkward position. I wouldn't even rule out war."

"War? But I'm my stepfather's ally . . ." Olof said angrily.

"You are, my lord," Asgrim agreed, "but Queen Sigrid has never allowed an insult to go unpunished."

Olof flinched and spilled his wine. Only now did he truly understand. If his mother returned and took back power—*his* power—then she would take her vengeance on him and Sven simultaneously. Wilkomir's words echoed in his ears: *You will forever be the son who betrayed.*

POLAND

Świętosława, her procession in tow, rode toward the bridge that led to the island. Warta hadn't frozen over. The beginning of the year had seen no snow, while the frost made it possible to travel along the roads comfortably. In a moment, they would open Poznań's gates for her.

Her thoughts kept returning to her children and parting with them. She was embracing Cnut's fair head and Harald's red hair. Astrid and Świętosława. "This isn't the last time, I swear it," she whispered to each of them. "I will never abandon you. I will never forget you. I will come back for you." She left them under the care of Melkorka, Vali, Heidi Goat, and even Arnora, who seemed to be immune to death. She'd have left Great Ulf and Wilczan with them, but Sven hadn't allowed any of her people to stay. "You won't wipe me from their memories," she'd shouted. "We'll see," he'd threatened. All the chieftains bid her farewell in Roskilde. Stenkil of Hobro, Haakon of Funen, Uddorm of Viborg who had whispered: "It's such a pity that our queen is leaving us." Ragn of the Isles had said: "I hope to host you someday on each of my islands, my lady." Gjotgar, the handsome one from Scania, had promised: "I will look after the church in Lund, and I'll pray that you visit it one day, my queen." Gunar of Limfiord had only said: "It's such a shame," while Thorgils of Jelling, along with Ulf, his young son, had barely nodded to her. She saw clearly who had sided with Sven, and she committed the division of power to memory.

She rode to Poznań with fifty armed men and her servants. The fair-haired Egil led the Bold One's men; there were thirty of them. Great Ulf commanded the remaining twenty, who had named themselves the Lynxes. Everyone knew why. And Wilkomir once more led her personal guard. He'd broken his word and abandoned Olof. She couldn't even hold that against him after what had happened. And she thanked him for bringing Helga with him. She'd missed her friend. Only Wilczan felt awkward in the company of his parents. He wasn't used to it anymore. He'd brought a servant called Ylva with him from Roskilde. She needed female servants anyway, but the more important reason was Ylva's large family: her five brothers all served Sven, and her three sisters all worked at the manor in Roskilde.

A few wagons loaded with her possessions clattered heavily at the back of her procession. She'd brought more with her than she had taken sixteen years ago when she'd left. At the very end, tied to the last wagon, with a collar around his neck, was Ion.

Her heart skipped a beat when she saw Poznań's powerful ramparts. She'd forgotten how massive they were. In the cold months, when the sun was low, there were eternal shadows inside the borough, and today was no exception.

Shadows and darkness, she thought. *The perfect surroundings for a queen in mourning. For Olav, for the lynxes, for the children that Sven is keeping from me.*

The horses' hooves were already clattering on the stones in the yard. They came out to greet her with a large, bright procession. Great Ulf blew the horn.

"Sigrid Storråda, queen of Sweden and Denmark!"

She denied the throne that was given to her after Olav's death, never letting anyone call her the queen of Norway.

"Świętosława!" her brother called.

"Bolesław!" she called back, Wilkomir already helping her off her horse. "Your stomach has grown," she teased. She couldn't help but notice when he embraced her. "Have you not been to war recently? Emnilda spoils you, doesn't she?"

"My queen," the duchess greeted her. "Don't mock him, please. He's been at his wits' end since last night."

"He has never been anything but, Emnilda!" She laughed and embraced her sister-in-law.

"Ah!" Emnilda looked at her face, unable to hide her surprise. "What happened to your eyes, Świętosława?"

"Something to remember Sven by," she replied grimly.

Bolesław was at her side in the blink of an eye.

"What are you talking about? Did he hit you? I didn't notice anything."

"Look," she replied, meeting his eyes.

She had always been told that her eyes were a golden-green, but the day after Sven had given her what remained of her lynxes, Heidi had pointed out the change. "My lady," she'd murmured. "Your eyes don't match. One green, one gold."

"Mismatched eyes," Bolesław said, and added reassuringly: "There are worse things. Did you know that I had a mare with two tails?"

"It's a good thing it wasn't a stallion with two . . ." She didn't have time to finish since Emnilda grabbed her elbow and dragged her away.

"Auntie, where are your lynxes?" Regelinda asked.

Świętosława leaned down and kissed her forehead.

"Here, my princess. Wrzask had green eyes, just like my right. Zgrzyt, with his golden eyes, lives in my left. I will never forget them, though they may be dead."

"I won't forget them either," Regelinda promised.

"Neither will I!" "Nor I!" Mieszko and Sława, the youngest daughter, chimed in.

"You didn't see them," the eldest reminded them haughtily. "Only I did. Mieszko was little and always asleep, and you weren't even born then, sister."

"Leave them alone, daughter." Emnilda caressed her youngest children. "They've heard the stories."

Świętosława straightened and moved her shoulders to loosen them.

"An exiled queen has returned to her family nest," she muttered emotionlessly.

"Don't say 'exiled,'" her brother whispered with a grimace, "because that implies that I should take my troops and march on Roskilde to punish Sven for the insult, and we both know it's a lot more complicated than that." He stood up straight and announced, "We welcome you, Świętosława. The Piast house has never stopped being your home. Come, please, we have much to discuss." He pulled her away quickly.

"Perhaps you'll manage to ease my husband's mind." Emnilda expressed her hopes aloud.

They sat together in the hall that evening. Świętosława had asked her brother not to hold a welcome feast for her.

"You have no idea how angry I am, sister!" he seethed.

"I can see." She studied him as he paced the room, unable to sit still. "Just because my eyes don't match doesn't mean they no longer work. You really cannot accept that Bezprym wants to be a hermit?"

"No! I cannot! It's nonsense. A duke's son can be a bishop, highly placed in the Church, but not a ragamuffin who lives on roots! What's the point in that?"

"Bolesław sent messengers to Emperor Otto," Emnilda explained calmly. "And to his firstborn. He asked that the emperor send the hermits to him along with his son. The hermits have come, but Bezprym has not."

"That bloody old man is responsible! Romuald!"

"Control yourself, Bolesław!" Emnilda looked frightened. "He's a holy man . . ."

"The hermit Romuald? I know that name. Ion, my treacherous monk, ran away from Romuald," Świętosława remembered.

"Did you hear that, Emnilda? It is possible to escape Romuald. Where there's a will there's a way. Evidently Bezprym didn't! I feel as if I've lost my son," Bolesław roared.

Świętosława walked to her brother's side. "Sven took four children from me, but I haven't once said that I lost them. Get a grip." Świętosława said this to him quietly but firmly, in a way that only his bold sister could get away with.

When they were children, they used to compete in everything. Bolesław had been better at losing his temper as well as controlling it again.

"Could Ion, the one you brought on a leash and named a traitor, help us in getting Bezprym out of the hermitage?" he asked, already calming.

"I don't know. I don't trust him. But perhaps he knows something useful about the pious hermit that will help get your firstborn back. He was with Romuald for long enough. If we trust what he says."

"Can I speak to him?" Bolesław asked, though they all heard the question he really meant. *Can I torture him?*

"Do what you want with him, but don't kill him. His penance is to see me every day," she said, and before she'd even finished speaking, Bolesław was striding from the room with his men.

"Świętosława," Duchess Emnilda began when they were left alone. "My husband's anger stems from deeper issues. Don't think that he doesn't respect God's will. Bolz has already designated two of our children for the Church. My beautiful Bogumiła, do you remember her? And Mieszko." She swallowed audibly.

Astrid had told her about Bogumiła, but she'd had no idea about Mieszko.

"When Mieszko was born almost four years after our wedding," Emnilda continued with a blush, "Bolesław was mad with joy. He carried him around everywhere. He even briefly considered"—she glanced at Świętosława, embarrassed—"whether he should change the line of succession and make Mieszko his heir instead of Bezprym. But he fought the impulse and said that he wouldn't break with tradition. Mieszko has been studying since he was five. He reads and writes in Greek and Latin, he knows arithmetic. Unger is beginning to introduce him to theology now, and apparently our son is gifted. You saw him today . . ."

"I did. He's just like Bolek. He looked exactly like him at his age."

Eric always used to say that Olof had dark curls just like he did. Sven always preferred the red-haired Harald to the fair-haired Cnut. Men were so predictable. She could understand her brother's dilemma when his son chose a hermitage that offered no chance for a career in the Church when another of his sons was already training to be a priest.

"What about your youngest . . . Otto, is it?"

"The little one. He was born just before the emperor's visit, hence the name." Świętosława waved a hand.

"You're right. The most difficult years of childhood are still before him. We must do all we can to bring Bezprym back."

Świętosława watched as Emnilda ordered the servants without saying a word. A raised hand or a meaningful glance was enough to have her servants fulfill her unspoken wishes. Even now, before Świętosława herself had had a chance to think about the fact that her goblet was empty, it was filled after only a glance on Emnilda's part in the right direction.

"Świętosława." Her sister-in-law's voice grew timid. "Let us talk about it openly."

"What?"

"Your arrival in Poznań . . . You're queen of two kingdoms, while I am only a duchess . . . I want you to know that I know my place, and I'm prepared to concede to you in everything."

"Emnilda, are you mad?" Świętosława laughed and stretched her legs out on the bench she was sitting on. "You're my brother's wife, and the hostess, there can be no talk of you conceding anything to me. Besides, you know that the royal titles held by my husbands are not the same as those given by the Church; they are not 'kings' in the same way as kings of Christian countries are. Leave it alone and tell me something else, Duchess." She leaned over the table. "How did you do it? How have you managed to keep my brother's heart for fifteen years?"

Emnilda had wide, honest blue eyes. She blushed, but not like Tyra used to do, at the right moment. She didn't flutter her eyelashes either but looked straight back at her.

"When Duke Mieszko sent messengers to my father, Duke Dobromir, to ask for my hand, they tried to scare me. They said that Bolz is impulsive, violent, temperamental, cunning, sly, and belligerent. They told me he would send me away quickly. Obviously, for my father this was such a good alliance that he couldn't possibly decline, so I accepted my role as best as I could. Every year, I treated it as if it would be my last, knowing that it very well could be. I still think, 'Nothing is given to me forever, I'm only passing through,' and it seems that I haven't passed through just yet." Emnilda smiled.

Świętosława studied her with her mismatched eyes. Emnilda was beautiful, and as serene as a lake's waters. There was nothing of the foam of ocean waves in her, no threat of a gathering storm. So that was her secret? She was only passing through?

"I hope you stay forever." She squeezed her hand. "If I were Bolesław, I would have fallen in love with you, too. But I always met men I fought with."

"You're like the wind, Świętosława," Emnilda told her. "You blow over a solid rock, you fan fires, and you make waves on water . . ."

"And I almost drowned as a result. I didn't notice the gathering storm."

Eric was the rock, she thought. *Olav was fire, we fanned each other. And Sven was the sea that almost killed me.*

"You're wrong." Emnilda smiled sadly. "Wind cannot drown. It's not the water that starts the storm, it's the wind. You. I hope that you have the chance to rest in Poznań after everything that you've been through. I hope that you can settle down as a breeze for a while, instead of a hurricane."

Świętosława could feel the tears gathering under her eyelids. A moment more and she would have fallen apart in Emnilda's warm hands. The walls she had built for so long to contain her emotions would have tumbled down. Her grief for Dusza, how wildly she missed Olav, the animal-like loss she felt at losing Wrzask and Zgrzyt. A mother's grief for being separated from her children. But at that moment they both heard the roar. Bolesław's wild, furious roar. He burst into the hall.

"Emperor Otto is dead!"

14

POLAND

Bolesław knew that the emperor's death changed everything, and he didn't hesitate for a second.

"Get the horses ready," he ordered his troops.

Jaksa, Zarad, and Bjornar were already with him.

"Wilkomir!" he shouted. "I charge you with defending Poznań and both my women, my wife and my sister. Be prepared for anything. Bold One, get the information we need out of Ion and send some men with Ostry to Pereum to fetch my son. Emnilda! . . ." He ran over to his wife and instead of leaning down to kiss her, he picked her up. "I will come back, I promise."

"Don't make promises, just come back," she replied.

"I'll take Duszan, if that's all right?" he asked, because Duszan had been at Emnilda's side, or rather his sons', more often than not in recent years. It was superstitious he knew, but he'd always had the feeling that wherever Duszan went, peace followed. He regretted not having sent him to Rome with Bezprym.

"That would be best, Bolz," his wife said.

He headed toward their Western border with thirty soldiers, all heavy cavalry. Their flags bearing a white eagle fluttered in the wind, against a clear, blue, early-spring sky.

He heard about his friend Margrave Eckard of Meissen's death on the way, shortly before they reached the border. He howled for a second time.

"The counts Udo and Henry of Kaltenburg, and Siegfried and Ben of Northeim," Eckard's brother Gunzelin's messengers reported. "They haven't confessed to anything yet, but there are witnesses. They lured him into a trap and stabbed him . . ." The messenger hesitated, as if he was afraid of sharing all he knew.

"Tell me what happened, or you'll be the one getting stabbed!" Bolesław roared.

"That's what happened," the pale messenger continued. "They killed him . . . they stole from the corpse to stage a burglary, and then . . . they beheaded Margrave Eckard . . ."

Bolesław felt his blood boil.

"I hope they all go to hell!" he exclaimed. "Those are Henry of Bavaria's men. It was an assassination."

Henry, Otto's cousin, had been a constant opponent of the late emperor. If he was behind Eckard's death, that meant he was eliminating any rivals to the Reich throne.

Does he know of my plans with Otto? Bolesław wondered as they crossed the border.

They crossed the Bóbr at Iława, then the Oder. They reached Łużyce, securing borough after borough as they went. Niemcza, Lubusza—he moved quickly. The enormous Budziszyn opened its gates to him and welcomed him as their ruler.

This is what Otto and I agreed on, he thought. *Połabie was meant to be mine. I was meant to rule the Slavs.*

He crossed the border at Łużyce, entered Strehla, and took the borough after a short siege. He then sent the victorious messengers on to Meissen, which defended itself for an even shorter period than Strehla, and soon welcomed him with open gates.

"Our duke! Bolz! Bolesław!"

"Hail Bolesław!"

Gunzelin, Eckard's brother, stood at his side. The Meissen March lay down at Bolesław's feet like a submissive servant. The Slavs of Połabie perceived him as one of their own, a contrast that was especially stark after the century of Saxon rule over the area.

Jaksa, trusted leader of his scouts, came to Bolesław's tent in the middle of the night.

"Duke," he murmured; he never spoke loudly. "There will be a council of the Reich lords held in Merseburg in a month. Henry expects them to support his claim to the throne. Tomorrow, or at the latest, the day after tomorrow, a messenger will come to you with an invitation. They know that after Otto raised your station two years ago, their decision will be invalid without you."

"Are they angry?" he asked Jaksa.

"Furious, my lord. Otto's decision was unacceptable to them."

He laughed wholeheartedly. Of course it was! The Reich lords and the love of sweet Germania. The land of the blunzen sausage with bacon, beer, and bragging at the dinner table. Oh! They couldn't understand Otto's plan to enlarge the empire without bloodshed, based on a confederation of the kingdoms.

"Bolesław—a king?" Giselher had squeaked. "But his father was a barbarian pagan! That's not possible, Emperor, it's just not."

But Otto had known otherwise. And Bolesław remembered their parting in Quedlinburg. Otto's eyes had burned like the brightest gold. "Bolizlaus, if I have no sons, I want you to succeed me as the lord of the Reich and emperor. And if I have no heirs, fight the Reich to get your way. Do you promise?" Bolesław had promised. He'd believed that Otto would have the time to marry sweet Zoe, the Byzantine empress, and that together they would have a child who would ally the two enormous empires. But his faith only did not shape reality. Otto had died of malaria. Bezprym was imprisoned in Italy by a mad hermit. And Henry was grimly fighting for the title of king of the Reich already. If he won, he would crown himself emperor, too. But he was about to find an obstacle in his path that would not be so easily cast aside: Bolesław.

There was enough time before the council for the duke to enjoy his journey to Merseburg, soaking in the summer as he went. He stopped frequently, talking to the people, admiring the beauty of the Meissen lands. For years, Bolesław had dreamed of joining the area with Poland, and now, after Otto's death, he had the chance to make this dream come true in an unexpected way. Bolesław was under no illusions—the Reich wouldn't give up Meissen without a fight simply because he'd taken borough after borough as he made his way toward the council, each faction hailing him as their ruler by the time he left—but that was also the reason Henry would find it difficult to claim the lands back. People here spoke his language.

"We are approaching the river Saale," Jaksa, the leader of the scouts, reported.

"It looks like molten lead," Duszan observed.

"The border with the March." Zarad pulled up his horse. "After that it's just Merseburg and the Reich."

The duke turned his horse in a circle.

"I can't ride into Merseburg for the council of the Reich lords with an army. I'll take only my personal guard."

"Yes, my lord," Zarad said.

"But I know that Duke Henry is watching us from the castle. Order the troops to ride into the river when I'm crossing it. Do you know what I want you to do?"

"Yes, my lord," Zarad said. "We won't move a step."

"Exactly," Bolesław said calmly, and put on his parade casque. The one with the golden forehead and decorated with eagle feathers. When he whistled, a dozen great warriors and Duszan followed him into the river.

He was reaching the western shore when he heard Zarad's orders:

"Drive in the stakes!"

He turned around and watched as his men drove their spears which bore his flag into the Saale.

That is the new border of my country, he thought, and rode on toward the borough, splashing water. Merseburg opened its gates to him and blew the horns in greeting.

"Bolizlaus! Bolizlaus! Bolizlaus!"

GERMANIA

He recognized the men in the audience hall: Archbishop Giselher of Magdeburg, Bishop Retar of Paderborn, Bishop Bernward of Hildesheim, Bishop Arnulf of Halberstadt, Bishop Ramward of Minden, Bishop Idzi of Messen, Bishop Bernhard of Werden, Bishop Hugo of Żytyce, the Saxon duke Bernard Billung, Margrave Henry of Schweinfurt, and Eckard's brother Gunzelin, whom Bolesław considered a blood brother. And Henry, duke of Bavaria. Slender, dark-eyed, dark-haired, and resembling a bird.

And a small bird at that, Bolesław thought pettily as he looked around. *But he's gathered quite the flock.*

"You kept us waiting, Duke," Henry of Bavaria observed sourly, but then, unexpectedly, he smiled. "Allow me to explain to you," and his tone gained a false note of caring, "that in our empire, when one duke goes to visit another, he doesn't have to . . ."

". . . steal the whole road he travels," Giselher finished for him, and everyone else laughed.

". . . or cut it with his sword," Henry concluded. "That just isn't acceptable among us, the Reich lords."

"But cutting off someone's head is fine? A preposterous murder of the most likely heir to the throne is acceptable to you?" Bolesław spit back. "You disgraced yourself with your actions against Margrave Eckard. You got rid of Otto's closest companion to ensure he didn't stand in your way to the throne, Henry. Save your morals."

"The king is dead, long live the king!" Giselher croaked, quickly addressing the real reason for which they had gathered. "Who supports Duke Henry of Bavaria? Our dear Otto's closest living male relative?"

"I do not!" Bolesław shouted, his voice booming in the stone-walled space, his refusal echoing on, *"Not, not, not . . ."*

"I do!" the old archbishop of Magdeburg exclaimed, his words similarly reverberating throughout the room. *"I do, do, do . . ."*

Retar of Paderborn, Bernward of Hildesheim, Arnulf of Halberstadt,

Ramward of Minden, Idzi of Messen, Bernhard of Werden, and Hugo of Żytyce dutifully repeated Giselher, "Yes, yes!"

Eckard's brother Gunzelin and Bernard of Billung followed Bolesław's lead. "No," they voted.

Billung surprised Bolesław. It was widely known that he had recently supported the Bavarian. Henry of Schweinfurt expressed no opinion. It seemed he might want to join the majority, but he waited.

That's not enough, they've outvoted us, Bolesław thought bitterly. He would have to risk everything now to press forward.

"My 'no' carries more weight, because I am above you," he announced. "That was Otto's will. He wanted me to rule the Slavs. All of it, including Połabie."

"You were more important, Duke, when Otto was alive . . ." Henry replied politely.

"He made a ruler out of a tributary," Giselher added.

"Tributary?" Bolesław repeated coldly. "Do you want a taste of my armies?"

"That's not what I said," the gray-haired Giselher replied, offended.

"I did," Bolesław whispered to him, blowing out the candles on the table in the process.

"We cannot do as my dear dead cousin might have," Henry said in a pained voice, "since he isn't among us. We have to therefore accept an ordinary majority, which means . . ."

"That you're giving yourself the title of king?" Bolesław smirked. "And where will you get the respect and loyalty that the office requires? Don't count on me. If you think you'll get it from these rats, then know that I'll be the cat that hunts them all down . . ."

"Duke Bolesław, that's barbaric," Giselher observed in an insulted tone. "The Hoftag is no place for such words. Maybe at your home, in the glades . . ."

"In Poland," Bolesław corrected him.

"Yes, yes," the archbishop mocked.

"That's enough, my lord." The duke had reached the end of his patience. "You haven't seen my country. Do you want to? I'll take you on a pilgrimage through Poland to visit Saint Adalbert's tomb."

"I am honored, but I suffer from gout."

"What?"

"It's a pain of the joints. Don't you know it? Oh, you're too young . . ."

"Or you're too old to rule, Giselher. Do not attempt to mock my country."

"Duke of Poland," Henry began smoothly. "I remember your father, Duke Mieszko, well. My own father told me much about him. Duke Mieszko sided with my father twice against the Otto family. Good traditions are worthy of being upheld."

"Indeed." Bolesław looked at the birdlike duke coolly. "My father sided with yours twice and sided against him twice when he supported Otto's family. Is that the tradition you want to uphold?"

"Otto is dead, and he had no heirs," Henry pointed out coldly.

That's what he'd been afraid of. That's why he said, "I want you, Bolesław, to be my heir." But those who side against me are too many, he thought as he looked around at Henry's followers.

"That is why this is the end of switching sides," announced Bolesław. "I'm telling you now that I'm not with you, Duke. Do what you want with that."

"I suggest a recess," Giselher interjected smoothly.

The men rose and walked slowly from the table. The Saxon duke Bernard Billung whispered as he passed next to Bolesław, "Don't let them buy you off."

Billung has never been my friend, the duke thought. *What's changed?*

"Duke Henry of Bavaria is inviting you to dine with him in a private chamber." A servant bowed to him.

They met in a modest stone cell. There were three places set at the simple oak table. The only decoration in the chamber was a heavy weave on the wall, and a blackened wooden crucifix. The thorn crown which adorned Christ's head gleamed golden in the light. A spear protruded from the dying Savior. As Bolesław entered, he found Henry standing by the window, which admitted little light. The servant swiftly cleared the third setting.

Two armed guards stood at the door.

"Wine?" Henry offered and smiled invitingly when Bolesław didn't respond. "I will drink from the same jug as you."

"I'm not afraid of poison," Bolesław said. "It's not the weapon of an honorable man. Besides, no one has ever been murdered at a council of the Reich lords. Yet."

"Don't link me with Eckard's unfortunate accident. Truly, I had nothing to do with it."

But you're the one who gains from it, Bolesław thought.

"Your health, Duke." Henry raised his goblet in a toast and drank. "Your loyalty to the dead emperor is touching. In fact, I admire it. I'd like you to be that loyal to me. I suspect that our dear Otto promised you something which inspires such loyalty. Perhaps I could fulfill some of those promises?"

"Withdraw your claim for the throne and support me."

"What?" Henry's birdlike, protruding eyes became round.

"In the case of his untimely death, Otto III intended for me to be his heir."

"But you have no rights to it! I do. I'm his cousin. Besides, that's just not possible, he could not have been in his right mind when he said that."

"You asked, so I'm telling you." Bolesław never took his eyes off Henry. "Did you hear he had opened Charlemagne's tomb in Aachen?"

"A sacrilegious act." Henry snorted. "And he took the emperor's throne . . ."

"And he gave it to me."

"Impossible!"

"Come to Poznań," Bolesław lied smoothly. The throne was still in Italy, but Henry didn't need to know that.

"That means nothing."

"Doesn't the Saint Maurice's spear mean anything either?"

Henry put down his goblet and placed both palms flat on the table.

"Bolesław, I'm a practical man, while my cousin Otto was a deluded dreamer. He dragged the Reich into a war in Italy that we don't want. His dreams are already costing us too greatly. The idea of renovating the empire, of four equal provinces of Gaul, Italy, Germania, and Słowiańszczyzna, it's ludicrous! It cannot work."

"If you start with war and murders, then you're right, it can't. Otto assumed that the four provinces are equal not just in status, but that they exist in peace, and the ruler of each works to maintain the external borders of the empire since the internal ones were meant to be safely established."

"Bolesław, the situation has changed. And I have no intention of continuing my predecessor's work."

"You are not his successor yet. And even if you get the Saxon crown, you still have a way to go before you wear the imperial diadem."

"Let's set aside our differences. I want to talk about what connects us." He nodded at a servant, who refilled their goblets and served a cold roast. "Make your peace with the facts, Duke," Henry continued. "The Reich crown is already mine."

"While Łużyce, Milsko, and Meissen are mine," Bolesław replied.

"That's not possible, Bolesław."

"But it's true. I've taken them." He took a bite of meat. "A royal crown and Połabie, those are my terms."

He watched Henry's reaction closely. The Bavarian duke wasn't prone to losing his temper; he was good at masking his emotions. He was slight, skinny, and though he showed no external symptoms of illness, he had to have been in some kind of pain as, every once in a while, he clenched his jaw and his features contracted in a grimace. He had a fondness for bishops, which was no doubt influenced by his having spent his youth in Saint Emmeram's abbey.

This council and the support they unanimously gave him was the best testimony to that. But Bolesław was thinking about something else as he watched Henry. The Bavarian duke had no children. They said that he and his wife had both taken purity vows, but Bolesław never believed it. The alleged vows were more likely masking the duke's real problem. And if that were the case, he could soon be negotiating with someone else entirely.

"I won't give you Meissen," Henry began.

"I don't want a gift. I will buy it from you. And I don't negotiate."

He knew that Henry needed his armies in Italy.

"It's not for sale. I want to give it to Eckard's brother Gunzelin, as a gesture of good will. He's your ally. The eastern part of the Meissen March will go to Herman, Eckard's son."

You want to wash Eckard's blood off your hands, Bolesław thought. *And you're clearly willing to sacrifice much to do so. But Gunzelin as Meissen's ruler is actually a good idea.*

"I won't take silver for Łużyce and Milsko," Henry continued. "You can be my vassal there."

"I already have them." Bolesław shrugged. "I took them."

"Illegally."

"No. Based on my agreement with Otto."

"Otto is dead, and he has left no documents that may confirm your words." Henry looked bored. "Be my vassal in Łużyce and Milsko. It's a good offer."

I know, Bolesław thought, but said, "And a royal crown."

"The time for your coronation will come once I'm emperor." Henry tried to smile, but it looked more like a grimace. He clenched his jaw again. "Do you accept?"

"Yes." Bolesław nodded and pushed his plate away. The cold roast wasn't very good.

"I knew we could reach an agreement." Henry held the edge of the table tightly as he stood up.

This isn't an agreement, but a temporary compromise, Bolesław thought as he turned to leave.

That evening, the bishops went to mass, but the margraves and dukes, other than Henry of Bavaria, made their excuses. Bolesław, along with Gunzelin, Duke Bernard Billung, and Margrave Henry of Schweinfurt, waited for their horses in the yard.

"Henry of Bavaria as king of the Reich . . ." Billung shrugged his shoulders and stretched his neck, which was tight from sitting for so long. "The German duke Herman would have been a better choice."

"They outvoted us." The margrave of Schweinfurt grimaced. "For now, Bolesław has negotiated the most advantageous arrangement. Łużyce, Milsko . . ."

"You know very well this is not what the emperor intended. If Otto were alive, things would have gone differently. Gunzelin, how much do you want for Meissen?" Bolesław clapped his back.

"Stop it, Bolz. It's not funny. Dividing the March between me and my nephew could lead to conflict."

"But the Bavarian skinflint has agreed for your nephew to wed Bolesław's daughter," Billung interjected.

The grooms brought their horses. Duszan held Bolesław's as he mounted. His twelve men stood to attention. Henry of Schweinfurt and Billung each had twice as many men as he did.

"I'll join you beyond the city walls," Gunzelin said. "We'll meet in your camp this evening."

The horns sounded when they reached the gates which opened for them.

"As you wish." Bolesław nodded.

On his other side, Billung asked, "Why do you only have a dozen men?"

"Why do you have more?" Bolesław asked in return as they set off.

His men headed the procession, while two rode on either side of the two dukes. Duszan, as usual, was right behind him.

"Henry's messengers told me I can only bring a dozen with me," he added with sudden unease.

Billung looked at him carefully and frowned. Led by instinct, Bolesław reached for the helm at his saddle and put it on. They rode through the city gates and along a narrow path between merchant stalls.

"Out of the way!" his guards shouted to some people who were trying to push a wagon loaded with flour and pulled by an ox.

"Have pity, my lord," the wagon driver groaned. "The cart is stuck, the wheel broke . . ."

The ox roared as it was struck by a whip.

"Make way for the dukes!"

People began to gather behind the cart which obstructed their path.

"What dukes?" someone in the crowd asked.

"Which ones?"

"Duke of Poland, Bolesław, and the Saxon duke Bernard . . ."

Suddenly, an arrow whizzed past from an alleyway. Bolesław and Bernard dodged it. The crowd, which moments before seemed to be composed of ordinary people, pulled out weapons: butchers' knives and axes. Archers appeared as if from nowhere and took shelter behind the wagon. This was intended to be a slaughter.

"It's an assassination!" Henry of Schweinfurt shouted behind them.

A powerfully built soldier who had pushed ahead of Bolesław to shield him fell as he was struck by multiple arrows. Another took his place, but his horse was wounded and crushed its rider as it fell. Bolesław turned, but Henry's and Billung's men obstructed the way back. His men in the front, faced with dozens of bandits, were falling one by one.

"Retreat!" Billung shouted. "To the side gate!"

They turned their horses around with difficulty. Bolesław's last men protected their backs as they pushed their way through.

Where the hell are Henry's guards? he wondered as they squeezed out of the alley and into a small square. None of his men, other than Duszan, had survived. The whinnying of horses and the shouts of the crowd mixed with the terrified screams of ordinary passersby who found themselves in the wrong place at the wrong time.

"Protect Duke Bolesław!" the margrave ordered his men.

They surrounded him with shields. Billung forced his way toward the front of their column and was leading the way to a side gate which led out of the borough. Bolesław realized that he didn't even know where this second exit was.

If I survive, I will learn the position of every gate of every borough I ever enter, he thought.

His horse squealed and almost reared. *They must have hit its hindquarters,* Bolesław thought as he quickly kicked the stirrups off his feet so that the falling horse didn't drag him under and crush him.

He leapt off his mount's back. For a second, he was outside the protection of the shields. Duszan was already with him; he was shorter than Bolesław, and he pressed his entire body against him to protect him. They retreated toward the wall. Someone wearing a gray hood ran toward them. Bolesław turned around as soon as he heard Duszan's whisper:

"It's me . . ."

But their assailant wasn't so easily tricked, and he hissed straight into Bolesław's face over Duszan's head:

"The empire only needs three pillars. The Slavs will never equal Germania, but they can be its subordinates!"

Bolesław took in every word as he reached for the long Saxon dagger he carried on his back. He didn't wait to hear more. Pushing Duszan away with his left hand so hard that his friend fell to the ground, he stabbed the cloaked man in the stomach. Billung ran toward him while his men regrouped so they were once again shielded.

"Bolz! What took you so long? He could have killed you!" Duke Bernard exclaimed.

"I wanted to hear what he had to say," Bolesław panted.

"Do you know him?" Billung kicked the dying man.

"No," he replied, and turned around. "Duszan, get up!"

"A horse for the duke!" the margrave shouted as he rode over to them.

"Duszan?" Bolesław, overcome suddenly with dread, rushed to his friend's side. "Are you hurt?"

Duszan was clutching his stomach as blood flowed from a wound in his abdomen. He was using both hands to try to stem the blood.

"Press harder. You aren't allowed to die. That's an order!" Bolesław shouted and picked him up as if he weighed nothing more than a child. "Duszan, can you hear me?"

"Yes . . ."

One of the margrave's men brought over a horse. Bolesław laid Duszan gently over the saddle, then mounted behind him.

"Follow me!" Henry of Schweinfurt called. "It's not safe here, and there's no sign of Henry's guards."

Bolesław set off after the duke and margrave.

"And there won't be," he said, nodding in the direction of the man he'd killed. "He gave me a message from Duke Henry."

They reached the small gate, which was usually used by servants, quickly. Henry of Schweinfurt's men began to hack at it with axes.

"It's boarded shut!" their leader reported. "It hadn't been this morning when I checked it."

"Duszan, can you hear me?" Bolesław kept his left hand on his friend's body.

They left Merseburg immediately, retreating to a safe distance at a canter. Nobody shot at them from the walls. Bolesław stood tall in his stirrups as he turned around to face the city.

"The Slavs will not be subordinate to Germania!" he roared.

This is war, he thought. *Is my son still in Italy?*

Duszan groaned. Bolesław leaned over him.

"I can't carry out your last order," he said hoarsely as his eyes misted over.

15

POLAND

Świętosława wasn't sure whether she should send Ion to Italy. She had no reason to trust him, but Unger convinced her in the end.

"He may have sinned, but the Lord requires us to forgive those who trespass against us. Ion knows Romuald, and he knows Pereum and the surrounding areas. He can write, so he can send us a message."

"He's not meant to send us a message, he's meant to send Bezprym back to us. What if he's lying about having been a hermit with Romuald?"

"There's nothing simpler, my lady. Have the duke's men take Ion to the hermitage in Międzyrzecz and show him to the monks from Pereum. If they recognize him, we'll know for sure."

And know him they did. Ion left the meeting trembling all over, as if only now realizing that he would be sent to face the old hermit, his old master.

"If Wrzask and Zgrzyt were still alive, they'd be able to smell your fear," she told him disdainfully. "But because of you, they're dead. Ostry"—she turned to the leader of the expedition—"if Ion crosses you in any way, kill him. You can leave his corpse by the road."

"My lady," Unger reminded her, "that's not acceptable behavior."

"And sharing someone's confession with a third party is?" she asked. "All right then. Leave him in the bushes. Tie him up when you stop and keep an eye on him. He's a cowardly rat. If Wilkomir and Helga agree, you'll take Wilczan with you. He's got a sharp mind and he'll be able to handle the damned monk."

"My queen," Ion pleaded. "If I do as you wish, will you consider forgiving my sins?"

"If you fail, I'll think of a better way to punish you than to drag you around with me," she promised as she turned to leave. Behind her, she heard him mumble, "There is no better punishment, my lady."

Three months had passed since their departure. Bolesław was already at the gates of Merseburg for the council of the Reich lords when the messenger from Italy arrived.

Brother Bruno of Querfurt, who had been charged with Prince Bezprym's care by Emperor Otto, has delivered the young lord into our hands. We are going to travel through the Alps and Bavaria to avoid meeting Duke Henry's armies. Since the Italians have chosen Ardurin of Ivrea as their king, we have to be careful, as he hunts Otto's friends as well as Henry's supporters. The roads aren't safe. Brother Bruno left for Rome today to be made a bishop and receive a pallium as soon as possible, which will enable him to be a missionary as Duke Bolesław had hoped. Bruno must go to the new king of Germania before he comes to Poznań for the investiture as soon as a king is chosen, though, so we cannot expect him in Poland very soon. The young prince is healthy and has agreed to return home under the condition that his father will keep his promise and allow him to stay in the hermitage in Międzyrzecz.

Unger finished reading and put down the parchment.

"Is the sign we agreed on there?"

"Yes, my lady. It is undoubtedly a letter written by Ion on Master Ostrowod's orders. Their journey comes at an unfortunate time."

Emnilda, with her youngest son Otto on her lap, sighed.

"Ostrowod took his best men," she said reassuringly.

"And the biggest coward," Świętosława added. "Ion always gets out unscathed, so perhaps he'll bring them luck."

"What will happen when Bezprym finds out that Bolesław has no intention of leaving him in the hermitage?" Emnilda asked, ignoring Świętosława's warning hiss.

"Doesn't he?" Unger asked sharply.

"Oh, my brother likes to change his mind," the queen said quickly, not wanting to anger the bishop. "Damn it! Didn't they say anything about the throne? Unger, would you be so good as to check again. Bolesław really wants to place his . . . self . . . could you check?"

Unger frowned. She wasn't immune to his bishop's charms and was better behaved with him around. There was something about him. He was as insightful as her father had been.

"Not a word," he said drily. "Tell me, please . . ."

But Sobiesław's entrance saved her from responding. He strode into the hall, a worried look on his face.

"There is trouble in Prague," he announced.

"Wonderful!" It slipped out of Świętosława's mouth before she could stop herself. "Perfect timing." She smiled at Unger apologetically before turning back to Sobiesław. "Or is it not?"

"Tell us, Duke of Libice," Emnilda requested, casting a frightened glance at the bishop. "Sit with us and speak."

Unger must still have been thinking about what Emnilda had let slip, because instead of looking at Sobiesław Sławnikowic, his attention was on the duchess and Świętosława. Uneasy under his scrutiny, Świętosława rose.

"Things aren't looking good in Prague. Duke Władywoj is never sober . . ." Sobiesław began.

Świętosława picked up a jug of wine as he said this. "Will you have some?" she asked Sobiesław, as if about to pour him a glass.

"Yes, my queen." He looked surprised that a woman of her stature would pour it for him herself.

Instead of doing so, though, she placed the jug back down with a clatter.

"Yes, Bishop." She turned to Unger and spoke in her brother's place. "Bolesław will not let Bezprym off the hook."

"He sent for him, but he doesn't think his place is in a hermitage." Emnilda joined the confession.

"Please, try to understand . . ."

"And forgive him before he returns . . ."

"If Bezprym has made his vows to God," Unger replied, "then the duke cannot place his own wishes above His will."

"But how do you know it was God's will and not a mere whim of a passionate adolescent?"

"A vow made to God cannot be broken."

"Really? Sven married me at the altar, but he still sent me away."

"My queen, please do not be insulted, but you are not the best example. Your life is full of details of which a confessor would prefer to remain ignorant."

"Oh, so I open up my heart and confess just once, and what happens? My confessor turns out to be a traitor. But what can one expect of a man who had a hand in Jarl Birger's murder and helped me burn my suitors alive? The man I love is dead; my husband has exiled me and killed my lynxes. You're right, Unger, I'm not a good example."

As she said this, Emnilda cried out and covered little Otto's ears with her hands. Sobiesław picked up the jug and poured a heavy glass of wine for himself. The blood had drained from Unger's face. And only then did Świętosława realize that not everything was discussed openly in Poznań.

"Ah," she muttered. "My apologies. I thought you knew. It's the northern bards' favorite topic. Let's not talk about me. Sobiesław, tell us the news you came with—Władywoj is a drunk, you were saying. He's one of our distant relations, is that right?"

"Yes, my lady. After your uncle's son, the Prussian duke Boleslav the Red, castrated . . ."

This was the last straw for Emnilda though. Burning suitors and castrations . . . She rose from her chair.

"I'm sorry, Sobiesław, but it's getting very late. I'm going to take Otto to the alcove. Please excuse me." She carried the toddler away so he would hear no more family stories.

"He castrated Jaromir, his younger brother, while he tried to murder Oldrzych in the bathhouse . . ."

"In the bathhouse?" she asked quietly.

She had always thought of herself as taking after her father, "*You are my daughter through and through,*" as he had liked to say. She'd forgotten that the blood of the Přemyslids ran through her veins, too. Was committing murder in a bathhouse some sort of family tradition? The bard's verses echoed in her memory: *Those who come at a wrong time were reprimanded by our merciful lady. The flames washed their soiled hands.*

"Yes. He completely lost it, and his mother fled from Prague with the two younger—"

"Wait. In order for him to be castrated, Jaromir would have had to have gone through puberty," she observed.

"A young one."

"Where did they go?"

"To the Reich, seeking Duke Henry's protection." Sobiesław shook his head. "Unfortunately, our rulers have always relied on the kings of the Reich when trying to resolve their issues. It's a mistake, and it has cost the Czechs dearly over the centuries. But coming back to the matter at hand . . . Your brother, wanting to punish the Red One for his cruelty against his brothers, abducted him and took him to Kraków, replacing him with Władywoj. The first is a brute by nature, the second is only cruel when he's drunk. But he hasn't been sober since the day he took the throne. I have had news from Prague that the people are rebelling against him. The nobles are considering bringing Jaromir and Oldrzych back, which would mean the end of your brother's political ventures."

"I assume that Bolesław sent his men to Prague to accompany Władywoj."

She knew that Bohemia had always been one of her brother's dreams. When they'd been children and sweet Dobrawa had told them about their grandfather, he'd called himself "duke of Prague" and he couldn't understand that he wouldn't be its heir.

"Yes, my lady, but apparently even Bolesław's men cannot control a single drunk brute. Besides, Jaromir and Oldrzych are spreading rumors that their older brother was following your brother's orders."

"That's nonsense," Unger interjected. "Surely nobody reasonable believes it?"

"Bohemia is in chaos, Bishop," Sobiesław said sadly. "Reason has evaporated since my family was slaughtered."

I don't believe that Bolesław would have tried to convince someone to castrate their family, she thought. *He may be impulsive and temperamental, but he isn't cruel. The revolts in Bohemia, though, might be used to his advantage if he hasn't forgotten his childhood dream.*

WOLIN, WOLIN ISLAND, POLAND

Astrid didn't want to meet with Sigvald's brother. She did what she could to forget that she'd ever had a traitor for a husband. But what did her efforts matter when she had to pass Jomsborg every time she sailed Dziwna? A constant reminder that he used to be there.

"Forgetfulness comes with time," Busla told her one day while folding canvas dressings. "My grandmother reached a point when she forgot she'd ever been married and had children and grandchildren. She wore chains of flowers in her hair and spoke to us like we were her servants."

"Is that meant to make me feel better?" Astrid snorted.

She got up and observed the wounded men around them. Omold the bard was the only one left from the battle at Øresund. The rest of Olav's men had left Wolin a long time ago. She now had only a few oarsmen and the helmsman from a Frisian cog which recently arrived in port. They'd gotten into a fight with the Jomsvikings when drinking at the port tavern, and they had lost. Dalwin had asked her to help them in any way she could.

"If the news spreads that Wolin isn't a safe port, ships won't come here. We'll all lose on it. Please, heal them."

"There'll be more," she said sadly.

"It's bad; it's never been like this before," Dalwin admitted. "We paid the Jomsvikings to protect Wolin and the merchants, but now? They do what they want in Jomsborg, and there's no one to talk to, no one to pay."

"Oh, haven't you heard? They recently threatened that we'd have to pay each one of them separately."

"That's robbery," Dalwin observed with horror.

Her grandfather was getting older; he wasn't the same energetic viceroy he'd been years ago. He had never said it out loud, but he regretted that

Astrid had no children. A son who might take over from him and ensure the survival of the great, wealthy port. There had been many willing and greedy suitors since Sigvald's death, but even Dalwin had liked none of them, and Astrid reacted almost hysterically to the word *husband*. None had been suitable to introduce to Bolesław either. Deep down, Astrid was glad that her brother had enough of his own problems to deal with and had forgotten about her for the time being. She knew that if it came to it, Bolesław would be as ruthless as Mieszko had been. He'd pick out a husband for her and that would be that.

Is he already plotting Świętosława's next marriage? she often wondered. *He has a queen with no kingdom at home. If he could find a suitable husband for her who could help him, he probably wouldn't hesitate for a second. Maybe he feels guilty though? Or perhaps he'll leave her alone and let her choose for herself?*

She found it hard to admit even to herself that Świętosława's silence made her even gladder than her brother's disinterest. She was afraid that her sister, lonely and in pain, would seek to meet as soon as possible. But Astrid didn't have the energy for it. She still wasn't ready to face her. Maybe later, once everything fell into place. Sometime. In a while. So long as it wasn't now.

But the fragile peace of mind she built with so much difficulty was crashing down now as Thorkel the Tall, Sigvald's brother, arrived in Jom and asked to meet with her.

"Hear him out," Dalwin pleaded. "It's his brother."

I want to forget I ever had a husband, she thought stubbornly, but she couldn't deny Thorkel and she certainly couldn't ignore Dalwin.

He lived up to his nickname and stood out because of his height.

He had a long, slightly asymmetrical nose, just like Sigvald. Shining dark eyes, like Sigvald. And slender fingers like him. *At least he's bald,* she thought with relief. *If he had the same beautiful, long hair as Sigvald, I wouldn't be able to say a word. It would have felt too much like talking to the jarl of Jom.*

"My lady." He bowed. "I've wanted to meet you for a long time. I was in Jom a few times when Sig was still alive, but my brother never introduced me to his beautiful wife."

"He was jealous of everyone," she replied, trying to provoke him. She wanted to find out as soon as possible whether Thorkel had come to blame her for his brother's death.

He nodded and said, "I couldn't have put it better myself. His challenging personality was the reason why I could never stay in Jom for long."

She remembered Sigvald mentioning once or twice, years ago, that Thorkel was busy in England.

"We never had children, as you are probably aware. So, if you came to arrange matters of inheritance, take all the lands you are owed. I don't want anything," she said.

"I came for men. Jomsvikings without a leader . . ."

"The iron wolves turn into furious, drunk dogs that attack each other for no reason now that they have no master," she finished for him. "But I don't know if those dogs are ready to follow Sigvald's brother. The ones who still have some honor consider the battle of Øresund to have been another betrayal."

"I know. Many of them are sorry that Jom's old laws have been broken."

He wasn't like Sigvald, she could sense that already. Perhaps he was playing his own game with her now, but he wasn't the same as her husband, the man who'd hidden his sharp edges within a cool demeanor. Dalwin listened to their conversation, just as they'd arranged. She knew her grandfather and suspected she could already guess what he'd say once Thorkel left.

"Do you want to be the jarl of Jom?" she asked.

"No. I want to take what's left of the Jomsvikings to England. I need crews, and they need something to do."

"I don't have the power to grant you permission for that. You should ask my brother, Duke Burizleif."

"The Jomsvikings don't meddle in royal affairs," Thorkel replied.

Astrid laughed humorlessly.

"Sigvald did little else. But despite that, you're alike."

"Don't insult me, Lady of Wolin. I think that the Jomsvikings' participation in the affairs of Denmark and Poland is the source of all this strife. I want to end that."

"You should ask my brother's permission to lead the crews out of Jom," she repeated.

"And if I don't? Burizleif has no fleet with which to chase me across the seas."

He was right, as she knew all too well. Besides, Bolesław was somewhere in the Reich with his armies, and undoubtedly had no time to trouble himself with the Jom fortress for the time being.

I can't force them to stay, she thought feverishly. *If I disagree, they will attack the same Wolin that they once guarded.*

"Tell me, Thorkel, are you going to sail to England as Sven's ally or rival?"

"If I were superstitious, I'd say that Sven's allies and rivals alike tend to draw the short straws. I mean Olav Tryggvason."

I know, she thought, hiding her anger.

"Sven is too powerful today for me to pose any threat to him. But perhaps a counterbalance in England, where he doesn't rule himself, only his chieftains do—why not? Does it matter to you either way, Lady of Wolin?"

Sven built a coalition against Olav and is responsible for his defeat, and you're asking me if it matters?

"The king of Denmark has exiled my sister," she replied with complete composure. "It should be no surprise that I'm interested to learn who his enemies are."

"He has many," Thorkel replied. "But don't count on anyone openly challenging him. He's too strong. He rules in Denmark, controls Sweden, and has conquered Norway. Who'd have thought, right?" Thorkel chuckled grimly. "I remember when Palnatoki sent me and Sigvald years ago to help Sven win back Hedeby. He started with nothing."

"You admire him," Astrid observed sourly.

"Which doesn't mean I want to serve him." Thorkel looked at her carefully, cocking his head just like Sigvald used to do and making her clench her jaw.

"I told you I don't have the power to give the Jomsvikings leave to depart from Jom. My brother, Duke Burizleif, would undoubtedly be against the idea. You'll do as you wish."

He nodded, still looking at her.

"We'll leave in two days," he said.

"I understand."

"And I promise that we will leave it untouched. The Jomsvikings wanted to burn it down, but I wouldn't let them."

Thank you, she thought, but aloud she said:

"It wouldn't have occurred to me, Thorkel, that you'd be capable of such a barbaric act. No one reasonable burns their bridges behind them."

He stood up and walked toward the door after nodding his farewell, but he stopped and turned around before he reached it.

"They say, Lady of Wolin, that you saw the end of the battle and the surrender of the *Long Snake*."

"Someone must have misinformed you, Thorkel. The *Long Snake* never surrendered. It defended itself until the last man fell."

Once Thorkel had left, Dalwin came to her, sat down, and sighed loudly.

"No, Grandfather." She beat him to it. "There is no way. You heard everything. Thorkel did not come here asking for my hand, promising to reorganize the fortress which would defend Wolin again, or anything of the sort."

"He didn't say it outright, but he's better than anyone." Dalwin shook his head.

"No. Thorkel lives to conquer. Being the fortress's guardian would bore him faster than it bored Sigvald."

"But . . ."

"There will be no bread from this flour, Grandfather. The most important thing is that they will leave us the fortress, and we can get the crews needed to fill it and protect Wolin. The only thing I don't know is who should lead them."

"Don't you?" Dalwin moved his shoulders with difficulty. "You should, my dear. You."

16

⚜

POLAND

Świętosława rode out of Poznań with Wolrad, Helga, Ylva, Great Ulf, and her guards. The men Bolesław had given her made up Duszan's funeral procession. The coffin with his body in it rocked on the wagon.

When the duke had returned from Merseburg and news of Duszan's death spread throughout the country, an old, gray-haired, pigeon-like man arrived in Poznań. It was Wolrad, their father's old flagbearer, who was living out his last days in Giecz. Bolesław had been busy preparing for the next expedition, so the old man asked to be seen by Świętosława. "My lady," he'd said, "Duszan's body should rest with the bones of his kin."

"Do you know who they were?" she'd asked with surprise, since Dusza and Duszan's origins had always been veiled in mystery. Wolrad had nodded, and now here they were, traveling east.

Wolrad urged his horse forward until he was level with Świętosława once Poznań was behind them. She smiled at the old man who seemed younger now that he was in the saddle.

"It won't do to complain on the road," he said, rubbing his forehead, "but we'll have to stop for the night before we reach Duszan's burial place. I sent a message to Siemir. He is our old comrade and used to be at your father's side. His son Tasław is now the castellan at Grzybowo. We'll stop there for the night."

"I won't argue with you," she told Wolrad.

"That's odd, my lady. You did little else when you were a child." He winked at her.

"You're older, so you probably know better than I do," she said politely.

"And the spell is broken." He chuckled croakily. "You let me have my way out of pity because you see in me a man with one foot already in his grave."

"It's Duszan that we are taking to his grave. I suspect you aren't heading there anytime soon if you've talked me into a journey to Bodzia."

The borough in Grzybowo appeared on the horizon in the late afternoon, soon after the castellan with some guards appeared on the road ahead to meet them.

"Hosting the queen of three kingdoms is an honor I never expected to have," Tasław greeted her, and the words caught in his throat.

"You blush just like when you were a boy and I a girl," she replied cheerfully. "I remember how Father chose you for my brother's first team that night they went into the ice hole. What did you feel then, Tasław? You regretted it, didn't you? The Old Hawk chose you to accompany a barely grown Eaglet."

"No, my lady." He looked even more embarrassed. "It was an important day in my life. It was the first time I heard the duke's daughter speak my name . . ."

"Oh, stop it, I knew all of you . . ."

"And the spell is broken," Wolrad repeated with a smile. "Don't worry, Tasław, the queen has inadvertently insulted me today, too. Beside my lady I feel as if Duke Mieszko were still alive!"

"May he rest in peace." The castellan bowed his head, then they set off toward the borough.

Grzybowo lay by the small river Rudak and was surrounded by swamps on three sides.

"I remember how Astrid and I would catch fish in the Rudak!"

"And I remember the summer that these wetlands turned into swamps with bubbling lakes." Wolrad nodded gloomily.

"Really? When was that? Father never said."

Wolrad and Tasław exchanged glances.

"Your lord father wasn't here then," the old flagbearer said, and fell silent with a grimace.

"Wolrad, if you begin saying something, then please finish. The curiosity will never let me rest. Ylva?" She turned to the servant. "Have you heard about the bubbling swamps?"

Ylva's pale face grew paler and she whispered as she crossed herself:

"Witches are drowned in swamps, Bold Lady . . ."

"So, Wolrad? Tell me. My Ylva is very curious."

"There's nothing to tell. It was the year that the lord duke was baptized."

"Are you saying that the old gods took their revenge?"

"The gods? I'm only a simple flagbearer, who am I to know such things?" He shrugged. "I only know that Ludmiła threw curses around like a madwoman."

"Ludmiła?" Świętosława recognized the name.

"His wife," Tasław reminded her, then quickly corrected himself. "One of the seven women with whom the lord duke lived before he married your mother, the lady Dobrawa."

She remembered. She'd often eavesdropped on conversations about his wives when she'd been a child.

"This Ludmiła . . . is she still alive?" she asked.

"No, my queen," Tasław replied. "But her younger sister is. Tomiła, but she's known as Tomka. Age has affected her mind though, and it's hard to talk to her. And here is Grzybowo's northern gate!"

A massive wooden guard post was erected over the gate. She could see the soldiers' gleaming helmets and glimmering spearheads. A flag bearing Bolesław's eagle fluttered in the wind.

The guards at the gate blew their horns in welcome as they were admitted and rode onto a stone-laid road that led straight to the large wooden manor. Tasław was faster than Great Ulf and he helped her dismount, blushing like a young man the whole time.

"We prepared the best room," he said. "The one in which the duke usually stays."

Huge hunting hounds appeared in the yard. A whole pack of them barked and nudged their hands with their enormous red heads, asking to be stroked.

"They look like the ones Bolz has," she called, patting the ones nearest to her.

"They are the same ones, my lady," Tasław said proudly. "The famous kennels of Grzybowo. Perhaps the queen would like a few puppies, too?"

"No," she replied quickly. "Thank you. I won't keep animals again."

Suddenly, one of the bitches howled, and the rest of the dogs joined in. They all sat down, as if following a command, and howled almost in unison. Świętosława looked around. A tall woman with rounded shoulders, dressed in white, approached them. She had a chain of ruth and chamomile flowers in her loose gray hair, and she held a small basin covered with clay in her hand.

"Tomka." The castellan shook his head. "Take her away," he ordered the guards, shouting over the howling dogs.

"No." Świętosława stopped them. "I want to meet her."

Tomka walked slowly, dragging her feet. She seemed to be looking at the ground she walked on instead of around her. She stopped and, never straightening her back, reached out a hand and waved it in the air. The dogs all turned around as she indicated and fell silent. The woman started walking again with difficulty. Her gray head bobbed around on her long, thin neck. Świętosława gazed at her, enchanted. Great Ulf appeared at her side, silent as a cat. The old woman stopped when she was within a few paces of them, and without straightening her spine, she lifted her head to look straight at Świętosława.

"If you fight with iron . . ." she murmured slowly, "iron you will break . . ."

She lowered her hand into the basin and lifted out a handful of clay. She lifted it as high as Świętosława's head and squeezed. The wet clay slipped between her fingers.

"Clay remains clay," Tomka said with an unexpected chuckle. "Nobody wants clay, everyone loves iron. The fools and the blind, the fools and the blind!"

"Don't insult the queen," Tasław snarled.

"I'm not talking about her," the old woman said sharply. "I'm talking about you!" And pointing a clay-covered finger at all the armed men in the yard, one by one, she turned around and shuffled away. The silence that fell when she left was broken only by the panting of the dogs.

They spent the night in Grzybowo, and left at dawn by the east gate, toward the Vistula. The morning mists hung above the wetlands surrounding Grzybowo. Świętosława was thinking about her father. What had he felt when he had to send away the women with whom he'd shared a bed and a table? When he died, he mentioned only one of them—Urdis, Astrid's mother. She knew that each one of them had been an alliance. Seven families, seven boroughs, seven wives. He gave them all up for one God and one Dobrawa. Had he known then that he was doing the right thing? Had he been afraid?

They rode out onto the east road and the sun began to warm them. And suddenly she realized that no matter what her father had felt at the time, it had been his decision and his move. His wives had been forced to comply whether they had wanted to or not.

It wouldn't be surprising if they'd all cursed him seven times over, she thought. *Thank the Lord that the curses never broke Father.*

She shook it off and moved closer to Wolrad.

"Tell me about the borough to which we are going," Świętosława said, hoping conversation would help clear her mind of darker worries. "Father sometimes mentioned Bodzia, but he never took us there."

"Because of them." He nodded toward Duszan's coffin. "He didn't want to hurt their parents by parading the children they'd given up in front of them."

"They said that he bought Dusza and Duszan, paying their weight in silver for them."

"He did, my lady, but he did not buy them from the poor. You'll see for yourself, there is a reason for which Bodzia is called the Golden Borough."

"Is it true that only exiles live there? Those who came here from neighboring lands?"

"Yes." Wolrad nodded his gray head. "The Rusyns who struggled with the Ruriks, Danes who were running away from Harald Bluetooth, your father-in-law, and others who could not make a life in the countries of their birth."

"And Dusza's family?" she asked with a tremor in her voice.

"They're dead," Wolrad said.

"Do you know who they were?"

"You'll find out in Bodzia."

The Golden Borough was built by the Vistula, guarding the wide river. A young, flaxen-haired youth greeted them at the heavy, carved wooden gates.

"My lady." He bowed. "I am Arne, Bodzia's castellan. The Golden Borough opens its gates to you."

Her heartbeat quickened when she saw the gates. A ship with a golden bow and slender mast was carved into them. A ship that looked so like the *Haughty Giantess,* the vessel which had taken her to her first husband. She was about to ask about it when the horns sounded in welcome and they rode in.

She looked around her in wonder, never having seen houses like this before. Some had more than one level and detailed carvings decorating their cloisters, making them look like wooden lace. Others had sooty wooden roof tiles that resembled reptilian scales and dragon heads emerging from their rooftops. There were also enormous round buildings with peaked roofs like the tips of nomadic tents.

"Here is our manor," Arne said, and she saw a building that looked like a boat turned upside down.

"I saw some like this in Denmark," she told Arne.

"The ones who built this one years ago probably carried a Danish manor in their hearts," the castellan said with melancholy as he jumped from the saddle and handed his reins to a stable boy. "Will you allow me, my lady?" He gave her a hand to help her dismount. "I'd like to invite you to a feast. It is a great honor to host Sigrid Storråda."

She walked into a spacious hall. A long hearth ran in the middle, after the fashion of northern manors, and a raised platform which ran around the walls and was laid with furs served as a seat. Colorful eastern fabrics, nimbly woven, hung from the darkened beams, and above them were the shields. Some of them were unknown to her. Small, round ones with spikes protruding from their centers.

"My lady," Ylva whispered. "Look. It's just like Roskilde."

She glanced at the carvings which ran along the only wall that was not covered with fabric. At first, she agreed with Ylva, thinking they were just like the ones in Sven's manor. But when she walked over for a closer look, she realized they these weren't carvings of animals, but a story.

"It's the legend of Sivrit!" Ylva squealed. "Look, my lady! The blacksmith Regin is making the hero his sword. There is the dragon which Sivrit kills, and the birds whose chirping he understands when he eats their hearts. Oh! . . ." Tears streamed down Ylva's face. She wiped them away with the back of her hand.

"And here, Queen Sigrid"—Arne proudly pointed at a silver crucifix that hung above the door—"is one of the treasures from Moravia."

The silver Christ watched her from the cross with open eyes and seemed to be smiling.

Many parts of the world met in this manor in Bodzia. *The entire world in a single drop of water,* she thought.

"We have a gift for you, my lady, and for your maidservants," Arne said, summoning a servant.

"These silver ear cuffs are decorated with gold, formed by our own goldsmith. Unfortunately, he is away at the moment, so he cannot give these to you personally."

She lifted the long ornaments out of the small box. Seven delicate chains were attached to a temple ring that was decorated with silver beads. Each chain ended with a leaf, and an animal stood in the center of each ring. *My God,* she thought, *it's not just an animal, it's a lynx. They all want to make me happy with some kind of lynx, but I only want the ones Sven killed.*

"Thank you, they are beautiful." She smiled so as not to hurt Arne's feelings.

Ylva and Helga put on their ear cuffs, which were decorated with flowers rather than lynxes.

I'll swap with Helga, she thought, and immediately felt better. She sat down on the carved throne that had been prepared for her.

It's so similar to Eric's tall chair, she thought. *The one he sat on in Uppsala, not Sigtuna.*

As she sat, she placed her hands on the armrests and her fingers reflexively moved lower to the carved stanchions.

"Whose are these?" she asked.

"Konung Lesir," Arne replied, and raised a toast. "To Queen Sigrid!"

She wanted to ask who that was, but when she took a sip of mead, the castellan sat beside her and called out:

"Ivar, come closer."

At first, she thought that a large, clumsy child was walking toward them. Then she noticed the long, gray hair and realized he was a dwarf, not a child. He bowed low before her, stood up straight, and she saw an old man.

"My lady," he said respectfully. "Master Wolrad. They had to die for Ivar to be lucky enough to meet the queen and see her with his own eyes."

Tears shone in the dwarf's eyes, but he wiped them away with the back of his hand and grinned. Gold teeth gleamed in his mouth.

"My queen." Arne turned to her. "Here is Bodzia's oldest inhabitant, Ivar Goldtooth."

It's a good thing they don't call him Ivar the Short, she thought, and invited the dwarf to sit beside her.

"Will you tell me who Dusza was, Ivar?" she asked after a moment.

He studied her with keen, bloodshot eyes.

"Your shadow, my lady."

"That I know." She shook her head. "Tell me of what was hidden from us. Who were her parents? Why did they give her to the duke?"

"They gave her up because she was born on the same day as you, my queen. They gave her up because they were in the konung's debt. As are we all," he added sadly.

She knew that her father harbored noble exiles. It had never been openly discussed, but when she'd been a girl, she knew how to eavesdrop on the discussions held at secret councils. And now, when she was an adult exiled queen herself, she understood. It was unlikely that her father did it out of the goodness of his heart. She'd known Lord Mieszko too well to suspect that. He had to have had something to gain.

But who was this Konung Lesir they kept talking about?

"I loved Dusza," she said. "I want to know where she came from. Is my friend's family still alive?"

"No, my queen," he said. "None of her family who were here, in Bodzia, survived. Her parents and grandparents are all dead."

"The Golden Borough," Arne interjected, "is home to the descendants of those who escaped Great Moravia. And the descendants of the Khazars, whose ancestors ran from the civil war which raged by the Khazar Sea when their khagan, the khan of khans, forbade the worship of many gods and brought in rabbis to spread the word of Yahweh. It is also home to Russians, Varangians, Czechs, Swedes, Danes . . ."

"Yes," Ivar interjected. "That's where Dusza is from. Her family had come from Lejre."

"What?" she exclaimed. "Arnora, the tribal queen who is Sven's prisoner in Roskilde, comes from Lejre!"

"Arnora . . ." The dwarf nodded. "They spoke of her. She is Dusza's father's aunt."

Świętosława recalled how much attention Arnora had paid her Dusza.

"Did Dusza know who she was?" she asked quickly, her fingers clenching on the goblet in her hand.

"No, my lady," Ivar admitted. "She was given to you and your father as a baby. She had no way of knowing. Although the great konung was probably already planning to tie your fate to the kings of the north. He talked to the descendants of the jarls who lived in the Golden Borough many, many times. Those families have died out now, but back then, the lords of Birka, Uppsala, Lejre, and Aros all lived here. The konung loved to talk to them. There were also descendants of those who came from places even farther north, from the Norwegian islands, the ones who had to leave rocky Norway when it was under the rule of Harald Fairhaired and had found a home here when they had had enough travel . . ."

"Did he only accept nobility here?" she asked through gritted teeth.

"Well, no one here is poor." Ivar shrugged.

"Poor men don't run," Arne said abruptly.

"I worked hard all my life," Ivar added.

"You're a master," the castellan said. "An outstanding master!"

The dwarf blushed and rubbed his cheeks with the back of his hand.

"I'm an armorer, my lady," he explained in a trembling voice. "I make helms, chain mail, that sort of thing . . ."

"Will you show me tomorrow?" she asked.

"It will be my pleasure, my lady. It's an honor for Ivar . . . but I know that Queen Sigrid has better things to do than to watch an old man in Bodzia fidget with things . . ."

"Ivar made chain mail for your grandfather, Siemomysł," Arne praised him.

"But I didn't make any for Lesir," the old man said scathingly. "I regret that."

She wanted to ask who this Lesir was, whose name she was hearing for the second time, but a toast swept through the hall, repeated by everyone. It sounded like a song.

"From Mora we come! From Mora we come! The wraiths are gone, but our people remain!"[*]

"The Moymirids! The Halperins! The Bożydars! The Bjornssons! The Ruriks!"

She leaned over to Wolrad and asked, "What does it mean, 'from Mora we come'?"

"Do you remember the remains of the burnt borough opposite Ostrów Lednicki?" he replied with a question.

The borough of Moira. Never mention it to the duke again. That moment from

---

[*] The translation of "from Mora" in Polish is "z Mory," while the word for *wraith* in Polish is "zmora."

twenty years ago came to memory as clearly as if it had happened only hours ago: she'd ridden to the top of the mounds, and Mieszko had called her back angrily.

"Queen!" The dwarf touched Świętosława's elbow. "I know a stonemason who will make a gravestone for your lost Dusza."

"To the memory of Konung Lesir!" someone called out from the middle of the hall, and everyone drank.

"Who was Lesir?" she asked Arne.

"Your great-grandfather, my queen," he replied, clearly surprised that she didn't know.

"Świętosława knows her ancestors by our names," Wolrad explained. "Duke Lestek."

His words transported her away from the noise of the hall in the Golden Borough to the stillness of a glade. It was night, and a dark oak tree spread its branches over four grass-covered mounds. She was a young girl once more, searching for the tombs of her grandmothers and great-grandmothers. Her father, Mieszko, refused to meet her eyes as he told her that they'd gone to the pyre with their husbands. The ashes of each one had been poured into their husbands' graves, and Świętosława could feel the solid-gray dust settle heavily in her chest as she listened. Her mother, Dobrawa, was the first in their family to have been given her own tomb.

She clenched her hands on the carved stanchions.

The vast cemetery lay alongside the borough. It was surrounded by a wall of wildflowers. The houses of the dead rose above the graves, each one different, just like the borough's inhabitants. Some had detailed carvings engraved in their cloisters; she knew now that these belonged to the Ruriks. Others had sooty wooden roof tiles and dragon heads emerging from the rooftops. The descendants of the Khazars from the Halperin dynasty were laid to rest under the round houses with peaked roofs. Some were guarded by large, sculpted slender dogs.

Duszan's coffin had been made by a Moravian carpenter. It looked like a long, squat chest with iron fittings. Arne admitted that Duszan was descended from the family of exiles from Great Moravia. Świętosława decided that neither Dusza nor Duszan would have their houses marking their tombstones. Instead, she ordered huge gray rocks to mark their resting places. Duszan— friend was what she commanded be etched into Duszan's stone, and on her friend's: Queen Sigrid thanks Dusza for her journey on earth.

The runes don't know the name Świętosława, she thought sadly as she gazed at their slender, feral image. She crossed herself, regretfully thinking about Dusza's bones which could never rest here, but were somewhere in the rocky depths of Øresund.

I will bring you back to life, Dusza, she promised as she placed a bouquet of wildflowers by the rock.

Helga sighed when they left Bodzia and headed back to Poznań.

"I felt almost as if I were back in Sigtuna."

"Or Roskilde," Ylva added.

We're going home, she wanted to say, but decided not to. To her friends, Poznań wasn't home.

When their procession approached Ostrów Lednicki, she ordered that they spend the night in the palatium on the island.

"Helga, Ylva, I have something special for you," she said. "You'll ride over the longest bridge in the world we know, and you'll see the hidden nest of the Piast dynasty."

"And you, my lady?" Helga asked warily.

I need to find out something that has long been hidden from me, she thought.

"I'll join you later. I need to see to something with Wolrad first."

Her father's old flagbearer shook his head and sighed. She rode over to him.

"I wasn't meant to ask Father about Moira, but you will tell me about it. There were too many secrets implied but never spoken in Bodzia."

They set off at a slow pace toward the wide, tree-covered mound.

"The borough of Moira," he said thoughtfully, looking around.

"Was it built before Father constructed the residence on the island?" she asked, seeing how perfect the position on top of the hill would be. "Its inhabitants would have had the perfect view of the surrounding areas. This was a watchmen's borough, wasn't it, Wolrad?"

"Yes," the old man confirmed.

"Moira," she repeated, and asked: "From the Moymirids?"

He glanced at her and nodded, smiling.

"From Mora we come! From Mora we come! The wraiths are gone, but our people remain!" She repeated aloud the chant she had heard at the feast in the Golden Borough. "If I understand correctly, it used to be called 'Moira' after the Moymirid exiles, who had come from Great Moravia. And then its name was changed to Mora and, to forget about the wraiths which haunted the ashes, my father moved everyone to Bodzia?"

"More or less," Wolrad agreed.

The horses had climbed the hill and now stepped carefully along what used to be the borough's ramparts. The place which once must have pulsed with life was now covered with thick, thorny briars.

"Moira was beautiful when it bloomed," Wolrad said, pointing at the part of the hill closest to them. "This is where the old borough stood, and over there they added a new one."

"Tell me about the people who built it," she encouraged.

"You were right, it was the people who escaped from Great Moravia. When the Hungarians attacked them, Duke Svatopluk's land was already weak and had no strength to defend itself. Its inhabitants ran from the Hungarians to wherever would take them—south, east. And the duke's youngest brother went north. They called him Dalmir, and your father's great-grandfather, Siemiowit, welcomed him along with his women, children, servants, and the few possessions they had. He gave them this place and let them cut out the forest to build a borough. It also gave him the chance to watch them, and he decided that Moravian carpenters knew how to build ramparts better than ours did. So he sent his men to learn from the Moravians, and that's how he got the knowledge which was then so useful to his son."

"Lestek, also known as Lesir?" Świętosława checked.

"Yes, my lady. In the north, people knew him as Konung Lesir."

She slid from the saddle and tied her mare to a tree. Wolrad dismounted carefully. They walked down the old ramparts and into the borough, steadying themselves on the branches. Red berries glinted on the branches like drops of blood.

"There was war in the time between Siemiowit's rule and his son Lestek's. Terrible wars. The Saxons made their way across the Oder and moved east like a fiery dragon. Old Siemiowit, knowing he could not defeat them, told all his people to hide in the forests."

"He was a coward? He didn't defend his lands?" she asked, tugging her dress from where it had caught on a briar's waiting thorns.

Wolrad laughed and for a moment forgot that she was a queen.

"He had no chance, girl!" he snapped. Her implication that Lesir was a coward had clearly struck a nerve. "He had a choice: allow the Saxons to murder the defenders and take the women and children as their prisoners, or hide in the unbreachable forests, just like those who had lived here for centuries before that had done. Do you know how many barbarian hordes from the east traipsed across our lands? Too many to count. And the people of old had one weapon against them—they disappeared. They vanished in the swamps, hid in the ancient wilderness, and dissolved in the fog. The invaders lost their trail in the woods, died in the swamps, and gave up on trying to conquer the land that they thought was wild and uninhabited. It used to be said that our ancestors were like grass—wind might push us down, but when the danger had passed, they rose up again. They didn't build boroughs so that they could disappear at any moment, and their gods didn't need rich temples because they worshipped in the woods, in glades, or on lake islands. They had no riches, and saw no value in them, because what was the point of owning something you couldn't take with you into the wilderness?"

"Who has nothing, has nothing to worry about," Świętosława said thoughtfully, looking at the remains of the borough through the birches. It had to be as large as the settlement in Sigtuna. "But it wasn't that Saxon invasion which destroyed Moira, was it?" she asked.

"No, no. The Saxons reached Poznań and turned back. They never got as far as here. But after that attack, Lestek decided that he had to build boroughs big enough to defend his country from another invasion from the west. He knew how to do it because the builders from Moira had shown him how to strengthen the construction of the great ramparts with hooks . . ."

"Such massive constructions cost a fortune," she interrupted. "How did my great-grandfather have money for this?"

"Lestek had been lucky"—Wolrad laughed—"and he was smart enough to make the most of it. Did you hear Arne talk about the Khazars who ran from their khan?"

"The Halperins who didn't want to accept the faith of the one and only Yahweh?"

The old flagbearer clucked his tongue.

"Faith's faith, my lady. The khan of khans wanted to rid himself of his opponents under the guise of spreading the new religion. The rabbis only helped him in this. Halperin was a noble who lived by the Khazar Sea. When he realized what was happening, he loaded two ships with his goods and, pretending to be a merchant, set off north along the Volga, and finally reached Novgorod. There he was apparently told that there are beautiful, uninhabited lands with plenty of forests in the east and on the southern shores of the gray Baltic Sea."

"Uninhabited, because the travelers didn't know that the people hide from foreigners in the woods and forests." She laughed cheerfully.

"That is most likely what happened." Wolrad nodded. "What we know for sure is that Halperin took his fleet and sailed to the Baltic. And here he was met with spring storms, and the Khazar's ships were stranded in the shallows. Lestek's scouts saw them and reported it to their duke."

"You don't mean to say that he robbed the shipwreck?" she asked, aghast.

"No, quite the opposite. He went to greet them. He wanted to see for himself the ship with the golden sail which his scouts had told him about. He took his troops with him, just in case, since he wasn't sure whether the ships carried merchants or warriors. When he stood on the shore with his men, Halperin realized that the information he had received in Novgorod had been right about the lands being beautiful and full of forests but had been wrong about it being uninhabited. The Khazars had no choice, since the storm had destroyed their ships. They came to an arrangement with Lestek . . ."

"I once heard Father laughing at a feast that Lestek had the gift of words," Świętosława recalled.

"And he had. Apparently, he told Halperin, 'You're not young. Do you want to spend your whole life running to protect your gold? What good will that do you when you die? Don't be afraid, we can share it.' The khazar tried to barter, but Lestek said, 'What has washed up on my shores is mine. Look at my troops, my warriors. Do you want me to kill you for your treasure? Gods be my witnesses that I don't want to do that. We, the Slavs, are a welcoming people. I welcome you, my guest, and I will give you a roof over your head, shelter, and your khan of khans will never find you in my wilderness. But you must give me something in return. I need your riches to build boroughs that will protect us against the khan of khans if we need it. Do you understand, my dear newcomer, that by welcoming you here, I may be putting my people in danger?'"

"Dear newcomer . . ." She laughed, repeating Wolrad's words. "Was this Halperin really that rich?"

"Yes, he was. Even though he gave most of what was aboard his ships to Lestek, he still had enough to live out his days comfortably. Apparently, he ordered one of his wives be covered with silver coins when she was laid in her coffin. Try to remember the women you saw in Bodzia. Did you see the rich clothes they wore? And that's the fourth or fifth generation since Halperin."

"And wasn't the 'dear newcomer' surprised to find that Lestek built these boroughs on the western borders, not the eastern ones?"

"When he settled in Moira for good, the duke explained to him that he has more enemies than just the khan of khans, and that he had to start on the other side. Besides, Halperin himself didn't live long. He was initially buried in Moira, but then, when things there grew complicated, his tomb was moved to Bodzia."

"What about the ship?" she asked curiously. "Our wet-nurse used to sing us a song, *'Lord Lestek sailed on a golden ship under a golden sail.'* I used to think it was just a story, but I hear now that apparently there really was a golden sail at our shores."

"Duke Lestek ordered the destroyed ships be taken apart so their wood could be repurposed, but he had a soft spot for the one with the golden sail. He didn't let anyone touch it. And it was the golden sail which drew the Vikings to us. Then, once again, Lestek proved that he excelled in his use of words. Instead of fighting them, he invited them for a feast and suggested that they set up a merchant settlement in Truso."

"But Truso wasn't within the borders of his lands," she said with surprise.

"That's what was so brilliant about Lestek, my lady. He didn't let them onto his territories, but he had them near the border. In one move, he protected himself from invasions from any of their allies, and set up a line of defense against the war-loving Prussians."

"Now I can see that Mieszko and Bolesław's political talents come from Lestek-Lesir. But I still don't understand why Moira burned. Who burned it?"

"That happened in my lifetime." Wolrad gritted his teeth. "While Lestek and his son Siemomysł were alive, relations with Moira's inhabitants were good. Those who escaped settled down in our land and never forgot who had given them shelter. Siemomysł took Świętomira for his wife, who was the granddaughter of Dalwin, the one who had escaped from Moravia. Her father was a man called Mojar. Świętomira gave our duke two sons: Mieszko and Dobronieg. Only Czcibor, as you recall, was born to a different mother. After Siemomysł's death, there were only three sons left, and someone who wanted power very much, although he had succeeded in hiding his ambitions while the old duke was still alive."

"Mojar?" she guessed. "My father's maternal grandfather?"

"Yes, my lady. He festered and plotted. He traveled around the land and tried to convince the chieftains to give power to someone older and more suitable than the young Mieszko. What was interesting was that Mieszko found out about his plans from Mojar's own people, the loyal inhabitants of Moira."

She looked at the outline of the walls of the old borough, which were marked by a dark trail of burned tree stumps. The ashes were covered with green moss, brambles, and pale birch trees. It was only then that she realized that she couldn't hear any birds. There was complete silence in the burned borough.

"Tell me," she commanded Wolrad.

"In return for a pledge of loyalty to himself, Mieszko had promised the people of Moira that they would not be harmed and that they would receive a new, safe place to live. They had to leave the borough quickly, making the most of the fact that Mojar had gone to Giecz and was trying to convince the elders there to support him instead of your father. When Mojar returned, never expecting a trap, he found the borough empty."

She could almost see it. She could hear the silence, the same one that surrounded her now, the same one that her ancestor must have heard when he stood in the middle of the empty settlement. The manor and the surrounding houses—abandoned. Individual chickens which had fallen off the wagons. The husks of dishes cluttering the yard, broken in the hurry to escape. Clay rattles which would have been lost by children, flattened straw, broken eggs, spilt milk. The descendants of runaways who had to run away themselves, and him, Mojar, the one in whom a thirst for power had awoken. It wasn't difficult to understand him; his ancestors had ruled Moravia, and he probably remembered the whispered family stories. But turning against a Piast, the heir to the realm and the grandson of the man who had saved the Moymirids, was like biting the hand of the one who fed him."

"Did my father burn him alive?" she asked with a tremor in her voice.

"No, my lady. He ordered Mojar be taken right there in the yard in front of the manor, and he sentenced him in front of the elders. In this way he also showed that though he may have been young, he could rule as well as any duke. Both his brothers stood with him. And all three Piast brothers passed the same sentence: death for treason. The elders supported this, and saw that the new lord would not show mercy to those who betrayed him. He was supposed to be hanged, but since he belonged to the royal family, he was beheaded instead. Mieszko ordered Moira be burned afterward so that everyone would remember the treason that stained this place. It burned for days, the pillar of smoke rose above this plain and was visible from afar. With time, the people from the surrounding areas began to say that Mojar's ghost haunted these lands, and they began to call this place Mora, and then Zmora. Besides, for your mother's sake it was important to your father that the infamy wasn't associated with the Moymirids. Weeds grew over the old borough, while Mieszko built the two bridges that led to the nest on Ostrów Lednicki."

"Anyone else would have left this place and never returned to better forget the bitter past," she said thoughtfully. "But my father preferred to see the treacherous ashy remnants of Moira, as if he wanted to remember."

"They say that you, Queen, keep the man who betrayed you on a leash, and order he be led around with you everywhere," Wolrad said, and cleared his throat. "The apple doesn't fall far from the tree."

"What happened to the people who lived here? Did they settle in Bodzia?"

"Yes, my lady. Mieszko's ancestors had accepted Halperin from the Khazar Sea, the Moymirids from Great Moravia, and the Vikings. And he opened Bodzia's gates to the reduced branches of the Ruriks, the ones who were less fortunate than Knyaz Vladimir in their bid for power. He invited the exiles of Lejre and all others who were chased away from their homes by war."

"It's thanks to them that he built such a strong web of spies in all the courts." She finally understood. "Was my marriage planned for a long time?"

"Your father liked to hear the stories from the north." Wolrad smiled. "You know everything now. Can we end our walk among these thickets? My old bones would be cheered by the fires in the hall and a cup of mead."

"These thickets have revealed their history to me today. My history," she said. "How many people know it, apart from you?"

"We are dying out." Wolrad nodded his gray head. "But the memories will remain."

17

POLAND

Bolesław sent troops to the boroughs on his western borders before he'd even returned to Poznań from Merseburg. He expected war with Henry—now Henry II.

"The Slavs will never equal Germania, but they can be its subordinates . . ." That will never happen, Bird King! *"The empire only needs three pillars . . ."* and it will fall over, like a bench with three legs. Did he curse him? Yes. He looked down on him.

If Henry had behaved like a real warrior after the unsuccessful attempt on his life, if he'd emerged from behind the Merseburg walls and fought his armies which waited across the Saale, Bolesław might have respected him. But Henry hadn't been capable of that. He tricked them, he acted like a coward, he was no more than a rat. He didn't respect the laws of the royal peace which was always announced for the duration of the council. He sent bandits to kill Bolesław. And then he closed the city gates and hid behind them like a rodent in its burrow. He hadn't expected that the Saxon and Schweinfurt dukes would risk their lives for Bolesław's, who vowed to have his revenge for Henry's blatant disregard for the laws and Duszan's death.

This was the end of Otto's beautiful idea for uniting the kingdoms of the empire and making them equal. It was the beginning of war. Of fire and tears.

"It's not true," he said to Sobiesław when he brought news from Prague in the late autumn.

"It is, even though it sounds awful. Władywoj, the Prussian duke, has gone to Regensburg and pledged his loyalty to Henry, king of the Reich. And then he received the Bohemian crown to rule as the Reich's vassal."

Bolesław could feel the bile in his throat. Since they weren't alone in the audience hall, however, and the entire court watched him receive Sobiesław, he bit back what he really wanted to say and snarled:

"A drunk on the throne is worse than a tyrant. I will go to Kraków immediately."

"Bolesław," Emnilda interjected gently, "what about our daughter's wedding?"

He'd forgotten about that, although he shouldn't have. The marriage was an important alliance against Henry.

"You can prepare the girl for married life."

"But . . ."

"Świętosława will help you. She's got the experience." He smiled to his sister.

"I'd prefer that our little Regelinda didn't follow in my footsteps," the Bold One replied.

"Why not?" He didn't understand. "You're queen of three kingdoms."

"And I refuse to accept the third since I received it over the dead body of the man with whom I wanted to share it." She smiled at him across the hall. He had never met anyone else who spoke so lightly of their suffering. "I am a widow, a divorcée, an exiled queen, but yes, you're right, I have vast experience. I will be happy to prepare Regelinda for her role as ruler, though I suspect that it is Emnilda who can tell her everything she needs to know to have a successful marriage."

"Oh, right . . ." He looked embarrassed and cleared his throat. "I need to go . . ."

"And you won't be back soon," Emnilda finished for him.

Back then he hadn't known just how long he'd be gone for. He hadn't set the events which followed in motion, although it would be a lie to say that they didn't suit him. Everything had happened so fast. The messengers who had found him on the road brought surprisingly good news, even if their information completely changed his perception of the situation. It made him head south in an even greater hurry. Unexpected events were his specialty.

He liked Kraków; the moment that he rode onto the empty plains from the Poznań road, after having traversed forests, fords, and the wilderness, and saw the gently sloping hills of Kraków on the other side. The people welcomed him, coming so close that they almost touched his stirrups. They still remembered the days when he'd lived there as Mieszko's vassal.

"Our duke, our moon, our lord!" they cheerfully called to him.

He could see Wawel Hill, surrounded by the Vistula like a ribbon; the small, round church; and the two-story palatium which had a brilliant view of the river.

"Everything is ready, although we didn't expect your lordship," Gnierad called to Reptile Eye, Wawel's castellan, and greeted him. "Should I summon Bishop Poppo? Would my lord like a welcome mass?"

"Yes, of course! I would like that, but have the bishop offer it in my intention . . ."

"Without the duke, I understand. Consider it done." Gnierad caught on quickly.

"How is the construction of the cathedral going?" Bolesław asked, heading toward the building site, where he could already see the stone foundations rising. "And how is my prisoner?"

"The cathedral is progressing according to plan, and the prisoner is healthy," replied Reptile Eye. "He's locked up and allowed one walk a day with his guards."

"Bring him to me," ordered the duke, and headed toward the palatium after casting a quick glance at the construction site.

Boleslav the Red was his uncle's, his mother Dobrawa's brother's, eldest son. She and her sister Mlada, a nun, had been the only sweet and innocent creatures born into the Přemyslid dynasty. "In my family, boys are always predators," her mother would say when he was little. "But the girls are very well behaved." She had thought then that he'd grow up to be a slightly less bloodthirsty predator, while Świętosława would be good and sweet. She'd avoided talking of her father, but they all knew why their grandfather was known as "the Cruel."

The Red One turned out to be cruel even without the nickname. He had been constantly afraid that his two younger brothers would steal away his power. He castrated Jaromir when the boy had barely hit puberty. And he'd tried to strangle the youngest, Oldrzych, in a bathhouse. He'd failed, and now both of them were under Henry's protection. Henry, king of the Reich! Bolesław felt the sting of anger at the thought.

Boleslav the Red was brought in front of him. He was thin and had long, dirty hair.

"You look awful." Bolesław grimaced.

"I'm doing penance," the Red One said hollowly. "Bishop Poppo has ordered me to pray and fast . . ."

"And the dirt?"

"I'm a prisoner." Boleslav raised his head defiantly. "Silks are hard to come by. You've taken them away from me."

"Penance should be clean. I won't give the Prague throne to such a dirty prisoner."

The Red One flinched.

"Throne? The throne from which you chased me away? Your chosen one sits on it now, Władywoj . . ."

"Come back to me when you've washed and changed your clothes. Then we can talk of Prague."

Władywoj had died the previous week. He had done the one good thing he could for Bohemia: he drank himself to death. He had been a bad ruler: cruel, with no conscience or regard for anyone but himself. He hadn't been the reason why the sun began to set on the Přemyslids, but he had been the event's culmination. A stop in the dark. Bolesław wished he'd never placed him on the throne in the first place. To give his country to the Reich? To surrender his country, no matter how elegant the form? He couldn't accept that, even though he knew that Władywoj had done it out of fear of the rightful heirs, Jaromir and Oldrzych, who had sought Henry's protection. He was thinking like a scared child, a cornered dog. He wanted to show Henry he could submit so that Henry wouldn't send the two Přemyslid pups after him.

That wasn't why I placed him on the Czech throne! Bolesław thought angrily. *I had a plan, a great plan, and that drunk ruined it all. Will the Red One fulfill my needs? Is he willing to give up his wild, cruel ways?*

He returned to Bolesław washed and wearing clean clothes. Only the trembling of his hands and the deep lines in his face testified to what he'd survived.

"Boleslav the Red," Bolesław began, "are you prepared to become a fully Christian ruler?"

"I have confessed and done penance, brother," the Red One replied. "I'm ready."

I don't believe you, Bolesław thought. *But I have no other choice.*

"Władywoj is dead," he finally said. "I want you to take back the Prague throne."

The Red One reddened and his entire body seemed to tremble.

"But you must know something. Władywoj did something unforgivable, from a true ruler's perspective."

"Something worse than I did?" the Red One asked hopefully.

"He didn't castrate his brother, since he didn't have one," Bolesław said vengefully. "He didn't hunt his mother and brothers like you did. Your sins were against your family, but he sinned against his country. He gave himself and his kingdom to the Reich. Do you understand what I'm saying? I don't mean just the lands that Bohemia took from the Reich, I mean the whole country."

"Damn it!" the Red One roared.

Thank God, at least this he understands.

"Don't curse, you're also to blame," he said aloud. "You hunted your brothers so that they were forced to seek shelter and they ran to the Reich king. Władywoj was afraid that Henry would return them to power, which led to his foolish decision. You contributed to this evil. If you can turn it around, I will give you back the throne."

"I can!" the Red One exclaimed.

"Just know that I'm not doing this for you. And now, try to understand something larger than your own backyard. I want to unite Bohemia and Poland into one strong country. Słowiańszczyzna. We are connected by blood. Our people are linked by their language and traditions. A strong Słowiańszczyzna is my dream."

A dream I shared with Otto, he thought. *But he's dead, and Henry wants a Słowiańszczyzna which is divided into small realms against one another. Ones he can control from the Reich. But Otto III woke a thirst within me when he gave me the Holy Spear and put his diadem on my head. I'll show Henry that the empire can be complete when it balances on four equal pillars, or it can fall.*

"Your Poland is powerful," the Red One said. "Invincible and strong."

"I want more, can you understand that? Poland and Bohemia, joined by an alliance that cannot be broken."

"I swear it!" the Red One shouted. "I swear it!"

It could not be accomplished just with the Red One's promise. Bolesław spent a week in negotiation with the Czech nobles, and he had to become the guarantor of the arrangement himself. He, the Red One, the eldest of the Wrszowce, and one member of each of the noble Czech families all swore an oath on the cross: "We will never again surrender our country to the Reich. God help us."

But God did no such thing. No sooner had Bolesław returned to Kraków than news reached him of the Red One having invited the Wrszowce for a feast at which he slaughtered them. Only a complete brute or fool could have done such a thing. He stabbed his son-in-law in the chest himself. The husband of a daughter who hadn't even had time to give him a grandchild! Bohemia resounded with disgust and anger.

Sobiesław whispered with horror:

"I hate the Wrszowce because they are the dogs who killed my family, but slaughter at a feast? There's no honor in that! To break the laws of hospitality? Good Lord, don't look down at this, you died for lesser sins on your cross . . ."

"The Red One has insulted me," Bolesław said. "He has pissed all over the understanding we had, on the oath which we all took. He's splattered it with blood. He's trampled over the great Słowiańszczyzna in the name of his own petty vengeance."

"My lord," Ciechan, his Czech comrade and the leader of his southern scouts, spoke up. "My brothers will now either overthrow the Red One, or they will summon Jaromir to take the throne. But Jaromir has as many enemies as he has allies. They say he is now Henry's man, and that like Władywoj he will give the country to the Reich."

"Jaromir is not Bohemia's only option," Sobiesław observed. "They can ask our duke Bolesław to take the throne. He's a Přemyslid after his mother, and he's the greatest Slavic ruler."

"They may want to do that," Ciechan agreed, "but they are afraid. A strong ruler provides an obstacle for nobles who want to fulfill their own ambitions."

"Ciechan, go to Prague. Extend my invitation to talk face-to-face to my cousin, the Red One."

"As you wish," Ciechan replied, and bowed and disappeared.

While he waited for the Red One's arrival, Bolesław did what he had always dreamed of doing. He entered the dragon's cave, hidden in Wawel Hill.*

"Will eat us, won't eat us, will eat us, won't eat us . . ." Zarad whispered as they entered.

"I prefer the Lucic, Veleti, and my cursed relatives the Redarians," Jaksa decided. "At least they don't have dragons. Sacred mounts, that's normal. But this time our duke has gone too far."

"I know the tale of Sivrit who defeated the dragon," Bjornar bragged cheerfully. "Dragons always guard treasure. Sivrit touched the dragon's heart and began to understand the language of birds. Wouldn't that be useful, Burizleif?"

"I'd lose my position," Jaksa snorted. "Along with all of the duke's other scouts. What are we doing here?"

"Making a dream come true," Bolesław whispered.

"Your dream. I don't need dragons to dream," Jaksa replied.

"If there's no dragon then it won't eat us up," Zarad panted from behind them. "If there's a dragon, there will be treasure and it will eat us. So what use is that treasure to us, if . . . ? You can't wear gold when you're a corpse."

"Stop it," Njornar reprimanded him. "Sivrit defeated the dragon with a sword that was called Gram. Burizleif, do you have a magic weapon?" he asked with hope in his voice.

"No," the duke replied, and hoisted himself up onto a rocky shelf.

It got narrower. He made his way forward on all fours along a corridor of smoky, moist rock. He thought he could smell human excrement, or vomit. His knees ached, and his knuckles were rubbed raw. He thought: *It's nonsense, an old superstition, no dragon ever lived here.* The rocky passage widened, and he could stand again. They reached the cave, on the floor of which thick, black water splashed. He leaned over and saw his own face staring back at him.

"A dragon," Zarad said, only just rising from his knees. "There had to be a dragon in here."

Light from the torch in his hand flickered around the cave, joined moments later by the light from Jaksa's torch.

Bolesław was still looking into the water. Its surface rippled, and the dragon

---

* The Wawel Dragon, or the Dragon of Wawel Hill, is famous in Polish folklore. Its lair was in a cave at the foot of the hill, and it was defeated, depending on the account, during the rule of the legendary Krakus, either by his sons or by a cobbler called Skuba.

wore his face. Two torch flames flickered in the places where his eyes should have been.

BOHEMIA

Bolesław rode into Prague on a white mare, holding the Holy Spear in his hand. The people greeted him on the Vltava's banks. He stopped his troops and waited for the shouts to cease before calling out:

"I am the grandson of your great duke, Boleslav. The one who never bowed to anyone! And I only bow to God! Bohemia will not be anyone's tribute. I will not allow the king of the Reich to call himself your ruler. I am strong enough to go to war with him if he tries to make you his servants!" He lifted the spear high above his head.

The crowed responded:

"Glory! Glory! Glory!"

"My Czech brothers!" Bolesław shouted once they'd fallen silent. "Glory does not come cheap. Even when it is a birthright, there is no certainty that it will endure. Fame must be won. You are a brave people, warriors, and I am a ruler who does not like to bow. I will lead you if you need to fight for your fame."

"What about the Red One? What about the cruel duke?" someone in the crowd shouted. "He has dishonored us!"

"Dishonor! Dishonor!" the people muttered.

"The Red One will not return," Bolesław swore.

POLAND

"You promised to become a Christian duke once you did penance! You lied, tricked, and betrayed!" Bolesław had accused him two weeks earlier, in Kraków.

"It was the Wrszowce," the Red One defended himself. "Evil people, evil . . ."

"Be quiet," Bolesław said as he strode toward him. "You're the one who's evil. You broke the promise that we both gave to your people. I supported you, and you dishonored us both. Zarad!" he called. "Come closer with that torch."

Its light filled the stone cell. The Red One paled. Spittle gleamed in the corners of his mouth.

"No," he groaned. His eyes widened as if he had seen a ghost, and perhaps he thought he had because he said, voice shaking, "You can't be the Dragon of Wawel Hill . . . it's only a legend, an old folktale . . . aaaaa . . ." He howled horribly and covered his face with his hands.

"It is done," Zarad announced tonelessly, and stepped back, still holding the torch. He had blinded the man.

"You will never again see the beauty of the world which you demeaned with your sin," Bolesław told the Red One. "But I will spare your life because I will not kill my family. You'll live here, and I'll make sure you're taken care of until you die. You'll have enough time to do real penance."

"Aaaa . . . dragoooooon . . ." the Red One howled in pain.

"I'm not the Dragon of Wawel Hill," Bolesław denied. "But I will tell you a secret: it is more than just a legend."

18

DENMARK

Sven watched his sons practicing on the training ground. Eight-year-old Harald was as red-haired as a squirrel, and as nimble as one. He was fast, agile, and loud. Cnut, a year younger, seemed in comparison to be slow, almost frightened. They were beating each other with wooden swords under Jorun's supervision.

"Cnut attacks only once for every five times Harald hits him." Sven shook his head, dissatisfied with his younger son.

"But Harald misses two in three times, and Cnut never does," Jorun pointed out. "They're different. The king's son and the queen's son." He shouted to the boys: "Harald! Not the head!"

Sven hissed. He hated that nickname. "*The queen's son,*" people said of Cnut, and it bothered him to be constantly reminded of the Bold One. She was gone. Gone!

Vali warmed his bed, and she'd taken over the responsibilities of the manor's hostess in Roskilde. Melkorka and Heidi looked after the girls. Cnut and Harald were old enough to be raised by men now, and they had no need of a mother.

But still, something was missing. Not a woman; Vali fulfilled those needs. He missed a queen. The empty throne in the great hall stood next to his own. He hadn't had it removed. He let his sons sit on it, and sometimes his daughters, but he'd occasionally catch himself glancing over to look at her and find only emptiness. He was drinking more.

He'd tried, at first. He reached out to the Saxon duke Bernard Billung, the ruler of the Northern March, because he thought it would be beneficial to secure Denmark's southern border. But Billung rejected the offer. He promised the beautiful Othelindis to someone else. He had two younger daughters, but when Sven's messengers insisted Billung give one of them, he resisted stubbornly: "*I would prefer to give both my girls to God than to have them marry a barbarian from Roskilde.*" When he found out that Billung was Burizleif's ally, Sven was furious. He understood the message.

He stopped insisting and thought that perhaps upholding traditions was also a good thing. His mother had been the daughter of the Obotrite leader Mściwoj. But he'd wed the best Obotrite princess to Olof. The one who was left was only the ruler's niece, so not the best match, and even so her father wasn't enthusiastic about the prospect. He was afraid of Burizleif. "The Oder is the border between our lands," he explained. "And Duke Burizleif has already reached across the Saale. I won't give him an excuse to come for me. I'm sorry, King Sven."

"If the queen hadn't given you children," Father Wulfric explained, "you could have sent her away for being barren and thus unfit for marriage. But as things stand, you did not act wisely, my king."

"The queen was plotting against me behind my back." Sven lost his temper. "Is that not reason enough to rid oneself of one's wife?"

"Where's the evidence, my king?"

"Her confession!"

Wulfric nodded his head thoughtfully and said, carefully:

"The church considers the seal of confession to be almost sacred. For Ion's account of it to be admitted, it would have to be shown that he is not the Church's son. To do so, you'd have to have a bishop's support. But the venerable Oddinkarr is not kindly inclined toward you. You won't go to the Saxon bishops, there's no point in that. Duke Bolesław received an independent diocese from Otto III. The matter is complicated, my lord. You parted with the queen at the wrong moment, that's all I can say. Her brother has gained both influence and significance, which he did not have before. King Henry II of the Reich would be the best choice, but we both know you won't go to him. You're left with the option of negotiation with the queen herself. If she agreed, we might be able to resolve the matter amicably."

Sven snorted angrily.

"It seems you didn't know my wife very well, Wulfric. The Bold One will not renounce her title of queen of Denmark voluntarily."

"Nobody lives forever." The monk nodded.

No. He killed her lynxes, but he could never touch her. Wulfric misjudged him. And so the queen's throne remained empty.

That evening, they were drinking in the great hall when the messenger arrived. His expression betrayed that he brought bad news.

"My lord! There is unrest in England. Our settlers have been attacked, a few villages have burned, and their people have been murdered."

"Damn it! King Ethelred guaranteed their safety personally!" Sven was furious. "Is he behind this?"

"No one knows," the messenger replied. "But the attacks were planned carefully. Settlements next to each other were attacked at the same time so their inhabitants couldn't help each other. It's hard not to think that a royal order might be behind it."

"This is because I haven't been to England personally since the great dane-geld," Sven said. "I haven't frightened London with fire."

"My lord . . ." Jorun's eyes shone brightly. "When, if not now? Let's gather the Danish armies, and the troops of our vassals Jarl Eric and Jarl Sven. We can get more men from Olof King of Swedes, and then we can sail to green England."

Sven's breath quickened. He waved a hand, and Vali poured him more beer.

"Not beer!" he shouted to her with a smile. "Wine, and my best goblet!"

"There's something else, my king," the messenger added. "One of your companions appeared in England a few months ago, leading a large army."

"Who?"

"Thorkel the Tall."

Of the two Zealand brothers, Sven had always preferred Thorkel to the treacherous Sigvald. What was Thorkel searching for in England? Easy money? Or something more?

"We'll manage Thorkel," he said. "We will defeat him if we must, to ensure he does not stand in the way of our invasion. Who knows? Perhaps Thorkel the Tall will want to join us."

"Another Army of the Two Kings?" someone from a distant table asked cheerfully.

Sven emptied the goblet in one go which Vali handed him.

"We defeated the second chieftain on Øresund's waters," he roared. "There will never again be an Army of the Two Kings! Do you understand?"

After a moment of silence, they began to beat their cups against the tables. He nodded.

"The time has come for King Sven to lead a massive army to England for the largest danegeld in history!" he shouted, and banged the goblet so hard against the table that it broke.

Glass shattered into many glittering shards. What did he care for glass! He would bring much more of it from London.

POLAND

Świętosława, right after Regelinda and Herman's wedding, told Emnilda:

"I'm going to Wolin. I want to see my sister."

"You can do what you want," Emnilda replied sadly.

Her sister-in-law already missed the daughter who had just been married. She stopped Świętosława with a question:

"Don't you think Herman, our son-in-law, is a bit too heavy-handed?"

"While your husband Bolz is a peaceful lamb?"

Emnilda sighed.

"Regelinda is so young. Fourteen . . ." Emnilda's eyes refused to stay dry.

"How old were you when they wed you to Bolz?"

"Sixteen!" her sister-in-law retorted. "Sixteen. I'm worried about Bolesław not having been at the wedding, and that . . ."

"He's the duke of Bohemia?" Świętosława asked mockingly. "You know he can't leave Prague because he's expecting King Henry to invade after he refused to pay tribute."

"This will lead to war." Emnilda only saw the dark side of everything today. "We sent Regelinda to her husband, to the Meissen March. Henry can attack them before he heads to Bohemia. Our little one will be in the first line of attack . . ."

"Thank God Bolesław can't hear you." Świętosława lost her patience.

Emnilda only looked at her with sad doe eyes.

"Listen to me, since I'm telling you this because you're like a sister to me. Do you love him?"

"I do."

"He loves you, too. Don't you realize that you're one from which he derives his energy? Don't look at me like that; I know what I'm talking about. My brother can conquer the world because he knows who he's fighting for. He knows that you're here, taking care of your children and ensuring that matters of state run smoothly."

"But he's not here," Emnilda whispered. "Isn't that a trap? You say that he wants to conquer the world for me, but I don't need that world. He, Bolesław, is all I need."

Świętosława sat down beside her and caught Emnilda's hands.

"Do you know what the Vikings believe in? Valhalla. That's what comes after death. The bravest warriors, the most courageous and most beautiful, will be snatched away from the battlefield straight to Odin's palace. It's a great honor for a warrior to reach Valhalla. And it works the other way around: if a man is unlucky and he dies in bed, lying in the straw, then that's a humiliation, no matter how brave his life was. I remember the women in Uppsala, after my Eric returned from the battle at Fyrisvellir. He was known as the Victorious after that, but many of his warriors had died. And do you know that none of the wives, lovers, or mothers dared to shed a tear? They stood by the funeral pyres of their men and their eyes shone. I spoke with them afterward. They said, 'My queen, the better the husband you are given, the less time you spend together. A great man must die in battle. Heroes never age. We remember our men as strong, young warriors. We don't know what groans and complaints would have come with age.'"

"I got the best one." Emnilda wiped her nose. "Even the pagans have something to teach us."

They sat like that in silence for a while, listening to the wood crackling as it burned.

"What happens next, Świętosława?"

"King Henry won't be able to start a war with Bolz straight away because he has to handle the unrest in Italy. He's offered Bolesław Bohemia if Bolesław offers it as tribute and rules as Henry's vassal. Bolz laughed at the idea, or if you prefer, he refused to pay tribute to Henry and will never change his mind because he has promised the Czechs their freedom."

"A strong Słowiańszczyzna?"

"Exactly. Henry has two of our cousins in hand, Jaromir and Oldrzych. As soon as he's in control of Italy, he'll lead the German army to Bohemia and try to chase Bolz out of Prague, to replace him with one of them on the throne as his vassal."

"Does Bolz have a chance against the Reich?"

"I don't know," Świętosława replied honestly. "But remember, he's ruled over Moravia for years. He can use their troops. Besides, Henry won't have the support of the entire Reich. The margraves of the Eastern March are Bolz's allies. Herman is his son-in-law, Gunzelin his blood brother. That will make war over Bohemia more difficult for Henry. I can tell you what I know for certain: my brother will sooner abandon the throne of Prague than break his word and bend a knee to Henry. What worries me is something else. We've had no news of Bezprym. The war which is about to begin might make his journey home more difficult. Horrible things happen on the roads in the middle of war."

Mieszko walked into the hall. They both smiled at him. The thirteen-year-old had Emnilda's pretty face and Bolesław's build; he was tall and broad for his age.

"You have a spearman's arms!" Świętosława praised her nephew. "I didn't know you can develop such a body while studying books."

Mieszko blushed.

"Father has let me train in my spare time," he mumbled. "He said that Poland's bishop should look like a warrior, not a weakling."

They burst out laughing. Emnilda embraced her son and kissed his forehead. Świętosława turned her head away to hide the tears which suddenly filled her eyes. Olof, Harald, Cnut, Astrid, Świętosława. She had five children, but she couldn't kiss a single one.

"What have you learned today, son?" Emnilda asked him fondly.

"The story of Cain and Abel. Cain killed his brother because he was jealous of the love their father bore him."

Świętosława bit her lip. She knew that the story with which her brother had struggled most had been the one about the firstborn son being sacrificed.

"Bishop Unger sent me to tell you, lady mother and lady aunt, that he wants to speak to you about an urgent matter."

"Invite the bishop in then if the matter is so urgent." Emnilda hugged Mieszko.

When the boy walked out, her sister-in-law brought her face close to Świętosława's and kissed her cheek.

"I have a favor to ask of you, if I can rely on your sister's love. Forget about this conversation. Forget that you ever had to explain the most fundamental things to me. And I promise that I will never let Bolz know that I ever had any doubts. Even if I will be petrified at my core, even if I have to pretend, I will be brave."

"Conversation? What conversation?" Świętosława feigned ignorance. "The one about Cain and Abel? Fascinating, indeed."

Emnilda smiled so beautifully that Świętosława couldn't stop herself from kissing her full on the mouth. Unger walked in.

"Am I interrupting a display of family love?"

"No! Love cannot be stopped by anything," Emnilda replied cheerfully. "Be so good as to sit down with us, Father, and tell us what's happened."

"I have no idea." Unger spread his arms wide and sat down at the edge of the bench. "I dare not pressure my hermit brothers in Międzyrzecz, but something's happening. A man I had sent on a pilgrimage to the hermitage has returned. Brother Remigius. He was also meant to find out whether the hermits need anything, since this is quite an awkward situation. Our duke insisted that they come here from Pereum, but when they arrived without his son, it's like he's somewhat forgotten them. I didn't want the pious hermits to think that the duke has abandoned them. I'm honored by their presence in the country . . ."

Świętosława adored Unger. He was the embodiment of God's power on earth to her. Humble, unyielding, and strong all at once. But now she sensed that he was stalling.

"What did Remigius say when he returned from the hermits?" she interrupted, hoping to help him reach whatever point he needed to make.

"That duke Bolesław has summoned Brother Benedict to Prague. He summoned . . . that is . . . armed men came for him."

"Oh!" they both exclaimed.

"Yes." Unger nodded. "Strange, isn't it? We've heard nothing about it."

"If my brother has some mission for hermit Benedict and he doesn't see it fit to confide in us, we should respect his wishes," Świętosława said, straightening her back. "Can you send this Remigius back to the hermitage on another pilgrimage?"

Unger's dark Hungarian eyes flashed.

"Of course, my queen. All I need is your permission."

"You have it," Emnilda announced.

Once the bishop left the hall, her sister-in-law grabbed Świętosława's hand.

"A secret for a secret. You'll keep mine, about a great duchess's cowardice, and I'll keep yours, about the queen's visit. Where do you really want to go, Świętosława? Because I know it's not to see your sister."

PRAGUE

Bolesław howled like a dog.

"That's not true! That's not possible!" he roared, kicking the benches in front of him.

Only a few weeks earlier, he'd given Benedict of Międzyrzecz a fortune in ransom money—ten silver grzywnas*—and now it turned out that not only was the money late, it was also no longer needed.

He was in Prague. He was guarding the gable by the Vltava from Henry, who was already mustering his troops, but he did not foresee what had just come to pass.

"No!" he howled. "It's not true!"

"It is, my lord," Ciechan replied. "Benedict didn't get there in time to pay the ransom for your son. Jaromir acted like a rabid dog that bites everything near him, and he hurt Bezprym. He let him go and ran away himself to escape the reach of your anger. The boy is in shock after what happened, but he hasn't lost his mind. He can relay the events to you in more detail than I."

Bolesław had been waiting for him for so long. Tearing him out of the clutches of Romuald of Pereum had taken so much effort. But in his worst nightmares, he would never have dreamed that this could have happened.

Bezprym walked into the audience hall of the Prague manor.

"Everyone, out!" Bolesław shouted. "I want to speak with my son alone."

---

* A grzywna was a unit of measure of a unit of exchange, so it was often used as money in medieval Central and Eastern Europe.

The Czech nobleman, Prague's castellan, Borzywoj, the priests, and one of the bishops all exited swiftly. His roar echoed around the hall, bouncing off the stone ceiling.

Bezprym was nearly as tall as he was. Long, dark, unkempt hair fell to his shoulders. He had still been a boy when they'd last seen each other in Quedlinburg three years previous, but now he looked like a man.

"Jesus," Bolesław roared when he heard his own thoughts.

He rushed to his son, grabbed his shoulders, and hugged him as tightly as he could.

"Jesus Christ," he groaned. "What have they done to you?"

"Don't you know?" Bezprym stiffly moved out of reach.

I know, he thought. *But I refuse to accept it.*

"Tell me," he asked his son.

"There's nothing to tell." Bezprym shrugged.

They stood facing each other, he and his seventeen-year-old firstborn. The son whom he had tried to retrieve from the hermitage in Pereum. Bezprym's dark eyes were just like his mother Karolda's. The Black Weasel peered out at him from this wild, untamed boy. His son.

"Ostrowod decided that we would go to Poznań through Bohemia when he heard about the war Henry is fighting in the mountains. We ran into an unmarked troop in the mountains. It turned out they were Jaromir Přemyslid's men." He spoke without a shred of emotion, though his voice was hoarse. "They outnumbered us two to one. Ostry tried to break away from them a few times when we'd stop to rest, but it was futile. They took us to their master. Jaromir was waiting in a forest glade. Do you know, even that wasn't lost on him." The corners of Bezprym's mouth trembled. "He said, 'The young prince of forest glades.'"

Bolesław snarled but said nothing at his son's glare.

"'Your father,' he told me later, 'first placed my elder brother on the Czech throne, and then he replaced him himself. Do you know what my brother, the Red One, did to me?' I didn't know, I had no idea, and when he realized that he just laughed. That's when I knew it wasn't good."

Bolesław clenched his fists.

"'Your daddy supported that torturer, the Red One,' Jaromir told me. 'So, your father supported what my brother did to me. Do you know the Bible, my boy? An eye for an eye. You know that's how it has to be.' His men tied me to a tree."

He fell silent for a moment and shut his eyes. When he opened them, he raised his voice and howled, "Father, I waited for him to gouge out my eyes, but he took a strap of rawhide and tied my balls with it. What was I supposed to do? Wilczan came forward and tried to pretend he was me, but it was too late. Ion threw himself in front of Jaromir and begged for his mercy . . ."

"And you?" Bolesław asked.

"Forgive me. I don't beg." His firstborn's eyes flashed. "An eye for an eye, I gave myself up to pay for your sins."

"No!" Bolesław screamed. "I had nothing to do with Jaromir's castration! Nothing!"

Bezprym frowned. His eyebrows were dark and thick.

"Are you saying that my sacrifice was in vain, Father?"

Bolesław howled like a dog. What was he supposed to tell his maimed son? His firstborn? That his suffering was unjust?

"Prepare for war!" he shouted to his chieftains.

I will avenge you, son! he thought. *I will drown out our pain.*

"Father," Bezprym said once Bolesław had finished giving out orders. "Keep your promise. I don't want to fight. I want to go to the hermitage."

The duke looked absently at his son. He'd forgotten. Yes, he'd forgotten that this is what he'd promised him. That he'd promised him he could go to the hermitage in Międzyrzecz if he only left Romuald's hermitage. He rubbed his face and blinked uncertainly.

"Listen, it's not safe now," he said. "You know that better than anyone. Stay in Prague with me, and when war is over, I will take you to Międzyrzecz myself."

Bezprym chuckled bitterly.

"Not safe? What else can they do to me?" He grimaced, and only in this expression could Bolesław see that his son hid pain and humiliation deep inside about what had happened. "I am useless as your heir now. I wanted to become a hermit"—he spread his arms wide—"and now that is all that I'm good for. Let me go."

Bolesław walked over to him, placed his hands on his shoulders, and said:

"Go."

19

❀

DENMARK

Świętosława shivered with cold in the nun's habit she wore. She glanced at the sky. The wind chased low-hanging, leaden clouds, the ones which usually brought rain. When they revealed the sun, its sharp autumn rays stung her eyes. She stood on the gray, reddening moor and gazed out toward Roskilde-fiord. Would they come? Would Melkorka keep her word?

"I see a ship!" Wilkomir called out. "It's them."

Świętosława's heartbeat quickened. Helga, standing beside her also dressed as a nun, grabbed her hand.

"Do you remember?" she asked, embracing her. "You cannot go nearer than fifty steps. And you cannot speak to them, no matter what."

"They won't recognize me?" Świętosława checked.

Helga studied her carefully again from head to toe. The white hood covered her hair entirely, sitting low on her forehead and high over her chin. There was a black veil over it, then the habit and gray cloak.

"I wouldn't have recognized you, Sigrid," Helga decided. "Stop shaking."

"They have reached the shore," Wilkomir said. "I'm going to hide. They're only supposed to see two nuns gathering herbs."

Wilkomir hid behind a large rock. Her guards were hiding in a low wood behind him. The ship was tied up on the other side, in a small bay. Helga gave her a basket.

"What if someone wonders what nuns are doing here? There are no nunneries in Denmark."

"Stop it! You came up with the idea, and now you're looking for trouble," Helga reprimanded her. "Melkorka was supposed to only take trusted people. Trusted ones who don't ask stupid questions. They're coming! Gather the herbs."

Świętosława leaned down. A seagull screamed as it circled above her head. Dried-out crab shells and claws lay on the ground around her. She stared at the path which led from the harbor, not paying any attention to what she was doing. Whatever her hand stumbled upon, she put in her basket absent-mindedly.

"Stop it." Helga caught her hand. "You're gathering stones."

Two guards led the group that neared. She didn't recognize them, but she knew Sven would have brought in many new people since she'd left. Harald came after the guards with a bow in hand, his hair gleaming like fire against the moors. Cnut was chasing him, his long, fair hair falling into his eyes. He brushed it away impatiently. Melkorka followed them, rocking from side to side as she walked, leading five-year-old Astrid. And then came Heidi, the Goat, carrying three-year-old Świętosława. Her view of the children blurred. The emotions were too strong, and her knees gave way. She kneeled, leaning on the basket. She wiped her eyes. This moment would be too short; she couldn't afford to miss a second. She didn't know which one of her children to look at. Her heart was pounding like mad. She saw Heidi trying to ignore the two nuns, Melkorka discreetly nodding to her as she wiped her face with the hand that wasn't holding the little one.

"Me!" Harald shouted in the distance. "I'll be the first to catch a hare!"

Cnut didn't respond to his brother's provoking call, but ran on the other side of the moor, and all she could see was his back.

"Calm down," Helga whispered quietly. "Don't cry . . . they'll pass by in a moment . . ."

The boys ran across the moor and out of sight. The two guards passed by the nuns so carelessly that they might as well not have been there. She could hear the girls chattering.

". . . I'd prefer a live hare to play with than a dead one we can eat . . ."

"I want a lynx. Cnut says that Mama had lynxes."

Her stomach clenched. She blinked quickly so that the tears didn't obscure her vision. Little Świętosława was wearing a hood, but her pale curls slipped out from under it. They passed by, following the path, led by their nannies. Thirty steps away. She was afraid that she'd lose control. That she would leap to her daughters and take them with her. This was the closest they were going to get. She could see the flush in their chubby cheeks.

"Oh! Who are these people?" Astrid pointed at them.

Melkorka wanted to say something, but her voice caught in her throat.

"Nuns." Heidi came to her aid.

"A priest but a woman? A lady?" Astrid persisted.

"Mhmm," Heidi confirmed, and burst into tears.

Little Świętosława stood and stared at them. When Heidi let go of her hand to wipe her eyes, the child started walking toward them. Świętosława's heart pounded even more violently. She froze; she couldn't lower her gaze.

"Come back!" Heidi shouted after her, but she stood still, motionless herself.

"Me too." Astrid pulled away from Melkorka, who only glanced toward the guards' retreating backs. They were already about fifty paces ahead of them.

Little Świętosława ran over to the kneeling Świętosława and Helga; she stopped shyly only a few steps away. Astrid was right behind her. The girls gazed at the nuns. Świętosława looked back at her daughters.

"What are you doing?" the younger one asked, cocking her head to one side.

"We're gathering herbs," Helga replied. "To heal people."

"You might be able to heal someone"—Astrid nodded seriously—"but the other lady can't."

"Mhmm," little Świętosława confirmed, and addressed her mother directly. "You picked stones."

"Stones can heal people, too," Helga said quickly.

"How?" Świętosława pushed a finger into her mouth.

"You boil them and place them wherever it hurts when they're warm," Heidi said.

"Are you a mute?" Astrid asked.

Świętosława shook her head.

"She's taken a vow of silence," Helga announced.

"She talked too much, did she?"

If you only knew, my love. I always talked too much.

"Yes, little princess," Helga said quickly. There was a tremor in her voice when she added, "But she can give you a blessing. Make the sign of the cross over your heads so that God is always with you."

"I'd prefer for our mama to always be with us, my lady," Astrid replied. "But God will do, I guess."

Świętosława raised her hand, and both girls stepped toward her. She couldn't help herself and touched their foreheads.

Mary, Mother of God, she thought. *Give these children a sign so they may know I didn't abandon them.*

She made the sign of the cross on both their foreheads. It remained there, imprinted by the gray earth from which she had picked stones instead of herbs.

"It's time we go," Melkorka called out in a trembling voice.

Astrid swiveled around on her heel and ran toward her. The little one, still studying her, lifted a finger and pointed at each of her eyes in turn.

You noticed, thought the queen, *so you'll remember the woman with the mismatched eyes.*

The girl, led by some trusting, childish impulse, threw her arms around Świętosława's neck and kissed her cheek. She let go just as quickly and ran back to Heidi.

"Boys! We're leaving!" Melkorka shouted. "Now!"

The guards had also turned back and were heading toward the harbor. Heidi, holding each girl by the hand, pulled them both with her. Świętosława was afraid that she wouldn't get to see her sons if they ran along the other side of the moor. She could only see the backs of her daughters as they walked away with the Goat. She stood up and brushed the dirt off her knees.

"I caught the hare first!"

"But I got a larger one!"

They ran, panting, holding their hares. Cnut paused for a moment and looked at her from afar, but Harald caught up to him and clapped his back, and with a laugh Cnut followed his brother down toward the harbor. The guards passed them and, before walking down to the ship, turned around and bowed to Świętosława.

They knew, she thought, acknowledging them with a nod. *My God, if I had really taken a vow of silence, maybe I wouldn't have lost everything that ever mattered. My children. The only man I'd ever really loved. The lynxes. Dusza.*

She took a deep breath and wiped her face with her sleeve.

WOLIN, WOLIN ISLAND, POLAND

Astrid was expecting Świętosława. She knew that there was no avoiding their meeting this time. When her sister had come to Wolin with her guards for a ship to sail to Roskilde, Dalwin had made excuses for Astrid's absence, saying that she had sailed to Kołobrzeg with cargo for Bishop Reinbern. Yes, she did sometimes go to him, but not then. Dalwin never failed her, though; he knew how to protect her from uncomfortable questions.

Now, she was ready to meet her sister. Or so she hoped, anyway.

She went to port to greet her as soon as they informed her the ship had arrived. No one knew who was really on it. "Two nuns from noble families," they said. A queen shouldn't travel without her husband, and her husband should be the last person to ever find out about this excursion.

They stood face-to-face. Her sister so changed by the nun's habit that if Astrid didn't know who she was, she wouldn't have recognized her. Świętosława's face, framed by the white hood and enclosed in the black veil, was ageless. Childish and old at once. They stared at each other while the crowd that was curious of the two extraordinary travelers grew around them. Astrid bowed to the two women and said loudly:

"Please accept our hospitality as our guests, venerable sisters! Accept my invitation to my home. Allow me to lead the way."

They didn't look away from each other for the whole meal though they spoke only of unimportant matters.

Świętosława kept her veil on while the servants were about, and convincingly played the part of a nun. When the time came for them to retire, Astrid led her to her alcove and closed the door.

Her sister pressed her whole body to hers. They embraced and didn't let go of one another for a long time.

"I have so little left," Świętosława said, tightening her slender fingers on Astrid's shoulders. "Sven has taken everything I cared about. Why didn't you come to see me in Poznań? I waited for you."

Her sister sighed as she removed the veil and hood. Only when she freed her hair, which fell in pale waves onto her shoulders, did Astrid notice her eyes. They didn't match.

"Ah"—Świętosława shrugged—"that's the least important thing that's happened."

"How is that possible?"

"How is it that people go gray overnight?" she replied with a question.

"I used to envy you that your eyes seemed to change color, sometimes green, sometimes gold," Astrid said. "Now they're both simultaneously."

"Help me out of this habit," her sister asked, and a moment later they both sat on Astrid's large bed.

"Why didn't you come?" Świętosława asked again.

"I was taking care of the wounded, and then . . . I was afraid. I feel responsible for Sigvald's betrayal. I failed you."

"Stop it, it's not your fault." Świętosława's fingers pulled at a loose thread on her sleeve. "My son didn't stand by Olav either. Everything went wrong. But could it ever have gone otherwise? Maybe God was trying to punish me for my sins. You know, for Jarl Birger, the suitors, betraying Sven . . . Do you believe in punishment for your sins?" she asked suddenly.

"No," Astrid replied. "I believe in destiny. Stop pulling at that thread, it's such a beautiful pattern and you'll ruin it. Will you have another drink? You've barely had anything while you played the part of the pious nun."

Świętosława giggled like she had as a young girl and shook her head, her hair tumbling down over her face. Astrid couldn't stop herself from laughing either as she stood and walked across the room.

"I have thick, sweet, heavy wine from Constantinople. Golden wine from Styria. White wine from the Rhein's banks. Amber wine from land near the Danube. Bloodred wine from Hungary. And ordinary mead."

"Oh dear." Her sister laughed. "You really indulge yourself! I've never had wines like these. I want to try them all!"

"Then help me, my lady, since the servants have retired."

"We can call them back. They can watch their Lady of Wolin amuse herself with her sister nun."

They dragged the chestful of jugs over to the bed.

"Oh! How does this open?" Świętosława asked curiously.

"Use your hands," Astrid suggested. "The wine merchants advise starting with the palest and moving on to darker ones by degrees."

"Let's do it the other way around then, shall we?"

Astrid didn't believe that time could turn back, but that was exactly what was happening now. Świętosława was once again her younger, annoying little sister, trying to convince her to break the rules.

"Constantinople! Cheers." Świętosława poured them each a full goblet. "Oh, Lady Mary, how sweet!"

"Oh, healthy Mary, you're right!"

"Don't twist around the name of Mother of God," her sister reprimanded. "You always do that to annoy me. If you keep being so disobedient, I'll convince Unger to baptize you before you notice it happening!"

"No one can be baptized in secret." Astrid wagged a finger at her and drank some more. The wine warmed her. "The person being baptized has to say their part during the ceremony."

"Oh! You've brushed up on your knowledge! Who told you?"

Astrid blushed and quickly replied with a laugh:

"Little Satan, Lucifer's child, half devil! That's what they used to call you, my pious sister! Reinbern, the bishop of Kołobrzeg, tells me something every now and then."

"Have you ever seen Archbishop Radim?" Świętosława took a sip of wine, and her cheeks burned, too.

"No. That's the brother of the saint who was killed by the Prussians, whose body Bolesław bought back with silver, isn't it?"

"Mhmm. But only his half brother. Oh, sorry! It's different with us, I have no sister but you! Imagine that when Otto came to Gniezno and gave Bolesław a diocese, he forced Bolz and Unger to agree to make Radim the bishop. They are furious because our brother had intended for the honor to be Unger's. And here the emperor surprised them both and made Radim the bishop of the sacred corpse."

"Your religion is horrible." Astrid grimaced and downed the rest of her wine in one go. "You eat your god's body, cut apart the bodies of your saints . . . I'm too sensitive to consider such barbaric acts!" She flinched.

Świętosława laughed, then pulled a somber expression.

"You blaspheme, sister!" she said. "Although as a pagan . . . I don't know, it's too hard for me. I'll ask Unger. Hey, my wine is gone," she complained.

"Your Christ changed water into wine at some wedding." Astrid gently knocked her shoulder with her goblet.

"Hey! You do know a lot. Reinbern is really working hard on you, Astrid! What's our next color?"

"The bloodred Hungarian. Give me a knife." She pulled out the jug and examined the blade her sister had just handed her. "Is this the same one you bought in Wolin all those years ago?"

"The same one. I wear it on a chain around my neck. Next to the golden cross. Oh! Do you remember the tall, red-haired boy who ran into us that day? You told me, 'Learn the tongue of the Vikings,' and he ran into us and you talked back to him?"

"Mhmm," Astrid replied, throwing the seal to the side. "Give me your goblet. I'll fill it."

"Do you know who that was?"

"The redhead? No. How am I supposed to know that?" But at the same moment, she realized she did know.

She'd seen him, but she didn't recognize him. He'd sailed up close to the *Long Snake* as it was in the throes of death. The last warriors were fighting on their knees. Dusza lay under the mast with an arrow through her heart. The wind blew, and she remembered the red hair that danced in the wind.

"That was my second husband. Sven Haraldsson," her sister said. "Let's drink!"

Astrid flinched.

"I remember only that you repeated the whole conversation word for word, in one breath," she said thoughtfully. "And I had a feeling that the 'tongue of the Vikings' would become your tongue. Let's drink."

"I saw my children," Świętosława whispered. "They are . . ."

"Yours," Astrid said, grabbing her hand.

"He stole them from me."

"I have no children." Astrid suddenly felt sorry for herself. "I could have had them, but . . ."

"But what?"

"I was afraid they would be like Sigvald. I drank herbs that stopped me from carrying a pregnancy to term. There was nothing I wanted less than to have his children." She took a deep breath, and tears spilled from her eyes. "You know, I regret it now. Even if they'd have been like him, I would have raised them myself and they would have been mine. I regret it so much . . ."

"Give me more of the blood," Świętosława said, holding out her empty glass. "Some things are too much to bear sober. My Harald is the spitting image of Sven, but I still love him. Cnut is like me, but only in his appearance. He's so . . ."

"Obedient?" Astrid suggested.

"Mmm. And the girls, fair-haired and blue-eyed . . . My God, they're so sweet that all I want to do is kiss their red cheeks . . . Both were conceived in anger. Astrid should be called Fury, Świętosława Betrayal. Olof, my firstborn, was Eric's child, the great, bald, bearded, stubborn Viking who never failed me. He kept every promise. And what happens? His only son betrays me when he's tested. Hey, do you know what? I want to cry over your unborn children. If you'd have had them . . . those girls with amber hair, wise and serene like you. Or the boys with beautiful eyes like your pretty traitor. We'd have loved them . . ."

They fell into each other's arms, sobbing as the rest of the bloodred wine spilled across the bed.

"Right, wipe your nose and open the next one," Świętosława commanded. "We need to get a grip."

"Give me the knife!"

"Did you know that this is the knife that Vali used to cut open my dress on my wedding night with Sven? The dress fit so snugly that . . ."

"I used to like tight dresses, too." Astrid was struggling with the amber liquid from near the Danube. "I don't like them as much now though. Oh! I've done it."

"Pour it out because I'm sad." Świętosława yawned. "Horribly sad. Astrid, please, get baptized, because life after death without you will be unbearable."

"I've heard that before," she said before she could stop herself.

"From whom?" Świętosława's eyes flashed.

"Oh, I don't remember," she lied, pushing away her memories of mourning Geira with Olav. Something else occurred to her. "Listen! Sven went to England. If something were to happen to him . . ."

"Yes!" Her sister clapped her hands, spilling more wine. "Oh, crap . . ."

"Don't cry, little one, your older sister is watching over you!" She leaned over to pick up the jug and poured more wine. "If only the war had ended as you wished it . . ."

"The last time I wished my husband dead, Olav died in his place. Damn it! I'm afraid to make the same wish a second time."

"Wish him well then for a change?" Astrid drank some wine. "If your prayers work the wrong way around . . ."

"Any good wish for Redbeard chokes me."

"Wash it down then. Drink up," she urged her. "Which one do you like best?"

Świętosława took a sip thoughtfully.

"I don't know," she said, considering. "When I was drinking the sweet one from Constantinople, I was sure there was no better option. The bloody one was also wonderful, tart and sharp. The amber Danube one is like mead, but it's wine. You know"—she lowered her voice—"I think the best one is whichever I happen to be drinking when you ask." She nodded and took another gulp. "But you're right! If God hears me and Sven dies, I could take my children . . . God!" she pleaded, raising her gaze.

Astrid interrupted her sharply.

"You were supposed to stop that because . . . you know . . . you bring misfortune!"

"Ah, yes." Świętosława remembered. "Right. But . . . can you give me some more? I'll tell you something if you do. A secret I told no other . . ."

"The Danube one again?"

"Mhmm."

More of it spilled onto the bed.

"Redbeard is a monster," Świętosława announced as she drank, "but I know that all of his monstrosity came from his love for me . . ."

"Sigvald was a monster, too," Astrid observed. "And he loved me, too. What of it? Loving monsters?"

"They caught Olav." Świętosława bit her lip so hard it bled.

She didn't wipe it away. Astrid, unsteady on her feet, stared at her sister. Her sister, with mismatched eyes and a bleeding lip.

"There really were human beasts there," she whispered. "I saw them. Berserkers. Warriors who gave in to the bloodlust." Her hand began to knead her dress compulsively. "Geivar . . ."

"Geivar Painted Fangs?" Świętosława asked.

"Yes. Do you know how my husband died? Sigvald the traitor?" Astrid's body shuddered. It was the first time she spoke of it. "Geivar bit him . . . he bit through his artery . . ."

"Like dogs," her sister said. "Did you see Olav's death? Tell me!"

"He jumped into the water. The red king . . ."

"Sven!"

". . . sailed to the *Long Snake* when the last warriors were dying. Olav didn't want to be taken alive. He covered himself with a shield and jumped into the water."

"Did you ever think that he might not have drowned?" Świętosława asked. "That he might have emerged somewhere?"

"Don't jest! That's a cruel thought. He was wounded. He was hit by arrows in his shoulder, thigh, and stomach. He was wearing chain mail when he jumped. He couldn't have survived! He couldn't have!"

"I know, I know . . ." Świętosława tried to calm her. "And the wounded?" she asked, hoping to distract her sister. "Did you save them?"

"Only some of them," Astrid answered softly. Those memories were painful as well.

She could smell the blood, salt, pus, the stench of entrails which spilled out of men's bellies. She had stayed, trying to heal them, for months after the battle. She'd cried over each one she couldn't save, while they cursed her for not leaving them on the *Long Snake* on the day of the battle so that they may have gone straight to Valhalla.

"There's one left," she admitted. "Omold, Olav's bard. I saved his voice, but he does not seem content with it."

"The bard?" Świętosława choked on the remains of her wine. "Give him to me, please! I beg you . . ."

"All right, stop that," she snorted. "You are a terrible beggar. We can ask him in the morning if he wants to go with you."

"I'll ask him," her sister said. "I know how to phrase the question to get the answer I want. The golden one from Styria next?"

"Yes," Astrid replied unthinkingly, and burst out laughing after a moment. "It's true, you do know how to ask."

"The girls have fair hair, so fair it's almost white . . ." Świętosława muttered as Astrid struggled with the seal on the jug. "They are pretty, so pretty . . . And the boys . . ."

"Drink!" Astrid interrupted her, throwing the seal away. "Give me your goblet, half devil! I'm pouring the golden one from Styria . . ."

"Ah! Isn't drinking Styrian wine treason? Our brother is fighting Henry . . . Bavaria and Styria . . . Oh Jesus . . . How delicious . . ."

"The best one for last!" Astrid announced as she took a sip herself.

"No! This isn't the last one! There was some white one . . ."

"White one," Astrid confirmed.

". . . white as Olav's hair!"

"Fool. The white one was from the Rhein," she corrected her. "Olav cut his hair. He shaved it all off."

"What? You lie!" Świętosława accused furiously.

"No! I thought I saw . . ."

"Leave the dead in peace. The golden Styrian one is wonderful." Świę-

tosława swayed, and her mismatched eyes seemed to pulse. "I will help
Bolesław in his conquests. He should take the country that makes such wine!
We can move there to be the vassals of vineyards . . ."

"My grandfather, Dalwin, isn't well . . . I have so many problems here,
Świętosława."

"Bolesław is in Prague. War . . ."

"I'm drunk," Astrid noticed with surprise.

"Only now? I've been drunk for a long, long time . . . I don't even know if
I've ever been sober since the battle of Øresund."

"The evil and mischievous god Loki had a hand in the ambush at
Øresund . . . What were we talking about?" Astrid's thoughts scattered.

"About Radim, the bishop," Świętosława reminded her. "You know, I think
I hate him. He's a coward. How could something like this happen . . . They
killed Adalbert . . . his brother, and he . . . survived! A witness to the tragedy, really? A normal man . . . a real brother would never have abandoned
his blood in need, right? He wouldn't have betrayed . . . Astrid? Think, sister!
Could you ever betray me?"

"Me . . . me . . . Me . . . ever . . ." Astrid repeated drunkenly.

"See? You couldn't. I could never betray you either . . . but this one? He
saw what was happening and he did nothing, and now he's a witness to the
tragedy . . . I feel like I'm going mad every time I see him . . . Unger loathes
him, too . . ."

"I feel sick," Astrid admitted.

Świętosława dragged herself from the bed and pulled Astrid off, too.
She took her to the side, let her lean on her shoulder and pulled back Astrid's hair.

"You can be sick now. Come on!" she ordered.

"No." Astrid rebelled. "I won't be. Give me water."

"Water? Where will I get you water? We have a chestful of wine, but
water? . . . Wait. Don't move."

She left her lying on the ground and walked out. Astrid had the impression, a horrible impression, that everything around her was spinning. She was
afraid that the ceiling would hit her head. The entire world whirled before her
eyes. It was as if she were aboard a ship that was tossed around by a storm.
She sailed on, wave after wave, as it dragged her under. It wouldn't be a bad
death, it . . .

"Drink!" Świętosława pulled her hair and put a cup of water to her lips.
"Drink!"

A sip of water, instead of clearing her head, only made her more aware of
her intoxication.

"Why did you name your ship the *Salty Sister*? Why? Why?" Świętosława questioned.

The question echoed around her skull. She knew that she shouldn't say anything else. Not a single word more.

"Because," she replied, and curled into a ball on the floor. She bit her tongue and tasted salty blood.

20

PRAGUE

Bolesław and Sobiesław Sławnikowic accompanied Margrave Henry of Schweinfurt and Bruno, King Henry II's brother, to the gates of Prague.

"Thank you, Bolz." The margrave embraced him. "I will never forget
what you've done for me. You sheltered me here, in Prague, during the worst
parts of the war."

"A life for a life," Bolesław replied with a smile. "You saved mine in Merseburg."

"These are dark times we live in, when brother hunts brother," Duke
Bruno said, putting on his travel cloak. "If fate had had her way and my eldest
brother had become a priest, like he was meant to, none of these monstrous
things would have happened."

When they were children, their family, under pressure from Emperor Otto,
had intended for the older Henry to become a priest, and for the younger
Bruno to inherit the Bavarian dukedom. But Henry had abandoned his path
as soon as their father had died and battled for his inheritance. Once the emperor died, he then fought for the highest position in the Reich. Now that war
raged, Bruno was forced to run from his country, so Bolesław had offered him
shelter in Prague, too.

"I'm going to go to Hungary as a pilgrim, a nomad," Bruno said. "To my
brother-in-law, King Stephen. I promise to speak to him about what we discussed. If I succeed, when Henry attacks Bohemia or Poland, Hungary will
remain neutral and not touch your southern borders."

They shook each other's hands. Duke Bruno added:

"Stay safe, Bolesław, and think about what I've told you. Turning sons
away from the paths from which they were intended has unexpected consequences. You have two wonderful sons and a third who will grow up
to be his brothers' equal. Don't make any rash decisions concerning their
futures."

"Go with God!" Bolesław said in farewell. He still struggled to think about
Bezprym without losing control of his emotions, so he preferred not to discuss
the matter now.

He and Sobiesław turned their horses and began their way back to the castle. The last dry autumn leaves crackled under their mounts' hooves. The people they passed bowed to Bolesław, but they glared at Sławnikowic.

"They don't like me," Sobiesław muttered.

"So what?" Bolesław shrugged. "It's a duke's duty to rule, not to be liked. And the people? They remember that you're Adalbert's brother, the bishop who had to abandon a cruel and thankless Prague. They have your family's blood on their hands. They see you beside me and they're afraid that I'll make you my vassal when I leave and let you take your revenge."

"I won't," Sobiesław said. "The Red One slaughtered the Wrszowce, and though I should be grateful to him, I am disgusted by what he did. I have had enough of this endless cycle of family revenge. It's not for me. Coming back to it all the time means that I cannot live. I don't even know if I want to be your vassal in Prague, Bolesław."

Bolesław bit back a curse. He had suspected as much. Sobiesław was loyal to him, and it would seem, as a duke of Libice, that he would be the perfect choice to be Bohemia's vassal, but it wasn't hard to see how uncomfortable Sławnikowic felt in Prague. As if the worst memories had caught up with him and wouldn't let him breathe.

"I can't sit here forever," Bolesław snorted. "I have to return to Poznań. Please, think about it. Don't turn me down rashly. Sobiesław, who else am I going to put on the throne? Bezprym?" He felt the lower part of his abdomen clench as if it were he who had been wounded by Jaromir. "How do you think my firstborn would feel, here, in the old house of the Přemyslids, the family who have taken away his . . . Ah!"

"Maybe that's not a bad idea?" Sławnikowic turned around to face him. "Maybe that would help Bezprym retrieve his dignity? Think about it. He'd be ruling over those who have wronged him. Wouldn't that be just?"

Bolesław remained silent for a while. They rode into the yard in front of the stable where he dismounted and, when the stable boys had led away their mounts, he whispered to Sobiesław:

"I have allowed Bezprym to go to the hermitage. He's probably settled down in Międzyrzecz by now . . ."

Jaksa walked out of the stable.

"When did you come back?" Bolesław called to him.

"Just now. You were bidding your guests farewell by the pilgrim's eastern gate, I rode in from the west."

One glance at Jaksa's expression was enough for Bolesław to know he didn't bring good news. The Redarian's fair hair fell into his eyes in dirty streaks. He had scratches across his chin and forehead.

"Did you get into a fight with a passionate lover?" Sobiesław asked in jest. "She left quite the mark."

"I wish. I was sitting in the bushes," Jaksa replied gloomily, and glanced at the people around them. "Can I ask the duke of Prague for an audience someplace other than a stable?"

Bolesław clapped him on the back and they made their way toward the castle.

"I like having you in my service, Jaksa," Bolesław said as they walked into the stony interior. "You announce good news with a gloomy expression, and bad news with an even worse one."

"What does that have to do with anything? Do you want me grinning like some fool? I don't like smiling men." Jaksa shrugged.

"Of course. A man must be grim. And dirty," Bolesław joked, but the Redarian had no sense of humor. "Are you hungry? Thirsty? What can I do for you?"

Jaksa had been skinny since he'd been a boy; he could go days with no food. Now, he looked like a skeleton with skin stretched over it. He waved a hand.

"My service first. Henry won't give up Jaromir. He did condemn the wrong that the young Přemyslid did your son, and expressed his regret for it, but he said that he absolutely won't give him to you for fear that 'Duke Bolesław may abuse his right for a father's vengeance.'"

"Bloody hell!" Bolesław banged his fist on the table. "Abuse? Jaromir's brother, the Red One, has already castrated him. How am I meant to abuse my right for vengeance? Cut his balls off again?"

"It wouldn't hurt to check that there's nothing left," Jaksa said soberly.

"Hold me, Sobiesław, or I'll hurt the messenger!"

"I'm not a messenger!" Jaksa replied scornfully, but momentarily regained his self-control. "Forgive me."

"I forgive you," Bolesław replied immediately. "It isn't your fault; it's Henry's. But Bezprym's suffering suits him just fine. Christ! A firstborn who cannot have an heir!"

"You still have Mieszko," Sobiesław reminded him. "The boy is thirteen soon, and so what that he's educated? You'll have an heir who can rival the king of Germania. He was also raised to be a priest and look at the warlike spirit he's displaying now. Besides, you've already allowed Bezprym to follow his heart to the hermitage. Make a trade with God. Give Him Bezprym, if he wants to go down that path so much, and take back Mieszko. Mieszko hasn't taken his vows yet."

Bolesław started pacing around the chamber. It calmed him, or at least it stopped him from seeing red. He had thought about it since the day that Bezprym had stood in front of him and told him what had happened. Yes, he'd thought about it, but his fatherly love told him that Bezprym's decision was an attempt to run away from what had happened, something that he would outgrow, like one grows out of acne. Earlier, he had wanted to reclaim his son from the clutches of Romuald of Pereum. He'd suspected that Bezprym would forget about the hermits, roots, and dreams which didn't suit his station once he returned home. That with time, he'd stand beside him as his heir. He had the blood of Hungarian warriors running through his veins. His mother Karolda's blood, and that of the nomad tribes who tamed wild horses. He was certain that that's what would have happened! But Jaromir's cruel attack, abducting Bezprym and taking away his manhood, it destroyed his plans. Bolesław's fatherly heart bled within his breast. Yes, he should focus on Mieszko so that his heir might have sons. But at the same time, he didn't want to do that lest it brought Bezprym down even further. He didn't want to take away what dignity the boy had left.

"When will we be at war?" he asked absentmindedly to change the topic of conversation. "When will Henry II set off?"

"In spring at the earliest," Jaksa replied tonelessly. "He's gone to Pavia to crown himself king of Rome."

They heard an uproar from outside the castle. Shouts and the clatter of horses' hooves on stones. There must have been at least a dozen riders. And Zarad's familiar voice:

"Out of my way or I'll strike you down!"

"Christ, what now?" Sobiesław whispered.

Bolesław could feel the blood drain from his face. Zarad was supposed to be in Poznań, but if he had ridden here in such a hurry, then . . .

"Duke!" His dark-eyed friend burst into the room, almost taking the door off its hinges. "There has been a crime in Międzyrzecz! The hermits have been murdered! There are no survivors!"

Bolesław rushed to Zarad and lifted him off the ground, as if he weighed no more than a child.

"No one?" he shouted.

"No one," Zarad repeated.

"Bezprym!" Bolesław howled. "Bezprym was in the hermitage!"

"Bloody hell . . ." Jaksa paled. "That's impossible. The young duke?"

"Put me down," Zarad ordered. "Put me down!"

Bolesław dropped him as if he'd been burned. The first thought that crossed his mind was that the boy must be cursed.

Zarad slowly picked himself up from the ground, clenched his jaw, and said: "Bezprym's body was not among the murdered men at the hermitage."

POLAND

Świętosława heard about what had happened to Bezprym from Ion, Ostrowod, and Wilczan. They had returned from Prague almost at the same time as she came back from Wolin. Unger, Emnilda, and Zarad were the only ones whom they told. Ostry's men had been sworn to secrecy.

"The young duke has been horrifically wronged," Emnilda told them. "There is no reason for you to make matters worse by gossiping. Silence is golden and I promise you that Duke Bolesław will reward you for it."

"While I will punish you severely if you can't keep your mouths shut," Świętosława promised. "I can be cruel as well as strict. Ion, your mission is over now; you can go back to your chain."

"My queen," Ostry spoke up in his defense. "Ion begged for mercy on Bezprym's behalf, he risked his life to do so. We wouldn't have managed to navigate Italy without him either."

"I have heard you," she announced, striking fear into Ostry's men. "Chain, now! And I hope that all of you"—she turned back to the witnesses to Bezprym's suffering—"remember your vow of silence."

"Yes, my lady," they whispered, horror-struck.

"You may go and rest now. The duke will pay for your drinks tonight," Emnilda said, smoothing things over.

They locked themselves in the hall: Świętosława, Emnilda, Unger, Zarad, and Ostry.

"Where is Bezprym now? Did he stay in Prague with his lord father?" the bishop asked.

"No, the duke has allowed him to travel to the hermitage in Międzyrzecz," Ostry replied. "We rode with him and left him with the pious Benedict before coming here."

"Has Brother Barnaby returned from Rome yet?" Unger asked. "They were expecting him no later than on Saint Martin's Day."

"I don't know. There were five of them. Pious Benedict, John, and our two, Isaac and Matthew. They have beards as long as their Italian brothers do, so you can't tell which ones are more pious anymore." Ostry chuckled but stopped when he saw Unger's disapproving look. "And the fifth was Chris, the brothers' servant. They welcomed the prince with joy, since Benedict and John knew him from Pereum. And Barnaby has apparently gone to bring back

Bruno of Quedlinburg, who was meant to lead the mission. If we'd known, we'd have brought him back from Italy with us."

They ignored his comment. Świętosława was stricken. She couldn't imagine what Bezprym must be going through.

"How old is he?" she asked Emnilda.

"Seventeen," her sister-in-law replied. Tears streamed from her eyes. She tried to wipe them away discreetly.

"God," Świętosława whispered. "He could be married by now . . ."

"May I remind you that Bezprym has chosen to pursue a spiritual path," Unger said. "And it seems that his resolve is strong, since he didn't stay in Prague with his father, but headed straight to the hermitage. Why . . ." Unger's voice trembled and rose higher and higher with each word. "Why do you continue to deny Bezprym his right to choose? Why do you keep trying to force a secular life upon him when he has chosen God?"

"Because, holy father, he is the firstborn son of the great duke of Poland," Świętosława replied sadly. "None of us have been allowed to follow our hearts, because ensuring the good of the dukedom has always been our duty."

They were silent for a long moment, listening to the crackling flames and Emnilda's quiet sobs. Unger finally spoke:

"I will speak with Bezprym. I'll go to the hermitage. Maybe the young man needs spiritual support. His mother was Hungarian, as was my father, so we have something in common."

"That's a good idea. I have nothing of the Hungarian in me, but I accepted help from you sooner than from anyone else," Świętosława admitted.

"You have more than you think you do." Unger smiled mysteriously. "Do you remember how you told me the legend of Gudrun? Gudrun and the wolf hair which was wrapped around the ring as a warning for her brothers that her husband Atli would betray them? And about the suffering that her warning failed to prevent?"

"I remember." She nodded. "You're a good listener."

"That Atli is none other than the legendary Attila, our Hungarian ancestor. We will talk of this again someday, Queen. We have much to discuss." Unger smiled.

A feeling of unease crept over her. Like the priest could see into her heart and read her need to confess written upon it.

But Unger didn't go to the hermitage. He woke up with such a high fever the next morning that he couldn't get out of bed. He asked Zarad to go in his place, and to tell Bezprym that the boy could count on his support. Emnilda added two wagons of viands for the hermits, while Świętosława, hurriedly searching for something that might bring her favorite nephew some relief, gave him a young owl in a cage.

"An owl?" Zarad couldn't conceal his surprise. "Why does he need an owl?"

"Tell him it's from me. It's a sign that I remember and that I cannot explain further because the messenger won't understand." She smiled cunningly. "If he ever lets me visit him, I'll tell him myself."

Zarad stared at her foolishly.

"What?" She shrugged. "Can't I have a secret?"

"You have more secrets than a confessor's head can contain."

"Says the saint," she reprimanded him. "Don't stare, you look as foolish as you did when you were fifteen and struggled with pimples." She tickled him under his chin and felt him stiffen. "Yes, I remember everything! Even the days when you blushed at the sight of every maidservant."

She gave him the caged owl and saw him on his way.

There was no reason behind her gift. But she knew that she couldn't give Bezprym a knife, sword, or any other weapon, in case the boy thought the gift was meant as encouragement for him to take his own life, or as trying to force him to be his father's heir. Giving him a beautiful brooch, ring, or cloak might be interpreted as a lack of sensitivity to his needs as a hermit. She had found the owl in the woods on her journey back from Wolin. It had tangled itself in a net left by the duke's hunters when they had been hunting young hawks. It was intriguingly beautiful, and Świętosława had accepted it as a gift from the hunters. She should have let it go, as the men had advised her to do, but she hadn't, because she found that staring into the enormous round eyes brought her a strange pleasure. She thought that Bezprym might feel the same.

The day after Zarad's departure, she and Emnilda found themselves drowsily wandering around the palatium.

"Maybe we are unwell?" the duchess wondered. "Like Unger, but without the fever?"

"No, my sweet," Świętosława disagreed. "We can't settle down anywhere because we are suffering on Bezprym's behalf. It was so cruel." She flinched. "The boy had just reached manhood . . . God!"

"I'm afraid, Świętosława, that this was a sort of severe punishment." Emnilda voiced the thought that had also taken root in Świętosława's mind. "Bolz wanted to take his firstborn away from God . . ."

"And God has clearly shown us His will," she finished for her, and inhaled loudly. "Did Bolz ever tell you about Abraham's sacrifice?"

"Bolz never did, but I heard the story from a priest when I was a child."

"Our father had a second wife, Oda. We called her Duchess Icicle. She was a remarkable bitch, but I learned a lot from her."

"You? Impossible. You're so kind . . ."

Świętosława looked at Emnilda and kissed her cheek.

"No, you are, and you see the world as a better place than it really is. Oda gave my father two sons and they named the first one after him."

"As did we." Emnilda smiled with her eyes.

"That's different. My brother grew up, feeling the pressure of his stepmother and Mieszko, Mieszko's son. He constantly thought that Father might sacrifice him to God, just like Abraham sacrificed Isaac. And he never blamed Father for it, he blamed Oda. He knew that if that ever happened, it would be her doing, that she would convince Father just so she might make space for her own son."

"I had no idea." Emnilda sighed.

"That's why Bolesław, even if he loves your children more, will never willingly deprive his firstborn of his inheritance," Świętosława said in one breath. "That's why he's been fighting so hard for Bezprym. So that his son never has to wonder about Abraham and Isaac."

"Do you remember what my son told us recently?" Emnilda recalled. "He mentioned Cain and Abel."

"Christ! Brother killing brother. That's his story . . . I hope it never comes true," Świętosława said. "I don't even know which one is worse . . ."

"They are both cruel," Emnilda said. "But as you've seen yourself, life can be even crueler. I'd rather you tell me about your meeting with the children. Did you see them?"

"Yes." Emotion leapt to her throat like a wolf attacks its prey. "They're wonderful."

A few days later, as she was crossing the West Bridge returning from a ride, she heard hoofbeats behind her. She turned around. And although she shouldn't have recognized him, she did. She knew him by his furrowed brow, hair black as soot, and eyes like molten lead.

"Bezprym?" she asked, pulling on her reins to stop her horse.

"An owl?" he replied.

He was angry, the emotion bubbling in him like water in a fjord during an autumn storm.

"Where are your lynxes?" he asked, riding up next to her.

"Murdered," she answered, looking at him carefully.

"So are they," he said, clenching his jaw.

"Who?"

"The hermits."

"My lynxes were killed by my husband. It was an act of powerless revenge," she told him.

"The hermits were killed by a man whom my father trusts completely," he said, and his horse's hindquarters touched her mare. The mare snorted.

"Betrayal?" she asked, and only then began to understand what he'd told her.

"Betrayal," he confirmed.

"How did you survive?"

"Because of your owl," he said, and the anger and despair flooded out of him.

He spat out a word that sounded like something between a spell and a whistle, and his horse leapt forward like an arrow loosed from a bow. He had already dismounted by the time she reached the palatium's yard. He was almost as tall as Bolesław. He had broad shoulders, black hair, and gray eyes. He looked like the embodiment of pain, forcefully enclosed within the figure of a man. A young man.

A groom helped her dismount. She took a step toward Bezprym.

"Don't say anything," she said, grabbing his hand as if he were her son and pulling him along behind her. "You'll tell us everything in the hall."

The servants must have recognized him, for two of them made the sign of the cross as they kneeled before him.

I will kill the one who talked when I find him, she thought.

They met at the foot of Unger's bed, since he was too weak to rise. Emnilda rushed in.

"What's happened, son?" The bishop's eyes gleamed in the dim chamber with a dark fire.

"The hermits have been murdered," Bezprym announced.

Emnilda groaned and made the sign of the cross.

"Christ, Lord, protect us in the hour of need," the bishop whispered.

"Master Zarad arrived with your message," Bezprym began, "with the carts from my stepmother the duchess and the caged owl. I wondered, 'Why an owl?' Zarad left. The brothers prayed in the chapel for Barnaby's safe return from Rome, but I kept thinking about the caged owl. I couldn't focus on the prayers, so Benedict said, 'Perhaps the queen sends you a bird so that you may set it free?' I took the cage and went deep into the woods. When I opened it, the owl didn't want to fly out. It sat inside its prison. I talked to it . . ."

He broke off. No one rushed him, even Świętosława found the patience she needed within herself. They waited for him to continue when he was ready.

"It got dark, and then I heard the riders." He picked up where he had left off. "I sneaked back through the woods, taking the owl that didn't want to fly away with me. I saw the duke's trusted man, and I thought that my lord father must have changed his mind and was going to try to convince me to return to court. It never even crossed my mind that something bad might happen . . ." He lowered his head and his dark hair obscured his face. "I was more interested in the owl," he admitted. "It just sat there, motionless, as if it were dead, but I could see its breast moving. I stood in the wood behind the hermitage and looked from the owl to the newcomers and back again. They dismounted and walked into the chapel. It was night, the brothers were asleep . . . I had no bad feelings, I knew who they were. But then, when I heard the screams, I realized that I knew nothing. I heard the furious threat, 'We really don't want to kill you,' but John just calmly replied, 'Deus vos adiuvet et nos' . . ."

"May God help you and us," Mieszko translated. No one had noticed him come in.

"The attacker had a candle in his left hand and a sword in his right," Bezprym said, as if he were inspired. "He stabbed Benedict in the chest, and he seemed to have been waiting for it. He didn't defend himself or try to stop it . . . His blood splashed over the wall. The brothers followed him like lambs led to the slaughter. Afterward, his men ran around the yard and killed anyone who was still breathing . . . They were afraid that someone would survive . . . and I realized that if the caged owl made a sound, it would be over for me. But it just looked into my eyes and stayed silent. The murderers tried to set fire to the chapel but it didn't take . . . They were furious because they couldn't find Barnaby . . . They didn't find him . . . They knew that he was supposed to have returned . . . Dawn was coming, and they melted into the woods when they heard hoofbeats. I was stricken. I hid behind a tree and one of them ran right past me. They went south."

"Who was it who came?" the feverish Unger asked in a whisper.

"Master Zarad. The same one who had brought us gifts the day before. He saw the corpses, ordered the fire be put out, and shouted curses before leaving, calling his men to follow him to Prague."

"Who killed the monks?" Świętosława asked.

"Didn't I say it was the scout?" Bezprym frowned.

"You did, but which one?"

"The fair-haired Redarian, Jaksa. My queen"—he walked over to her—"I owe your owl my life, even though I'm not yet sure whether I'm grateful for it."

"It's not my doing." She solved his dilemma by refusing to accept any potential gratitude. "Ask the owl what you should make of it."

Unger raised himself as much as he could.

"We have to inform the duke as quickly as possible," he said. "Jaksa controls all of the scouts in the west, and war approaches our borders in strides. The Redarian doesn't know that Bezprym saw him. He might have gone back to Bolesław; he may be planning even worse treason at his side. The hermit brothers must be given an honorable burial. They died martyrs. Perhaps their death, like that of Bishop Adalbert, will bring the fruit of holiness?"

"Bishop Adalbert, our Saint Adalbert," Mieszko spoke again, moving to the center of the room, "died while on a mission among the pagans. According to what you've taught me, Father Unger, that was different. He died while spreading the word of God."

"It does not make their death any less of a loss," Bezprym snarled, turning to face his brother. "You didn't know them or who they were!"

"And I didn't wait in the woods while they died," Mieszko retorted.

"Do you wish that I'd let myself die alongside them?" the elder brother asked sharply.

Świętosława held her breath as she watched them. Her eyes met Emnilda's. For a second, she thought the brothers would leap at each other, but they both placed their hands on their chests instead. Mieszko's hand was open, Bezprym's was clenched in a fist.

"You misunderstood me, brother," Mieszko spoke first. "How could I desire your death? I am glad that you survived, even though I know what misfortune you have suffered. I stand by you in your pain."

Bezprym inhaled so loudly that Świętosława felt a chill on her spine. She saw no sympathy in Mieszko's eyes, only the flash of scornful pity.

"But I don't want you beside me, brother," replied Bezprym slowly.

21

BOHEMIA

Bolesław sent Jaksa west. The winter was so warm and dry, with no snow, that if Henry had already returned from Pavia, he could attack any day. Discontent spread in Prague, and he suspected that Jaromir had sent out messengers to sniff out potential allies among those surrounding Bolesław.

"When the nobles supported you, they thought you'd take the throne, set everything right, return to Poznań, and they would rule themselves," said Sobiesław.

They rode along the Vltava. Bolesław's dogs chased each other, leaping over patches of dry grass.

"I disappointed them." Bolesław shrugged. "Do you know what would happen if I left? Henry would arrive the day after, with Jaromir and Oldrzych in tow. That will be the day!"

"Why haven't we heard anything from Jaksa?"

The dogs turned around and, barking, ran back toward them.

"Because there's probably nothing to report. You know what the Redarian is like. He can disappear for weeks before reappearing suddenly with news."

Bolesław turned around to see who his dogs were barking at.

"Ciechan is coming!" Sobiesław noticed the approaching man.

"Duke, it's difficult to find you at the castle." Ciechan's usually cheerful countenance looked worried.

"I didn't come here to sit still." Bolesław smiled at him. "What news?"

"There is unrest on the roads. People say that gangs of bandits have begun to appear in the mountains. One, which attacked Bishop Unger's messengers, has been broken up."

"Are they all right?"

"The messengers have not been found. The band's leader claims they escaped at night."

"None of this reached me." Bolesław rubbed his forehead. "And I pay them well enough that they know they won't find a better position."

Only now did he realize that the last news he had received from Poznań had been from Zarad; there had been none since. He had sent Emnilda and the children Christmas gifts and orders for the hermits' funerals, but he had heard nothing for two months.

"Sobiesław, give the orders. Increase the number of guards by the roads, they must be safe. And send messengers to Poznań immediately. What the hell is this?"

A small armed guard approached them, but they were not his men. They rode to meet them.

"We come from Margrave Gunzelin to see the great duke Bolesław!" their leader announced, looking at them carefully.

"You stand before the duke," Sobiesław informed him. "Do you have the margrave's seal?"

"I do," the leader replied uncertainly, glancing between Bolesław and Sobiesław. "But I will only show the duke."

Bolesław burst out laughing. He was wearing simple riding clothes. Of the two of them, Sobiesław looked more like a duke than he did.

"Come to the castle," he shouted, and turned around.

He changed before he saw the messengers to avoid embarrassing them. He strode into the audience hall wearing an embroidered red tunic, a cloak lined with fur, and a royal diadem on his head.

"My name is Derwan, Lord Gunzelin's servant. Please forgive me, my lord." The leader bowed. "I didn't recognize you on the road . . . I didn't expect . . ."

"It's all right. Don't waste time now, you were riding so fast that you left clouds of dust in your wake."

"Because the matter is urgent. Your brother Gunzelin sends us to tell you that the Redarians and the Veleti have made an alliance with Henry."

"Damn it!" Bolesław cursed. Jaksa should have been the first to know. Why had they not heard about this?

"Do you know any details?" he asked the messenger.

"King Henry used you to scare the pagans, Duke. He told them that you brought missionaries to Poland, men who will baptize them by fire and burn the woods down to the last temple. They agreed to send their troops against you, on the condition that they get . . ."

The hermits from Międzyrzecz, Bolesław guessed, and Derwan confirmed it.

"They are ready, Duke. Since the winter is dry and warm, they will march at any moment. The pagans will probably attack from the direction of Milsk."

POLAND

They did attack, but before the two armies met, early spring storms hit and lasted for a week, making battle difficult. Bolesław pulled back his heavy cavalry; the horses sank into the soft ground. He sorely missed Jaksa and his knowledge of all the fords, swamps, and passages. He suspected that something must have happened, because how else could Jaksa's absence be explained? He was worried that his childhood friend had been tripped up. Perhaps he'd fallen into the hands of the Redarians? They knew that their relative had served him for years.

"There is only one division from the king's army, and it's at the back," Derwan reported. "Henry's men are afraid to enter the woods."

"We'll send two of our divisions at night, and attack them from behind," ordered Bolesław. "The pagans won't want to fight us alone. When they see that we've broken up Henry's men, they'll scatter. The infantry can go through the woods to catch the Redarians and Veleti. I want their leaders alive," he snarled. "They are the only ones who might know what happened to Jaksa."

Zarad led one squad while Bolesław led the other. Derwan stayed in the woods and hunted the Redarians who walked into their trap.

It was dark and pouring with rain. Their guide, riding a light, stocky horse, led them down a path along the edge of the immense wilderness. Bolesław's mount stepped quietly. They surprised those of Henry's men who were standing watch as they warmed themselves at a small, covered fire. The duke ordered them to be taken alive.

"They can lead us to the squad," he said quietly.

With knives at their throats, the soldiers didn't fail them. They led Bolesław and his men straight into a small camp. There were barely a dozen tents, Bolesław counted no more. A short, chaotic fight ensued.

"Take everyone alive! Maybe they can tell us where Jaksa is."

"They don't need to," Derwan called out as he rode toward Bolesław.

He held a torch in his left hand, and a bound man lay across the saddle in front of him. Derwan threw him off the saddle. The prisoner fell into the mud, but he raised himself onto his knees, and stayed there with his hands and feet tied.

"Jaksa?" Bolesław couldn't believe his eyes.

"You ordered us to take the pagan leader prisoner," Derwan said. "Here he is. He's yours."

They stared at each other until Bolesław said bitterly, "No, he isn't, not anymore. Chain him up!" he ordered.

Jaksa angrily spat at his feet. The duke turned away. He didn't even want to look at him.

ENGLAND

Sven watched as his people packed away their camp on the Isle of Wight. They pulled the canvas tents off their poles, rolled them up tightly, and carried them onto their ships. Leather sleeping bags, a chest with weapons, barrels of valuable seal fat, and supplies. They covered the fires and excrement pits with soil. They left a small crew behind, but he suspected they'd return to the island the following winter; he liked a clean camp.

The short spring storms had passed, and it was time to warm up their bones after winter. The past year had been busy. They attacked Wessex and conquered Exeter without much difficulty. He'd stood face-to-face with Earl Elfric, a man he knew from years ago. He was as ineffective today as he'd been in the past. His men defeated Elfric's without losing a single man, and they invaded Wilton, which they "conquered, plundered, and burned," as Jorun liked to report. They took the nearby Salisbury just as efficiently. He'd dissolved his army before winter, sending back the men his stepson Olof King of Swedes had offered, and allowing some of his own to return to Denmark. He kept the Norwegians with him, though; while he had nothing against his son-in-law Eric of Lade, he nevertheless felt more secure when he knew that his vassal was not in command of all of his forces back in Norway.

About thirty ships rocked on the water in the harbor. Not enough to take London, but just enough for the eastern parts of England, which was the target he had chosen this winter.

"*Anger* is waiting for you, my king!" Jorun bared his teeth in a smile and stretched, his joints cracking.

"Have the horses been loaded?"

"Yes, one on each ship, as you ordered."

"Then let's go!" Sven clapped his shoulder and boarded the ship.

It's so good to have the deck under my feet again, he thought as they pushed away from the shore and *Anger*'s dark sail filled with a gust of wind from the west.

After three days, they reached a small bay where he ordered the ships to put up. The horses were led onto dry land, and they set up camp. He sent a few men to discreetly capture some locals who they could use as guides and invited his chieftains for a meal that evening.

"We have nine hundred men and thirty ships to guard. We have to leave at least a hundred in the camp. I'll take the riders and ride ahead. We will split the rest up into three divisions. They will be commanded by Stenkil, Thorgils, and Jarl Haakon of Funen. You will each have a hundred infantrymen. You'll move through the forests so that our visit remains a secret for as long as possible. We'll meet in the woods which surround the town in the south."

"Visit?" Stenkil asked. "Tell us, King, who are we visiting?"

Sven laughed as he lifted his horn and raised a toast:

"Norwich! The second largest city in England, after London!"

"That's what we drink to!" Jorun called out. "To a rich city that will open its gates to us!"

"I will spread its legs!"

"Scatter silver!"

"And wine!"

"Beautiful women!"

"Enough drinking!" Sven decided. "We can only conquer the city if we have the element of surprise on our side. We set off at dawn."

Before the infantrymen had reached the woods in which they were meant to meet, his men were already waiting with ladders and a battering ram intended to break open the gates. He allowed the infantrymen to rest, and only gave the signal to attack once night had fallen. They were first noticed when they were already within range of arrows.

"Shields! Protect the men with the ladders!"

Sven and his riders attacked a small side gate with their axes, drawing the defenders' attention away from the great gates at which Jorun's men were running with the battering ram. The church bells began to ring. How he loved that sound! The sound of fear. He counted the rings. Three, four, six! The high-pitched voice of a small bell was the last one to join. It was fast and piercing, almost like the strokes of a sword.

"Fire!" he shouted to Stenkil, and a moment later, burning arrows began to fly over their heads.

The defenders fell for the ruse and threw themselves at the fires to put them out. The regular beat of the battering ram, followed by the sound of wood cracking as the gates fell, and the triumphant shout of Jorun's horn which carried over the noise told Sven that his comrade was forcing his way into the city through the main entrance.

That was enough for the defenders of the side gate to retreat to help those fighting by the main gates. Sven swung his axe one last time and the gate fell.

He rode into the city with his sword raised high. The first thing he smelled was something burning. The smoke rose from side streets and the flames from the arrows which had found their mark in thatched roofs spread from house to house. The bells were still ringing, though there were fewer of them. People screamed as they ran from under his hooves. He didn't chase women, searching for armed men instead.

"This way!" he shouted, recognizing the way that led to the main gate.

They fell on the defenders from the back. It was slaughter. They faced Jorun's axemen on one side, and Sven's riders on the other. The last bell had fallen silent by the time they had finished.

"Norwich surrenders!"

* * *

They plundered the city until noon the following day. Sven ordered his men to round up all the surviving horses and load them with their spoils.

"We need to hurry." He rushed his chieftains. "Once the ealdorman hears of this, he might try to cut us off from the ships."

"What is your master's name?" Jorun asked one of the prisoners, a monk.

"Ulfcetel, my lord. The ealdorman of East Anglia," the monk replied.

"Is he brave?"

The monk sighed and shook his head. Jorun laughed loudly.

The days that followed revealed the truth in the monk's assessment of the ealdorman. He did attack their camp, but the one hundred men they'd left behind were enough to push him back. When Sven returned to the shore with the rest of his army and all their plunder, Ulfcetel's messengers were waiting for him.

"Our lord, the noble Ealdorman of East Anglia, wants to make peace, King Sven."

"How much will he pay for peace?" the Redbeard asked.

"A fair amount," the messenger replied.

"Then tell your ealdorman that I invite him to a feast at my camp."

He knew that the messenger would negotiate for a neutral meeting place, but he wanted to frighten him now, so that the negotiations might conclude more successfully for him. Before Ulfcetel arrived for their meeting, he had another visitor.

"Our meeting, King Sven, must remain a complete secret," said the slender man with shoulder-length gray hair.

Two younger men stood beside him, so alike that they could only be his sons. They were dressed in gray cloaks like ordinary travelers.

"Who are you, guest?" Sven asked.

"My name is Elfhelm of York. I'm the ealdorman of south Northumbria, and these are my sons, Ufegeat and Wulfheah."

"How can I be sure that you're the man you say you are?"

"If our discussions are of benefit to us both, I hope that you will accept an invitation to my castle," replied Elfhelm.

"Tell me then, Ealdorman, what do you suggest first?"

Elfhelm did not look like a cunning man, but Sven was under no illusions that he understood people. He had been mistaken so many times! His own wife was the best evidence of that. His sweet Sventoslava, a traitor.

"Many Danish settlers have lived in Northumbria for years," Elfhelm said. "They are honest people. We don't get in each other's way. I respect them and they respect my rule."

He's afraid that I will attack his lands and the Danes who live there will support me, Sven thought.

"I'd like us to understand each other," the ealdorman continued. "I am loyal to my king, but I believe that Ethelred has made many mistakes. Not when he paid you and Olav Tryggvason the great danegeld years ago, but since then."

He wants to overthrow Ethelred, Sven realized. *And he wants me and my armies to help him.*

"Are there more people who share your views?" he asked the ealdorman.

"Yes, King Sven."

"Then, Elfhelm, we have something worthy of discussing. I will gladly accept your invitation to York and see your castle and your country. I suggest that you leave your sons in my camp as a guarantee that I will return here safely. Are these your only sons?"

"Yes," Elfhelm confirmed. "Apart from them I only have a young daughter, Elfgifu."

"Elfgifu," Sven repeated thoughtfully. "Don't be afraid!" He turned to them. "I also have two sons, and I love them more than life itself!"

He pictured London as he had left it years ago as he'd sailed away from its walls. He could almost smell the Thames, the riverbank and the scent of fear wafting over the walls from its inhabitants.

I promised you, London, that I would return, he thought. *And here I come, even if the road to you, great city, leads me through York.*

POLAND

Bolesław was taken by surprise. He still hadn't rebuilt his networks of spies in the west, and when he received word in early summer that Henry II was gathering armies in Merseburg, he was sure that the king of the Reich was going to attack Poland. He sent forces, two thousand heavy infantry and eight thousand light infantry strong, from Poznań, Giecz, and Gniezno, to defend the western border. He had doubled the troops stationed in the boroughs by the borders a long time ago. He was prepared to push Henry back from his country. But the German king, with Jaromir Přemyslid at his side, didn't march west; he marched south. Bolesław received word from Gunzelin of Meissen, his son-in-law Herman of Strehla, and Margrave Henry of Schweinfurt at the same time, all reporting the same news: "Henry II is marching on Prague."

Bolesław immediately sent a messenger to Kraków to gather reinforcements, even though he knew there was but a slim chance that he would manage to regroup his troops in time.

"Don't expose Poland," Sobiesław warned him during their council of war. "Henry might have another trick up his sleeve. Will you send your troops to Bohemia and leave your home undefended?"

"Great duke," began Sławomir, the Moravian duke who was Bolesław's guest while they were threatened by war, "will you not consider abandoning Bohemia?"

"Sławomir, can you see any other Czech leaders beside me, other than Prague's castellan?"

"No, my lord," Sławomir admitted. "But Moravia's chieftains stand with you."

"If we can verify that Jaromir Přemyslid marches with Henry, what will the Czechs do, Castellan?"

"You already know, Duke," Borzywoj answered. "They will side with Přemyslid."

"And you, Borzywoj?"

"I will defend my city, then my castle and my duke Bolesław inside it. I was among those who called for you to sit on our throne, and my mind hasn't changed since then. Jaromir will be a bad ruler, the worst of them all. He has been hunted since childhood. Before the Red One took away his manhood, he allowed the nobility to mock him. Did you know that when he was hunting with the Wrszowce when he was a young boy, before the Red One slaughtered them all and castrated him, even they humiliated him? They laughed at him, at their duke's brother, they undressed him, tied him up, and jumped their horses over him. The Wrszowce weren't the only ones responsible; there were others with them. I'll be honest: the men who were there are the same ones who are calling for him to take the throne today. What kind of duke could he be if they remember how disrespectfully they once treated him?"

Borzywoj's long, soot-black mustache quivered in anger. He grimaced as he added:

"If Jaromir and Henry arrive together, Jaromir will probably bend the knee to the king just like Władywoj did. I don't like it. This past year in which you've ruled Prague, my lord, there has been peace on the roads, royal audiences have returned, and you refused to bow to Henry twice now. I like that. What does it matter if the nobles don't like it that they can't steal because you watch them too carefully? Before you, we had Boleslav the Cruel, Boleslav the Red, and twice now the drunk and harsh Władywoj." He shook his head.

"And now I am to wait for the next one in line? Jaromir the Odd? I'll defend you and your claim, my lord, because I want Bohemia and Poland to be one!"

Bolesław embraced the castellan.

"If our cause becomes a hopeless one, you'll come back to Poznań with me. I'll take you and your whole family."

"No, my lord," Borzywoj snorted. "I would prefer to die for you here."

"No," Bolesław replied firmly. "I don't want you to die for me. I want you to serve me, there is a difference between the two. It is no feat to lose your life in war. It is a challenge to keep it without losing your honor. Ask Sobiesław how he likes to serve me in Poland."

Borzywoj thought about the duke's words as he pulled on his mustache.

"Sławomir, go back to Moravia. Gather the troops and hound Henry with some skirmishes. I don't know what plans he has for Bohemia, or how long he intends to stay, but I want him to remember this journey as particularly unpleasant thanks to my Moravian subjects. I say the same to you, Moravian chieftains. That's the end of the council, we have enough to do. Borzywoj, prepare Prague to defend itself." He rose, and they followed his lead. He started toward the door but stopped before he reached it and turned back. "I will pay the man who captures Jaromir Přemyslid alive so much that he will never need anything for the rest of his days."

He hadn't expected there to be a tremor in his voice as he spoke.

That evening he and Sobiesław inspected the city's ramparts. His two red hunting dogs scampered between them. The enormous bloodred sun was setting, reflecting off the Vltava's surface.

"A bloodred river," Sobiesław said thoughtfully. "It has seen so much cruelty, so many slaughters. Bohemia is a beautiful country. I know that for you, Bolesław, it may be a small one, but for me it is home. When we first came here and you said you wanted me to be your vassal in Bohemia, I was touched. And when you rode onto the pastures on the Vltava's banks on the white mare, holding the Holy Spear, my heart almost burst with joy. You spoke of 'a strong Słowiańszczyzna,' just like Otto did at the Congress of Gniezno. Those were the most beautiful moments of my life."

Sobiesław suddenly stopped and turned around, placing his hands on Bolesław's shoulders.

"You have stood by me in my darkest moments. After your uncle hunted down my family—God Almighty, if you hadn't forced me to accompany you to Połabie all those years ago, I wouldn't be alive today! They would have slaughtered me alongside my family in Libice. I have been granted what can only be described as divine rather than human mercy twice now because of you. The first time was when you helped make my brother Adalbert a saint. The second time was a year ago on the fields of Prague, when you promised the Czechs that you would not bend the knee to Henry and that we would become one united power. What did I do to deserve such happiness? Such a friend?"

"You're like a brother to me," said Bolesław, feeling a lump rise in his throat. "Like a brother I never had."

"You had more than one!" Sobiesław laughed, but tears shone in his eyes. "You chased them away with Oda."

"Oh, you don't know how to just enjoy the moment, do you?" Bolesław clapped his back.

"Brother, I'd like to ask something of you, but I worry I may be overstepping. Let's agree that if you find my request inappropriate, you'll refuse me, and I will hold no grudge and never speak of it again."

"Speak."

"I want to ask for your sister Świętosława's hand in marriage."

Bolesław cursed himself. How could he not have thought of it before? He had been secretly wondering whom the Bold One should marry so he might gain the most from the alliance. Dissolving her marriage with Sven should not be too difficult for Unger to arrange, especially since he knew that Sven had been asking at neighboring courts for a suitable wife. His red-haired brother-in-law had had no luck. All those he asked were Bolesław's allies. But if they were the ones to offer such a solution, Haraldsson would agree without hesitation. He had considered one of Knyaz Vladimir's sons, but dismissed the idea when he'd heard that she'd already burned one of the knyaz's bastards in her bathhouse. Why hadn't he thought of Sobiesław sooner? If they were married, he could place them both on Prague's throne and he could rest easy knowing the Bold One was managing the spoiled Czech nobles. He slapped his forehead, and then slapped Sobiesław.

"Sorry," Sławnikowic apologized. "Forget about it."

"You fool!" Bolesław blustered. "You fool! Why are you only telling me of this now, when Henry is marching toward us with his armies? We should have done this a year ago, the moment I took Prague. Oh, Sobiesław! Damn your shyness!"

"Do you think that such a queen as she will agree to marry a duke of Libice?" he asked as his cheeks turned red.

"No, not a duke of Libice," Bolesław replied honestly. "But she'd marry the ruler of Prague. Whether you could manage her, that I don't know. But maybe she will soften with age. Stranger things have happened. Promise me something."

"Anything!"

"Next time you have such excellent ideas, share them immediately and don't hold back."

"I swear, my great duke. I swear it!"

"Oh, I wish you could call me brother-in-law already!" He embraced him, and they both turned back toward the castle. "First . . . start with capturing a wild animal for her. You can see the grief she feels for her lynxes in her eyes."

"That isn't for the lynxes but Olav Tryggvason, you know that."

"You have to impress her," Bolesław continued, excited by the vision. "I don't know what, maybe a bear? Or a bison? Will she give you children though? I don't know, thirty-five is not young . . ."

"I don't need to have children with her, Bolesław. I'd feel alive with her beside me. It's something more. Your youngest son Otto could inherit Prague from us. Wouldn't that be better than having many heirs for whom you then must divide the country? After all, it's your wish to have a strong, united Słowiańszczyzna."

Bolesław wanted to strangle him. He hadn't heard such a good idea in a long time. Once they reached the castle, he lay in bed, unable to sleep. His sister beside Sobiesław, with little Otto, stood in front of him as if they were really there. He could see her as she paced her chamber, as her laughter echoed within the gloomy castle stones. How she pierced the Czech noblemen with her gaze, a mixture of green and gold, showing them their place. Raised beside him, she had learned the same lessons he had from Mieszko, and then more in the mysterious courts of the north. She could handle the thick-skinned Vikings, so she would be more than a match for the Czechs. Their mother Dobrawa's beloved daughter, a Přemyslid by blood. Jesus! Why hadn't the damned Sobiesław shared his idea before now? He trusted him as if he were his brother, and she was his sister. And then there was the thought that they might pave the way for little Otto to take Prague's throne! . . .

He got up, too excited by the idea. He wanted it to come true so badly. At first, he didn't even hear the banging on his door. When he did, he thought it was Świętosława. Only when he recognized Borzywoj's voice did he return to reality.

"My lord!" The castellan was carrying a torch. "Jaromir Přemyslid is at the city gates. The Saxon army marches behind him. We cannot hold Prague; there are too many of them."

He shook off the wonderful dream as he realized that Sobiesław had been too late. He spoke as a sober chief and warrior.

"Borzywoj, we must leave Prague. Those who decide to follow you will be safe in Poland."

He pulled on his chain mail and picked up his weapons. The dogs followed him to the stables, barking as they went. He ran into Sobiesław in the doorway.

"Put your helmet on," he told him. "There will be a fight on the bridge. Squad!" he called to the men who were already mounted. "Retreat from Prague! Leave behind whatever you don't need. We head north!" He pointed in that direction with the Holy Spear.

They clashed with the enemy as soon as they left the city's perimeter. Bolesław's warriors passed through them as easily as wind through fields of rye, but that was only Přemyslid's first squad. They raced away, their horses' hooves thundering over the bridge. They were crossing the Vltava. Jaromir's men gave chase, the Saxons alongside them. Bolesław turned around without slowing his horse. He saw Sobiesław pull up his horse. Bolesław rode on as he watched his friend stay behind, as more and more of his men passed him.

"No!" he shouted. "Sobiesław! You're supposed to be my brother-in-law!"

Bolesław's dogs whined as they ran. The Czechs chasing them were gaining. The bridge's narrow throat could easily turn into a deadly trap. He caught sight of Borzywoj's black mustache, his head hanging low over his horse's neck.

"Call him back!" he shouted. "Call Sobiesław back! It's suicide!"

"Go!" he shouted to Borzywoj, and to the men who followed him. "Go! Go!"

"It's a wedding gift!" He heard Sobiesław's shout behind him. "For you, brother! Brother-in-law!"

He watched as Sobiesław tried to throw a looped rope over the youth who led the Czech and Saxon armies. He watched as Sobiesław froze, motionless. Two, then three arrows found their mark. The duke of Libice crashed down from his horse, and a rider behind him finished him off with a thrust of his sword.

Bolesław groaned and doubled up as if he had been the one who was struck. The rider who was probably Jaromir turned back.

Wait, you bandit! Bolesław thought, forcing his horse to turn back. *I'll get you. I'll have my vengeance for Bezprym!*

Someone rode in front of him and caught his horse's reins.

"Duke, you said you wanted service, not death," Borzywoj, Prague's castellan, shouted into his face. "Well, I'm serving you now!"

And he led him across the bridge as the arrows rained down around them. Bolesław kept turning around, shouting:

"Sobiesław!"

Borzywoj kept his lips pressed together and said nothing.

Once they reached the other side of the river, he shouted:

"Farewell, free Prague! Farewell, free Bohemia, great Bohemia! Farewell, great Słowiańszczyzna!"

22

WOLIN, WOLIN ISLAND, POLAND

Astrid first heard about the troubles which faced Bishop Reinbern of Koło-brzeg by chance. She stood in port, waiting for Dalwin to complete his business with the salt merchants, and listening to their conversation.

"There were days when he didn't leave the church at all. He would barricade himself inside, afraid."

"He was afraid?" She walked closer to them. "Afraid of what?"

"Not what, but who, Lady of Wolin." The merchant bowed. "Strosz."

She knew Strosz, she'd even spoken with him two or three times. He was an odd old man; seventy, maybe eighty years old, and his long hair had never turned gray. It earned him the name of Crow's Wing. He had once had a temple in the woods on the peatlands by Kołobrzeg, he was Swarożyc's priest. Strosz had been forced to move when Bolesław established a diocese in the salt settlement.

"I haven't seen Crow's Wing in years," she said. "I'd assumed he was dead."

"No, my lady." The merchant chuckled. "Men like him don't die so quickly."

"A bad thing never dies, as they say," another one added.

"Was Strosz really all that bad?" Astrid asked. "Odd, certainly, maybe stern, but not cruel."

The merchants exchanged a glance.

"The salt settlement has its secrets," the taller one observed.

"Salt is expensive," the other one recited the words with which they began every transaction. "And it values silence."

She reflected on this. It was no secret that the income from the saltworks was exorbitant, but she had never heard of the owners fighting amongst each other over access to the brine. Of course, Bolesław was the one who controlled the profits from the salt sales, and since he'd funded the diocese he passed these on to Reinbern, but nobody doubted that the saltworks' owners gained something on the side.

"It values silence," she repeated after the merchant. "Tell me quietly, then, what is this secret that Strosz has which frightens you as well as the bishop?"

"Crow's Wing has power," one of the merchants replied reluctantly.

"Brine flows from salt springs, my lady," his companion explained. "And Strosz says that there is no such thing as an inexhaustible spring."

"He's just trying to frighten you," Astrid said.

"Yes, he is. But he has shown that he has power to stop the water from flowing. He's done it twice since I've been alive, and once before that," the merchant replied grimly. "You won't find a man in Kołobrzeg brave enough to argue with Strosz."

Astrid realized that since Reinbern had appeared in Kołobrzeg four years earlier and Strosz's temple had disappeared from the peatlands, the saltworks owners had been giving Strosz refuge, and likely keeping this from the bishop.

"What's happened to make Strosz angry with Reinbern now?"

"What's happened, what's happened! . . ." The merchant scoffed. "As soon as the bishop arrived he began to preach that the reign of the old gods and their priests is over. He showed us those miracles of chasing the spirits of the seas and stones, and Crow's Wing grew angry."

Astrid had a soft spot for Reinbern. The bishop's religious zeal reminded her of Olav. After her conversation with the merchants, she realized that he had stepped on the tail of a far larger beast than he'd expected. And with Dalwin's permission, she took a troop of soldiers with her and set sail for Kołobrzeg.

POLAND

The port was quieter than usual. Leszko tied up the *Salty Sister* in a way that allowed for a swift retreat if it was needed.

"Lady of Wolin," Bogusz of the port guards called to her, and added his usual greeting: "The *Salty Sister* has come home. Welcome to our salt springs."

Why do some men insist on saying the same things all their lives? she wondered. *Do they think it amusing?*

She had no intention of explaining that her ship was named for tears rather than salt, because nobody in Kołobrzeg would understand. Everything here revolved around salt. She smiled at Bogusz and asked innocently:

"Where is Bishop Reinbern?"

"Where should he be, my lady?" Bogusz replied defensively. "He's guarding the church."

"Isn't it strange that he must guard it himself? Where are the duke's men?"

Only now did Bogusz notice the armed men on her ship.

"I can't allow soldiers into the borough. Not unless they leave their weapons with me. Those are Duke Bolesław's orders."

"This is my personal guard. I was advised not to come to Kołobrzeg without them as the settlement is apparently a dangerous place."

"No, my lady." He blushed. "You have been misled."

"Is that so?" she asked sharply, but then laughed. "Oh, I suppose I will find out soon enough. Will you give us horses? I won't walk."

She usually paid for a wagon when she arrived with cargo, but the few times that she came without heavy goods, Bogusz had just given her a horse from the stable which belonged to the soldiers who guarded the port and the nearby saltworks. The city itself was farther inland, on the river Parsęta banks.

"I can give you a horse, Lady of Wolin. But I have none for your guards."

"Of course you do, you're only teasing. Twelve horses and mine's the thirteenth, that should be easy enough!"

"Thirteen horses?! That's half my garrison!"

"I don't want to take them from you, only borrow them. There and back again. You're not planning any long journeys today, are you?"

She could have just said: "Give me the horses because you're my brother's subject," but she wanted to keep in his good graces for as long as possible while she remained on lands that were under his control.

"Come, Bogusz, time is of the essence." She took his arm and started to walk toward the watchtower. "Don't dawdle. You welcome me by saying that I've come home, but then you don't want to give me a horse? Would a mother really refuse to give a horse if a stepmother did it freely?"

He gave them to her, and she suspected he knew exactly why she needed them. She noticed that the guards by the saltworks had been doubled. *They're afraid for the springs,* she realized. The merchants weren't exaggerating; they'd taken all the precautions in the salt settlement.

"My lady." He stopped her as she was mounting her horse. "Don't leap to any conclusions based on what you see. Salt is expensive."

"And it values silence," she added, looking down at him from the saddle.

They rode out by the watchtower's gate that led to the settlement. Ordinary life continued on along the road. Oxen pulled loaded carts while sheep and cattle grazed in the wetlands on Parsęta's banks. Children squealed as they chased ducks, women did their laundry in the river and stretched out their sheets to dry. A fishwife was selling flat-cakes from a basket—salty ones, of course.

If not for the armed men who guarded the saltworks and salt springs, there would be no way of telling that anything out of the ordinary was happening.

They rode into the borough. Although it wasn't market day, the crowd and noise which greeted her was greater than in Wolin. Her mounted squad was observed with surprise, since there were fewer guards here than around the saltworks.

At least they make their priorities clear, she thought sourly.

About a dozen men stood in the square by the small wooden church. They were gathered in a tight group, and two dozing guards stood watch in the shadow of a nearby tree. When they rode into the yard, the guard leaped up and walked over to Astrid, glancing at a group of gawkers.

"Lady of Wolin." One of them recognized her with relief and held her horse.

"Who are these people?" she asked as she dismounted.

"Strosz and his followers," he replied carelessly. "There's nothing going on, they've been standing here for a week. They're harmless."

"What? The bishop hasn't left the church in a week?"

"No, he has; we take him back to his house for the night," the guard replied reluctantly.

"Why don't you chase Strosz and his followers away?" she asked, barely restraining her anger.

"We have, my lady, but they always come back."

"Are you trying to say that you, a duke's soldier, in my brother's service, are afraid of a handful of fishermen and one old priest?"

"I come from here, my lady, just like you do from Wolin," he replied, meeting her eyes. "The duke is far away. We serve him faithfully, but we serve here, in this place. There are some matters which cannot be resolved with an order from Poznań."

"It's not one old priest," the second guard added. "It's Strosz Crow's Wing, who swore that all the salt springs would dry out the moment he died."

"And everyone here remembers that he's already shown us what he can do."

She nodded. There was nothing she could say. Strosz had made himself untouchable with a single sentence. She walked over to a group of people. They made way for her, and Crow's Wing stepped out of their shadow.

"Astrid, Lady of Wolin," he croaked.

"You're looking well, Strosz," she replied.

"Salt is a good preserver," he replied, and added as he looked into her eyes: "Are you in such a rush to see Reinbern because you've been baptized?"

"No. Are you preparing for baptism? Is that why you're sitting outside a church? Have you stopped guarding Swarożyc's temple?"

"If you came to see me as often as you did the bishop, you'd know that they burned it."

"It wasn't the only one. If you're angry about it, go to Duke Bolesław. He'll hear you out."

"Don't mock me, Lady of Wolin," Strosz hissed. "He's strong today, but who knows what will happen tomorrow? The old gods haven't had their last word yet. The Redarians and the Veleti have sworn they will have their vengeance for the night in the woods by Milsko. The Great Old One of Radogoszcz has already begun to paint his puppet with soot . . . Do you know what that means?"

He's threatening me, she thought, and felt a stab of fear.

"There's a different world beyond the Oder," he whispered, never taking his eyes off her. "Freedom marches toward us from the west. Just like years ago our armies burned their stone churches, cathedrals, and dead god hanging on a cross, so will we burn them again. The Bird King respects our gods. The Bird King respects our leaders. Your brother is born of a woman and may die like any other . . ."

A chief will be born of woman and man,
He will rise from the seed and the mead.
A warrior and a lord, a hero and a king,
He will win fame and glory when he leads.

As she sang the words, Strosz hissed like a snake and covered up his ears to stop himself from hearing.

"An old song," he snarled.

"Old but strong." She smiled triumphantly. "Why do you grimace, Crow's Wing? Did you not sing it? You did. On the day he was born, it was sung in all the temples between the Baltic and the mountains. That's why you're so afraid of him. That's why none of the priests will challenge him. You've hidden yourselves away in woods and devilish marshes because you're afraid."

"Not anymore." Strosz's eyes shone, but not with the same fire she had seen there years ago. His hair was no longer black, and she could see gray roots showing by his skull. She could advise him to add some dry lady's mantle to the oak bark he used to dye it, but she didn't want to humiliate him in front of his followers. She felt pity for him. She turned toward the church.

"May health be with you." She threw over her shoulder, knowing he would curse her if she didn't say something first.

"And you," he whispered drily.

She ordered four men to remain outside and entered with the rest.

"Reinbern!" she called out in the darkness. "It's me, Astrid."

He was kneeling in front of the altar, praying. She had to wait for him to finish.

"Welcome, Lady of Wolin," he said when he finally stood up. He glanced at the men standing behind her. "Have you brought me my own guard?"

"I've come for you," she replied.

"I didn't call you." He shook his head stubbornly.

She sighed.

"You will be of no use to your god if you're dead."

"How do you know?"

"That you'll be dead? I spoke to Strosz and the people in the borough. They won't tell you the truth, so I must: salt is more precious to them than their bishop. It's hardly surprising, though, since they make their living off salt, not you."

She sat down on a low bench by the church wall. She knew him, and knew he'd need time to accept the sad truth.

"I cannot abandon my diocese." He walked over and sat down beside her.

"It's your choice," she replied. "I won't rescue you by force. I will only say again that you'll be of no use if you're dead."

"Bishop Adalbert accomplished more with his death than he did with his life."

"It's your choice," she repeated.

"He was killed by the Prussians for spreading God's Word." He sounded as if he were trying to convince himself. "And I will be the first bishop in history to be slaughtered for salt." He laughed hoarsely. "Such fame!"

"Mmm." She nodded. "When word of it spreads, others will try, too. Of course, the glory of the salt martyr will be yours, but if it turns out that you can be killed without punishment and for personal gain, there will be market martyrs, wool martyrs, port martyrs . . ."

"Ox martyrs, oak martyrs, pitch martyrs." The bishop laughed. "You've convinced me. Fame there would be, but it will not serve the Church."

"Leszko!" she summoned her helmsman. "Undress. You're going to switch clothes with Father Reinbern."

"There's no way," Leszko began in his usual way. "He's not my father. I'm not baptized."

"That's why you're staying behind. Crow's Wing won't touch one of his own." She smiled. "Besides, he's known you the longest, and he's always seen you with me. If you want, we can tie you up so he doesn't suspect you of helping the bishop."

"All right," Leszko agreed.

She didn't think that Strosz would be angry. Rather, he should be happy that she was solving his problem for him.

"When they let you go, tell Bogusz that my brother will send the horses back. Take the *Salty Sister* to Wolin and don't forget to recite those poems about salt to them when you're leaving."

Leszko was already undressed except for his undergarments. He gave his clothes to the bishop and waited for the priest to change. Astrid turned away.

"Oh, I always want something sweet when I'm in Kołobrzeg to get rid of this salty taste," complained Leszko.

Astrid walked over to him and kissed his cheek.

"There you go."

"If I had known before today that the Lady Astrid would be so warmed up by me in my underclothes I would have steered the *Salty Sister* with no clothes . . . Ouch!" He put a hand to the cheek she'd just slapped.

"Don't cry, that was only a warning." She wagged a finger at him.

"Here you go, young man," Reinbern said as he handed over his habit.

"I don't know if I can fit in this dress," Leszko bragged again. "The bishop's shoulders are far narrower than mine."

"You'll fit," Reinbern assured him. "We always have larger ones made so that there is space for our bellies in the future."

She studied the bishop carefully. Once he put on Leszko's helmet, it would be fine.

"Please stay close to me, and don't speak a word to anyone," she told Reinbern. "We'll ride out by the southern gate and they will probably stop us to ask about the horses. It would be best if you forgot who you were for the entire journey back and only returned to being yourself once we reach Poznań. Who knows what will happen on the way."

"The bishop has to straighten his back, like me," Leszko interrupted.

"Tie him up," she ordered her people.

"Here!" the helmsman decided. "I want to lie right by the altar. Sorry, but does the bishop have a cloak or some fur hidden somewhere here? The stones are cold, and there's no way of knowing how long Crow's Wing will take to realize I need to be freed. Some food would be nice, too, in case my bishopping drags out . . ."

Reinbern found him a cloak.

"Ready?" she asked the bishop.

"With God." He nodded.

She had to turn away because she felt a lump in her throat. She'd had a conversation like this before. Except back then, she'd lost everything. Now, she couldn't care less about what was to come.

23

POLAND

Świętosława was furious with her brother when they found out that Bishop Unger had been detained in Magdeburg.

They were sitting in the hall—she, Bolesław, Emnilda, and the children. Little Otto was playing with a wooden horse. Świętosława was playing hnefatafl with her brother, and Emnilda was embroidering one of Bolesław's shirts with a golden thread. Zarad was cleaning his sword.

"I told you not to send him! Henry knows how important Unger is to you; he'll keep him out of spite. Couldn't you have sent Big Head?"

"Gaudentius," Emnilda corrected her discreetly, cutting the thread. "Archbishop Radim Gaudentius." She tied a perfect knot.

"Oh, what great kin he is," Świętosława snorted. "Even his half brother didn't like him, and anyway, Sobiesław is dead."

"Because of you," Bolesław snapped.

"What do I have to do with this?" she hissed, leaving the board game and walking over to her brother who, instead of replying, waved his hand. "Sobiesław died protecting your back."

"Wanting to catch Jaromir alive," Zarad corrected.

"Please don't bicker," Emnilda requested, speaking louder this time as she threaded the needle. "We need to find a way to get Unger out of Henry's grasp."

"I couldn't have sent Bishop Gaudentius because he can't be relied on to do anything." Bolesław seemed not to have heard his wife. He spoke loudly to his sister as he pushed more pawns off the board. "You need to realize that the pope closest to Otto, Pope Sylvester, is dead. Gaudentius was Otto and Sylvester's man, and today his networks are useless. Henry will do whatever he can to stop me from receiving the crown. Our only hope lay in Unger, in him succeeding to gain Pope John XVIII's favor before Henry does. That's why I sent Brother Barnaby with Unger, the only survivor of the hermitage . . ."

"Yes, all right," she conceded. "And those hermits who were so well positioned in Rome died at Jaksa's hand."

"Don't remind me of that traitor," Bolesław exclaimed, sending the board and pawns flying across the floor. Little Otto abandoned his horse and started to pick up the pieces.

Świętosława understood her brother better than anyone. She still felt the weight of Ion's betrayal on her shoulders.

"Do you always have to shout at each other?" Emnilda asked.

"We aren't shouting at each other," they replied in unison. "We're shouting to each other."

"It's easier to think like this." Świętosława smiled at her sister-in-law, but she lowered her voice. "What will you do with Jaksa? Will you keep him on a leash like I do my monk?"

"No," Bolesław muttered. "I'll send him to an abbey."

Bishop Reinbern of Kołobrzeg, who had recently been brought to them by Astrid, had been listening quietly to their conversation. He stood up and walked over to Bolesław.

"Duke, before you lock up the Redarian in an abbey cell, I advise you to question him again. It's obvious that news of Henry hosting the Redarian and Veleti leaders in Quedlinburg has resulted in widespread horror. But I think that if a man like the Reich king, who is so wholly loyal to the German church, can commit an act so heinous as meeting pagan leaders during Easter, then perhaps there was more agreed between them than an alliance for one battle. You don't have to forgive him if you're not ready, but you need to hear what he has to say. Please."

Świętosława studied Reinbern carefully. He didn't have Unger's strength or his stern charm which buckled knees and inspired confessions in those who saw him, but he certainly looked more trustworthy than the endlessly frightened Gaudentius. Of medium height and slender, Reinbern wore a simple gray woolen dress which he always called the "habit of the exiled bishop," and he never took salt with his food.

She walked over to Bolesław and pulled his arm so that he leaned down to her.

"If you decide to speak to Jaksa, I'll find the courage to face Ion."

Her brother looked at her with surprise.

"Haven't you talked to him yet?" He raised his eyebrows. "Even though Bezprym has spoken in his defense? Why not?"

"For the same reason you haven't spoken to Jaksa." She smiled sadly.

"Bolesław? Świętosława?" Emnilda lay down the unfinished shirt, stood up, and walked over to them. "Why are you whispering?" She studied them fearfully. "I think I prefer it when you shout."

* * *

They left the palatium holding hands. Like the brother and sister they used to be as children. When one of the housekeepers saw them as she was crossing the yard, she fell to her knees and sobbed like a sheep.

"War, there'll be war . . ." she wept.

Bolesław put an arm around his sister and whispered affectionately:

"They feel safer when we shout."

"Mmm." She rested her head on his shoulder. "Is that surprising? They're used to us shouting. Who's first?"

"Jaksa," Bolesław said.

They walked toward the buildings by the ramparts, one of which was the most heavily guarded prison holding. It resembled an enormous barrel because the beams from which it was built were encased in iron fetters. Fully armed men guarded the fitted doors.

"Do you want to speak to him alone?" she asked in a whisper once they'd entered the damp hall. "I can wait outside the door."

"No." He shook his head. "Come with me. I need . . ."

"I'll have your back, I promise."

They walked into the cell with a torch, lighting up the small dark room. It stank of excrement. A rat squealed as it ran from the light, and Świętosława flinched. Bolesław put the torch in the sconce and ordered the guard:

"Leave us. We'll speak to the prisoner alone."

A few months of imprisonment had altered Jaksa beyond recognition. He had always been slender, but now he looked like a skeleton with skin stretched across his bones. His dirty, uncut fair hair fell into his face in matted tangles. His beard reached his chest and covered his cheeks with a whitish-yellow growth. He had thick iron manacles on his wrists and ankles which were attached to the wall by chains. He lifted his head and blinked as the light blinded him.

"Why did you do it?" Bolesław asked.

"What?" Jaksa replied firmly.

Bolesław took a step forward, but Świętosława held his hand and he spoke instead.

"How could you betray me, brother? Have you forgotten who snatched you out of enslavement in Magdeburg all those years ago?"

Jaksa laughed hollowly.

"Have I forgotten?" he said. "No, it's impossible to forget that. Yes, you snatched me away from being a slave in Magdeburg so I might serve you faithfully to repay you for what you'd given me. And so overnight I became your servant."

Bolesław hissed. That wasn't fair.

"Do you know what it's like to be abandoned by your own?" Jaksa adjusted his chains. "First, the Saxons forced my father to hand me over as a hostage. Then they baptized me by force, as if they were raping a child. When the priest of Magdeburg asked me, 'In what language will you declare your faith?' all I could think was: 'A foreign one.' When you released me from Hodo's clutches and sent me back to my father, he sniffed me like a dog and turned me away like a bitch does a pup when she smells a stranger on it. You took me in a second time and I roamed around here like a stray dog."

"That's not true! You were a brother to me."

"By name only. You saved Jaksa's body, but not his soul. You never even realized it, did you? I was always just a servant to you. One of many. But . . . I served you with fervor. Over time, I started to enjoy tracking my own and reaping my revenge. Though I would never have called it sweet. Do you remember when your father forgot himself and called me his 'Redarian wolf'? He touched something deep within me. He had called upon someone I used to be. But then I continued to serve you for years, and all I felt was empty, like a hollow tree. But while you sat in Prague and sent me to Połabie to track . . . I met a boy who looked just like me. Thin, fair-haired, suspicious, and small. Wojrad, son of Wojbor."

"Your nephew? The son of the chieftain who dishonored Bishop Dodilon's body when the Redarians took Bremen?" Bolesław remembered.

"Yes. My brother had fallen, and Wojrad was too young to rule. The Redarians are like a pack of wolves, sometimes they chase away the young of their old chieftain. I didn't go to them to take Wojbor's place, I went to fight for Wojrad's rights, to fight for the boy who made my cold blood boil. And they welcomed me like one of their own. As if I had never served you, as if my father had never exiled me. As if I were one of them."

His pain was almost tangible. Świętosława could feel it like a pulsing ball of air between them. In that moment, she was ready to understand him and forgive him his betrayal. She sighed. She wasn't the one who could forgive him. That was Bolesław's task.

"Seven of our elders were already negotiating the terms of our alliance with Henry. The monks of Międzyrzecz were a sacrifice made as a show of good faith."

"And Henry agreed to it?!"

"It was his idea." Jaksa laughed cruelly.

"Christ!" her brother groaned.

"From what I was told, the Redarians wanted the hermits gone because they were worried the hermitage would become another nest for a crusade against them. And Henry thought that if the hermits who were under your care were harmed, then he would succeed once and for all in severing your ties with Rome. With Otto's empire, the same one that died with the young emperor. Henry knew . . . someone told him that Otto had given you Charlemagne's throne."

"I told him about it myself," Bolesław snorted. "Answer the questions based on your information, not your hatred. Would it be possible to unite the Slavs of Połabie into one great Słowiańszczyzna?"

Jaksa thought about it for a moment.

"No. They're a thorn. Like me."

Bolesław breathed loudly for a moment, and she watched his profile in the flickering torchlight. He couldn't make up his mind. Jaksa kept talking.

"An owl screeched when we were killing them, though I was the only one who heard it. An owl in my head, I thought. Believe me, I wasn't cruel to them, and they acted as if they'd been waiting for death, as if they were ready for it. King Henry? Henry is mad. Firm. There's something about him that cannot be described in words. That's why the Redarians will follow him, and this time they won't back down."

"Do you have any regrets, Jaksa?" Świętosława asked.

He bowed his head and stayed like that for a long time. Eventually, he raised his eyes again.

"I wish that I'd never been born. But I don't regret becoming the man that I am." His lips twisted.

The Redarian wolf no longer wants to attack, she thought.

Bolesław leaned down so he could look directly into Jaksa's eyes.

"Don't regret it if you cannot," he said. "I'll do it for you. I'll mourn for you for the rest of my days, friend."

He stood up and called for the guard. The fitted doors opened with a metallic crunch.

"Unchain the prisoner," he ordered. "Take him to a brighter cell."

He turned back to Jaksa and added:

"I won't condemn you to death. I'll give you a chance to repent for your sins."

They walked outside. Świętosława felt as if she was suddenly hearing dozens of different sounds. Birds, dogs, children playing, and wagon drivers shouting.

The taste of imprisonment is strongest when you're free, she thought, and said aloud:

"Go to Emnilda. I will hear Ion out alone."

She hadn't had the monk kept in a dark cell. She wanted others to see him, so she'd locked him up in a cage where people passed by all the time. It was a humiliation for them both. For him, because children would throw mud and rotten apples at him. For her, because she knew she had trusted this debased creature with her most precious secrets. She had imagined cutting open his throat with a knife many times. Or stabbing him in the heart. Or throwing him into a dungeon that was overrun with rats. She wanted to torture him and have her vengeance. Vengeance for Olav's death.

"Kalle, Hauk!" She greeted the axemen who were guarding him today. "It's almost sundown. Who's replacing you?"

"Egil and Ake, Bold Lady."

"Fat Egil and Loud-Mouthed Ake. My favorites. After you two, Smooth Hauk and Long Kalle. Although . . . why are you called long if you're as tall as Hauk?"

"It's my hidden weapon, Bold Lady. That's why." Kalle nodded, happy she'd asked.

"Hidden weapon, you say? And how do your comrades know about it? Do you show each other your toys before you go to sleep?"

"Ehm . . ." This time, he blushed.

She didn't really want to hear the answer anyway.

"Open the cage, Long Kalle. I'm taking Ion out for a walk."

"My lady," Hauk protested. "You made us swear that we wouldn't let you lash out at him and hurt him . . ."

"That's why you're coming with us. Or behind us, at any rate, at an acceptable distance. Give me the leash. Ion, move your arse. We're going to the banks of the Warta. I find the reeds calm me."

Ion reluctantly got to his feet and cast sullen glances at her. She wrapped the leash around her wrist without thinking, just like she used to do with the lynxes' leash. She pushed the memory away. Wrzask and Zgrzyt.

They walked through the gate and over the bridge. She turned toward the damp fields crisscrossed with streams. How was she meant to begin this conversation?

"Ion," she said eventually, once she felt the soft, damp grass under her shoes. "I want the truth."

"Whose truth, my lady?" he asked.

"Yours. I want to know why you betrayed me."

I won't tell him that I can't sleep because of him. That every night I wonder what might have been had I not poured out my heart to him. That I accuse him and forgive him every morning and every night.

"I'll tell you, my lady," replied Ion, quietly and tonelessly. "Although I'm not sure that my answer will satisfy you. You don't like to hear about Sven."

"Don't tell me what I do and don't like," she snarled. "What did Sven promise you?"

"Nothing. He promised me nothing," Ion said almost sadly, and sighed heavily.

"Nothing?" she asked helplessly. "You betrayed me for nothing?"

"No, you misunderstand. I owed Sven my life. I didn't mention it, because what was the point? Before your husband Eric captured me at Hedeby and brought me back with him as a gift for you, I spent a year in Denmark. I traipsed around the country. I met young King Sven in Roskilde when he came there with his father Harald's body. He arranged a funeral and feasts in his honor. I ate at them. At one of the feasts, when Sven's warriors were as drunk as hogs, one of them grabbed me and said: 'This is a monk! Let's throw him on the royal pyre so Harald may have a priest to serve him up in heaven.' As you can imagine, this amused many of them and encouraged them to entertain themselves at my expense. There was a great fire burning in the yard, but Harald had been placed on a pyre in the royal crypt. They wanted to have some fun, they were drunk, but I was terrified. I wet myself. Sven walked outside just as they were about to throw me into the fire, swinging me by my arms and legs. My habit had started to smoulder. Sven shouted: 'What are you doing, fools?' and ordered them to untie me. One of them, a tall and broad-shouldered bandit, was so drunk that he disagreed with the king. Sven pulled out a knife and killed him. He shouted: 'If I say that someone is to be freed, no one will disobey me!' I was shaking with fear that there might be a brawl because of me, but they all submitted to him, and there was only one corpse by the fire that night. Sven gave me a coin and said: 'Go in peace, monk. Don't let them notice you.'"

She briefly wondered whether Ion was telling the truth. Sven had never bragged about having saved the monk's life. But those words, *"If I say that someone is to be freed, no one will disobey me,"* that was Sven through and through. She could almost see his long red hair dancing in the firelight. The spittle in the corners of his mouth.

"Later, when King Eric invaded us, I met Sven at Hedeby. He was gathering an army. He was asking rich merchants to give him ships with which he could defend the country. They gave him some, but not many. He was boarding the *Bloody Fox* to sail to the Jomsvikings and ask for their help. I was in port searching for a ship that would take me away from the looming war. Sven recognized me and said, 'Monk, now you can repay me. Eric won't kill a holy man. Let him capture you and take you to Sweden, and I'll send my messengers to you. You can . . .'"

"Spy?" she guessed.

"Yes," he answered.

They walked in silence. She could hear the clinking of the metal rings on his collar on which the leash was fastened.

"After Eric's death, you said, 'Your king is already sailing to you,'" she recalled. "You knew it would be him."

He nodded. Moments of their lives flashed before her eyes. How he saved Olof's life by pretending to be a drunk fool. How he stood beside her as she burned the suitors alive. How he looked at Olav Tryggvason when he was her guest in Sigtuna. He had been Sven's spy all along, standing at her side.

"We're turning back," she announced tonelessly.

The rings clinked louder, as if he was trying to move sideways, toward the meandering stream. She'd have preferred him to do it.

"And?" she asked after a while. "Sven came to you after I confessed, and ordered, 'Tell me, Ion, what is it that burdens my wife's conscience?' And you just told him, without pausing to think how many lives you were sacrificing? Without pausing to realize you were destroying my life? You just told him?"

"Yes, my lady," he replied.

"You know what, Ion," she said, "I was probably too harsh to you. The servants probably didn't spoil you. Of course, you surprised me with your tale of Sven the generous, who saved your life all those years ago, but it still isn't enough for me to understand why you did it. If it weren't for the fact that Bezprym has pleaded with me to spare your life, Bezprym whom I love as if he were my own . . . If it weren't for Ostry's assurances that you faithfully aided their mission, I would strangle you with my bare hands, because until this moment I thought there was a reason for your actions. Something. A great reward Sven had promised or given you. I would bear the betrayal better if I thought you'd sold me out. For silver, privileges, women, anything. But you have hidden too many secrets under your monk's habit. Under the guise of serving God, you shared my deepest secrets and in one stroke condemned so many to die. You could have lied to Sven! You, who never tried to hide the women you had in your hut by the church, could have added this one more to your list of sins. If you wanted to humiliate me, you could have lied to Sven and told him something awful. That I have a lover among the servants or guards, anything to avoid betraying me. I don't have enough strength to deal with you, Ion. God will judge you. I refuse to pass sentence."

24

POLAND

Bolesław was in his element—the element of war. He had lost the white mare on whose back he'd ridden into and out of Prague, and now he rode a majestic snowy stallion he called White.

He had summoned nine companies of heavy infantry, each one counting three hundred warriors and as many shield-bearers. He hadn't deprived his country of its defenses; he wasn't naïve. His Moravian crews protected it from the south. The Hungarians remained loyal for Bezprym's sake and thanks to his hosting Bruno, the emperor's brother, in Prague. He had taken two-thirds of his troops to war, and he left the rest to guard the eastern and northern borders. He couldn't be sure of the north after Astrid and Reinbern's reports. The east had never been safe. Of course, he had never admitted to the Bold One that he had considered marrying her to one of the Russian knyazes after Sobiesław's death. It was easier to make plans while away from home than tell her in Poznań when he was forced to look into her mismatched eyes. He gave it up, deciding that he didn't have enough time.

Henry had chosen to gather his army at the borough of Leitzkau, by the river Elbe, not far from Magdeburg. Bolesław tripled his defenses on the border and waited in the middle of them, in Krosno by the Oder. He sent scouts out to the west, and he waited. He divided up the companies equally, three to each line of defense. He kept Bjornar, sent Zarad to the first line, Stojgniew, son of Mieszko's flagbearer Wolrad, to the third. He stayed on the second.

I'll manage without you, Jaksa, he thought every night before he fell asleep and every morning when he awoke. He had Derwan, who had come from Gunzelin; the scout from Meissen had wanted to serve Bolesław since the night of the fight in the woods anyway. Bolesław had paid for him in silver; he knew how much it cost to raise and train a good warrior. He didn't regret it. He paid for Jaksa's loss in bile. Derwan moved between the soldiers and the scouts like living silver.

"My lord!" he reported, stopping his foaming horse. "Henry and his men have crossed the Elbe, and the Czech duke Jaromir has joined them on the other side. We have a moment to breathe. Their guides are Margrave Gunzelin's men."

"They won't fail?"

"They will!" Derwan laughed. "But not us. They'll fail Henry's troops."

They led them through the forests on along the river's banks, into wetlands and marshes. The heavy infantry sank into the soft ground.

"Apparently, they can hear the rusałka's* garish songs," Derwan whispered. "The ones which make your eyelids heavy and stop your limbs from obeying you. The guides disappeared as soon as they led the troops into the bogs. They dissolved as if they had been nothing but mist."

Bolesław didn't want to celebrate too soon. He knew that in their war of fears, Henry had strong allies. He had imprisoned Unger and surrounded himself with bishops even while in his war camp. Maybe he thought he'd protect himself from the charms of the marshy maids by reciting the litany out loud? Besides, he could count on new guides to be supplied by his pagan allies.

Three days later, it turned out Bolesław had been right. Derwan brought news:

"They reached the river Spree. Exhausted and frightened, but they reached the bank and have made camp."

Good, thought Bolesław. *They have reached my first line of defense. Now Zarad can play his part; he loves this.*

Zarad had hidden a troop of heavily armed soldiers and a few hundred archers in a solitary little wood by the river. He had built fences to hide them. It hadn't been long before Derwan came back.

"My lord! Master Zarad has struck a blow!"

"Tell me!" Bolesław ordered with satisfaction.

"The vassals of Bishop Arnulf of Halberstadt, the four lords Thiedbern, Bernard, Bennon, and Izys, led their squads into the wood. They wanted to impress King Henry and had heard from the locals that one of your companies was hidden there. They went in without sending scouts first. The cut trees looked so innocent when they rode in, but they were sitting ducks for Master Zarad's men. Thiedbern was the first to fall, and the rest soon followed. Nobody survived, and now there is mourning in the royal camp. The king has ordered that nobody is to make any unsanctioned moves."

Bolesław thought deeply about Zarad's next orders. Should he leave him on the backs of Henry's army? It was tempting, but dangerous for his friend.

* A rusałka is a creature of folklore, a female associated with water who is often malicious toward mankind, though they used to be associated with fertility. They are sometimes said to be the souls of women who died near water, come back to haunt their place of death. They often resemble mermaids in popular culture.

Zarad loved to take risks, but he had a hundred men under his command, and he was a responsible leader.

Derwan brought more news that night.

"Duke, Henry has new guides. He's found a ford across the Spree and his army is marching toward the Oder. The Redarians and Veleti are approaching from the north. Their forces will join Henry's any day now."

"I need to see this!" Bolesław shook his head.

He rode out beyond Krosno's ramparts with a dozen men. They crossed the river Bóbr and entered the woods. He kept the second line of defense on the right bank of the Bóbr and had lookout points hidden among the trees on its western banks. Set up to be just within sight of each other, they were used to pass on any orders or information about the enemy's movements. They reached the lookout point farthest to the west, by the river Lubsza. He left his horse and climbed the rope ladder until he reached the platform nestled in the crown of an enormous beech tree. A tall, slender scout who was standing watch almost choked when he saw the duke in the branches.

"What's your name?" asked Bolesław.

"Przebor," he whispered.

"Then move over, Przebor, unless you want me to fall."

The view from the top was impressive. The beech towered over the other trees.

"A sea of trees," Bolesław said to himself as he gazed around him at the crowns rippling in the breeze.

Lubsza looked like a narrow ribbon from his vantage point. It was more of a stream than a river. The camp stretched along the other bank as far as the eye could see.

"White sheets," Przebor spoke up shyly. "It's Henry's camp. The royal tent is there, between the trees, you can recognize it by the gold sheets. The pagans have set up in the south, it's hard to see them because they hide their tents between bushes to avoid open space. They'll be coming out soon . . ."

"How do you know?"

"If you look at that birch, my lord"—Przebor pointed—"you'll see the lookout there signaling to us."

The powerful branch was moving up and down.

"Does that mean they are going to attack?" he asked with interest.

"No, my lord." The boy blushed. "They're just going to talk. To signal that they're preparing for battle, there will be spades pushed out among the branches."

Bolesław heard them before he saw them. The water carried their song, at first quietly, but it grew louder when the singers emerged from the bushes.

"That's a battle song, Duke," Przebor said.

"I've heard it before." He nodded.

A woman dressed in white, carrying a huge circular sieve, walked in front of the soldiers, with two others on either side of her carrying jugs of water that they poured through the sieve every few dozen steps. A priest with long, almost black hair carried Swarożyc's statue over his head.

Strosz Crow's Wing, he thought, remembering Astrid's news.

A group of boys followed him, dressed in white just like the woman. A high-pitched, unearthly whistle emerged from their pipes. The priests riding white horses came after them. He counted seven. Then came the soldiers, singing their battle song like wind passing over a field, forcing the grass to bend under its strength.

"Look, Duke, the king is riding out to meet them."

He recognized Henry by his scarlet cloak. Henry II, the Christian ruler of the Reich, the one who was fighting for the sacred imperial crown, rode out to meet Swarożyc's followers on a black horse. Flagbearers rode before him, bearing the royal flag and, of course, a great cross.

It's happened, Bolesław thought. *The cross and Swarożyc have united against me. I would never have believed it if I weren't seeing it with my own eyes.*

"Przebor, can you point out the duke of Bohemia, Jaromir?"

"The Bohemian tents are on the edge of Henry's camp." The scout pointed. "The three men over there always move together. They are the only ones who attend the councils by the golden tent, so one of them must be Jaromir."

The Redarian army came to a halt. The boys stopped playing their pipes. The seven priests rode over to the king and his procession. They discussed something aggressively for a long time, after which Henry and his men whirled around their horses and returned to their camp.

Have they argued? Bolesław wondered hopefully.

He saw their strength. He counted their troops. Even without the pagans' help, facing them would be a challenge. Henry had twenty companies of heavy infantry to match his nine. The Redarians and Veleti were comprised of light infantry, but they were fierce, wild, and cruel adversaries. His hope that they would leave Henry evaporated when he saw that the priests and Swarożyc's statue followed Henry.

"Oh my . . ." Przebor groaned. "I'd never have believed it . . ."

The king dismounted, the priests did the same, and they all walked into the golden tent together. Strosz Crow's Wing, holding Swarożyc's statue, and the flagbearer with the royal flag stood on either side of the tent of the war council.

"It's time for me to go, Przebor." Bolesław clapped the boy on the shoulder. "Are you afraid?" he asked, looking into his eyes.

"No, my lord. I'm not afraid now."

Bolesław returned to the heavily fortified Krosno and sent messengers to Poznań with orders for Emnilda and the children: *go to Ostrów Lednicki immediately*. They would be safe there, in the family nest his father had built, on the island connected to the mainland by only two bridges that could be burned at any moment. His second order was for Poznań's castellan: *be prepared to defend the city*. The third was for Stojgniew, who had command of the final line of defense on the right bank of the Obra River: *It's not good. We need a mass mobilization*.

Henry and his allies had walked over to the river Bóbr. Bolesław could almost see them from Krosno's ramparts. He was sure that their supplies were running low, and while their horses found plenty to graze on nearby, the people would find nothing to sustain them. That's how Bolesław started every war; he ordered the peasants to bring any supplies they had to the boroughs and to burn the rest. A hungry enemy grows less fierce; there were many armies who surrendered for the simple reason that they were famished.

"They're building bridges," Derwan reported. "They're making large rafts. They're determined to cross the Bóbr as quickly as possible."

"Have they found the ford?"

"No."

There was a ford, and it was wide and shallow. The warm, dry summer had lowered the water levels and Bolesław was afraid that they would find it any day now.

Bjornar woke him at dawn. He had been sleeping deeply but dragged himself out of the darkness of dreams as soon as he felt a hand on his arm.

"Duke . . . they found the ford."

"Are you sure?" he shouted at Bjornar as he leaped out of bed and pulled the leather caftan onto his shirt.

"The first legion is already on its way."

"Where's my helm?" He couldn't find anything in the half darkness.

He ran out of the chamber without it, heading for the ramparts. The sun hadn't risen, but the first thing he saw were Henry's infantrymen crossing the river.

"My horse! The white one!" he shouted, running back down into the yard. "Attack!"

Henry's archers protected the troops who marched across the river. The camp on the other side was almost entirely packed up. Bolesław was under no illusions that he could stop the Reich's armies, but he had a plan. A risky one, but since the united forces of Henry and the pagans were marching against him, he had no choice.

He had already mounted White and was riding out to lead his troops with his sword in his hand. Bjornar rode beside him, holding the Holy Spear.

"The Spear with the cross's relic against Swarożyc!" he shouted to his men, standing up in his stirrups. "Who has everything to lose, loses nothing by fighting for it! Face the enemy!"

"Glory!" they replied loudly, and they followed him.

He tightened his grip on the sword and squeezed White with his knees.

"Glory!" he said through gritted teeth.

The first of Henry's infantrymen had reached land. As soon as they stepped out of the water, though, they were felled by spears and swords. Bolesław moved through them as easily as a knife through butter. He led his men through the shallows, pushing Henry's men into the water. The river turned red with blood. Two shield-bearers rode in front of Bjornar and the Spear, protecting him from arrows. Bjornar held the spear high over his head. There was a bustle on the other bank. The archers sent arrow after arrow their way from behind a wall of shields, but Henry stopped any further troops from crossing the river.

He wants to pull me onto his side of the river, Bolesław thought as he realized he was already halfway across. *I'd do the same thing if I were him.*

His men were almost finished slaying the heavily armed infantrymen who had tried to cross.

"Shields!" Bolesław shouted, and a wall of shields rose in front of him and Bjornar.

"You're not wearing a helm!" Bjornar hissed at him.

Only now did Bolesław realize that himself. At that moment, the Redarian priests began to sing their battle song. The bishops surrounding Henry responded to its wild sounds with a psalm. The Saxon army joined in.

Who may ascend onto the hill of the Lord?
Or who may stand in His holy place?
He who has clean hands and a pure heart,
who has not lifted up his soul to an idol,
nor sworn deceitfully.

Bolesław felt his blood boil. *Liars,* he thought, and sang out:

Truly God is good to Israel,
to those who are pure of heart.

Then he took the Spear out of Bjornar's hand and lifted it high above his head as he screamed:

"Your alliance will do you no good! This Spear has a piece of the cross in it, bishops! Have you no shame? Henry! Are these the actions of a Christian king? Spearmen," he hissed, and they understood what he wanted of them.

They threw twelve spears which soared through the air together, hitting the western bank like a symbolic barrier.

"Retreat!" Bolesław shouted, and White whirled around on his haunches.

The arrows flew after them, but they were fast. They lost only three men.

Only? he thought bitterly as he rode out of the water. *What if those are the three men I need in Poznań?*

White meandered agilely between the bodies of Henry's slain infantrymen. Bolesław looked down. Some of them were still alive. They were in their death throes, choking on blood from their pierced lungs. He felt nothing. Not even pity.

"We need to retreat back behind the third line of defense! Behind the river Obra!" The command spread among the troops and his soldiers set off.

They had a head start; for an army that big to cross, even through the shallows, would have to take Henry a day or two. Bolesław suspected that the Reich king would try to stop for the night at the abbey in Międzyrzecz to repent for his sins and pray for forgiveness for his role in bringing about the hermits' deaths.

How does it feel to have ordered the death of monks? he wondered. *Do his bishops know the price he paid for his alliance with the Redarians?*

"Are you sure that Bezprym heeded your orders and went to Ostrów with Duchess Emnilda?" asked Bjornar when they had stopped to rest.

"No," Bolesław admitted honestly. "I suspect he's in Międzyrzecz because he would have insisted on escorting Jaksa and Ion there personally. That's why I will give you command of the troops. You'll take them to cross the river Obra and join forces with Stojgniew. I'll take a squad to Międzyrzecz to fetch my son. If he'll listen to anyone, it'll be me. I will not allow him to stand face-to-face with Henry. I don't trust a king who has struck a friendship with pagans."

"After what happened, Henry should have sent you Jaromir bound in chains," Bjornar observed.

"He would gain nothing in doing that," spat Bolesław. "Jaromir is an obedient vassal. My God, when I heard the stories about how he bent the knee to Henry with all of Prague watching as he accepted his new position . . ."

"And now we have the enemy's great army in our country." Bjornar shook his head.

Bolesław slapped the redhead's shoulder.

"Great and hungry." He laughed. "Go to Stojgniew. Do you know what to do?"

"Yes, my lord!" His friend nodded.

He'd been wrong. Bezprym wasn't in Międzyrzecz. What was once the hermitage had been rebuilt into an abbey. Brother Barnaby, the only survivor of the slaughter because he had been fortunate enough to have been delayed on his journey back from Rome, was now rotting in some Magdeburgian cell alongside Unger. Father Remigius had stepped in to fill his shoes for the time being.

"The young prince didn't come," he announced. "The castellan's men were the ones who brought us Ion and Jaksa."

"Father Remigius, war is raging. In two or three days, King Henry and his bishops are likely to come here. If you want, I can give you an escort to take you to Poznań."

"No, my lord." The monk shook his head. "Our Lord forgave His pursuers as He hung on the cross. We will not fear to face them either. We'll stay."

"I want to ask you something, Father," began Bolesław. "Don't let the king speak to you alone. Mention what happened, and to what Jaksa confessed, in front of his bishops. If you're not afraid, that is."

"Will you stay the night, my lord?" the monk asked. They were walking out of the church.

"No. War is calling."

Father Remigius nodded and, walking over to the wood alongside the duke, added:

"We can hear the hoots of an owl from dusk until dawn every night. It's the same owl." He pointed at a powerful ash nearby. "It's somewhere there. It calls out in time for the litany. It's very accurate . . ."

Bolesław was in a hurry and glanced down at the monk from his saddle.

". . . just like Brother Benedict, may he rest in peace. The martyrs are watching over us, my lord, so how can I be afraid? I will not meddle in the affairs of this world, but I will not refuse you. I understand that I should also mention the need to free Bishop Unger and our Brother Barnaby within the bishops' hearing?"

"Yes. And about Brother Bruno of Querfurt if you can. Henry and Bishop Tagino were meant to give him permission to come to Poland as a missionary, but they really don't want to do that, though they must know we won't let them forget about Bruno. They can't keep him in the Reich forever. Tagino may be with Henry, so you'll be hosting the elite," he added sarcastically.

Remigius's silver eyes looked steadily at Bolesław.

"It is an honor for me to host my duke," he replied. "I will admit the elite of Rome because it is a Christian thing to do, to host people, but I would feel much better if you stopped them at the border."

"Sometimes the situation requires you to let an intruder into your home," Bolesław said in farewell. "Just so you can slam the door shut behind him."

Henry's armies met no resistance once they crossed the river Obra. Abandoned villages with empty cowsheds and troughs. Chicken coops with no chickens or eggs. Fields with no wheat. Covered-up wells. Stray dogs barking at them as they passed. The harvest had been gathered before the war had begun.

"I'd poison the apples in the orchards if I could," Bolesław said when Derwan was giving his report.

"Zarad crossed the river Oder with his three companies a day after Henry's men. They're plaguing him with skirmishes every night."

Bolesław joined Stojgniew's companies with his own and split them into two final lines of defense, a mile and two miles away from Poznań. He gave Stojgniew command of the mass mobilization and Bjornar led the shield-bearers. Neither of them left Henry's flanks untouched. The tired and hungry army of the Reich lords began to slow. The Redarians and Veleti were furious that there was nothing for them to plunder on the way. They would set empty villages on fire out of sheer helpless rage.

"The peasants won't have to concern themselves with burning fields this year," joked Bolesław, though he wasn't particularly amused.

Despite their hunger and exhaustion, despite the attacks they had to parry each time they stopped to rest, the army of invaders marched onward. Bolesław summoned his chieftains.

"We have to lure them into a trap. Tonight. Stojgniew, are the villages ready?"

"Yes, my lord. The villagers have left, and armed soldiers wait in the huts with torches ready. They're burning fires so the smoke from the chimneys makes it look like the people are still there. The peasants from the mass mobilization are wandering in the yards and chasing cows back and forth to make them roar all the louder and attract Henry's men. They even have some goats to act as bait."

"How many villages like that do we have?"

"Seven, my lord. If a troop goes to each one, then we'll deprive the main army of a few hundred men. The peasants are fierce enough to march on Kiev when they're protecting their own," Stojgniew bragged.

"Later"—Bolesław laughed—"I'll wait in the front of our last line of defense. Hurry up. I want prisoners, the nobility and the wounded. This could be the best way to end the war quickly. Don't take the pagans, kill them where they stand, other than their priests. Go with God!"

Ostry greeted him when he returned.

"We have guests, my lord."

"Who?"

"The Bold One's axemen."

"Brilliant!"

"And . . ."

"Speak faster. I'm in a hurry."

"And your sister, my lord, but she's not alone. Bezprym is with her."

"Christ! Don't I have enough to deal with?" he groaned. "Take me to them."

As he might have expected, Świętosława felt no embarrassment. She laughed aloud when she saw him and rode over to him, stroking her mare's black neck. White neighed as if he were happy to see her.

"You look like a bandit!" she greeted him. "You have a Viking's beard, and you haven't washed your hair either. Do you even change your clothes anymore?" She sniffed as she kissed his cheek. "No, you don't."

"This isn't a suitable place for a queen and young prince."

"Nonsense! Where is your son to learn how to fight wars if not at his father's side?"

He'd rather not think about that. He had no idea what would happen to Bezprym next. Świętosława seemed to sense his quandary because she pulled him closer and he leaned in to hear her whisper:

"Jaromir may have tied up his testicles, but he left his vitals intact. If you keep avoiding him, it will be like you're cutting it off yourself. Do you understand?"

He was speechless. Perhaps the Bold One was right.

"All right, Bezprym can stay, but you're going back to Poznań."

"You'd have to escort me yourself. I'm not going anywhere."

"Did Emnilda listen to me at least? Did she go to Ostrów Lednicki?"

"Of course she did," replied his sister. "Along with Sława, little Otto, and Mieszko. They are safe in the palatium on the island. The nest of the Piast dynasty has welcomed back its children. Although thankfully Mieszko wasn't happy about it, so we know the boy doesn't lack courage." She narrowed her eyes cheerfully. "You should have let him come, too. The boy is fifteen and has more than water running through his veins. He would get along better with Bezprym if you just gave them a chance . . ."

"Stop!" he shouted at his sister. "War is not the time to discipline children."

"Isn't it?" she asked. "Did Father keep you locked up safe and sound? Do you think you'd be half the warrior you are if he hadn't dragged you along with him from camp to camp? Or maybe you're such a great duke that you think you were just made this way, huh?"

"Jesus, Bold One! Will you shut up? I don't have time to argue with you."

"When do you want to talk then?" She shrugged. "You spent a year in Prague. Believe it or not, time didn't stand still while you were gone."

He wanted to retort that he finally understood why Sven had sent her away, but he bit his tongue. It was better not to bring up certain things, especially as his sister was still blessedly unaware that Olav and Tyra's marriage had been his idea.

A fair-haired warrior he didn't recognize rode up to Świętosława. He had a scar which ran across his cheek from his forehead to his throat. They spoke briefly in the tongue of the north, and Bolesław didn't understand a word. His sister introduced her guest.

"This is Omold, Olav's bard. Astrid saved him from the battle. He doesn't speak our tongue yet, but he's learning. I bought him from the Lady of Wolin."

"A bard? Why the hell do I need a bard?"

"Not for hell, for fame! How do you expect to be remembered if there will be no songs written of your battle outside Poznań's gates?"

"How will he sing about it if he doesn't know our tongue?" he retorted.

"He'll write his verses in his own and I'll translate."

He'd had enough of his sister and the havoc she had already wreaked with her arrival. At least he didn't have to worry about her safety, because as soon as she rode away, Great Ulf and his axemen surrounded her. Wilkomir approached him.

"How did you survive with her for so many years?" he asked his old friend.

"I had a long break when Sven carried her off." Wilkomir shrugged. "When are you expecting the first of Henry's men?"

"Tomorrow. We have to wait for Zarad, Stojgniew, and Bjornar to close their pincers. We can attack the first group he sends, scatter them and let a few ones escape to report to the king, and then return to our positions to await the main body of the royal army."

"What if Henry sends in the Veleti first?"

"He won't. They slowed him down so much that Derwan says he doesn't even want to talk to their priests anymore. His rest in Międzyrzecz did its job, too. Apparently, he was crying over the brothers' graves, and the bishops turned their noses up at his alliance with the pagans."

"He cried," repeated Wilkomir disdainfully. "Right on time. That's royal logic for you. Kill, then regret the act."

Bolesław said nothing. He thought about himself. About how he hadn't had a chance to go to confession since he'd blinded the Red One.

There were one hundred heavy infantrymen in the troops Henry had sent ahead, but when Bolesław attacked, a third turned and ran without even waiting for the battle to begin.

"Archers!" commanded Bolesław. "Stop them!"

"They're really tired," said Bezprym, who stood next to him on the hill.

"Individual battles can be won with strength and courage. And sometimes with good tactics and cunning," he told his son. "But the outcomes of war are often determined by illness, exhaustion, and hunger. I knew he'd send a big army, but I didn't think it would be so big."

"The dukes of the Eastern Reich are still sympathetic to your cause, although even among Otto's men I heard some of the ones farther in the country call you a 'conceited braggart' and 'a duke who reached beyond his station.'"

Bolesław couldn't focus on his conversation with his son. He was watching the fighting, which was only beginning. He hissed when he thought he saw Ostrowod wounded by a spear. Bezprym fell silent and they both watched the soldiers. The duke breathed a sigh of relief when he saw Ostry sit back up in his saddle. Świętosława and Omold suddenly appeared beside them.

"The bard has to have a better view of the battle," she announced. "Oh, Bolesław! I'm so happy! Father could never have dreamed up a better moment. Look at that oak tree. How often did we race toward it while Father watched?"

He glanced at the majestic, lonely tree which stood a fair distance from the road. There was an enormous eagle sitting on its branch, watching the chaos of battle.

That's when he realized that nobody, and especially not the Bold One, even considered that they might lose. He didn't either, in fact. Though he knew he hadn't won yet, he was certain he had exhausted Henry, who would soon be forced to adjust his expectations.

As the sun set, the king's messengers appeared with a white flag mounted on a spear and met Bolesław's men in the middle of the road. Henry's wounded were loaded onto carts and taken away. Crows circled above the corpses.

The eagle took off and flew toward Poznań.

25

⚮

POLAND

Świętosława was content. She was riding Thorhalla. She gave all her mares the same name, in honor of the horse she'd been riding when Olav had arrived in Sweden aboard *Kanugård*. This black mare was the fifth Thorhalla. Świętosława recalled her father's words as she watched the Reich army hurriedly erecting their camp by the road leading west out of Poznań: *"Do I expect danger? I'd be a fool if I wasn't always prepared for it,"* he'd told them that midsummer's night on the bank of the Warta. He'd spread his arms wide while the hawk hunted in the sky above them. Mieszko had laughed as he'd added: *"I'm not afraid of it. Fear takes away a person's freedom, it's a paralytic more effective than any wound."*

Yes, Father, you were right. And thanks to you, I don't fear threats. Henry's armies may be a mere two miles from Poznań, but they are the ones who are wounded and weak from hunger. Your son risked everything because he could have lost everything. I don't know what we might gain by negotiating for peace, but Bolz won't rest until he's crushed Henry. This is his Theophanu, Father. You competed with the empress for as long as I can remember; Bolz has Henry. The golden emperor, Otto, awoke the king inside my brother when he gave him the Holy Spear, his own diadem, and Charlemagne's throne. Ostry may have chopped the throne to pieces to stop Jaromir from laying his hands on it, but who cares about an old chair? What matters is that my brother feels worthy of the man who used to sit on it, because that's how Otto saw him. By fighting Henry, Bolesław is fighting for a great Poland. For a country which will unite the Slavs under its wings and will refuse to bow to the empire. Isn't that what you wanted, Mieszko? If Otto were still alive, Bolz would probably already be wearing the crown and the empire might have made the dream of a country with equal kingdoms and no borders come true. Italy, Gaul, Germania, and Słowiańszczyzna would be an edifice supported by four columns. But visionaries and mystics die young, like Olav, and Otto succumbed to death while God placed Henry the Bird King on Bolesław's path. Henry, the man Bolesław hates and despises. It gives him the strength that standing up to Theophanu gave you. But you betrayed her as often as you sided with her, while Bolesław will never stand beside Henry, he will always oppose him. Their fates have been woven together forever; I will make sure Omold writes the song that will be repeated long after grass or trees grow on our graves. You wanted me to be queen of Sweden. I said, "Very well, Father," never suspecting that the first throne would lead to a second, which would conquer a third. I received the crown of Norway over the dead body of the man with whom I wanted to share it.

I am not wallowing in self-pity as I know you would not feel sorry for me in your afterlife. You probably raised a triumphant toast to the queen of three kingdoms. We were not born free, but we can rejoice in being alive sometimes. And today, when the bloodred sun is setting over a wounded and hungry enemy camp that is singing mourning songs outside Poznań's gates, I am proud to be a Piast, Mieszko's daughter and Bolesław's sister. Świętosława. Sigrid Storråda. The queen of three thrones of the north. I thank God, you, and Dobrawa. I thank my husbands and my lover. Amen.

Two days later, the horns in Poznań announced the arrival of guests. Świętosława sat beside Bolesław in the palatium's audience hall under the golden cross and Saint Peter's sword as Henry's messengers approached. Bolesław had had time to shave and wash his hair, and he was resplendent with his red tunic stretched over his wide chest and a white cloak fastened with a golden brooch shaped like an eagle. Świętosława also wore bloodred and snowy white fabrics so that they might look like the royal siblings they were, and Helga had arranged her hair into a crown of braids.

Neither Duszan nor Dusza are with us, she suddenly thought, childishly.

"Archbishop of Magdeburg, Tagino, Bishop Arnulf, Margrave Udo, and the canons Thomas and Ederam."

"Perhaps my guests are hungry?" the cunning fox, her brother Bolesław, asked, knowing it had been a long time since they'd eaten. "I would be pleased if you agreed to share a modest meal with me."

"We have come to talk, not eat"—Tagino swallowed—"but if the duke insists . . ."

Bolz clapped his hands and the servants brought in trestles on which they put tables and spread fabrics woven with gold thread over them. It took no more than a moment. The guests sat as the servants brought in the dishes. There were roasted piglets on enormous platters stuffed with apples or grits; deer thighs laden with wreaths of summer pears; rabbits roasted with carrots and bacon; tenches and pikes in thick cream; chopped boar meat with junipers and berries; hot, fragrant bread; fresh butter; jugs of mead and the wines they received from Astrid. The scent of roasted meat spread across the hall and Tagino was already reaching out his hands for a piglet when Bolesław ceremoniously announced:

"Let us pray before feasting! Do my guests no longer feel the need to pray?"

She could have giggled.

"I do not have Bishop Unger of Poznań with me"—Bolesław's pained tone sounded sincere—"but Kołobrzeg's Bishop Reinbern is here on a pastoral visit. Noble Reinbern, as a host I ask you to lead our prayers."

Reinbern, knowing what he was really being asked, prayed for a long time. Long enough for everyone to hear the guests' stomachs growling.

"Amen," he finished.

Bolesław encouraged them:

"Eat and drink from my table, everyone!"

"Golden Styrian wine." She smiled at the pretty servant. "Fill it to the brim."

Neither she nor Bolesław ate. They redirected the platters to their guests, who could no longer contain their hunger.

"Only bread and water for me," her brother announced loudly, sweeping hair from his forehead.

Tagino froze mid-bite. He swallowed and asked:

"Is the great duke fasting?"

"In the intention of regaining Bishop Unger," replied Bolesław. "You, Archbishop, have the pleasure of seeing him when you're not accompanying your king to war. I cannot feast knowing that my beloved shepherd may be sitting in Magdeburg with nothing but bread and water to sustain him. I will therefore join him in fasting."

"I can deny that," said Tagino. "Unger is coming to no harm in Magdeburg."

"Really?" asked Świętosława. "Then why do you keep him there against his will? Why has he not yet returned to his diocese?"

"There are still some matters of a canonical nature which must be resolved, Duchess," he replied.

"Queen," she reprimanded him gently.

"No." The archbishop shook his head, disgruntled to be dragged into a conversation before he'd had a chance to eat his fill. "My lady, your husband is not a king. We heard about the situation with Otto's diadem, but that was not a coronation!"

"Bolesław is not my husband," she replied in between sips of wine.

Tagino was dumbfounded.

"Why?" She acted surprised. "Does a man have to wed a woman if he wants to share a house with her where you come from?"

"My lady . . ." the archbishop of Madgeburg whispered with horror as he gazed at Bolesław, his cheeks burning. "I thought you're hosting us in the company of your wife, Duchess Emnilda, but I see you wanted to dishonor the messengers with the presence of your con . . . con . . . concubine."

"I wanted no such thing," replied Bolesław. "This is my sister, Świętosława, Queen of Sweden, Denmark, and Norway."

She smiled radiantly at them and raised her goblet.

"To our guests!" she called out.

Magdeburg's canon Ederam covered his mouth to stop himself from laughing aloud.

"Oh," Tagino whispered. "I am honored . . . Forgive me, my queen, I didn't know . . ."

Bolesław nudged her under the table as if he were worried she was going to confess that her husband had exiled her because she'd conspired with her lover to kill him and take his kingdom. She gave him a look to ease his mind.

They waited for their guests to sate their hunger, which took a deliciously long time. Eventually, Archbishop Tagino began to speak.

"King of the Reich and of Italy, Henry II, is generously offering you peace, Duke."

"That's nice," replied her brother without a shadow of a smile.

"He wants to establish a new border, at the place his army has reached . . ."

She snorted in laughter while beside her Bolesław laughed long and hard.

"Bohemia will not be ruled by you, and it is the king's wish that you accept his appointment of Duke Jaromir," Tagino continued, hesitantly, once Bolesław had stopped laughing.

"I can agree to that. But I will not change my borders," her brother replied coldly, and added: "Give me back Unger! Let my missionary bishop Bruno go free. Leave here and go back to where you came from. If you don't, my sated and rested troops will attack you like wolfhounds tomorrow!"

"We will fight," the archbishop replied.

"Fight then!" Bolesław shouted.

Silence fell.

"The king will not accept these terms," Tagino announced quietly. "Retreat from the lands across the river Elbe. Stop stirring up the lords of the Reich in the east against the king. Forgive . . ."

"Forgive us our sins, my Lord," Świętosława said sweetly.

"My sister is right. Only God can forgive us our sins," Bolesław said firmly. "He will judge you for your alliance with the pagans. For murdering the hermits. For trampling all over God's commandments. I do not forgive you."

He negotiated with them. He let only Łużyce and Milsko go. They swore to let Bruno and Unger go free, though it pained them to do so. And they were to leave before dawn.

When a disgruntled Tagino rose from the table with his companions, Świętosława approached Canon Ederam.

"My lord," she said to him, "I watched you all evening. I don't believe what they say."

"What does my queen mean?" He frowned.

"That someone like you could have allied himself with a king and pagans to stand against my brother."

Ederam said nothing. He looked at her, and it was enough.

"There is so much food left over from the feast," her brother worried. "Would you like to take some with you for your lord?" he asked with what could almost pass for concern and snapped his fingers at a servant.

One appeared with a basket momentarily and gathered the food from the table.

They were left alone. Sister and brother.

"What are you thinking?" she asked as she poured herself more wine.

"This peace will choke him like the leftovers from the feast," he said, stretching. "I will fight him for Milsko and Łużyce for as long as it takes to get them back. This agreement won't last forever. If Gunzelin dies, I will take Meissen without hesitation. And then I will be satisfied. But I will not be content until he's dead. I will feast on his corpse."

"Stop that!" She hit his arm. "Have a drink. You saved your country today."

26

ENGLAND

Sven did not stay in England for long. The locals called that year "the year of the hunger." The breadbaskets were almost empty, and he had an enormous army to feed. "Silver cannot sustain men and that's all we have!" Jorun said after having returned from another village with merely a bag of rotten apples and a single chicken.

After Sven pillaged the wealthy Norwich and received danegeld from East Anglia's ealdorman Ulfcetel, he accepted an invitation to York from Elfhelm, the vassal of southern Northumbria, and his two sons Ufegeat and Wulfheah. His host insisted that Sven's visit remain a secret because he claimed that "King Ethelred has eyes everywhere." He rode out to meet Sven and his men with a procession that hardly resembled an ealdorman's retinue.

"I want to prove to you that I'm your friend, King Sven," he said. "I want to show you the country and convince you that here, in Northumbria, your countrymen live with us in peace. The Danish settlers are frugal and resourceful. They are hard workers. There was even once . . ."

"There was even once a Danish vassal in York. My father's brother-in-law, his sister's husband Eric Bloodaxe," Sven interjected.

"That may not have been the best example," the vassal said with embarrassment. "Eric was exiled because of his quick temper . . ."

"It's all right, Elfhelm." Sven laughed. "We all know that he didn't earn his name thanks to a love for chopping wood." *What are you getting at?* he wanted to ask. *What are you offering me?* He saw no purpose in this small talk and wanted to get to the point.

The ealdorman was clearly uncomfortable being rushed and wanted to lay a stable foundation for whatever he was going to offer, but Sven didn't want to be managed.

"I want to make a deal with you," the ealdorman said eventually. "I have many rich lands, and places where you can build watchtowers on my shores. All I need are good men and excellent chieftains. Someone I could entrust with defending us . . ."

"Against the Vikings?" Sven smiled.

The English had been trying to hire the invaders to protect them from other invaders for years. It suited the younger sons waiting at home, who never had a chance to inherit their own land, to come and fight on this coast, but even they soon grew bored with playing the role of faithful protectors of a foreign kingdom. And sooner or later, they always clashed with the locals.

That's why he's showing me around the area. He chuckled to himself. *He wants me to see the peaceful settlements to convince me that this time, it could work.*

"Why are you talking to me about it? If you had any sense, Ealdorman, you'd have approached one of the lesser chieftains, one of the ones who would be impressed with your offer. But me? There is nothing in it for me. I'm the king of Denmark, I conquered Norway, and my stepson rules Sweden. Why would I want to be York's guardian?"

Elfhelm took a deep breath and replied:

"You have daughters, King Sven. I have sons. Does that not interest you? I propose an alliance between our families. To marry my two sons to your two daughters."

"You still stand to gain more than me." Sven smiled, seeing through the offer. "By placing my daughters here as the wives of an ealdorman's sons, I'd be guaranteeing peace. And if your king challenges you when he hears of this, as he very well might do, you'd call on me for help, isn't that right? If you know so much about my children, you also know that I'm a good father and I wouldn't leave them in need."

Elfhelm said nothing. After a moment, Sven reassured him.

"It's not a bad proposition, Ealdorman. But it's an offer to be made in the future. Astrid is seven, Sventoslava five, and we are not in the habit of marrying off little children. Speaking of daughters . . . how old is yours? Elfgifu, is that her name?"

"She is ten, but I have already promised her," Elfhelm said quickly.

"To someone better than the king of Denmark?" Sven smiled, placing a hand on his shoulder.

Elfhelm narrowed his eyes as Sven's meaning reached him.

"She's the same age as your sons, King Sven."

"The same age as the younger, Cnut. Forgive me, but I have already promised Harald to someone more important than the vassal of Northumbria." Sven clapped him on the back.

Elfhelm gave him three wagons of food when he left, but it was still only a drop in the ocean of the hunger his army suffered that winter. They had no supplies on the Isle of Wight, and after holding council with his chieftains, he ordered everyone to sail back to Denmark. "It is better to take the silver back home than to keep it in chests and die of hunger in a foreign land," the men said on the way back.

Sven kept thinking about the ealdorman's offer. He knew that Elfhelm risked the anger of the king of England by tying his family to his, and that he was doing it with full knowledge of the potential consequences. He probably hoped that Sven would pay the dowry for his daughters in the shape of an army which would protect his shores from other invaders and support him in the war against Ethelred. A war which the ealdorman would win, and which might lead him to reach for England's crown.

"It's not a bad idea," Jorun commented when Sven shared his thoughts. "Our girls would have a king for a father-in-law. Who knows, maybe one of their husbands would reach for his father's crown. It's not a bad idea, but I wonder, as a simple helmsman might: if there are rocks on the starboard side, and a storm brewing on the port side, there must be a third way through."

"That's exactly it, Jorun, that's exactly it. And I know what that third way is."

A cheerful noise welcomed them back in Roskilde's port. Jarl Stenkil of Hobro sailed in first, and his horn was so loud that the people waiting to greet them had no doubts that they'd been victorious.

"Conquered, pillaged, burned!" Jorun shouted as he leaped down onto the pier.

"King!" Uddorm of Viborg greeted him. Sven had left him in charge in his absence. "King! I beg you, I have had enough of having the reputation of a land rat! Let me come on the next voyage."

Sven spotted fair-haired Vali at the end of the pier, with his daughters beside her. But amongst the crowds of people, the wives greeting their husbands and children searching for their fathers among the disembarking crews, he could not see his sons.

He patted Uddorm on the shoulder and pinched his cheek.

"Uddo! You're fatter than when I left you." He laughed. "Look at how thin your king is. Salt and veins! Are you sure you'd like to switch?"

"We were chewing on leather straps by the end of the journey!" Jorun pushed his way over to them, carrying two large chests under his arms.

"What do you have there?" asked Uddorm.

"Silver!" Jorun bared his teeth. "Skinny, hungry silver."

The welcome feast was just as it should have been. Loud, hot, full of laughter and rhymes. Vali served him the choicest pieces all night.

"My lord has fasted." She shook her head.

"Yes, my dear Vali. I will do nothing but eat and drink for the first three days. Only then will I take care of you. Forgive me, but we weren't short of women in England, only food! Where are my sons?" He wiped grease off his chin.

"Hunting rabbits." She shrugged. "We didn't expect you back so soon."

"Rabbits?" He looked surprised. "Was there hunger in Denmark while we were gone, too?"

"No." Vali laughed. "Uddorm manages to get what we need. But your sons cannot sit still, and archery training in the square is no longer enough for them. Do you want to speak to your daughters?"

"Bring them here! Have Melkorka come with them."

They walked into the hall, shy amid the noise, crowds, and laughter. His own laugh died in his throat when he saw them. Fair-haired, they both looked like their mother, except for his blue eyes. They gazed at him with those eyes, standing two steps away from the throne and showing no inclination to approach closer. Stubborn too, no surprise there.

"I don't know these girls," he said soberly. "I think they're changelings. My daughters would have kissed their father immediately."

Astrid stiffly kissed his cheek, but Sventoslava pointed an accusatory finger at him.

"I'm afraid of your beard," she said. "I don't want to kiss you because it will sting me."

He laughed, grabbing the braids of his beard in one hand.

"How about now, little lady? Is this better?"

"Yes." She nodded and kissed him.

He grabbed her and sat her down on his lap. It made Astrid bolder. She climbed up beside her sister.

Melkorka watched this uncertainly, but she sighed with relief once they started talking.

"What did you bring us?"

"Do you have gifts?"

"I want my own animal, because Cnut has a snake and Harald has a dog."

"I'll take this ring from Father. It's very pretty, but it's too big for me."

"I want this necklace. And that one."

"I want lynxes, like Mother had."

"When will she be back?"

He froze.

"She won't be," he replied quietly.

He didn't have to think about her when he was away, when he was at war. Although that didn't mean he hadn't. But at least he didn't have to answer his children's questions. He tried to push the thoughts away now. He preferred to kill than to take prisoners, but life wasn't as simple as that.

"Let's not talk about her," he said, and added: "Vali, fill my cup!"

Winter passed calmly and quickly. Spring brought with it a visitor.

"Thorkel the Tall! It's been so long! I'd have known you by your broken nose even at the other end of the world. Are you still sailing the *Zealand Falcon*?"

The Jomsviking had grown older, but in that way typical for sea warriors, where his skin was preserved by wind and salt. Taller than most, broad-shouldered, slender, and lean, he had dark eyes which gleamed with hidden laughter.

"My brother Sigvald took the *Zealand Falcon* when we parted ways years ago. My ship is *Nidhog*."

"Biting Fear." Sven nodded, inviting Thorkel closer. "Sit down. You won't bite me?"

Thorkel grinned to show he still had teeth and laughed.

"I'm honored to sit beside the greatest king in the north, but I bring bad news from England."

"What's happened? Has King Ethelred suddenly grown strong and power-ful? Is he building a fleet to face me at sea?"

"That's a close guess. An Eadric Streona is building a fleet for the king. He's the new ealdorman of Mercia. He has great plans, and many trees are falling under his axes. They say Streona was paid enough to build one hun-dred ships."

Sven whistled and asked:

"Are any of them fit to sail yet?"

"No," Thorkel replied calmly. "They say that they have only just cut down the trees to build them."

"But the silver has been paid? Oh, what a thrifty king! When I hear such news, I want to raise *Anger*'s sail and set off for England! To my endlessly full treasure chest."

"Streona shouldn't be underestimated, he has more influence over the king than any of the ealdormen before him. He's a cunning fox and a master of court intrigue. Heads rolled after you left."

"Whose?" Sven asked curiously. "Apparently the ealdorman of East An-glia, Ulfcetel, negotiated the value of the danegeld on behalf of the king. At least, that's what he told me, and I'm not in the habit of asking my silver what vault it comes from."

"Yes, Ulfcetel was following the king's orders. But the vassal of York was not. The king beheaded Elfhelm . . ."

There goes my daughters' father-in-law, Sven thought.

". . . and blinded his two sons," Thorkel concluded.

There go our big plans. Blind sons-in-law will be of no use to me. How did the king know about their meeting? And, more importantly, how did Thorkel know about it?

"What do you say to such news, King?" the Jomsviking asked after Sven remained silent for a while.

"Nothing." Sven shrugged. "Let's talk of something else. What are your plans? They say that you led the rest of the iron boys out of Jom."

27

POLAND

Świętosława listened to Bishop Bruno of Querfurt, and she was entranced by what he said as much as by how he said it. He was her age, perhaps a little younger. He had dark curly hair, a dark, evenly trimmed beard, and eyes that burned like two coals. Even his skin seemed darker. He was slender and surprisingly agile, which made her think of an exotic animal. He had been raised by a wealthy noble family of Saxon lords in Querfurt, and he had no trouble navigating the names and places of all the most important people in Italy and the Reich. King Henry had let him leave Magdeburg, honoring the agreement he'd made in Poznań. Bruno had been ordained by an archbishop before the war had even begun.

He had found a common ground with Bolesław immediately since, like her brother, he had admired the late Emperor Otto. Besides, it was Bruno who had looked after Bezprym at Romuald's hermitage at the emperor's request. He was sorry to hear of what had happened to the prince.

"God has His own plans for us," he said. "Those of us who are able to recognize the path on which we should be suffer less than those who go through life blindfolded."

"What about you, Bishop?" she asked him. "How did you know where your path lay?"

"I was led onto it by the death of my master, Saint Adalbert," he replied. "We met at Otto's court before Adalbert came to Poland, from which he set off as a missionary. When we spoke of spreading the Word of God to pagans then, I didn't understand him. I was Otto's chaplain, and the royal court has charms which are hard to ignore. Even the bars seem beautiful when they're part of a golden cage." Bruno sighed. "And Adalbert spoke of how he was going to go into the unknown, into the land of uncharted forests, wilderness, and lakes. I could almost see the mud through which he'd have to wade, the bushes and the swamps . . . and believe me, when I returned to my chambers after speaking to Adalbert, I pulled the clean, fragrant sheets over my head with relief. But since the moment that Radim Gaudentius came to us to tell us of the bishop's martyrdom, I haven't been able to stop thinking about it. Meeting Romuald in Pereum and feeling the ancient pious man's power for myself staggered me. I understood that it was in the evangelical simplicity that his power lay, in the renouncement of all worldly riches . . ."

"My Ion has never felt it." Świętosława shrugged. "He ran from Romuald and Peter Orseolo because he claimed the roots stopped him from standing to attention. And now he is doing his penance in the abbey in Międzyrzecz. He ran from the roots only to come back to them, that was his fate."

"Did he choose it for himself?" Bruno asked.

"Mhmm." She nodded.

"After a while," their new missionary bishop continued, "I discovered that my path lay somewhere between Romuald's and Adalbert's. The hermits deny themselves any part in the life of this world so that they may dedicate their entire existence to the contemplation of God. That's why they shut themselves away in seclusion, to separate their lives from what happens in this world, as well as from the people in it. So that they are left alone with God. A missionary gives his life to serve God, knowing that he can give it in a literal sense. To be a missionary is to serve those who do not know God, so it forces one to open himself to the world."

"What about forcing pagans to let themselves be baptized?" she asked. "Forcing them by placing a blade at their throats to abandon their old gods and accept Christ?"

"Well . . ." Bruno spread his arms wide. "There are those who would say that any path that leads to God is a good one."

She thought of Olav. She could see his white hair and his pale, stubborn eyes. His intention to christen the entire country even if the world was against him.

"And you?" she pressed. "What do you think?"

"Don't tire the bishop out," Bolesław interrupted.

"But Bishop Bruno himself has just said he wants to suffer like Adalbert did," she replied.

"Yes, and you're worse than the Prussians!"

"No, I'm merely curious. Bishop?"

Bruno's dark eyes closed for a moment, as if he'd gone to sleep.

"Bishop?" she asked quietly.

He opened his eyes. Tears ran down his cheeks.

"Thank you, my lady," he whispered. "You've brought me back down to the earth from which I so often fly when I think about my mission. You're right, Świętosława, I want to follow in Adalbert's footsteps."

"Forgive me." She understood the reason for his tears. "I didn't mean . . . I thought you realized that Adalbert didn't die swiftly or painlessly. Forgive me."

"No, no. You're right, and I know about that; I wrote about his life. It's just that I usually think about the joy of meeting our Lord, not the pain, so that when my turn comes to be tested, I might maintain my honor. A martyr must give his life with joy. He cannot kick and scream, because that's like giving a gift with one hand while taking it away with the other."

"You've received the pope's permission to go to Połabie," Bolz said. "War rages there just as it did in Adalbert's day. You'll die not because you'll be preaching the Word of God, but because you'll step foot in the lands of the furious Veleti."

"I have permission only to go to the east of the empire. I can go to the Prussians like my master did."

"There are other lands. The country from where Bezprym's mother came, the home of the Black Hungarians. They have had contact with the true faith for years and nobody has been able to save their souls. There are also the lands of the Pechenegs on the border with Russia. If you managed to tame those madmen, you'd have done the Church credit."

"I understand"—Bruno nodded—"that the priests of the eastern empire have reached that far?"

"Even if they have, they have gained nothing by it. The Pechenegs worship horse heads just like they've always done. Besides, you could meet with Kiev's Knyaz Vladimir."

Świętosława didn't interrupt her brother, knowing what he intended. He wanted Bruno's mission to give him something, too. The Słowiańszczyzna in Bolesław's head had never stopped growing, and the loss of Bohemia and peace in the west had turned her brother's attention to the east. All the messengers from Russia praised their prince, so Bolesław had dragged Daniła, a Russian loyal to him, from a family of Kiev exiles in Bodzia, and sent him east, where he'd established a whole network of spies in Kiev. Bolesław was mainly interested in Vladimir's problems related to his successor. Bruno's visit to the knyaz's court would be a good opportunity for them to try to tip the scales. Bruno clearly took no issue with becoming her brother's man.

Bruno does everything like his master, Adalbert, she thought, waiting for them to finish.

"Do you want to go for a walk around the borough with me?" she asked Bruno once their discussions concluded.

"I will not turn you down, my lady," the bishop said, though he looked tired.

They walked out of the palatium, leaving the cathedral behind them as they headed toward Poznań's western gate. She led him onto a bridge from which they could enjoy a majestic view of the river Warta.

"My brother knows how to suck a man dry like a phantom, although those only work at night while he never sleeps." She saw Bruno's startled look and reassured him: "I'm joking! But I do want to talk to you about a matter of some gravity. My firstborn son, Olof King of Swedes, has never been christened. When Father married me to Eric, he gave me a priest to accompany me aboard the *Haughty Giantess*, but the poor man didn't survive the journey. The only Christian in my husband's court turned out to be a schemer and . . . he had to give his life for committing treason. And the monk Ion that my husband brought back as a gift from war, who used to be a companion to your Romuald, has never been ordained and then, as I've already mentioned, it turned out he was a traitor all along. Eric may have built me a chapel in Sigtuna, but Ion claimed that it was worth no more than a boat shed if it stood on unconsecrated ground . . ."

"Why haven't you sent your son any of Poznań's priests?" Bruno studied her carefully.

"There is a thorn in our relationship," she explained reluctantly. "Betrayal."

"Who betrayed whom?"

"What is this, a confession?" she snapped.

"And if it is?"

"I have a bad experience with that. When I finally decided to confess, Ion broke his word and told my husband everything, you see."

"No, I don't." Bruno shook his head. "First you say that Ion hadn't been ordained, but then you tell me he heard your confession. You must admit that sounds odd."

"I know, it does." She shrugged, angry at herself for ever having begun this conversation.

Bruno grabbed her elbow unexpectedly, hard enough that she hissed.

"We speak of missions and pagans. Of widening the horizons, of great plans! But I'm beginning to see that the first mission I should focus on is right here in Poznań, with you. And perhaps with your sister whom Bishop Reinbern mentioned."

"I won't give you the satisfaction of a martyr's death," she snarled.

"You misunderstand me, my lady," he replied coldly, locking eyes with her. "I'm not searching for a meaningless death to gain fame. I'm searching for the meaning of death as a passageway to eternal life."

He let go of her elbow and asked with complete self-control:

"When was the last time you confessed your sins properly?"

She thought about this.

"Twenty years ago, right there, in the palace chapel," she replied. "The night before I left for the home of my first husband."

He looked at her. She saw the dark, flickering outline of his pupils.

"Let's make a deal, Świętosława. I have the power to ordain new missionary bishops. I will prepare a man who will sail to Sigtuna while you teach him the language and give him one of your men."

"All right." She sighed with relief.

"I'm not done." Bruno laughed, flicking back his hair. Only now did she notice the dimple in his chin, as deep as if it had been cut with a knife. "I'll only do it if you prepare for confession."

She grimaced. She really did want to do it. She'd thought she would ask Unger, but by the time she'd decided she was ready, he had left for Magdeburg and never come back. But if King Henry let Bruno go after the peace talks in Poznań, perhaps he would let Unger go next? Yes, she would prefer to wait for her favorite bishop to return.

"I don't want to offend you, Bruno of Querfurt . . ." she began, but he interrupted her.

"This isn't a negotiation."

They fell silent, sizing each other up like wolves preparing to pounce.

"All right." She sighed. "I'll trust you. But not today. Tomorrow at the earliest."

"Naturally." Bruno nodded. "You have to prepare and think on the last twenty years, feel some remorse for your sins . . ."

"I feel remorse every minute of my life," she told him. "I've been wearing a crown of thorns for the past six years."

Bruno pulled her close and kissed her right on the lips.

Bolesław asked her to see him in the late afternoon. There was a jug of wine on the table, and her brother was pacing the chamber like a wildcat.

"I have a new idea."

"I don't doubt it. You wouldn't have summoned me to discuss an old one." She sat down and poured herself some wine.

"I didn't summon you, I asked to see you. Why are you so sour? Has Bruno refused to ordain someone to go to Sigtuna? He doesn't usually turn me down. I'll ask him myself."

"There's no need; it's all been settled." She flinched at the memory of that strange kiss. "What's this wine?" she asked, feeling as if it had stung her tongue.

"Hungarian. Listen, I want to build Bruno a cathedral."

"I won't talk to you if you keep pacing. My head hurts and I don't like talking to your back. Sit down."

It was a lie. It wasn't her head that hurt but her breasts, which had been squeezed by a man's hand for the first time in years. Bolesław sat down, but she could tell by his expression that he wouldn't sit still for long.

"The diocese of the north," he said with gleaming eyes. "On the northeast border of Poland, in Kałdus. What do you think?"

"Kałdus? Where is that?"

"On the right side of the Vistula, near our border with Prussia. He will be close to the place of his master's death. A missionary center, not just a hermitage. I will build a cathedral as great as the ones in Poznań and Gniezno."

"Bolz, wait. Do I understand correctly that you want to imprison Bruno in Kałdus?"

"No!" He slammed a fist on the table.

She was certain she was right.

"He wants to be a martyr, like Adalbert. Can't you understand that? He won't be kept in a cathedral, no matter how great it is. He'll want to go to the Prussians."

"Damn it!" her brother shouted. "He'll go to the Black Hungarians, the Pechenegs, and to Russia. But if he goes to the Prussians it will be with my armed troops. I won't let him die." Bolesław's green eyes seemed to pulse with anger. "Bruno of Querfurt is more valuable alive than dead. He's an educated, well-adjusted man who has experienced Henry's two-faced politics himself. His voice in Rome will mean more than the voices of one hundred other men! I'll build him a cathedral, a monastery, an abbey, whatever he wants, but I won't let him die for nothing."

She drank more of the tart Hungarian wine which stung her tongue again. Maybe that was the only thing that stopped her from saying that Bruno would not be stopped.

"It's the most disorganized part of the country," she said after a moment. "The network of boroughs is sparse, and there is always the threat of invasion. Is it a good idea to build great cathedrals there?"

He patted her hand as if she were a child and said:

"It's the best place I can think of."

POLAND

Bolesław watched the light flickering on the colored glass on the chapel wall, reflecting in shades of amber. Bezprym's voice broke into his thoughts.

"You summoned me. I'm here."

He turned around to face the entrance. The brilliance of the light on the glass had been blinding, which for a moment made his son's figure appear to be no more than a dark silhouette.

Like a hole of darkness amidst the light, Bolesław thought, and flinched at the simile.

"Close the door," he asked Bezprym, "and come here."

His son followed his instructions and stood before him tall, broad-shouldered, and dark-eyed.

"We are standing on the graves of our ancestors," said Bolesław. "Your grandfather and grandmother lie under this floor."

"Everyone dies one day," Bezprym replied tonelessly. "And some people die while they're still alive."

If he were still a boy, I could hold him or take his hand, Bolesław thought. *But it's too late.*

"Son," he said, and heard the hoarseness in his own voice. "This can't go on. I need to choose."

"What?" Bezprym clenched his jaw.

"My successor," replied Bolesław. "You're my firstborn, but you won't be my heir."

Bezprym's eyes narrowed. He exhaled loudly and hissed:

"Because Jaromir Přemyslid deprived me of the ability to father sons when he took his revenge on you? Why won't you just say it, Father? Do the words stick in your throat? That a randy bull like you has a son who is no longer a man? You're wrong!" he shouted, and spittle flew from his mouth. "You're judging manhood by the number of children one can have or the length of . . ."

"Enough!" snarled Bolesław, grabbing his wrist.

Bezprym tugged his arm free.

"I'm furious, Father! I know that you weren't the one who castrated my executioner, but I am the one who paid for your ambition, for your plans for Bohemia! Me! You garner the praise while I pay for it every single day. Do you think I can't see the way they look at me in court? The pity in the servants' eyes? Are you surprised that I prefer to stay away from here, that I want to be in the abbey in Międzyrzecz? At least over there nobody stares at me as if I were a cripple!"

Bolesław let the boy shout all his pain out. He watched his son's dark eyes blaze with anger, and as a father, he felt every shade of the anguish and fury inside himself as well. When Bezprym fell silent, he spoke in a calm voice.

"I have never thought any worse of you after this happened. All I know is that you cannot have children, and a ruler must have heirs. It's a brutal truth, but it's the truth. We cannot change what has happened, but if I could turn back time, I never would have tried to take Prague."

"I don't believe you." Bezprym grimaced.

"What can I say? That sooner or later, I will avenge the wrong that has been done to you? You know I will. But it's not what I want to speak to you about. I have a proposition."

"You've already made it." Bezprym's voice was colored with disdain. "You're removing me from power."

"You didn't want it anyway. You preferred the hermitage."

"Yes, and you refused to accept that."

Bolesław had always struggled to control his temper, and Bezprym wasn't making it any easier in this conversation.

"Son, I won't repeat myself. We cannot turn back time. What's done is done. Mieszko will be my heir as duke of Poland, but I want to give you your own borough. And a task. Listen to me, don't interrupt," he commanded, seeing Bezprym's mouth open. "The northeastern parts of the country, close to the Prussian border. It's a wild and untamed land. A virgin land. I want to give you the difficult task of subduing it, because I believe you can do it. And I have great plans for it: a diocese in Kałdus."

"Kałdus?"

"Yes, Kałdus. The hill on which the borough is built looks like Veszprém, which is where your mother Karolda has been laid to rest. When I saw it for the first time, I thought I was dreaming about the Hungarian lands. I want Kałdus to have a cathedral as great as the one in Gniezno and Poznań. For Bruno. And you, my son, would be my vassal and Bruno's right-hand warrior in his conversion of the Prussians and Yotvingians to Christianity. Only think of the challenge. You may never be a husband or a father, but you can be a monk and a warrior in one. Your soul is wild and restless like your mother's, from the nomadic tribes you come from." He grabbed his son's shoulders, and Bezprym didn't draw away this time. "There is a wilderness there, so if you want to build a hermitage, you can do that. But I expect you to become a missionary warrior. You'll defeat the Prussians and aid Bruno in his mission. Fight! Because those who fight win. I'm telling you this here, standing on the graves of our ancestors, in front of the altar and the holy cross!"

Bezprym pulled away now and bit his lip until it bled.

"Don't order me, Father," he said, barely keeping his anger in check. "Let me make up my own mind."

They sized each other up for a moment. His son's eyes were like vortexes of hot molten lead. Bezprym turned on his heel and ran out of the chapel.

28

WOLIN, WOLIN ISLAND, POLAND

Astrid was given Bjornar by her brother, who had the reputation for being one of the duke's most trusted men. The awe-inspiring procession which arrived in Wolin with Bjornar also included her nephew Mieszko. All this to negotiate with the merchants of Wolin. Dalwin hadn't risen from his bed in six months. His days were numbered.

"Before I close my eyes," he'd say, "I can still tell my merchant brothers what I want of them. Will they follow my wishes? I don't know, although I'm hoping that they found the long years of my rule as vassal to have been favorable for them . . ."

She walked the length of Wolin's port with Bjornar and Mieszko at her side. She could see her nephew's eyes shine.

"The port is full of ships from spring until autumn," she explained to him, just as Dalwin had done for Świętosława all those years ago. "You'll find the ships of Arabian, Russian, and Flemish merchants here. And vessels from the north, from the land of the northern lights. Only a few spend their winters in Wolin, those for whom it is a stop on a very long journey from east to west or north to south. Some of the foreign merchants have their homes here, others stay in the sailors' homes or rent rooms in the inns. There are inns which rent alcoves covered in fabrics woven with gold and with guards posted at the door."

"What about the church, Lady of Wolin? Where is the church?" Mieszko glanced around restlessly.

Since his early childhood, the boy had been raised to join the Church. He read and wrote in Greek and Latin. Nobody could have anticipated the cruel chain of events which had led them to this moment in which he was to become the heir to the Polish throne instead of a bishop. Now that Bolesław had made and announced his decision, Mieszko was being introduced to all the duties he would have as a ruler. She looked at him. Bolesław had looked just like him when he'd been seventeen. Tall and slender, with gleaming amber hair. They looked alike, but they were so different. As different as a smooth summer sea and a violent autumn storm. Bolesław had been untamable since he'd been a child. He had been kept in line only by their father's iron will, but his restless energy had always been visible churning right below the surface.

Young Mieszko seemed calm and well-mannered, as if he had an untroubled soul. Even their eyes were different. Mieszko saw the world through Emnilda's blue eyes, while Bolesław's whirled with colors.

"So where is the church in Wolin?" he repeated stubbornly.

They passed the merchant port and walked toward the piers intended for the fishermen. It was empty here at this time, the morning catch had already been sold, and the fishermen's wives untangled the nets while their children cleaned the baskets. Three or four seagulls circled overhead in the hopes of easy prey in the shape of a dead fish forgotten in the nets.

"It's not that simple, nephew," replied Astrid after a long moment of silence. "You must understand the nature of this place. It is the port for people of all nations, of many different faiths and gods. Each one of them seeks peace after their long and dangerous journeys, and they want to feel comfortable here. We want them to bring their business here, to Wolin, rather than Hedeby or Trust. That's why, many years ago, an agreement was made to allow people to pray to any gods they wished here, without raising any faith above the others."

"I understand. So where is the church?" the young prince asked again.

One of the women threw something into the water and the shrieking seagulls dived toward it. Mieszko turned around, watching the wild, screeching fight.

"Christ's priests were the only ones who did not agree to the pact of religious equality," Astrid replied. "Allah's followers meet in the home of the eldest Arabian merchant while the Jews gather in the hut by the shores. There is a small shed behind the workshop of one of the merchants who deals in arms where men worship Odin and Freya. The Slavic temple has been by the Dziwna for years. My grandfather Dalwin wanted to give Christ's priests some land close to that temple, where there is a beautiful sandbank that would be perfect for a small church. But they requested exclusivity, which is the enemy of the kind of settlement that Wolin needs to be."

She didn't say anything else. She didn't tell him that Christ's priests had been prepared to start a religious war over this, that they wanted to remove the temples and clear any sign of the other gods from Wolin.

"Did you chase them away?" Mieszko asked, watching the victorious seagull escaping toward some bushes nearby with the fish clamped in its beak.

"No, young prince. They left of their own volition."

"You should have invited them again," her nephew said, turning to her. "My father, as a patron of Christian missionaries, cannot allow Wolin to remain unchristened, no matter how wealthy a port it may be."

"Mieszko, think about it," she interrupted, struggling to contain her irritation. "Doesn't your father buy his silks from the Arabian merchants? Doesn't he drink the wine that is brought to him over the seas? Doesn't he rely on the information brought to him by the Jews, Normans, and Arabs from all over the world? Some matters require tact."

Mieszko studied her and she couldn't shake off the feeling that there was a sense of superiority emanating from his gaze, as if he were the adult speaking to a child.

"I understand that, Astrid, but you should also understand my father. When he stands against King Henry and wants to show the entire Christian world that it is the Reich king who strikes up alliances with pagans against him, he cannot allow himself to risk similar accusations."

She pressed her lips together.

"Does the young prince have to be present for our negotiations with the merchants?" she asked Bjornar on the side once Mieszko had walked away.

"Yes." Bjornar nodded. "But the final decision will be mine."

"If Mieszko speaks the way he just did, I'm certain that the majority will support Racibor."

The merchants of Wolin chose their leader themselves. If Mieszko had forced someone on them all those years ago, that man would never have lasted. To support Dalwin, Mieszko had married his daughter Urdis, Astrid's mother. Then, when he'd allowed himself to be baptized and he sent all his wives away so he might marry Dobrawa, none of his old wives or their children had suffered, so the alliance which relied on Dalwin's position continued, and passed on to Bolesław after Mieszko's death. Now, though, it was at risk. Dalwin's life was coming to an end, and with it Bolesław risked losing Wolin. The iron boys had deserted Jomsborg to follow Thorkel the Tall, and it was no longer Poland's armed sea fortress. Yes, Astrid had filled it with warriors under Sambor's command, but their only task was to protect Wolin from any invasions that might come by land or sea.

"Tell us about the people who are fighting for power in Wolin," her nephew asked when they met in the hall of her manor after their walk.

Busla served fried sturgeons, fresh cream, and salty onions that had been picked from the fields by the sea.

"There are two main contenders," she began. "Tomir is a friend of my grandfather Dalwin, and he would continue Dalwin's work. Racibor may respect everything Dalwin's accomplished, but he wants something different. He has earned a fortune in trading arms. English blades, Danish aces, Frankish and Frisian steel. He is surrounded by the best craftsmen, blacksmiths in Wolin, as well as the richest men—goldsmiths. Racibor was among those who loudly complained that the Jomsviking fortress fell, since they were its clients as well as suppliers. The Jomsvikings sold Racibor the weapons they took from their enemies then bought better arms from him. They brought back the newest kinds of blades and Racibor's blacksmiths used these as an example to follow when they fashioned their own weapons. They also say he had a workshop of forgeries, where he had steel hammered into the same shapes as the products of a certain English blacksmith's, marking them with his name, but perhaps those are just nasty rumors. Racibor has never made his peace with the fact that those times are in the past. He would like to bring the iron boys back to Jom so that his business would prosper again."

"The man who profits on trading arms will always support war," young Mieszko observed. "Who is Tomir?"

"He grew up among the fishermen. His grandfather started out with one boat and some ripped nets, as so many others, but Tomir's father commanded a dozen fishing boats which caught herring, codfish, and all kinds of larger fish. Tomir used the silver he earned to build a weaving mill. He began with sails but quickly became the leading merchant in sheets, wool, cloth, and leather. He employs ropemakers, weavers, embroiderers, and a host of other craftsmen."

"In other words, the hard arms trader against a soft man dealing in fish and cloth?"

"I assure you, nephew, that a man who attains the wealth Tomir commands is not soft. But you're right in one thing: Tomir is open to discussions. Racibor is more difficult."

"Astrid." Busla came back to the table and halted the flow of conversation with a solemn look. "You need to go to Dalwin. It's time."

"Forgive me." She bowed to her guests, took a woolen scarf from Busla, and walked out.

Despite his illness, Dalwin hadn't agreed to live with her in Wolin's manor, the one he'd given her when she'd married Sigvald. He'd preferred to stay in his hut overlooking the port. As she walked toward it, she heard the horn blown three times, the sound bouncing off the water.

"I wonder who has come to Jom," said Busla. "Do you know whether Sambor was expecting visitors?"

"That's none of my business," she replied, covering herself with the scarf. The wind which blew from Dziwna was cool and damp. "How is he?"

"You'll see for yourself." Busla sighed. "As my aunt used to say, 'It's all the same to him if he's dead or alive.'"

"But it's not the same to me," Astrid said as she pushed open the door to the hut.

Dalwin was propped into a half-seated position on the large, ornately carved chair covered with reindeer furs. His head was tilted back, and his gray hair fell over his shoulders. His closed eyelids trembled.

"Are you asleep?" she asked, kneeling beside him, and taking hold of his cool thin hand.

He didn't respond, but he moved to indicate he was still alive.

"I told you," Busla announced, moving pots around. "It's all the same to him."

"Be quiet, please," Astrid said. "And if you can't do that, leave."

"But he doesn't care if I talk or make noise. Everyone must die, and it's better that he hears me to know he's dying in his own home, isn't it?"

"Leave, please," Astrid requested.

"As you wish." Busla shrugged. "You're the mistress here."

Perhaps not for much longer, Astrid thought bitterly. *But at least I can give our orders to ensure Dalwin dies in peace.*

When the door closed behind Busla, Dalwin moved. She placed a small pillow under his head and stroked the gray beard and hair. He opened his eyes with difficulty. His eyes were like hazy water, washed-out and unclear. He moved them as if he were watching images quickly passing in front of him. He moved his lips as if he wanted to speak. *No,* she realized, *he is speaking, but his words cannot be heard here. He's speaking to his dead family, those who have come for him.*

She closed her eyes and listened to the silence. At first, she heard the wood crackling on the fire, the distant calls of the sailors in port, a baby crying in a nearby house. A man's laughter. But all these faded into the background when Dalwin spoke, and all she heard was his whisper:

"Urdis, my daughter, at last I see you again. Are you still crying for Czcibor? Have you not met him where you are? Oh, of course, you're right, he was baptized, he's elsewhere. No, I haven't been. I will be with you soon and we will speak then. I still need to say goodbye, wait for me, wait . . ."

Dalwin's fingers tightened on her hand and she heard his hoarse whisper: "Astrid . . ."

"Oh." She realized that he was back and that she was the one he had to say goodbye to.

For a long moment, she wanted to feign sleep, to keep him with her for longer, but he was breathing so heavily that she didn't have the heart to let him suffer.

"Yes, Grandfather? I'm here. I'm watching over you."

"I want . . . to die . . ."

"I understand."

"I want you to let me sail off on a boat and burn it . . ."

"I will make sure of it. The black horn will sound for you when you sail to Nav."*

He nodded, and his features began to smooth out and settle.

"Grandfather, may I ask you something?"

He grimaced. She sensed that she had interrupted his dying, but since she'd already done it . . .

"Please, tell me of my mother and Czcibor . . ."

"That's in the past . . . Czcibor loved Urdis, but she was Mieszko's wife. She guaranteed his alliance with Wolin, you know that . . . and only when Dobrawa . . . and all that . . . then . . ."

This was the first that Astrid had heard of it. She felt a sudden stab of fear.

"Who's my father?" she asked. "Is it Czcibor? Is . . ."

"Mieszko, Mieszko . . ." Dalwin reassured her.

"Then why is my mother searching for Czcibor in Nav?"

Dalwin's eyes were misting over, but they moved as if he'd seen something.

"Pain . . ." he whispered. "Czcibor's pain hurts her even in death . . . Child . . . those who are unloved suffer so terribly . . . She . . . he . . . took her, when Mieszko gave her up . . . but Urdis didn't . . ."

"Oh." She understood.

We keep spinning in this cursed circle of brothers and sisters, she thought. *We inherit everything from one another, even love.*

"Dalwin," she said, though the emotion choked her. "My life with you has been so good . . ."

"We will meet again . . ." He smiled at her with white lips and inhaled for the last time.

What is it like? she wondered as her tears fell. *Geira died fearing the darkness that consumed her like a swamp. Mieszko walked into the light of eternal life which baptism gave him. And Dalwin's death was as calm as a breath of wind in the sails.*

She had been almost ready to be baptized after having seen her father's death, and the difference between the light which enveloped him and the darkness into which Geira had been sucked. But now, she wasn't so sure.

She didn't call for Busla or the gray servants. She wanted to prepare Dalwin's body herself. She dressed him and arranged his beautiful gray hair and beard. She fastened the silver beads he had liked so much into it. She slipped his rings onto his fingers. And then she watched over his body while Leszko prepared the boat.

---

* In Slavic folklore, Nav is the name for the underworld, ruled over by the god Veles.

"Call for Sambor and have him bring the black horn from Jom," she said. "I want to send Dalwin off tomorrow."

"As you wish, my lady."

Those who had accompanied him in his sailing days carried Dalwin's body from the hut to port. The ones who were his crewmates, those he hosted under his roof, the ones with whom he'd traded, negotiated, and drank. Wolin's narrow roads were full of people. Everyone wanted to send off their old vassal. Young duke Mieszko waited on the pier, alongside Bjornar and the rest of her brother's men. Sambor, the fortress's leader, sailed over on *Jom's Wolf*, and blew into the black horn when Dalwin's body was laid in his last vessel.

"Wolin bids its vassal farewell!"

The low sound of the horn spread over Dziwna's waters like thunder. Astrid stood at the top of the pier beside Dalwin's boat. She looked at him resting on the bottom. Someone touched her shoulder and she flinched. Thorkel the Tall, her dead husband's brother, was leaning toward her.

"Will you do me the honor of letting me loose the arrow?"

At first, she didn't understand what he was asking of her. Then she remembered the horns sounding out in welcome from the gates of Jom on the day of Dalwin's death.

"If Sigvald were still alive, he'd have the right, as your husband," Thorkel said gently.

"He's dead, and you're not my husband," she replied. "But yes, you can set the boat on fire."

He pushed it off skillfully and sent it into Dziwna's current. Sambor blew into the horn again. Thorkel lowered the arrowhead into the flames then let loose the burning arrow. The fur covering Dalwin's body caught fire. The flames slowly spread across the boat until it reached the sail and, with the help of the wind, set it ablaze.

"Why have you come, Thorkel?" Astrid asked, wiping her tears away.

"For many reasons," he replied evasively. "One of them is to deliver a message to your sister, Sigrid Storråda. I assume I can count on you to convey it, my lady."

"Tell me."

"King Sven intends to make one of their sons ruler of England by marrying him to the daughter of Northumbria's ealdorman. It can be the beginning of a great conquest."

"I see." She nodded. "Can we talk of this later? I am still bidding my grandfather farewell."

"I would like to speak to you alone, Astrid," he whispered into her ear, standing so close to her that she felt his hot breath. "But I have seen to my affairs in Jom and Wolin, and I must leave today. So, if you want to speak to me as much as I want to speak to you . . ."

"I will not interrupt my mourning just because you're in a hurry," she replied firmly. "Goodbye, Thorkel."

"Until next time, Astrid," he said without a shadow of a smile, and walked away.

She didn't turn to look after him. Mieszko appeared beside her moments later and, looking at Thorkel's retreating back, asked angrily:

"Are you conspiring with that man, Lady of Wolin? You let him set fire to the boat? Who is he to you?"

"What's it to you, nephew?" she snarled, angry at him for interrupting her in looking after Dalwin's boat.

Bjornar pushed his way over to them.

"Astrid, we have heard that Racibor, the arms dealer, has taken control of Wolin while you have been here preparing Dalwin's final rites. The merchants voted on the night of Dalwin's death, and Sambor of Jom joined them at the last minute, bringing Thorkel with him. Their presence swayed the vote in Racibor's favor."

"It's happened, then." She sighed. "It is out of my hands now."

It might not have been had I not just refused him. She had understood Thorkel's proposition, but she had no intention of mentioning it to Bjornar.

"Have you managed to reach an understanding with Racibor?" she asked. "Will he accept Bolesław's rule?"

"He says that he will consider it, but I think he's contemplating the opposite," Bjornar replied. "I must return to Poznań immediately. You should come with us; I'm not sure that you'll be safe here."

"I won't be," she replied. "But I'm not afraid. I need you to deliver my sister a message."

29

POLAND

Bolesław had felt like a spinner for a month now, and he swore to himself he would never thoughtlessly unravel any fabrics again.

"Apart from tearing Emnilda's shirt off," he muttered to himself. "Daniła! Welcome, friend!" he called out to the Russian.

Świętosława entered alongside his guest.

"Will Emnilda be joining us?" she asked her brother.

"No, she's gone to Gniezno with the children," he replied impatiently.

He already regretted sending her away because as soon as she'd left, he'd begun to miss her terribly.

"To Gniezno? And Big Head? I guess I should also pay the archbishop a visit. What's the use of having him around if he can't free Unger? All he does is sit in Gniezno and watch over Adalbert's relic, stuffing the treasury with donations from the pilgrims . . ."

"Sister, we have a guest," he reminded her. "Daniła, how is Bishop Bruno faring at Knyaz Vladimir's court?"

When she'd heard that Emnilda wasn't in Poznań, Świętosława had taken her sister-in-law's seat in the audience hall. She had her own, of course, at Bolesław's side, but she rarely used it, claiming that it "makes me look like a second wife, mistress, or concubine to my own brother. Disgusting." She laughed aloud.

"Control yourself, brother, at least while the messenger is present. It's not the bishop's mission to the knyaz, but an official voyage with the intention of converting the Pechenegs to Christianity."

"Daniła is our man." Bolesław ignored her objections.

"Yours, great Duke, yours. Bishop Bruno has won Knyaz Vladimir's favor, and he ensured Bruno was well-protected on his journey to the Pechenegs. Once he arrived there, the reverend Bruno negotiated peace between the Pechenegs and the Russians. Vladimir's son Światopołk was brought as a hostage to ensure the treaty."

"That's the one Vladimir wanted me to marry." Świętosława laughed. "His eldest, am I right?"

"Yes, my queen," Daniła agreed. "They say that since he gave his eldest to be a hostage, he may be trying to replace him with Jarosław as his heir. Jarosław is devoted to his father."

"This Świętopołk . . ." Bolesław moved his fingers. "What's he like?"

"Headstrong, greedy for power, demanding his father give him a borough of his own. It's no surprise the knyaz chose him to be a hostage."

Another thread, another plot, thought Bolesław.

"What are you doing with your hand?" Świętosława noticed.

"I'm weaving." He laughed and thanked Daniła for his news. "Go and have a drink with my men. They've been awaiting their Russian friend with impatience."

Once they left, he turned to his sister.

"Has Astrid sent word from Wolin? Have they made a move?"

"Mhmm." Świętosława couldn't look away from his fingers. "They have, they've left. Do you want to marry Sława to Świętopołk?" she asked bluntly. "Why not Jarosław?"

"A headstrong son might become an obedient son-in-law. And an obedient son tends to be a bad son-in-law."

She laughed at him.

"You know, a lot depends on the father-in-law. Look at Herman. He's a good husband to your Regelinda, but not a great son-in-law to you, right? Apparently, he complains that you're difficult and unusually demanding for a father-in-law. You keep insisting that he turn his back on the Reich . . ."

"Herman's loyalty hasn't been decided yet!" He lifted his hands, moving his fingers. "I'm still weaving, sister."

"For yourself or for the king?" Her voice was laced with irony.

Herman, the margrave of East Messien and the son of Bolesław's late friend Eckard, arrived in Poznań a month later on a mission that was uncomfortable, to say the least.

"I wish you'd brought our sweet daughter Regelinda with you." Bolesław greeted him from the throne in the audience hall under Saint Peter's sword. His son Mieszko stood behind him. Emnilda sat on his left, and his sister on his right. He had also invited Reinbern, Poznań's priests, and his trusted advisers. Both long walls were lined with identically clad warriors wearing silver helms, chain mail, and red cloaks.

"I also wish that we were meeting under better circumstances, my lord." Herman bowed stiffly.

He's like Eckard, Bolesław thought as he studied him. *But not quite. His father was a great warrior, but Herman turned out to be no more than a pawn. If he'd brought my daughter with him, I would have taken her back. They have no children, so it would be no loss, but I could wed such a pretty and well-connected girl again for another alliance.* Bolesław knew why his son-in-law had come and was playing with him like a cat does with a mouse.

"What news do you bring from your beloved lord and master, King Henry?" he asked.

Herman grimaced as if Bolesław had told him to drink a broth made of wormwood.

"I have never said Henry is my beloved lord," he replied stiffly. "I would appreciate it if you could understand, Duke, that my loyalty to the king stems from a desire for peace and respect for an old tradition. The marches belong to the empire . . ."

"So young and yet so traditional," mocked Świętosława, and asked with feigned concern: "Do you think it possible that our Regelinda is bored with him?"

"I don't believe she is," Herman protested. "My lady wife is expecting a child."

"Finally!" Emnilda clapped her hands.

"Thank God," Świętosława agreed with her as if Herman wasn't there. "Because I was beginning to think there was something wrong with him."

"When will she give birth?" asked Bolesław.

Herman blushed.

"I don't know much about these matters."

"I was right!" Świętosława exclaimed.

"What do you mean?" Bolesław asked with surprise. "You'll be the father of my grandchild and you don't know how that happens?"

"I will send a messenger when my son is born." Herman wanted to change the topic. "In the meantime, perhaps I'll come back to the matter of . . ."

"King Henry's good news." Emnilda smiled radiantly.

"Just news, Duchess," Herman corrected her carefully. "It is not, unfortunately, good."

"Some courts still observe the old traditions of beheading the messenger," Świętosława whispered loudly to Emnilda, who was sitting on Bolesław's other side. "Not all barbarian traditions were all that bad, right?"

"That's cruel," Bolesław observed, and was silent for a moment. "It's cruel of King Henry to send you, my son-in-law, of all people, to give me bad news. Why do you think the king picked you, Margrave Herman?"

"Because he hoped that you wouldn't rip your daughter's husband apart?" Świętosława's words elicited a muffled chuckle.

"Because he was wrong?" Emnilda asked. "He thought that he might push a wedge between you, husband, and Herman, to ensure there was bad blood between us all . . ."

"As my father always pointed out, sons-in-law are not family." Bolesław smiled at his wife before turning back to Herman with a stern expression. "Or perhaps nobody else wanted to accept this mission?"

"That I don't know," Herman replied, looking pale. "I didn't argue with my king."

He has a vassal's personality, Bolesław thought coldly, regretfully. *Why does the apple sometimes fall so far from the tree? His father was made of different material altogether.*

"There have been important developments"—Herman spoke so stiffly that it sounded as if he was reciting from memory—"which have led to Henry needing to change the terms of your agreement."

"Why?" Bolesław asked, although he knew the answer. What's more, he was the one who had instigated all these developments.

"There are many reasons."

"Name them!"

"Duke Jaromir's Czech messengers have complained to the king that you tried to bribe them with promises and money to turn their backs on Henry . . ."

If you knew me better, boy, you'd know that I have had no dealings with Jaromir since he hurt Bezprym. But it's true that I have men close to him. My faithful friend and Prague's old castellan Borzywoj made contact with them, while Ciechan, the leader of the Czech scouts, hid his communications. They are tired of Přemyslid's rule. There are those who would give me the throne because I've sowed the dream of a great Słowiańszczyzna in their hearts and it has bloomed into a flower. But they aren't the ones who would complain to Henry. That was Jaromir because he wants to start a war with me. A war which he is too weak to fight alone, but would like to fight under the black wing of the Bird King.

". . . the Veleti have asked Henry to protect them from your fierce troops . . ."

And the doves have been found. Bolesław chuckled inwardly. *It bothers them that I have Strosz Crow's Wing locked in a cage, that I caught the ugly bird but am keeping him locked up rather than killing him.*

". . . and Wolin's powerful merchants have also turned to Henry for help, claiming that you want to overthrow their leader, Lord Racibor, who was justly elected, and replace him with Lord Tomir, who follows your orders . . ."

They are no lords, boy, thought Bolesław. He had increased the merchants' unease with Astrid's help. *One of them trades in arms, the other in fish and cloth. Henry must really despise me if he has been hoodwinked so easily. That's a good sign. Fighting an opponent who is too stubborn is easier, especially if so many of my old friends are on his side.*

". . . and after taking all this into consideration . . ." Herman took a deep breath to say what he had been sent to say, but Świętosława interrupted him.

"Christ, I'm so touched . . ."

"King Henry II is forced to terminate the peace agreement you made in Poznań two years ago."

"Well, now I'm angry. Daddy heard some snotty snitches and now he wants to break the peace that he didn't even negotiate himself but that was agreed upon by the noble Archbishop Tagino?" Świętosława shouted. "And coincidentally he's doing it at the exact time at which he promised to free Bishop Unger. Herman, I hope that you don't actually believe this lesson they have forced you to memorize? Because if you do then that's evidence enough that we wed Regelinda to a fool."

"I'm not here to believe or disbelieve, Queen of Sweden . . ."

"Denmark and Norway," young Mieszko interjected quickly.

". . . I'm just here to deliver the words of Henry, king of the Reich."

They let Herman go that evening. Emnilda invited him to stay for the evening meal despite the bad news he'd brought, but thankfully he'd had enough tact to decline. Bolesław sat at the table with his closest friends. He raised his goblet and called out:

"King Henry has terminated the peace agreement we made in Poznań! And good riddance. As you all know, I have never made my peace with the loss of Milsko and Łużyce. I wish that we had Bishop Unger back, but I suspect that is the one promise he had never intended to keep. Our arch-Christian Henry feels a vengeful satisfaction knowing that he has deprived me of my friend and trusted adviser, and my beloved city of its shepherd. I don't believe that Unger would have betrayed us, as Henry's people would have us believe. His court may be full of traitors, but he doesn't know the kind of man Unger is. Friends, let us drink and rejoice. My hands are free again. The king has terminated our peace agreement so I am not the one who is starting this war—even if I do intend to set off to fight it the day after tomorrow."

"Bolz, no . . ." Emnilda groaned, gazing at him, doe-eyed. "I've only just returned from Gniezno . . . Give us at least one more night . . ."

"Let us drink to my wife!" he shouted, taking a sip. "And let us drink to the surprise we will spring on Henry."

"What surprise, my love?" asked Emnilda. "He must expect war if he's the one who broke the peace treaty."

He took her white hand and kissed her delicate fingers. He slipped his tongue between them and caught her ring in his teeth.

"Emnilda," he whispered. "I have loved you for the past twenty years, and I love you more with each passing year."

She replied with a blushing smile as he looked into her eyes and whispered:

"Henry's understanding of war is based on his position. He will begin to gather armies now, attempt to convince the lords to leave their comfortable houses, wives, children, and other benefits of a peaceful life to meet me in the marshy lands by the river Oder. But I won't wait for them to muster their forces. I'll set off the day after, like you asked me to. And I'll meet them not by the Oder but by the river Elbe. I'll be a hungry wolf which attacks the fat Reich's belly, not its leg. What do you say to that?"

"Come with me," she said, pulling him by the hand.

They made love in the great bed covered in soft wolf furs. The warmth of the fire left its mark on their backs. He tracked each of their children across her stomach: Bogumiła's groove, Regelinda's purple line, Mieszko's scar, Sława's stretch mark, and Otto's furrow. She was as juicy as an apple, and full when he lifted her buttocks and drank from her. He stood to attention beside her, a warrior and tactician and excellent archer. He used his weapon skillfully, not shooting blindly like a child. He squeezed the breasts which had fed his sons and daughters. He occupied her like a land he'd longed for; he besieged her like a soldier does a borough. He waited for her surrender, for the moan of opening gates, but she unexpectedly turned the tables on him and conquered him instead. He shouted and howled. And Emnilda, the generous duchess, crowned him with her thighs. She wrapped them around him and allowed him to sleep in glory. When he awoke, he was ready to invade her again, and she gave in to him without any opposition. He took her, opening her gates and riding into her at a canter.

Bolesław led five companies of heavy infantry, and thrice as many companies of light infantry followed. They moved quickly, crossing rivers at the well-marked fords. They hit the Reich like a well-aimed arrow, and they were outside Magdeburg less than two weeks after Herman delivered Henry's message. They didn't plunder any villages to gather supplies for the troops because the people supported them and fed them freely. They didn't burn or loot, but marched onward purposefully like a knife cutting bread. He heard the sweet sound of the city's bells ringing out in alarm. He couldn't conquer the city, but he felt Unger's pain from somewhere deep within its walls, and he thought:

You will understand me, my bishop friend. You will understand me better than anyone.

They set up camp around Magdeburg's high walls, waiting for a response. Archbishop Tagino, accompanied by a small troop, rode out toward them on the third day. He rode around the city to see how many men he had and where they'd been positioned. Bolesław's heavy cavalry numbered one thousand five hundred and his heavy infantry added up to three times as many. Bolesław rode toward them on White, and Tagino's small troop moved back toward the city.

"Tagino!" the duke shouted. "Tagino! Come back! I wish to speak with you."

The archbishop pulled his horse to a stop and waited for Bolesław, surrounded by guards.

"Archbishop of Magdeburg, noble Tagino," he said loudly as he neared. "Don't run from me. It is your king who has broken the peace agreement we made in Poznań. I do not want a new war. I want Unger!"

"I cannot!" Tagino shouted. "The king . . ."

"How can this be?" Bolesław called back. "Can a man who breaks peace treaties still be your king? A man who allies himself with pagans?"

Tagino flinched.

"Unger comes to no harm, I swear," he shouted. "To Magdeburg!" he ordered his men. "Go!"

The archbishop turned his horse around as his men set off and made the sign of the cross in the air, as if he were blessing Bolesław. Then he rode off after his men toward the gates of their city.

Bolesław returned to his armies.

"Pack up camp!" he ordered.

They rode off to recapture Łużyce, which barely opposed them at all. They traveled from settlement to settlement until they reached Budziszyn.

"Defenders of the city!" Bolesław shouted. "Here I am! Look at me!"

He cantered back and forth in front of the gate. He knew that the men defending Budziszyn were under his son-in-law Herman's command, even though Herman himself wasn't there.

"Surrender the borough and open your gates! I don't want to take your lives or your property. Accept me as your master!"

"Give us some time!" the castellan called back after a few moments.

So Bolesław ordered his men to set up camp. He knew that they had sent messengers to Herman in Strehla and to their king, Henry. His armies rested as they surrounded the borough, while the defenders awaited a response. When two weeks had passed with no replies, he mounted White again and his men took their positions. He rode around the ramparts again, shouting:

"Surrender the city! Surrender the city!"

Silence answered him. Derwan told him the rest in the evening:

"Your son-in-law Herman went to the Reich king's court and begged him for help. He shouted: 'My lord, you were the one who started this war. Help them. Duke Bolz has Budziszyn surrounded.' But all Henry apparently did was rip at his beard and kneel at his feral black cross, studded with one hundred nails."

"In front of what?" Bolesław felt his hair standing on end. There was not much that Henry could surprise him with since he'd heard about his alliance with the pagans, but desecrating the cross?

"Have you not heard about your enemy's tastes, Duke?" Derwan smiled crookedly. "He has a crucifix cut from a black oak with an equally dark figure of the Savior hanging from it. It differs from other crosses, however, by the holes in Christ's body, as if someone had been driving and removing nails from it . . ."

"Perhaps termites have damaged the wood?" Bolesław flinched.

"Perhaps," said Derwan, unconvinced, and continued his report. "Your son-in-law reminded Henry that he'd been the one to break the peace treaty and bring this misfortune on Herman's head. He begged for help."

"And?"

"And Henry did nothing, Duke. The bishops refused to help him. Your blood brother Gunzelin has ordered a message be delivered to the king: '*The one who sows the wind must reap the storm.*' Budziszyn is at your mercy."

"I will show it!" declared Bolesław.

He allowed the inhabitants to leave the borough with all their goods. He rode in on White after they'd left, then he feasted, and checked the strength of the ramparts. He drank mead with his comrades: Zarad, Stojgniew, Derwan, Bjornar, and the Czech Borzywoj. The last always had a wet mustache from all the drinking. Bolesław wished that he didn't love Emnilda so much that he had no desire for any of Budziszyn's women. But a leader cannot show any weakness, and so he took a girl and spent the night with her, all the while thinking: *This is tradition.* She had a young, supple body, a pretty face, and soft pale hair.

She could be my daughter, he thought.

He left some men in Budziszyn and raced back to Poznań, to his dukedom and his duchess. He turned around in his saddle as he left and shouted:

"You've lost, Bird King! This time you lost with no negotiations, peace, or alliances!"

30

POLAND

Świętosława's royal procession that accompanied her when she left Poznań may have been small, but the Bold One's axemen, led by Great Ulf, came with her. Wilkomir had stayed with Bolesław, though his son Wilczan was by her side. So were Omold the bard and Helga, who, like her, was also growing restless in Poznań. No further opportunities for a secret trip to Roskilde had arisen. Sven was sending crews to England under his jarls' command, but he himself stayed in Denmark. She missed her children. The knowledge that Sven wanted to marry one of their sons into an English family brought with it the nagging thought that she might never see her child again.

She was going to Gniezno to speak to Archbishop Gaudentius, and then to meet Bezprym in Kałdus. Bolesław's eldest son had taken the northeastern territory his father had given him, but he hadn't said goodbye to anyone when he left Poznań. He'd ridden out like a ghost in the night, so she'd decided to see for herself what was really going on with him. *My children are far away*, she thought, *but perhaps I can help him?*

"Wilczan, look!" She pushed her way to the front when Gniezno came into view at the end of the road. "Bolesław, Father, and I used to ride here when we were your age."

"I doubt that, Sigrid." Helga rode up alongside them, looking from her son as he rode next to the queen. "Wilczan is twenty-two! Oh, my boy, where has all that time gone?"

It was true, Świętosława still treated Wilczan as if he were a child, but he'd been a man for a long time. And Olof was a year older than him. The lack of news from Sigtuna weighed on her. Though she did know, thanks to the merchants who traded in Wolin and passed news to Astrid, that her son had four children of his own already. Two with his Obotrite wife, and two with his beloved mistress. She also knew that he constantly faced opposition, and that his hold on the throne wasn't as secure as Eric's had been.

The horses climbed the gently sloping hill, and they stood outside Gniezno's gates.

"This is a great honor!" Castellan Gosław greeted them, studying her axemen with some trepidation.

"We won't stay for long," she announced. "Where is the archbishop? He's the one I've come here to see."

Even if he doesn't want to see me, she thought, but kept the suspicion to herself. "He's indisposed. He's in his manor."

"I hope he won't deny an audience to the sister of his duke and master." She smiled at Gosław and ordered him to lead them.

He took them to the royal palatium, passing the cathedral and the archbishop's home on their way. Although more modest than the one in Poznań, the palatium was just as comfortable. Once there, Świętosława changed quickly out of her travel clothes and summoned Great Ulf.

"You'll take Wilczan and go first. Tell Gaudentius that I'm on my way and I want to speak with him."

The two had barely left when she herself set off, surrounded by six axemen. She didn't want to give the archbishop too much time to think. She stopped outside the cathedral, studying it. It was no less impressive than the one in Poznań. The enormous stone walls reached high toward the sky. Bridges and scaffolding still surrounded it as construction continued, though there were no stonemasons there today and the yard outside the cathedral looked deserted.

"It will be crowded tomorrow," Gosław explained. "Today is Monday, the only day without pilgrims."

"I understand." She nodded, watching Wilczan and Great Ulf walk out of the archbishop's house, supporting him between them.

"I see that your men have healing powers," muttered Gosław.

Radim Gaudentius was not as handsome as Sobiesław. The dead brother had been a duke and a leader, while the man before her was slender, bald, and stooping.

How strange it is, she thought as she watched the men approach, *that it is the bravest men who leave us first. He's the only one left out of that entire family; a half brother. His entire career has flourished only thanks to the great bishop Adalbert's death. Am I prejudiced? Have I been deceived by the rumors which claim that Radim ran away while his brother was murdered?* She shivered.

Relations between the archbishop and Bolesław had been awkward from the start. At the Congress of Gniezno, Emperor Otto III had wanted to take Adalbert's body to Rome to establish it as the center of Adalbert's cult. When Bolesław defied the emperor's will and said that he wouldn't give up the body because he needed the power that Adalbert's cult would give Poland, the imperial plans had to adapt. The relics remained in Gniezno, so this was where the emperor established the new Polish ecclesiastical province, with an archdiocese in Gniezno, and dioceses in Kraków, Wrocław, and Kołobrzeg which answered to Gniezno. It had been no secret that Bolesław wanted to bestow the highest honor on Unger. Unger had stepped aside for the good of the dukedom, and his diocese in Poznań had been made independent of Gniezno. By keeping him in Magdeburg they were forcing him to acknowledge the authority of that archdiocese over Poznań.

"Archbishop Gaudentius," she greeted him.

"Duchess Świętosława," he replied, his eyes narrowed against the sun's glare.

"Queen," she corrected him.

"The royal titles of the rulers in the north are invalid, my lady. None of them received his crown from the pope, so their power does not differ from the power held by ordinary dukes."

"I don't pay as much attention to titles as you do, Archbishop. You may call me the duchess of Sweden, Denmark, and Norway if you prefer."

He had dark eyes which watched her suspiciously from under swollen eyelids. His cheeks sagged as though he had never once smiled. Świętosława tried to push away the distaste she felt for him, but failed. He cast a critical eye over her procession.

"Please, come to the cathedral," he said. "God's house is a good place to talk. Except that one cannot enter bearing arms."

"Wilczan, Ulf, leave your weapons with your comrades and come inside with me."

The heavy doors creaked as they were dragged open. The interior was dim. The small windows, high on the walls, didn't let in much light. There were no laborers inside, but there was scaffolding erected by the walls. The work on the interior had barely begun.

There was a beautiful martyrium carved into the center of the cathedral for Bishop Adalbert. They walked over to it. There were silver-plated doors built into the bloodred sandstone. Gaudentius ran a trembling white hand over them. His slender fingers hovered above the keyhole.

"You have come to ask me why I haven't done anything to free Bishop Unger." He sighed. "That's not the case. It's not difficult to accuse someone, cruel words slip out easily enough . . ."

"Tell me what you have done, then. And why has Unger not been returned to us?"

"I keep sending messengers to the pope and to Archbishop Tagino, but to no avail. I have received no clear answer, but everyone blames our duke Bolesław for Unger's imprisonment in Magdeburg. His aggressive and possessive actions against the Reich king . . ."

Świętosława snorted with laughter, the sound echoing off the stone walls and ceiling.

"Radim Gaudentius, you're the archbishop of Poland! You should be taking action on behalf of the country that has been entrusted to you."

He shrank away from her. Both his hands pressed against the doors that guarded the coffin where his brother's body lay. He turned to her without moving his hands and whispered:

"Your brother has tricked me. Do you think I wanted to stay in Gniezno? I didn't. I wanted to protect the saint's bones and spread my brother Adalbert's cult in Rome, like the emperor had planned for me to do. But Duke Bolesław, of course, had different plans. He didn't give my brother's bones to Otto, and in doing so he tied me to Gniezno like a dog tied to a kennel, giving me no power whatsoever. I accepted it as a challenge God has placed on my path, and I will pray at my brother's feet for the rest of my days, but . . . you can't imagine what they did to me . . ."

His whisper sounded horrified, and there was nothing but despair in the eyes which looked at her.

"What?" she asked quietly.

"The key . . ." He whispered while his fingers gently stroked the empty keyhole. "They ordered me to guard my brother's bones, but Unger took the key that opens the doors beyond which they lie."

She froze. She had to admit that even she could not have come up with a better idea. She felt an instinctive admiration for Unger.

"If you thought, my lady, that I don't wish for Unger to return, now you know that is not the case. I want him back more than anyone, so he may return what was not his to take."

There was nothing else to say. It was clear Gaudentius was overwhelmed with this thought, and Świętosława turned to leave. Halfway across the cathedral's awning, though, she looked back.

"Radim! Your family was slaughtered in Libice. Sobiesław fell while protecting my brother. Adalbert gave his life for the mission that Bolesław had given him. If you want to be worthy of them, do something. If God has decided to save only you of the entire Sławnikowic line, then make sure you have not been spared for nothing. Do you not appreciate that you're alive? You are stubborn. You refuse to create anything new, giving yourself wholly to the deaths of others. Open your eyes, Archbishop Radim Gaudentius! There is so much left to do."

Ulf and Wilczan stood by the door. As she approached, Wilczan reached for the handle to pull open the door, but froze as Gaudentius chuckled and raised his arms, his fingers spread wide.

"Beholdest thou the mote that is in your brother's eyes, but considerest not the beam that is in thine own eye, Bold Lady . . . Is it better that way? Is it easier?" he asked, his head cocked on his scrawny neck.

She held her breath. In that moment, it was as if the old woman from Sigtuna stood before her, the one who had thrown bones for her and presided over Eric's pyre.

"They repeat the ancient evils of the past . . ." he whispered, moving his long fingers in the air as if weaving invisible yarn. "An ancient evil which deprives the heirs . . . ha, ha, ha . . . The Piasts break the rules, ho, ho, as if they were above the law . . . Mieszko wanted to disinherit his firstborn and failed, but his son, his power-hungry son, has turned away his first pup . . . Woe! Woe! A broken law, a broken tradition, and the punishment for removing the rightful heir from the throne will be paid by the country. Others will commit the sin, and others after them . . ."

"Be silent, old man!" Świętosława shouted, interrupting the dark predictions, trying to stifle the ghastly feeling that had come over her. "Who do you serve, God or Satan? Your duke or your own pride?"

"Ide, ide, ide . . ." he repeated as if he were laughing and clicked his fingers at her.

Świętosława turned to the basin beside the door, the one that held the cathedral's holy water, and quickly submerged her hands within. At that moment, Ulf swung open the heavy doors and clean, bright light burst inside. Świętosława made the sign of the cross and walked from the cathedral. Wilczan barred the archbishop's way and closed the door behind her.

It was late autumn, so the weather was still good enough to travel. The roads were dry, and the heavy rains hadn't yet begun.

Świętosława decided to stop in Bodzia on her way to Kałdus to pray at Dusza's symbolic grave.

Arne the fair-haired castellan greeted her at the gates to the Golden Borough. A woman stood beside him.

"My wife, Irbis," he introduced her. "The duke has given us permission to wed."

"Ibris, where are you from?" asked Świętosława.

"My grandparents came over with Halperin from the lands by the Khazar Sea. Great Duke Lesir was their benefactor," she replied as she bowed.

Świętosława studied the girl carefully. She had beautifully sculpted cheekbones, dark eyes, and dark hair on which she wore a loose silk turban. Jewel-encrusted silver bracelets clinked on her wrists, and colorful glass beads interspaced with gold swung from her neck.

"It is a pleasure to meet you, Irbis, Arne's wife," she said, thinking that Halperin's treasure must have been great indeed if it had been enough to fund

Lestek's enormous building plans as well as to supply his descendants with such jewels.

She had the opportunity to study more of Bodzia's women at dinner. She met Irina who wore the famous Byzantian silver beads interlaced with large gemstones.

"Irina!" She laughed after they'd already had a goblet each of the delicious wine from Constantinople. "Do me a favor and walk up and down the table again."

"My lady." Irina blushed. "I'll do as you ask, but why?"

"Oh, Irina! You're used to it, so you don't hear it anymore, but when you walk your necklaces clink so beautifully together!"

After they'd finished, Świętosława visited Ivar Goldtooth's workplace, and the old dwarf showed her his treasures.

"I'm an armorer, my lady," he said as he opened a chest, "but I love beautiful weapons more than anything in the world. I collect them," he confided.

"Like my husband," she replied with a smile. "The second one."

"The queen is too kind to old Ivar." He shook his head. "Your husband bought weapons to use them in battle."

"And you?"

A blush appeared on the wrinkled cheeks.

"It's enough for me to look at it. See for yourself, lady of the north! Here is an axe decorated with silver, the beloved weapon of the Great Steppe! The greater the warrior, the more beautiful the blade he had forged for himself."

"And I thought that it was the weak warriors who tried to make up for their deficiencies with pretty weapons."

"No, my lady, not on the Steppe! The east loves beautiful weapons. If you must take a life, do it with the most wonderful blade. Look, my queen. I bought this ice axe with a hole in its blade from Halperin himself. It's a famous Khazar weapon. I've seen your men's axes, which are of a similar type, but the ice axes are smaller and easier to wield . . ." Ivar smacked his lips like a child eating a juicy plum as he showed her the weapons.

Sven would have given you a piece of his mind for that sound, Świętosława thought.

The dwarf opened another fitted chest.

"I have wide blades from Normandy. I can show you a sword from the days of Charlemagne, if that would interest my lady."

"My goodness, Ivar, you have collected so many treasures!"

He blushed at her praise and reached inside.

"Here are maces decorated with silver, straight from Russia. They are called bulavas. I quite like them. Did you know, my queen, that a single blow

from a bulava is enough to punch a hole through one's head? Providing the
warrior is strong and knows how to use the weapon."

"And what's this, my dear?" she asked the dwarf about a large stone with
a hole in its center.

"That's my wife's." He waved a hand dismissively.

"A hand mill? Can a blacksmith's wife not afford a servant?"

Ivar blushed and blinked.

"Jaruna doesn't grind corn with that, but fates. She's a fortune-teller," he
replied reluctantly.

Świętosława was about to summon this Jaruna, but she bit her tongue.
She'd had enough visions of the future. She hadn't bent the knee and confessed
her sins to Bruno of Querfurt only to try to outsmart God again.

She prayed at Dusza's and Duszan's graves and asked to see Halperin's tomb
before she left.

She and her men crossed the river Vistula on comfortable wide rafts and
rode along its far side toward Kałdus.

"It seems," Great Ulf said as he looked around, "that young Duke Bezprym is managing well. The roads are peaceful and there has been no news of
bandits. The woodsmen have their work cut out for them, though." He pointed
at wide expanses of recently felled forests.

"I hope you're right." She patted Thorhalla's neck.

Kałdus was built on a hill in one of Vistula's meanders. It was spread out
over the foot of a breathtakingly steep slope. She couldn't help but think that
this place, protected on the one side by the river, and on two other sides by
the steeply rising hills, was unreal in its beauty. It grew out of the river like
some phenomenon. Ramparts were being erected around the borough where
it faced land and the parts that had already been finished loomed impressively.

"Queen Sigrid Storråda!" Bezprym called out as he rode to meet them.

He still looks like a nomad, she thought as she watched her nephew. There
were two braids framing his face to keep the strands out of his eyes, while the
rest of his hair streamed down his back. He wore a simple leather caftan and
tall Hungarian riding boots, a wide belt, and a knife. He wore nothing that
might disclose his noble birth, save for the Piast ring on his finger.

"Prince Bezprym!" she shouted to him. "What do you say to my visit?"

"I can put up with you, I'm sure." He smiled. "Please, come to the manor.
I'll show you the cathedral's foundations if you want to see what I've been
doing here."

He pointed toward piles of gray stones as they rode side by side.

"We have more than enough materials. I want to transport as much as possible here before winter. We started to build the foundations in spring, so with a little imagination you get an idea of what it will look like once we've finished."

"It's the same size as the ones in Poznań and Gniezno," she observed.

The wall reached no higher than a horse's belly. She looked around.

"But the other two were built within the ramparts of a borough, while you're constructing it in the wilderness. Aren't you afraid that the Prussians will arrive at night to destroy what you built during the day?"

"No." Bezprym laughed. "There is only one route by which you can get here, and as you can see, I'm working on the ramparts. There were remnants of some here when I arrived, but I've started anew. For now, armed guards stand by the construction site at night. My lord father has sent me into the middle of nowhere and is probably waiting to see me fail. I won't give him the satisfaction."

"You're wrong about Bolesław," she said.

"Are you saying we aren't in the middle of nowhere?" he retorted.

"You're the one who wanted to be a hermit. He took that into consideration."

The peasants they rode past bowed not to her, but to their master. The entire village was one great construction site. Bezprym's manor was new and smelled of fresh wood. That evening, they sat in the hall over a simple supper.

"I am expecting Bishop Bruno's return any day," he said, staring into the fire. "I've sent men after him to Russia's border. He said that he wanted to be back in Kałdus in time for the anniversary of the slaughter of Międzyrzecz."

"Does he know you're building a cathedral? Is he expecting it?"

Bezprym nodded and she saw the flames reflected in his eyes.

What's going on inside that head of yours? she wondered as she looked at her nephew.

"Why do you never come to Poznań?" she asked.

"Why would I? This is where my lord father sees me. Apparently, he intends to settle Otto in Mazowsze when our brother comes of age. Let Mieszko look after Poznań." He shrugged and pulled his knife out of its sheath. He began to clean it. His dark hair fell into his eyes and covered his face. Bezprym's enormous shadow danced on the wall.

"Are you angry with your father, Mieszko, or with God?" she asked bluntly.

"None of them did this to me," he replied firmly. "Jaromir was only a tool in the Lord's hands. I must have been cursed since the day that Father pulled me away from Romuald."

Dogs began to bark somewhere in the distance.

"Curse, curse," she snorted, thinking of Gaudentius. "Where did you get that idea from? If your father hadn't fought for you, you'd be sitting in Pereum right now, eating roots and convincing yourself that the Piasts abandoned their firstborn. Maybe your soul needs revenge to know peace? If that's the case, you can take my axemen and go to Prague. Capture Jaromir and . . ."

The door opened and revealed a hooded man who raised a hand in blessing.

"In the name of the Father, and the Son! At the foot of the future cathedral of Kałdus, a good Christian queen was trying to convince a young duke to spill blood!"

"Bruno!" she exclaimed.

"Bishop Bruno!"

He pushed the hood off his head to show them he was laughing. He had a long unkempt beard and his hair fell to his shoulders in heavy locks. His teeth shone in his sunburnt face as if he were a wolf.

A wolf? He should be a lamb, she reprimanded herself.

He embraced Bezprym warmly and faced her.

"Won't you kiss the bishop?" he asked.

"Like last time?" she replied, shaking her head. He didn't even blush. "It's a good thing that you're back in one piece. Have you baptized all the Pechenegs?"

"Only the ones whom I managed to convince that praying to a horse's head is as useful as trying to raise the dead using nettles. Will there be space by the fire for a few tired pilgrims?"

A few monks walked into the hall after Bruno, pulling off their travel cloaks and silently spreading themselves around the room.

Omold recited:

Greetings to the hosts, where should the guests sit who have entered your home?
Impatient is the one who seeks relief by the fire.
Flames are desired by the pilgrims who come in with cold knees.

"What is your bard's song about?" Bruno asked.

"It's the 'Song of the Mighty,'" she replied. "A pagan song, 'the Mighty' refers to Odin. Don't worry, Bishop, its message is Christian enough. It's about making a guest feel at home by the hearth."

"Do you remember our agreement?"

"I have kept my side." She nodded. "You heard my confession yourself, Bruno. It's time for you to keep your promise."

He looked at her so intensely that she felt uncomfortable.

Am I interpreting his intentions correctly? she asked herself.

"I left Tankmar and Rodbert with the Pechenegs to continue spreading the Word of God," he said. "I will ordain Bishop Theodulf for you so he may sail to Sigtuna to baptize your son and his people. Theo"—he turned around to his companions—"come here."

It was difficult to guess how old he was because it had been a long time since any of the monks had cut their hair or beards, and they were all covered with dust from the road. But his pale eyes met hers bravely.

"Will you teach him the northern language, my lady?"

"I have a better idea. Wilczan!" She turned, searching for him.

The boy put down the sword he'd been cleaning and joined them.

"You will go to Sigtuna with Theodulf. You'll meet with my son, your old friend Olof. You'll help Theodulf with his task. What do you say to that?"

"As the Bold Lady wishes." Wilczan nodded. "I love all voyages."

"Wilczan was born in Sigtuna, then he came with me to Roskilde and Poznań," she told the bishop.

"And he accompanied my father's men to fetch me from the hermitage in Pereum," Bezprym added. "I can confirm that he's uncommonly brave."

Wilczan had tried to protect him from the fate Jaromir had planned for him. Świętosława had never forgotten it.

"It will be my honor." Theodulf nodded. "Although I would like to learn the language regardless, just so I may use my own words as well as yours."

"I will give you some of my men, and Bolesław has pledged some of his . . ."

What will I say to my son? And through whose lips, Wilczan's or Theodulf's?

She listened to Bruno as he recounted the mission among the Pechenegs, and she reflected on her relationship with her son. She thought about the thirteen years which had passed since they'd last seen each other. *We were lucky,* she thought. *We spent his first ten years together. I didn't have as much time with Harald, Cnut, Astrid, and little Świętosława.*

"My queen?"

Bruno's voice broke into her thoughts.

"Yes? Forgive me, I was miles away."

"I was saying that I would like to relay news of my mission to Duke Bolesław personally. Is your brother in Poznań or has he set off to fight Henry?"

"There has been a semblance of peace since last year's conquest of Budziszyn," she replied. "Henry has made no move against us. It seems that he has other problems, in Italy and the Reich. As I'm sure you know, he hasn't been able to get the imperial crown, and that's keeping him up at night. He's probably still licking the wounds he sustained from Bolz last year. Not many of the lords in east Germania want to fight my brother."

"Then perhaps we can travel to Poznań together? Do you want to hear more of Russia?"

She nodded carelessly. Right now, when Theo's mission was so close to being realized, Olof had all of her attention.

"We met remarkable pilgrims there. They walk to Constantinople, and from there to the Holy Land. They walk so many miles in the hopes of seeing the Savior's tomb that their pilgrimage is, in itself, the beginning of the soul's journey to the Lord . . ."

What if Olof refused to allow himself to be baptized? Or that he decided it was a bad time, that he might lose more than he'd gain by being christened? But who knew if there would ever be a better time for Sweden to open itself to the world and to God.

". . . there are also those who serve the Lord differently. They spend all their wealth on buying out Christian slaves from traders. Chief among them are the Arabs who call the Volga Nahr-as-Saqaliba, that is, the Slavic River. The people I'm telling you about buy out entire ships of slaves and set them all free in God's name. There are also bold pilgrims on the Dnieper who cross the river and its famous rapids to reach the holiest of Christian places through Constantinople. They count among them Vikings who have converted to our faith. One of them impressed me with the strength of his faith. A barge full of ordinary people who were heading to Kiev for the market began to sink right in front of our eyes. The barge had too many people aboard and after rocking from one side to the other, the wagons began to slide off it, followed by frightened horses and eventually the people themselves, screaming and lamenting. Some woman shouted: 'Lord have mercy!' and the pilgrim standing next to us, whom I recognized as a past slave by the mark on his shoulder, threw off his shirt and jumped into Dnieper's current. He surfaced beside the barge and saved that old woman. He then displayed almost inhuman strength by pushing the barge level again. People began to kneel and thank him when he reached the shore, but all he said was: 'God is the one who saved you, I was merely his tool,' and he walked away, refusing to accept any gifts of gratitude . . ."

"I'm tired after our journey," she interrupted Bruno's tale. "Forgive me, but I must retire."

"Let us speak in private, my lady." The bishop stood.

"As you wish," she replied, and bid the others good night.

They walked outside into the cool autumn air.

"Why are you telling these tales?" she asked.

"You know why," he replied, moving closer to her.

They were silent for a few moments, though she was uneasy feeling his presence so close at her back. She stared into the huge round moon hanging over Kałdus.

"We are all of us God's tools," Bruno said.

She felt his breath on her skin.

"What will you do when you leave my brother?"

"What I was meant to."

"Bolesław wants you to live, not die."

"Your brother is the best ruler I have ever met," he replied, and she felt every word tickle her scalp. She was afraid to turn around. "Sometimes, when I think about the archangels, the leaders of Heaven's armies as they defeated Satan, I imagine that Michael wears Bolesław's face." His whisper grew heated. "I can almost see him strike the Prince of Hell from astride his white horse with the spear. The great and terrible Bolesław. But not even he can interfere with God's plan."

"You remind me of a man I loved."

"You attract mystics."

"Or madmen."

She heard his breath again. He was closing in on her.

"If you take another step, which one of us will be confessing our sins?" she asked.

"The one who sins," he replied, touching her hair, before turning on his heel and walking away.

31

⚭

DENMARK

Sven sat on his wolf-fur-covered bench by the shore, watching his sons learning to fight on a ship. The *Bloody Fox* had dropped anchor a fair distance away from the fjord's shore, just enough for the deck to rock under the boys' feet and make them realize how different fighting at sea was to fighting on dry land.

"The *Bloody Fox*'s second youth," Jorun observed cheerfully, sitting down beside his king. "What's it like to watch your sons grow? Do you envy them? I don't know what it's like; Hildigun has only given me daughters."

"All I see are their missteps, and they make me twice as angry," Sven replied honestly. "Look at them. Harald is so impatient and stubborn that he keeps repeating the same mistakes. Do you see that? He moves too quickly, and he keeps losing his balance. He'll fall overboard any moment now!"

"Don't be angry, my king." Jorun tried to calm him down. "The boy is learning. It's a good thing that he's fast."

"And Cnut is too slow. Oh!"

"Do you remember what you were like? I can see it as if it were yesterday now that I watch them aboard the *Bloody Fox*. And then there was the old king. You fought your father so he might give you some power. And now you have not just one but two sons. But then again you have more than enough to leave them! You control two kingdoms."

"One less than is needed." Sven smiled as he looked at the gleaming waters of the fjord. "A king and two sons need three kingdoms, my friend. I have no intention of leaving for Valhalla just yet."

"I wonder what will happen to us." Jorun sighed. "Will the beautiful Valkyries take us to Odin's palace once they realize we've been baptized?"

Sven started to laugh so loudly and openly that his sons stopped fighting and raised their heads, thinking he was laughing at them. Harald flicked his red hair out of his eyes, offended. Cnut took advantage of the fact that his brother exposed himself and struck him in the chest.

"Do you really care about such things?" Sven asked when he'd stopped shaking from laughter.

"Don't you?"

"I don't care what happens to me after death," he replied firmly. "So long as songs about me stand the test of time."

And so long as she, that treacherous Sventoslava, hears the verses about King Sven and cries with remorse for not being with me.

The seagulls above them screeched furiously. One of them fell like a snowy arrow and snatched a fish from right under the surface. The others circled around it, hoping it would drop its catch.

"Have you spoken with Thorkel's messengers?" Jorun asked. "How is your hound faring in England?"

"Brilliantly." Sven nodded. "He gathered the rest of our men from the Isle of Wight and attacked Sandwich with Heming and Eglaf's troops."

"Bravely done." Jorun smacked his lips and a jug of mead appeared in his hand, seemingly out of nowhere. "Will the king drink?"

"No, the king will control his sons." He raised his sword and pointed its tip at Cnut and Harald as they struggled against each other on the ship's rolling deck. "But Jorun should drink."

"Your wish is my command!" His friend poured himself a cup.

"After the attack on Sandwich, Thorkel called the army the Predatory Shoal and they set off toward Canterbury. The people of eastern Kent collected three thousand pounds of silver and brought it to Thorkel, asking him to leave them in peace."

"Those English are so well mannered." Jorun took a swig of mead. "But three thousand isn't enough."

"That's what Thorkel said, too. He moved to the Isle of Wight, from which he launched attacks on Hampshire and Berkshire. King Ethelred has called the entire nation to arms."

"That's new. It's always been the entire nation that has begged the king for protection." Jorun laughed.

"And it turned out that this new way of doing things was no good either. Thorkel ordered the Predatory Shoal to make a series of attacks on Kent and Essex."

"On both sides of the Thames," Jorun pointed out. "That's a good idea."

"Mhmm." Sven nodded, and exhaled impatiently. "Look! Again! Harald is throwing himself around blindly while Cnut keeps waiting for his brother to expose himself before striking!"

"You're exerting excellent fatherly control." Jorun poured himself more mead and said: "Tell me more about Thorkel. It angers you less and interests me. The boys aren't going anywhere, they know that Daddy is watching."

"Daddy?" Sven snorted with a frown. "Thorkel approached London a few times, trying to take the city by surprise, but he failed. But he paralyzed the city and intercepted the merchant ships which sailed along the Thames, so he did achieve something."

"We must remember that!" Jorun burped. "What about the great fleet on which the king has spent so much silver? Do you remember? Thorkel told us about it the last time he was here."

"Oh, the fleet!" Sven laughed. "I almost pity King Ethelred. Just imagine the misfortune: the storm destroyed most of the vessels before they'd sailed on their maiden voyages."

"Bad luck." Jorun stretched out so much his joints clicked. "For Ethelred, I mean, because it sounds to me as if Thorkel is uncommonly lucky. He received the army and instructions from you. He is meant to pave the way for your great expedition. But . . . has it not occurred to you that Thorkel might forget who sent him and whom he serves with all these successes raining down on him?"

Sven said nothing. He watched as the seagulls grabbed their spoils from each other and stroked the long, stiff braids of his beard.

32

POLAND

Świętosława stood in her room by the open window, looking out into the yard. She heard the horn blown in welcome, signaling the arrival of someone from the dynasty. A single glimpse of the dark, muscular silhouette of the rider was enough for her to know who had arrived and what news he brought. Her heart pounded with fear and tears blinded her.

You cannot cry, she told herself. *This was what he wanted!*

Bezprym dismounted outside the stable as lightly and nimbly as a large cat. She saw the servants bow to him, noticed the glances he attracted, curious and frightened all at once. Two young, pretty washerwomen carrying baskets of dry underclothes gazed after him, enraptured. He walked across the yard with his long dark hair gleaming as it fell down his back. He looked like a warrior monk dressed in black wool. He didn't wear a habit. He was clad in trousers, a simple caftan, a black cloak lined with wolf fur, tall boots of dark leather, and a belt. One of the servants who evidently didn't know who Bezprym was froze when she saw him and stared, forgetting about the basket full of apples in her arms until it shifted and the apples began to fall one by one. There was something predatory and noble at the same time in his figure and his movements. He walked looking straight ahead, as if he didn't see anyone. Świętosława noticed that her favorite stable boy Dobrut approached the servant who was still staring after Bezprym. He whispered something to her, and she flinched, looking as if she'd just awoken from a wonderful dream. Dobrut laughed and nodded.

You think you're better than him, Świętosława realized with disgust. *You, a mere stable boy, finally feel like you're better than a Piast prince, just because you can father little dirty screaming brats and he cannot. Did you have to tell her straight away? Do you not realize that when you take her tonight on the straw in the stables, she'll close her eyes and see only Bezprym while you fill her with your seed? The black prince, the warrior monk.*

Bezprym had almost reached the door when Mieszko appeared in front of the palatium.

Light and darkness, she thought. *What will they do?*

She couldn't hear their conversation from her vantage point. She saw

Mieszko spread his arms wide in greeting. She saw that Bezprym didn't even slow down his pace as he passed his brother and walked inside.

Świętosława ran down to the audience hall and met her nephew in the doorway.

He opened his mouth to tell her his news, but she placed a finger on his lips. They looked at one another briefly before she observed:

"He made his dream come true."

Bezprym nodded and walked into the audience hall beside her to face Bolesław.

"Bruno set off to meet his death. He got what he wanted," Bezprym announced to everyone bluntly. "He absolutely refused to take an escort because he didn't want to spread the Word of God with a sword. As a bishop, he achieved the highest goal of his life," he added, "spreading faith in places that had been ignorant of it before his arrival."

Świętosława didn't cry, but her heart felt cold and empty. But when Bezprym described the details of the bishop's death, she tightened her hold on the armrest and kept asking herself: *Bruno, were you afraid?*

". . . the Yotvingians killed his companions, too. Only Wibert survived. Do you remember him, my queen? But they gouged his eyes out so that he wouldn't be able to lead anyone to where they buried Bruno."

Świętosława kept looking from Bezprym to Bolesław and back again. Her brother was trying to control his emotions with all his might. It was no secret that he'd had great plans for Bruno, and though he supported his mission, he never wanted the bishop to venture among the Prussian warriors himself. He wanted a living Bruno, not another dead martyr like Adalbert.

Bolesław rose from the throne and walked over to the wall. He took Saint Peter's sword off the wall and lifted it above his head.

That's how Bruno imagined you, she thought as she felt the emotions choke her. *That's how he saw you when he said that you reminded him of the archangel Michael.*

Bolesław kissed the sword and placed it back on the wall. As he turned around to face them again, he recited:

"What harmony is there between Christ and Belial? Or what fellowship can light have with darkness? What agreement is there between the devil Swarożyc and the leader of the saints, yours and my Maurice?"

She recognized the words. Bolesław was quoting the letter that Bruno had written to King Henry II. A brave, passionate letter in which he condemned Henry's alliance with the pagans against Bolesław.

"How is it that the Holy Spear allies itself with the devilish flags of the ones who drink human blood? Do you not consider it a sin when a Christian—it horrifies me to even say it—is killed as a sacrifice to the demons?"

Her brother's eyes shone with tears. He waved a hand as if he wanted to chase them away. He stepped off the platform and stood by Bezprym. Mieszko walked into the hall.

"And so, Bruno has been killed under the demons' flag!" he said melodically.

Bezprym flinched, but he didn't turn around to look at Mieszko as he walked closer.

"And you, my brother," the younger prince continued, "have witnessed the death of holy martyrs for the second time. Isn't that strange?" he asked, trying to provoke him as he stopped, standing beside his father and Bezprym.

Light and darkness, Świętosława thought again.

They stood beside each other: Mieszko, with his curly amber hair, dressed in a blue tunic embroidered with a gold thread, and Bezprym, wearing a simple black outfit. The only ornament he wore was a small silver cross hanging from his neck. The firstborn son, the heir, denied what should have been his by right of birth, and the second son, intended for the Church, unexpectedly pulled back from that path.

The brothers turned to face each other, and their father stepped between them, with Bezprym standing on his right. He was watching his sons as carefully as she was, as closely as everyone else.

It was here, in this hall, that Bolesław fought Oda and her sons for power after Mieszko's death sixteen years ago, Świętosława thought.

"Were you unable to follow our father's orders," Mieszko continued, "and keep Bruno from Querfurt alive? Our lord duke's wishes were clear. You were meant to be the bishop's right hand, warrior monk, you were meant to protect him, not allow him to go among the untamed pagans to get himself killed . . ."

She saw a tremor run over Bolesław's face, and she saw her brother force himself not to react, to see what Bezprym would do. Her nephew clenched his fist and lifted it in one fluid movement. She held her breath. No! Bezprym didn't hit Mieszko. He placed his hand on his chest, and the Piast ring on his finger glimmered.

"Our father does not stand above God," he said in a choked voice. "Even if you might think so, little brother. The duke's wishes and commands are not enough to impede our Lord's will. Bruno followed in his master Adalbert's footsteps, led by the Savior's voice. But perhaps you, Mieszko, cannot understand the meaning of true sacrifice."

Mieszko opened his mouth to reply, but then he just placed a hand on his chest like his brother and bowed his head to Bezprym. Bolesław, still standing between them, turned to the elder.

"Son, Wibert has been blinded so that he may not lead us back to our friend's grave. Will you find it for me? Get his body back from the Yotvikings, with force or money, I don't care, do whatever it takes. If you need to pay them, take as much as they want. Will you do this for me, son?"

"I will, Father," he said, looking not at Bolesław, but at Mieszko.

Bolesław grabbed Bezprym's head and kissed his forehead before pulling him close. Bezprym stood stiffly for a moment, but then he reached out his arms and returned his father's embrace.

The manor felt empty after Bezprym's departure. Bolesław stalked around angrily. He was worried about the conflict in the west between Gunzelin and Herman. Gunzelin, the late Eckard's brother, and Herman, his son, were two very different men. Bolz had considered the former his blood brother.

"Time has shown that my blood mixed with Gunzelin is worth more than the family ties we have made with Herman when he married Regelinda," he snorted angrily one evening over dinner. "Blood and blood! Do you think that Mieszko and Bezprym will make their peace?" He changed the topic as if he'd just remembered something.

Emnilda sighed and said:

"I'd like them to."

Your wishes aren't enough, thought Świętosława.

"You can take your daughter back by force," she suggested, returning to the first topic. "But that would give Henry an excuse to start a war, since he'd be able to argue that he has a duty to his vassal."

"Don't give him such ideas," whispered Emnilda.

"If I wanted a war, I could find a hundred reasons for it," Bolesław reassured his wife. "Now I just need some peace to work out the details of our dear Sława's marriage to Świątopołk."

Sława, their youngest daughter, sobbed loudly. She had known what her lord father had decided already, but she kept fighting him on it.

"Father . . . I don't want to go to Kiev . . ." she sobbed, smearing the tears over her face. "I don't want to . . ."

"But I want you to go," Bolesław replied.

Emnilda exhaled loudly and shook her head at him. She walked over to her daughter and put her arms around her.

"Kiev is beautiful." She stroked the girl's fair hair. "You'll like it there."

Bolesław was already preparing to begin another story about Kiev which was bound to frighten his daughter more when they heard the horn announcing the arrival of guests. Derwan walked into the hall.

"Duke!" He dropped to one knee in front of Bolesław.

Bad news, thought Świętosława.

"King Henry has captured Gunzelin and accused him of conspiring with you and offending the king."

"Where is he holding him?" Bolesław quickly overcame his surprise.

"In a stone cell in Halberstadt. Bishop Arnulf is responsible for the prisoner."

"That's not good," Bolesław observed.

"There's more, my lord. The king has taken the title of margrave from Gunzelin and given it to Herman instead."

"Meissen in my son-in-law's hands?" Bolesław was furious. "Fox!"

"Consider carefully whether it isn't worth getting your daughter back from Herman, so you don't end up with your hands tied. You can attack the Meissen March once the girl is with us, and take the land back from your disloyal son-in-law," suggested Świętosława.

Her niece, hearing what was facing her wedded sister, began to cry louder. Emnilda led her out of the hall.

"If I do that, they'll kill Gunzelin." Bolesław leaped up from his seat. "They'll hold him to weaken my blows."

They could hear Sława's hysterical crying from another room.

"Let's split up, sister. I'll figure out what to do with the March, and you figure out how to calm down my daughter. Do something to stop her from howling and make her see the benefits her marriage might give us. Światopołk doesn't need a virgin who marries him under duress but a strong and decisive wife to help him fight his father for Kiev."

"Then marry him yourself!" snarled Świętosława before storming out of the hall.

She found them in Emnilda's alcove. Her niece's face was red and swollen from tears. Her beautiful fair hair was in tangles and her dress was covered in creases.

"It's worse than I thought," whispered Emnilda.

Świętosława sat down on the bed next to the girl.

"Sława, what are you afraid of?" she asked gently.

The girl said nothing.

"You're fourteen. You'll be fifteen before the marriage takes place. That's the same age I was when my father made me board the *Haughty Giantess* and sent me to Sweden. My husband was my father's age, but yours is much younger. Mine was a stubborn Viking who sacrificed people to his gods and eventually had himself killed in offering to Odin. Your Światopołk is a Christian. He's a good match."

Jarozleif would have been better, she thought, but she didn't say it out loud. Neither did she mention Świ:atopołk's numerous and fierce brothers, or the fact that wars among family members were an unofficial Russian tradition.

"I'm afraid," the girl whispered, "that I'll never see any of you again."

"Sweetheart, look." Emnilda stroked her daughter's hand. "Świętosława came back home. Fate is unpredictable."

"I know, I just heard all about that!" Sława burst out. "You're already planning to take Regelinda back from Herman. Has anyone asked her what she wants? Maybe she's happy with him, has that even occurred to you? No. We're like mares to you, like cattle that you can do with as you wish. Give away, swap around, sell, and breed!"

"How dare you!" The blood drained from Emnilda's face.

"She's right," said Świętosława firmly. "That's exactly what it's like. We are like mares. Our lives are never our own, they belong to our fathers from the day we are born. That is the price we pay for being part of the royal family. And you're right, some of us are sold at a better price than others. Some of us start our own herds where each new foal extends their mother's life. Have you visited your sister Bogumiła in the abbey? No. I've spoken with her. She was asking after you, and I was under the impression that she would happily switch places with you and go to Kiev. Think about that, perhaps we can discuss that with your father."

"No," Sława whispered quickly. "I don't want to be a nun."

"Then at least that's settled." She patted her hand. "Now, listen to what I tell you, what I learned from my stepmother Duchess Oda. You have to be cunning, patient, and strong to outlive your husband. Being a widow and the mother of royal children is a good position to maneuver yourself into."

"I know better ones." Emnilda smiled, kissing her daughter.

"Oh, you don't count," snorted Świętosława. "You and Bolz are an exception. But, of course, your daughter might be an exception, too. Maybe it will turn out that Świ:atopołk is a strong, handsome man and they will fall in love with each other."

"I want to . . ." whispered Sława, "but I'm afraid of strangers."

"That's why you'll have an entire court going with you. Your father will even give you Bishop Reinbern . . ."

Sława stopped crying and began to listen, relaxing in her mother's embrace.

Świętosława could leave them now. She went to her rooms on the first floor, closed the door, and took out a piece of parchment. She traced the words with her finger. She had never learned to read, but she had memorized the letter Bezprym had brought her from Theodulf.

Olof King of Swedes sends greetings to his mother, Queen Sigrid. He thanks her for sending the bishop and for thinking of him, since he recollects her with the warmest affection. Amen.

SWEDEN

Olof King of Swedes rode around Sigtuna wearing the white robes Bishop Theodulf had given him. He wanted to show his people that he was proud of the fact that he'd just been baptized. He threw small silver coins to them, following the tradition of Christian rulers as Theodulf had described it to him. His son Anund Jacob sat in the saddle in front of him. The three-year-old was small for his age and he kept close to his father, shy in front of the crowds of strangers. Ten-year-old Ingegerd sat confidently in the saddle, keeping her back straight and her head held high. She looked like a born princess. *"She gets that from me,"* his lady wife, the Obotrite princess Astrid, would say. *No, my queen,* he'd think, though he never voiced his thoughts. *Ingegerd looks like my mother.* Wilczan and Theodulf's arrival had brought back countless memories.

"Long live King Olof!" the crowds chanted.

"Long live Anund Jacob and Ingegerd!" someone added.

His wife Astrid, riding next to him, snorted angrily, but she reined in her temper and greeted her subjects. Nobody mentioned her name. The Obotrite mistress had a talent for slighting people. She seemed to think that the size of her dowry bought her the right to arrogance. She surrounded herself with wealth and introduced practices into the simple manor in Sigtuna that nobody liked but her.

Olof searched for Edla in the crowds. He didn't have the strength to send her away. His mistress, lover, and friend gave him everything that his wife could not. Tenderness, understanding, and unconditional love. Astrid wanted to be a queen so badly that she didn't realize that he needed a woman, not just a lady. And Edla, modest, sweet, passionate, and loving, never forgot that she was a woman. He built her a house by the water in Sigtuna. He surrounded her with servants. He visited her whenever he could. His lady wife knew about Edla. At first, she'd been furious, and then she demanded that he send their daughter, who was a few years older than Ingegerd, away from Sigtuna. He'd agreed. When his wife had given him a son, she grew quieter, feeling more secure now that she had given him two children while his mistress had only given him one. But Olof knew that it was just the calm before the storm that would come when Astrid learned that Edla was with child again.

Maybe I should move her to a safer place? Away from the queen? he wondered, feeling a stab of sorrow at the thought of being away from the woman he loved. He didn't see her in the crowd and suspected that she was probably trying to avoid Astrid.

"Is it nearly over?" Anund Jacob asked.

"Yes, son. We have ridden across Sigtuna so that our people have the chance to celebrate the royal baptism with us. We can go home now."

Wilczan was waiting outside the manor. His childhood friend stood by the shield at which the sons of his lords were shooting arrows.

Like we used to do. Olof sighed. He wasn't sure which life he preferred: the one he led now, as an adult ruler, or the time when he'd been a boy.

"I want to pee," his son whispered, and Olof forgot his doubts. One couldn't turn back time.

He picked the boy up under his arms and lifted him from the saddle, handing him to the servants. He heard his wife say to someone:

"I need to change before dinner."

He sighed with relief. That meant that she hadn't seen Edla either and she wouldn't want anything from him.

"Will you walk with me, King Olof?" Wilczan suggested.

"With pleasure! Although what I'd like to do more than anything is to dress up as a servant and run away with you for a day." He nodded toward the yard full of people and horses.

He took his cloak from a servant to cover the white robes. He'd been wearing them for a week, but tomorrow would be the last day he dressed in white.

"What next, Wilczan? You said you didn't want to stay in Sigtuna with me."

"But Bishop Theodulf will stay. I need to go back; the queen may need me. There is much happening in Poland."

"In Denmark, too. Does the queen know that Sven is gathering forces to invade England?"

"Yes." Wilczan nodded.

"She has many friends," Olof guessed, but Wilczan didn't say any more.

"I remember that she told me once," Olof broke the silence after a moment, "that you can judge a ruler's strength by the number of his enemies."

"Now she claims they should balance each other out. Do you wish me to pass on any message to the queen?"

Olof took a deep breath and said:

"No message for the queen. But I have much to say to my mother."

Then he opened his heart to Wilczan and his confession flowed out. He was back in Øresund, rocking aboard the *Golden Shield*, giving out orders.

"We only live once, and we cannot turn back time," Wilczan said eventually, once Olof had finished. "Do you want me to tell my mistress that her firstborn son will never betray her again?"

"Yes, Wilczan. I have understood Theodulf's teachings. I cannot make up for what I've done. I cannot bring Olav Tryggvason back to life, but I regret my sins and I ask my mother's forgiveness for my part in what happened. Do you think she will give it?"

"She already has, Olof. She sent me to you."

33

POLAND

Bolesław hated traveling with a procession. The dozens of supply-laden carts and throngs of servants slowed the journey down. He could have covered the distance between Poznań and Przemyśl in ten days if he'd been alone with his squad. Now, he was riding alongside Sława's entire household, escorting her to her future husband, Światopołk, the son of the grand prince of Kiev. This was their third week on the road.

"Boring, isn't it?" Świętosława appeared beside him.

He had taken his sister with them because she knew how to keep his daughter calm.

"But the country is beautiful," he replied curtly.

"You've ridden this way on your expeditions to Moravia." She nodded.

Świętosława had brightened up considerably since Wilczan returned from Sigtuna, relaying news of Olof and the Swedish court.

Olof, the one who betrayed her at Øresund, is the thorn in her heart, just as Bezprym is mine, thought Bolesław, studying his sister's profile. There was nothing matronly about Świętosława. Age suited her. Her hair still shone like the clearest amber, and her short height and slender figure made her look like a young girl. *Or perhaps I only think that because I feel as if I were still a boy when I'm with her? Bolesław, the lord duke's son. Our father had also thought he'd live forever. I remember that winter night when he took off his clothes and led me to the ice hole.* The memory was enough to make Bolesław shiver with cold. *Mieszko was as old then as I am now. Forty-five. Where has all that time gone?*

"Lift up your chin so it doesn't start sagging." He heard Świętosława's voice behind him.

He turned around with a snort of laughter. His sister who had been beside him only moments before was now alongside Sława, giving her advice.

"When will we get there?" She rode up beside her brother again. "I want to see the beautiful Przemyśl."

"And I want to see the far more famous and beautiful Kiev," retorted Bolesław.

"Knyaz Vladimir would drop dead if he heard that you want to visit his daughter-in-law so close to his home."

"That's a shame." He sighed.

"I know, I know. If you didn't have to guard the western borders, you'd find an excuse." She laughed. "Your Daniła says that there are plenty of lynxes roaming the area. If you loved me as much as you say you do, you'd catch me some young ones."

"Make up your mind!" He scowled. "Is it your children that you miss, or your lynxes? I can't keep up with you sometimes."

"You lack imagination, brother dear. You're getting soft. Are you sure you're not beginning to rot of old age? Has Emnilda checked recently?"

She does so less and less frequently, he thought sadly.

"Emnilda hasn't been feeling well," he confided.

"I know, she told me," replied Świętosława softly.

"What do you think about it?"

"She'll pull through." His sister shrugged.

"You're a bad liar."

"I know. That's why I'm here and not in Roskilde."

They both laughed because what she said was as tragic as it was foolish.

"She's my whole life," he said when he caught his breath.

"And you are hers. You are both lucky, Bolesław. Most rulers aren't. You've had so many years of a great, passionate love . . ."

"Stop," he said through gritted teeth. "One can never have too much love."

"You're speaking to someone who almost died for lack of it," she replied tonelessly. "Fate had a different life in store for me."

He didn't tell her. And seeing the sadness in her face as she spoke, he knew he never would.

"I've sent for our sister," she said after a moment. "Astrid knows her herbs and she's a healer. Some say she can heal even when all hope is lost. Emnilda will find it easier to allow Astrid to help her while you're not there."

"Thank you," he replied.

He grasped hold of the hope this thought gave him. Astrid, their loyal sister. A strange woman. She hadn't left the port island once since Dalwin died and Wolin backed out of their alliance. He'd asked her to accept her place at Poznań's court as his sister, but she'd refused. *"If I cannot breathe the ocean air, I'll die,"* she'd said, and he had to admit that he understood her. But it was true, Astrid had hidden powers. *God willing, she will be able to use them to help my Emnilda.* He could see his beloved wife caving in on herself, shrinking. She was hiding how weak she was. She painted her lips and her cheeks so that nobody would see how terribly pale she'd grown. But he did see. He loved her anyway. He loved her even when she was helpless because her soul hadn't changed, and though he had taken her body years ago, it was her soul he loved.

The Reich king had sent Duke Bernard Billung to him last spring, the same one who had saved Bolesław's life from the assassins in Merseburg ten years ago. Bernard had conveyed the purpose of his visit in the simple words of a soldier: *"The king wants to use me to ask you to retreat from Połabie. I do his bidding, but I tell you: don't listen to him. You have more hidden allies than enemies there. The people and the borough's leaders are on your side. That's all I have to say. I didn't save you from his thugs only so that you may satisfy him by doing what he wants you to now."*

"What do I think about it?" He repeated the question. "The Bird King has wandered into a swamp. That's the easiest way of putting it. My people are as unyielding to the actions of the wild Veleti as they are to the Saxons. My word is law. And though I know that Henry will take the imperial title for himself sooner or later, it won't change his position on the river Elbe's banks. He could of course drag all of the Reich's army over, or even the entirety of the imperial forces, and grind me to dust, because I could not defend myself against such numbers. But he will not be able to convince the people there that they are his subjects. Pride and arrogance make for poor advisers, sister. The war has been raging for ten years, and he, the great Reich king, can do nothing about that. I'm prepared to make as many illusory alliances as I need to, but I won't back down."

"I know that. You still want Otto's dream to come true."

"I wish you had met the emperor. There was a light inside of him. He wanted to build on the foundations of peace, not of war."

"If the master of war that you've become can be seduced by such an idea of peace then you're right. I wish I could have met him, too."

They reached Przemyśl two days later. The border borough greeted its duke with delight.

"It is an honor for us to host our duke and his household, and it will bring us glory," Castellan Rosław greeted them.

"Have the Russians arrived yet?" Bolesław asked.

"They've been waiting for a week." Rosław winked. "Duke Świątopołk with his household. I told them to set up camp by the river San. The weather has been good and dry. The palatium awaits my duke and his daughter. I will throw you a feast tonight! I want my duke to see what our hospitality looks like."

It was boundless. Rosław poured them such delicious mead during the feast, so strong and full of flavor, that Bosław was drunk before he'd thought about how much he was drinking. They ate bear paws braised with herbs, beavers baked in cream, roasted deer, and stew of wild boar and berries. There was a selection of other dishes after that, but Bolesław didn't remember those. The evening meal became breakfast.

"Brother." Świętosława nudged him. "I beg you, tell Rosław that he is the best of castellans, otherwise he will never stop giving us food and drink."

He ordered a bucket of cold water be poured over his head to sober him, and he shook himself off.

"Enough!" he shouted.

Rosław froze in the middle of giving his servants orders to bring in the next dish. Bolesław saw Sława, trembling and hunched over under her cloak.

"Enough feasting," he said calmly, and walked over to his daughter. "Are you ready?"

She shook her head. He felt a headache coming on.

"Świętosława?" He searched for his sister, seeking her help, but she'd disappeared. Either that, or he wasn't seeing clearly.

But eventually he saw them all. Bishop Reinbern, Daniła, his men, Sława, her servants, his sister, and Great Ulf with his gray beard on his scarred face.

"Rosław, tell the Russians that I will give them my daughter at noon tomorrow."

They met as custom dictated in the middle of the river.

Sława was dressed in gold silk and a white cloth covered her head. She rode a gray mare whose mane was interwoven with pale flowers and pearls. She couldn't see anything from behind the veil, so Bolesław's squad of men led her horse. He rode in front of her with his sister. Świątopołk rode out to meet them. He was tall, with curly hair and eyes that glowed like hot coals. He was lavishly dressed. Gemstones and plates of gold glimmered in his caftan and cloak. He had a rich, fur-lined military cap on his head.

"Pretty boy," commented Świętosława when she saw him.

"Do you wish you'd married him when Vladimir offered?" Bolesław asked maliciously.

"No. I prefer warriors. Chain mail, caftans, helms, the stink of seal fat and unwashed hair—you know all about that. But this one here is a real prince. At least he looks like one. Sława"—she turned her head back to speak to her niece—"your lover is beautiful."

"Who goes there?" asked Bolesław when the procession was within earshot.

"The groom comes for the bride!" the young prince called back.

"What's his name?"

"Światopołk, son of Knyaz Vladimir, lord of Russia between Novgorod and Kiev."

"Who accompanies him to take his bride?"

"A procession of his sisters and maidens and a squad of warriors!"

Only now did Bolesław look beyond Światopołk, and he was blinded. Not by the gold and riches which seeped from the prince's procession, but by the deep blue eyes which peered out from behind him. Among the girls who accompanied the prince, there was one dressed in green. The green of moss and of ferns which only bloom once a year. Could it be Jaga, the girl who had given herself to him on that midsummer's night? No. The girl from his past had been beautiful in her shameless nakedness. This one blinded him with her maiden beauty.

"Who gives away the bride?" the prince shouted.

"Bolesław, the duke of Poland."

"It is an honor for me, the man who will take her!"

Bolesław's men walked Sława's mare over to Światopołk. He rode up to meet them and raised her veil.

"As beautiful as a dream!" he announced, throwing the fabric over her back. "I will take her as my wife."

He placed wide silver bracelets on her wrists as he spoke. Sława didn't cry. *Maybe she likes him?* he thought with relief. *But how can I find out who is the girl in the moss green cloak?* He felt himself blush like a boy.

"I, her father, give her to you in good faith," he called out, squeezing his knees into White's sides. "But if any harm should befall my daughter, I will take her back and I will punish you."

"I accept those terms," said Światopołk. "Her procession can follow us."

Bishop Reinbern made the sign of the cross to send them on their way. The women in waiting, servants, and maids Sława had been given sobbed as they crossed the river San. An armed squad followed them, men who were intended to guard her day and night. Sława turned around to look back. Tears were streaming down her cheeks, but she made no sound.

"Sława!" Świętosława shouted after her. "Remember everything I told you!"

"About the chin?" he asked.

"You may be a duke, but you're also a fool," she snorted, and called out again: "Make your herd!"

Sława waved a hand clad in a golden glove. The silver bracelet glimmered on her wrist.

The girl in the green cloak turned around to look back at Bolesław with her blue eyes.

"Jesus," Świętosława groaned. "What's that? Who's that? An elf?"

"I have no idea," he replied.

34

❀

DENMARK

Cnut, according to his father's custom, sat on the throne on his left. His older brother Harald was on Sven's right. Their sisters, Astrid and Sventoslava, sat beside them, the younger beside him and the older beside their brother. The queen's throne, his mother's old seat, had disappeared barely a year ago. He and his brother had defended the empty place, but they had backed down eventually.

"This is what our family looks like. Me and my two sons and two daughters. That's it," Sven had decided, and there was no more discussing the matter after that.

"I prefer this than if he tried to take a new wife," his older brother had confided in him. "Mother's memory is sacred to me."

"Me too," Cnut assured him, though it was getting more difficult with every passing year to keep the image of her that he carried in his heart from blurring.

They argued about her with Harald sometimes.

"She had green eyes."

"No, they were gold!"

"It was her hair that was gold!"

"No, red!"

"Your hair is red but that's because of Father!"

"She had lynxes."

They always agreed on the memories of the two predators on a leash walking beside her. Sometimes Cnut worried that that was the only thing about his mother that he knew for certain. Father made sure they had no time for reflecting on the past. The entirety of Denmark was focused exclusively on one thing: the preparations being made for the great excursion to England.

Today was no different. They sat in the great hall of Roskilde's manor house and listened hungrily as Ragn of the Isles shared his stories of Canterbury.

"Thorkel the Tall's Predatory Shoal is choking England, my lord. They robbed and burned the place for the entirety of last year. Thorkel is making the most not only of the camp on the Isle of Wight, but he has also set up a number of other bases on land where he keeps the horses he's stolen."

"That's why he's so fast and he can attack from the land as well as the water," Sven said, and Cnut was under the impression that his father was pleased with his chieftain's work. Sven was coiling his long red hair around his finger, and he never did that when he was angry.

"Our siege of Canterbury began in the autumn of last year," Ragn continued. "It dragged on and on, and I was sure after the third week that we were just wasting our time. But that fox Thorkel somehow found a way to get to one of the priests inside the abbey, and he bought him off. The man opened the gates for us."

The men in the hall laughed loudly at this, praising Thorkel's cunning. Cnut felt a twinge of unease. He glanced at his father. Sven had let his hair drop, and he placed his hands on his knees.

"Continue," he said to Ragn, silencing the others.

"We took our time pillaging the city since there were many treasures to find." Ragn smiled. "But Thorkel wasn't searching for riches. He ordered us to take prisoners. His men brought him the nun Leofrun first. She was the abbess of the abbey of Saint Mildred, if I recall correctly. Thorkel praised them for the capture, but he ordered the search continue. Bishop Godwin of Rochester was brought before him next. The man had chosen a bad time to visit Canterbury. They also brought him Eldred, the royal sheriff. Thorkel spoke to these two and then set off to continue the search himself. He came back with the greatest of treasures: the archbishop of Canterbury."

"Odd man. I would have been looking for beautiful English ladies, preferably maidens!" Uddorm exclaimed.

"Keep listening, Uddorm, and you'll find out why Thorkel preferred the archbishop to women," his father replied.

He probably wanted to trade him for ransom, Cnut thought. He was right.

"We kept the prisoners with us all winter while King Ethelred's messengers rode back and forth. The ransom grew each time, but Thorkel kept raising it anyway."

"How much did he take?" his father asked impatiently, interrupting Ragn's narrative.

"Forty-eight thousand pounds of silver."

A murmur of admiration passed around the hall, and it quickly grew into loud shouts.

Cnut saw his father's jaws stiffen as his fingers clenched on the throne's armrests. The song about the Army of the Two Kings, Sven and Olav, and how they took the greatest danegeld England had ever paid, had been recited in this hall numerous times. But that had been three times less the amount that Ragn of the Isles had just given. Cnut knew his father's quick temper and he knew that Sven would never forget this, not even if Thorkel shared the silver with him. It wasn't about the riches, it was the fame that mattered.

Ragn of the Isles lifted an arm to stop the chanting.

"Wait, that's not all. Before the messengers reached our camp to tell us how high a ransom their king was willing to pay, and to stop us from invading again, strange things began to happen. The Predatory Shoal fell apart. People got tired of waiting. We took Canterbury in autumn, but it was Easter before Ethelred and Thorkel had finished their negotiations. One night, a drunken brawl broke out. Men, impatient to get their hands on the ransom money, began to threaten the prisoners. Thorkel tried to smooth things over and explained that the king was bound to send an offer any day. But then the archbishop joined in from his cage and announced that he wasn't a horse that could be bought. That was all the spark it took to ignite the fire. Fighting broke out, and the furious warriors slaughtered the prisoners. The archbishop died first."

Silence fell over the hall. Cnut could feel his heart pounding. He looked at the faces of the warriors and chieftains around him, and he tried to understand what was behind their silence. Did they pity the dead? Or regret losing the enormous ransom they might have been paid? Were they angry that the events which unfolded had been so barbaric?

"Chaos ensued. Thorkel managed to regain control. He didn't allow for any desecration of the bodies and he went to King Ethelred himself."

He's either extremely brave or completely mad, Cnut thought.

"Wasn't he afraid?" his father asked.

"I don't know, my king, I didn't ask him. I know what happened though, and it surprised everyone. King Ethelred paid the ransom despite the prisoners' deaths."

Another wave passed over the hall in Roskilde. Laughter, shouts of joy, and, above all, expressions of admiration.

"Thor-kel! Thor-kel!" the people chanted, while Cnut watched his father grow redder and redder.

"Stop praising Thorkel until I've finished!" shouted Ragn of the Isles. "Yes, he got the silver even though the prisoners had died. He gave back their bodies, and then dissolved the Predatory Shoal after having paid everyone their share. Listen to me! Because then he, and forty other crews, switched sides to serve King Ethelred."

Cnut saw Sven let out the breath he'd been holding.

"Betrayal!" Jarl Thorgils of Jelling shouted, and his son Ulf, like his father's shadow, joined in.

"Betrayal!"

"When he was dissolving the Shoal, Thorkel announced that from now on, anyone who stands against the English will have to face him. And that he will not hesitate to kill his old comrades in the king's name."

"Betrayal!" The word traveled around the hall. Thorgils and Ulf were the loudest. "Revenge!"

Sven stood up, and silence fell. Cnut and Harald rose up quickly, too, standing behind their father like a shield.

"Chieftains!" King Sven called out. "Prepare your sons, brothers, cousins, and fathers. This is the end of the Predatory Shoal! The fleet that we will build and which will sail to England next year will be known as Sven's Anger."

"*Sven's Anger! Sven's Anger! Sven's Anger!*"

"I will lead it, with my son beside me!"

Harald, flushed with emotion, stepped forward. His father turned around and said:

"No, Harald. You'll remain in Roskilde. You will rule Denmark in my absence as my eldest son. Cnut will stand beside me as we sail to England!"

Cnut felt dizzy. He looked at his father. *Yes!* Sven reached out to him. Cnut took a step forward and grabbed his king's left hand. Sven raised their arms together. Cnut felt giddy with happiness at the unexpected turn of events. He glanced at Harald. His older brother, still flushed, was glaring at him angrily, as if their father's choice was his fault. Sven took his eldest son's hand and raised it, too. And so there they stood, all three of them, holding hands. Their father eventually let them both go and embraced them.

"I have decided," he announced. "There will be no arguments over this."

"Yes, Father," they replied in unison, before sitting back down.

Jugs of mead were already circulating around the hall. The warriors chanted all their names in turn. All of Roskilde was ready to go to war. Cnut caught Ulf, Thorgils's son, staring at him with malice as the bard began to recite the "Song of the Mighty."

Silent and thoughtful
should be the royal son.
Brave in battle
and unyielding in giving orders . . .

Silent and thoughtful—that's about me. Christ! Can I do this? Harald is better suited for this kind of excursion. Cnut's thoughts raced feverishly in his head, but he managed to maintain a calm exterior. The bard, having paused to take a sip of mead, continued:

Fortunate is he who gains for himself
wisdom and fame during this life;

Among the general laughter, uproar, screeches, and happiness, his father leaned over to him. His red hair gleamed in the firelight, and the long braids of his beard stuck out threateningly. There was no reflection of the joy which pervaded the hall in Sven's blue eyes.

"Don't let me down, son," he snarled.

35

POLAND

Świętosława returned from her journey to Przemyśl entirely satisfied. Daniła had caught her a young lynx on their way back.

"Why did you only get one?" she reprimanded him at first, but then kissed him and rewarded him richly. "Daniła, Daniła, it's a female!"

Her beloved lynxes, Zgrzyt and Wrzask, had both been male. The newly captured animal rode in a cage and Świętosława fed it every time they stopped, wondering all the while how to tame a female.

"I have no idea," she confided in her brother. "I had ten years with Olof, six with Harald, and five with Cnut, but the girls were taken from me so quickly . . ."

"You'll be fine," Bolesław told her distractedly. He was thinking about something else.

They found Astrid in Poland.

"How is Emnilda?" she asked in a whisper when she greeted her sister.

"I did what I could. It's not terrible," Astrid replied.

Świętosława studied her sister carefully as she held her at arm's length.

"How are you?"

Astrid's dark hair was streaked with gray and her face seemed tense, tired, and unhealthy.

"Me?" She grimaced. "There's nothing wrong; I'm just getting old, sister."

"Don't say that because then I'll have to get old, too!" Świętosława snorted and kissed Astrid's cheek. "Don't go back to Wolin. Please, stay."

"It's not that bad." Astrid laughed drily. "I don't need to be looked after just yet."

"Bolesław needs you," Świętosława lied smoothly. "Don't go."

Astrid stayed, though it probably wasn't because she believed what Świętosława had said about their brother. Astrid had an amazing ability to disappear and appear exactly when she was most needed. She could remain almost invisible for days at a time.

Shortly after midsummer, the same day that they heard of Strosz Crow's Wing, Swarożyc's priest, fleeing his cage, Świętosława spotted Astrid's dark blue cloak by the river Warta while she was returning from a walk in the nearby glades.

"Sister!" she called out and felt a stab of fear when Astrid didn't reply.

She walked close to her.

"Astrid, what are you doing here?"

Her sister turned to her. She looked straight through Świętosława as if she couldn't see her. Her hands were shaking. Świętosława embraced her tightly.

"I'm looking for the living among the bones of the dead and drowned," she muttered after a moment.

The Astrid that Świętosława held in her arms was fragile, stiff, and absent. She felt as if she were holding a stranger. The reeds rustled and shifted, parting to reveal her lynx's flaxen muzzle.

"Down, Dusza!" whispered Świętosława.

Her sister softened in her arms, flinched, and pulled away.

"Świętosława and the lynx." She chuckled, and corrected herself, "She-lynx. Were you out walking? Are you teaching her to hunt?"

"She's a predator; hunting is in her blood."

"What did you call her?"

"Dusza." Świętosława studied her sister's face carefully. "Can you really not remember what you just said?"

Fear flickered in Astrid's dark eyes.

"No. What did I say?"

"You were searching for the living among the bones of the dead and drowned."

Astrid shivered. She sat down on the grass, pulling her cloak more tightly around herself.

Is she cold? Świętosława wondered. *It's the middle of summer.*

"Sit down next to me," Astrid requested.

Dusza ran in the direction of the glades while Astrid ran her fingers through the dry grass.

"It happens rarely, but it does happen. The first time was when our lord father told me about his marriage plans for us all and told me to marry Sigvald. I begged him to change his mind, but he wouldn't. You know what happened. He said that Sven might pose a threat to us if he joined forces with the Obotrites or the Veleti. He said that if we all did as we were bidden, then although Sven might inherit a great Denmark, he would leave behind a kingdom no larger than a fishing village."

"He was wrong," Świętosława observed tonelessly.

"At first, I just started shivering. Then I felt the tears stream down my cheeks, even though I wasn't crying. I couldn't feel my fingers, as if I'd thrust them into a bucket of ice. And that's what I told him: 'You're mistaken, Father,' and then it passed."

"I always knew you were special, Astrid. You have the gift of Sight. You were the one who was right, not Father. Has it happened since?"

"A few times," Astrid answered evasively.

"And now? Whose bones were you searching for?"

"I don't know, sister. I felt as if I were searching for someone holy."

"Are you cold?" Świętosława asked, holding her sister closer. "My special, beloved sister." She kissed Astrid's shoulder.

"Why are you telling me that now?" Astrid asked in a choked voice. "Why now?"

Świętosława looked carefully at her. Astrid's chin trembled, as if she was trying to stop herself from crying.

"Give it a rest." She laughed, patting her shoulder gently. "You're a big girl now. Let's go back. Dusza, heel!"

The sound of horns came from Poznań's ramparts.

"Come on, don't dawdle. That was the western gate. It's probably important news. Let's go."

Awaiting them was news Świętosława would have preferred to never have heard at all.

"Bishop Unger is dead," reported Derwan.

Świętosława exchanged a glance with Astrid. Could these have been the holy bones that Astrid had seen in the river?

Bolesław rose from the throne, and Derwan braced himself for his anger.

"They murdered him?!" her brother roared.

"It's still a mystery, my lord," the scout said. "Because if they did, they killed Bishop Tagino, too."

"What?!"

"Your bishop Unger and the host of the place in which he was imprisoned, the archbishop of Magdeburg, Tagino, died on the same day. Magdeburg is buzzing with rumors."

Świętosława was horrified. Astrid grabbed her hand and began to laugh hysterically.

"And to think that I was about to get baptized! I told myself: 'When Bishop Unger returns, I will come to him so he might baptize me.'"

"How could this have happened?" Bolesław paced the audience chamber. Dusza growled.

"No one knows. Apparently, they were both found dead one morning."

"Had they eaten together?" Emnilda asked.

"Even if they had, so far it's all just speculation, and nothing is known for certain."

"Tagino was an ally, brother." Świętosława wrapped Dusza's lead around her wrist. The young lynx still struggled with obedience at times. "Sit. The duke will pace for as long as it takes him to come up with a plan. In the worst case, they got rid of an archbishop who supported you, and your own bishop, Unger. In the best case, someone wanted to kill Unger and accidentally poisoned them both."

"Or," Bolesław suggested from the other end of the hall, "Tagino was the intended victim and Unger was an unexpected witness and victim. It's no secret that Tagino wasn't a supporter of Henry's alliance with the pagans, and though he may not have expressed his views as bluntly as our Bruno the martyr did in his letter, he still refrained from supporting that endeavor."

"There is another rumor," Derwan interrupted. "Apparently Unger was being pressured to accept the authority of Magdeburg over Poznań's diocese."

"Gaudentius mentioned it in Gniezno." Świętosława remembered. She also realized that Unger had been the only one with the key to the martyrium which held Saint Adalbert's bones. "What if it was him?" she wondered aloud. "What if Gaudentius is behind Unger's death? He wanted to take back the key . . ."

"My queen!" Emnilda reprimanded her. "You're speaking of the archbishop of Poland!"

"I'm not speaking so much as thinking out loud."

I'll go to Gniezno, she decided immediately.

"I'm going west," her brother announced. "If Henry is behind both of these deaths, then we are standing at the precipice of another war."

She and Bolesław set off on the same day. He rode White across the West Bridge, with Mieszko at his side, three companies of heavy cavalry and six companies of heavy infantry following them. She crossed the East Bridge on the black Thorhalla, followed by the Bold One's axemen, Great Ulf and Wilczan, and Dusza on a leash. Bolesław was seen off by Emnilda clad in a beautiful honey-colored dress, with the fair-haired twelve-year-old Otto standing at her side. Świętosława was accompanied to the gate by Astrid wrapped in her dark blue cloak.

"See you soon, Astrid!" the Bold One called to her.

"Farewell, my salty sister." Astrid waved as her hair danced in the wind.

She swept it away from her face with a slender hand that was covered with spots. "Świętosława! I put something in your saddlebag."

"A live snake? Poison?" she joked, riding past her sister.

She froze when she saw that there wasn't a trace of laughter in Astrid's eyes.

"Open it when I'm gone," said the Lady of Wolin.

So, we are never to meet in this world again, thought Świętosława, feeling as if someone was clutching her heart, stifling it. *Or the next.*

They raced away. Gosław, Gniezno's castellan, stood at the gates holding a torch, even though it was nearly midnight, having been informed of their impending arrival by a messenger. A night of the new moon, as dark as they come.

"My queen . . ." He yawned. "With a wild animal on a leash and the Vikings at her side."

"Such are the times that I must ride hard enough that I arrive at night. Where is Gaudentius?"

"I haven't checked." The castellan's eyes widened.

"Has he been anywhere recently, or met with any strangers?"

"My lady, crowds flock to us every day of the week except Mondays. The archbishop has many visitors . . ."

"Including me," she hissed. "Wake him up if he's sleeping. Tell him the Bold Lady has arrived."

They didn't dismount. Gosław quickly established that Gaudentius was watching over the martyrium, despite the late hour.

"Open the cathedral gates, Castellan," she ordered.

Gosław's men followed her directions. Wilczan and Great Ulf took their torches. Świętosława moved Dusza's leash from her right hand to her left and crossed herself.

"In the name of the Father, the Son, and the Holy Spirit. God Almighty, strike me down if I'm mistaken. Axemen! Let's go!"

And she rode into the cathedral.

"Oh!" Gaudentius exclaimed.

"I was right!" she called out.

The archbishop was kneeling by the open martyrium. The horse hooves clinked on the church floor. The axemen surrounded the archbishop in a tight ring so he couldn't escape. Wilczan leaped down from the saddle and took Dusza from her.

My God, she thought. *It's just like it used to be with Wrzask and Zgrzyt.*

He offered her a hand to help her dismount, and she took the leash again.

"The door to the relics of your brother is open while the man who had the key, Unger, lies dead. How do you propose to explain that, Radim Gaudentius?" she asked as she approached him.

"That's none of your concern, sinner," he hissed at her.

"Are you sure about that?" She walked closer while Dusza soundlessly walked so close to him she was almost touching his feet. "I accuse you of Bishop Unger's murder."

"I did not kill him." The archbishop laughed, his face transformed into a horrifying mask in the torchlight.

"But his blood is on your hands."

"No . . ."

"Dusza, now!"

The lynx pushed herself off the floor and pinned Gaudentius to the ground in one fluid movement. Świętosława closed the distance between them and tore the silver necklace that held the key from his neck. Fat Egil helped her rise. Loud-Mouthed Ake held Gaudentius down while she walked over to the martyrium to make sure it was the key she thought it was. Yes. It turned in the lock with a crunch. She was about to close the door when she heard Long Kalle's voice:

"Bold Lady, please, let us see the relics. You have told us so much about the saints, and I've never seen wonders such as these before."

"I ask this, too," Smooth Hauk joined in. "You have promised us Heaven, so give us a taste of what that will be like."

She shivered.

"Don't ask then, help me," she said to Hauk.

Together, they pulled the silver coffin out of the martyrium. The key fit perfectly. They turned it and Hauk lifted the lid.

"Christ!" Great Ulf fell to his knees with a clamor.

A headless body lay inside the silver coffin. The head, preserved so well that he looked as if he'd been dead for less than a day, rested on his stomach, held there by his hand with the thumb locked into the empty eye socket.

Ake allowed the archbishop to sit up on the floor, though he held him with his arms twisted back.

"Dead for fifteen years but he looks almost as if he were alive . . ." Gaudentius whispered.

"Without his eyes," Wilczan pointed out.

"The Prussians gouged them out right after he died . . . If you look closely you will see the scar on his cheek . . . He's had it since we were children . . . We were slinging rocks and Sobiesław hit him with one. He never told on him, though, and when Mother asked him where he got it he said he tripped and fell . . ."

"That's why he was the saint while you . . ." Świętosława didn't finish the thought. The word that danced on the tip of her tongue was too cruel.

She stared in wonder. Not at the man, though the body was naked. At the miracle, because he truly did look as if he were alive. A leaf was rotting in Adalbert's hair.

"Axemen," she said quietly, "if any one of you has lost faith, let him touch the holy limbs."

Only two of the twelve stood up. The others greedily took in the view.

"Close the coffin, Hauk. That's enough."

They slid the coffin back into the martyrium with a clang. She closed the door herself, turned the key, and hung it around her neck.

"No!" Gaudentius tore himself out of Loud-Mouthed Ake's grasp. "You cannot!"

"But you can kill for the key?" she replied.

He hid his hands behind his back.

"I didn't . . ." he lied.

"No, you only gave the order," she said.

"Give me back the key, my lady. It doesn't belong to you."

"Nor to you," she said firmly.

"I curse you!" he shouted.

Ake and Hauk grabbed him immediately. Dusza growled, and the sound bounced off the stone floor.

"For taking away my ability to see my brother, for leading a wild animal like this into a house of worship! A terrible curse will fall upon this country . . ."

"Don't try to frighten me," she interrupted him. "What you did was petty and cruel. If the Lord is just, which I have never doubted, your curse has as much power as last winter's snow. I'm taking the key with me, Radim Gaudentius, so that you may understand that God takes away whatever it is we want more than Him. Mount your horses, axemen. Dusza, leave him. He's not worth your pretty fangs. Let's go!"

36

ENGLAND

Sven was fuming as he sailed the ship he'd named for this very emotion, *Anger*, to England's eastern shores. He was moving against an ally who had betrayed him. Thorkel, who had robbed England instead of giving it to his king, had now switched sides. He knew that York's vassal was dead, but he remembered the numerous noblemen of Northumbria who were of a similar mind to him, and after a few days' rest at Sandwich, he set off north. He reached the estuary of the river Humber and sailed into Trent's currents, reaching the wealthy city of Gainsborough. He didn't need to besiege it; it was enough that he made sure its inhabitants saw the army he led. The gates opened for him and the new vassal of Northumbria walked out to meet them.

"My name is Uhtred!" he shouted. "King Sven, welcome to my city. We accept your rule because we respect the arrangements made by our late ealdorman Elfhelm. Welcome to Gainsborough!"

A feast was held in their honor in the main town square. Cnut sat beside the vassal, as surprised by what had happened as Jorun and the rest of the chieftains. Each dish the servants brought in and placed on the roughly set-up tables was more delicious than the last.

"What do you know about my arrangements with the late ealdorman, Uhtred?" asked Sven, taking a gulp of bloodred wine.

"Everything, King Sven." He smiled. "I know that you intended to join your families. Elfhelm is survived by a daughter, Elfgifu. A marriage with her would provide a solid base for an alliance between you and northern England."

"I'm not looking for a wife." Sven chuckled. "Elfgifu was meant to be my son Cnut's wife. What do you say, boy?"

"I don't know her," Cnut said bluntly.

"We can change that!" He lifted his goblet, but didn't quite raise it to his lips. He turned to the ealdorman and said: "Your assurances of standing with me against King Ethelred bring me joy, but I'm too old to trust your word."

"What would convince you, King?"

"Hostages," he said, gulping more wine.

The blood drained from Uhtred's face.

"You must know that ever since news of what happened to the archbishop of Canterbury has spread, the word *hostage* has acquired rather threatening associations. Murdering highly influential men despite a ransom being paid . . ."

"That's your problem, Ealdorman, not mine. I'm not the same as that commoner Thorkel. I'm the king of Denmark and Norway. I may fight bloody but I fight clean. Give me one son from each noble family, and I give you my word they will be safe if you remain loyal to me. I also need supplies for my army. That will ensure that my men will not burn your villages or steal your sheep. I will set up camp here, and my son Cnut will rule."

He could see his boy clenching his jaw. Every young man his age wanted to fight. They all thought that war was no more than waving a sword around and spilling blood.

He moved closer to Cnut and whispered into his ear:

"You're my son, and you will do as I tell you whether you like it or not."

"Do you want me to marry some local girl?" His son grimaced.

"I don't recall you objecting when we discussed who your sisters should marry."

"That's different," Cnut hissed.

"Is it? I don't think so. You are my child, just as they are."

"Your father never forced you to marry. You chose Mother yourself."

"Old Harald was dead by then." Sven chuckled into his ear. "You're out of luck, boy! I'm in perfect health. You're angry that you have to guard the camp? It's harder than it seems. You will have to look after our ships, guard the prisoners, and ensure that the men under your command don't rise up. Did you think that battles are won with swords? Yes, that's true. But wars are a different thing altogether. Do you know why I left England eight years ago? I took the wonderful danegeld and struck an agreement with York's vassal. Everything was going smoothly—until we got hungry. Who knows what would have happened if it hadn't been for the hunger. Perhaps today it would be King Sven, not King Ethelred, sitting on the English throne."

"I'm to have your back, is that right?"

"Yes. What have you learned today?"

"That wars are won by alliances," Cnut replied.

"Almost." He patted his son's cheek. "But before you begin to negotiate terms, there must be a show of force."

He drained his goblet, put it down, and rose from the table.

"Son . . ." He turned to Cnut. "My chieftains! Jorun, my closest friend. Thorgils of Jelling, Ragn of the Isles, Uddorm of Viborg, Gjotgar of Scania . . . and my friends of northern England! Here is my son Cnut. He is eighteen, but every one of you who has seen him throw off his clothes to swim knows he's a man!"

A chuckle of appreciation spread around the hall. Cnut, though it embarrassed him greatly, carried a sword rather than a mere knife in his trousers. He blushed. Sven put an arm around him.

"I am making Cnut the chief of our camp in Gainsborough. And if the Valkyries should come for me during our journey across beautiful England, remember that King Sven has named his successor!"

They hooted happily and drank.

"And now, my chieftains and my new English friends, it is time for us to show England just how strong we are!"

He showed off their strength in Mercia, which fell without putting up a fight. He then set off for Oxford, and its inhabitants gave themselves and their entire wealth up to him, too. He took supplies for his army and hostages from both places and sent these last ones back to Cnut. Winchester was next. The city didn't wait for him to arrive; they sent messengers to meet him on the road and announce that the city would be waiting with open gates and the noblemen had already chosen the sons they would give as guarantors of their alliance.

"There's only London left!" Jorun said, stretching as he woke up the morning after their feast at Winchester.

"Only London," young Ulf, the son of Thorgils of Jelling, snorted.

"Are the children mocking you?" Sven asked, rubbing his eyes.

"No, my king," Ulf retorted. "But I doubt that we will be able to take London. That's where Thorkel the Tall, the defender of the king of England, is waiting for us."

"If you have doubts then go and hide behind your father's back," Sven snarled.

The jarl of Jelling appeared, ready to stand up for his son.

"Ulf is right," he had the guts to say. "So far, we have only fought the English, or rather accepted the keys to their city gates that they willingly gave us. Our meeting with Thorkel is what will really test the strength of *Sven's Anger*."

"Do you want the first taste of it?" Jorun stood beside his king. "Unless you do, I suggest you go sharpen your sword, take your shield with you, and be quiet."

But that brat, Ulf, had been right. London did not give in. Thorkel's ships lined the river Thames and fought for Ethelred, the king who had bought his services. They turned back to save their strength, and Sven, controlling his anger, ordered them to leave their ships.

"We march west." He pointed.

"Revenge is a dish best served cold, my lord." Jorun was always at his side. "London is not the center of the world."

"You're wrong there. It's the center of England. But it will mean nothing if it stands alone while the rest of the country surrenders."

He knew what he was doing. The inhabitants of London whom they happened upon on their way by the Thames told them that all the king did was pray and call for a public penance. "Our lord has announced that your invasion is God's punishment for our sins. He has ordered us all to fast, pray, and offer donations to fund the defense of the city." He suspected that apart from Thorkel the Tall, the only other defenders of the city consisted of the king's royal guard.

"Ethelred doesn't believe in victory," Sven observed to Jorun. "He sent his wife, Queen Emma, to her brother in Normandy, along with their children."

"That's a shame." Jorun sighed. "A queen like that with her children would have made a good hostage."

When they reached Wallingford, they found the city followed Oxford's example. It opened its gates. They moved on to Bath and Devon.

Ealdorman Ethelmer summoned all the nobles and rode out with them to meet Sven.

"The south and west of England accept you as its ruler, King Sven, just as the north and east has done. We will no longer serve Ethelred."

He felt almost dizzy with the triumph that seemed to have fallen into his lap so effortlessly. He heard the whisper of the jarl of Jelling behind him:

"London."

"Did you hear the jarl, English nobles?" He turned around and met Jarl Thorgils's gaze. They studied each other for a moment before Sven turned back to the ealdorman. "He's right. I will give London a chance. It can follow in your footsteps and open its gates to invite me in as its ruler."

POLAND

Bolesław rode to Merseburg with Emnilda and Mieszko at his side. After everything that had happened recently, he had accepted Henry II's offer of peace.

"Not for long," he'd promised Świętosława before they left. "Only for as long as it takes for me to get back my daughter."

The riots in Kiev, led by his son-in-law Świętopołk, had broken out after Knyaz Vladimir had tried to change the line of succession and force his eldest sons to accept their younger siblings, the ones he'd had with Anna, as his heirs. The Principality of Turov and Pinsk that Świętopołk had been given by his father was not what Bolesław had hoped for when he made his plans for an alliance with Russia. When he'd heard about what was happening in Kiev, he'd told his son-in-law to defend what was his by right. Światopołk had stood up to his father, which had quickly led to him being thrown into a dungeon alongside Bishop Reinbern and the sweet Sława, the girl who was so afraid of strangers. It gave Bolesław an excuse to march on Kiev. A duke's daughter in a dungeon? The very thought made his blood boil with anger.

He knew that Henry wanted peace largely because he needed to set off to Italy to crown himself emperor. Unable to fight Bolesław out in the open, he tried to plot against him, but had exercised poor judgment when picking his allies. Henry of Schweinfurt, though still a subject of the Reich king, was still loyal to Bolesław. His son-in-law Herman's younger brother Eckard, named for his famous father, had recently sided with him, too.

"So long as this marriage is successful." Emnilda smiled to her husband as she rode beside him. "So long as Mieszko does not meet the same fate Sława has. An alliance with the Lotharingians is truly extraordinary. Our future daughter-in-law is the niece of Emperor Otto III!"

And Ezzo's daughter, the man who's the main opponent to Henry II's rule, thought Bolesław with satisfaction, but he didn't remind his wife of this fact. He was happy that Emnilda felt better and endured the hardship of travel without complaint.

The marriage of Mieszko and Richeza was the result of many years of discreet communications held behind Henry's back. Ezzo was related to the Carolingians and the Liudolfings, and his marriage to Otto's sister Mathilda had raised his family to the peak of imperial royalty. He had fought Henry for power and he'd lost, but he never abandoned his ambitions. An alliance with Bolesław was, for Ezzo, a natural partnership between two predators who cannot catch their prey alone but hope to at least surround it by working together. Henry would never have agreed to this marriage had he had another choice. In deciding to finally reach for the imperial crown, he had to appease Ezzo in some way. The Lotharingian duke had recovered some of his wife's lands which Henry had taken for himself during the wars, and he'd been given new territories so that his lands now stretched from the rivers Rhine and Moselle as far as Turingia in the east. Henry had also agreed to Mieszko's marriage to Richeza on the condition that Bolesław made peace with him. It was a fair price to pay, made fairer by the fact that although Ezzo and Mathilda had seven daughters, they had given as many as six to the Church, leaving only one to forge an alliance through marriage: Richeza, their future daughter-in-law.

"The river Saale dead ahead!" Zarad shouted from the head of the procession, and Bolesław was unexpectedly overwhelmed by memories of the council at Merseburg from eleven years ago.

"This is where we planted our spears, young prince." Zarad rode over to Mieszko and pointed to the middle of the river.

Henry's servants waited for them at the ford to help them cross. Derwan leaned over to the duke and whispered:

"We know this ford better than anyone, but if he insists . . ."

As they reached the other side, a procession set off from the gates of Merseburg toward them.

"Hostages," Bolesław muttered, pleased.

He had given Henry a number of conditions, among others that he supply hostages to ensure the duke's family's safety in the city. Zarad was already giving instructions to set up camp. Duchess Emnilda wanted to rest before she continued. Her golden tent gleamed on the bank of the river Saale.

Here he was, riding into Merseburg again, for the first time since the assassination attempt on his life. He rode White, and Mieszko carried the Holy Spear beside him. Emnilda wore gold and blue. This time, he had one hundred men with him, not a dozen. He glanced at the side gate which the margrave's men had chopped to pieces that day to give him a way out of the city. It had been walled up.

"That's where Duszan died." He pointed it out to his wife.

"It won't happen again," she replied quietly.

"No, my lady. These are different times."

Trumpets sounded over the gate.

"Duke Bolizlaus of Poland with the noble Duchess Emnilda and Prince Mieszko, heir to the throne."

Henry's guards led them straight into the castle yard. Two lords held Emnilda's horse for her and wanted to help her dismount, but he got there first. He wasn't going to trust these men around his wife with even as simple a task as helping her off her horse.

Henry II sat on the royal throne in the audience hall. He looked even smaller than he had eleven years ago. The German crown rested on his temples. His dark hair was streaked with gray.

Have I also aged so much? wondered Bolesław.

They faced each other. Mieszko went down on one knee before the king, while Bolesław and Emnilda both bowed. Henry bowed slightly without standing up.

"Duke! I have waited so many years," he said quietly. There was no triumph in his voice. "So many matters have divided us."

"Do you want us to name them all, beginning with my leaving the Hoftag here years ago?"

"I hope that all that has been discussed by our messengers so that we, the rulers, can focus only on the good between us. This is the dawn of a new era. We will soon join your son with Princess Richeza in marriage; there is much to celebrate."

"I have brought you gifts, King." Bolesław nodded at Stojgniew and Zarad. "Generous gifts."

Zarad and Stojgniew placed two chests full of gemstones at Henry's feet. "Thank you."

"But I also have a spiritual gift which is, as I understand it, more valuable than gemstones, silver, or gold."

He nodded to Bjornar, who walked over to the royal throne and handed Henry a small box.

"It's a relic, King," said Bolesław. "The finger bones of our noble martyr Bishop Bruno of Querfurt."

Those same fingers held the quill with which he wrote that letter to you, calling on you to cease your alliances with the devil, thought Bolesław as he watched Henry open the box.

"This is a precious gift," the king observed, closing the box quickly. "I duly accept it."

They sat opposite one another that evening at the feast. Bolesław could hear the din of conversation, laughter, and singing. He saw the flickering candlelight and smelled the heavy scents of wine and food. But it all felt like nothing more than the wind which rustled the leaves as he rode by. He and Henry stared at each other across the long table.

They had returned to the issue which had divided them before. Eleven years ago, Bolesław had taken Milsko and Łużyce by force. Now, after years of fighting, Henry II gave them to him to rule over as vassal. Back then, Bolesław had wanted to buy Meissen from him, but he couldn't do that now because it was ruled by his son-in-law Herman. Back then, they had agreed to a ceasefire. Today, Henry promised him an entire troop to support him in his venture to Russia. Bolesław promised to back him with the same number of men when Henry set off to Rome. Nobody could give Unger back his life, but Bolesław was given Ederam in his place. Ederam had been a canon in Magdeburg once, and Bolesław had hosted him during the peace agreement discussion in Poznań.

Otto's beautiful niece Richeza sat beside Mieszko. She was as fair-haired as her late uncle.

Does Henry make a list of gains and losses as I do as he stares at me across this table? Does he believe that we will both hold up our ends of an agreement with which neither one of us is satisfied? We are like to hunters who both want the deer's heart, but now that the catch is before us it is clear that the animal has already been disemboweled.

Henry's dark eyes narrowed when he raised his goblet.

"To the peace treaty of Merseburg!" he called out and drank, never taking his eyes off Bolesław.

Bolesław froze with the goblet in his hand. He watched his son and daughter-in-law drink, along with the Reich lords, bishops, archbishops, and nobles.

"Bolesław," Emnilda whispered, "everyone is watching."

"To our joint venture to Kiev this autumn!" he said, and drank.

37

ENGLAND

Sven switched from *Anger* to the *Bloody Fox* when he led his fleet down the Thames to London.

"You're getting sentimental," Jorun muttered, glancing up.

The wind filled the *Fox*'s sails triumphantly.

"And you aren't?" Sven retorted. "I saw you cleaning your sword, the same one you had when we failed to conquer London twenty years ago. The same one you used to chop us a way into Bamburgh."

Jorun shrugged and patted the sheath of his sword.

"It's good to have trusted friends by your side."

Sven unexpectedly embraced him.

"You're right, my friend."

Thorkel the Tall's fleet, the same one that had recently opposed them, had left the port in Greenwich for the Isle of Wight, taking King Ethelred with them. The ruler had been defeated.

"I think Thorkel must be the most brazen man I have ever met," said Jorun as he freed himself from Sven's embrace.

"No." Sven spat into the Thames. "Thorkel is the only true Jomsviking. That's what they were meant to be. Devoid of a conscience."

The day that the south and west of England surrendered to Sven was the day that Thorkel woke up his Predatory Shoal and his crews began to plunder and burn the same men they had been defending. The chaos which took hold of London's surrounding areas forced King Ethelred to pay Thorkel handsomely to stop. Only then did the Jomsviking agree to protect the king again and took him to the Isle of Wight.

"We're nearly there!" Sven called out, and Jorun blew the horn.

The rest of his crews blew their horns, too, and the sound filled London's port. Sven stood at the bow with Jorun at his back. His red hair, heavy with the mist that hung over the river, lay still on his shoulders. He breathed in. It was the same smell he remembered. The smell which London gave off as it greeted its new ruler was that of human fear.

The ones who had first offered him their services were waiting for him: Mercia's noblemen with Ealdorman Leofwin, and Ulfcetel representing East

Anglia. The archbishop of York, the noble Wulfstan, stood between them, as did the new archbishop of Canterbury, Lyfing. The bishop of London, Elfwig, was missing. The courage he'd shown while defending the city was legendary.

"Long live King Sven!" someone shouted from the crowds that waited on the banks.

The Londoners kept close together in a tight, antagonistic group.

"Long live!"

"Sven, king of England!" shouted Ealdorman Ethelmer.

Jorun took a deep breath and roared:

"King of Denmark, Norway, and England, Sven I Haraldsson!"

They don't need to love me; they just need to serve me, thought Sven, looking around at the terrified inhabitants of the city as he leaped down from the *Bloody Fox* onto dry land.

The first weeks he spent in London felt like a dream. They feasted, accepted tributes, and drank to their victory.

"I promised London that I would return, and I've kept my word!" thundered Sven.

The red wine tasted like blood, and though he drank and drank, his thirst never abated.

"Now what, King?" Jorun sat down on the bench beside him.

"What do you mean?" Sven didn't understand.

"You've made one more of your dreams come true." Jorun clinked his goblet against Sven's. "You need to find another."

Sven laughed hoarsely and patted Jorun on the back.

"Oh, my friend! Being a king is like being married. It's easy to get a wife, but much harder to keep her happy!"

He rose earlier in the mornings to make his days longer. At first, Sven received subjects who came to air their complaints, following the archbishop's claim that this was custom for English kings, but after the third day of endless lamenting, he'd had enough.

"If I ruled Denmark the way that Ethelred ruled England, I would go mad," he complained to Jorun.

He began to try to put matters of state in order, starting with the collection of taxes for the armies and strengthening the neglected garrisons.

"Everything here is old," he groaned. "Whatever the Romans didn't build the English never thought of themselves. The old fortresses are drowning in heathlands."

"No one knows the weaknesses of this country as well as we, its invaders, do. Besides, King, we need to rebuild the bridge," pointed out Jorun.

"Bloody hell!" Sven cursed, then began to laugh. "We got stuck on that bridge so many times and now that it's been destroyed, we are the ones who must rebuild it. Damn it! But now this is our London and the bridge is the key to its defense."

"There's something else, King Sven." Thorgils of Jelling joined the conversation, though nobody had invited him. "The English Church is as rich as the Crown, if not richer."

I hate him, thought Sven, *but he's right. We need to tax the Church.*

And so he did, immediately. This gave rise to complaints from the bishops as if he were taking away their last goat.

"Think of Saint Edmund!" thundered Archbishop Lyfing.

"Why?" Sven asked. "Shouldn't it be the other way around? Shouldn't the saints look after the kings?"

The archbishop was horrified.

"King Edmund the Martyr died at the hands of your countrymen over a century ago. You cannot tax his abbacy! That would be a dishonorable thing for a Christian king to do."

"And what your Christian king Ethelred did was honorable?" Sven shrugged. "He ordered common people to fast, pray, and repent sins of which they were innocent. At least I state my conditions clearly: everyone must pay to see the country defended. I don't understand why the abbacy should be treated any differently. After all, they are the first to attract foreign invaders."

The archbishop gritted his teeth.

"You know much about barbarian invaders."

"Don't force me to become the devil you see in me, Archbishop." Sven smiled so coldly that his guest began to gather his things to leave immediately. When he was at the door, Sven added: "My people will come to the abbacy to collect the taxes in one week. Tell the monks."

"Me?" the archbishop froze. "Why me?"

"Because you're their leader. Do I understand the hierarchy of the Church correctly? Or would you prefer if I changed it?"

He missed the wind at sea, the way it caressed his face and lifted his red hair. It made him feel like a bird about to take flight. Here, in London, he felt like an endlessly damp crow.

Christmas was rainy, and he was glad it passed quickly. The walls of London's castle protected its inhabitants from the water, but not the damp. Eye-watering smoke always hung in the rooms and it soon began to choke him.

"Your son, King, has sent a messenger asking if he should send the hostages home yet," Jorun said. They were alone in Sven's stone chamber.

"No." The king cleared his throat, feeling as though the smoke were stinging it. "There's no air with which to breathe here."

"True." Jorun nodded. "A king's life is a hard life indeed."

Sven waved away his attempt to provoke him.

"What else does my son say?"

"His wife, Elfgifu, is expecting a child. She will give birth within a few weeks."

"Ha! I told you that Cnut had everything he needed."

"And he knows how to use it." Jorun chuckled.

"Don't brag, don't brag. We'll have to wait and see whether he has followed in my footsteps and fathered a son first."

"That's hardly his fault, is it?" Jorun scratched behind his ear.

His Hildigun only gave birth to daughters.

"Boy or girl, it will be a child that ties us even more closely with the nobles of Northumbria. The lords of the south and the west are here in London, and it's clear that they can't be let out of our sight. The bishops especially are still treating me like a usurper. Oh, damn them!" He choked on his own saliva. "That's why we still need the hostages. They ensure the nobility's loyalty. Tell Cnut to keep them comfortable but secure . . ."

He had to stop speaking because he suddenly felt breathless, and when he tried to take a deep breath, he coughed so hard that his entire face turned red.

"Damn it, my lord!" said Jorun. "I haven't heard your cough since . . ."

"Bloody hell . . ." he choked out once he could speak again. "I thought I was going to cough out a lung."

"Melkorka would have a lime brew to help with that. Vali would give you mulled wine," said Jorun.

"Do you miss Denmark?" Sven asked, clearing his throat.

Jorun didn't say anything.

"Summon . . . what's her name?"

"Mary?"

"Yes. Have her bring us some mulled wine."

He crawled into bed still wearing his shoes and caftan and pulled the royal silk sheets over himself. He was still cold.

"Throw me a cloak, Jorun," he requested.

The quiet, fair-haired Mary brought them cups of mulled wine. Jorun made himself comfortable next to the bed. Sven wanted to drink the wine, but at the second sip realized he couldn't swallow. The royal chamber was blurring before his eyes. He felt a warm presence beside him and turned to look at it with difficulty.

"It's a vision," he whispered.

"What?" asked Jorun.

"Can you see her? The Bold Lady beside me . . ."

Jorun didn't say anything, and Sven, even though he knew it couldn't be real, gave himself up to her small hands and felt the touch of his wife, the one he hadn't seen in over a decade. She sat beside him and said: "Don't worry, I'll look after our children." He felt something warm between his legs. The cup tipped over and the wine spilled out.

"My lord? What's wrong?" Jorun leaned over him, but his voice sounded as if it was coming from a distance, through a mist of fog.

Two lynxes leaped up onto the bed. Wrzask and Zgrzyt approached him. *No,* he pleaded, *no . . .* Wrzask leaned down and licked the spilled wine.

Who blew out the candles? he wondered impatiently. His father Harald emerged from the darkness. He wore a blood-soaked bandage across his chest. Sven knew that it flowed from a wound which would never heal. A wound he himself had given him.

"My malicious son," wheezed Harald. "Come on! You're all equally furious. Pups who bark before they're even born, when they're still in the pregnant wombs of the bitches. What are you afraid of? Come on! Father's waiting for you."

Harald laughed aloud, displaying his painted fangs. Pus and blood seeped from his eyes.

"No!" Sven shouted. "No!"

"My king . . ." Jorun appeared before his eyes again. "What's wrong?"

"I don't know. I can see the dead." Sven shivered and wiped the sweat from his forehead.

"Stop that, Sven." His friend patted his shoulder. "You're just seeing things. A moment ago, you said you could see the Bold One, and she's still among the living."

Sventoslava. He clutched onto the idea of her.

"Is she here?" he whispered to Jorun because he couldn't see anything. The bed was surrounded by darkness that was as thick as the gray fog.

"No." Jorun's voice drifted across from behind the fog. "It's just me."

"But I can't see you," Sven admitted, and understood. "All I see is fog and darkness."

"Friend," Jorun said after a moment, "I think you're dying."

The clink of iron pulled from its sheath reached him from beyond the fog.

I'm on the battlefield, fighting for my life, thought Sven. Jorun pushed the sword into his hand and wrapped his fingers around the hilt.

"Sven, do you want me to call anyone?" Jorun asked.

"My wife," he demanded.

"That's not possible. Queen Sigrid is in Poland. You exiled her." Jorun sounded sad. "Sven . . . you're the king, who is to take the throne once you're gone?"

He realized that Jorun truly believed he was dying. He wanted to laugh. Wasn't it funny? Instead of laughing, he coughed. He felt his lungs rip apart. *Odin! Christ! I cannot die of a cough!* He held onto the bed as tightly as he could. A lynx sat on his chest, while he, the great Sven, was trying to throw off the predator. He felt the bed he was holding onto as if it were his enemy shift. He was still strong enough to move it!

"I'll open the windows . . . You're choking, friend," he heard.

A moment more and he was breathing in the cold, damp Thames air. And the smell of human fear.

"Come to me, son," Harald growled from the gloom. "I'll tell you what it feels like to be stabbed by your own son."

An army of the defeated stood behind Harald. He saw tens of faces of men he'd killed. He hadn't remembered them until this moment, until they stood before him, stabbed, with missing arms, drowning in blood after being pierced by spears, desperately grabbing at icy decks with stiffening fingers.

Olav! He called out to the army of the dead which surrounded him. *Face me. The second king, the second chieftain. Come, let us fight for the danegeld paid in silver!*

Instead of Olav, a black rider appeared and threw severed heads at his feet. Black Ottar, the exile from Lejre, and his sons. He could hear the clinking of Arnora's chains, but the tribal queen was nowhere to be seen on this side of the darkness. A voice pierced the gloom again.

"Who is to be king after you? Who do you name your successor?"

"The son of the queen . . ." he whispered. "Cnut . . ."

His father's cold fingers were taking him. His lungs stopped fighting. He walked confidently now, treading on the soft clouds. He saw the army in London below him light the torches and thunder:

"Long live King Cnut of Denmark and England!"

He saw the Valkyries' white wings above him, soaring toward the battlefields, calling out to him: "We cannot take you with us because you did not fall in war. Go, go, you cannot stray. The High One is waiting."

He walked on. His red hair floated in the breeze again. The stiff braids of his beard stuck out before him, pointing due north. His father, Harald, marched beside him, laughing as he revealed his painted fangs to the darkness.

PART III

THE FOURTH KINGDOM

1014–1018

38

DENMARK

Warm, sticky mist hovers above the surface of the sea in the last moments before dawn. The moon has melted like a piece of ice thrown into water, and the sun hasn't risen yet. The peaceful depths rock the boat gently as if it were trying to extend the night's sleepiness. The sail, heavy with moisture, hangs limply at the mast, waiting for the gust of wind that will bring it back to life. The sun rises without warning, with no ringing of bells or blowing of horns. It emerges from the waters, slicing it in a single moment with a sharp golden ray. The seagulls rise from a rock with a screech. The fish freeze in fear under the surface. The rigging sighs as wind fills the sail.

Cnut stood at the bow of the *Queen's Son* and watched Hrani nimbly steering the ship as they sailed through wide but shallow straits. His brother Harald walked over, his red hair braided in thick plaits.

"You look like our sister!" Cnut laughed when he saw him.

"I hate it when the wind blows hair into my eyes." Harald shrugged, then looked at him carefully. "When did you name the ship the *Queen's Son*?" he asked, mistrust coloring his voice. Cnut's hands tightened on the gunwale.

The past few weeks had been hard on them both. After their father's death, things in England had happened so quickly. King Ethelred had shown more initiative than ever before. He returned from his exile in Normandy with Thorkel the Tall and the Predatory Shoal, while the great lords of the south and the west, the same ones who had sworn allegiance to Sven, turned away from Cnut and returned to serve their old master. His father's army named him king, but Cnut, stationed at Gainsborough, was cut off from the main forces. He'd gathered the entire fleet and sailed out to sea. By the time they reached Sandwich, he knew that he had no allies left.

Before he'd stepped foot on land, he could already hear the edict issued by Ethelred and Wulfstan, the archbishop of York: "Any Danish king is henceforth banished." He was furious, and he acted without thinking. He didn't like to think about it, because every time he did all he could see was a bloody mist. True, he'd previously thought of himself as honorable, just, and brave, but in Sandwich something happened to him, something he wasn't expecting.

"Any Danish king is henceforth banished." That's what Ethelred's heralds screeched, and the hostages aboard his ships, the same ones he had looked after for so many months, stared at him defiantly, with disdain. Yes, he did it. He gave the order and didn't look away for a second. And then he left the hostages on Sandwich's empty shore. He left them there as a painful reminder of their fathers' betrayal. Afterward, he had had no choice but to return to Denmark.

His wife Elfgifu couldn't come with him. She was in the advanced stages of her pregnancy. Her relatives hid her, while he gathered his forces and sailed home, to Roskilde.

"I asked you something." Harald dragged him out of his memories. "When did you name the ship the *Queen's Son?*"

"When I was in Gainsborough," he replied, walking over to his brother. "I was angry with Father that he left me in Northumbria with the hostages and everyone else while he set off to conquer England. And one evening, Hrani reminded me of the story Father disliked so much."

"The one about your birth?" Harald sighed with relief. "You should be happy it was forgotten, otherwise the boys would have called you a mommy's boy." He chuckled, but quickly grew serious again to make sure he understood his brother's motives. "So, you named the ship to make Father angry, despite the fact that, as you all claim, he made you his heir?"

His brother's eyes were still filled with distrust. Their meeting after a year of Cnut's absence in Denmark was difficult, as there was a cold fog hanging between them. Cnut had sent Hrani ahead with news of his return to Roskilde. There were horses and a procession of people to welcome him home at port, but his brother wasn't among them. Harald did not come out into the yard when Cnut reached the manor, either. He was waiting for him in the great hall, sitting on their father's throne. The chieftains who had returned from England with Cnut walked in with him: Thorgils of Jelling, Ragn of the Isles, Uddorm of Viborg, and Gjotgar of Scania.

"Where's Jorun?" Harald asked in greeting.

"He'll bring back Father's bones when they're ready."

"You remembered how much he hated rot . . ." His brother smiled.

"Yes. Won't you embrace me?"

Harald stood up and asked:

"Are you coming here as a brother seeking help?"

"And as a king," Cnut added, voicing what had so far remained unspoken between them.

"King," Harald repeated. "But if Hrani's report is to be believed, you just lost your kingdom. England."

"But not Denmark, brother."

"Father made me vassal of Denmark when he left."

"But he named me his heir in England."

"We can attest to that," the chieftains said. "We were there."

"And the army has named me king, like Father wanted," added Cnut.

Harald's face grew red.

"Wait." Cnut tried to reassure him. "I don't want to take anything from you."

"I am not a child who will allow you to take anything from me," Harald shouted, and disdain dripped from his words. "You're the one who lost a kingdom."

Cnut let it slide.

"Help me get England back, brother," he said.

"And if you can't? Then what?" Harald cocked his head.

How like Father he is, Cnut thought.

"Then we will divide Denmark between us."

"I'm older than you," Harald pointed out.

"But Father named me." Cnut refused to back down.

Two groups stood facing each other. Harald had the new young bishops of Ribe, Gunar of Limfiord and Oddinkarr, beside him, as well as Jarl Haakon of Funen. Cnut was backed by the chieftains who had returned with him from England. Ragn of the Isles, Uddorm of Viborg, and Gjotgar of Scania. Thorgils of Jelling stood to one side, waiting.

"According to custom, the name of the new king is given by the council of Viborg," a flushed Uddorm exclaimed. "The nobles should gather on the rocks overgrown with red moss and vote."

"Viborg! Viborg!" shouted voices from around the hall.

Oddinkarr, the nephew of the late bishop of Ribe after whom he was named, stepped forward. He spread out his arms and said:

"Choosing a new king is one thing but anointing him is another. Your father, King Sven, took power after killing his father Harald. He was not afraid to strike out against the Church and cut the roots of faith. But the young prince Harald is different. He is a Christian ruler who will want to be crowned and anointed as king."

Oddinkarr has already made his choice, thought Cnut with horror, and reacted quickly.

"Don't divide us, Father Bishop. Don't position me beside my father in opposition to my brother."

Their sisters, Astrid and Świętosława, held each other's hands as they fearfully watched the tensions rise between their brothers.

That's when they heard the clanging of chains in the farthest corner of the hall. Arnora, the tribal queen, as dry as rotten wood, leaning on Vali's and Melkorka's shoulders, emerged from the shadows.

"Fighting for power. The eternal curse of kings!" she said in a loud, raspy voice. "But you, the young heirs of Roskilde, have someone who can help you choose. You have your mother."

They looked at each other with surprise.

"In the face of King Sven's death, Queen Sigrid Storråda should return to Denmark," Ragn of the Isles said, and the chieftains backed him, even those who supported Harald's claim.

Even Oddinkarr.

"That's true. The king is dead, but the queen still lives, and she is now the guarantor of peace in our country."

Cnut now understood the mistrust in his brother's eyes when he saw what he'd named his ship. Harald had likely been afraid that he had chosen the name now, to sway their mother in his favor. But that wasn't why he had done it.

He looked at the sea fields which surrounded Dziwna. The wind kept flattening them, but they wouldn't stay down. Blue, gray, green, and silver.

"The famous island of Wolin is dead ahead!" Hauk shouted, skillfully steering the *Queen's Son* as they sailed into the port.

"What do you think?" asked Harald as he walked over. "What is she like? How will she greet us?"

"I don't know, brother." He embraced him. "But whatever happens, she's our mother and the queen of Denmark."

39

POLAND

Świętosława and Bolesław walked out of Emnilda's alcove as quietly as they could. The herbs had sent her to sleep.

"Oh, if only Astrid were with us, she'd think of something better than a sleeping draught." Bolesław sighed as they closed the door. "She's a stubborn old woman. She's hidden herself God only knows where."

"She might no longer be alive, Bolz," said Świętosława, taking Dusza's leash from a servant. "And don't call her an old woman, she's not much older than we are."

That made no difference though. Something strange had happened to Astrid, as if old age had suddenly sat down on her chest and blown straight in her face. The year since the last time they'd seen her in Poznań had aged her by years.

"I don't know what hit Emnilda harder," Świętosława wondered as they set off toward the stairs. "That first Udalryk and then Henry imprisoned Mieszko, or that we haven't freed Sława."

"Stop!" shouted Bolesław, forgetting that they were meant to be keeping quiet. "You were supposed to support me, not . . . Oh! I'll go back to Kiev, this time with more men."

"Tell me, Bolz, is it your daughter you want or the throne of Kiev?" she asked, grabbing his sleeve.

His eyes shone like a wildcat's.

"I want everything," he said. "I always want everything."

She laughed briefly, but quickly grew serious again. They stood at the top of the stairs.

"Be careful, brother. You almost lost a son. Bezprym has already met a cruel fate at Jaromir's hands, but you still didn't hesitate to send Mieszko to Udalryk."

She could speak about it calmly now that Mieszko was back in the country, but just a few short weeks ago the situation seemed dire. Since Henry II had changed his mind about the Přemyslid dynasty and decided to support Udalryk in his quest for the throne of Prague, Bolesław had been weaving an intricate web of intrigue. First, he hadn't given Henry the troop he'd promised him in Merseburg to march with him to Italy for the imperial crown. Yes, Henry had finally forced the pope to crown him emperor, but her brother had only ever recognized Emperor Otto III, and he never had any intention of supporting Henry. He'd dared to make such an unfriendly gesture, despite the fact that Henry had kept his word and sent him troops to help him in his venture in Russia, even though that had failed. Bolesław had then sent his heir Mieszko to Udalryk, the new duke of Prague, to propose an alliance against the emperor. Udalryk had feigned interest, but when Mieszko was leaving Prague, he'd sent men after him and captured him. Bolesław had raged with anger and pain, howling, afraid that Udalryk would do to Mieszko what Jaromir had done to Bezprym. The idea that both his sons might lose their ability to father children terrified him. He sent messengers to the emperor who pleaded as much as they demanded. He wanted Henry to act like a Christian ruler would and order his vassal in Prague to return his son to him. The emperor fulfilled his wish, but his people took Mieszko to Magdeburg rather than bringing him to Poznań. War was a hairsbreadth away. Emnilda, though already unwell after hearing of what happened in Kiev, was unable to eat or cry, and the knowledge that her firstborn son had been taken from the cruel duke of Prague straight to the emperor gave her no solace. Bolz had led two companies to the border and only then did Henry return Mieszko to him, unharmed. But tragedy was only one step away, and Emnilda had grown weaker every day since then. By the time Mieszko returned, she was unable to rise from bed. She held her son's head and whispered prayers of thanks.

"*Be careful, be careful,*" Bolesław mocked her as they walked downstairs. "If I were always so careful I'd never be ruler of such a large dukedom! You said yourself that one cannot teach sons to rule by keeping them safe at home."

When they reached the bottom of the staircase, Dusza snarled and pulled at the leash.

"What is that?" asked Świętosława. "Can you hear that?"

The horns from the gate were being blown, as signal of welcome to returning family members.

"Bezprym?" wondered Bolesław. "Or Mieszko with his wife?"

"Bezprym would be coming from the east. It might be Margrave Herman with sweet Regelinda, hmm?" She elbowed him.

"Excellent! I can chop up my son-in-law and we can have him for dinner."

They walked outside. The sharp spring sun reflected off the chain mail and helms of their guests. Dusza raised her head and sniffed.

"Who is it?" asked Bolesław, shading his eyes.

Two men took off their helms and dismounted. Świętosława dropped Dusza's leash.

My God, you're so big! she thought, and immediately ordered herself: *Don't you dare cry.*

She recognized them like an animal in the wild recognizing the scent of her pups, even though they were grown now and so unlike the children she'd left behind in Roskilde. She knew them at once. Harald by his red hair, Cnut by his blond locks. She looked around for her daughters, but all she could see were soldiers.

"These are my sons, Bolz," she told her brother, and took a step forward. "Harald and Cnut."

They approached her uncertainly, as if they weren't sure whether they had come to their queen or their mother. They finally reached her and stopped. She gazed at them for a moment, before embracing both of Sven's grown sons as tightly as she could.

"Queen Sigrid." Ragn of Isles spoke up from behind them. "When you left Roskilde, you said you would come back . . ."

"I said that I would come back and gouge out Sven's eyes if he ever hurt any of my children," she corrected Ragn, and for a moment her heart stopped. Why weren't her daughters here? But Sven had said: *"Over my dead body."*

"It's happened, Queen Sigrid. Sven Haraldsson, King of Denmark, Norway, and England, is dead."

DENMARK

Świętosława took out the pins which held her hair in place as soon as they sailed out into the open sea, letting the wind unplait it. She stood at the bow, holding onto the gunwale, and she waited for the salty wind to hit her with her eyes closed. She said nothing. She wanted to listen to them, to her sons. She listened to them as they spoke together, separately, in turn. They sailed to Roksilde aboard the *Queen's Son*, and they had the entire voyage to themselves.

This may not give us back the years we lost, she thought, *but it's still more than I ever dared hope for.*

She learned them. They both had Sven's stubborn blue eyes. Harald looked like his father so much, with his long red hair, that at times it made her uncomfortable.

If I'd seen them every day when they were growing up, this wouldn't be so painful, she thought. *He gets as red as Sven did when he's angry. Is that his fault? No, he's just his child. And Cnut? He's got my hair, but he's not like me. He's calm and levelheaded. Secretive. They are both mine, but they are both their father's sons, too.*

"Mother," said Harald, once he'd finished telling her about himself. "I need you, and so does Denmark. I don't want to fight my brother, but if the

council at Viborg tries to remove me from the throne, I won't stand down."
She heard anger in his voice.

Cnut watched them from the stern of the *Queen's Son* gloomily. When she
walked over to him, he didn't ask for her help. He just glared at the sea.

She asked Ylva to braid her hair again before they arrived in Roskilde, and
she changed her dress.

"What's this, my queen?" Ylva took out a small box from between her
clothes. It was fitted with sea lion teeth.

"A gift that I don't want to open just yet," she replied. "Put it at the bottom
of my chest. Astrid might still be alive."

She looked at her people. The ones who had been in exile with her, who
were now on their way home. Ylva was bubbly with joy. Wilczan was curious
to see what came next, as usual. Great Ulf, with his long gray beard, said that
his service would end in his death and that he hoped he wouldn't die lying on
straw. Only half of the Bold One's axemen returned with her; she had sent ten
of them to Bezprym in Kałdus. They enjoyed being with the monk prince and
were excited for the missions he planned to undertake.

"We couldn't forgive Father for killing your lynxes," Harald said, stroking
Dusza's head.

"Why did he do it?" asked Cnut, standing on her other side.

He never told them that I betrayed him. She felt grateful to Sven, though she'd
never have thought it possible.

"I'll tell you one day, my sons. It's too long a tale for now, and we must focus
on other matters. What are the girls like?"

"They look like you," said Cnut. "You'll meet them soon."

When the ship got closer to shore, when she saw the multicolored crowds
in port, she felt emotion choking her. She tightened her sweaty fingers on the
leash.

"There they are," she whispered.

They stood right by the water. Two fair-haired girls. One in a blue dress, the
other clad in rusty red. Świętosława's tears made them blurry. She wiped them
away. She saw the gray-haired, stooped Melkorka. And Heidi Goat, and the
still beautiful Vali. She recognized them all, one by one. Uddorm of Viborg,
Haakon of Funen, Thorgils of Jelling, Stenkil of Hobro, Gjotgar of Scania, Gunar of Limfiord, and others. She trembled when she saw Jorun. He had always
been Sven's companion in her mind, his shadow.

"Who's that?" she asked, pointing at a tall, dark-haired woman with a
baby in her arms.

"Mother, brother," Cnut said, "you're about to meet my wife, Elfgifu of Northampton. And my child, whom even I haven't met yet. A son or a daughter?" He laughed nervously.

The ship hit the pier.

Her sons leaped off the deck and helped her off. Her daughters walked over to her, and she placed a hand on each of their shoulders. They gazed at each other.

"I saw you," said the younger one, touching her chest with a finger. "I must have dreamt of you, because I remember a woman with mismatched eyes."

"It wasn't a dream, child," Melkorka interjected from behind her. "Don't you remember the nun on the moors?"

"The one who was collecting rocks!" Astrid remembered now.

"Mother," they both said.

"Daughters!" She embraced them.

"My lady . . ." Elfgifu approached them, holding her child close. "Cnut has told me about you. I see that you have a lynx once more."

"A she-lynx." Świętosława smiled. "Welcome, Elfgifu and her child!"

"It's a son," Cnut's wife said proudly, handing him over to her husband.

Świętosława saw the shadow which crossed Harald's face as clearly as she saw Cnut's pride. He lifted him above his head.

"My son! I name him Sven."

The crowds around them began to chant.

"Sven! Sven! Sven!"

She took Harald's hand so nobody could see. He stiffened but held on to her.

That evening, they sat in the great hall in Roskilde. She sat in the middle with her sons on either side of her, and her daughters on either side of them. Elfgifu had given the child to a wet nurse and didn't step away from Cnut for a moment.

She's new here, thought Świętosława. *She doesn't know anyone yet.*

The chieftains occupied the best places. A tired Melkorka sat to the side, with Heidi beside her. Vali sent rows of maidservants to walk between the tables with jugs of mead and wine.

Harald stood up with a horn in his hand, like a host would. *My God, I remember that horn!* she thought.

"Queen Sigrid Storråda! Mother! Welcome home."

The bard began:

Sigrid Proud, Sigrid Ruthless,
to whose bright home

suitors doggedly come,
from the rocky borders along a swampy path . . .

She interrupted him with a laugh.

"That's enough, Skuli! Stop there. My children are listening."

"Bold Lady! Bold Lady!"

"Can you hear that? They haven't forgotten you despite the years," Uddorm said.

"And I remembered you, too," she said, hearing the tremor in her voice. "Anything we say right now will sound sentimental. We drink to remember King Sven, and to celebrate my return. And to Cnut's safe return from England, along with all his chieftains. And to his wife Elfgifu, and little Sven. It's wonderful that you chose to name your son after my late husband." She hadn't used that word in so long, but it rolled off her tongue surprisingly easily. "Let us drink to the memory of the dead, and then toast the living!"

Lifting the horn Harald handed her to her lips, she closed her eyes.

I wish you eternal rest, Sven, or if you prefer, Ragnarök in Valhalla! she thought, passing the horn to Cnut. She could almost hear his loud laughter. It was an illusion, she knew that, created by the memories of feasts that mingled with the present din and laughter. Sven wasn't here. He was somewhere else, in the place he'd chosen or that God had given him. She had never been certain if he had really believed in Him.

When the guests had sated their hunger, she gave the sign that she wanted to speak.

"My sons came for me so that Denmark might have its queen during this time of grief. As you know, it is not our intention to find me a new husband to rule the country, but to decide what is the next best course of action."

"Why not?" a flushed Uddorm of Viborg asked. "The queen doesn't look too bad yet!"

"Is your Thordis dead that you make such advances?" she replied, and the hall resounded with laughter. "Besides, dear Uddo, a queen who has survived two husbands will outlive a third, so if you want to enjoy the delights life has to offer, I suggest you stay away."

"Our lady is back!" Ragn announced joyfully.

Uddorm refused to give up.

"We will sail to Viborg tomorrow and hold a council there. Who can host the queen better than the owner of Viborg's manor? I will happily give up my alcove for you, my lady."

"As long as its owner leaves, I accept. I want to say something to you all before you stand in Viborg to make your decision. Don't let yourselves be influenced by emotion." She grabbed her sons by the hand and lifted them. "They are both my sons! And they are both Sven's. I have returned as your queen, but I have also returned as a mother. Let us rejoice today, and judge tomorrow."

They drank another three toasts before the silent Cnut spoke.

"Mother, do you remember when you gave birth to me?"

"I haven't forgotten the births of any of my children."

"They called me 'the Queen's Son.'"

She didn't miss the glance that Harald cast his brother.

"That's how it happened," Melkorka croaked. "Our lady gave birth to you standing up!"

"While you were drinking wine," Świętosława retorted.

"Yes." Melkorka's toothless gums appeared in a smile. She lifted her goblet.

"And you, Harald," Świętosława continued quickly, "were always hungry."

"And the first royal son I ever nursed," Heidi Goat reminded them.

Harald blushed as he lifted his goblet.

"The first!"

"You sucked like a blacksmith's son," the Goat continued, staving off the argument that was hanging in the air. "The other one was quiet, but you were either eating or screaming!"

The servants circled the room under Vali's directions. The feast continued. She rose from her seat and walked around the hall with Dusza. She looked at the carved beasts running around the hall. She had admired them so much all those years ago. The beasts that caught each other.

She grabbed Wilczan's shoulder and whispered:

"Bring me a hammer from the forge."

He raised his eyebrows but said nothing and left to do her bidding.

She spoke with every chieftain, but she wouldn't let any one of them stop her for long. She finally reached the dark place by the door which never admitted the light from the hearth. She sat down on the bench beside Arnora.

"Welcome back, Queen of Thorns," the old woman hissed from the darkness.

"Greetings, Arnora. Tell me a secret. Has time forgotten you, or has God?" She giggled like a little girl.

"The gods I worship are unknown to you, Bold Lady."

"Will you tell me about them?" she asked, stretching leisurely.

"Why, do you want to include them in your confession?" she asked disdainfully. "How is Ion?"

"He's eating roots and drinking nothing but water in the hermitage."

"I don't believe that."

"Blessed are those who do not see but have faith anyway," replied Świętosława.

"I'm no good at such blessings." Arnora moved and her chains clinked. "But it's not unwise of you to come. These are good boys, and your Sven didn't ruin them."

"I know, Arnora. I want you to agree to something, you stubborn old thing."

"What?" She looked surprised.

Świętosława nodded in Wilczan's direction. He was waiting nearby with the hammer.

"For me to take those chains off."

She didn't even flinch, and Świętosława interpreted that as a silent agreement. When it was over, she knelt beside her and slipped the cuffs from her ankles.

"Even while you were in chains, you were still free, Arnora. Your strength increased my own every single day."

The old woman said nothing. She moved her legs, and stamped hard on the ground, once, twice, a third time.

"I have worn iron for twenty years. I don't know if I remember how to dance, Bold Lady."

"Dance if you will, Arnora. Your legs are your own. You can do whatever you want to now, even trip."

Świętosława twirled around her and then walked toward the platform with a light step. Jorun grabbed her arm as she passed. She looked him up and down and felt as if time had turned back and she was face-to-face with Sven.

"Bold One," he whispered into her ear, "I have brought his bones."

She sobered up immediately.

"You know how he hated rot. I boiled them to cure the skeleton. The king's bones have returned home."

Jorun's blue eyes gleamed wildly. She understood what he was saying.

"Did he want us to burn them?" she asked.

"No, Bold One. He didn't say anything about that."

She placed a hand on his shoulder. He stiffened. She grabbed a jug with mead from a passing servant and drank straight from it before handing it to Jorun. He emptied it.

"Bring them here," she ordered. "I want to touch them."

She was sitting on her throne when Jorun walked back into the hall with a chest. He carried it to her and opened it.

"Vali!" she shouted. "Come here."

The fair-haired servant hurried over to her side, uncertainty written all over her face.

"Did you love the king, Vali?" she asked.

"Yes, my lady," she replied.

"Then stand beside me. We will touch his bones together."

Jorun pushed the chest closer to them. Vali sobbed. Świętosława reached out and grabbed Sven's naked shinbone.

40

DENMARK

Cnut didn't sleep that night, and the great camp surrounding Viborg's twin lakes pulsed with life. Elfgifu insisted on coming with him, though his mother had tried to convince his wife to stay in Roskilde with little Sven.

"Our presence will help you. The chieftains will see a man with a family and a son," Elfgifu had whispered to him, and he agreed.

Now, baby Sven and his wife were fast asleep while he tossed and turned. What if the chieftains supported Harald tomorrow? Oddinkarr evidently did. *He will make me an enemy of the faith because Father named me heir.*

Hrani woke him from a doze in the morning.

"My lord, it's time."

He washed his face and dressed quickly. Elfgifu was waiting for him with Sven in her arms.

"You won't be able to come into the meeting itself," he warned her.

"I know." She nodded. "But your mother is going, so I see no reason why your wife shouldn't."

"Mother will speak after the mass Oddinkarr will hold before the council."

"I don't intend to compete with her. I saw for myself in Roskilde the power her words have. All I want is for everyone to see your son."

A rocky hill rose between the two lakes of Viborg. The moss that covered it looked like dried blood. Oddinkarr had an altar erected at the foot of the hill, by the water, where he held mass.

The church in Viborg is too small to hold everyone who came for the council, thought Cnut. *Oddinkarr wouldn't be able to hold it against those who might be absent. But here, he can see everyone. He knows who is praying and who hasn't come.*

He stood with Elfgifu beside his mother and brother. The Bold One's henchmen were all in attendance. Almost all the chieftains who had been with him in England had come, too. Only Jorun was absent, but Cnut could see his fair head nearby and he knew that when the time came on the rusty moss, Jorun wouldn't let him down.

Bishop Oddinkarr was just over thirty years old. He had a square jaw and puffed-up chest. He didn't resemble the weak monks that his comrades enjoyed mocking so much. He spoke in a voice that was as clear and strong as a bell.

His uncle and the previous bishop of Ribe lived in a state of war with Father all his life, thought Cnut. *When did Harald get young Oddinkarr's support? What happened in Denmark during that year that we were gone?*

The bishop concluded the mass.

"Let us go to the hill," he said, "and may God guide your choices."

Świętosława stepped forward and asked:

"Will the father of Denmark's church allow the mother of the future king to speak?"

He didn't dare refuse her.

She turned toward the crowd.

"When you reach the hill, you will hear men speak for Harald, and others for Cnut. As their mother, I want to speak on behalf of them both."

"Two kings?" asked Thorgils of Jelling skeptically.

"Thorgils," she replied sternly, "don't provoke me. Denmark may not have a king yet, but it has a queen, and it is not appropriate for you to interrupt your ruler."

She lifted her chin and called out to all of them:

"Since you sent for me to hear what I have to say, listen to me now."

Elfgifu clung to his arm and he felt her tremble. He took a deep breath.

"I accept that the chieftains and the army hailed Cnut as their king after Sven's death following his wishes."

He breathed out with relief. He glanced at his brother. Harald's face was red, and his fists were clenched.

Their mother continued.

"My husband, in pointing to Cnut in his last moments, was undoubtedly thinking first of England, because that is where they were, together, and that is the kingdom they conquered. We cannot know whether he wanted Cnut to rule Denmark as well, because he never got the chance to voice his thoughts. But even if he had done so, then I, as Denmark's queen, would be the first to challenge him."

Mutters spread through the crowd.

Now what? he thought in a panic. Elfgifu stiffened beside him. He saw Harald's head move.

"Yes," Świętosława said clearly. "Harald is our firstborn son, and he has never given anyone reason to forget that. The throne of his father's land is his by right."

The muttering grew louder.

"That's what your mother's help looks like, Queen's Son," Elfgifu hissed.

"King Sven indicated the fate he had in mind for each of our sons on the day he decided to take Cnut with him to England instead of Harald," the queen continued, her eyes flashing. "The firstborn son should take Denmark's throne, while the second needs to conquer his own kingdom. The kingdom we know as England!"

Cnut felt as if he were standing on a ship that was heaving violently underneath his feet. He felt his stomach turn.

Some of the chieftains exclaimed in agreement, others muttered angrily. Świętosława stood up straighter and raised her voice.

"Yes, I know that King Ethelred has returned from Normandy and announced that all Danish kings are banished. So what? Sven defeated him before with you at his side! Stand by the son as you did by the father. I will help you with the fleet of my firstborn, Olof King of Swedes. And with my brother Duke Burizleif's forces. That is Queen Sigrid's input into this voyage. Danes have been invading England for over a century. They burn, rob, and plunder, bringing back danegeld. But my husband was more than just a wild barbarian. He was the king of England. Let's gather our forces and attack Ethelred next year with an army so strong that he will never rise to oppose us again. Let us conquer our new kingdom once more!"

Elfgifu embraced him.

"How mischievous! She played that well. We can return to England! Home! My love, you will be king of England."

"Not yet." He tried to calm her, though he felt happy, too. "The rest of them have to agree to it first. And . . ." Only now did he realize the uncertainty of the situation he found himself in. "I need to conquer it again."

He turned around. Harald was beaming.

Bishop Oddinkarr nodded to his mother and said:

"My queen, it is a good thing that you have returned to Denmark. Chieftains, it is time for us to go to the red hill."

When they took their places, the vote was merely a formality. Harald was hailed king of Denmark, and it was decided that in spring the Danish army and its allies would set off to take back Cnut's kingdom.

DENMARK

Świętosława stood at the altar of the church in Viborg beside Harald during the coronation mass, wearing a dress that was green and gold, matching her eyes.

Harald had come to her the day before and said:

"My lady, your husband Sven was king, but he didn't want to be anointed a

Christian ruler. That deprived you of the same honor. Do you want to change that? The people of Denmark adore you and acknowledge you as their queen, but I think you want more than that. Now that you've returned from exile, now that your voice has swayed the nobles, is a better time than ever to hold the mass your husband refused."

"Yes, I want that," she told Oddinkarr.

So it was happening. She stood at the altar with Harald.

Cnut may be known as the Queen's Son, but my real coronation is with Harald at my side. My God, how unpredictable you can be, she thought at the same moment that lightning forked across the sky. The growl of thunder followed close on its heels.

"Sigrid Storråda," Oddinkarr called out. "Dowager queen and mother to the new king. Our Christian lady. It is God's will that you be anointed as only those He chooses can be. Sigrid, the rite is now complete."

"Świętosława," she politely corrected him.

He frowned.

"Sss . . . Shhhh . . . Siii . . ." he tried.

"Świętosława," she repeated, slower this time.

"Shhh . . ." Droplets of sweat appeared on Oddinkarr's forehead.

"Mother," Harald whispered. "He won't be able to say it."

"I want to be crowned under the name that was given to me at birth," she said stubbornly.

"You should be grateful, Bishop, that she hasn't insisted on bringing the lynx with her." She heard Jorun's voice from the depths of the church.

A furious storm broke out. The thunder echoed off the stone walls.

"Santaslaue," a seminary student whispered to Oddinkarr.

"Santa?" he repeated, looking into her mismatched eyes.

"Sventoslava," Cnut prompted from where he stood behind her.

Oddinkarr breathed out deeply and said:

"Sventoslava, I hereby anoint you queen of Denmark by God's will . . ."

He dipped his fingers in the dish with the oil and touched her forehead as if he were leaving a fiery track there.

"Amen," she said. "By accepting this sacrament, I reject myself and become the servant of servants. In the name of the Father, and the Son, and the Holy Spirit. Amen."

"Amen," all the clerical students said, and the storm ceased.

They anointed Harald next. Her son's pale face was flushed when Oddinkarr announced:

"Here is the king of Denmark!"

Oh, Sven, she thought, *I wish you could see him now. Our firstborn son is a magnificent red-haired king.*

They walked out of the church in a ceremonial procession led by Odd-inkarr. The king and queen. She and her son. Cnut and Elfgifu followed with little Sven, then came the chieftains and nobility.

The air smelled of the storm that had just passed. Fat droplets of water glimmered in the sunlight like the most precious of gemstones. She breathed in deeply, basking in the moment.

Uddorm, their host in Viborg, organized the coronation feast.

"Long live the queen!" he shouted, standing at the door to his manor, his face turning red with the effort. "Long live the king!"

His maidservants carried meat and mead around the hall. They drank from silver goblets and from Sven's horn. Once they'd finished, Jorun spoke.

"Thor himself attended the Bold One's coronation!" His blue eyes flashed. "When Sven was crowned at Winchester, it rained, too."

"Jorun," she called to him, "the rain has stopped."

"I know," he snarled, taking a sip. "They're just memories."

Oddinkarr did not drink much, but his laugh carried. Harald was happy. Elfgifu was cheerful; it seemed that the prospect of going home suited her better than the thought of staying in Roskilde. Cnut looked as if he were lost in thought.

The chieftains began to chant:

"Sigrid Storråda! Our Bold Lady! And our king Harald!"

Skuli was preparing to recite a poem when Cnut stood up to speak:

"Mother, I'm not afraid to fight for England, but I must admit that I am inexperienced in what my father excelled at. In making treaties and alliances, in politics . . ."

"I'll tell you, young prince, what Sven thought," Jorun interrupted. "He said: *'Being a king is like being married. It's easy to get a wife, but much harder to keep her happy!'*"

Everyone turned to look at Świętosława and, after a moment's silence, the room erupted with laughter. She laughed, too. Only Elfgifu remained silent and frowning.

"Mother," Cnut continued when they fell silent again. "Come to England with me. I will do the fighting, but you can help me with the alliances and negotiations. You can teach me."

She hadn't expected that. She felt like a horse struck by a whip. She understood what it was to be challenged. She saw Jarl Thorgils's snakelike eyes as he snorted. And Elfgifu who was pulling Cnut's sleeve, trying to communicate to him that she wanted him to take it back.

Don't be afraid, girl, she thought. *I don't want to take away your husband, I only want to help my son.*

"Harald?" she asked. "What do you think?"

"What can I say?" He laughed, and the crown glimmered on his red head. "The Queen's Son doesn't hesitate to use his position. I have no problem with it, though I would also appreciate your help in managing Uddorm of Viborg and Ragn of the Isles. You have no idea how petty they've grown in their old age, Mother."

"I can help, my lord!" Uddorm shouted. "I've decided to sail to England with the queen and Cnut!"

"And I will create a new problem for you, Sigrid," roared Ragn. "My ships and my men are yours to command, as am I. The fat one and I will argue in front of your eyes. Ha, ha!"

"My lynx is talented at solving such problems." Świętosława smiled. "All I need to do is let her off the leash."

"I'd be happy to pet the pussycat." Uddorm chuckled, drinking.

She looked at her sons. They both looked content.

"Very well, my son," she replied, turning to the younger one. "Your brother has received his father's beautiful kingdom. I'm used to changing thrones. Since you have need of me, I will come with you. I don't like shiny things, but they say that English silver is uniquely attractive. I will go to see it for myself. To touch the treasure won by you, your father, and Olav Tryggvason, the one your father defeated in the Battle of the Three Kings."

Her heart pounded unevenly.

You have given me a challenge, Cnut, she thought. *And I will try to be worthy of it.*

The feast grew louder. The mead and wine were poured generously.

She caught Wilczan's eye and summoned him.

"Will you go to Uppsala?"

"Aren't you afraid that my meetings with Olof bring you bad luck?" he asked with a smile as crooked as his father's.

"No, Wilczan." She kissed his forehead. "The message you brought back last time was most beautiful. I believe that my firstborn won't fail me this time and will send the ships I ask for."

"Very well, my lady. I will go at dawn."

"Don't you want to rest after our journey from Wolin?"

"No, my lady." He looked at her as faithfully as Helga did. "I love to serve you."

41

DENMARK

Cnut was in port checking the ships when he saw the flag bearing the wolf of Jom appear on the horizon. He asked for his mother and Jorun to be sent to him.

"That's *Nidhog*, Thorkel's ship," said Jorun, when the ship had come closer.

"Sigvald's brother," his mother said thoughtfully.

"Traitor," said Cnut.

"Why is he coming here?"

"Maybe King Ethelred is dead?"

"A dream." His mother laughed. "Although who knows? From what you have told me, it's clear that the king is old and weak. Son? Maybe that flag is bringing you the crown of England."

He felt a tightness in his chest. *"The second son needs to conquer his own kingdom."* That's all he'd been able to think about since she'd said the words. Conquer, not receive. The crown was not going to arrive by ship.

Thorkel's men moored the ship and he leaped onto the pier. Lean and broad-shouldered, he was bald and had piercing eyes. He reminded Cnut of a snake.

How does one greet a traitor? he wondered.

"Mother," he said, "this is Thorkel the Tall, the Jomsviking who once served my father and your husband, before he switched sides to protect King Ethelred."

"And has he come to switch sides again?" she asked.

"Or to find out who will pay him more?" Jorun added.

"Since I have already been introduced, allow me to inquire about the ships being built on the shore," Thorkel spoke up. "Is the young King Cnut preparing a fleet to win back England?"

"Yes."

Thorkel studied Cnut carefully. He was twice his age, and he was taller and bigger. Cnut knew that he was facing the man before whose Predatory Shoal England had already surrendered once before. And that this was the same man who had betrayed his father. He wasn't a fool; he knew that if they'd met in battle, he wouldn't stand a chance.

"In that case, young king," Thorkel finally broke the silence, "what would you say to joining forces with the Predatory Shoal?"

I need to choose my words carefully, thought Cnut.

"I would ask you why I should trust someone who has betrayed us once before."

"I'll reply with a question: Why would I risk coming to you to Roskilde if I didn't mean what I said?"

"People betray their promises for any number of reasons," his mother said. "Love, fear, greed, power, fame . . . Tell us, Thorkel, what was your reason?"

"Not fear or love," he said.

"Then any alliance with you is like a negotiation at the market. It's all about the price."

"No, my lady. We can reach an agreement today. The price may be high, but my knowledge of England and the strength of my fleet are worth it."

"How much do you want?"

"It's not about the money," said Thorkel. "I want my own piece of the kingdom."

"Well considered. Riches and power," Jorun pointed out.

"A regular income and fame among my men," Thorkel corrected him.

"You're sharing out the skin of a bear that's still alive." His mother laughed.

"No, my queen," Thorkel said. "This bear is soon to fall."

DENMARK

Świętosława watched Bolesław's men disembark. The heavy cavalry, unbeaten in battle on land, the same warriors from whom Emperor Henry's troops ran, looked exhausted by their journey. Only Wilkomir, their commander, looked as he always did.

"It's impossible to tell whether you're happy or angry, ill or healthy, when you grimace all the time." She greeted her friend on the pier in Roskilde. "What about them? Did they spend their whole journey drinking? They look as if they are battling never-ending headaches."

They leaped onto dry land, stretching their stiff legs. The port was filled with the clinking of chain mail, sheaths, and belts. Their faces, gray and green and swollen, were slowly regaining a regular appearance.

"They're riders, unused to traveling by sea," Wilkomir replied. "They'll come back to life once they feel dry land beneath their feet again."

"My brother should have built his own fleet a long time ago," she muttered.

"The duke has many things on his mind," Wilkomir replied evasively. "And his most important wars are fought on land."

A warm, gentle breeze quickly dried their wet cloaks. The eagle feathers which decorated their helms waved slowly in the wind. The soldiers straightened their muscular backs and formed two lines on the shore. The flagbearers unfurled their flags and Bolesław's eagle fluttered on the Danish shore. Her heart pounded.

"Your presence fills me with more joy than a chestful of riches would," she shouted to the three hundred men. "In times of war, each one of you shines as brightly as gemstones laid in sharpened iron."

"Oh, no!" She heard the bard groan behind her. "I was so happy that the Bold Lady had returned, but she's stealing my job!"

"Skuli! Greet the guests instead of grumbling," she reprimanded him.

Skuli shouted out:

The snake of the sword knows how to find the bloodstream,
The beetle cut down follows the paths of thought to slaughter's warm rivers . . .

"My lady, we know our military commands in every language, but we don't understand a word of what he just said," the flagbearer said, shaking his head.

"That the fight will be bloody," Wilkomir translated briefly.

"That's obvious." The flagbearer nodded. "What else would it be?"

"What's your name?" Świętosława approached him.

"Kalmir."

"Kalmir, the bards have two hundred different metaphors and synonyms for battle, and one hundred others with which to describe a sword. They can say as much about a ship, a shield, or one's courage. Warriors may win battles, but it is the bard's talents that ensure your victories are remembered. I suggest you make friends with Skuli if you want a couple of lines to describe the undefeated Kalmir."

She saw both her sons arriving to greet the warriors.

"My mother knows what she's talking about," Cnut said. "Her name appears in many songs."

"Though not all of them are appropriate for her children to hear." Wilkomir cleared his throat.

"Either way, you're the best present I have ever received from my brother." She smiled radiantly at the soldiers.

"Please, accept our hospitality," Harald added. "Tonight, Roskilde will celebrate the arrival of its Polish guests."

Barrels of mead and beer, roasted piglets, smoked eels, slabs of cheese, fish sauces—all these and more were carried into the hall by the maidservants under Vali's directions and placed before Bolesław's men. Skuli recited poem after poem, trying to nurture a love of verses in Kalmir's heart. The more the flagbearer drank, the more he enjoyed the bard's words.

"I have a gift for you from Duke Bolesław and Duchess Emnilda," Wilkomir said from his seat on her right.

"They are the best gift," she repeated, watching the warriors eat. "I still wonder why my brother was so happy to give them to me. I thought he would try to negotiate, like he did before Øresund."

"That's exactly it, my lady."

She turned to look at him carefully.

"My brother feels guilty," she realized.

Wilkomir raised an eyebrow, but he didn't grimace like he usually did.

"I'm not the duke's confessor."

Something gave her pause. An unclear thought, no more than a feeling.

"Is my brother feeling guilty about something he did to me? A wrong he wants to right by giving me these men?"

Wilkomir held her gaze.

"Don't ask me about events I didn't participate in," he said after a moment.

She fell silent. When Bolesław had given Otto III one hundred armed men after the Congress of Gniezno, every court buzzed with news of the generous gift. He sent her thrice that number even though he hadn't won his war against Henry yet, and he was still preparing men to march on Kiev.

"Do you want to see what else your brother sends you?" asked Wilkomir.

She nodded, still lost in thought. Wilkomir's men brought over a few chests. He nodded to them, and they lifted the lid off the first one. Initially she thought they were showing her a short silver dress, but after a moment she realized it was chain mail.

"Apparently, you were struck by Ivar Goldtooth's work while you were in Bodzia," said Wilkomir. "The old armorer hasn't accepted a commission in years, but when he learned that it was for the Bold Lady, he didn't dare refuse. It is possible that you will wear the last thing that Ivar ever makes. Your brother wishes for you to be protected."

She stood up and walked over to the chest to examine the metal rings up close. It was delicate but tightly knit. Unlike men's chain mail, this one was cut at the back and had a web of silver hoops through which she could thread a ribbon or string to tie the chain mail tightly around herself.

"Goldtooth swore that he remembered the queen's figure well and claimed it would be a perfect fit," Wilkomir added in a voice that sounded almost cheerful, though she knew her old friend never expressed his feelings, even when he was happy.

You cannot hide anything from me, she thought sadly.

"Beautiful work," she said loudly. "But I'm not a warrior and I don't need armor. I go to England as my son's adviser."

"You're sailing to war, Mother," Harald and Cnut both said.

"But I'm not about to pretend to be a Valkyrie! Besides, I'm not a virgin." She smiled to her sons and sat down again. She turned to whisper to Wilkomir: "No chain mail can protect me from a wounded heart. Some gestures come too late."

"Do you believe in God Almighty, my lady, or the Fates?" Wilkomir asked. "Because if it's God, then you need to accept that He chooses the paths we tread. And if it's the Fates, then you know yourself how good they are at tangling up our lives."

She took a gulp of strong mead. Why hadn't she just asked Bolesław directly when she'd had the chance? She'd spent so much time at his court, so many evenings in Poznań's hall. They'd had so many long conversations, but she'd never asked him what part he'd played in the battle of Øresund. Not the battle itself, of course, but in the events which had led up to it.

Her lynx growled in her sleep, and Świętosława shivered.

It was not my brother who stirred the waters of Øresund, she thought. *Even if he isn't innocent in all that's happened, it is not for me to judge or forgive him.*

"Let us celebrate." She clapped her hands. "The feast continues!"

"Open the next chest," Wilkomir said, and turned to her again. "As you know, my lady, the symbol of the English dynasty is the dragon of Wessex. Duchess Emnilda spent many nights worrying that her beloved sister-in-law was going to set off to war in a country filled with dragons. That's when Prince Bezprym came to Poznań, and when he heard about the preparations being made for the invasion, he said: 'I pity those dragons. They have no idea that the Bold One is coming for them.' And that's how the idea for your flag was born."

The servants lifted a colorful material out of the chest when he nodded to them. An intricately woven eagle was in mid-flight with a dragon clutched in its claws.

"The eagle and the dragon!" the chieftains exclaimed.

"The eagle and the dragon whose proud life is coming to an end because . . ." roared Skuli, drunk, trying to climb onto a table.

Kalmir grabbed him and pulled him back. He put a horn in his hand.

"Drink, poet, drink."

"That's not just an eagle!" the chubby Uddorm of Viborg pointed out. "It's a female! It looks just like our lady! The sharp claws . . ." He smacked his lips. "The wings like our lady's cloak . . . I can see it! And a beak . . ."

"Shut your beak!" Ragn of the Isles shouted at him. "Otherwise the queen's lynx will walk you to bed."

"Mother." Her daughters moved closer to her. "It's so good to have you home."

42

⚛

ENGLAND

Cnut sailed to England with a fleet that numbered more ships than the Army of the Two Kings or Sven's Anger ever had. His half brother Olof King of Swedes had sent him twenty longboats with crews that were his to command, just as their mother asked. Thorkel's Predatory Shoal was comprised of fifty ships that all had experience of fighting the English. His father's loyal Norwegian vassal Eric of Lade arrived with forty ships when he was summoned. His mother's brother, the powerful Duke Burizleif, might only have given him two ships, but they carried unmatched treasure: three hundred warriors of the famous heavy cavalry forces, led by Wilkomir, Wilczan's father. Additionally, Denmark gave him seventy ships which were going to help him win back his kingdom.

They reached Sandwich at the start of autumn, just as they'd done two years earlier with his father. The same Sandwich to which he had been forced to retreat afterward, when Sven had died. And where he'd left behind evidence of his cruelty. The maimed hostages. He wished he could take it back, but he'd punished the sons for the sins of their fathers when the English nobles deserted him. He had ordered their hands, ears, and noses cut off, and he hadn't looked away for a second.

"Cnut the Cruel!" muttered the people in port when his ship arrived. "Cnut the Cruel has returned!"

He grimaced and felt his mother's hand on his shoulder.

"It is better that they mistake you for a cruel man than see you for a fool," she said.

"But they're right, Mother. What I did was beastly."

"We are at war, Cnut. Blood is bound to flow."

Last time, his father had gone north, to Northumbria, where he had allies. Now, following the advice of his chieftains, Cnut decided to do something different. He divided his forces to attack multiple places simultaneously. "We'll bring in chaos so that they won't know where the main army is. Let them think the enemy is everywhere," the chieftains suggested. "Check the value of the Jomsviking," his mother advised, so he sent Thorkel to face the forces gathering around Sandwich. He had Jarl Eric sail to conquer Kent and led the rest of his men on land toward the heart of England: Wessex. They didn't have many horses, having only brought one hundred with them from Denmark, so the first thing they had to do was capture more. They marched west quickly, their progress slowed only by the oxen-pulled cart which contained Elfgifu with little Sven and their wet nurses.

"Your lady bears the hardship of travel well," observed Hrani one day, attempting to divert his attention from the frustration he felt at having to wait for the cart to be ready before they set off.

"You should send her and the child to her relatives," his mother told him. "Surely you don't want to give the impression that the Jomsviking and Jarl Eric are more effective warriors because they aren't distracted by their families."

He retorted sharply to that:

"Do you believe in me, Mother?"

"Yes, you I believe in," she said, unnerving him with those mismatched eyes.

"Fine." He sighed, giving up. "Hrani, you'll go to Northampton with my wife and son. Take a squad of men with you."

"As you wish, my lord," replied the helmsman. "But I won't be the one to tell Lady Elfgifu. There is nothing in the world that I would do to risk her wrath."

He spoke to his wife himself. He accepted her fury, waited for it to simmer down into grumbling, cool into regret, and finally settle in sadness. This hurt him more than her curses.

"It's your mother's doing, isn't it?" she sobbed. "She told you to send me away?"

"No, Elfgifu. I'm concerned for your safety, and Sven's, so I want to hide you away in a safe nest." He kissed her wet cheeks and smoothed her dark hair. "We'll see each other again soon."

They moved faster now. They crossed pastures and fields. The peasants ran away into the forests when they saw the approaching army. Every large village was surrounded by a palisade guarded by a few young men who blew horns or rang bells when they saw the invaders, calling their people back from the fields. They passed burned villages which looked frightening with their charred chimneys reaching to the sky. Uneven mounds surrounded these, sparsely covered with grass, occasionally marked by roughly built crosses. Murders of crows flew overhead.

His mother crossed herself anytime they passed such places.

Where are the defenders? he wondered. *Where are the men who should ensure these people's safety?*

"They are hiding in their fortresses and their castles," his scouts reported. "They're rushing to muster their forces."

Jarl Eric in Kent defeated troop after troop. Thorkel the Tall scattered the armies around Sandwich and joined Cnut in time to march alongside him into Wessex. He couldn't have picked a better time since they were shortly faced by two different armies. One flew flags bearing a golden cross, while the other marched under a proud, clawed dragon.

"That's the dragon of the Wessex dynasty. Those are the armies of Ethelred's heir and eldest son, Edmund," said Thorkel. "The ones with the cross are Ealdorman Eadric Streona's men. They come from Mercia."

"I remember that you warned Father about him." Cnut frowned.

"Because he's the man who has the most influence on King Ethelred," said Thorkel. "He's a master of intrigue. Although he doesn't come from an influential family, he's climbed his way into the highest spheres of society by plotting and manipulating others. I suspect that half the kingdom is tied to Streona in one way or another. Edmund, the king's son, despises him. That's why we are facing two armies rather than one; although it would be in the kingdom's best interest for them to join forces, those two don't know how to work together."

"So Streona thinks himself equal to the king," his mother observed.

"Yes, my lady," Thorkel agreed. "And not without reason, since the old king seeks his counsel more than he does his own son's."

"What about Edmund?" asked Świętosława. "What kind of man is he?"

"Not as spoilt as his father." Thorkel laughed. "At least, not yet. Many of the king's current troubles were born in his love of feasts, wine, and women. Queen Emma is his third wife."

"If I understand correctly, she's not Edmund's mother, is she?" He heard something in Świętosława that gave him pause.

"No, she isn't," Thorkel confirmed. "I suspect that Edmund's troops will be the only ones actually fighting since for him this is a battle for the throne."

"It's a battle for everything," Cnut said. "Do you think we should invite Streona to negotiate with us?"

"Let us fight Edmund, young king. Streona will come to us himself."

Thorkel was right. They fought Edmund's men day after day, with neither side gaining any advantages. Edmund had a strong cavalry, while Cnut commanded an undefeated infantry. They clashed together and leaped apart. They tried to set traps for each other, attacking at night or at dawn. The enemy was vigilant and wouldn't be surprised. The army of Wessex might scatter under the Danish wall of shields on the battlefield one day, but they would regroup and stand to fight again the next. Cnut noticed, however, that by the third day there were fewer men returning to face them.

Streona didn't help Edmund. He packed up camp and retreated into the woods. A week later, he sent messengers to Cnut. The men fighting for the heir to the throne, under the flag of the Wessex dragon, disappeared that same day.

Cnut and Streona met on a moor in front of the Danish camp. Eadric Streona approached him surrounded by guards.

"My God, that's a groom dressed up in silks," whispered Świętosława when Streona was close.

"I would warn you not to underestimate this groom's abilities," Thorkel snorted.

The ealdorman of Mercia had none of the dignity with which English nobles seemed to be born. He was a large man with eyes that disappeared in rolls of fat.

He controls the nobles, thought Cnut as he watched him approach. *And I need to take that control from him.* He felt his mouth go dry and suddenly felt a strong desire to fight rather than talk. He turned and looked behind him at the flags his men flew. Agile snakes, proud horses, leaping fish, Jom's wolves, and his mother's brother's Burizleif's eagles. *I have brought the greatest army of invaders this country has ever seen,* he reminded himself. *I am their leader. I will not be afraid.*

"Make him speak Danish," whispered Thorkel. "He knows our tongue well."

Streona had almost reached them, and he was looking at Cnut greedily. He greeted him in English, but Cnut didn't even nod to acknowledge him. He was silent, still gathering his thoughts. Streona seemed to find this disconcerting, and he switched to Danish:

"Greetings, King Sven's son."

"You should greet his widow, too," Thorkel observed. "You are in the presence of Queen Sigrid Storråda!"

Streona smiled lewdly at her as he said:

"I have heard stories of the beautiful Viking goddess Freya whose carriage is pulled by white cats, but here I see a glorious queen with a lynx! Does the young lord always travel with his mother?"

"We are not here to travel," replied Świętosława mildly. "We've come for the English throne."

"I see you have a strong ally. He used to stand by King Ethelred, but it seems Thorkel the Tall has decided to switch sides!" Streona laughed as he adjusted his position in the saddle. "Will we talk without dismounting?"

"You're the one who wanted to talk," Cnut finally spoke. "You have one moment to convince me that you're worth my time. If you fail, I will give my men the order to attack."

"Oh, the wonders of youth! Always so impatient to fight even though so many matters can be settled without lifting a sword."

"What do you propose?" asked Cnut bluntly.

"An alliance." Streona's pale lips stretched into a smile. "A sweet alliance."

"Why should we want to join forces with you, my lord?" his mother asked provokingly. "My son's army can conquer England without your help."

"I have no doubt," Streona hastened to agree. "But why destroy England if you want to rule it once you've won? If you have come for the throne, as you say, my lady, then why seek to burn it?"

He offers us nothing, thought Cnut. *Could he be playing for time? Did he lure us out here for his allies to target us?*

He glanced at his mother with worry. She'd refused to wear the chain mail.

How could he find out what Streona really wanted and why he'd asked to speak with them?

Streona must have felt more confident since he let go of his reins and patted his protruding belly.

"I don't know if my noble guests have heard that I am married to King Ethelred's daughter Edith," he said, running a hand over his bald head.

"We are not your guests," Cnut snorted.

"We've returned to a country that has already been conquered by Sven," his mother added, but changed her tone quickly. "Is it your wife who has sent you to betray your king and her father?"

Streona didn't even blush. He flicked his fingers as if he were trying to rid himself of a stray hair.

"My wife knows the king's weaknesses," he replied curtly.

And you want to replace him, thought Cnut.

"People become traitors for all kinds of reasons," Świętosława observed, repeating what she'd said to Thorkel all those months ago.

"I'm no traitor." Streona lifted his chin. "I'm merely returning to . . ."

"You're switching sides," Cnut interjected.

"Just like he did." Streona didn't smile as he pointed a chubby finger at Thorkel. "The Jomsviking who defended, betrayed, and robbed England. He invaded London, then defended London. If you've accepted his help, why not accept mine? Oh, I see, a Danish traitor is better than an English one. Forgive me, but you would do well to consider, friends, that I hold the keys to the castles and cities in this country. Who will the nobles listen to, Thorkel or Eadric? Besides, I'm sure you've noticed that Edmund's forces were gone by dawn. Surely you must have guessed that it was I, Eadric Streona, who convinced the lords of Wessex to retreat so that I may negotiate with you?"

Cnut noticed his mother loosening her hold on the lynx's leash so that Dusza could approach Streona while he conducted his monologue. *Oh, Mother! That may have been enough in Poland or Denmark, but it is not enough to gain the English throne.*

The lynx sniffed Streona's stirrups, snarling when his mother smiled brightly and said:

"I am so glad, Eadric, that you have come to offer us your services on this wonderful sunny day!"

That evening, when Streona finally left, Cnut sat in his tent with his mother and chieftains.

"I'd prefer a three-day battle at sea in pouring rain than having to meet with Streona again," confided Jorun. "I need more mead to wash away the bad taste he's left in my mouth. It's a good thing that Sven isn't here to see it. An alliance with a man like that is disgusting."

"But thanks to this alliance you'll have a supply of mead that will last you through winter." Thorkel laughed, taking a sip of his own drink.

"I just said I would prefer to win a fight to get this mead then negotiate for it," snarled Jorun.

"Especially since we have no way of knowing for certain that Streona won't betray us," Cnut pointed out tiredly.

"Jorun," his mother said, "get ready for a long period of drinking, because the Groom will be beside my son when we go north. We cannot let someone like that out of our sight."

"No!" Cnut exclaimed. "I don't want him near me!"

"Listen to me, son," his mother said. "Streona promised you the support of Wessex. He gave you hostages and supplies for everyone for the entire winter. That means that if he keeps his word, you won't have to plunder and burn the homes of the peasants."

The memory of the dirty, skinny children who fearfully herded sheep into villages whenever they caught sight of Cnut and his men made him feel nauseous.

"If you have decided with Thorkel that you need to conquer the north, Streona must be beside you, otherwise he will betray you as soon as you leave for Northumbria," argued Świętosława.

"The queen is right, Cnut," Thorkel agreed.

He never calls me "king." It's always "young king" or "Cnut," he realized.

"He makes me think of a great fat spider," Cnut grumbled.

"That's accurate," his mother agreed. "He's a spider who has woven its web across the entirety of England. Keep him close. Learn about his agreements with nobles, the layout of his web."

"Streona's web," burped Jorun.

Świętosława stood up and kissed his forehead as if he was a boy. The chieftains were all watching him, and for a moment all he wanted to be was the Queen's Son, to feel the relief that her tender touch brought him.

"When you take over control of the web, you can get rid of the spider," she said, breaking the spell.

Jarl Eric of Lade joined Cnut after completing his mission in Kent, and they all marched to Northumbria together. Autumn was over before they knew it, but the English winter was mild and didn't interfere with warfare. The small troops they encountered along the way were not difficult to defeat. Cnut learned from the prisoners they took that Earl Uhtred hid in York. The same one who had given Sven Gainsborough three years ago without putting up a fight, the same one who held a feast in their honor and then betrayed Cnut by attacking his camp as soon as his father was dead.

The earl must have felt confident since he rode out to meet them with only a small number of guards. He stopped just outside York's walls, and the gate remained open in a gesture of friendship.

"King Cnut!" he called out. "I want to give you control of the city as a sign that Northumbria is yours to command."

Eadric Streona, riding beside his mother, was already preparing to answer when Świętosława gestured for him to stay quiet.

"Uhtred," Cnut called back, looking at the archers who lined the city walls. "Northumbria is already mine to command, unless you're hiding an army bigger than mine inside those walls." He indicated Eric of Lade's Norwegian soldiers with a sweep of his arm. When Eric gave the sign, the Norwegians hit their swords across their chain-mail-covered chests. He then pointed to Burizleif's warriors gathered around the flag with the eagle, and he knew that the city's inhabitants were seeing more of his men marching to join them.

No, Uhtred can't have more than five hundred men, Cnut thought. *He must see that I have twice as many soldiers. What is he counting on?*

That was the moment he realized that he, his mother, and his chieftains had approached close enough to the walls to be within range of their arrows. He saw Streona retreating discreetly, and he felt like a child drawn into a trap.

Uhtred was already close, surrounded by a dozen guards.

He's not afraid of me, he thought. *He betrayed me when I was in Gainsborough when he heard of my father's death, and he's not afraid of me.*

He turned around and whispered to the Jomsviking as he glanced again at the archers who lined the city walls:

"Thorkel, you're our shield."

He gave Eric a sign. The jarl of Lade and his men immediately moved to surround Uhtred's squad, which the earl quickly noticed.

"You shouldn't be killing messengers who bring you good news, young king." Uhtred laughed without a shadow of discomfort. "You cannot hurt me when I come to you to surrender. Look, the city gates are open. I will also give you hostages and swear fealty to you."

Streona emerged from where he'd been hiding behind the men and joined them again.

"I hate men who break their word," Cnut replied, looking from Streona to Uhtred. "I thought you understood my message."

"What message?" Only now did Uhtred's composure crack.

"I left the hostages maimed on the beach when I left Sandwich to prove that I will not tolerate betrayal."

"But, my lord . . ."

"Take them!" he ordered Eric.

"I'm not just a lord, Uhtred," Cnut replied firmly. "I'm a king. You gave the royal title to my father Sven three years ago, and he named me his heir with his dying breath. You're speaking to King Cnut!"

"Yes . . . of course . . ." Uhtred groaned, immobilized by Jarl Eric's men.

"Execute him for the treason he has committed against his king," ordered Cnut.

"You cannot execute the earl of Northumbria!" protested Uhtred, struggling to free himself.

"Will you die with him or will you side with your king?" Cnut asked Uhtred's guards.

Seeing they were outnumbered and outmaneuvered, the guards handed over their weapons. Uhtred was pushed from the saddle at the same time as Jarl Eric turned around and shouted, his hand pointing at the walls:

"Archers!"

Thorkel lifted his shield to protect Cnut, obscuring his view of Great Ulf throwing himself in front of Świętosława to protect her from an arrow. His mother found herself in her protector's arms in the blink of an eye. Cnut pushed away Thorkel's shield and shouted at Uhtred, who was lying on the ground, his humiliation witnessed by his men:

"As the rightful king of England, I relieve you of your duties as the earl of Northumbria. There is only one punishment for traitors: death."

Eric's men dragged Uhtred over to a tree stump as people begin to spill out of the city gates.

Executions always attract gawkers, like crows to a corpse, he thought gloomily.

York's defenders squeezed themselves through the growing masses and stood in front of Cnut. Streona, having recovered his confidence once he saw how the events unfolded, was beside him again.

"On your orders, my king," a skinny, short chieftain said, "the city voted last night to surrender." He glanced at Uhtred, who had been forced to his knees by the tree stump.

"Bring me the man who shot the arrow at my mother," demanded Cnut.

"I don't know which one it was," the chieftain replied uncertainly.

"What's your name?"

"Guthlac."

"Are you Danish?"

"My grandfather is from Jutland."

"Bring me the archer who shot that arrow, Guthlac, otherwise I will hold you, the chief of York's garrison, personally responsible."

Mutters spread across the crowd of onlookers. Eric's men pushed back the soldiers as Guthlac turned around and said:

"Bring him here!"

Two soldiers dragged over a young, pimple-covered, sullen boy. He couldn't have been more than sixteen. His mother approached him with Great Ulf at her side as her mare snorted.

Don't let her ask me for mercy now, Cnut thought as he clenched his jaw and asked:

"Why did you want to kill Queen Sigrid?"

The boy dropped his head and didn't answer. Eric's men struggled to keep the mob at bay, pushing them back with their shields. Cnut leaped down from the saddle, walked over to the boy, and lifted his chin, forcing him to look him in the eye.

"Speak!" he hissed. "Who told you to target the queen?"

"The earl," the boy replied. "He said the witch is more dangerous than you."

The boy's eyes were filled with anger. He knew he was about to die, and it made him brave. Cnut had no choice.

"Great Ulf," he said, turning to his mother and her guard. "Deal with him."

Świętosława was pale, but she didn't ask for mercy for the boy. Ulf dismounted, unsheathed a long knife, and sank it into the boy's chest without hesitation. His ugly, pimply face twisted and froze in a grimace of pain, his mouth wide open.

Ulf stabbed him straight in the heart, thought Cnut.

"Execute Uhtred," he ordered.

The executioner lifted his axe. A murmur flew across the crowd and Cnut saw people pushing and shoving each other, trying to get a better look, as he climbed back into the saddle. When the traitor's head rolled across the ground, he looked at Streona's back and his sweating bald head.

Cnut the Cruel, he thought grimly.

"The new earl will be Eric of Lade," he announced.

ENGLAND

Świętosława focused her eyes on Eric to avoid looking at the dead boy's body stiffening nearby. The jarl of Lade heard what Cnut had just said, but he didn't seem to understand the meaning of his words. He frowned, took off his helm, and swept his hair off his forehead. She looked over at Streona. The fat man couldn't hide his surprise, and he seemed to be swallowing convulsively as if he were choking on something. Thorkel's expression remained stony and unchanged.

She had remained in the tent with her son the previous night, after the chieftains had all left. They had heard the reports of the scouts and were certain of Uhtred's presence in York. She had been the one to suggest this plan to Cnut.

"If you take Northumbria, you have to leave a vassal here whose loyalty cannot be questioned. Jarl Eric is your only option. In killing Uhtred, you will show the people the face of Cnut the Cruel. Streona will see that you show traitors no mercy. Thorkel will realize that he doesn't deserve your trust yet, since you did promise to give him power eventually. Besides, you cannot take London without Thorkel, so for now the Jomsviking must stay with you. In naming a new earl, you'll be acting like a king. That will be Cnut the Just."

"What about Cnut the Genuine?" he snorted.

She looked at him sadly.

"He's here now." She pulled him to her. "Now, when he's in pain at the thought of being cruel to others in order to regain power. You're a good man, my son. But good men lose, and they don't get the crown."

"Mother," he whispered, and she saw tears in his eyes. "Is the crown really worth all these sacrifices? Blood, betrayal, lies . . ."

My sweet little son, she thought. *Maybe I should have sent you to an abbey instead of telling you to fight for the crown?*

"It is the destiny of royal sons to rule," she said, stroking his shoulder.

"You'll understand once the crown is yours. And when it is, you'll be able to afford to be good."

That night, she hadn't known that siding with Eric would save her from a traitorous arrow by the walls of York the following day. She'd picked him because despite the fact that not a day went by when she didn't remember that Eric of Lade's ships were the ones which had caused Olav's fleet the most harm in Øresund, she knew also that he had been the only one with pure intentions in that battle. He faced Olav to fight for the Norwegian throne which had been his own father's once. The rest of them all played dirty. Sven fought to defeat the despised "second chieftain" and the man who stole his wife's heart. Olof fought to impress Sven and to show his mother how independent he was. Sigvald fought to forget his own defeat and humiliations at Hjørung Bay. That was why, although she hadn't forgotten what Eric had done, she didn't hold it against him. As a chief and a warrior, he was just as effective as Thorkel the Tall, but unlike the Jomsviking, he was predictable in his loyalty and fairness.

They departed York swiftly, moving south toward the camp at the river Frome where their fleet awaited. From there, they would sail to London, to Edmund. Cnut never let Streona out of his sight.

"You can't treat him like a dog, even if you see him as no more than a mutt," she said, riding beside him.

"I can barely stand him," Cnut snarled.

"And he knows it. Have you ever trained a dog?" she asked her son.

"No."

"It's simple. When he does what you want, reward him. When he doesn't, punish him. Men like Streona are sensitive. You have to show him some respect, otherwise he will begin to think he made a mistake by standing by you." She patted her mare's neck. "Are you beginning to regret taking me along?"

"No." He chuckled. "But I'm beginning to see why Father couldn't keep you with him."

She wanted to say something, but she only took a breath and fell silent. Cnut spoke again after a moment, but his voice had turned harsh.

"Mother, I am grateful for all your advice, but allow me to give you some of my own."

"Do you want to give me advice or orders?" she asked, noticing his tone.

"It wouldn't suit a son to give his mother orders, but know that I don't want to see you beside me again . . ."

She froze.

". . . without your chain mail," he finished, and she let out her breath.

They joined forces with the men who guarded the ships and stopped to rest in a large stone manor house in Southampton.

"Mother, I want Elfgifu and little Sven to join us. My wife and son shouldn't be in the camp any longer if I'm here."

"Are you asking for my opinion?" she asked, stroking Dusza's large head. The lynx purred and laid her tufty ears flat along her head.

"You know what I'm asking."

She looked at him carefully without a flicker of tenderness.

"You won't want to hear this. I don't think you should have taken them with you at all. It would have been better if they had remained in Roskilde under your brother's care and sailed to join us once this is all over."

Cnut bit his lip.

"I know, you're right. But Elfgifu insisted. She never felt comfortable in Denmark, and she wanted to come home as quickly as possible."

"That's not a good thing. A woman who wants to be queen must accept her husband's country for her own."

"My home will be England. Surely you don't doubt that?"

"No." She smiled and kissed him before walking away with Dusza at her side.

43

❧

ENGLAND

Cnut may have secretly agreed with Świętosława, but he still summoned Elfgifu and Sven to join him in Southampton in spring as soon as they could travel the roads again. His reunion with his wife was passionate but short. The council with the other chieftains took up most of that evening, and when he finally escaped them, all he felt was exhaustion. Elfgifu gave him little Sven to kiss before sending him away with a wet nurse.

"How are we progressing?" she asked him as she unbraided her hair.

"We?" He looked surprised. "It's slow. The English nobles are like . . . well, I've never known a man like Streona before." He sat on the edge of the bed, feeling tension that bordered on pain in his neck and shoulders.

Elfgifu sat down next to him and placed a hand on his knee.

"I missed you," she whispered.

"I missed you, too," he replied, trying to loosen his shoulders.

"Do it for me," she said, kissing his neck.

"Do what?" He reached for her, but she slipped through his fingers.

"Defeat them," she replied. "Defeat them and take the throne," she demanded. "For me and for our son. King Sven I Cnutsson of England."

"Sven I was my father," he reminded her.

"We should have a real wedding," she said.

"We pledged ourselves to one another in front of witnesses, what else do you want?" he asked with confusion.

"Cnut, we're in England now. We should be married in a church, say our vows before an archbishop."

"I think you mean God." He sighed. "There'll be time for that. Right now, the bishops are my enemies. I'm so tired. Streona and all his plotting . . ."

Elfgifu knelt behind him and began to knead his shoulders. He closed his eyes and exhaled.

"The most important thing," she whispered straight into his ear, "is that we stay together."

"We are in the middle of a war," he replied.

"Your mother accompanies you everywhere you go."

Elfgifu pressed herself against his back and he felt the softness of her breasts. Her hands roamed his chest and stomach as she kissed his neck. His exhaustion disappeared as quickly as her dress. They joined in an embrace like two animals. He confessed his love for her to her soft thighs, her nipples which their son sucked, her belly button. Elfgifu wrapped her arms around him and gave herself to him. She was like the promise of the kingdom he wanted to conquer. They fell asleep holding each other, and the next thing he knew, Jorun was waking him up by banging on the door.

"A messenger, my king!"

"Is it urgent?" he groaned, rubbing his eyes.

All he heard in response was Jorun's loud laughter and raised voices in the yard. He kissed Elfgifu's sleepy face, pulled on his clothes, and entered the room where his mother, Eadric Streona, Thorkel, and the rest of the chieftains were already waiting. He swept his hair out of his eyes and looked around at them all.

Świętosława nodded to the messenger.

"King Ethelred is dead!"

At first, Cnut thought he was still dreaming. But then he realized he was wide awake, and that his mother and everyone else had already heard the news before he arrived. Streona stepped toward him first. Beads of sweat glistened on his bald head.

"King Cnut! You must take London as fast as possible."

The king is dead, Cnut thought. *Dead. I couldn't have planned this better myself.*

"Edmund has locked himself in London with his army under the dragon flag. He will fight for the city like a lion now that his father's dead," said Thorkel.

Ethelred's eldest son, Edmund. Brave and fierce. To him, his father's death meant the English crown was his. Cnut looked at his mother and sensed that she wanted him to speak rather than to listen to the others.

"If he plans to fight like a lion then we will surround him like a pack of wolves," he announced confidently.

"I know the best way to do that," the Jomsviking announced without a flicker of emotion. "But we need to leave immediately, and we cannot be slowed down."

Elfgifu will be angry. She and little Sven, the wet nurses and the servants, he thought. *I can't allow for the chieftains to blame my wife for slowing us down.*

"My queen." He turned to his mother. "This time, I will ask you to stay in Southampton and support Elfgifu." He hesitated before adding: "You will join us when it's over."

She understood. They looked at each other briefly before he kissed her forehead. *I hope you can forgive me.*

The first ships set sail at dawn. He knew they had to be swift because they could not afford to waste the element of surprise that was on their side now. Thorkel's idea was mad, but it could work.

"The key to gaining London is the fortified bridge across the Thames. That's where all the armies fail. The bridge was ruined in the fights which broke out after Sven's death, but it's been reconstructed since. The garrison guarding it is the strongest part of London's defense. But if we dig a ditch from the west, we can surround the city and attack from both sides."

"Has anyone ever tried that before?" he asked Thorkel.

"No." The Jomsviking rubbed his bald head.

Thorkel knew the Thames as well as if he'd been raised on it, and his *Nidhog* led the way, followed by the smooth hull of the *Queen's Son* and the rest of the fleet. They reached the wide mouth of the river with the tide, so all they needed was a gentle push of the oars to drift upriver. Hrani, Cnut's friend and the best sailor he had, skillfully navigated the waters now that he'd been saved from accompanying Elfgifu again. Cnut watched the muddy banks. He saw gaggles of geese rising from the reeds with warning screeches. He saw the graceful, slender swans, and their long necks reminded him of kissing Elfgifu's neck. He noticed a hill on the right where the charred remains of a fortress stood. He had Hrani signal Thorkel and the *Nidhog* slowed. The Jomsviking stood in the stern of his ship while Cnut stood on the bow of the *Queen's Son*.

"What's that?"

"Benfleet," Thorkel shouted back.

"Who burned it?"

"I did!"

"For my father or against him?"

"It was after his death." Thorkel shaded his eyes as he looked up at the ruins.

"I'm asking you to tell me who you were fighting for," Cnut insisted.

"Ethelred," the Jomsviking replied without a shadow of embarrassment. "Look, my lord! The bay by the fortress is a good place to berth a large army. It could fit more than one hundred ships."

"Why has Edmund not hidden himself here to catch us off guard?"

Thorkel spread out his arms.

"I'll ask him when we meet. For now, all I can say is that I doubt the new king has enough ships to stop us under the Benfleet remains."

Cnut nodded, allowing the Jomsviking to turn away again. The ruined fortress looked abandoned.

Jorun stood beside him.

"Did my father look at that fortress when he sailed into London?" he asked.

"Everyone looked at it. I stared at its palisade when I was on my way to Roskilde with Sven's bones, and do you know what else? I pissed into the Thames as I stared at that bay. The Jomsviking is right. This is the best place from which to defend the city, but you have to have a large enough fleet to do so. The king's son doesn't command enough ships."

"When I take London, I'll build a new fortress here to guard the city for me," Cnut decided.

Jorun spat and laughed hoarsely.

"I like you, my king! You haven't even taken the throne yet but you already know what you're going to do when you will. Your old man didn't like London much."

"You never told me that," Cnut said with surprise.

"Does it matter?" Jorun shrugged. "Whether he liked it or not, he took it and that's the end of it. There are many cities more beautiful in England than London, but without London you cannot claim this green kingdom as your own."

He and Thorkel split up before they reached London. The Jomsviking left to dig the ditch while Jorun took command of the troops left to storm the city. The famous bridge forced them to stop, and that's when they saw the fortress of Southwark.

"That's new," Jorun snarled angrily. "That wasn't there when Sven and I took London."

They fought on the Thames for a week, to no avail. The city refused to surrender. Cnut's fleet was unable to use its numbers to its advantage because the bridge barred their way and the defenders used it to pour hot oil and shoot burning arrows at them from above. Unwilling to keep dozens of ships on the river for no reason, he ordered camps be built on the banks to which he sent the wounded, and the men fought in shifts.

"The spies say that Bishop Elfwig is responsible for London's refusal to surrender," Hrani reported.

"Elfwig." Jorun narrowed his eyes. "I remember that name, he left the city when Sven took the throne. He never pledged himself to your father."

"And he clearly doesn't intend to side with the son," Hrani observed.

Cnut inwardly cursed the Jomsviking, regretting ever having taken his advice. Thorkel's plan had engaged a large number of the men in building the ditch that had proved to be of no help at all.

"What if he did that on purpose, and betrays us now?"

"Calm down, my lord." Jorun spat into the water. "We can take London by starving it out. Our ships are blocking the route by which they get their supplies, and we have plenty to last us a long time."

Once again, he realized that he was only twenty years old, too inexperienced to have undertaken such an ambitious mission. So, he followed Jorun's advice and tried not to worry.

That didn't last long.

While he focused on the promising thought of starving out the city, the enemy attacked them from behind.

"The English struck at dawn, storming the camps farthest from the bridge," reported the messenger as he leaped onto the *Queen's Son*'s deck. "Our men are fighting, but the enemy is trying to push them into the water."

"They managed to set fire to some of the ships. The Swedes have suffered the greatest losses." A second messenger appeared soon after.

"The attacking army is determined and fierce," a third added, arriving at the same time as Eadric Streona. He crossed a plank to board Cnut's ship, stepping carefully to avoid slipping.

"It's Edmund. He's been spotted in the front line," he said, failing to hide his fear.

"How did he manage to leave the city?" Cnut exclaimed, and his chieftains echoed his anger, muttering as they glared at Streona.

The Fat Spider, Mutt, Groom—he had a dozen offensive nicknames that were used behind his back. Nobody ever trusted him. Cnut was furious with his mother for forcing him to bear the company of this disgusting man. He should have broken his neck on the moors when Streona had first arrived, offering his services.

"I have nothing to do with it," Streona tried to defend himself, and proceeded to use the coward's favorite defense. "I have more to lose than you do if Edmund wins."

"It's possible that Edmund left the city before we arrived," Thorkel pointed out. "He knew that London would stand long enough for him to gather his forces in Wessex and return. Walk with me, my king."

"Wessex?!" roared Cnut. "Streona negotiated an alliance with Wessex for us! He promised that the nobles wouldn't stand against us!"

The Jomsviking pulled him to the bow of the ship, out of Streona's earshot.

"Just because the fat one hasn't betrayed us yet doesn't mean he won't try. He's waiting to see which is the winning side, and I've told you already that if anyone will put up a real fight for England, it's Edmund. I see another danger though. His men are trying to pull us away from the city. If we lose sight of its walls, it will be harder to make our way back."

"What do you suggest? Leaving some of our forces behind? That will weaken us." Cnut's suspicions grew.

"I suggest we leave about a dozen ships here who will keep an eye on the city and stop the inhabitants from feeling too safe. We can leave the ships we don't need in the bay at Benfleet."

"All right. Let's go and face Edmund."

It was the middle of summer by the time they clashed at Brentford. Ethelred's son demonstrated the strength of his cavalry, which tore through Cnut's infantry. Cnut saw the lords of Essex stand beside Edmund and felt despair. They had promised to serve him. Cnut fought, trying to give vent to his fury at the nobles for constantly switching sides. He left so many dead on the field at night that he cried like a child in his tent when he was hidden from the eyes of his chieftains. He thought of the fathers in Roskilde who had sent their sons to fight with him with such enthusiasm. He thought of the red-haired Harald, his brother, safe to govern Denmark in peace. And he heard his mother: *"We are at war, Cnut. Blood is bound to flow."* In the morning, he washed his face with cold water and stepped outside to his men.

"We are going to burn and plunder the neighboring villages. We will strike fear into them and destroy everything in our path. And most importantly, we will steal their horses."

They nodded, accepting the order, but when they began to disperse to gather their men, Hrani arrived. They stopped to listen to what he had to say.

"King! My king! Eadric Streona is gone. His tent is empty."

Jorun spat on the ground. Thorkel narrowed his eyes and cocked his head. His father's friends, Uddorm and Ragn, both wore an expression which could best be described as trying to say: *Your father had better luck, boy.* Cnut ignored it. He knew that the traitor had just decided who he thought was going to win. And he felt Cnut the Cruel wake up inside him.

"I won't forgive him for this," he said, and walked back inside his tent to put on his armor.

They tracked Edmund and Eadric Streona, along with a few hundred heavy infantrymen, to Essex.

"How many horses do we have?" Cnut asked Thorkel.

"A herd." The Jomsviking smiled. "We brought one hundred with us from Denmark. Jarl Eric sent us another hundred from Northumbria, and we took another two hundred. A few of them are cart horses, useless in battle, but we have enough for two lines of cavalry."

"I remember when you took control of England. You refused to back down. I made the same decision on the night we fought in Brentford. This country will bow to me."

Thorkel the Tall looked at him as a brother-in-arms, not a boy. He said:

"Ake. Fat Bue. Kalle. Vagn. Gunnar the Slender. Karl the Cheerful. Haakon Thin-Faced. It's been years and I still remember the faces and names of the friends I lost. But the ones I remember most clearly are those who were with me in the first fights. I know you fought beside Sven. And since we landed in Sandwich, you've been reaching for your sword. You're a good warrior, King Cnut."

"No longer the young king, then?"

"No. You aged that night."

Edmund's armies, marching under the Wessex dragon, faced Cnut near Ashingdon in the autumn sun and the vibrant purples of the heathlands. When they rode out of the forest toward the battlefield, Cnut saw a few nuns gathering herbs at the edge of the woods. He made the sign of the cross, and they responded in kind, even though they were frightened at the sight of his soldiers. He interpreted it as a good omen. In his mind's eye he saw Świętosława again as she'd appeared when she'd come to see them near Roskilde dressed as a nun. He remembered that day. It was autumn, like now. It had been the first time he'd ever seen a nun, and he'd thought she was as beautiful as she was strange. Did he wish he'd known sooner that it had been his mother? It didn't matter anymore. She was with the queen's son now.

Edmund seemed to be a short man when Cnut spotted him riding out in front of his armies proclaiming, "For England!"

Cnut brandished his sword and lifted it over his head as he turned his horse to face his people.

"For our new kingdom!"

And then he charged without looking to see if his soldiers followed. He could hear the hoofbeats of their mounts, though. Two hundred of them, half of his previous horses, were ridden by his uncle Burizleif's precious cavalry. "Their men are used to fighting on horseback," his mother's brother had told him when they'd met in Poznań. "They are unafraid of Saxon armor or enemy riders, and they fight with sword and spear alike. Half of them have Russian bulavas. A large piece of iron mounted on a handle. They keep them at their belts and use them if they lose other weapons in battle. The horses do the biting and my boys can break a skull open with bulavas. Remember that they can form a wall of shields on horseback and push your enemy in whatever direction you choose. All you need to do is show them what you want."

He couldn't help himself from glancing back. They rode behind him in an even line, side by side. The feathers on their helms didn't bend with the wind, cutting the sky like blades. The powerful Kalmir held the flag bearing the Piast eagle. Cnut heard Wilkomir give the order:

"Shields!"

And they all shifted their shields from their backs onto their left arms, moving together like one man. Wilkomir didn't lean forward in his saddle but urged his horse onward sitting tall, keeping an eye on everything like a falcon eyeing its prey.

"Spears!" he shouted, and Cnut saw the spearheads gleam in the sunlight.

There were another one hundred paces between them and Edmund's armies when Wilkomir shouted:

"Ostry!"

A warrior with white feathers attached to his helm rode out before the others, overtaking Cnut as he shouted in passing:

"Forgive me, King!"

He leaned forward in his saddle and his horse sped up into a gallop, stretching out its head. Ostry moved his body fluidly as he took aim and threw the spear.

The weapon flew so fast that it looked like an arrow shot from a bow.

What is he doing? wondered Cnut without slowing down.

But then he saw the spear fly through the center of the dragon flag carried by Edmund's flagbearer. They heard their enemy's cries of dismay at their symbol's defeat.

"The dragon is dead!" Ostry shouted and blew into the bone whistle that hung from his neck.

The horses of their foes all reared up at the high-pitched sound, while Burizleif's warriors roared:

"God is with us. To battle!"

They threw their spears into the approaching opponents. Every other horse fell, pulling their riders with them. But Edmund had thrice as many horses as they did, and the fallen were replaced in the blink of an eye.

They clashed. Cnut searched for Edmund, but a large warrior in gleaming chain mail appeared before him, thrusting a sword. Cnut protected himself with his shield without thinking and heard the clang of steel on the iron fittings. He struck back. The whinnying of horses, clanging of iron, and furious screams of the soldiers pierced the air. Cnut cut down anything in front of him blindly.

He attacked anyone who was in his way. He saw the horses' flared nostrils and their bared teeth. He didn't think, couldn't think, he just acted. He raised his shield and cleaved the air with his sword. That's when he heard the roar of his men behind him.

The infantry, he thought.

An army of Vikings experienced in warfare, men who preferred to fight at sea than on dry land, had followed his orders and acted like madmen. Their strength lay in the fact that they weren't fighting blind. They were as disciplined as if they had had a rolling deck beneath their feet. Before the battle, he'd told them: "We will take this kingdom today. Imagine that Edmund's army is the enemy vessel. We will throw our hooks over their gunwales and cut their ship in half."

He knew that they had a larger cavalry, but he had enough to push back the first attack. His infantry proceeded to cut down Edmund's horses to reach his soldiers. It was just like throwing grappling hooks. They outnumbered Edmund's men, so they pushed between the English soldiers as if they were leaping aboard a new ship. They took no prisoners and asked for no mercy. Cnut kept searching for Edmund, but he couldn't see him. He felt a blow on his shoulder, but he managed to weaken the impact by raising his shield. His horse was racing forward and Cnut couldn't take out his anger for that blow until the next enemy soldier crossed his path. And the next one. Someone struck the bottom of his shield, which slammed upward into his chin and almost cost him his teeth. He tasted blood but not even that slowed him down. He rode on, and even if he'd wanted to stop, the raging battle had driven his horse into a frenzy, too, and it was impossible to control him. He saw Ostry, or at least the handful of white feathers which streamed from his helm. He cut down a soldier, slicing him from shoulder to midriff. He saw one of Burizleif's men grimace in pain as his entrails fell out of his belly. His horse sped on. A small man encased in steel gave a shout from up ahead and took aim with a spear which he sent flying at Cnut's head. His shield protected him, but the force of the blow almost pushed him out of the saddle.

Jesus! he thought. *Jesus, what a slaughter!*

He suddenly realized he'd ridden so far among the English troops that he couldn't see his men anymore. He tried to rein in his horse, but the animal struggled to respond to his commands. He heard a familiar voice screaming, a voice he'd recognize in the depths of hell, because it was none other than Eadric Streona:

"King Edmund is dead! Edmund is dead! We need to surrender!"

He could hear him, but he couldn't see him. His foes froze, turning around and retreating, leaving behind a battlefield of corpses.

"Archers!" he shouted back to his men. "Chase them with arrows!"

He turned and rode back toward them quickly, leaning low over his horse's neck to avoid becoming a target himself.

The face of Ulfcetel, the ealdorman of Essex who had once sided with his father, flashed past as he rushed by. He lay on the ground with his eyes wide open as blood seeped out of a wound in his neck.

He's still alive, thought Cnut, *although he's already passed through Death's gates.*

The arrows whizzed over his head. He caught up to Wilkomir's retreating men. When he reached his troops, he began to look around for his companions. He spotted Thorkel quickly, since the Jomsviking stood out by his height. Hrani, his best helmsman, had already galloped over to stand beside him. Jorun was approaching slowly, wiping blood from his face. Old Ragn of the Isles and dark-haired Gjotgar of Scania were still alive, too. Wilkomir raised his right arm to show he was still undefeated, and Kalmir raised the flag with the eagle above his head:

"Under the wings!"

"How many have we lost?"

"I don't know yet, my lord," replied Thorkel. Blood dripped from his forehead.

"You're bleeding!" they said to each other at the same time, and it was only then that Cnut felt the wound under his collarbone. He took off his helm and wiped his sweaty face.

"My trick worked!" He heard Streona's voice behind him. "Edmund's men believed he'd died!" The Spider, Groom, Mutt was laughing cheerfully as if it were the best joke he'd heard.

Cnut pulled on the reins to turn his horse around when Thorkel leaned over to whisper to him:

"You don't have the net in your hand just yet, my lord. Control yourself."

Cnut heard him, and loosed the reins again, remaining where he was.

"So Edmund is still alive?" he asked.

"Yes!" Streona laughed again. "But he knows he's been defeated, and he has no chance of winning now. He wants to negotiate."

"Excellent trick, Eadric Streona," said Cnut through clenched teeth. "I'm happy that you haven't betrayed me after all, only crossed to the other side to give us an advantage. You're a true friend, Earl of Mercia."

"At your service, my lord." Streona smiled.

His chain mail had not a single drop of blood on it, though sweat beaded on his forehead.

44

ENGLAND

Świętosława left the stone manor in Southampton with overwhelming relief. Her time with little Sven revealed that she had no patience with children. She felt nothing at the sight of his face sticky with berries or his "sweet clumsiness," as Elfgifu called it, and it drove her mad that he kept pulling Dusza's short, protruding tail. Her lynx was very tolerant and only snarled at Sven when he was being particularly annoying. When she heard Elfgifu encourage him to "play with Grandma's pussycat," she wanted to bite her daughter-in-law herself. She needed a few days to realize that it wasn't little Sven who was irritating her, but his mother. And what Cnut had wanted her to do. Elfgifu was the last person who needed help or taking care of. That girl knew exactly what she wanted. She was demanding of her servants, regal in her demeanor, and more than anything completely devoted to her child. "My son will be king of England," she'd chirp. "Daddy will return soon and bring you back the crown." Whenever she heard such nonsense, Świętosława took Dusza and went for a walk along the moors which surrounded the manor. Wilczan and Great Ulf usually accompanied her.

"Ulf," she'd ask once they were out of earshot of the manor, "am I getting old?"

"No, my lady," he'd say. "You're always going to be younger than me!"

"But apparently women turn bitter and mean with age," she worried.

"Not all," Wilczan replied one day, and it was almost enough to calm her, when he continued: "Some are bitter and mean when they're young and mellow with age."

"How do you know?" she asked angrily.

"Father told me."

She shrugged it off, thinking that if Wilkomir wasn't mistaken then it was a sign that she wasn't old yet. She was still far from mellow.

She awaited news from Cnut every day while she was in Southampton, and she analyzed every one of them with care. When her son asked her through a messenger to join him and the chieftains, she was ready to go in a matter of moments.

"What about us?" asked Elfgifu suspiciously. "Why is the king only summoning his mother?"

"Because she's a queen," Great Ulf retorted, and his expression too revealed the relief he felt at the prospect of leaving Southampton behind them.

She rode toward the Danish camp on the banks of the river Severn with Great Ulf and Wilczan beside her, surrounded by her axemen. She'd heard about her son's victory on the moors of Ashingdon. The messenger had told her that "the flower of English knighthood died on those moors," and Edmund decided to negotiate. He'd had no other choice. Her son was unbeatable in battle, but he still didn't rule England. This game had proven more difficult than either of them had suspected, but there was no turning back now. She didn't want to believe in Gaudentius's cruel curse about firstborn sons being pushed off the throne, and so she'd pushed Cnut into battle instead. *"The firstborn son should take Denmark's throne, while the second needs to conquer his own kingdom. The kingdom we know as England!"* That's what she'd said in Viborg, then Cnut had asked for her help. She couldn't fight for him, but she could support him.

"Cnut!" she greeted her son as she rode into the camp on the banks of the river Severn.

"Mother!" He rode over to greet her. "How is my son?"

"Little Sven can say your name now," she replied. "And Elfgifu is with child again. You're a good shot, Cnut, since you only had one night together." She stopped her horse.

He blushed.

My boy, she thought. *I'll spare you the stories of Elfgifu's follies.*

"You're well dressed, Mother," he praised her.

"I take the king's advice," she replied offhandedly.

The chain mail that her brother had sent her, Ivar Goldtooth's handiwork, was a perfect fit. Ylva had struggled to learn to tie it properly, but she managed eventually, and now Świętosława did indeed feel safe in its embrace. She wore a simple wool dress underneath. The steel circles clinked together every time she moved, but they protected her from any stray arrows. She wore a cloak fastened with a brooch, and a soft wolf fur. She also accepted high leather boots from Wilczan, with steel plates sewn into the shafts. And she now had new-found appreciation for the warriors who wore all this iron every single day.

"When are you speaking with Edmund?" she asked. "And on whose side is Streona today?"

"In two days," replied Cnut. "Streona will be there as our ally."

She glanced at the sky and smiled.

"It will be a new moon. That's a good sign. Can you be patient?"

"Can stubbornness replace patience?" he asked.

"Yes!" she replied, letting the lynx off the leash.

"I caught the hare first!" Harald shouted in her memories. *"But I got a larger one!"* Cnut had replied. The moors here looked just like the ones that day, violent in their purple hues. She didn't need to pretend to be a nun anymore.

"Bold One!" Jorun sounded genuinely pleased to see her as he ran toward them but checked himself before he reached them and blushed. "The Bold Lady, our queen, has returned!"

"Sven would drop dead if he saw you, and his bones would tremble in a hellish dance," Ragn of the Isles called out. "Bloody hell, our lady in armor. Damn it, the queen has tits . . . breasts . . . Jesus, forgive me, I just mean, in front . . ." The old chieftain blushed like a boy, but he didn't look away.

"Will there be a feast?" Uddorm of Viborg appeared from his tent. "With the lynx hunting his prey?"

"How have you had so many children, Uddorm, without learning how to differentiate between boys and girls?" Świętosława reprimanded him. She was always sensitive about people forgetting her lynx was a female.

"I'd be happy to show the queen how I've made so many children." He brightened up.

"Why not?" she replied. "I'm sure the entire camp is curious!"

Uddorm cleared his throat and backed down while she greeted the rest of the chieftains.

"How did Edmund's men fight?" she asked Wilkomir as he helped her dismount.

"Bravely," he said carelessly. "They did better than Emperor Henry's troops."

"And my son?"

"He's not a boy anymore," Wilkomir replied. "He's learning to be a ruler."

"But . . . ?"

"What?" He grimaced.

"You tell me. I can see there's something else."

"Thorkel the Tall," Wilkomir whispered. "He's the real leader of this army."

"He is more experienced than Cnut," she said thoughtfully. "Warriors adore men like him. Does he act superior when he's with my son?"

Wilkomir shook his head.

"Does he urge the men to rise up against Cnut? Or question his orders?"

Wilkomir shook his head again.

"Thank you, Wilkomir," she said, and walked to the tent that had been prepared for her.

Cnut's and Edmund's camps stretched along opposite sides of the river as far as the eye could see, but it was clear that the Danish camp was larger. There was no chaos; her son's chieftains ensured the camp looked fit for a king. Flags bearing wild boar heads, leaping deer, serpents winding themselves around their own tails, Polish eagles, and Jomsborg's wolves were frayed and faded from their exposure to wind, salt, and water. Flags bearing the proud Wessex dragon flew over Edmund's camp. Most of them looked new and clean.

"Wilczan," she called out. "Fly the flag I received from Duchess Emnilda."

"Right away, my lady," he replied, and within moments the sky was obscured by the image of an eagle in flight holding a dragon in its claws.

They met on an island in the middle of the river.

Świętosława, Thorkel, and Jarl Eric stood behind Cnut, with Streona nearby. Her son's chieftains lined up behind them. Edmund was a short, stocky man with smooth dark hair and light eyes. He surprised them by arriving with an infant in his arms.

"My son, Edmund," he introduced the child, handing it over to the wet nurse. "A second child is on its way. My wife, Edith, is healthy and fertile," he added.

Does he want our sympathy? she wondered. *No, it's more likely that he wants us to know he leaves behind heirs even if he dies in battle. He wants to show us that his dynasty won't die with him.* She looked at Edmund carefully and decided that he looked more like a warrior than the lazy king his father had been.

His companions were introduced.

"Lyfing, the archbishop of Canterbury, the murdered Aelfheah's successor."

"Martyr Aelfheah," corrected Edmund, looking at Thorkel.

The Jomsviking didn't even flinch, as if the matter discussed had nothing to do with him, even though the archbishop had been slaughtered in his camp and had been the spark which had set the entire country ablaze.

Is he trying to reach out to Thorkel by naming Aelfheah a martyr? Is he telling him that a crime which results in the victim's sanctification offers the Jomsviking a chance for forgiveness?

"Leofwin, earldorman of Mercia."

"He was among the nobles who greeted Sven in London," whispered Jorun into her ear.

"And he was a victim of the Groom's plots. Edmund set him free of those," Thorkel whispered into her other ear.

"His son, Northman."

A young, confident man stepped in front of his father after being presented and forgot to step back into his place. She didn't miss the glances he kept casting at Streona.

Either he mistrusts him as much as we do or he is part of his web, she thought.

"And his second son, Leofric."

This one bowed from where he stood behind his brother without moving closer to them.

"And the noble Godwin, son of the great Sussex family."

"The wealthiest," Thorkel added in a whisper.

A young man with closely cropped hair nodded to them gravely.

The servants of both sides erected a tent and brought in benches while the introductions were made. Earlier, when Edmund had suggested before their meeting that his people would prepare a place worthy of two kings for them, Cnut hadn't agreed. He wouldn't let Edmund play the role of host.

"We witness here today the meeting of two kings," Eadric Streona began, struggling not to rub his hands together triumphantly. "King Edmund, who is the rightful heir to the throne now that King Ethelred is dead. And King Cnut, King Sven's successor, who was invited to take the throne of England when Ethelred ran from the country. Archbishop Lyfing was present . . ."

Because you were beside the old king then. You thought he'd be triumphant in the end, but you were wrong, she thought. *There is no king that you wouldn't betray.*

Jorun, when he had told her about Streona's last betrayal on the battle-field, had been vulgar but accurate: there is no ass he wouldn't lick or face he wouldn't spit into. But he was leading one of her son's most important campaigns: the one that could give him the country. The nobles were as divided as England itself. Every alliance, agreement, or pledge of fealty could be broken in the blink of an eye. Calling on Edmund's right by blood as opposed to Cnut's right by strength resolved nothing. If her son used all his forces today, he would defeat Edmund, but what then? Without all parties unanimously accepting him as king, he wouldn't be in power for long because someone like Streona or Leofwin or any other of the ealdormen could rise up at any point, produce a blood heir, and start another war. That's why they'd decided, before coming here to see Edmund, that a division of the country would be an acceptable solution.

"If we acknowledge that King Edmund's right to the throne, as King Ethelred's heir, is equal to King Cnut's, as King Sven's son," Archbishop Lyfing said carefully, "then the only solution is to divide the kingdom into two."

She watched Edmund. His expression didn't change, so he and Lyfing had probably considered the same option earlier. A division was the obvious solution. That's what King Alfred had done a century before when the Danes continuously invaded his kingdom. To save his country from destruction, his people from exile, and his language from extinction, he'd created Danelagh in the southwest of England, giving it to the invaders so that Wessex, which had been much larger then, could remain English. The Danish rulers died out in time, and though the settlers remained, it all seemed to resolve itself peacefully, if one didn't count the small fighting which always broke out between the different parts of the country when the nobility sought independence from the monarchy. King Alfred saved his kingdom by dividing it, and now they were asking Edmund to do the same. *Will he think of himself as Alfred's successor if he agrees?* Alfred was already beginning to be spoken of as "the Great."

"I will stay in the north and middle England, but I won't leave London," said her son.

"You haven't taken London," Edmund pointed out calmly.

"But I will, if you want it to burn. Fire wins many battles. But will the wealthy London merchants forgive you for letting their fortunes go up in flames?"

"No," Streona whispered. "They won't."

Edmund flinched when he heard Streona's voice.

How is it, thought Świętosława again with admiration, *that the man who is despised by all still leads the most important of negotiations?*

"Wessex stands with me," said Edmund, pausing for a moment before he continued. "I will accept this: you keep Northumbria and Mercia, like you said, while I keep the west and the south. And London."

"Not London," Cnut replied.

Neither one used the royal title when addressing the other. She watched the game carefully, noticing that Cnut maintained perfect control over his emotions.

"Well then, maybe we should fight for London?" suggested Edmund with hostility. "But not with fire, not by destroying everything that Londoners own. We should fight with the sword. The battle of two chieftains. Two kings."

The Spider had spoken the truth! He claimed he suspected that Edmund would suggest a duel to settle the outcome of the war.

"I won't send any of my men to fight for me," said Cnut calmly. "And I won't soil myself with royal blood, not even in a duel. I've not come here with an army which has already forced England to its knees only to be provoked into such a dangerous game."

If she didn't find him so disgusting, she would have kissed Streona's sagging cheek. Knowing beforehand that Edmund would propose a duel was key to gaining the upper hand in the negotiations. Streona had brought news of it the night before, having heard of Edmund's plans from his inner circle, gleaning the information in a way known only to himself. Her fierce, young son would have fallen for it, but thanks to Streona, they'd had enough time for Thorkel, Jorun, Ragn, and everyone else to convince him that this wasn't about honor but about victory.

Northman, Leofwin's son, didn't look surprised, even though according to the division upon which Cnut and Edmund had just agreed, his father lost his position as Mercia's ealdorman. That convinced her that he must be working for Streona. Who else was?

"Royal blood," Edmund repeated, his eyes flashing. "So you acknowledge my claim to the throne."

"I understand it. You used the title of king to describe me first." Cnut smiled. "The battle of two kings."

"If we settle on King Cnut taking Northumbria and Mercia, and King Edmund keeping Wessex and the south, then London is our only point of disagreement," the archbishop interjected. "I suggest we divide London, too. Make the city open to both kings."

"No, noble Lyfing," Streona interjected, fulfilling his mission. "London is not all we have left to discuss. There is the matter of the danegeld. If King Edmund wants to keep his power, the inhabitants of his parts of the kingdom must pay for his privilege."

The negotiations were stopped, but when Edmund returned, he agreed for London to be open to them both, and for some of Cnut's men to spend winter within the city walls, although he would be the ultimate authority in the city. He also agreed to pay the danegeld.

"All that is left for us to do is swear on the cross to uphold everything we agreed to today," the archbishop of Canterbury announced dejectedly.

A cold, humid wind made the fabric of the tent flutter as it blew in from the river. She looked up at the sky and saw the rain clouds gathering.

Cnut and Edmund faced each other and grasped one another's hands. Leofwin stood behind Edmund with his son in his arms. Świętosława stood behind Cnut.

"Here are the two kings: Edmund, son of Ethelred, and Cnut, son of Sven. Like two brothers they have sworn to uphold the peace in the country, and now give their word never to break it."

"You have my word," said Cnut.

"And you have mine," replied Edmund.

They embraced stiffly.

Świętosława watched them through her green and golden eyes. And she watched Thorkel. And Streona. And Edmund's infant son.

45

⚮

ENGLAND

Cnut charged Thorkel with the task of bringing his wife Elfgifu to her family home in Northampton, while he himself set off to York with Jarl Eric to meet with Archbishop Wulfstan and strengthen his hold on Northumbria. His mother led three strong companies of seasoned warriors to accompany Eadric Streona to Worcester, where he claimed he had business to attend which could not wait and which would be of great benefit to Mercia.

Even after they'd announced that the peace negotiations had been successful, Cnut refrained from telling his chieftains which land he was going to give them, though he hadn't yet taken away Streona's position in Mercia which he'd received from the late Ethelred. And although he knew Thorkel was waiting for the lands and title he'd been promised, he didn't take Northumbria from Eric, either. When they were leaving to go their separate ways, he invited everyone to spend Christmas with him in York. "That will be the time for us to divide the spoils," he announced, and they all set off in their designated directions.

"Hrani . . ." He rode up beside his friend. "I'm beginning to wonder whether I should bring my sisters over from Denmark."

"I would think that's a good idea." The helmsman's pale eyes gleamed.

"My lady mother says that we need many of our beautiful maids here now."

"The queen is wise indeed." Hrani grinned. "I need them! I'll be first in line!"

"Stop that!" Cnut laughed. "My lady mother has something different in mind than you do. She thinks we need to marry our daughters and sisters into the English nobility."

"Oh no! They won't be coming here for us?" Hrani groaned. "But I miss our girls so much! I can't seem to come round to the locals . . ."

"Knowing my mother, you won't have a choice. She'll find you a daughter of some Leofwin or a Godwin's sister and then what? The queen knows how to get people to agree with her."

"I hope Streona has no daughters," Hrani said gloomily.

"I don't know about that, but I know his wife is King Ethelred's daughter, so you'd be marrying into a royal family!" Cnut laughed and added, though he wasn't sure whether he was addressing Hrani or himself: "Elfgifu will soon give birth to another child. I haven't seen her since spring."

"Why did you send Thorkel for her, of all people?" asked Hrani. "Do you trust him that much?"

"No." Cnut sighed. "But my mother suggested it, saying that it will convince Thorkel that I do trust him. After all, I'm relying on him to protect my wife and son."

He didn't like it, but he saw the sense in his mother's words. And it was his idea, after all, for her to accompany him to England. Diplomacy. The art of saying no to someone in a way that made them believe you said yes. He was learning the game, but he still wasn't entirely certain he wanted to play. What had he been thinking when he left Roskilde over a year ago aboard the *Queen's Son*? That Cnut had been a dreamer, thinking he would arrive, fight, and win his kingdom. Instead, he'd been taught a bitter lesson of betrayals, alliances, and treaties. Somewhere between the failed attempts to storm London, the bloody battle by Brentford, and his negotiations with Edmund on the river Severn's banks, he'd realized that there was no turning back from the road onto which he'd stepped. That he couldn't just turn around and say: "I was wrong. I want to go home." What home? His brother, the redheaded Harald, sat upon the throne in Roskilde. He'd been crowned Denmark's king.

I have been victorious at Ashingdon and I lead the greatest army that has ever invaded England. How could I return to Roskilde and ask Harald to let me have Funen or Scania? He felt a cold sweat break out on his neck whenever he thought about it. *Those lands are taken already. Gjotgar is Scania's vassal and he stands beside me now. Jarl Haakon rules Funen under Harald's authority. How could I take that away from either of them? I couldn't do that. Every one of the men who boarded their ships and came here with me believed that I could conquer England. I have taken half of it. It's enough to give them all lands and silver. I haven't let them down.* He tried to reassure himself with these thoughts, even though he never forgot that he was surrounded by men who wanted something from him and could betray him in the blink of an eye if they found themselves dissatisfied.

"I think that Thorkel won't be content until he has more power. You'll have to share that with him, friend," Hrani gave voice to Cnut's own thoughts.

There is still a month until Christmas. I'll think of something, Cnut told himself.

Peace reigned in York. Archbishop Wulfstan was in a nearby abbey, so they waited for him, resting after the eighteen months of war they had just finished waging. Cnut knew that Wulfstan didn't support him, and although he had to agree to the terms on which he and Edmund had settled, he didn't accept that his diocese now answered to the Danes. Before he had parted ways with his mother, she had left him with the task of winning over the archbishop. It was easier said than done.

Skuli, his father's bard before he'd moved to Jarl Eric's service, was preparing a poem about "Cnut, king of England."

The moors flowed with the blood
of English knights
when King Cnut struck victorious blows with his sword . . .

Cnut sat on a tall chair with his legs on the bench, lazily cleaning the sword he'd fought with in Ashingdon.

"My lord, have you heard the nickname that King Edmund has gained after his war against the 'horrifying, bloodsucking Danes'?" the bard asked, pausing in his struggles with the poem to pour himself some mead.

"You're getting old, Skuli," Jarl Eric announced as he reached for a cup. "You've already described us as the 'horrifying, bloodsucking Danes' in a different poem."

"I'm not getting old, I'm just quoting myself," the bard corrected him archly. "Good words should be repeated," he added proudly. "They call him Edmund Ironside."

"What?" Cnut didn't understand the significance of the name.

"Ironside. Like he's their great hero for defending England from us. And to think that he owes his fame to our refusal to retreat."

"Ironside? That's an exaggeration, but there is no doubt that he's brave; he did stand his ground and fight us. The only such man in this nest of plotters." Cnut was grateful to his mother that she'd decided to manage Streona herself. He couldn't stand to be around the man for a moment longer.

"My lord, Archbishop Wulfstan of York is approaching." Hrani stood up to look into the torchlit yard.

"Now?" Cnut was taken aback. "It's almost nightfall."

"What's more, he's running!" Hrani added with surprise, smacking his lips.

"Don't do that, I hate that sound!" Cnut reprimanded him.

He dropped his legs from the bench and put down the clean sword. Wulfstan ran into the chamber. Rainwater streamed from his cloak and his face revealed the emotional turmoil he was in. Cnut stood up.

"Archbishop," he greeted the newcomer. "What happened?"

"King Edmund is dead," announced Wulfstan. "He's been murdered at the Winchester castle."

Cnut could barely believe his ears.

"Who did it?"

Wulfstan looked at Cnut carefully as he replied:

"They say it was you."

ENGLAND

Świętosława sent one messenger to her son and another to Elfgifu and Thorkel as soon as she learned of Edmund's death. She asked the Jomsviking to come to London immediately, leaving Elfgifu and her son in Northampton.

She might get angry, but Cnut might not think to tell her to stay in a safe place for the time being, she thought.

She left a third message for Eadric Streona to be delivered as soon as he returned to Worchester, telling him to join them. She set off to the river Thames with Ragn, Uddorm, Jorun, and a company of soldiers. Edmund may have died at Winchester, but London was the key to the kingdom.

"Wilczan, take Dusza and all of our things. Follow us. We don't have time to wait; we must go immediately," she decided.

"As you wish, my lady." Wilczan smiled, barring her way.

She wanted to walk around him, but he wouldn't let her.

"You can leave immediately, but I cannot let you go without your chain mail."

"I prefer to see you carry out my orders than give me your own," she hissed, turning around to get dressed.

Ylva tied it securely around her torso.

"It will get hot," Jorun warned her as he helped her mount her horse.

"It already is," she said, adjusting her seat in the saddle. "I hope we won't be too late."

They rode side by side. The pouring rain didn't make their journey any easier.

"Jorun?"

"Yes, Bold One?" He never bothered with titles when it was just the two of them.

"This steel is pinching me," she complained.

"Your breasts?" he asked bluntly.

"Fool. It's heavy on my shoulders, like I'm carrying around additional weight."

"You should be glad that you don't have a shield, two belts, and a sword . . ."

"Oh, stop that, you'd brag all day if you could."

"You can always hunch, I won't tell anyone."

"As if," she snorted. "A queen never hunches."

"Do you think Streona had anything to do with this? He left a week ago. Who's to say he didn't go to Winchester instead of Nottingham?"

"He's too clever to get his own hands dirty in something like this," she replied, and rode out in front of him.

She knew that regardless of who was truly responsible, her son would be blamed. *He made an agreement with Edmund and then quietly got rid of him. That's what people will say.* Yes, Cnut gained more than anyone by Edmund's death, but he was also the last person who would commit such a cowardly act. She knew the stakes had just been raised, and she wasn't about to lose.

They met with Thorkel and his men in front of London Bridge.

"Did you do it?" she asked bluntly.

"No," he replied.

She nodded.

"Do you know where Edmund's sons are? The infant that was by the river Severn and the other one that was meant to have been born right after we finished our negotiations?"

"No, my lady. But I do know where Queen Emma is," said Thorkel with narrowed eyes.

"So you did what you set out to do?"

He nodded.

"Then take me to her. You said she knows some Danish, is that right?"

"Yes, she learned it in Normandy. That's where she's from. You'll find common ground with her, my lady."

"We have no other choice."

When Cnut's troops left Southampton in spring to march on London and her son had ordered her to stay with Elfgifu, she had secretly asked Thorkel to ensure that the dowager queen didn't leave London. She wouldn't have trusted Streona with the task, and Thorkel knew the court and its people just as well after his time spent serving King Ethelred. She knew that if there was anyone who might be able to influence Emma, it would be Thorkel.

Night was falling when they rode into the city, hurrying across the bridge over the Thames.

She thought of how this was the bridge that had stopped the Army of the Two Kings all those years ago. This was the bridge which Sven must have crossed when London surrendered to him. This was the bridge his son had fought for and failed to take.

And now she was the one crossing it in such strange circumstances, on this night that brought with it a taste of both autumn and winter.

Dusza will go mad when she smells all these different scents, she thought, instead of rejoicing that she had made it into London at last.

"I will gladly show you the city by day," offered the Jomsviking.

"For now, just show me the queen."

"She's in there." He pointed at the poorly lit castle.

She had expected something grander. The castle may have been surrounded by a stone wall and it was larger than Poznań's palatium, but it looked stifling and gloomy. The gates opened at Thorkel's command, and the guards led them across the yard to the stables.

"The last time I was here, I was leaving with Sven's bones," Jorun said grimly.

"Are you saying that to worry me or reassure me?" she asked.

"I'm just saying." He shrugged.

"Thorkel the Tall, at this time of night?" a small man in a green hood greeted them coolly. Servants bearing torches walked by him.

"Has Streona been here recently?" asked Thorkel.

"Not that I know of," the man replied, glancing curiously at Świętosława and her men.

"My queen," Thorkel addressed her, "allow me to introduce Ethelweard, London's castellan."

She nodded to him, trying to commit to memory his rather unmemorable features. Ethelweard was shamelessly staring at her.

"I suggest you bow," Thorkel said to him. "The queen is known for having an excellent memory and I'm sure you don't want your inhospitable behavior to make a lasting impression. You stand before Sigrid Storråda, queen of Sweden, Denmark, and Norway, and mother to Cnut, king of England."

"Welcome, queen of the Vikings," said Ethelweard in English, but she understood him all the same.

"I am now also your queen," she replied in Danish.

He bowed to her, but when he raised his head, his gaze was defiant once more.

"Is Elfwig, the bishop of London, in the city?" Thorkel asked the castellan.

"I don't know, my lord, though I'm sure he wouldn't welcome the news of your arrival. He defended London as well as he could."

Thorkel ignored the comment.

"Has your arrival got anything to do with King Edmund's death?" Ethelweard asked, cocking his head.

"That's none of your concern," said Thorkel, before addressing her again. "My queen, allow me to escort you."

"Should I have the rooms prepared for you?" the castellan called after them.

"Yes. The best ones you have," the Jomsviking ordered.

"He wasn't here in Sven's day," Jorun said once they'd walked out of earshot of the castellan.

"Because he was beside Ethelred with his father when he ran from you to his brother-in-law in Normandy," Thorkel explained, leading him up a narrow staircase. "Just because he was a trusted adviser of the old king doesn't mean he is trustworthy now."

"We need to find out the whereabouts of Bishop Elfwig," Jorun added. "The old man doesn't like us much."

My God, thought Świętosława. *Nobody trusts anyone over here.*

She knew what life at court was like. She knew the intrigues, dangers, and rumors. Her father used to say that even when he bedded Dobrawa or Oda, he was never certain of anything. She herself had experienced manipulation and betrayal at Birger's hands, and then Sven's and Ion's, but despite all that, what she learned of England increased her distaste for its people. But she was here to help Cnut cross these stagnant waters, and she intended on doing just that. But what would her son say when he learned of her current plan?

"We're here," said Thorkel, stopping outside a fitted door.

She heard the sad sound of a harp.

"We're in a tower," observed Jorun, looking around.

"The west tower," the Jomsviking confirmed before turning to the guard. "Open the door."

Within moments, Świętosława found herself face-to-face with a dark-haired woman with big blue eyes.

"Queen Emma, you have a visitor," Thorkel said softly. "Here is King Cnut's mother, Sigrid Storråda, queen of Denmark, Sweden, and Norway."

Emma blinked uncertainly. She laid down the harp gently, as if it was a sleeping child.

"Where are your sons, my queen?" asked Świętosława. "I've heard that you have two little boys."

"The elder is twelve, the younger three," Emma replied, sweeping hair from her eyes with a cunning smile. "You won't get them. They're safe with my brother in Normandy."

She's fast, thought Świętosława. *But you had no need to fear us. I would never hurt a child, not even if it was the last obstacle standing in Cnut's way to the throne.*

"I'm glad to have the chance to finally meet you, Emma," she said out loud. "Because I have something that I need to speak to you about. Thorkel, leave us."

"Yes, my lady."

She turned to him and whispered:

"If Ethelred's sons are no longer in England, find Edmund's children. And let no harm come to either of them."

The Jomsviking's dark eyes flashed in the gloomy chamber.

She walked over to Emma and took her arm.

"The music you played is sad."

"I'm a widow. Sadness is my constant companion."

"I have never met a queen who could play before." Świętosława smiled. "Most of them hire musicians or bards."

"I've never met a queen who wears chain mail," Emma replied. "The ones I've met hire soldiers."

"Then we are curious about one another, Emma. Let's talk. How old are you?"

"Almost thirty, and you?" Emma began to play the game.

"Almost fifty. I could be your mother!" Świętosława laughed. "Would you like that?"

46

ENGLAND

Cnut arrived in Winchester with Wulfstan, the archbishop of York. He needed Wulfstan to act as witness to his presence in York at the time of Edmund's death in Winchester.

He felt the suspicious glances everyone cast him as he walked through the cloisters with Wulfstan and his guards at his side. He summoned everyone to the audience hall and stood before them.

"How did the king die?" he asked.

Godwin, a young Sussex noble and one of Edmund's trusted companions, one who had been present at their peace negotiations, came out to face him.

"He was strangled in his room," he said quietly.

"Where is his body?"

"In the chapel."

The horns sounded in the yard.

"The archbishop of Canterbury has arrived," a servant announced, and Cnut said:

"Let's wait for the noble Lyfing to join us."

This death is attracting a lot of scrutiny if the Church leaders are coming to Winchester, he thought, wishing his mother or Thorkel were with him. He'd left Jarl Eric in York to ensure that he didn't lose control of Northumbria. Where was Eadric Streona?

"King Cnut is present at the place of King Edmund's death." Lyfing nodded as he entered and looked around the room.

"I've only just arrived from York with Archbishop Wulfstan. We are trying to find out what happened, because so far all we've heard is speculation."

"Me too," replied Lyfing, meeting his eye.

I cannot start explaining myself, Cnut thought feverishly. *Even if Edmund's death benefits me, I've had nothing to do with it.*

"Then tell me what happened, Godwin." Cnut turned his attention to the young noble again.

"As I said, the king was found by a servant strangled in his bedchamber in the morning."

"How is it possible that nobody knows anything else?" Cnut asked furiously.

"How do you know he was strangled?" asked Lyfing.

"His face," Godwin replied uncertainly. "And the scarf tied around his neck."

"Who was the last to see him alive? Who did he meet with? My God, have you not asked yourselves these questions? Kings don't just drop dead!" Cnut exclaimed.

"The last person who went to see our lord was . . ." Godwin fell silent.

"Who?!"

"Someone too close to him to speak his name with any suspicion . . ."

"Who?! Tell me!"

"His half brother Eadwig Etheling," Godwin replied, glancing up at Cnut.

Eadwig? Cnut searched his memories. *Ethelred's youngest sons, the ones he had with Emma of Normandy, are still children. And Edmund's brothers are all dead; that's why he was the heir to the throne. But Edmund's father had had three wives, so there are still the sons of the second. Eadwig Etheling. Jesus, he also has a claim,* he realized.

"Your words reveal the murderer, Godwin," said the archbishop of Canterbury firmly. "Are you aware of the value of your testimony?"

Silence fell across the hall. They heard a dog howl somewhere outside. A long voice to which no other replied. Godwin's handsome face looked fearful as he replied:

"We all know it, that's why nobody wanted to say it out loud. Eadwig Etheling is next in line . . ."

"That's not all." Someone else who had been present at the negotiations stepped forward.

"Speak, Leofwin," the archbishop urged him.

Leofwin, the ealdorman of Mercia. Streona pushed him into the shadows when he replaced him, Cnut remembered.

"When the king's younger brother left his chamber, he said the king ordered him to take his sons, Edward and Edmund . . ."

"And none of you asked your master before handing over his children?!" roared Cnut.

"Forgive us, my lord," said Leofwin. "We had no reason to mistrust him. He adored his nephews and often took the older one for walks . . ."

"He abducted Edmund's heirs," the archbishop of York announced gravely.

"Lyfing, archbishop of Canterbury," Cnut called out. "Godwin and Leofwin. You were all present when Edmund and I made our vows on the cross to uphold our peace. *'Two kings.'* That's what you called us, Archbishop. *'Two brothers.'* Now, the other king is dead, and I am duty-bound to punish his murderer. Godwin, send men to find Eadwig Etheling and bring him back to me. And tell them to find the sons of the murdered king. They are not to be harmed."

"Amen," said the archbishop of Canterbury.

"Where is his widow?" asked Cnut calmly. "Where is Edmund's wife, the mother of his sons?"

Godwin and Leofwin exchanged a glance.

"She left after the king's death," said Godwin. "She was afraid. She has no family here. I don't know if you've heard, my lord, but Ethelred murdered her father, acting on . . ."

"Streona's advice," Leofwin finished.

"Is she not searching for her children?" asked Cnut with surprise.

"She thinks they're already dead," Godwin said gravely.

"Let's hope she's mistaken." The archbishop made the sign of the cross.

"Oh, my!" said Hrani when they were alone again. "What a king! As if you'd been raised by these serpents yourself. What a talent! Streona couldn't have played that role better."

Cnut stood by the narrow window, looking out at the dark night. He suddenly missed Roskilde. He missed his brother Harald, as red-haired and nimble as a squirrel. He missed his sisters, the fair-haired girls who laughed so melodically, argued so loudly, and embraced him so tenderly. He missed his father, King Sven, and his mother, whom he had only regained recently. He saw his father in his memory, spittle sticking to his beard as he said: *"Don't let me down, son."*

ENGLAND

Świętosława met with Queen Emma in the palace chapel. She was praying for clarity of thought and good advice. She didn't notice Emma's arrival at first, spotting her only when Emma lit a candle and slid it into a tall silver candlestick. Świętosława flinched and turned toward the light.

"Emma?"

"Forgive me, Sigrid, I didn't expect to see you here."

"You see in me a barbarian Viking queen," Świętosława realized, remaining where she was on her knees.

Emma lowered her head.

"For whom are you lighting the candle?" asked Świętosława, although she knew it was an intrusive question.

"It is Saint Dagobert's Day today," replied Emma. "We had his sanctuary in Normandy, where I was born."

"My father took his name when he was confirmed."

Emma took a step toward her.

"Isn't it strange, my lady," she said quietly, "that though everything divides us, we are connected by the saints?"

Świętosława moved to make space for Emma beside her. After a moment's hesitation, Emma kneeled on the prie-dieu beside her.

"I was born on the day my father was confirmed," she said to Emma after a moment. "On the very day that the great duke Mieszko gave himself into Saint Dagobert's care. My sisters tell me that I was a child straight from Hell, but as you see, I haven't forgotten the name of the saint who brought me into the world. Our first bishop, Jordan, was an Irishman. He'd been a novice in Slane and he worshipped Saint Dagobert. He said the saint looked over the Piasts, over the family into which I was born."

"In Slane?" Emma twitched. "Do you know what his name was before he joined the Church?"

"No." Świętosława chuckled bitterly. "He was the son of an Irish ruler who fought the Vikings and turned to the emperor in the hopes that he'd aid the Irish against their barbarian invaders. He didn't get the help he needed, but he met my father and saw that his life's mission was to turn Mieszko into a Christian ruler. Jordan never returned to his kin, but I know he exchanged letters with his brother. What was his name?" Świętosława searched her memories. "Jordan's father was called Cennétig mac Lorcáin, so his brother, the one who ruled after him, was . . ."

"Brian Boru!" exclaimed Emma, and immediately covered her mouth, but it was too late. The stone chapel echoed her words back at her: *Boru . . . Boru . . .*

"Forgive me, my lady." Emma was staring at Świętosława as if she'd seen a ghost. "But this is the strangest coincidence . . ."

"We think we make our own decisions about what paths we tread, but in time it becomes clear that the Lord has guided us all along," replied Świętosława. "What is it that you find so strange?"

"Brian Boru, Brian the Bold," whispered Emma. "We all prayed for his victory because, my lady will forgive me for saying, his plight reminded us of our own. The Irish king, though old, spent his entire life fighting the Vikings who landed on Dublin's shores and tried to take away his kingdom piece by piece . . ."

Świętosława studied Emma's profile as she listened to her speak. A straight, shapely nose, round chin, and high forehead. The flame of the candle she had lit climbed the wall and reflected off the silver candlestick in dozens of different directions, sending flickering lights dancing above the widow queen's head.

She's brave, thought Świętosława. *She's not afraid to speak of Viking invasions.*

"Your husband, my lady," continued Emma, "the red-haired Viking with the forked beard . . . Forgive me for saying, but he was the sort of man with whom we frightened our children . . ."

"You're right." Świętosława grimaced. "That beard was horrible. It was even worse when it was covered with wine or grease! But the rest of it? I don't know, he used to be a handsome man, although I hadn't seen him for the last twelve years."

Emma looked at her with surprise, and Świętosława shrugged.

"He sent me into exile after our children were born. We argued all the time. But, forgive me, we weren't speaking of my marriage to Sven but about the Irish king."

"Shortly after your husband died and your son escaped back to Denmark . . ."

"He never escaped," Świętosława corrected her. "He returned for reinforcements."

"Naturally." Emma inhaled. "We came back from our exile in Normandy with our children. We spent Easter in London once more." There was a note of longing in Emma's voice for a time to which she could never return. "And after Easter we heard the news that Brian the Bold began an open war with the invaders. He set fire to their sacred tree, Thor's tree . . ."

"Thor's tree?" Świętosława interrupted her. "That's nonsense. Odin was the one who hung from the tree. Thor was more of an adventurer. Why would he need a tree? I must ask my bard . . . wait, no, I can't! I left him with my brother in Poland. Well, anyway, continue, I didn't mean to interrupt again."

"The Irish armies faced the invaders on Great Friday. Brian's son and grandson fought beside him . . ."

"That Brian must be quite old if his brother Jordan died forty years ago. Maybe he bathed in that famous spring the bishop used to tell me about when I was a girl, hmm? It's incredible how long some men last . . . Well, did they win?"

"Yes, my lady. They defeated the Vikings." There was triumph in Emma's voice. "But the old king fell . . ."

"Thank God!" Świętosława crossed herself. "Not that I wished him ill, but if he was such a warrior it would have been bad for him to have died in his bed. Heroes should die on the battlefield so that fame may never forget them. And yours? How did yours die?"

"Ethelred was no warrior," replied Emma evasively.

"But he rejoiced to hear of Brian Boru's victory, didn't he? He must have felt better knowing that they could be defeated. And? Did he summon his troops? Stand to fight?"

Emma turned her head away and said quietly:

"No. He took Eadric Streona's poor advice and argued with his son Edmund, who wanted to fight. He paid Thorkel the Tall to protect us."

Świętosława unclenched her hands and slapped her open palms on the armrest of the prie-dieu on which they were both kneeling.

"Exactly, my dear Emma. Old Brian Boru put on his chain mail and helm, mounted his horse, and even though his joints were probably twisted with arthritis or . . . well, you know the secret illness that ails old men . . . he led his army with his son and grandson. And your Ethelred . . . all right, let's not speak of it. You're an extraordinarily rational woman and it probably bothers you to have your name linked to such a helpless king. Sometimes widowhood offers us another chance."

"I am in mourning for my husband," Emma announced proudly.

"Yes, well, that is what one would expect from a widow. At first, of course. Tell me, because I'm curious, what did your husband look like? Because we've already established the appearance of mine." Świętosława cocked her head. "I only saw King Edmund. He was handsome enough, though not as tall as my Cnut. Did he resemble his father?"

"No, my lady." Emma's voice was low.

"Then, just between us women, you haven't exactly had your fun, have you?" Świętosława asked with pity, and patted Emma's hand without waiting for an answer. "It's time for me. I've prayed for good advice and you've told me a wonderful tale. I'll have a letter written to my brother Bolesław. I want him to learn of what happened to our beloved bishop Jordan's family. Praise Saint Dagobert. Isn't it amazing that we have so much in common, Emma? The same holy patron for both our families. Two queens, like you said, from two different worlds, both of whom have learned so much from one Irish family. Although you were fascinated by Brian Boru, the warrior king, I was entranced by his brother Bishop Jordan. And by the way, Jordan showed me the book he'd brought with him from Ireland. A masterpiece. Archbishop Lyfing says that there are beautiful manuscripts in London, too, although Bishop Elfwig does not care for me much."

"Would you like to see them, my lady?"

"If you had a way of convincing Elfwig to let me." Świętosława smiled as she stood up.

Before she walked out of the chapel, she placed a hand on Emma's shoulder and thought to herself about Emma what Ion had once said to her: *"Your king is coming to you."*

47

POLAND

Bolesław watched his son Mieszko riding, thinking of how well he held himself in the saddle. Mieszko was twenty-seven now, and one of Bolesław's best chieftains. They inspected Poznań's ramparts together to make sure the flooding of the river Warta wasn't sabotaging them.

I was already a ruler by his age, he thought, his mouth twisting. *Is my son counting down the days until I die? No, he can't be. He knows how much he has. Even though he's not my firstborn, he will be my heir. I removed Bezprym from the line of succession for him.* The reason he'd had to change the line of succession struck him anew. The memory overwhelmed him like a howl of pain. For his Black Hungarian, as he often thought of his eldest son. Bezprym had taken Kałdus, strengthening their northeastern border and chasing away the pagans. He, Bolesław, ordered that a white eagle be woven onto his flags. Bezprym rode under the image of a black eagle. *He wants to be different. If I choose white, he will be black. He carries the night inside him. The wildness leaps out of him like darkness did from his mother.* He shook the memories off. He loved Emnilda, but sometimes when he thought of Karolda, his untamed lover, as wild as a Hungarian warrior, he felt a stirring in his loins.

And Mieszko? Mieszko was just like him.

The war they had waged on Emperor Henry together had brought them closer. Father and son, like an old and young wolf, fought together. The emperor was furious because Bolesław had humiliated him in refusing to send a troop to accompany him to Italy. Henry gathered his forces by the river Elbe and pushed forward to Krosno instead. The same Krosno from which Bolesław had escaped all those years ago. This time, it had been Mieszko who barred the emperor's path by the river Oder. They both knew that ever since the emperor had retrieved Mieszko from the Prague duke's grip, he would try to call in his debt of gratitude. Which was exactly what he'd done. He sent messengers, but Mieszko, a cunning fox fluent in Greek and Latin, responded to the emperor in no uncertain terms. "Great Emperor, some things are more important than others. I may have pledged myself to you, but of what value is that word when you attack my home? When you lift a hand to strike a parent, a son's first duty is to protect his father. I will not choose you over him."

They knew the size of the army that marched toward them. This time, the emperor had risked everything. He had renewed his alliance with the Veleti and had called on the Bavarians and Czechs to join the German forces.

When Henry, raging from his failed exchanges with Mieszko, sent men to cross the river Oder, Zarad led troops to the south to fight the Bavarians and the Czechs, led by Uldaryk.

Bolesław faced the Veleti and the Saxons, who fought under Duke Bernard's command, in the north. Bolesław rode Red into battle, not White. Red was a huge stallion strong enough to carry the duke in his armor. And he defeated them in a single battle, after which Bernard retreated to his lands, abandoning Henry and breaking his word to join his forces with the emperor. He ran because he was afraid.

After his triumph, Bolesław redirected all his soldiers to the south to help Zarad against the Czechs. They forced the enemy to turn back. When the emperor learned of this, he stopped trying to cross the Oder and pulled back his troops. As he watched Henry ride away, Bolesław thought that if he led his men like that, he'd be left with no one but slaves to fight for him. No warrior wanted to risk his life for a king who abandoned his soldiers. He himself refused to back down, urging his men to chase the retreating foe. They crossed the Oder and forced the imperial army to fight. They cut down an entire company of heavy infantry. The battlefield looked gruesome when they had finished. There were heaps of maimed corpses. Henry sent Meissen's bishop to him to ask his permission to bury the dead. Bolz allowed it. What use were corpses to him, even if they had been margraves in life? But when the bishop's men began to carry the rigid bodies off the field, he called Mieszko to him and ordered him to chase down the survivors. His son wiped the blood from his face and, laughing, galloped west as far as the river Elbe.

Enough of these memories, he told himself, though it was tempting to lose himself in them.

"Mieszko, let's go back!" he shouted to his son when they had completed their inspection.

He saw messengers crossing the bridge.

"Russians!" his son called.

Bolesław's heartbeat quickened. His affairs in Kiev hadn't stabilized. When the great Vladimir had died over a year ago, Sława and Światopołk had finally been freed from the dungeons. Reinbern, unfortunately, hadn't survived imprisonment. Światopołk pushed his two brothers, Boris and Gleb, off the throne as soon as he was free, and prepared to face his most dangerous foe, his brother Jarosław.

Bolesław met the messengers in the palatium's yard without getting off his horse. The guest bowed low, giving him a silver coin bearing the mark of his son-in-law.

"What news of Kiev?" Bolesław asked.

"The Orthodox churches are burning. There is a war, an evil war, between the brothers."

"Oh, speak faster, I know there's a war! Who's winning?"

"Knyaz Jarosław, my lord . . . He has chased Knyaz Światopołk out of Kiev to the west, he's taken Pińsk, and . . ."

The messenger's face was ashen from fear.

"Speak, man." Mieszko laughed at him. "It's not true what they say about my father killing messengers."

"He's kidnapped Lady Sława, my lord." The Russian fell to his knees, wrapping his arms around his head to protect it.

"Who did?" demanded Bolesław.

"Jarosław. He abducted her, took her from Światopołk . . ."

"Jesus Christ! And my son-in-law?"

"He escaped to Brzeźce with his army and has settled in the borough there. He awaits your help . . ."

Bolesław dismounted. He turned the news over in his mind, unable to accept it. Once more, he had chosen a weak man for a son-in-law. How could he have allowed Sława to be taken from him?

"Don't tell Mother," Mieszko whispered.

"Too late," said Zarad, nodding toward the palatium door.

They turned around to see Emnilda, white as milk, supported by the servants.

"Wife!" Bolesław leaped toward her.

"Mother!" Mieszko got there first.

Emnilda rarely rose from bed these days. She was fragile and slender. They both caught hold of her. She blinked and whispered:

"She really didn't want to be married . . . She was so afraid of strangers . . . my youngest daughter . . ."

Bolesław carried her back to her bed as if she were a child. He laid her down gently. Emnilda's face was covered with beads of sweat, like dew on a rose. Her lips were growing paler, and she was breathing with more difficulty.

"Bring me Bishop Emeram," he said to his son, refusing to let go of his wife's cold hands.

"Emnilda, I'm with you," he whispered, carefully lying down beside her.

She smiled. She had been unwell for a long time. For so long as Astrid had been with them, she could dull Emnilda's pain and return her strength to her, even if only sporadically. But Astrid had vanished, she'd disappeared into thin air, and nobody knew where to find her. Emnilda grew weaker with every month that passed. Yes, he knew what it meant, but that didn't mean he could accept it.

"Only the Almighty God knows the secrets of life and death," said Emeram as he walked in. "If you believe in God, my lord, surrender yourself to His will."

"I can surrender myself, but not her." He put his arms around her.

"You cannot keep her with you by force," the bishop argued.

"Only a man who has never loved a woman can say that," snarled Bolesław.

"Shhh . . ." Mieszko implored them both. "Don't raise your voice near her . . . Let her go, you'll strangle her like that . . . Maybe she wants to tell us something?"

Bolesław was afraid that if he stopped holding on to her, she would escape and float away from him. But he loosened his hold and looked at her face. Her eyes were closed, but she was still breathing through parted lips.

"Emnilda . . . you're alive, and you will live," he promised, stroking her cheek.

"The good duchess has already taken her first step into the immortal life she is about to begin." Emeram made the sign of the cross above her. "The procession of angels is already on its way to meet her."

Bolesław missed the moment she stopped breathing. He just missed it. Each breath was shallower, and then she just didn't let one of them out. She didn't give it back. He kissed her lips to keep them warm. He kissed her cheeks and her forehead, he kissed her hair. Her hands. Finally, he ordered everyone to leave the room, and he sobbed, realizing that this was the end. That he, the powerful duke who decided who lived or died on the battlefield, had no power here. He watched over her until morning. Then he washed, changed, and walked into the audience hall.

Emperor Henry's messengers were waiting for him. He sat down on his throne under the sword of Saint Peter with his son beside him. He ordered that Emnilda's throne be covered in black.

The duke's mourning embarrassed the messengers.

"Our lord, Emperor Henry, sends you an invitation, great Duke, to Merseburg, to speak of peace. It is the emperor's wish to find terms to which you can both agree after the most recent terrible war."

"I won't go to Merseburg," he replied bluntly.

"Of course, we understand the exceptional circumstances you find yourselves in. The emperor will understand, and will wait until after the duchess's funeral . . ."

"I won't go," Bolesław interrupted the messenger, "and that has nothing to do with my being in mourning. I am not the one who lost the war, the emperor is. If he wants peace, he is welcome to come to see me here, in Poznań."

"I will be happy to greet the emperor as he crosses the Oder," Mieszko added firmly.

ENGLAND

Świętosława wrapped her cloak more tightly around herself, but the rain was falling at such an angle that the stinging droplets found their way underneath her hood no matter what she did.

"We're here, my lady," said Godwin, the young nobleman Cnut had sent to London on a rather delicate mission. "Northampton lies before us."

"It's gloomy here," observed Świętosława.

"The queen is never wrong," he replied politely. "But if we had arrived in the blooming spring, perhaps she would see things differently."

She snorted with laughter.

"Do you have a bard in the family?" she asked.

"No, my lady."

"Then you must come from one of those famous noble English families who have been at the royal court for generations," she decided. "Is there any blood still flowing through your veins or has politeness replaced it all?"

"I'm not quite sure what my lady means"—Godwin looked worried—"but I agree with whatever she says."

A stone manor began to take shape through the deluge, though it was difficult to discern anything past its large size. It was blurred by the rain. A drowsy guard stood at the gate which creaked on a broken hinge, loosely tied in place by a rope.

"Godwin." Świętosława stopped her horse. "I know the delicate task my son has set for you."

"I expected as much, my lady," the young man replied gravely. "Locating Edmund's widow is a sensitive matter, and her rights need to be respected."

Especially since Thorkel the Tall demonstrated ruthless firmness and a complete lack of tact when he took her children away, she thought guiltily. *I ordered him to find them and bring them to London, and he followed my commands without harming the boys, but their mother Edith escaped.*

"That's true, Godwin," she said, looking directly at him. "And I know that my son made the right choice in asking you to complete such sensitive tasks. You seem to have a talent for them. But . . ." She hesitated briefly before continuing, "Allow me to make the decision with regards to the second matter."

If Godwin was surprised, he hid it well.

"My lady, I promised the king I would bring his wife to London," he replied.

"My son doesn't yet know how many matters await his attention," she replied evasively. "His decision to bring his family to him has been rash. Elfgifu, little Sven, and the second boy she gave birth to barely a month ago should spend some time away from the nest of serpents that is London's court."

"I do not disagree with you, my lady, but . . ."

"We are doing it for their own good, Godwin," she interjected, and rode off toward the gate.

"We are?" groaned Godwin. "But I've been protesting . . ."

"And your concerns have been noted," she threw over her shoulder.

Although the manor's surroundings were pitiful—the shape of the broken gate, derelict stables, a yard drowning in mud with pigs parading around it—the inside of the house was clean, fragrant, and warm. Elfgifu greeted them from where she sat in a great chair by the hearth, feeding her baby.

"The queen and Master Godwin!" she said, lifting her head to look at them. "That must mean my king has sent for me. Forgive me for not rising to greet you, but I have an heir to the throne at my breast. Prince Harald."

"You named him without waiting for Cnut?" asked Świętosława with surprise.

"Well," Elfgifu began haughtily, "my lord husband is so busy with affairs of state that he hasn't seen him yet, and what was I meant to call him in the meantime: 'boy'? Do you think Cnut will be pleased? It is, after all, his grandfather's name, and his brother's. A family name. A royal name."

"Indeed," said Świętosława evasively, taking off her dripping cloak and sitting down.

Elfgifu gave out orders for supper and turned back to them.

"When are we leaving?"

Godwin smiled sympathetically and said:

"The weather is horrible, awful to travel in with small children."

"Oh, don't worry about that," Elfgifu replied drily. "I've survived worse than some winter rains."

The baby had fallen asleep and his mother's nipple slipped out of his mouth. Godwin looked away discreetly. Elfgifu, however, didn't seem embarrassed and she didn't cover herself, as if she didn't feel uncomfortable by her nakedness, which was, after all, justified by her new state of motherhood.

"Do you want to hold your grandson, Świętosława?" she asked, and without waiting for a reply, offered her the baby.

Świętosława, having been left no choice, stood up and took the child from her. She looked at the red face. *He even looks like little Harald,* she thought. The boy started to cry without opening his eyes. She started moving her arms, wanting to rock him, but he cried even louder.

"He doesn't like to be rocked," said Elfgifu.

Her breast was still bare.

"Take him then." Świętosława pushed the child back into her arms. "Feed him or settle him."

He stopped crying immediately, and Elfgifu sent her a triumphant smile.

"He doesn't like to be rocked," she repeated, "but he adores his mommy, isn't that right, little one? My prince, my sweet prince."

"My lady," Godwin began, "we are searching for the noble Edith, King Edmund's widow."

"And you think you might find out something here?" Elfgifu asked with surprise. "I have nothing to do with her."

"That's not true," observed Świętosława firmly. "Edith's first husband was your kin. What was his name again?"

"Sigeferth," Godwin reminded her.

Elfgifu hissed like an angry cat.

"You have the audacity to speak to me of Sigeferth? What do you know about me?" She flushed, looking as if someone had just slapped her. The child in her arms remained asleep, even though she spoke loudly.

"We know that Sigeferth looked after you after your noble father Elfhelm's death," Godwin said calmly. "And we know that when Sigeferth died, young King Edmund married his widow Edith. That's why we think you might know where she is, now that Edith is a widow for the second time. Do not fear, Elfgifu," Godwin reassured her, "we do not want to harm her. In fact, we want to ensure her safety."

When the young noble had finished speaking, Elfgifu laughed. At first it was just a chuckle, but it grew into a hysterical fit during which she threw her head back, her mouth wide open, her white teeth gleaming like a cat's. Świętosława and Godwin exchanged a glance.

A servant entered, carrying little Sven. Elfgifu fell silent, stroking Harald's head, and wordlessly reached out a hand to her eldest son. He looked shyly at the guests before hiding himself behind his mother. She kissed his fair hair and sat him beside her on the wide chair. Then she straightened her back and lifted her chin.

The queen mother with her two sons, thought Świętosława. *That's what she wants us to see when we look at her.*

"Since you seem to know so little about Sigeferth and Edith, allow me to enlighten you," she said haughtily.

She's always been proud, thought Świętosława, recalling the day she'd met her daughter-in-law in Roskilde's port, *but when did she grow arrogant?*

"My father, Elfhelm, the ealdorman of south Northumbria, was one of the first sacrifices made on Cnut's path to power. He died because he was a visionary. Because he realized sooner than others did that England's future was in accepting the Danes as our rulers. It was my *father*"—she emphasized the word—"who came to King Sven, long before my noble father-in-law took London and the title of king of England for himself. And it was my father who offered him help when everyone else still saw him as nothing more than a wild Viking and barbaric invader. As proof of his honorable intentions, he suggested my marriage to Cnut to ally our families." She placed a hand on her elder son's head and turned to him, softening her voice. "Your daddy, honey." She spoke firmly again when she turned back to them. "But Elfhelm paid for his vision of a strong and proud England with his life. When Sven left for Denmark, Eadric Streona came to our good, peaceful home. Remember what I'm about to tell you, my lady"—she addressed Świętosława—"because you are the one who talked my husband into forming an alliance with that monster."

If she wasn't the mother of two of my grandsons, I would set Dusza on her, thought Świętosława.

Elfgifu continued:

"My father received him at dinner. I was still a girl, but I joined them. I ate and drank with Streona, with my father, Ufegeat and Wulfheah, my beloved brothers, and the fire crackled brightly and cheerfully just like it does tonight. I had no idea that was the last night of my childhood."

Little Sven looked at his mother with pale eyes and pressed himself closer to her. She put an arm around him as she continued:

"The following morning, Eadric Streona invited my father and all of us to London. 'King Ethelred would like to speak to the ealdorman of southern Northumbria in person, and to meet his wonderful family.' That's what he said. Father was uncomfortable, and he suspected the invitation hid a threat. He couldn't refuse, though, since Streona spoke for the king. He gave me some berries in secret and told me to eat them. When I did, I got a fever, and I couldn't accompany my father or brothers."

Little Harald shifted in her arms. She gave him her breast and kissed his forehead.

"My father's maimed body was sent back home two weeks later. My brothers returned with it. Ufegeat and Wulfheah. My father's body was dragged back on a cart while they were brought back in a cage. They both wore bands over their eyes which were covered with dried blood, pus, and dirt. Streona had ordered them blinded."

Świętosława's heartbeat quickened. Harald was an infant, but little Sven was old enough to understand what she was saying. Should she be telling such stories in front of a child?

"The country was horrified to hear of it," said Godwin carefully. "Your father's death was intended as a warning to other nobles who might have considered supporting the Danes. King Ethelred suspected that all of Northumbria would aid their cause."

"Of course," Elfgifu quipped carelessly, returning to her narrative. "I was sent to my father's relative, Sigeferth. You asked me if I knew his wife, Edith. I knew her as a strict and cruel mistress who didn't spare me, a young, hurt little girl, any cuffs or reminders that I endangered them all by being in their home. Sigeferth threatened to take me for himself if the Danes didn't come for me soon. I praised the day that Sven returned at the head of a large army and took me from the home of my cruel protectors, giving me to Cnut. Yes, son." She turned back to her eldest son. "I'm talking about your grandfather, Sven, and your daddy, Cnut. King Cnut." She patted his cheek. "When I heard, while we were still in Roskilde, that Streona was responsible for imprisoning Sigeferth and Edith, I was glad of it. They deserved no better. Sigeferth was executed, but Edith was more fortunate than that. Edmund took my dead relative's lands and as a sign of protest against Streona's politics, because I don't think anybody can doubt that he was the man who really ruled England at that point instead of that hapless Ethelred, he dragged Edith out of prison and married her. The beautiful Edith, who so passionately insisted on her love for Sigeferth, had no qualms about getting into the bed of the next king of England."

"How do you know that?" asked Świętosława tersely. "How do you know she had no qualms? That she went voluntarily?"

"Because she had two children so quickly, one after the other," Elfgifu hissed.

"So did you," Świętosława retorted ruthlessly and coldly.

Elfgifu was speechless. So was Godwin.

"How dare you?" she shrieked at Świętosława. "How dare you compare me to that whore Edith?"

"That wasn't my intention," the queen replied calmly. "I was merely stating the facts."

"You have no right to compare me and Cnut to Edith and Edmund!" Elfgifu refused to calm down. "Do you hear me? Grandmother has insulted Mommy!"

"Control yourself, Elfgifu," Świętosława said firmly.

"You're speaking to a queen, my lady," Godwin reminded her.

"Forgive me," she snarled at them. "I raised my voice because I love your son Cnut with all my heart, and that comparison felt like an insult to my feelings."

"Then you don't know where we might find Edith?" asked Godwin.

"No. What do you want with her anyway? She means nothing anymore. Edmund is dead and you have her children. Her family won't ask you for her."

"She should be with her children," said Godwin.

"Why?" Elfgifu shrugged as she smiled almost tenderly at Harald, sleeping peacefully in her arms.

She's unstable, Świętosława realized as she watched how gently she spoke and touched her own sons while simultaneously expressing a complete lack of sympathy for the plight of a fellow mother. *What she's been through has twisted her mind.*

"Yes, little ones." Elfgifu stroked the heads of both her sons simultaneously. "Mommy has named you after your Danish ancestors, though I could have named you after my father or brothers. But your mommy understands the needs of the dynasty. The sons of the Danish king of England must have Danish names."

She lifted her head and looked straight at Świętosława.

"I lost everything because of Cnut, and that's why he and the children are everything to me. Do we leave for London tomorrow?"

"Godwin and I do, yes," replied Świętosława. "You and your sons stay here. We will send for you when the time is right."

A shadow crossed Elfgifu's pretty face. She pressed her lips together to control her emotions. Świętosława was prepared for another outburst, but it never came.

"We'll leave you a few men to help you rebuild the gate," added Godwin. "King Cnut, my lady, wants you to be safe."

"Does he want to lock me up in a fortress?" she asked.

"Northampton doesn't resemble a fortress in the slightest. It's a beautiful country manor, although it may look somewhat worse for wear after recent events," Godwin replied evasively. "We should return it to its past splendor."

"Of course," Elfgifu replied, and smiled. "Make it splendid enough again so it is worthy of the presence of the king's sons and his wife, the future Queen Elfgifu."

48

ENGLAND

Cnut rode to London. He didn't conquer it from the river Thames, as he had tried to do six months earlier. He just rode in by the bridge at the end of which his mother and Thorkel waited for him.

"King Cnut!" Świętosława greeted him.

He saw that his mother wasn't wearing her chain mail and was about to reprimand her for it when he noticed Great Ulf standing behind her, holding up the flag with the image of the Piast eagle holding a dragon in its claws.

"Queen Mother," he called. "Thorkel."

He knew that it had been the Jomsviking who had captured Edmund's half brother Eadwig Etheling, then brought the murdered king's sons to London. Thorkel was growing to be one of the men he relied on most. This should have made Cnut feel secure, but instead it frightened him.

He rode through the gates, dismounted, and walked like a pilgrim to the castle, followed by his procession. He looked around as he thought: *My God, is this the city for which so many of my friends have died?*

The road was soft and muddy in the wet winter weather. The merchant stalls crowded upon one another on a nearby hill like mushrooms growing on a tree stump. The alleyways he passed stank. London looked far more noble from the other side of its walls than it did on the inside. Winchester was far more beautiful, but this was the city into which the merchant ships sailed, thanks to the Thames. This was England's heart of trade. He pretended not to be disappointed. When he entered the city, the horns sounded in welcome. He finally felt stones under his feet. The old Roman residence was not as wondrous as it had been in the past. The simple but beautiful walls crumbled in places while the builders clearly didn't trouble themselves to match the stone slabs when they fixed the damage. They used clay on wicker plaiting, making it look like the old stones were rotting.

"Is Elfwig, the bishop of London, here?" he asked his mother.

"No," she replied. "He's holed up somewhere. He appears every now and then to lead mass in the cathedral and speak out against you. He knows that Thorkel's guards won't seize him in the middle of mass, and he always disappears right after it's over. He vanishes in the crowds, probably having dressed up as a commoner."

Cnut sighed. A war with the bishop was the last thing he needed right now.

"Where's the prisoner?" he asked Thorkel when they reached the yard.

The nobles and guests stood deeper in the yard in two lines. He felt as if he'd swallowed a stone when he saw them.

"In a room in the west tower, my lord," the Jomsviking replied.

"Bring him out here!" Cnut announced, sweeping away his hair where it stuck to his forehead. "Justice should not be kept waiting. Mother, where are Edmund's sons?"

"Under the care of some wet nurses," replied Świętosława. "The older one, the one who was there with Edmund when you swore you'd both uphold the peace, is already walking. The other is just an infant."

Cnut tucked a stubborn curl behind his ear and, fighting with himself, said:

"I know they're only children, but they should be here. I'll be passing sentence on their father's murderer. Mother, summon the children and their nurses."

"As you wish," she said, though he could tell she didn't like it. She gave the orders to the servants.

"I'm with you, my lord," said Eadric Streona, hurrying out of the shadows. His cloak was spotless even though the yard was full of mud.

"Just in time!" hissed Cnut.

"I've been working on something that will take your breath away, my king. You will learn the extent of my loyalty to you today when we meet with the nobles."

The Spider's intrusiveness made him feel impatient. He nodded to him and stepped into the middle of the yard, looking around. The lords of England and his chieftains all watched him, awaiting his decision. A moment later, two women walked into the yard, one with an infant and the other carrying Edmund's older son. He nodded to them and asked them to stand beside him. The guards dragged in the prisoner.

Eadwig Etheling was the same age as Cnut. Slender, with a pockmarked, unhealthy face, wearing soiled clothes. He looked pitiful, not frightening.

"Eadwig Etheling!" Cnut called when the bound prisoner was placed before him. "You've been accused of murdering your half brother, King Edmund. You're the only one who gained anything by his death. You wanted his throne! What do you have to say in your defense?"

Eadwig made some incomprehensible noises.

"Did your uncle take you from Father's castle to go for a ride?" Cnut asked Edmund's eldest son gently.

The child nodded, hiding his face in the nurse's shoulder.

"Did you want to kill them, too?"

Eadwig made another noise but said nothing.

"I see no extenuating circumstances here," Cnut shouted to the people. "I see an unfortunate man who killed his brother. According to the law, such a crime is punishable by death. Enough time has passed. The sentence will be carried out immediately."

"Confess your sins," said Lyfing, the archbishop of Canterbury, from where he stood beside Cnut.

Eadwig snorted angrily, and Cnut nodded to the executioner. Nobody protested when he approached the condemned man, holding a gleaming axe over his head. Eadwig was forced to his knees and his neck was bent so that his head rested on a tree stump. Silence fell over the yard. Cnut could hear his ears ringing, and for a moment thought he could hear the sweet sounds of a harp. The hollow sound of the axe striking wood wrenched him back into the present and he saw Eadwig's head roll across the ground. Archbishop Lyfing made the sign of the cross and began to pray:

"In the name of the Father, the Son . . ."

Edmund's older son shouted out in fear while the infant began to cry. Cnut leaned over them both.

"You have nothing to fear. I am your father's sworn brother, and I will protect you."

His mother walked over to them and touched his shoulder.

"The children aren't safe here," she said. "We should send them away from England, to good homes."

"Where?"

"One of them can go to your half brother, Olof King of Swedes, while the other can go to mine, Bolesław, in Poland. The boys will be well taken care of there and treated with the dignity and respect to which their birth entitles them."

She looked at him with her mismatched eyes and he shivered. The eagle clutching the Wessex dragon in its claws spread its wings stiffly on the flag. The head of the Piast bird was facing east.

"You're right, Mother. This isn't the best place for the royal children," he replied, nodding to Wilkomir. "Chief, although I would like to, I cannot keep you here forever. I promised Duke Burizleif to send you all home once you've helped me secure the throne."

"Are you sure you won't need us anymore, my lord?" Wilkomir's face twisted, but Cnut had already learned this grimace was not a sign of distaste.

"Good warriors are always needed, but I think that you fought the most important battle for me on the fields of Ashingdon when you scattered Edmund's cavalry. The fight I might face now is a game of alliances and patience." Cnut placed a hand on Wilkomir's shoulder. "You will deliver the duke gifts from me, and I will send both royal sons with you. Let them leave London immediately. I cannot get rid of the feeling that someone here still wants them dead."

The servants had almost finished cleaning the yard after the execution. Eadwig's head was thrown into a wicker basket while his body was thrown onto a cart.

"I'm not a nurse." The chief grimaced.

"Wilkomir, you're speaking to a king," his mother reminded the warrior.

"I will take care of the children on the journey home." Wilkomir nodded. "But the nurses will come, too. I'm not about to change any nappies."

"Go now, my old friend," said Świętosława sadly. "I'll come to see you before you set sail, and I'll deliver the gifts for my brother."

Cnut walked out of the yard of the London palace, heading for the audience chamber. His mother walked beside him, holding her lynx on a leash. He grabbed her hand once everyone else was out of earshot.

"Was this your doing?"

"No," she replied.

They walked on. His mother, who had been here for two weeks, seemed to know the castle as well as if she'd been born and raised within its walls. She avoided the holes in the stone floors effortlessly.

"The roof is leaking," she observed as they turned left.

"It's a ruin." He shrugged.

"Hmmm. London is . . . not what it's made out to be," she admitted.

He grabbed her hand again and Dusza suddenly stopped and glared at him with the steady golden gaze of a predator.

"Who tore out Eadwig's tongue?" he asked.

"I don't know," she replied, and pulled Dusza along beside her. "Come on, kitty! The lords of England are waiting for us. The Groom has worked so hard to get everyone here." She glanced him. "There are many suspects, and first in line is Edmund's real murderer."

The English nobles waited for them in the hall. The lords from Wessex, Essex, Mercia, and Northumbria. Eadric Streona, dressed as richly as a prince, stood before them, waiting for the king's arrival. As soon as he spotted Cnut he shouted:

"King of all of England! God bless the king!"

Lyfing, the archbishop of Canterbury, took his place by the king's side and said:

"King Cnut has fulfilled his duty to King Edmund. He has avenged his brother's death. He didn't stop until he found the murderer."

"And as a sign of the respect we feel for this act of justice," said Streona, and his eyes gleamed from within the folds of skin on his face, "I have our unanimous answer for the king. All of England's nobles have agreed to dismiss any claims that Edmund's heirs may have on Wessex and the southern parts of England. King Cnut is king of all England! Long live King Cnut!"

Cnut was so taken aback by this turn of events that his initial reaction was to frown. But Streona and the others stood and took up the chant:

"King Cnut! Long live the king!"

My God, he thought, *the serpents' nest has just proclaimed me their sole king.*

"Maybe our decision to send the boys to our brothers was premature if they've just been disinherited?" he whispered to his mother.

"We can never be too cautious," she replied, and they both sat down.

"Where is Godwin?" he asked.

"Searching for Edith, though it looks like a hopeless pursuit at this point," she whispered back.

"You were meant to bring my wife and sons to London with you," he reminded her impatiently. He was tired, and the gruesome execution made him feel grimmer than ever.

"Are you sure that the place in which an unknown perpetrator rips out people's tongues is a safe place for your children?" she asked.

Inwardly, he agreed with her again.

The lords all began to approach the king one by one, introducing themselves. In a pause between two of them he whispered to his mother:

"Streona has just shown that nothing in this country happens without his say-so."

"There is a way to change that," Świętosława whispered back. "And I will tell you what it is as soon as this performance ends."

ENGLAND

Świętosława led her son to the west tower.

"Cnut, meet Queen Emma, Ethelred's widow. Emma, you should probably know that Edmund's sons have been disinherited. They have no rights to the English throne. My son is the sole ruler of the entire kingdom."

Emma wasn't frightened, although the dark green dress didn't suit her. Shadows played across her face. She put down the harp and bowed stiffly to Cnut.

Like a queen bows to a usurper, thought Świętosława.

Her son looked surprised; she hadn't told him where she was taking him.

"I can assure you, my lady, that I will not harm you or your children," he said to Emma.

"I would prefer not to have to rely on your assurances," she replied proudly. "After what you did to Eadwig today . . . how can you pass sentence on someone who cannot defend themselves? I do appreciate your cunning, though. In a single move, you showed the people that you're a just avenger, and you got rid of a potential threat to your rule. Oh!" she snorted. "I sent my sons to Normandy. I feel better knowing they are under my brother's protection than under the care of a victor such as yourself."

"You lose your temper with me unnecessarily," Cnut told her coolly. "I was not the one who pointed to Eadwig as the murderer, Edmund's noblemen did. Speak to the archbishops, they were there when I was told."

Emma frowned and took a step toward the window. Świętosława stepped between them.

"I'm glad you like each other." She smiled, stroking her lynx. "From what I've heard, Emma, you admire my son's courage, self-control, and efficiency."

Emma opened her mouth, but Świętosława didn't let her speak.

"And you, Cnut, are surely impressed with the dowager queen, the daughter of Richard, Duke of Normandy, and with the courage and wisdom she shows."

"What are you getting at, Mother?" asked Cnut, rubbing his forehead.

"A happy ending." She walked over to her son and took his hand. *When did the skin on his hands grow so hard?* she wondered. She grabbed Emma's, too, and said:

"You two should marry."

And she joined their hands together, taking a step back.

Cnut was more surprised than Emma. He let go of the queen's hand and addressed them both:

"I already have a wife. Elfgifu has just given me a second son."

But he didn't lose his temper, or even raise his voice.

"I do not deny that you have sons with Elfgifu, but you were never married before God. You made vows to one another, that's all," said Świętosława. "According to the law, then, Elfgifu isn't your wife."

"I have no intention of sharing my bed and my life with a barbarian," Emma announced haughtily.

"My sweet girl, was your father so innocent?" Świętosława laughed. "Don't use such unpleasant words when you address your king. You cannot deny the facts, even if you don't like them, Emma. My son's army has taken the entire kingdom. Edmund is dead, and his sons have no rights to the throne. There is only one king, and he stands before you now. I have introduced you to one another and given you both something to think about, my dears. I won't be in your way any longer." She turned toward the door, her lynx by her side.

"I'm not staying," announced Cnut coldly, following her.

Well, Dusza, we're in for it now, she thought.

She heard his steps behind her. He was silent, although she would have preferred for him to lose his temper before they reached her rooms. She didn't avoid the confrontation once the door closed behind them. She turned and faced him. He was white with fury. The stubborn lock of hair slipped from behind his ear and fell into his eye.

"How could you do that?" he hissed. "You should have spoken to me first!"

"No, because that would have led Emma to believe that you're just like Streona, just like everyone else. This way, I look like the plotter and you look like an honorable king."

"Absolutely not, Mother. I will not marry Emma and break my word to Elfgifu!" He was trembling with rage.

"See? You are honorable."

"Stop playing games!" he roared.

This is the first time he's raised his voice at me, she thought, but she didn't hold it against him. In fact, it made her respect him more.

"Think about it," she replied calmly. "Streona has handed you all the English nobles on a platter today. They all swore in front of the archbishops that they accept your claim to the throne. You now have to change the way they perceive you, from a usurper who has taken power from their kings into a worthy heir of their previous rulers. Marrying the widow of the last king is the final move that ends the wars in the chain of events you set in motion when you came back here. Do you understand?"

He was breathing heavily and still looked just as angry.

He understands, she thought. *He just doesn't agree with me yet.*

She walked over to the table.

"Do you prefer wine, like your father?" she asked.

"Mead," he snarled.

She poured mead into two goblets and handed one to him.

"Do you love Elfgifu?" she asked softly.

"Yes," he replied, though there was no passion in his voice.

"I will tell you the story of how your father married me," she said.

"I know how it happened. He came to Sigtuna after your first husband died . . ."

"And married the widow queen, bringing peace to two kingdoms that had been at each other's throats. Beautiful! A bard might have written that, hmm?" She chuckled hollowly and took a sip of mead. "Has anyone told you that instead of the barbarian Sven, I wanted to marry the king of Norway, Olav Tryggvason? That I denied the man I loved more than my own soul? That Sven came for me with a fleet and threatened my country? I had a choice: a war and my son's death, or peace and Sven's bed. Nobody remembers that anymore because your father's plan worked: he made our two kingdoms allies in our marriage. You have proof. My son Olof's ships helped you take England."

Cnut was staring at her as if he'd never seen her before.

"Why did Father exile you?" he asked quietly.

"Because he discovered that I still loved Olav," she replied quietly.

"I had no idea." He rubbed his forehead again.

She sat down and placed her goblet on the table. Dusza laid her great head in her lap.

"I have no intention of trifling with your feelings and I'm not trying to get you to do anything out of pity," she said. "I just know that if you marry Emma, treat her like a queen, and have children with her who will inherit the crown after you, then the nobility and the commoners will all acknowledge you as their king. Not even Eadric Streona will be able to challenge that. Thanks to Godwin, Thorkel, and Archbishop Lyfing, we know the identity of about half of his spies. The Spider's days are numbered."

49

POLAND

Bolesław knew who the girl in the moss-and-fern-colored dress was. He learned that it was Predsława, one of Knyaz Vladimir's daughters and Jarosław's sisters. The first in the procession that had accompanied Świątopołk to take Sława when they had met in the middle of the river San near Przemyśl. It had been almost ten years ago! His daughter hadn't known much happiness in that time. He suspected she probably cursed him for arranging her marriage to Świątopołk, since it had led to her imprisonment, abduction, and endless running. Ten years, and he could still see that girl's slender figure, her eyes and lips. His enemy's sister.

"Do you want to bring Sława back or take her to Predsława?" Zarad asked him one evening, when he was drunk enough to ask so directly.

Bolesław had chuckled, and Zarad, falling back on the bench, answered his own question:

"My duke always fights for it all."

That was true. He had paid scouts and spies through Daniła to bring him any information that might help him find his daughter. When the Russians had returned from the eastern borders, he'd said:

"Jarosław keeps Princess Sława near him at all times and watches her like a hawk. Only the maidservants he handpicked can see her, and there are guards at her door day and night."

"Bloody hell! He treats my daughter as if she were a hostage," Bolesław swore, glad Emnilda hadn't lived long enough to see this.

"My lord, we can reach people who will serve you without requiring payment. People who already have enough silver as well as enough of Jarosław's ruling."

"What are you saying?"

"Only that Jarosław is forcing his younger brothers to fight Świątopołk. Not all of them see Jarosław as their ruler. There is Briaczesław, for example. They say he is the handsomest of Vladimir's sons . . ."

"From which wife?" he interrupted Daniła.

The Russian laughed.

"They say he and Jarosław share a mother. Rogneda. But Briaczesław is dark, like the Greek Ewodia, Świątopołk's mother."

"Maybe he's a mistress's son? Old Vladimir had hundreds of them."

"If he were a mistress's son, my lord, he wouldn't be walking around in a caftan embroidered with gold thread, and Jarosław wouldn't keep him so close."

"Does he want to side with me?" Bolesław wanted details. "Will he free Sława from his brother's imprisonment? Promise him whatever he wants. I'll give him whatever it is as soon as the girl is brought home."

The tireless Daniła returned to Russia, not just on a secret mission to Briaczesław, but also with an official message for Jarosław. Bolesław, whose memories of his daughter kept getting mixed up with images of Predsława in his head, found a way to have them both, and ordered Daniła to say: "The great duke Bolesław, having suffered the loss of his beloved wife Emnilda, asks Knyaz Jarosław for his sister Predsława's hand in marriage. He intends to marry her and to make her Poland's queen. The duke asks that his daughter Sława be included in the procession which will accompany Predsława to Poland, since he intends to take her away from Świątopołk as he has proven himself unworthy of a duke's daughter in his inability to protect her."

But instead of sending Sława and Predsława, Knyaz Jarosław sent Daniła back empty-handed.

"Did you see her?" asked the duke.

"No, my lord. Jarosław is as cunning as a fox, and he didn't receive me in Kiev. He rode out to meet me with his attendants outside the city walls and heard me out without dismounting. He said that he's going hunting and has no time to listen to messengers. It doesn't bode well for us, my lord. I didn't have a chance to speak to Briaczesław either since he didn't accompany his brother."

Bolesław's blood boiled.

"He insulted my messenger and so insulted me! How dare he?"

He paced around furiously, sending servants away. A week after Daniła returned, a Russian messenger arrived in Poznań, exhausted but well dressed.

"Who are you?" asked Bolesław, receiving him in the audience hall.

"Igor, Knyaz Briaczesław's servant," the young man replied. "I escaped across the river Bug."

"Do you have my daughter with you?"

"No, my lord. I bring news. Knyaz Jarosław has made a secret alliance with Emperor Henry. They've exchanged messengers, gifts, and signs. They want to attack you simultaneously from the east and the west."

Silence fell across the audience hall. Bolesław's laughter rang out like thunder.

"Rise from your knees, Briaczesław's servant!" Bolesław exclaimed. "We celebrate my first grandson's birth today, Mieszko's son. Do you know what we'll name him? Charles. Casimir Charles, for Charlemagne. Emperor Otto III gave me his throne, and my firstborn son, Bezprym, was with him when they opened Charlemagne's tomb."

Igor watched him tensely, as if he suspected that Bolesław may have lost his mind. It only amused him further.

"My guest," the duke continued. "Wash the travel dust off you and put on some clean clothes. Then come and join us to celebrate my grandson's arrival."

"But, great duke . . ." whispered Igor. "I hurried to you to tell you what they are planning so that you may have time to prepare your defense . . ."

Bolesław rose from the throne and stepped off the platform. He put an arm around Igor and patted his back, leading him to his courtiers.

"Igor!" he called after them when they were leading the messenger out. "We are celebrating the birth of my grandson. A feast!"

And then he was left alone with Zarad, Daniła, Stojgniew, and Mieszko.

"The army must be ready. We leave the day after tomorrow, after the feast. Mieszko, you'll go where you usually do, to the river Oder. Take two troops and station them on the border. I'll go east. If they want to surround me, they're in for a surprise. I'll tear their pincers apart before they have a chance to clamp them!"

Recent years had proven the strength of his troops. Always at war somewhere, his men were incredibly experienced. They had polished their speed to perfection, traveling across the wide country like lightning. Having fought such diverse foes—Saxons, Bavarians, Czechs, Veleti, Russians—they had trained hundreds of strong, young, and experienced warriors.

The messengers, changing horses multiple times a day, hurried ahead, delivering reports. Bolesław reached the river Bug within two weeks with three companies of heavy cavalry.

"Your son-in-law Świiatopołk is locked up in Brzeście. Knyaz Jarosław's camp is a day's travel away. They are preparing to mount a siege and have sent out spies to inform them when you arrive," reported Daniła.

"Are they guarding the ford?" asked Bolesław.

"Strangely enough, no," replied Daniła.

"That's not strange at all," said Igor. They had kept him close all this time. "Jarosław knows how to set a trap. That's what he's trying to do."

"Let him try." Bolesław shrugged.

"They might set fire to Brzeście in the hopes that you will come to your son-in-law's aid," Igor warned.

Bolesław snorted angrily.

"Sława isn't in Brzeście so they can do what they want to it. I don't care if it burns. Prepare to cross the river!" he ordered.

"Just like that?" asked Igor, raising the duke's suspicions, and not for the first time.

Daniła and his men knew the ford. The three companies of soldiers crossed the river swiftly; Bolesław knew that moving quickly was his strength. When he'd defended himself in the west against the emperor, the duke had lured Henry into traps in the wetlands and swamps with guides he'd paid off to lead the enemy off the safe paths. If Jarosław and Henry were working together, it would be the Kiev knyaz's task to tie him up in the east for as long as possible. That was why, instead of allowing himself to be trapped, he wanted to act as swiftly as possible. His scouts had told him of Jarosław's spies, who rode back to their knyaz frequently, warning him that the Polish duke's soldiers were already on the other side of the river. He didn't give them much time, and the Russian knyaz had barely received the news when Bolesław blew the horns.

They met by Brzeście. Bolesław saw the ladders and platforms that the Russians had put in place in preparation for taking the village. They were abandoning them now, rushing to form a line of defense. He took stock of their numbers. There couldn't have been more than five hundred cavalrymen. He had nine hundred.

"Where is the knyaz?" he asked Igor, turning his horse around in a circle.

The young Russian searched the opposing troops.

"I can't see him," he said eventually. "The flag with the trident is flying on that hill, but I can't see the duke anywhere near it."

"Let's go!" ordered Bolesław. "Zarad, lead the charge."

Three riders with a white flag emerged from between the enemy soldiers, riding toward them.

"Zarad! Charge!" the duke repeated his order.

"They want to talk!" Igor shouted, pointing at the approaching messengers.

"But I don't," the duke replied firmly.

Reading his master's mind, Daniła nimbly took Igor's sword out of its sheath while two of his men pulled the young man from his horse. He shouted that he was not a spy, but nobody paid him any attention.

"Don't kill him, just tie him up and throw him next to our supplies," ordered Bolesław.

"To battle with God!" the cavalrymen of the first company shouted as clumps of earth flew from under their horses' hooves.

Zarad led the charge. Bolesław waited until he heard the sound of metal clanging on metal and quickly reorganized the two companies he had left.

Daniła was told to surround Brzeście and attack from the back while he led the soldiers to attack from the side.

They wanted pincers, and here they are! he thought vengefully as his horse broke into a canter.

He attacked the flank of the desperately fighting Russian force.

He saw the feathers in Zarad's helm across the battlefield. His friend was finishing off the wounded, severing the enemy lines like a spearhead. Bolesław found himself locked in combat with a stocky soldier.

Jarosław's personal guard, he thought, noticing the trident on the soldier's helm.

"Who are you?" he asked as he lifted his sword.

"Awija," the man snarled, taking a swing at him.

Bolesław parried the blow and moved to attack.

"Where is your knyaz, Awija?" he asked, pulling the sword out of the guard's body.

"None of your concern!" the soldier shouted, then began to choke on his own blood.

I killed him too quickly, Bolesław thought to himself angrily.

He turned around, looking for someone else to fight, but within the ring of steel that his three companies had formed around the Russians there were only the wounded left to slay. He heard the sound of a horn he didn't recognize and lifted his shield as he stood in his stirrups. A small squad was calling the Russians to retreat from a hill far away from the battlefield.

That's where Jarosław might be, he thought.

"Who is the knyaz summoning?" Daniła asked cheerfully, riding up to him. "Does he think that corpses might rise up from the field?"

He was right. The last Russians were falling under the swords of Zarad's men. They saw a lone rider split off from the group on the hill and gallop toward them, hunched low over the neck of his horse. Bolesław shielded his eyes to see better.

"Daniła!" he shouted before even thinking of what he was going to say. "Take your men and shield the rider. Bring him to me."

The rider was flying toward them like a wild warrior, trying to outrun the arrows that chased him. Bolesław's heartbeat quickened. Could it be a woman dressed as a man? The rider wasn't wearing a helm, only a colorful hat. They seemed quite small. No. At one moment the rider was forced to lean so far out to the side in the saddle that Bolesław grew convinced it must be a man. Apart from his first wife Karolda, he knew no woman who could complete such a maneuver. His Sława most certainly couldn't do that.

Daniła's men surrounded the rider in a tight circle while Jarosław's guards rode down the hill and headed east. They left a cloud of dust behind them.

"And the battle is over," said Zarad as he rode up to the duke and took off his gloves.

"They left their camp and supplies," added Stojgniew.

"Losses?" asked Bolesław.

"A few wounded horses, but my men are catching the ones from which the Russians fell," Zarad replied.

Daniła and the rescued rider had almost reached them. The young man was wounded: one of the arrows had scraped his temple. He was strikingly handsome, with dark eyes and prominent cheekbones. He was also lean and muscular.

That's not just a hat. That's a royal military hat!

"Great duke," Daniła said when they stopped their horses in front of his. "May I introduce the knyaz's brother, Briaczesław."

ENGLAND

Cnut stood by the fire in the large hall of Northampton as he waited for Elfgifu to stop screaming.

"You're just like your father!" she shrieked hysterically. "You're no more than a barbarian!"

They both say the same thing about me, he thought bitterly. *The one I'm leaving and the one I'm marrying.*

"You'll trample on everything! You'll dishonor yourself by breaking your word to reach your goal."

"My father never broke his word," he said, staring into the flames.

"Liar! He exiled your mother, just like you're exiling me now. Can you deny that?" She lifted her chin defiantly.

You see it, but you don't understand it, he thought, but it made him feel no better to know that he couldn't explain the real similarities between what he was doing and what Sven had done.

"Your blood is soiled by the dirty and wild. The blood of invaders!" She was searching for new words with which to insult him, not for the first time that day. "The Vikings who come at dawn to destroy, burn, and plunder . . ."

"Most of my blood is Slavic," he said quietly. "I inherited it not just from my mother, but also my paternal Obotrite grandmother."

"Mongrel!" she hissed. "A dog that cannot be trained!"

"Elfgifu, be quiet, or you'll end up saying something you're never going to be able to take back."

"Why? Will you kill me and my boys? The sons you've just disinherited?"

He didn't let the children listen to their conversation. He had ordered the nurses take Sven and Harald out and had his guards ensure his orders were followed.

"Don't talk nonsense," he said. "You know very well that I could never do anything like that."

"How am I supposed to know that?" Elfgifu rose and walked over to him slowly. "You're Cnut the Cruel. The one who cuts off his prisoners' ears and noses."

"Stop, please. That has nothing to do with this," he said angrily.

She placed her hands on her hips and faced him.

"I'll take the boys and run away. You'll never find us. You'll never see them again."

"Don't threaten me." He raised his voice. "You know I would never let you do that."

"Indeed!" Her eyes flashed wildly. "So, you intend to follow in your red-haired father's footsteps, do you? You'll take my children away from me! You'll tear the infants from their mother's arms and then send them far away, like you did with King Edmund Ironside's sons."

That's the first time she's called him a king, he realized, but he didn't hold it against her.

"I have a different proposition for you. Calm down, sit down, and listen to me."

She did as he asked, though he was fully prepared for another outburst at any moment.

"Our sons will not inherit the throne of England," he said bluntly. "But when they grow up, they will take the Norwegian throne as my vassals. And you, as their mother, will accompany them."

"No," she said. "I want England."

"I can't give it to you, Elfgifu, or to our sons. The English crown will belong only to the children I have with Emma."

He thought that she would start shrieking again when he said that, but she didn't. She was perfectly composed.

"What if Emma won't give you children?" she asked. "She's not exactly young."

"The marriage agreement insists that I remove our sons from the line of succession. I will uphold that until I die."

"I understand." Elfgifu nodded. "What am I meant to do and where am I meant to go while our sons are growing up?"

"You will receive lands and a castle in Northumbria. Jarl Eric, as its vassal, will look after you and the children."

"And what did he say when you told him our sons would take away Norway from his?"

As their conversation continued, he couldn't help but admire her for the self-control she exhibited after the initial outbursts. They discussed every detail of her future, and that of their sons. She brightened. Her face remained pale, but not as ashen as it had been at first. Her features returned to their gentle, attractive state.

He began to take his leave and told the servants to bring in the boys.

"I will bid them farewell and leave before dusk," he told her.

"Won't you stay and eat supper with me?" She looked worried, as if nothing between them had changed. "I had the fish soup you like so much prepared."

He didn't reply because the nurses had just brought in the children.

"Sven, Harald," Elfgifu said coaxingly. "Mommy and Daddy have something to tell you. Mary, Ursula, leave us, I can manage the children myself."

Cnut picked Sven up and looked into his blue eyes. The boy hid his face in his shoulder. The smell of the small child brought a lump to his throat. Elfgifu walked over to them, holding Harald in her arms.

"Daddy will be leaving soon, and we won't see him for a long time." She spoke in a low, sensual voice. "We'll live in a beautiful castle by the sea, and if Daddy has time, he will come to visit us. Promise that you will always love him, even if he's far away."

Harald was too young to have learned to talk yet. Sven kissed him instead of answering. Cnut felt as if his heart was about to break. He took Harald from Elfgifu and held both his sons close. He stood there like that with his children for so long that he lost track of time, until he felt Elfgifu wrap her arms round him and press herself to his back. Her hand began to stroke his stomach. It slipped under his belt and rested on his hip. He sighed and moved away.

"It's time for me to go," he said quietly.

"Won't you stay the night?" she purred.

"No, Elfgifu. Thank you for your understanding, but I need to go. I will leave men under your command who will help you in your travels north."

He leaned down to put Sven on the ground. She moved closer again, pressing her stomach to his buttocks.

"Stay, it can be like the old days," she urged in a low voice.

His hands were occupied with holding his younger son. Elfgifu's hand slipped from his hip to his side and touched the hilt of his dagger. He didn't want to frighten Harald, so he straightened back up slowly. Elfgifu ripped the dagger out of its scabbard.

"Don't do anything you can't take back," he told her again, without turning around.

He felt the blade press against his side.

"Listen to me," he said, still keeping his voice level.

Harald whimpered in his arms.

"Mother, what are you doing?" Sven asked, and Cnut saw the child's eyes widen.

"Mommy is only playing with Daddy." Elfgifu laughed, dropping the knife.

It fell to the stone floor with a loud clang. Cnut spun around and stepped on the blade. He looked at her. Elfgifu's expression wasn't wild or raging. She laughed, as if what had just happened had been nothing but a joke. He kissed Harald's chubby cheeks, tousled his red hair, and gave him back to his mother.

"Goodbye, Elfgifu. See you soon, my sons," he said.

He leaned down to pick up his knife, replaced it in its scabbard, and left the room without looking back.

50

POLAND

Bolesław took the less direct route so that he might ride through Bodzia on his way from Brzeście. He calculated that it shouldn't cost him more than a week, so it should be worth it. He sent messengers ahead to summon Bezprym to meet him in the Golden Borough, and they arrived at the gates at the same time.

"The flag with the black eagle," Myślibor announced. "The monk prince is waiting for his father outside the carved gates."

Time had been kind to Bezprym. He was thirty years old, and there wasn't a single gray hair on his head. He was slender and muscular.

The roots must be good for him, thought Bolesław. *Either that, or the endless fights with the Prussians.*

When Jaromir Přemyslid had captured his son all those years ago and deprived him of the possibility of having children, Bolesław had worried that his son would go soft and grow odd with age. In Bolesław's mind, his son was neither a man nor a woman. But time had passed, and Bezprym looked as masculine as he'd expected of any his soldiers.

Maybe it wasn't true after all? Maybe Přemyslid's leather thong hadn't done its job? the duke wondered, but he didn't know how to start such a conversation with his son. Especially since he had already changed the line of succession and named Mieszko his heir, sending Bezprym to the northeast borders to conquer more lands there. But the question bothered him like a thorn beneath his skin.

The Bold One had told him about Gaudentius's curse. He remembered the confusion which surrounded Mieszko's final words, the uncertainty about his intentions when he wrote that final document under Oda's supervision. Mieszko's parting words had not been clear. As murky as the ghost of death. On the night he died, Bolesław hadn't stopped to think about what his father had wanted, he just took the most direct path that lay between him and the throne and maintained unity in the country, since dividing it would have undone the Piast's life work. But did he take power with his father's blessing, or without it? He wondered about it every night that he lay down without having drunk wine or mead before bed. Sober as a child, going through every possibility like an old man. He always reached the same conclusion: he had saved Poland.

Was Gaudentius's curse true? The Bold One laughed at it, but she laughed at everything. She laughed at her own suffering just as well as at her triumphs.

He envied her, secretly. She was stronger than him. That predator had always seemed to have some invisible armor protecting her, even when they'd been children. She accepted only the things that were good for her, and rejected anything she didn't want. She had lived through twelve years of exile as if she knew she was only wearing a mourning dress until the right day came along and she could throw it off again. And now his sister, the golden-haired rascal with the lynx at her side, was helping her son take the throne of England. Any other woman in her position would have given up long ago. She would have died after her lover's death, after the failed plot to give him the throne and herself in one fell swoop. Any other woman, but not her. The only thing that was holy about Świętosława was her name; the rest of her had been forged from the most noble steel. She was a Damascan blade, pierced hundreds of times, forged in fire and water to make it undefeatable and shape it into something that delighted everyone who saw it. The mistress of three thrones who prepared to pounce like a lynx on the fourth.

He had raged at himself so many times. He was still just a duke. That mischievous minx had three crowns and would soon gain a fourth. He raged because he envied her as much as he loved her. He loved her because they were of the same blood and bone. A pair of hunting dogs who had come out of the same womb, the products of the same loins, predators who were so alike, who had walked out into the world to hunt for everything. He secretly wished that she was still with him, that they were still hunting the same prey together.

"Son!" he greeted Bezprym outside the gates of Bodzia.

"Father." The Black Hungarian, the monk prince, bowed his head. "Congratulations. You scattered Jaromir's army to the four winds."

I'd like to embrace him, thought Bolesław, but he didn't know how. Bezprym rode over to him but kept his distance.

"I heard that you killed the Prussian leader," he replied.

Bezprym didn't move any closer as their horses stepped side by side, their stirrups next to each other.

"He screamed to the skies, calling on the god of thunder and fire when I skinned him, but believe me, the one he called for didn't come. The flies got the body."

"There are no other gods outside of the one true God of the Trinity," said Bolesław with a shiver.

He stopped his horse just outside the gate.

"Son, I rarely come here, but there is a cemetery on the hill by the borough."

"I know." Bezprym nodded. "Dusza and Duszan lie here. Can I come with you?"

They turned in that direction without a word.

Mieszko, his father, had had the cemetery surrounded with a wall of field stones. They left the horses and walked past a blooming briar bush. They passed the houses of the dead built for all the noble men who had died in Bodzia.

"There are more dukes here than anywhere else in the world," said Bezprym. "Exiles, nomads, the ones who had been forced out of power . . ."

"Or they left because they didn't want to kiss the hand of a master who was at best their equal," added Bolesław.

They turned right and saw the twin rocks.

"Who were they?" his son asked.

"Duszan was a descendent of those who ran from Great Moravia. A branch of the old and excellent Moymirid dynasty."

"Did his parents not protest when your father chose him to be your servant?" Bezprym looked surprised.

"I don't think so. They were grateful that my father had given them a place where they could live in peace. Their duchy no longer existed, and their ancestors had fled north through the mountains. They gave up their son because he was born on the same day as I was. They thought the boy would have as great a fate as I was meant to have, but instead he died protecting me from a knife in Merseburg."

"Did he know who he was?"

"No. I only found out after his death."

"Did you ever think that he may have been why you took Moravia so easily?"

"Because of Duszan? No. My grandmother was a Moravian princess. They saw one of their own in me."

"What about Dusza?"

"Dusza was Danish. My father had mapped out Świętosława's life for her long before she was born. Dusza came from some noble family that Harald, Sven's father, had defeated. They were called 'the exiles of Lejre.' Her family is buried there, in the oldest part of the cemetery. Isn't it strange? Her parents fled Harald's wrath to Poland, but she was killed by one of Sven's arrows."

"There is no escaping one's fate, Father," his son said, and Bolesław felt every syllable resound deep inside him.

He made the sign of the cross in front of the rock which marked Duszan's resting place. They said a prayer for the dead. Bezprym crossed his arms, placing his palms on his chest. He made the sign of the cross once they'd finished.

"Son!" Bolesław turned to him and reached out a hand, wanting to touch him.

Bezprym took a step back.

"Why didn't you buy a Dusza or Duszan for your children?" his son asked, meeting his eye.

"Because it is a pagan tradition," Bolesław replied thoughtfully. "Barbaric." He nodded toward the graves. "Although if I could have foreseen what happened to you, I wouldn't have hesitated to pay with gold . . ."

Bezprym's eyebrows met in the middle of his forehead as he frowned. His son shook his head like a horse when it feels the bit in its mouth.

"It's a good thing you didn't do it," he replied firmly.

He turned and started walking away. Bolesław sighed as he followed him. He smelled the strong scent of roses as he mounted his horse.

Arne, Bodzia's castellan, was waiting in front of the carved gates. He greeted them and led them to the manor.

"The feast is ready, and Omold, the Bold Lady's bard, is impatient to sing for you," he called.

"I'm curious to hear if he's learned to rhyme in our tongue."

Bodzia's manor was different from any of his houses. It had been built by people who missed their homes. People who had found the Piast court to be their safe haven since his father's time. The Vikings and Russians, the ancestors of the people of Great Moravia. Those who fled Bohemia. Bodzia was the Golden Borough. A safe haven for the nobility of different countries.

The columns which supported the porch were carved with spiraling weaves, as if depicting serpents chasing one another. The manor itself wasn't made of stone, like the ones in Poznań, Ostrów, or Gniezno. It was made entirely of wood, specifically the great Piast oaks. It looked like an enormous ship with its hull facing upward.

They don't sail anymore, he thought, *because they've found a safe port.*

He gave his horse to a groom and threw off the cloak that was stifling him in this heat. An old friend stepped into his path as he was about to start walking.

"Wilkomir? You, here?" Bolesław exclaimed with surprise.

"In England they said that my lord is going to Kiev, so I gathered a company of men and followed as quickly as I could, but we were late." Wilkomir laughed as they embraced each other.

"Wait!" Bolesław tapped his forehead. "If the Bold One has sent you, that means . . ."

"Yes, my lord. Your sister now commands the London castle and her lynx pisses into the Thames. Cnut has taken England."

His heartbeat quickened.

"What a minx! And she tells me off for wanting everything!" He laughed. "Her firstborn is the king of Sweden, Harald rules Denmark, and her youngest, Cnut, has just conquered himself a new kingdom!"

"Yes, my lord. You have three nephews on three different thrones, but your sister is queen of four. That's not all." His friend grimaced. "She's sent me on a somewhat sensitive mission."

"Tell me."

Wilkomir nodded at two women who were standing in the shadows of the stable, and they walked over to them with children in their arms. Two boys. Bolesław looked at them carefully. They were small, the younger one was still a baby. They were pale, frightened, and clearly exhausted. He frowned.

"This is Edward and his brother Edmund. They are the sons of the late King Edmund Ironside. One of them is to stay in Poland, the other to go to Sigtuna."

"I suppose there are Russians, Swedes, Danes, and Czechs in Bodzia already, we can have the English, too. We need to wait before sending them on another journey; they need rest. Well, boys! My grandson Casimir will have playmates!"

Wilkomir sent away the nurses with the boys and indicated that he wanted to speak to Bolesław in the stable. The duke followed him. The gloomy interior smelled of straw and manure. Wilkomir led him to the farthest corner and leaned down to open his chest. He wore the key around a chain on his neck. Bolesław heard the metallic crunch of the key turning in the lock and Wilkomir straightened up again. A stallion neighed furiously and kicked a wall.

"She asked me to give you this along with the boys. She said you'd understand, my lord."

He glanced inside and flinched.

"Absolutely not," he said without hesitation. "I won't allow it."

"You're the ruler here." Wilkomir bowed to him and closed the chest.

"Come on." Bolesław grabbed his elbow and pulled. "Let's drink to your safe return and the conquest of England. And don't mention this again. It's good to have you back, my friend. We will leave for the river Oder in the morning to face Henry. Where is the company you came with?"

"I sent them to Poznań."

"Are they rested?"

"They stopped throwing up as soon as they felt dry land under their feet, my lord. Kalmir submerged the flag with the Piast eagle in the Thames for you, but Ostry yelled at him for it, saying it's a river of blood. They are ready to face the imperial army because the English fought like lions at Ashingdon."

They walked into the hall together.

"Konung Burizleif!" the people inside greeted him. "Konung Burizleif!"

Master of swords, lord of the battle, noble ruler of the fight.
He leaped over the silver ribbon of the Bug and plunged
his blade into the bellies of his foes.
He ripped out their purple intestines
and the knyaz cried when he fled east,
away from the dust of battle, toward the sun rising.

"Omold? Show yourself, bard. Your lessons haven't been in vain, I see," Bolesław praised the poet. "Who taught you those words? *Blade, plunge, leap?*"

"She did, Konung Burizleif," the bard replied, grabbing a woman in a shimmering dress. "Her name is Wszechmiła, and I would like your permission to marry her."

Wszechmiła? thought Bolesław. *One of my father's wives had that name, before he married my mother. But she taught Omold to speak our tongue. He speaks so well that he could pass for a Polan. Oh, women! They can get so much out of us.*

"I will be a witness at the ceremony," he called out. "And I'm taking you both back to Poznań. I need a bard. Briaczesław!" he addressed the Russian knyaz. "Meet your companions. Arne, a newcomer has arrived with us in Bodzia. Son of Knyaz Vladimir and Światopołk's brother. He fled the Russians outside Brzeście."

Bolesław placed a hand on Briaczesław's back and led him to the tables.

"Can you vouch for Igor?"

"Yes," the Russian replied.

"I thought he was a spy," said Bolesław with surprise. "He kept warning me."

Briaczesław smiled.

"If that's what makes you suspicious then I'm afraid you won't trust me either. I want to help you, great duke, in defeating my brother Jarosław, and I'm afraid that will involve warning you."

He missed the Bold One again. She hated caution. Or perhaps time had changed her?

They drank the mead Arne served them.

Briaczesław spoke:

"Knyaz Jarosław met with King Henry's messengers. They agreed to attack you from both sides, and they celebrated by drinking a ten-year-old mead. Jarosław doesn't despise you, my lord, but he is afraid of you. He fears the fame you have garnered."

Bolesław snorted.

"He keeps my youngest daughter in a cage!"

"That's not true." Briaczesław shook his head. "Your daughter travels in a wagon decorated with fabrics woven with gold. She is given the best rooms wherever they go. He looks after her as one would after a golden bird. She is unharmed."

"That's what you think," Bolesław shouted. "Golden threads and rich rooms are not evidence of my daughter's safety."

She suffers; she's afraid of strangers, he thought, and saw the dying Emnilda in his mind's eye.

"She sends this to you, my lord," Briaczesław said.

He gave him a piece of silk. Bolesław unrolled it carefully.

It was embroidered with a pale Piast eagle, pierced by a trident.

"She didn't have any thread," Briaczesław whispered. "She did that using her own hair."

51

ENGLAND

Cnut stood in front of the altar of Canterbury's cathedral, dressed in white-and-gold ceremonial robes, while Archbishop Lyfing anointed him king of England. The choir of deacons held up candles as they sang a psalm. Cnut had felt clean and light since Ethelnoth, whom he had made his personal confessor, had heard him out and absolved him of his sins. The horrific images of the prisoners he'd left on the beach in Sandwich finally evaporated from his mind. The people without ears and noses. Eadwig without his tongue. His comrades lying in a field of blood at Ashingdon. His men drowning in the Thames when he tried to take London. Elfgifu, Elfhelm's daughter, with little Harald in her arms, as red-haired as his brother, and fair-haired Sven at her side. The girl who had wanted so much for him to make her queen of England, the woman he had been forced to send away so that he might become its king. He still felt torn, still felt that part of him loved Elfgifu and wished he had never abandoned her for Emma, the woman who was the key to winning his subjects' hearts. The key to the kingdom. Which of the two Cnuts was the one who had sent Elfgifu away? Cnut the Cruel? How could he be certain that it was Cnut the Just that had married Emma? *"You'll understand once the crown is yours. And when it is, you'll be able to afford to be good."* He heard his mother's voice in his memories.

"Amen," the deacons sang the last of the psalm.

He kept seeing Elfgifu turning around to look at him. He knew that all he had to do to stop seeing her was close his eyes, but he didn't blink. He stared at the cathedral's stone altar because there, on a red pillow, lay the crown of England for which Archbishop Lyfing had just reached.

"I crown you, Cnut, son of Sven, king of England, before God. He has chosen you!"

As he spoke, Lyfing placed the crown of English kings on his temples and covered him with Edgar's cloak.

"The good King Edgar, King Cnut, symbolically embraces you. May you be as pious and wise a king as he was."

"So help us God!" the crowd shouted.

"Here is the king chosen by God and chosen by the people. King of Denmark, Norway, and England, Cnut I!" Lyfing announced, and Cnut turned around to face his subjects.

"Long live the king! Long live the king! Long live the king!" they shouted in unison as he looked at them. He saw Jarl Eric of Lade, Thorkel the Tall, and Jorun with his bright blue eyes, the man who'd never left Sven's side. He saw Ragn of the Isles and the chubby Uddorm of Viborg. He saw the younger chieftains: cheerful Hrani, Eilif and Ulf, the sons of Thorgils of Jelling, Urk, Halfdan, and Tored. He saw his English nobles: Godwin, Leofwin, Leofric, the brothers Ethelweard and Ethelnoth, the great Wulfstan, archbishop of York, Northman, Brithric, and Eadric Streona. He looked at them all and felt the crown lie heavy on his head.

"It is our king's wish to marry the widow Emma of Normandy," the archbishop announced, and although this was no longer a surprise to anyone, some of the men flinched. Cnut made sure to remember each one. Emma was brought to him in a dress embroidered with little gold plates, and he married her in the eyes of God, vowing to be faithful to her and to make their future children heirs to the throne of England.

A cleric stood at the entrance to the cathedral and repeated each word to the crowds of commoners gathered outside in a booming voice. The sailors and soldiers, the merchants and cobblers, the bakers, grooms, washerwomen, and beggars. His subjects.

ENGLAND

Świętosława was happy to have her daughters present at the coronation feast. The girls were looking around curiously as they talked with her son's younger chieftains.

So long as they don't fall in love too soon, she thought with concern.

She watched Emma and Cnut. Her daughter-in-law had looked splendid in the cathedral, and now she was trying not to show how much the dress weighed; it could not have been light with all those golden discs. Emma smiled to mask her exhaustion from the marriage negotiations. She hadn't sold herself cheaply. She'd fought like a lioness, though Cnut could have taken her by force if he'd wanted to. But he didn't.

Sven always liked to pretend he was a Christian king, thought Świętosława. *It was a game to him. But Cnut wants to be a great ruler, and Emma can help him be that. She's older than him, more experienced, and not as spoiled as the rest of the English court. Besides, she's on his side now, since she insisted that their son would be the one to inherit the crown. She didn't insist on him cutting ties with Elfgifu, but those boys had no rights to the throne.*

She didn't doubt that Emma would have a son. She wanted to revel in the success of this conquest, but she knew that it was still too soon for them to let down their guard. Eadric Streona was still present.

Skuli moved closer to her and whispered, though it was unusual for a bard to speak quietly.

"I have finished the poem, my lady. Would you like to hear it?"

Before she had time to say no, he began to whisper:

"Now that the difficult battles we have fought are ended, we can . . ."

"We cannot, Skuli," she interrupted him. "And I will be the one to say when the battles are ended."

"The Bold Lady doesn't understand a bard's soul," he complained. "Cnut's coronation has changed you, my lady. Here is the queen of Sweden, Denmark, and Norway, the mother of the English king. A queen four times over! What if I recited the poem about the suitors in the bathhouse in front of the archbishop of Canterbury?"

"Are you threatening the queen?" Jorun asked the bard.

"No. But I have composed a poem and I want to be heard."

"Enough!" Ragn of the Isles said. "King Cnut is about to speak."

Świętosława looked at her son. His golden hair was held off his face by a gemstone-encrusted band. His fair, neatly trimmed beard gleamed like silk. Cnut looked radiant in his white-and-gold robes. She again recalled her two sons as she'd seen them that day on the moors. Red-haired Harald shouting: *"I caught the hare first!"* and Cnut replying: *"But I got a larger one!"*

You caught it, son, she thought tenderly. *I am the mother of two anointed kings.*

Edgar's ceremonial cloak had been left at the cathedral. They had Emma to thank for it having been used during the ceremony. She'd reminded Lyfing that Ethelred had worn it when he'd been crowned king. Edgar had been his father, after all.

"The time has arrived for me to thank all those who have been through the good and the bad with me. My most loyal companions. I have no intention of changing the kingdom by force. I want to strengthen what is most noble about it, and reform what has failed in recent years. But today is not the time for work. Today, we celebrate my coronation and marriage to the wonderful Emma, my queen." He kissed the tips of her fingers.

Maybe they'll be happy? thought Świętosława.

"The kingdom of England can be divided into Northumbria, Mercia, Essex, and Wessex. I want my friends to help me rule well. Eric Haakonson of Lade will be the earl of Northumbria. He's been an honest and loyal vassal in Norway . . ."

Świętosława watched Eric. She'd never forgotten that he'd been the one who had struck the final blow at Øresund. And that he'd been the one to take power in Norway after Olav's death, as Sven's right-hand man. A part of her despised him, but the other part of her remembered that when everyone else had betrayed someone, he had remained loyal.

"Eadric Streona will rule the beautiful Mercia," continued Cnut, "while Thorkel the Tall will be earl of Essex."

Thorkel, Sigvald's brother, she thought. *Who would have guessed? He betrayed Sven, but not Cnut, and my son owes his victory to Thorkel. None of us knew England as well as the Jomsviking. Who is he really? And will the power and the title he wants so badly change him?*

"The three earls will answer to me. I will rule over Wessex myself."

"Excellent choices!" Streona was the first to speak.

Cnut raised a toast to his three earls with his wife and guests. Someone asked Emma to play the harp. She didn't refuse. She touched the strings with her hands and Świętosława heard the same sad melody that Emma had played in the west tower on the night they first met.

"Do you ever think about your wedding day, Mother?" Astrid asked her quietly.

Świętosława only smiled in reply.

"I attended both of the queen's weddings," Great Ulf bragged. "But I'm not sure I'm allowed to talk about it."

Emma fluidly changed the melody, and the notes grew light and cheerful. Świętosława sighed with relief.

She has bid her late husband farewell, and is greeting the second, she thought.

Skuli appeared at her side again.

"Now that the difficult battles we have fought are ended, we can . . ."

"Not yet. I promise you, the battles we have won were not the final ones we must fight." She dampened the bard's joy.

ENGLAND

Cnut waited for Emma in his alcove. She was brought with a procession of ladies in waiting following her. The archbishop of Canterbury blessed their bed. Skuli recited a poem about a beautiful lady and a young king. His sisters blushed as they took the heavy, richly embroidered cloak off Emma's shoulders. Hrani was telling him that it would all go well while the chieftains pushed and shoved each other to make space. Jorun turned to Uddorm and whispered:

"I remember the wedding night on which the maiden bride's dress was cut off her with a knife."

Emma heard him and shivered. Cnut placed a hand on her shoulder and said:

"Don't listen to them, my lady. They talk nonsense."

"Of course it's nonsense," his mother said to Jorun dismissively. "The bride was no maiden, she was a widow!"

The old chieftains all burst out laughing as Emma looked at him questioningly. He shrugged.

"I have no idea what they're talking about. It has nothing to do with us."

"It does a little," drawled Uddorm. "You were born a year later. It was your mother's wedding!"

"It wasn't him, Harald was first. Enough of this! Do you intend to stay and watch? I assure you, they both know what they're doing. Dusza, come on! Bard, out!"

Once they were finally alone, Cnut thought about how much depended on this night. He didn't want to turn Emma against him. He walked around the chamber, gathering his courage or his thoughts, until finally his wife stopped him by standing behind him and placing her arms around his waist. She pressed herself to him, stroking his stomach.

"Do you not like me?" she asked. "Is that why you're running from me?"

"No, of course not," he replied, grasping her hands to kiss them.

"Then why do you only kiss my hands?"

"I want to show you respect."

He could feel her quickened breath on his back.

"Respect," she repeated. "Like a matron?"

"No! Like a queen, a wife . . ."

"Did you show Elfgifu the same respect in bed?"

"Are you jealous?"

"Yes."

"Of what?"

"Her youth. And the fact that you fought for her and your sons . . ."

What am I supposed to say? he wondered, but then he understood. She had been Ethelred's wife for years, and he'd been a sick, bitter old man. *She's afraid of my youth.*

He turned around and picked her up as if she weighed no more than a child, carrying her to bed. He undressed quickly and helped her take her nightdress off. He touched her full breasts, her stomach and the womb which had given birth to two sons that weren't his. He found their marks there, like tracks left by prey in the snow. He forced himself into her, wanting to leave his own mark, his own seed. She moaned and covered her mouth with a hand as if she was frightened of her own voice. But her body had already given in to him. Emma moved her hips in time with his.

This is only the second woman in my life, he thought. *I know nothing about them,* he realized, and felt like a child.

The boy in him touched his lips to her nipple. He licked it shyly. Emma wrapped her legs around him greedily. She held him close. She wasn't the cool, haughty lady he had expected her to be. She was swiftly transforming into a passionate woman, as unsated as he was.

When he woke up in the morning, he saw Emma sitting beside him. She'd covered herself with a cloak but was looking at his nakedness. He covered himself instinctively.

"I have to tell you something, Cnut."

"Mhmm?" He turned over onto his side.

The smell of their night's passion emanated from the bedsheets.

"Eadric Streona hasn't been honest with you," she said, moving her hair off her face.

"I don't doubt that." He stretched.

"He probably hasn't told you that he was the one who organized my sons' escape to Normandy. He came to see me the day after Edmund died. He knew about it already and offered to take the boys away."

Cnut leaped up, rubbing his forehead.

"Ethelweard, the castellan, is one of Streona's men. He must have hidden his visit from Thorkel and Queen Sigrid."

And his brother Ethelnoth is my confessor, Cnut thought feverishly.

"Why are you only telling me this now?"

"Because only now do I feel like your wife."

He kissed her and began to dress hastily.

"We still don't know who ordered Eadwig's tongue to be ripped out," he said.

"Many people wanted Edmund dead, and Eadwig was the most obvious scapegoat," she replied, rising from the bed.

She adjusted his caftan. He slipped the cloak off her shoulders and took a long look at her body. He kissed her breasts and ran out of the room.

52

❈

POLAND

Bolesław's stay in Bodzia wasn't long. He had destroyed one enemy and the second was already waiting for him. He marched to the river Oder the day after the feast. This time, Henry was setting off to war from a camp near Magdeburg.

"He has the Veleti and Udalryk, the duke of Prague, with him," the scouts reported.

"Udalryk . . . Udalryk again . . ." Bolesław shook his head and turned to his son. "Mieszko, you'll take one thousand men and attack Bohemia, to show Udalryk that every time he supports the emperor against us, he will suffer the consequences. You, Zarad, go to Moravia and lead the Moravians against the Bavarians. That should make them less bloodthirsty."

"Yes, my lord," they replied, and soon, all that was left of the companies were clouds of dust.

Bolesław received Henry's main attack near Głogów. He could have dragged the emperor's men into a trap in the swamps surrounding the river Oder or on the Wzgórza Dalkowskie, but he didn't want to do that. He wanted to face Henry's armies head-on. The armies stood opposite one another on a large, flat plain.

"It's hard and dry," Wilkomir reported in the morning. "The summer sun has dried up the earth."

"Good." He patted his friend on the shoulder. "It'll be easier for the horses."

Now, he sat astride Red. The stallion snorted and shook its head a few times. Bolesław watched Henry's companies take their positions. He could see the imperial flag, but he wasn't naïve; he knew the emperor wouldn't be fighting himself.

"Such a shame," he said to Bjornar. "It would be nice to finish this war in a duel, wouldn't it?"

His friend laughed.

"My duke the dreamer."

"I will dream for as long as I live." Bolesław sighed as he stretched. "Do you think they've finished yet? Are they ready? I don't want people in Magdeburg to be saying later that I attacked an unprepared army."

"Since when does my duke care what people say about him?"

"You're right." Bolesław shrugged. "We're not going to stand here and boil alive in the July sun."

He stood up in his stirrups and drew his sword.

"God is with us. To battle!"

"God is with us. To battle!" a thousand voices answered him. "Victory with the duke!"

The powerful Kalmir unfurled his flag with the Piast eagle behind him, and Myślibor rode out in front of the soldiers with the Holy Spear. He lowered its ancient head and the duke kissed the steel that hid the relic of the Holy Cross.

"Let's go!" called Bolesław, hearing the silk fluttering in the wind. He urged Red onward.

He saw the emperor's flagbearers ride out with the second Holy Spear.

God will settle this, he thought without fear.

He allowed Wilkomir to lead the first charge. His old friend led the men in an even line. Head to head, shield to shield, the horses sped up. He loved the sound of their heavy hooves thudding on the ground. He loved the whistle of the bone flutes which they used to startle the enemy's horses. He used to love war and Emnilda; now all he had left was war.

"Shields!" Wilkomir shouted, and the first line shifted their shields from their backs onto their arms in unison.

Wilkomir was measuring the distance. One hundred paces. Sixty.

"Spears!" he shouted, and a shower of blades fell upon their foe.

The horses that had been struck by spears squealed wildly and fell, pulling their riders behind them. In every battle, they had to skillfully navigate around the kicking horses that lay on the ground. They broke through the enemy line. Bolesław lifted his sword and brought his shield close, up to his chin.

It's a good thing that Herman isn't here, he thought as he fought a strong, stocky Saxon. *I wouldn't want to make my daughter a widow, even though her husband is a sop.*

He lifted his shield to parry a blow and immediately cut downward with his sword, aiming for the shoulder. The Saxon fell from the saddle, under the hooves of his own horse.

Bolesław spun his horse around in a circle. He spotted a tall, dark-eyed man who he'd once seen beside Henry.

"Count!" he shouted. "Fight me!"

The other man leaned down in the saddle as he sped toward him. Bolesław held his sword close to his body, waiting for the German count to raise his arm and expose himself. He heard a horse behind him. *Someone is too close,* he thought. *They're right behind me.*

He moved Red sideways, not wasting time looking behind him, and attacked the lord from the right. Their blades clashed together. Bolesław could see that his opponent was looking behind him.

Who's there? Am I about to be stabbed in the back?

He didn't have a moment to lose. He squeezed his thighs around Red and, throwing his arm out, reached the count. Bolesław's blade connected with the man's chin, but the count didn't even sway in the saddle. He parried quickly, and Bolesław spun his horse around as he lifted his shield to protect himself. He found himself face-to-face with a pale-eyed young man who was aiming a gleaming axe at his head.

Bloody hell, he thought, *he's close enough. He'll get me.*

The count's horse approached him from behind.

I'm caught in their pincers, he realized. *I'm about to die with the sword in my hand.*

Red kicked, pushed the Saxon away from him for a moment. The pale-eyed man swung the axe straight at his face. And, in a second that to Bolesław felt like eternity, the young man straightened and his grip on the handle loosened. The axe fell from his lifeless fingers onto the ground in front of Red. Wilkomir stood behind the pale-eyed man, still holding the spear with which he'd stabbed him.

"You saved my life!" Bolesław screamed at him and realized that Wilkomir wasn't riding.

"Behind you!" Wilkomir shouted to him, letting go of the corpse and drawing his sword.

Bolesław turned. The wounded count was about to attack again while blood streamed from his teeth and onto his beard. They crossed blades once more. Bolesław shoved him away and buried his sword into the man's neck. His foe fell with a groan. Bolesław felt the sweat pouring into his eyes. He heard Wilkomir scream. He turned Red again, searching for his friend—there!

He was kneeling, holding on to his arm which had been almost completely severed from his body. He howled like a wolf.

Bolesław glanced around the swiftly emptying battlefield and leaped from his horse. He tripped over the pale-eyed man's body, Wilkomir's spear still embedded in its back.

"Brother!" he exclaimed when he reached him. "Brother! You saved me!"

"Warriors give their lives for their king," Wilkomir said hoarsely.

Bolesław handed him his sword.

"Take it!" he ordered. "I'll hold your arm."

Wilkomir's face looked as pale as if all the blood had drained from it. He wrapped the fingers of his left hand around the hilt of the sword. Bolesław was pressing his right arm into his shoulder as hard as he could. Blood pulsed from the wound. They looked at one another.

"Death has come for me," Wilkomir whispered, his eyes growing dim. "It's riding Thorhalla . . ."

"No!" Bolesław didn't want to accept his death. "Come back! I order you!"

He shook Wilkomir's dead body. He let him go. Wilkomir's right arm fell, now completely detached from his body. Bolesław lifted it and howled like a wolf himself.

"Victory!" Bjornar was shouting. "Victory! The survivors are fleeing! There's barely a handful of them!"

His voice died in his throat when he caught sight of his king kneeling on the ground.

They held a funeral for Wilkomir in Głogów. They blew the horns to honor everyone who had fallen that day. After this first devastating battle, Henry's troops retreated. Bolesław reinforced Wrocław and Głogów, but the emperor avoided any open fighting. Scouts soon brought news that Henry's troops were marching south. They were no longer attacking Poland.

"It could mean that Mieszko has decimated the Czechs," Bolesław mused. "Udalryk is going south to help his own. Or perhaps Zarad has overwhelmed the Bavarians and their allies are going to their aid."

The imperial and Veleti forces were delayed at Niemcza. When the city's people saw the approaching pagans, they placed large wooden crosses above each gate.

The world has turned upside down, thought Bolesław when he received messengers in Głogów. *The emperor should be the most avid defender of the Christian faith on earth, but instead he attacks Niemcza, which defends itself under the cross, with pagans at his side.*

Niemcza was besieged for almost three weeks, to no avail. Niemcza remained unconquered. Mieszko returned triumphant from Bohemia, towing a mass of prisoners behind him. The emperor and his armies hastily retreated, losing their supply trains and abandoning their wounded as they fled. Bolesław insisted on chasing them. Bjornar, furious after Wilkomir's death, led their pursuit as far as the river Mulde. He returned with almost one thousand prisoners.

"We will see the money we spent on this war in sales and ransoms," he told the duke as he counted the captured men.

Bolesław grabbed his shoulders and spun him around like a feather.

"Bjornar, my friend! We've defeated the emperor! Do you understand? Him and all his allies! The Bavarians and the Czechs and the Veleti! Ha! We crushed them! The war is won! Don't you worry about money now."

"I know, I know. Duke Bolesław values his soldiers. We are always paid on time."

"Yes, yes, but Bjornar, now that we have vanquished Henry and his army is licking its wounds, we can set out to fill our treasury."

"Where do you want to go? Should I even bother unsaddling my horse, or are we going now?"

"Unsaddle it, of course. I'll give you time to rest. Then, we go back to Kiev. We march on the wealthiest city in this part of the world."

"What if Knyaz Jarosław isn't keeping Sława in Kiev?"

"Then we take Kiev first and find my daughter afterward."

"So I thought. The spoils of war come first. For the soldiers."

Bolesław turned away. He didn't want his childhood friend to see him now, the man who knew him better than anyone. He didn't want anyone to see what he was thinking or feeling. Since he'd had the idea to marry Jarosław's sister as a way of getting his daughter out of his clutches, he hadn't been able to think of anything else. He hadn't wanted any woman as much as he wanted that girl since Emnilda's death. The blue-eyed beauty in the fern-and-moss-colored dress. She meant more to him than Kiev did.

53

⚯

ENGLAND

Świętosława walked through the streets of London with her axemen at her side and Dusza on a leash. Godwin was usually her guide. She was interested in everything. When they had more time, they would examine the remnants of the Roman castles on the hill.

"The Romans laid the stones in these streets, too, but as the years go by even the stone has crumbled," Godwin would tell her as they climbed.

The nobles had made their homes in ancient, crumbling castles, just like the royal family. The holes in the brick walls were filled carelessly, but when she half-closed her eyes, she could still imagine the wonder that these buildings must have inspired in the past. She kept asking her guide to find her old, Roman marble columns and statues to see. She liked to touch their cool, veiny surfaces. She liked to touch things that lasted even once their day had passed. *What will be left of us once we're gone?* she'd wonder.

She liked to look over London from the top of the hill or the castle tower. The city looked like a colorful, shimmering mosaic from up high.

If they didn't go up the hill, they would begin their walks by going to the small walled church of the Virgin Mary that stood opposite the castle. It was laid with old Roman slabs. They would then walk from Billingsgate, the stone city gates, through alleys full of seamstresses, Flemish market stalls, and German merchants, along the river Thames. They would walk the street of bakers where Godwin bought her warm, crunchy bread rolls. They would walk the milk street where Dusza would be given a bowl of cream, then they'd turn into the street full of rabbits where Godwin walked ahead and paid in advance for what the lynx stole on her way. They would walk through the streets filled with butchers—at that point, thankfully, Dusza would usually be sated and lazy—and cross the loud, noisy market where Świętosława fed stray dogs and orphaned children alike. They walked around Saint Paul's Cathedral. She admired it but she didn't like it much. They still struggled to see eye to eye with the bishop of London.

"Elfwig," Godwin began, "manipulates the citizens using the relics of Archbishop Aelfheah, the one who was killed by Thorkel's men. The martyr's bones make people listen to him."

"I have no idea how to fight our battle with the bishop," admitted Świętosława.

"If I may give the queen any advice . . ." began Godwin carefully.

"You may." She encouraged him with a wave of her hand.

". . . I would suggest using Ethelnoth, King Cnut's confessor."

"It's not exactly honorable to use men of the Church for one's own means." Świętosława laughed.

"The queen knows what I mean. The disagreement behind the priests of Canterbury and the bishop of London. Ethelnoth is the dean of Saint Augustine's Abbey, the Benedictine monastery, in Canterbury. Archbishop Lyfing also loyally serves the king. Perhaps it might be worth rewarding Canterbury with some wondrous relic," Godwin suggested with a smile.

"What a thoughtful idea, Godwin." Świętosława laughed again. "Are you suggesting we steal Aelfheah's relics away from London's cathedral?"

"I wouldn't dare! No theft, nothing like that. Merely a ceremonial relocation of the relics."

She knew it wasn't a bad idea. In one fell swoop they could ensure Canterbury's gratitude and take the holy bones away from the archbishop of London.

They walked down a road she liked, as far as they could, until they reached the city walls and gate.

"Is the gate from Roman times, too?" she asked. Godwin nodded.

They walked over an unused, overgrown moat.

"There will be an unusual church built here, my lady." He pointed at a small slab of a building that stood over the gleaming dark waters of the river Fleet. "The oldest Londoners call it 'Saint Bride.'"

"Saint Bride?" She wasn't sure that she understood his meaning.

"Saint Brigid of Kildare, my lady. Saint Bride is just what the people call it. She was Saint Patrick's student and companion."

She looked at the building carefully and shook her head.

"It doesn't look as old as you say. The wall, maybe, it's crumbling, but the roof looks brand new."

"The Danes refurbished it a century ago . . ."

"That's nice of them." She smiled.

". . . because they destroyed the old church when they plundered the city," Godwin finished.

She made a noncommittal sound. She wouldn't feel responsible for all the Danish invasions on London. All that mattered was that they fixed what they'd broken.

"Look, my lady." Godwin pointed at an uneven pavement made of red and brown tiles which ran along the east wall of the church.

"This wall is different," she realized.

"It's the only one that survived the fire. It belongs to the old Roman villa in which Christians prayed and worshipped. Their home became the first church, dedicated to Saint Brigid, because she visited London during one of her many voyages. That was when, according to legend, she prayed near a local spring, the waters of which were afterward known for their miracle-bringing powers."

"Does it heal?" asked Świętosława with interest. "Like Saint Patrick's spring?"

"Yes." Godwin smiled. "It heals the soul. It is said that the waters bring luck in love, so Londoners drink its water at weddings."

She couldn't help herself and she approached the small spring hidden in the timber. It gurgled quietly, falling in a small stream. She knelt down and stuck a finger out but snatched her hand back as soon as the water touched it.

Godwin will think me mad. An old queen interested in a spring that brings fortune in love.

Her companion's expression remained unchanged, always polite, regardless of what he might be thinking. He pointed at the back of the church.

"A Roman cemetery used to lie here, but the tombstones have been eroded by time and the Londoners have built a wall from them on the other side of the temple, though, as you can see, even that is crumbling now. Sometimes you meet inspired monks nearby, preachers and pilgrims who have come here from all corners of the world. The ones who are returning from the Holy Land or Rome. Saint Brigid traveled the world like they do, so they come to pray at her altar on their way back."

Dusza pulled on her leash and Świętosława followed her without paying Godwin any attention. A thin pilgrim in a tattered gray habit sat on the wall built of old tombstones that were eroding with time like everything else around them. Judging by his veiny, liver-spot-covered hands, he wasn't young. He sat like an old cat, with his legs curled under him and the hood thrown over his face, right down to his chin. His head was turned toward the sun.

A disciple of the Light, she thought, not daring to disturb him. His small wooden bowl lay at the foot of the wall, with a few coins inside. He wasn't guarding them at all, wholly consumed with the sun. She dug a coin out of her pouch and threw it into his bowl. He didn't even flinch, although the sound of silver hitting the bronze coins was clear.

"Oh, thirty silver coins would be better than one!" She laughed sarcastically, returning to Godwin. They walked on, crossing a plank to reach the large market in the Danish settlement of Aldwych, also known as the Old Market. They walked down toward the river to look at the ships that were berthed in the canals which ran near the houses. She stopped to speak to the

Danes who had lived there for years. Every family had arrived with a different invasion, at a different time.

"Aldwych is a peaceful area full of merchants and craftsmen. But we should go, my lady." Godwin gently directed their steps back toward the city walls. "London's council is meeting tonight in the old Roman theater. Would you like to see them?"

"I'd like to hear them"—she smiled as they walked through the gates—"but preferably without betraying myself as the queen."

A sound that made her heart stop ripped through the air from a nearby alley. The scream of a falcon. Dusza flicked her ears and dragged her mistress behind her. Queen and lynx sped toward the sound.

"My lady!" Godwin shouted, following, but Great Ulf was already at her side.

A sailor was carrying a cage with two falcons.

"Norwegian?" Świętosława asked feverishly.

"No, my lady. Icelandic."

"Trained to hunt?"

"Of course!"

"I'll take them."

"They aren't for sale, my lady."

"I'm not asking you if they're for sale, I am buying them from you," she announced firmly. "Godwin! Pay for the falcons because I threw the last of my money into the monk's bowl."

"I can go back for it," suggested Great Ulf. "There were some bronze coins in there, too."

Godwin dug out silver from his pouch and pressed it into the hand of the confused sailor. The man scratched his ear as he said:

"If it wasn't for the fact that we have a poem in Iceland about a queen and her two lynxes, I wouldn't let you have them. But I like that song. '*Sigrid Storråda flies in a golden sleigh pulled by two wild cats*,'" he recited, and sighed. "You, my lady, have only one . . ."

"My man, you're speaking to . . ." Godwin began, but Świętosława nudged him and he fell silent.

"Thank you, Icelander," she said politely. "Let's go."

Great Ulf carried the cage and the birds beat the bars with their wings.

"Why didn't you want to grant that man the happiness of knowing who you were?" asked Godwin once they were out of earshot. "He would have been proud to know he sold the birds to Queen Sigrid."

"The poem about the sleigh pulled by two cats is only one of many which are recited on the isles," she replied evasively.

"I don't understand." Godwin shook his head.

Great Ulf turned to him and winked.

"There is one about a plucked falcon the queen returned," he said, before she had a chance to protest. "'*A falcon without its feather cloak. Helpless and naked. A gift returned at a bad time. Let no one cross Sigrid, as the queen's anger is a storm that rips the sails.*' It went something like that."

"Is that why you bought the falcons?" Godwin asked fearfully. "Your guard is in jest, isn't he?"

"Of course," she reassured him. "Now, what about the amphitheater? Should we go and hear the discussion?"

"If we go, we must find some common cloak to cover you with and take the lynx back to the castle . . ."

"She-lynx," Świętosława corrected.

"Of course, my lady, that's an important distinction. The queen would never walk around with boys on a leash."

"Yes, she should, if they were still alive."

"I'm very curious, but I daren't ask for the tale."

"Is this amphitheater far?"

Wilczan gave her his cloak and she gave him Dusza to take back to the castle. She also sent away the axemen with the falcons. Great Ulf was the only one who went with them. She took Godwin's arm. She liked this young man because he was different from anyone she knew. He was full of self-control and tact. The kind of man she imagined Cnut would have become if he wasn't a king. They walked northeast, away from the cathedral, and she told him about Wrzask and Zgrzyt, leaving out only a few details.

"You are the only person I have met with mismatched eyes, my lady. I am honored to have heard this story."

"Were you also this polite when you were a child?" she asked him.

"My lady mother is dead, so I have no one to ask." He shrugged with a disarming smile. "London's council usually meets on Fridays, but I discovered that this time it would be on a Thursday."

"Thursday," she repeated thoughtfully. "Thor's day. Isn't it odd that the Christian inhabitants of the kingdom still use the names of the old gods to describe the days of the week?"

"Force of habit," he replied with a smile. "Our old king Alfred, the one who divided the kingdom, wanted to name the days of the week after the saints, but the people never used them. We're here. These stone benches were built by the Romans in the days when London lay on the edge of the empire. Today, London's council sits here and debates. This is where all the decisions were made about how best to defend the city against the Vikings, how much of the danegeld would be paid by Londoners . . ."

"Should I feel touched or guilty?" She pinched him. "Neither will happen, you know. What happened here when the Romans ruled London?"

"Gladiator battles, hunts for wild animals. The same as today, only without the council."

"Do you see what I see?" She pointed at Streona who had just emerged from a doorway at the far end of the amphitheater.

"Yes, my lady. Look there." He pointed discreetly at the benches lower down. "That's Brithric."

"None of us have seen him near the Spider yet," she observed.

"Neither of them should be here. This isn't a gathering for the nobility but a council of the common people. Great Ulf?" Godwin turned to him, uneasy. "Send a messenger after Wilczan and the axemen and have them return immediately. We may have need of them."

"What are they talking about?" she asked.

She had learned the local language, but she still struggled to follow the conversation when people spoke quickly or unclearly.

"About London's mint, my lady . . . Let's go back before Brithric sees us."

They walked down the narrow alley that led from the amphitheater into the street that was crowded. A lame beggar was loudly arguing with a fishwife. Godwin was nervous.

"I didn't think that Streona's grasp reached as far as the city representatives," he said. "He's more influential than I supposed him to be."

"Let's go to the king." She pulled his arm.

It's time to break the Spider's web, she thought coldly.

She caught sight of a tall figure in a gray habit and hood-covered face out of the corner of her eye. She turned, wanting to get a better look. Running blindly from the fishwife, the beggar threw himself at them and she let go of Godwin's arm. She saw the beggar's cane right in front of her. She felt hot, as if he had already struck her cheek, but then Great Ulf stepped in front of her. He turned around and lifted her like a child, pressing her to him. She instinctively threw her arms around his neck. She heard Godwin's frightened exclamation:

"My lady!"

Ulf carried her out of the crowd. She felt him stumble after a few steps.

"I'm heavy," she said straight into his broad chest.

"No," he whispered, falling to one knee.

She let go of him and stood up. She heard Godwin's voice again:

"Guards!"

"Ulf?" She leaned over him. "Christ, you have a knife in your back! What do you need me to do? Should I take it out?"

Great Ulf was panting, still on his knees. A crowd was gathering around them.

"No," he said. "Don't take it out. I'll bleed out."

She fell to her knees in front of him. They faced each other, and she could see he was quickly losing color. She looked at his bald, scarred face and into the eyes which were already growing dim.

Her axemen and Godwin ran over to them, but she stopped them with a wave of her hand.

"Get these people away," Godwin said quietly, realizing what was happening.

The furious axemen pushed the onlookers away with their shields and soon there was nobody left in the alley. Świętosława moved closer to Ulf. Tears streamed down her face. She leaned down to his belt and drew his sword. It was the first time that she felt the weight of the steel that had protected her for so many years. She placed the hilt into the hand of the enormous man before her, and he leaned on it.

"I die on my knees before my lady," he said with difficulty.

"You die with the sword in your hand," she said through her tears. "And I'm kneeling beside you, Great Ulf. Do you have a dying wish?"

"Yes." He moved his lips, and died.

Godwin held him up so that he wouldn't fall. Without rising from her knees, Świętosława kissed him. She rose only when Wilczan reached them.

"I killed the false beggar," he said, looking at Ulf with grief in his face. "He might have been anyone, but he wasn't the cripple he pretended to be. He ran as fast as a hare. If it wasn't for a hooded monk, I never would have caught him."

"The monk helped you? Where is he?" asked Godwin.

"The corpse? By the gutter."

"I mean the monk."

"I don't know. He vanished."

"Axemen, Godwin, Wilczan," she called them all close to her as they waited for the cart that would take Great Ulf's body away. "I forbid you from telling anyone what happened here today."

"Even the king?" asked Godwin, raising his eyebrows.

"No one. We won't hold a funeral. Find a place where Great Ulf's body can wait until we can bury him."

"My lady, there will be rumors."

"I know," she said firmly, "but only the one who is behind this . . ."

". . . assassination," Godwin finished for her. "Only they will know that Great Ulf is dead."

"I had two of them," she said quietly. "Wilkomir and Great Ulf. I felt safe between my two wolves. Your father has sailed to Poland . . ."

"So take his pup," said Wilczan, and took his place behind her.

ENGLAND

Cnut invited many of his nobles to a feast he held after Christmas. Emma assisted him for as long as she could. She was visibly pregnant. He walked the queen to her chambers when she got tired, asking his sisters to keep Emma company while he returned to his guests.

His mother sat on her throne with the lynx at her feet and Wilczan at her side. Thorkel, the earl of Essex, and Eric, the earl of Northumbria, sat facing one another on opposite sides of the table. Eadric Streona, the earl of Mercia, sat between them. Ethelnoth, Cnut's confessor, and his brother Ethelweard, London's castellan, were talking to each other on the side. The old chieftains were beside them, Ragn of the Isles and Uddorm of Viborg, eating a roasted partridge. Northman drank with Jorun, Brithric with Godwin, and the two brothers Eilif and Ulf with Hrnai. Skuli recited a poem:

Silent and thoughtful
should be the royal son.
Brave in battle
and unyielding in giving orders . . .

"Your northern songs are beautiful," praised Streona. "So simple yet insightful."

Godwin laughed at one of Brithric's jokes as he drank with his companion, making motions as if kissing someone. Cnut saw that his mother paled when she noticed, and Wilczan clenched his jaw.

"Skuli!" shouted the queen. "Recite the English song."

"The First Song or the Second Song?"

"The first, bard!" his mother said firmly as she wrapped the leash around her wrist.

After the great battle on the moors,
the blood soaked into the stones.
The Mysterious Warrior won the war.
Praise his name,

for he changed the path of Fate.
The one who was always there, the Guardian Spirit.
That is the name under which he will be remembered.

The guests drank in silence as they listened to each of Skuli's words. Cnut nodded with a smile. Streona spread himself comfortably on the bench and sipped his wine, satisfied that when the mysterious warrior was mentioned, most eyes looked to him.

Where would the Light King be today
And where would he be resting his head
if it hadn't been for the Guardian Spirit
and his modestly given advice. His hidden actions.

Streona motioned his heavily ringed hand at a servant to pour him more wine. He was drinking greedily now.

Who watched over the alliance of the two kings
when it was made on the island in the middle of the rushing river?
Who ensured they kept their words?
The Spirit, the Guardian Spirit.
And today, instead of two kingdoms,
there is one powerful realm.
The land of the Light King.
Who should he reward, the king wonders . . .

"The Guardian Spirit!" Streona yelled, banging his goblet down on the table so hard that wine spilled. "And his helpful souls."

"Tell us who!" His mother the queen smiled graciously. "I already have a reward for Ethelweard for Eadwig's tongue. And one for Northman for the alliance on the island. Who else?"

"Brithric!" Streona asked. "For . . . his help."

"For helping get the silver out of the royal mint," Godwin suggested politely, putting down the goblet from which he'd been drinking with Brithric moments before and grabbing his neck.

Jorun pushed Northman's goblet out of his hand at the same time and caught him in an iron grip. Ethelnoth, Cnut's confessor, kicked the bench from under his brother, Ethelweard the castellan, who found himself lying on the stone floor with Ragn and Uddorm pouncing on him. Thorkel and Jarl Eric held on to the surprised Streona.

"Skuli, the poem." Świętosława's voice pierced the air.

Skuli, his voice trembling, began to recite:

Sigrid Proud, Sigrid Ruthless,
to whose bright home
suitors doggedly come,
from the rocky borders along a swampy path . . .

"Not that one!" his mother interrupted. "The Second Song!"

"Forgive me, my lady . . ." The bard blushed.

A Guardian Spirit or an Evil One? The king asked himself.
His sworn brother stands within the blood-soaked circle of blood vengeance.
It is a sacred law that calls on him to avenge Edmund's death.

Cnut stood in the middle of the great stone hall. He watched his men lead the four tied-up prisoners toward him. Their confused expressions betrayed how little they had suspected this turn of events.

"Ethelweard, you are hereby accused of maiming Eadwig in order to hide the truth about the circumstances of Edmund's death. Northman, you are hereby accused of stirring up the people of Northumbria against me. Brithric, you have been stealing from the royal treasury, and you've been inciting unrest in Essex . . ."

Godwin, standing beside Cnut, finished for him.

"And you arranged and carried out an assassination attempt on Queen Sigrid Storråda."

Cnut frowned.

His mother stood up and walked over to Brithric with the lynx at her side.

"What assassination attempt is Godwin talking about?" asked Cnut. "We were sure about the theft of silver from the mint. What don't I know?"

"Forgive me, son," she said. "The mint is one thing, but the assassination attempt is another. Great Ulf died protecting me."

"My king, we weren't certain who was behind it," said Godwin apologetically. "That's why we hid it from you. It was only when Brithric asked me whether Wilczan is a better personal guard to the queen than Great Ulf had been that we could be certain. The man who asks about Great Ulf in the past tense knows he should be dead."

"I will never forgive you for my friend's death," his mother said to Brithric, and he saw the threat in her eyes.

"And I will not forgive anyone who tries to kill my mother," Cnut hissed through gritted teeth, and turned to address the earl of Mercia. The Spider. The Mutt. The Groom who had hidden his pawns for so many years.

"Eadric Streona, you are responsible for the most heinous act. You led to the death of King Edmund, son of Ethelred."

"But . . . my lord . . . b-but . . ." stammered Streona.

Świętosława walked by Brithric without looking at him, as if he no longer existed to her, and stood in front of the earl of Mercia. Her great lynx snarled, leaped forward, then pissed on Streona's feet.

"Even my Dusza is disgusted by you," the queen observed coldly.

"Ethelnoth, my confessor," Cnut said, "I will not blame you for your brother's sins, because I am certain you had nothing to do with them. To prove that I name you my chaplain from this day forth."

The pale Ethelnoth nodded.

"Leofwin! I know that you were once Edmund's loyal ally, and you've been hurt by Streona, too. I do not blame you for your son Northman's betrayal. To show you that I know one black sheep in a family is not the standard by which its kin should be judged, I name your other son, the loyal Leofric, earl of Mercia. The punishment for betraying the king is death. You, Eadric Streona, have betrayed many kings, so the sentence will be carried out immediately, and your quartered body will rest at the bottom of the Thames to serve as a warning to all traitors."

"The Bold One's axemen!" the queen called out. "Do your duty, in the name of God! Skuli, continue the Second Song. I don't want to listen to the screams of a coward."

His sworn brother stands within the blood-soaked circle of blood vengeance.
It is a sacred law that calls on him to avenge Edmund's death.

54

WOLIN, WOLIN ISLAND, POLAND

Astrid rose from the bench with difficulty.

"Leszko!" she shouted, but her voice was weak and quiet, barely breaking the silence.

As if it were making its way from under a pile of leaves already, she thought, fighting the urge to laugh at herself.

She struck her cane on the floor and, by the third thump, her helmsman arrived.

"You called . . ."

"Leszko, get the boat ready."

"No!" He flinched. "I won't do that!"

"You will," she said. "You always do as I ask . . ." She coughed, struggling to catch her breath.

"But not this . . . not this . . ."

"Leszko." She sighed heavily. "Speaking is more difficult than moving . . . Don't argue with me or I'll go get it myself . . ."

He blew his nose on his sleeve, nodded, and walked out without another word. Busla appeared a moment later. Her sagging cheeks were trembling.

"Are you sure you don't want anyone to come with you?" she asked.

"Not you," Astrid snorted. "Speaking tires me."

"At least take a jug." She took out a jug of wine sealed with wax.

"What is it?"

"Golden Styrian wine."

"It'll do. Don't walk me to port. I don't like farewells. My time has come."

She rose from the bench. Busla wrapped a cloak around her shoulders and placed the jug in one hand, the cane in the other.

"Stay well," Astrid said to her, and walked out without looking back.

There was a light breeze in the port, and the salty smell of the ocean filled her nostrils. Spring was still far away, but the Baltic Sea was already awaking after the short, mild winter. The harbor was empty; her *Salty Sister* was the only vessel there. Leszko stood by the pier with an offended expression on his face. He was fidgeting with a dirty rope.

"I can see every hole left by your missing teeth when you pull that face," she said to him, and unexpectedly kissed his stubbly gray cheek. "Goodbye, my friend. But help me in before you go."

When the deck rocked under her feet, she unexpectedly recovered some of her old energy. She put the jug to one side and grabbed the helm. Leszko untied the ropes and shouted:

"The Lady of Wolin's final journey!"

She turned for a moment to look at him. He was crying openly, smearing his tears like a child. The hardest part was navigating the Dziwna when it widened and flowed into the open sea. She felt the sweat streaming down her back as her arms and knees trembled.

A moment more and you can rest, she thought, calming her breath as she reached the Baltic. *Finally . . .*

She rolled up the sail and berthed the *Salty Sister* in one final effort. She then collapsed and for a while couldn't move. Once her heartbeat returned to a regular rhythm, she forced her muscles into action one more time and reached for the jug. She barely managed to pry the wax seal off because her hands were so cold, and she couldn't keep hold of the knife. She cut herself and wiped the blood away on her cloak. She lifted the jug, but her hands were shaking and she spilled the wine over herself.

If this continues, I won't be able to get drunk and I'll go down stone cold sober, she thought.

She had envisioned that once she had sailed away far enough from the shore, she'd berth the *Salty Sister* and a storm would arrive and drown her with her vessel in the blink of an eye. She glanced at the sky. There was nothing to suggest there would be a storm at all, but this was the season for them.

Wait and see, Dalwin's voice echoed in her memories, but she was here because she didn't want to wait anymore.

I'm the traitor, and yet I feel betrayed, she thought, pulling the cloak more tightly around herself. *A betrayed, abandoned, bitter old woman. That's me. The daughter of the great duke Mieszko, who had the misfortune of being born to the wrong mother and at the wrong time. Oh!*

If it hadn't been for the fact that Mieszko had been baptized soon after she'd been born and married Dobrawa, he never would have sent them away.

We'd all have been equal. Geira, Świętosława, and I. The same. But he divided us into the better and the worse, the more and the less valuable!

She took a gulp of wine and laughed bitterly.

"*My most precious daughter.*" He only spoke of the Bold One like that. And Świętosława? The Bold One had accepted it, of course. She had even embraced it. How many times had Świętosława spoken of others who were related like she was with Astrid and Geira, and she'd emphasized how it was "only" a half brother or half sister. Only! Only. A half sister. That meant worse, did it? *Oh, Bold One! You only ever thought about yourself. You may have looked at me, but you never saw me, as if I were nothing but air. You treated me as if I were one of your loyal servants. Didn't you see my love for Olav? That I was the one who brought him to Father's court? No. You only cared about what you felt. You even asked for my help in getting him back! But the Battle of the Three Kings ended differently. Yes, I was there. I was afraid that Sigvald might betray us, and I took the* Salty Sister *to help them. But Olav ordered me to stay away, to rescue the wounded. I hauled them out like fish . . .*

She saw it again as if no time had passed. She shivered. But her memories sped onward, to the moment she saw Dusza fall with an arrow in her heart, to Olav standing on the *Long Snake*'s gunwale with a bloodied Vigi at his side. "You won't take me!" he'd shouted. She saw it all, heard it all. And then he'd leaped into the waves as she'd clutched her heart and screamed. That was the only time she had admitted out loud that she didn't want to live without him. She'd wanted to jump into the water after him, to end her life, but she'd stood frozen as if she'd been turned to stone. She couldn't move. She'd just stood there. She'd seen Jarl Eric take the *Long Snake*, the ship full of corpses. The vessel of the dead. The wounded groaned all around her aboard the *Salty Sister*—and then she'd seen him. She'd thought she was hallucinating or dreaming, but no. He had swum to her underwater, leaving a trail of blood behind him. "Leszko!" she'd called. "Help me. We need to pull him out." Her strength came rushing back as she'd run to the gunwale. They'd pulled him onto the deck as he lost consciousness. They couldn't undress him, and blood had seeped from under his chain mail. She had never moved so efficiently, so quickly, she had never felt so strong. Her fingers had stiffened with the cold, but she'd slipped her hands under the chain mail and found his wound anyway. She'd stopped the bleeding and covered him with everything she could find while Leszko had taken the helm. She'd been afraid he wouldn't make it to Wolin. They'd stopped in a small bay near Rügen's stony shores, a place sailors and merchants didn't know. She'd known she must hide him, because if any one of the wounded men aboard her ship realized that Olav had survived, the news would spread. She had friends near Rügen who worked for the priests of Arkona, and they'd helped her, letting her use their hut. She'd sent Leszko and the rest of the wounded to Wolin to be looked after by Busla while she'd stayed with him. She'd pried the chain mail off his body and warmed him with her own. She'd washed his wounds. He was hers. She hadn't known whether he'd survive, but the short time she'd spent caring for him had been the most beautiful days in her life. Love and fear mixed in her heart, but all that had mattered was that the man she loved had been in her arms. Hers. She'd learned every part of his body. Every scar, every protrusion, and every dent. He had the slave's mark on his left shoulder, clear and black, in the shape of a chicken's foot. She'd kissed that mark, just as she'd kissed every single scar on his body. She'd touched his thighs and calves, his stomach, his chest. If she fell asleep it had only ever been for a short while, and when she'd awaken, she would massage him again. She'd seen his beard growing longer every day, and she'd touched it with the tip of her finger. The blood had begun to flow quicker in his veins again from her caresses. His wounds had healed. He wasn't healthy yet, but the worst was over. Then, one morning, he'd opened his eyes.

She'd had to leave him under the care of the locals to return to Wolin and look after the others they'd rescued from Øresund. And she'd needed to find better herbs for him. "I cannot heal you with what I have here," she'd said. She sailed between Wolin and Arkona for a full year. It had been the most important year of her life. Świętosława had called her. Bolesław had called her. She hadn't cared what either of them wanted. She was finally putting herself first. But Olav had changed, that battle had altered him. He was silent and thoughtful. The stronger he'd grown, the further he'd drawn from her. Until finally, when she'd come to see him, she hadn't recognized him. He'd shaved his long white hair. She'd known it was a sign of something, but she hadn't wanted to know what it was. They'd argued. "My life belongs to God," he'd said. "To God?" She'd been furious. "I'm the one who saved you, not some god! Me! You owe your life to me!" *And you should give it to me,* she'd wanted to add, but she didn't dare, because he'd looked at her as if he'd never seen her before. She'd felt cold all over. "You want to leave," she'd realized. "Leave?" She'd missed him again from that moment onward. She'd wanted to turn back time to when he'd been unconscious and she could do whatever she wanted with his body. "Yes, Astrid, I want to leave," he'd said, and there hadn't been a single note of sadness in his voice. As if he'd felt nothing. She'd remembered some old tale about drowned men brought back to life, about how they were no longer human. "I'm grateful to you for saving my life. But I would have been just as grateful had you allowed me to succumb to my wounds." She hadn't understood. "If it is God's will that I live, then I must give the rest of my days to God. I must submit to His will. I want to go to the Holy Land and to stand atop the hill of Golgotha. I want to feel the pain of crucifixion and the strength of resurrection." She'd been certain her heart would break, but instead, the old Astrid had emerged. The loving, helpful sister. She'd found some Russian merchants who would take him to Novgorod. She'd watched him as they'd sailed from Arkona to Wolin. Tall, slender, and bald. He'd taken the helm of the *Salty Sister*, and it had been just the two of them, but that had changed nothing. He'd already been gone. In Wolin, only Dalwin and Leszko had known the truth. No one had recognized him, no one had known anything. He'd taken off his brooch and given it to her before he'd left, as if in payment. A fish being torn apart by two eagles. He'd nodded to her as he'd sailed away, pulling up his hood.

She'd almost broken down and confessed everything, once. Just once. To Świętosława. The Bold One had stopped in Wolin on her way to Roskilde, when she'd gone to see her children dressed as a nun. They'd gotten drunk. When she'd heard her sister's pain as she mourned Olav, she'd wanted to badly to tell her the truth. But she hadn't.

I spent so many years lying, she thought. *I lied to the Bold One first, believing that Olav would stay with me. I thought that I was finally doing something for myself. Not for her, or for Father, or for my brother—just for me. And what was I supposed to say afterward? I saved him and he left me? What? I pulled him from the sea twice, but neither time for myself . . .* Finally, she sobbed. *I'm the traitor, but I feel betrayed. I lied, but I'm the one who feels like she's been lied to . . .*

She lifted the jug. The wine was as cold as ice. The waves rocked her.

I'm drunk, she thought. *It's nearly finished.*

The memories haunted her. They were both sitting in her huge bed and the chestful of wines was open nearby. They mourned the same man, though only the Bold One could admit to it. She talked about Radim Gaudentius and Adalbert: *"A real brother would never have abandoned his blood in need, right? He wouldn't have betrayed . . . Astrid? Think, sister! Could you ever betray me?"*

"Me . . . me . . . Me . . . ever . . ." Astrid repeated drunkenly, just as she had that night.

The Bold One, through and through. *"Me, mine, the most precious daughter, the most important, the most valuable."*

"Damn you, Bold One!" Astrid howled, lifting her head.

Everything grew darker as the wind hit her face. Waves rolled under her ship.

"My storm is coming!" she wanted to shout, but all that emerged was an old woman's hoarse whisper. *"Salty Sister,"* she called to the mast of her vessel, and spoke as if the Bold One was there: "Beloved. Sharp. So good. So bad."

She stood up, led by impulse, and held on to the mast. The waves were surging onto the deck; the water already reached her knees.

I want to die standing up, she thought, and saw her sister in her mind's eye again. With Olav beside her. They had both said the same thing to her: *"Astrid, please, get baptized, because life after death without you will be unbearable."*

"Ha!" she screamed, and a gust of wind almost threw her into the water and overturned her ship. "That's the only thing I never did for you! The only one! And the only one of my wishes that has ever come true is the storm that will kill me!"

And then she began to laugh, without knowing why. She laughed as the waves broke over the ship's gunwales and tossed it around. Astrid let go of the mast.

Nothing can be kept by force, she thought, and although her lungs filled with the freezing, salty water, she still wanted to laugh. She heard thunder somewhere in the distance.

Perun has struck the Baltic Sea! She heard Dalwin's voice in her mind, and she saw him reaching out for her. *I knew it would be you, honey, because I saw the empty wine jug fall in, and I knew you'd follow it. And what do I hear? My Astrid, laughing under the waves, laughing at everyone . . .*

And with everyone, she replied, embracing him.

55

RUSSIA

Bolesław led his army to Kiev, trying not to think about Predsława. He'd just gotten married. He had made peace with Henry. He'd signed an excellent, triumphant peace agreement that he had dictated, and which had been sealed by his marriage to Oda. She had the same name as their stepmother, the one the Bold One called the Duchess Icicle. Oda was young and pretty, and the daughter of his friend, Margrave Eckard of Meissen. This war that had lasted for the past sixteen years had begun with his murder, and now it had ended with Bolesław's marriage to Eckard's daughter.

After a horrific defeat, Henry had sent messengers to offer peace. He'd tried to convince Bolesław to go to Magdeburg, but he soon set aside his imperial pride and agreed to negotiate at the place of Bolesław's choosing. Budziszyn. The emperor had sent those for whom peace was most important; Bolesław's son-in-law Herman, margrave of Meissen; the Saxon lord Theodore; Archbishop Geron of Magdeburg; and Bishop Arnulf.

The emperor had been left with no choice but to give Bolesław what he wanted: Milsko and Łużyce. Not to rule them as Henry's vassal, but to rule them as their duke. They were parts of Poland now. Henry had also given him a company of heavy cavalry to help him on his journey to Russia, just like he'd done five years earlier, after they'd made peace in Merseburg. In doing so, Henry had buried his alliance with Knyaz Jarosław, an alliance which was intended to tear Poland apart, but which instead shattered both the knyaz and the emperor. Of course, there was no talk of Bolesław lending any men to Henry.

"Praise be to God," said Archbishop Geron afterward, "that this war which has destroyed so much has finally ended."

"Praise be to God"—Arnulf crossed himself—"that there will be no more alliances with the worshippers of fools to soil our reputations."

"Praise be to God," Theodore added, "that I won't have to hear any more cries from the widows and orphans left behind by our brave warriors."

Bolesław had promised to release some prisoners as a wedding gift. *Like my lord father had once done for Oda,* he'd thought, wondering what his Oda would be like.

She was pretty, polite, and nice. She wasn't afraid of him because she'd been raised almost in a cult of adoration for "Duke Bolz, Uncle Gunzelin's blood brother." The strangest thing was that, though a young, pretty girl should satisfy a man who hadn't had a wife in a long time, she couldn't fill the hole inside him. Bolesław didn't have anything against her. She smelled nice, moved gracefully, and even had her father's catlike eyes. But it turned out not to be enough.

He'd left the bedchamber with a sigh of relief and shouted to his men what he had so frequently roared to them recently:

"God is with us! To battle!"

This time, he commanded a truly enormous army. Ten Polish companies. Three thousand of the best trained warriors. Men whose caftans bore the imprints of their chain mail. Heavy cavalry forces, men who had fought beside him at the rivers Elbe, Saale, Mulde, Vltava, and Oder. The same soldiers who had been at Ashingdon with Wilkomir.

Henry had also loyally supplied him with a German company of three hundred heavy cavalry, led by Lord Zygfryd, Hodo's son. The same Hodo that Bolesław's father and uncle Czcibor had defeated at Cedynia. Bolesław's forces were joined by the Hungarians in Kraków: five hundred excellent riders, sent to him by King Stephen and led by Prince Honta. When they reached the river San, they found the Pechenegs waiting for them: wild, fast light infantry.

Bolesław tore across Poland like a hurricane in two weeks. His allies joined him gradually, but thanks to Zarad's brilliant planning, there were no delays; they joined him like wolves joining a pack, one by one. The last of them, with his tail between his legs, was Światopołk. Jarosław had chased him out of Brzeście. Bolesław met him outside the fortified borough of Wołyń on the banks of the river Bug.

Bolesław refused to exchange a single word with his son-in-law. He sent Daniła to speak to him instead.

"Knyaz Światopołk says . . ." Daniła began when he returned, but Bolesław interrupted him.

"He may or may not be a knyaz one day, but he certainly hasn't earned the title yet, other than by being born into it. Did you tell him that if a single hair falls from Sława's head . . ."

"Yes."

"Right, what else?"

"Światopołk claims that Jarosław's best troops are the Varangians. And the Russian cavalry: they're fast and fierce. He says that Jarosław called half of Russia to arms, but . . ."

". . . we both know that he's lying. Half of Russia is comprised of common-ers, we'd be able to hear the horses from here if he spoke the truth. Did you send scouts to the Bug's ford?"

"I did, my lord."

"And?"

"I only just sent them. I'll remind you that we've only just stopped to speak to Światopołk. But my scouts are fast, they know how much the duke despises being kept waiting . . ."

"Oh, Daniła, you're a smart man! The older I get, the less I like to wait, as if I was afraid that Lady Death will come for me too soon. I'm in such a hurry; the world is wide . . ."

"My duke will have time to conquer it if he has come this far in two weeks leading such an army . . . Emperor Henry would only just be heading to a council by the river Elbe right now, slowly, enjoying the view."

"That's why the emperor lost." Bolesław laughed.

The scouts reported that Jarosław set up camp by the river Bug and was waiting for the remainder of his forces to join him.

"Excellent! We won't wait," announced Bolesław. "God is with us! To battle!"

He didn't have to tell his men to mount their horses because most of them hadn't even had a chance to dismount yet. The wet sand on the riverbank was flying from under the horses' hooves within moments. He was riding Gold today. He had ridden Red to death; it had turned out that the stallion hadn't been as resilient as he'd expected. Gold snorted happily as he scented the wa-ter, and Bolesław rode into the shallows by the ford, allowing his horse to take a drink while he looked around.

Jarosław's camp stretched out on the opposite bank in either direction, as far as the eye could see. The knyaz's tent was marked by a flag with the gold trident. Bolesław turned and summoned Zarad. His dark-eyed friend still wore the same helm, after all these years, the one with the black horsehair flying from the top. It was dented and scratched, but it still brought him luck. Bolesław had no love of rich helms, ornately decorated swords, or gemstone-embroidered tunics either. He preferred leather, fur, and steel. The nomadic spirit was still alive within him; even his stirrups were more richly decorated than his necklace was. Apart from the golden cross he wore with the red ruby to symbolize the Savior's blood, he didn't wear any other jewelry unless he had to. It was enough to know he had chests full of gemstones waiting for him; there was no need for them to get in the way of warfare.

"Zarad, how much time before the last of our forces reaches the Bug?"

Zarad blew into the bone whistle that he always wore around his neck. Another whistle sounded in the distance a moment later.

"They're already here, Bolz. Right behind you."

"Ready?"

"If they're here then they must be."

"Excellent. Let us goad Russia into battle!" He urged Gold into the river before he'd even finished speaking.

Chaos broke out on the other side. A richly dressed man rode out to meet him.

Jarosław? he wondered.

"That's the governor of Kiev," said Daniła, appearing beside him.

"Hey, you!" the governor yelled. "We will shed your blood! We will pierce your belly! We will scratch out your intestines and feed them to the Bug fish!"

"Is he drunk?" Bolesław asked Daniła.

"He might be." The Russian nodded. "I don't know anyone who would dare insult you sober."

Bolesław turned to look at the four thousand soldiers standing behind him.

"The governor of Kiev has insulted me! Do you want to listen to him, or will you come with me to shove his insults back down his throat?"

"We are with you!" they roared.

"God is with us! To battle!"

"Wait for the Eagle's Wing!" Zarad shouted after him, but Bolesław didn't want to wait any longer.

"Tell me, Bolz, is it your daughter you want or the throne of Kiev?" He remembered the question his sister had asked him the day before she sailed to Roskilde.

"I want everything," he'd said. *"I always want everything."*

He saw the panic that took hold of his enemies, and heard the hurried orders: "Stand, stand! Mount your horses!"

"Daniła!" he yelled without turning around. Water reached Gold's belly. "What's this governor's name?"

"Błud!"

The stallion's hooves struck rock. He had reached the ford, and it wouldn't get any deeper than this. Gold was already emerging into shallower waters. Bolesław drew his sword. Another twenty paces and they would be on the bank. Out of the corner of his eye, he could see his guard, also known as the Eagle's Wing, catching up with him. He was first to reach the riverbank and Gold needed no more than a moment to shake the water off his tail.

"Błud!" yelled Bolesław. "Come on! I want to pierce your belly! You coward! Come and face me!"

He could hear his soldiers splashing out of the water behind him and the battle cry they were all repeating: "God is with us! To battle!"

He urged Gold forward to ride among the Russian troops, and he fell on them with his sword swinging. He didn't strike blindly; every blow landed with deadly accuracy. The royal guards had reached his side. They didn't get in his way to try to protect him. He hated it when someone did that. They rode on either side like an eagle's spread-out wings. The best of the best, the sons of his best men. Bjornar's, Zarad's, Ciechan's, Ostrowod's, Stojgniew's, Derwan's, and Borzywoj's. The boys who had been raised by the squad, who had been shooting arrows before they learned to talk. Today, they were men who knew all military commands in Polish, German, Czech, Hungarian, Russian, Danish, and English. They were warriors who could fight for three days and three nights without sleep, two without food. His undefeatable Eagle's Wing. Jaksa's sons were missing, but the Redarian wolf had become a monk, Father John, and he had no children. *Good,* thought Bolesław vengefully. *There is no need to breed the cursed.* Mieszko wasn't beside him either. He'd stayed behind to rule the country in his absence.

The first line of defense fell easily; they cut through it like an axe slicing through dry wood. He stood up in his stirrups.

"Ostry!" he yelled.

He heard the bone whistle from under the clamor of blades striking blades.

I can see him! Bolesław thought with relief as he watched Ostry split away from the fight and head toward the knyaz's tent. The light spear soared across the sky and pierced the trident flag. It collapsed onto the tent's sloping roof. The Russians roared. Ostry turned back and joined the main forces again as they broke through the second line which was mainly comprised of Jarosław's Varangians. Mercenary Vikings. He finally felt like he was fighting. He crossed swords with a tall, steel-covered man who bore the image of a tangled reptile on his shield. He protected himself with it well as if he knew where the next blow was going to fall.

I know that reptile! Bolesław realized as he swung his weapon. *It's the Yngling snake! Olav Tryggvason! Could it . . . ? No, he died at Øresund.*

He found a gap between the sword and the chain mail and pushed his blade into the man's flesh. His opponent screamed in pain before collapsing over his horse's neck. The helm slipped from his head, revealing long white hair that was swiftly reddening with his blood. Bolesław rode on. He saw the governor of Kiev fighting Bjornar.

"Give him here!" he roared. "I want to feed him to the fish! Come here, Błud!"

He took over from the redheaded Bjornar and cut the governor open from his shoulder to his waist.

"Knyaz . . ." the Russian hissed, refusing to accept this was the end for him.

"Throw him under the hooves!" ordered Bolesław, watching as the dead man fell from the saddle. "Gold, trample him!"

He twisted in the saddle and, led by some primal instinct, turned to the side. Just in time to avoid the axe of an approaching Varangian. Bolesław had just enough time to raise his shield. He heard the crunch of the blade strike the shield's iron side as Gold leaped toward another foe. Bolesław struck a broad-chested warrior wearing chain mail in the side and didn't even have time to pull out his sword. The man fell from the saddle. Bolesław let go of his weapon to avoid falling with him. He pulled out an axe that he had by his saddle, clutching the handle tightly because he could see another madman heading straight for him.

What a shame it is to ruin such a beautiful thing, he thought, looking at the gold-encrusted Russian helm.

And he swung his axe at it. The blade hit the nosepiece and slid down, cutting off the chin. His would-be attacker howled briefly before he fell to the ground.

Bolesław looked around. He could see the horses baring their teeth, trampling the wounded.

"Jarosław! Come to me! We will cross swords like a knyaz with a knyaz!" he roared, seeing the Russian troops melting away. "Jaroooosław! Jaroooosław, you coward!"

He spun his horse around, seeing that only bloodied corpses surrounded him. A few riderless horses raced around the battlefield, neighing wildly. He heard Zarad's whistle, and a moment later, his friend was beside him.

"We suffered only small losses. Jarosław has been vanquished. He took no more than two companies with him and he's fled."

"To Kiev?"

"No, northeast."

"Novgorod?"

"I expect so . . . We shattered his army and he cannot see a way to defend himself now. He's already given up Kiev, because who will defend it if the great knyaz himself is running away?"

"Leave a handful behind to collect our dead and the spoils. Reorganize the rest and let's go to Kiev."

Once more, there was no need for him to shout at anyone to mount their horses, because nobody had dismounted yet.

Three weeks later, they reached the river Dnieper. Gold had survived; he hadn't collapsed like his earlier horses.

I'll breed you, he thought, stroking Gold's neck. *I'll find you the most beautiful mare and I will ride your foals for the rest of my days.*

Kiev didn't fight. Daniła sent men everywhere to announce to the people that "great Knyaz Jarosław has fled to Novgorod in fear and plans to sail away." He remembered everything that Olav had told him about Kiev thirty years earlier. But he also remembered all of Daniła's stories, and those he heard from the merchants and Bruno of Querfurt. Despite all that, though, he was still awestruck by the city's splendor. Its beauty was greater than words could convey.

"My lord! Great duke!" a monk with a white beard wearing a gold ceremonial cloak called to him. He was standing in the gates with an icon of Christ in his hands, using it to shield his head.

"You speak to Bolesław, duke of Poland, monk!" Zarad informed him.

"Duke Bolesław! Draw your sword and hit the gates of Kiev. I'm telling you the city won't defend itself, but I'm also telling you that you will conquer it if you hit the gates."

They would prefer to be a virgin who defends herself than a wanton woman who spreads her legs, thought Bolesław, but he did as the monk asked.

He drew his sword and touched it to the carved archway. Gold neighed.

"Take these off!" Bolesław pointed the tip of his sword at the flags bearing the golden trident which hung on either side of the gate.

His flagbearers were already passing his own flags forward. He watched as the Piast eagle was hoisted up to fly over the city.

"Where is Knyaz Jarosław?" he asked.

"He's not in Kiev," said the monk. "He went to fight with you and he never came back. He's abandoned Kiev, abandoned us!"

"And who are you?"

"Anastazy of the Orthodox Church, the provost of the metropolitan cathedral."

"Anastazy, lead the way!"

The priest started to sing a song as he walked ahead of them. As soon as they emerged from the archway, monks dressed in black joined them. Each one carried an icon or a candle. They sang the same Greek psalm. He wished that Mieszko was with him. At least his son would have understood the words.

Gold lifted his knees high as he walked. He adjusted his speed to match the monks who led them. Bolesław looked around greedily, wanting to absorb all the sights around him. All the houses were wooden, piled on top of one another, the boundaries between them blurring. He saw the round, gold roofs of Orthodox churches all around, and bells rang out from every one of them. He couldn't count them all, he stopped after he'd reached one hundred. The city filled with their sound. They passed a square, a second, a third.

"There are eight in total," whispered Daniła.

Men, women, and children all peered out at him from alleys. Some fell to his horse's hooves, as was the eastern custom, while others only bowed as he rode past. He looked back and saw that they didn't rise from their bows until his entire army had ridden by.

They finally reached the royal manor. It was enormous and carved in such intricate detail that it looked like lace. It was decorated with cloisters and supported by stilts. Richly dressed servants had placed fabrics threaded with gold on the ground before his horse's hooves as soon as he rode into the yard.

Gold has walked over gold, he thought.

A procession of women waited for him. He looked over them and didn't see either his daughter or the beautiful blue-eyed Predsława. Anastazy stopped in front of him.

"The most noble women of Russia are here to greet you. Jarosław's wife Anne, his stepmother Allogia, and his half sisters."

"Where is my daughter?" he yelled. "Where is my Sława?"

He felt empty.

The eldest woman stepped forward. Allogia. Her slanting dark eyes gleamed under a sable hat. Golden necklaces with half-moon pendants hung from her temples. The aged lady bowed to him and the servants helped her stand up straight once more.

"Duke, great duke," she murmured melodically. "Jarosław keeps Sława with him at all times. He won't harm her. She travels in a golden wagon; no hair on her head will be harmed. But he will not give her up. He keeps her close because he knows she is the one you've come here for."

"I want Sława!" His voice echoed off the wooden cloisters.

"Accept Predsława from us," Allogia sang out. "My daughter by Vladimir. My beautiful daughter."

The door opposite him opened and there she was. The girl in the dress the color of moss and ferns. She wasn't a child, she was a women in her bloom. She had gemstones in her golden hair, and wore a green dress now, too, darker at the bottom than at the top. She bowed to him, spreading her arms wide.

"Predsława . . ." he whispered.

"Jarosław's sister, my daughter by Vladimir," Allogia introduced her.

Predsława danced off the steps and into the yard. She stopped by Gold's head and bowed again. When she straightened her back, she looked directly at him.

"If the great duke prefers one of my younger sisters," she said in a voice that pierced him to the core, "he can choose any one he likes. I stand before him because I know that the great duke asked Jarosław for my hand in marriage. I will not deny him. I give myself to him. Jarosław isn't here; he has fled from your might, your sword, and your army."

Christ! thought Bolesław. *I've married Oda!*

He leaped down from Gold's back after so many days of battles, galloping, and dirt. He took Predsława's hand and said:

"Lead on, girl."

She took him to her alcove. His hobnailed boots touched the soft furs strewn on the floor. Her small fingers helped him take off his helm, chain mail, belt, leather caftan, and shirt.

"Would my great duke like some wine from far-off kingdoms?" she asked. "Or Russian mead?"

"No," he whispered. "Girl of my dreams, all I want is you."

And he took her as if he were still riding Gold into the Bug. As if he were breaking through enemy lines. He defeated row upon row of troops and rode through Kiev's carved gates. Predsława gave him her virgin blood with a sigh, as if she were relieved. She wrapped her white arms around him, overwhelming him with the fragrance of the east. In taking her, he felt that he had taken Kiev completely.

"Russia is mine!" he yelled as he came.

"And I'm yours," moaned Predsława.

56

ENGLAND

Świętosława needed to feel clean after the bloody Christmas feast. Her son found solace in the Benedictine abbey in Canterbury, but women were not allowed inside, so she couldn't go with him.

"We have many beautiful churches, my lady," Godwin said, keeping her company. "I'm sure you'll like Westminster Abbey."

She grimaced.

"Maybe the abbeys of the pious abbesses?" he suggested, and she felt she was growing tired with his politeness. She didn't think that a visit to an abbey was going to help her. But an unexpected visit from the Jomsviking, now the earl of Essex, brightened her mood considerably.

"Jorun says that you feel unwell, my lady," Thorkel said bluntly.

"Because he's so familiar with the concept of a soul," she snorted.

"Do you know what your husband used to say?" Jorun asked her.

"Which one?" she retorted.

"She's not that bad if she still stings back," observed Wilczan.

"Sven used to say that the best cure for sadness is a deck under your feet," Jorun continued. "He felt all choked up in London . . ."

"Because he drank too much," she pointed out before asking: "So where are we going?"

Jorun and Thorkel exchanged a glance before answering in unison:

"Bamburgh."

They took *Nidhog*, Thorkel's ship. The bald Jomsviking stood at the helm himself. Dusza lifted her head and sniffed the air, and once they reached the North Sea, Świętosława did what she'd been dreaming of doing: she slipped the pins from her hair and let it loose in the wind. Jorun stood behind her.

"Sven did the same thing. I could never understand what went wrong between you. You were made for one another. You and him."

"I never loved him," she said honestly. "But today, when I look at Cnut, I respect him."

"That's good, too. Though, to be honest, Cnut is your son."

"I didn't make him alone."

"Maybe if Sven had shown you more . . ."

"Drop it, Jorun. You're a good friend." She placed a hand on his veiny forearm.

He took her hand and they sailed on, staring at the waves.

Bamburgh had stood on a rocky outcrop for years. The waves broke over it furiously. They approached at high tide. The haughty fortress reached up into the gloomy, rainy sky, constantly buffeted by the wind. Świętosława's dress was drenched by the time they'd arrived. Thorkel walked on her right, Jorun on her left, while Ragn and Uddorm followed with Wilczan.

"The two kings rode up these stairs and into the castle hall," said Jorun hoarsely. "Olav and Sven. The wall has been fixed"—he waved an arm at the patched wall—"but the night we took Bamburgh, there was a gaping hole here instead of stone. And they sat on their tall chairs, rested their feet on the bench, and drank, staring out to sea."

Świętosława's heart beat wildly when Jorun found the two thrones. She sat down on one of them. She let Dusza off her leash, and the lynx ran around the room, smelling all the corners. Wilczan started a fire.

"We all got drunk," Jorun continued. "Olav's right-hand man Varin and I played comparisons. The drunk Varin shouted: *'My dear king has hair like pure silver, while yours like common bronze.'* The warriors chanted: *'Sil-ver! Bronze!'* And I said that can be described better, but I don't remember what I came up with. But I know the men were shouting: *'Fla-ming ice! Fla-ming ice!'*"

He doesn't know, thought Świętosława. *Jorun doesn't know anything. He's lost in his memories.*

"That was an excellent plan, my lady," said Thorkel, sitting down beside her.

"But it wouldn't have worked without you. Or Jarl Eric. Or Godwin, or Lyfing, or Ethelnoth," she said honestly.

After the execution of Streona and his men, they had taken over his network of spies and destroyed it. Cnut hadn't named a new earl of Mercia to replace Streona. Instead, he'd divided Mercia between a few different people, English and Danish alike. He rewarded his loyal helmsman Hrani and Jarl Thorgils's son Eilif. By keeping Eilif close, he kept his father in check. He gave part of Mercia to Leofwin and Leofric, Northman's father and brother respectively.

"By dividing the power between men you'll make it impossible for another Streona to emerge," said Thorkel.

"Are you afraid of losing your influence?" Jorun teased him. "That your Essex will be the next in line to be cut up into pieces?"

Thorkel shrugged.

"Do I look like I'm scared?" He turned to Świętosława and said: "Getting Emma was a stroke of brilliance."

"I know." She smiled.

"Cnut is wiser than Sven was when he went to claim you for his wife," the Jomsviking said.

"Emma is not the Bold Lady," Jorun interjected, taking out a skin of mead.

"Are you trying to insult me?" she asked, reaching out to take a drink.

"No." He took a sip before handing it to her.

Thorkel laughed and said:

"Emma gave Cnut the archbishops Wulfstan and Lyfing as part of her dowry."

"That's true," Świętosława agreed. "Lyfing worked with my son, but he's only started working for my son since the day of the coronation and the wedding. And she was the one who broke through Wulfstan's mistrust and convinced the old stubborn man to create a code of law for King Cnut. But you, Thorkel, are the one who created a martyr!" Świętosława laughed.

"I didn't want his death," the Jomsviking replied glumly. "Believe it or not, but I did everything I could to stop Archbishop Aelfheah's murder."

Jorun snorted disbelievingly.

"The most important thing is that thanks to Godwin, Ethelnoth, and Lyfing, we've managed to take the martyr's bones out of London. Bishop Elfwig protested, of course, as did the people, but the relics are already in Canterbury."

"Old Elfwig will lose much of his power without the bones." Jorun shrugged.

"It's a good thing you're here to advise your son," said Thorkel. "Recognizing Aelfheah as a saint has shown the king to be a man who values the blood that was spilled before he took the throne."

"Blood spilled by your men," Jorun pointed out. "Blood which almost cost Sven his life!"

"Give it a rest," she interrupted. "Let the one who is without sin be the first to cast a stone."

"At whom?" they both asked.

The lynx appeared at her side.

"We've replaced the traitors with our own," she said. "We've destroyed Streona's web. Let's be good to one another, because we cannot build a kingdom on foundations of mistrust."

She knew that if it weren't for Thorkel and his Predatory Shoal, they would never have taken England. Jarl Eric of Lade may have been just as strong, but it was the Jomsviking's experience and contacts among the nobility that had won them the war. Thorkel and Jorun both sat in silence, offended.

She looked around the empty castle hall.

"I knew one holy martyr," she said after a moment, thinking about Bruno of Querfurt. "They carry light within them."

"Before death or afterward?" Jorun asked, trying to provoke her.

She didn't reply. Thorkel broke the silence:

"I also saw a martyr before he died. And just like you, I saw the radiance beaming from him. But it wasn't Aelfheah. I mean Olav Tryggvason."

Świętosława's heartbeat quickened, but she didn't say anything. Jorun didn't either, handing Thorkel the mead instead. The Jomsviking drank and continued:

"When he sailed into Øresund, I thought that he must want to play hnefatafl. It was foolish because although the king's defenders can win the board game, they have no chance when they are faced with so many enemies. But he didn't know that my brother Sigvald, the jarl of Jomsborg, would betray him. I didn't either. I thought I was sailing to fight beside Olav. When Sig told us to stab him in the back, I was against it. And then I saw the Lady of Wolin's vessel."

"The *Salty Sister*?" she asked.

"Yes. Sigvald said it was an enemy ship, and I realized that he and his wife were fighting for opposing sides. But I didn't let my men attack the *Salty Sister*."

"Why did Sigvald betray him?" She asked the question that had haunted her for so many years.

"I don't know." The Jomsviking shook his head. "My brother always wanted to be the most important one. He wanted to control everything. Maybe he thought this was the way in which he could decide who won the Battle of the Three Kings?" Thorkel sighed heavily. "Your father made a mistake when he married Astrid and Sigvald. Your sister was special, and she could never have loved a man who'd been defeated."

"You loved her," she realized.

"I still do," he said, blushing. "That's why I serve you."

"Couldn't you have told her?" she reprimanded him.

"I didn't dare. Jorun, give me that mead!" he demanded angrily.

Świętosława felt as if she were standing in front of a Roman mosaic in one of the rooms of the London castle. As if she were looking at the colorful plates that someone else had arranged into a pattern many years before. Some of them had fallen off, leaving empty gray spaces behind. She was beginning to fill the gaps after having heard Thorkel's story.

"What does *Nidhog* mean?" she asked.

"*Biting Fear*. The snake eats the bodies of the dead." He drank some mead. "The second death, and the final one. There is nothing left afterward. Emptiness lurking in the depths."

"Give me back my mead!" Jorun demanded.

* * *

A storm caught them on their way back from Bamburgh. Wilczan begged her to take shelter in the tent that had been pitched for her between the gunwales.

"Absolutely not," she said, holding on to the bow. "Let the seas take me!"

Wilczan didn't wait for that to happen. He forced her away from the gunwale and dragged her into the tent. The last thing she heard was Thorkel's order:

"Put down the mast!"

After that, all she could hear was the furious roar of the waves.

The water was calm by the morning. She stood at the bow, wet and cold, feeling as if she was nobody. Nothing. But when the sun came out from behind the leaden clouds, she lifted up her face to it so the rays could dry the salt water from her.

"My lady!" Wilczan shouted. "Did you see that?"

She rubbed her eyes.

Far away in the distance, an enormous lead-colored body rose from the sea.

"A whale!" Thorkel yelled.

She wanted to shout "Let's go after it!" but she realized it was an incredibly foolish idea.

Grow up, she told herself. *You're about to have another grandchild.*

The memory of the whale stayed with her when they returned to London.

She went to see her daughter-in-law.

"How are you feeling, Emma? They say you will have the child by Easter."

"Archbishop Lyfing spends every day praying for a royal son," the queen said with a smile. "I have to feel well to avoid calling into question the strength of his prayers."

"What about Wulfstan?" she asked after the archbishop of York.

"Oh, he has no time to spend lying down. He's working with Cnut on a new code of law. My husband would like to announce it as quickly as possible, probably before the child is born."

"I have a present for you, Emma," said Świętosława. "I bought a pair of hunting falcons from Iceland."

"Falcons?" Emma looked surprised.

"You'll have to regain your strength as quickly as possible once you give birth. Riding will be good for you. And my son has never hunted with falcons before." She winked.

"Me either," Emma admitted. "Will you teach me before I teach Cnut?"

"Of course," promised Świętosława, and she walked out.

She sat alone on the throne that evening, with Dusza at her side, staring into the fire.

The kingdom of England under my son's rule is like a fallow field on which its master has just arrived. It's starting to bloom, she thought. *It's such a beautiful thing to see as I begin to wither.*

"Skuli!" she called the bard. "You can recite it now."

The bard choked on his own spit and had to cough to catch his breath before he began:

Sigrid Proud, Sigrid Ruthless,
to whose bright home
suitors doggedly come,
from the rocky borders along a swampy path . . .

"Not that, you fool. I've grown out of such bloody tales by now. You said you had written a poem about England's throne."

"Forgive me, my lady." The bard blushed. "But you always keep saying you don't want to hear it."

"Well, I do now." She closed her eyes.

Now that the difficult battles we have fought are ended,
we can settle, my lady, in beautiful London.

When he'd finished, she went to her chamber and ordered Ylva to take out Astrid's final gift. She looked at it for a long time before her fingers closed over it, clutching it so tightly it bit into the skin of her palm.

ENGLAND

Duduc waited for the congregation to leave Saint Brigid's after the Easter mass and walk home to have their own simple suppers. The holy Paschal Triduum had begun; it was the twenty-third since he'd become a priest. He remembered every one.

The holiest days of the year, he thought. *The time of your death and resurrection, my Lord, and I'm forced to spend it among these baaing sheep.*

He knew that the Lord was the shepherd and his congregation comprised his lambs, but what did that matter when he felt no spiritual bond with any of them? He was lonely here, nobody wanted to share in the secrets of God. His sheep all wanted to confess their sins and be forgiven, and be given as light a penance as possible . . .

"With God, go with God, Anna." He hurried the last of the women and walked out into the little square outside the church. He dragged his cane along the mosaic on the pavement. *It's crumbling,* he thought with distaste.

"I'll just take some water," the woman squeaked, taking a jug out from under her cloak.

"Why?" he muttered.

"Not for me," the woman said, embarrassed. "For my daughter . . ."

Better donate something for the announcement, he thought, but aloud he said only:

"Take as much water as you want. Let Saint Brigid guide you." He made the sign of the cross after Anna as she scuttled away.

He inhaled the cool evening air.

He only had one eye, and the one he had left didn't see well at all, but his hearing was excellent. And he heard someone jump down from the wall which surrounded the church.

"Who's there?" he asked reluctantly. So long as it wasn't someone wanting a confession.

"A pilgrim," a voice answered him, and a tall, thin, broad-shouldered man emerged from the twilight. A hood shaded his face.

"Oh, it's you." Duduc nodded. "You've been sitting on the wall many a day now . . . Do you know you're sitting on old tombstones?"

"It's a good thing I'm not sitting in a grave," the pilgrim replied hoarsely, pushing back his hood. "I'm drawn to this place," he said, running a veiny hand over his bald head.

"Have you traveled far?"

"Yes, Father. I've been to the Holy Land."

Duduc felt the stirrings of curiosity.

"Today is Great Thursday," he observed.

"Yes. The eve of the Last Supper." The newcomer nodded.

"Then please accept my invitation. Let us eat a simple meal together like our Master once did."

"I will accept anything the Lord places in front of me," the pilgrim replied, and he may even have smiled, but the priest couldn't be certain of that.

Duduc walked with difficulty, dragging his feet as he led his guest to his house behind the church.

"What's your name?" he asked as he started the fire.

"The Arabs called me Ghareeb. It means Stranger."

"Sit down, Ghareeb." He indicated a place at the table.

Two goblets and a loaf of bread lay on the wooden slab.

"We eat with the grace of our Lord, modestly like he did with his apostles," croaked Duduc.

"With His will for ever and ever. Amen."

They broke the bread and drank the wine.

"Where are you from, Duduc?" Stranger asked.

"From nowhere." His host coughed and wiped the sticky crumbs from his lips. "From Viken in Norway. I was there many years ago when the mad King Olav Tryggvason baptized the country. That's when I learned the Word of God. The king went north and I sailed to England to learn more after I was enlightened by my baptism . . . Ah, youth! I was interested in everything. The Scriptures . . . I wanted to learn the Scriptures more than anything. The monks of Canterbury took me in. Oh, I can tell you, Ghareeb, they used to tell me I was talented, that I was a quick study. And then they sent me to filthy London." He chuckled. "I took over the church of Saint Brigid and here I am leading the souls like a herd of foolish sheep. Do you know something, pilgrim? I sometimes miss the bloody days of Olav Tryggvason. Baptism from a sword. Fire from a spark. God's anger and Hell with which the king frightened us. There was power in that. But now? I tell the congregation here about the spiritual union of Brigid and Patrick, about how those two blessed souls lived to serve God, and what do they do? Stand to take some water from the spring as if that will solve all their problems. The seamstresses betray their husbands. The sailors betray their wives. The bakers cheat with the flour they use, and the cobblers lower the quality of iron. Each one of them negotiates like a merchant to ensure their penance isn't too high. God, what boredom!"

"The Lord challenges us," the Stranger replied.

"Tomorrow, as He has done for almost a thousand years," Duduc croaked, "our Lord will die on the cross. Tell me, pilgrim, what does the Holy Land look like? Is it the miracle of the world that so many say it is?"

"No, Duduc. The Holy Land looks like any other."

Duduc coughed, feeling fearful, and asked:

"Are you saying that what we believe in isn't even real?"

"That's not what I said." The guest shook his head. "I went to Jerusalem a year after Caliph Al-Hakim bi-Amr Allah destroyed the temple that had been built on Skull Hill. I'm only saying that when I got there, the temple was a ruin, just like London was three years ago. But what it looks like isn't important. All that matters is what we see under the ruins."

"Amen." Duduc coughed again, and raised his goblet. "Let's celebrate the Lord's Last Supper as modestly as it has been described in Scripture. You're no Judas, are you?" He laughed.

"Even if I were, the Lord has still given me a seat at your table."

57

ENGLAND

Cnut invited nobles from the entire kingdom to attend the great gathering in Oxford. Wulfstan, the archbishop of York, stood at his side.

"Archbishops and bishops! My lords, the time has come for the final resolution."

They all looked at each other uncertainly.

Most of them don't know what I'm about to say, he thought. *I've only confided in the ones I'd trust with my life.*

"The beautiful Denmark from which I come, and the beautiful England which I now rule with God's grace, should ensure there is peace between them. The time for war and revolt is over. The great army with which I arrived on England's shores three years ago should go home."

Joyful mutters answered his announcement.

Armies may win wars, but they don't do well in times of peace, he thought, looking around at his old and new chieftains alike. *Brave warriors get bored and drink too much, starting brawls and fights too easily. Some of them have started families here and begun to lead the peaceful lives of commoners, but not all.* He took a deep breath and continued:

"I suggest that the kingdom pays the Danish army one last danegeld. Then, I will keep only my personal guard with me, and send everyone else back home. My presence here as your king will ensure they will not return to wage war on England. I will be its guarantor."

They all looked baffled. The English nobles muttered angrily about the danegeld, but he knew his army wouldn't leave without it. His men had not been allowed to plunder and rob anywhere since he was named king.

"Think of it as one final gift," the archbishop suggested.

It worked. Seventy-two thousand pounds of silver. The greatest danegeld history had ever seen.

"I suppose we must make the men feel it's enough to make parting with the beautiful England worthwhile," Godwin observed tactfully, then asked in a whisper: "How many ships comprise the personal guard that remains with our king?"

"Forty." Cnut smiled.

Godwin blinked. That had been the size of the fleet with which Thorkel had begun his invasions before he'd put together the Predatory Shoal that was fifty ships strong.

"Considering that my king sailed to England at the head of one hundred and ninety ships," Godwin observed, tactful as ever, "that is indeed merely a personal guard."

"I see that a great future awaits you at court, my dear Godwin." Cnut laughed.

He raised a toast to the soldiers' safe journey home to Denmark, Norway, and Sweden.

"The time of war may be over, but it is the king's duty not only to guarantee peace but also to enforce a law which will allow all of his subjects to look to the future. On mine and Queen Emma's request, the noble Wulfstan, archbishop of York, has prepared a new codex of the law which we wish to announce today."

Wulfstan appeared and began to read out the codex with a gravity befitting the situation.

Emma, reassured by the child that was growing in her belly, had helped Cnut, ensuring that Wulfstan linked Cnut with the good king Edgar in the codex, creating the impression of continuity between the two kings. He was thus presented as preserving what had been best about the past to create an even better future.

How many years will I have to spend undoing their perception of me as a usurper? he thought, looking around as Wulfstan spoke.

". . . we ban the sale of Christian prisoners into slavery because human life should not be a source of profit for anyone . . ."

Their marriage could have turned out a thousand different ways. He knew that Emma was still comparing herself to Elfgifu, that she kept asking about her younger rival.

Is she still a rival though? wondered Cnut. *I haven't seen Elfgifu since the day I told her I was going to marry Emma. But I will not abandon my sons. I will keep my word and not name them my heirs if Emma has a son. But will she?*

That question haunted him more and more, because while Emma felt wonderful in the first days of her pregnancy and accompanied him wherever he went, recently he had grown more doubtful. She was weak and didn't feel well, leaving her alcove less and less frequently. She couldn't come to Oxford with him. Sometimes, during the sleepless nights he spent staring at the dark, gleaming current of the Thames, he thought that God had already given him so much that His grace might end at any moment. By marrying Emma, he had sacrificed Sven and Harald's fates in the name of an unborn child. He flinched.

". . . God, in giving the crown and power, surrounds King Cnut I of England with his grace and protection." Wulfstan had almost finished. "And this grace flows through the king to the entire kingdom and all his subjects. Amen."

"Do you want to uphold these laws?" he asked.

"We do!"

"Then swear fealty to the king and let us accept this codex," Archbishop Wulfstan called out.

As Cnut was leaving Oxford with his household the next day, heading back to Westminster, Godwin, holding his stirrup steady, said:

"My lord, I admired you on the battlefield at Ashingdon, even though we fought on opposing sides that day. I was proud of you when you avenged King Edmund's death. But yesterday, when you announced that the king is beginning to rebuild the kingdom instead of just conquering it, I gave you my heart and soul. I have never felt so enlightened, my king."

"Ride beside me, friend," replied Cnut, and waited for Godwin to mount his horse.

Cnut had two favorite places in England: Canterbury and Winchester. He prayed in Canterbury, at Saint Augustine's Abbey as well as at the cathedral, before he went to Oxford to make his announcements. The monastery gave him strength. Now that the codex had been accepted, now that he had shown the people that he wanted to be Cnut the Just, he wanted to thank God in the cathedral at Winchester, at Saint Swithun's tomb.

When he stood by it and looked at the two tall towers of Old Minster as they rose toward the leaden sky, he thought: God's Keep. And then he thought of the wooden temple in Roskilde.

He realized that about fifty Danish churches would fit inside the English cathedral.

"My king!" his confessor Ethelnoth greeted him. "Congratulations!"

"I wouldn't have managed it if it hadn't been for Wulfstan."

"But the archbishop is on your side. They say that you're sending him to Rome. Are you?"

"Rumors!" Cnut laughed. "They're mixing up the archbishops. Lyfing will go. Do you know that every time I stand at this cathedral, Ethelnoth, I feel my legs go weak in the presence of God's work?"

"It was built by men," the confessor replied quietly.

"But they were inspired by a desire to worship the Lord. Odin and Thor, Perun and Trzygłów, the gods of my grandfathers, never pushed their followers to build such splendid temples."

"After the time of the gods of war has come the time for the God of peace." Ethelnoth bowed as he pushed open the cathedral's great doors.

They walked in silence, listening to the echoes of their own footsteps. Sunrays seeped in through the half-oval windows situated far above them. Dust motes spun in the air. The candles flickering in great iron candelabras gave less light than the radiance which streamed in from above.

They walked toward Saint Swithun's altar.

"My lord," whispered Ethelnoth, "did you know that the bishop ordered himself buried in front of the cathedral rather than inside it? Even after death he hadn't lost his humility and he wanted the faithful to trample his earthly body. When the cathedral was extended years later, his grave was moved, but his wishes were still fulfilled."

"Are you saying that we are standing on top of the saint's bones right now?"

"Yes."

Cnut felt a shiver run down his spine as he knelt on the cool stone floor.

Emma had told him that Saint Swithun had been a teacher to the old English kings. And now he was one of them.

"My Lord," he prayed in a whisper. "You have given me so much. Allow me now to give You what is the symbol of earthly kings. You redeemed us on the cross and You conquered death. I am not worthy of wearing gold if You won with thorns." He took off his crown as he spoke and placed it at the foot of the altar.

"Amen." Ethelnoth wiped away his tears and offered Cnut his arm to help him stand up.

"I will pay for a church to be built on the battlefield of Ashingdon," Cnut decided. "Not as a symbol of gratitude for our victory, but as a place in which people can pray for those they lost. Nothing as great as Winchester's treasure!"

He lifted his head. The wooden coffers, painted gold and red, had a dark gleam to them. The choristers began to arrive. The deacon began to sing in a high voice.

"The sext," said Ethelnoth as they stepped out of the shadows of the stone walls into the daylight. Cnut narrowed his eyes.

"The sun is out," he observed.

"My lord, my lord!" Godwin was hurrying toward them. "My lord! I bring good news! Queen Emma has given birth to a son!"

Cnut gasped and grabbed the light, slender Godwin and tall Ethelred and lifted them both up, spinning around.

"My God, your work is great," Ethelnoth groaned.

"What will you name your son, my lord?" Godwin asked.

He put them both down, thinking quickly. *I already have a Sven and a Harald . . .* "Harthacnut!"

ENGLAND

Świętosława, led either by instinct or by Dusza, walked to Saint Brigid's church, beyond the Roman wall and beside the river Fleet. She glanced at the spring and the crumbling wall built of old tombstones. The pilgrim monk wasn't there, but his bowl lay by the wall. Empty. The sun was hidden, too. Leaden clouds hung low above London, heavy with rain. She walked inside.

"Is anyone here?" she asked.

"That depends on who's asking," an old man's hoarse voice answered her. "I see fish merchants on Tuesdays and whores on Fridays."

"What about queens?" she asked mockingly.

"A sense of humor!" The old man coughed as he emerged from the shadows of the church. "Queens wouldn't come here; they go to the cathedrals and their bishops."

He was old and bent over at the waist. He leaned on a cane which he used to check that the way ahead of him was clear, though every step came with difficulty. A few strands of gray hair grew from his bald skull, and his one good eye was seeping pus. The skin had closed over the other one. He looked horrifying.

One-eyed like Odin. Perfect for me, she thought, tightening her grip on the leash. *And almost blind. He's got no idea who he's dealing with. Good.*

"Will you hear my confession, Father?" she asked.

"Has she examined her conscience?" he asked.

"Are you the only priest at Saint Brigid's?"

"Why, were you expecting someone better?" he replied provokingly.

"The wall outside is crumbling. It needs fixing," she said.

"The lady with a cat at her side has come to give me advice, has she?" His mouth twisted. "Maybe she'll leave a donation?"

"I will," she promised. "Please, Father, hear me."

"Don't think that I will lower your penance just because you'll pay me something. I'm a strict confessor."

"Good." She nodded.

The old man hobbled over to a bench by the wall. He sat down heavily, wiping the sweat from his forehead with his sleeve. She knelt by him and began.

"I confess that I always wanted to have more than I had, that I didn't understand the concept of boundaries. That I kept pushing the horizon farther and farther away . . ."

"Stop it, girl," the old man croaked. "Those aren't sins. Don't mock the Lord."

"But you order us to be humble . . ."

"Then confess to your pride, not your courage!" he shouted at her. "Don't mix up your sins or the Lord will think you're bragging."

"I've often walked blind. I had to make quick decisions in a wilderness of intrigue. I may have caused harm by making rash choices, but I was never motivated by vengeance, only by a desire to protect my son . . . Why are you silent?" she asked, worried.

"Because you sound like you're reading from a book, and I'm waiting for details. Sins, mistakes, lies . . . Hurry up before I fall asleep or this cough kills me."

"I hate my son's lover," she confessed. "Even though she's the mother of my grandsons. It bothers me that she hides behind her children as if her womb were holy and everything that comes out of it will be blessed. Young women only see themselves through the prism of their perky breasts . . ."

"Oh, says the one who was never young! He, he." The priest chuckled lewdly. "Born old straight away . . . You judge others quickly, don't you? A lover is a wicked thing to have. God requires a man and woman to swear loyalty to one another at His altar. But it isn't for you to judge, leave that to God. What else? Did you steal? Wish someone ill? Spit in your neighbor's milk?"

"No, Father, I didn't steal anything. And if I wished anyone ill, they deserved it."

"Oh, here we are! How wise. She knew herself who was good and who was evil. You need to confess to the sin of pride, cat lady."

"Very well, Father. I have felt proud more than once, and I have often been bold."

"Those are sins . . ." He coughed. "But as the songs say, it is a queen's son who should be silent and modest, not the mother."

Does he know me? she thought fearfully. *No, he can't.*

"There's something else, Father."

"Tell me."

How do I say it without being too direct but to ensure I'm still truthful? she wondered.

"I wished someone dead."

"Who?"

"Two innocent boys."

"Did they steal your goat? Beat up your child?"

They were born at the wrong time. She thought about both of Edmund's sons, sent away from England. And about the two swords she'd given Wilkomir so he would pass them along with the children. She knew that both Olof and Bolesław would understand the iron message. It weighed down her conscience like a stone. She remembered every day that she'd condemned those children to death.

"Why doesn't she speak?" the priest urged her.

"A mother can do much for her son," she replied evasively.

"But don't forget, woman, that it was the Son who died on the cross while the Mother looked on. You need to know your place!"

"I do, Father," she whispered.

And that's why I did it.

"If you did something bad for the good of your son, who knows, maybe God will forgive you?" he croaked.

"And you?" she snorted. "Can't you absolve me in His stead?"

"I can." He shrugged. "The Lord on the cross forgave the rogue because he repented. That's how the rogue became the first saint. The Lord's mercy is infinite."

He made the sign of the cross in the air.

"What about my penance?" she asked. "You said you were a strict confessor."

"Oh, yes. It's a good thing you reminded me, though you might regret it." He nodded and chuckled. "From this moment onward, cast aside anything that was more important to you than God."

"I swear I will," she whispered as she crossed herself.

The priest raised an old hand, covered with liver spots. At first, she didn't understand, but when he shoved it in her face, she realized what he wanted. She kissed it.

"Thank you, Father."

He cleared his throat and said in a bored voice:

"Go and pray at the feet of Saint Brigid. The bride. Did you know that she and Saint Patrick shared a friendship so great that it was almost as if they shared a heart? All my congregation wants to do is drink water from the spring, but it doesn't seem to occur to them that love isn't just feeling each other up and having children. Love is God's mystical secret that the saints sometimes reveal to us. Souls like that only find each other once in a thousand years, no more . . ."

He'd fallen asleep mid-sentence.

She stood up, untied the pouch from her belt, and put it at Saint Brigid's altar. It would be enough to fix the wall, though her confessor was paying no attention to what she was leaving behind as he snored on the bench.

She walked out of the church. Dusza meowed. The leaden clouds had disappeared. A bright spring sun almost blinded her. She narrowed her eyes. When she opened them again, she saw something that made her start.

Souls like that only find each other once in a thousand years, no more, the old man croaked in her head.

He sat on the wall with his head covered by the hood. The disciple of the Light.

But she had just promised to abandon everything that had been more important to her than God, so she unfastened the brooch that Astrid had left her. The fish torn apart by two eagles. A drop of old blood dried on a silver scale. She kissed it one last time, thinking: *Lord, I am not worthy.* She dropped it into the pilgrim monk's wooden bowl.

"Go with God," she whispered.

"And you. Thanks be to God," the pilgrim replied.

THE NAVE OF KINGS

⚭

First there was darkness, and she thought it was eternal. Then, she heard hushed voices. Sighs. Sobs. A woman whispering a psalm. She started to cry and couldn't finish. Świętosława wanted to help her. She kept saying "amen, amen," but no sound left her lips.

The unfinished prayer bothered her, like a door that hadn't been properly closed. There was only darkness again, and beyond that, only chaos. And the light of a candle which was too bright, hurting her eyes. Part of her thought: *If I hadn't told them to place me on the throne to die and let them lay me out like a lady, I wouldn't be blinded by the candle now.*

But it was done now and could not be undone. She heard a song:

We go in darkness,
in darkness we go to the source of Your life.

She didn't know whether they were singing the song in this world or the next. The voices she heard were distorted, as if someone had placed wax in her ears.

Only desire is the light,
only desire is the light in the darkness, O Lord.

Finish it, she thought. *Just let me die. Come on, it's not like I can turn back now.* She felt angry with the living for meddling with death. They held on to her as if her life could belong to them.

And then she heard a lynx's howl. *My Dusza howls,* she thought, and the sound slammed the door to the world of the living. Darkness surrounded her. She sighed with relief. Darkness was better than hovering between two worlds. The lynx meowed restlessly.

"Are you here?" asked Świętosława.

The lynx touched her hand with a wet nose, and she began to walk forward slowly.

"Lady, Bold Lady . . ." The walls whispered in voices that she recognized, though something told her she shouldn't respond. She pressed her lips together, but she didn't cover her ears.

"Sigrid Storråda . . . the widow queen on the throne . . ."

"Have the fires been lit in the bathhouse?"

"Harald of Oppland and Wsiewołod of Russia are asking whether the fires in the bathhouse are burning!"

"I'm on fire!"

"This is to be a proper apology," Wsiewołod roared somewhere next to her ear.

"I died for the single hair that fell from your son's head . . ."

She lengthened her step and whispered without stopping:

"Eternal rest grant unto them, O Lord."

"You wanted to take over the web, but you had the Spider killed." Another voice chuckled unexpectedly.

"Eternal rest," she repeated firmly.

"Don't mock!" Streona snarled at her. "You sent me into eternal darkness."

"Mine . . . You'll be mine yet . . . I did everything for you, and how did you repay me? By stabbing me in the chest with lightning steel."

The hair on the back of her neck stood on end when she recognized Jarl Birger's voice.

"Mine . . ." he insisted. "I will rest only when you're by my side." His whisper chased her, until it changed, until she recognized her voice.

"Lie down. I want to show you what a queen's gratitude looks like."

She didn't walk any faster, but she shouted:

"Lead us not into temptation!"

"Finally, you're here. You're . . ." She heard the voice everywhere. Above her, below her, and from all sides.

I am a queen, and I will not be afraid, she told herself.

"May God be with you," she said, and Birger fell silent.

Is this Hell, or only its entrance hall? she wondered. *Or is it purgatory's front yard?*

She fell into water. She swam through a thick, cold liquid with Dusza snorting at her side. Something touched her. A drowned man appeared. Then another, and another. Men killed in battle, without their arms, with wounds left by spears.

"Loki stirred the waters of Øresund." A corpse vomited something as he spoke.

She realized that these must be the victims of the Battle of the Three Kings. She swallowed some of the water by accident and tried to spit it back out.

Don't drink from the river of the dead, she thought.

Enormous hands with peeling skin grasped her clothes with blue fingernails. She jerked away. There was a corpse full of arrows ahead of her. Slippery serpents oozed out of his skull where his eyes should have been.

Nidhog, she thought. *Biting Fear. The snake consuming the bodies of the dead.*

A headless body was chaotically slapping the water. His chain mail was rusty. Dusza snarled. Dark beads dripped from the tufts of hair at the ends of her ears. Świętosława felt as if something was choking her. She reached trembling hands to her lips and took out a coin. A denar with a cross on the other side. A new pile of bloated bodies was drifting toward her. She threw the coin over her shoulder without looking back. The river dried up and she and Dusza ran out onto dry land. Świętosława stood up and tried to squeeze the water out of her heavy cloak. She heard soft singing from afar. Two or three voices.

Light the fire that will never die in the darkness, O Lord,
light the fire that will never die in the darkness.

She saw lights up ahead. The lynx began to move toward them, trying to catch them as if she were a young cat. Where did they come from? Nowhere. They just leapt around the walls like sunlight streaming into a hut through a smoke hole. Świętosława walked toward the lights, feeling the wet material of her dress sticking to her legs. She realized that each light was a voice when she reached them. Not the singing she had heard a moment ago, but a prayer that chased away the shadows. There were many of them, their number growing all the time as new passionate voices joined the old ones from years ago.

Prayers are forever, she realized, and moved closer to one of them. She recognized the voice immediately.

"Lord Almighty. If the pleas of a sinner and traitor mean anything to you, then hear me. I pray for the immortal soul of Queen Sigrid Storråda. Save her, sweet Lord, from the fires of hell and lead her to the light that flows from Your Word. To eternal life and light. Amen."

The traitor Ion was praying for her. The same Ion that she had condemned to humiliation, to wearing a collar and a leash; the one she'd sent away to a monastery, forgiving him his sins years ago when she understood that it wasn't he who betrayed her but the Lord who had made him a Judas. Her anger evaporated.

She stood in the darkness, feeling the tears stream from her eyes. She wiped them away and when her eyelids lifted again, there was light.

Light the fire that will never die in the darkness, O Lord,

The whispering voices repeated the chorus for the last time and Świętosława began to move to the light. It grew brighter, as if it were trying to absorb her.

The traitor's prayer has led me out of purgatory, she thought gratefully.

Her dress and her cloak, both of which had been heavy with the waters from the river of the dead only moments before, were now dry. She stepped along stones that gleamed like polished marble. She heard her shoes click with every step, as clearly as Dusza's claws. The floor ended unexpectedly and Świętosława found herself at the edge of a cliff. She inhaled sharply, staring in awe.

She was inside a majestic tower. She looked down and saw the open nave of Winchester cathedral. A funeral was in progress. When she looked up, she saw different stories winding upward in all shades of glittering radiance. One above the other, and another, as if the building never ended. Silver and gold pulsed with light. Each one was another kingdom.

She could smell the incense from below and hear the choir sing the Litany of the Dead.

"Dusza! Should we go to the funeral?" she asked, and they began to descend.

She stopped at the top of Old Minster, in the cloisters, where a great column ended. The archbishop was performing the liturgy down below, singing a funeral song.

My God, my Eternal God,
Lord, have mercy upon her!
You, who are the Father of compassion,
show her grace in your goodness.

"Is that Lyfing?" She stared at the priest disbelievingly. "How his voice has improved since he met the pope in Rome! As clear as a bell." She shook her head in awe. "It seems the pope's blessing he brought back for Cnut has affected him, too." She saw her coffin and sighed with relief.

"Thank God, it's closed!"

A flag was wrapped around the lid. The Piast eagle clutching a dragon in its claws.

Why is it only now that I see how unsuitable that is? she wondered. *Like a barbarian who just flew over here to steal.* She felt embarrassed. She lifted her head and saw a glimmering figure on the other side of the tower, holding an archbishop's staff in his hand. *Aelfheah.* She sighed. *Lyfing's predecessor and the martyr who fell victim to Thorkel's army.*

Opposite her, Aelfheah was gesturing, pointing at the flag covering her coffin.

"What do you want me to do? Tear it apart?" she asked.

He shook his head and shrugged. She felt a cool breeze. The window behind her was open.

"My Lord!" she prayed. "Is remorse possible after death?"

Another gust of wind blew into the cathedral and lifted a corner of the flag on her coffin, folding it over so that it covered the dragon and only left the eagle visible.

What a good thing the Almighty has a sense of humor, she thought gratefully.

She saw Cnut.

"He's so beautiful, Dusza. He's no longer the Queen's Son. He's a king."

Fair-haired and without a crown since he'd left it at Swithun's altar. Emma stood beside him, holding his hand. He tightened his grip, his thumb working its way inside her palm.

"She's pregnant!" discovered Świętosława as she studied the queen's profile. "God, let it be a girl!" she hoped, though she suspected that she shouldn't want anything in the place she was in now.

I'd like a girl, Heidi Goat squalled in her memories.

She saw little Harthacnut in Godwin's arms. Harthacnut had one blue eye and one green eye. The boy twisted and waved to her. She blew him a kiss then hid herself.

They shouldn't see me at my own funeral, she thought.

Godwin turned around to see who Harthacnut was waving at. He nodded, polite as always. She saw tears shimmering in his eyes.

"You're a big boy," she told him off from up high. "Don't cry. Ah!" She held her breath, only now noticing Wilczan kneeling at her coffin with his sword bare in his hand.

And the chieftains. Jorun, standing up tall like a spear, with gray hair falling into his eyes. *He washed his hair!* Thorkel the Tall. Old Uddorm who was crying openly. Ragn of the Isles who kept wiping his eyes discreetly. Thorgils of Jelling who glanced around every now and then with a smirk.

"Be happy now if you want. One day you'll be swimming through the river of the dead and you never know who might grab your sleeve," she whispered.

The deacons singing the funeral song suddenly sounded off-key, and she thought that even after death, one had to exhibit some self-control.

"Especially after death!" Great Ulf warned her, appearing beside her.

"Forever," added Wilkomir, joining them.

She felt so happy to see them that she squealed like a child.

"Together again!"

"Be better in death than you were in life," Wilkomir said.

"Be the same. Don't change," demanded Great Ulf with a smile.

He still had his front tooth, though she'd never seen it when they'd been alive. His skull gleamed like a lake on a sunny day.

"Do you want to wait to see them bury you, or should we go?" he asked.

"Let's go!" she said, not knowing where they were headed.

They climbed the spiral staircase around the tower. She heard more singing. Drunken voices. The clash of weapons. Eric's loud voice and Sven's laughter.

"What's that?" she asked.

"Valhalla, my lady," Great Ulf replied.

They reached a stone platform and she saw an enormous manor with its doors flung wide open. Warriors trained together in the large yard, their chain mail gleaming, swords and axes flashing as they fought. Steel clanged against steel, but there was no blood. The manor's walls were lined with spears with smooth ash handles and glittering metal heads. The ceiling was constructed from golden shields. A feast for the fallen was in progress. Fitted black horns were blown as the mead flowed.

"Such things are only possible after death!" She laughed.

Eric Segersäll and Sven Forkbeard, two enemies, two husbands, bald and red, sat side by side, drinking and laughing together.

"Eric!" she yelled. "Sven!"

They didn't react, as if she were nothing but air.

"This isn't your afterlife, my lady. Don't force yourself where you're not wanted," Wilkomir told her.

"But Sven was baptized!" she protested.

"So?" Wilkomir snorted. "He'd have to have believed that the water actually washed his soul."

"Oh my!" she exclaimed, interrupting him.

Arnora, the tribal queen, with her silver hair braided, sat on Valhalla's throne with gemstones glittering in her brooches and necklaces. Her husbands drank to her health while she laughed so loudly that she drowned out the noise with which the berserkers burst into Valhalla. The bloodthirst had transformed them into lizards, wolves, bears, and wild dogs. A never-ending river of guests flowed through the doors. She saw Jomsvikings with the square wolf head on their shields. She saw the beautiful fair-haired Vali. Melkorka and Heidi Goat sat in the corner and drank mead, giggling madly. Heidi kept nudging Melkorka.

"Should we go on?" asked Great Ulf.

"Yes," she said, touched that she was seeing them all.

She skipped steps and suddenly felt the wind, as if a storm's wing had kicked the legs from under her. Wilkomir held her up.

"She can't see you," he warned her.

She saw her sister Astrid holding on to the helm of a ship. The sail was billowing in the wind and the ship tore through the waves. Her sister was drinking wine and laughing. Her beautiful hair had recovered its amber hue, and water streamed from the cloak around her shoulders. Her grandfather Dalwin was beside her, and an entire crew from Wolin. Leszko was leaning over to her, whispering something Świętosława couldn't hear.

She felt regret. She wished she could have met her sister again. But regret was replaced with relief when she realized that Astrid had found her place.

They walked on, and when she skipped another few steps she heard Dusza's voice.

"Finally!"

They fell into each other's arms.

"Tell me everything!" said Świętosława.

"Slow down," Dusza said, "we have eternity together."

Only now did she see the leash in Dusza's hand.

"Wrzask and Zgrzyt!" Świętosława exclaimed joyfully, tousling the two big heads.

Her female lynx walked over to them and sniffed them. Świętosława unclasped their leashes and all three leaped up the stairs.

"Will you let me take you to the home of the Piasts?" Dusza asked, grabbing her hand.

They walked up, passing through the forest mists. She could smell tree sap, old trees, and woodsmoke. She passed by Slavic temples hidden in the wetlands, Trzygłów's statues leered at her around corners while vilas, rusałkas, and vampires laughed, until finally the mist thinned, and they walked out into a glade.

Her mother greeted her in a heavenly blue palatium. Sweet Dobrawa wore a dark blue dress and an amber necklace. Silver temple rings framed her face. Świętosława bowed to her mother. An unborn child whimpered in Dobrawa's womb. She stroked it through her mother's dress.

"I couldn't carry it," she explained.

"Was it a girl or a boy?" asked Świętosława.

"How am I supposed to know if it was never born? Go up, daughter, your father is waiting for you." She pointed at a throne that stood nearby. "But don't be unkind to your stepmother!" she warned.

"She's here?" Świętosława asked with surprise but fell silent when she caught Wilkomir's warning glance.

Duke Mieszko sat on his throne with the hawk on his shoulder and Oda at his side.

Ice can be beautiful, too, thought Świętosława when she saw her, and they nodded to one another like highborn ladies.

She sat down at her father's feet. He touched her hair. His hand didn't feel warm.

"Children are their parents' challenge," he said.

"Was I yours?" she asked.

"I underestimated you," he admitted.

"Stop it, there was no emperor looking for a wife!"

He laughed.

"You did well, Bold One," he said after a moment. "Better than I'd hoped you would. I was afraid that you would lose everything because of that sharp tongue of yours, but instead you brought Piast blood to the nave of kings."

"Stop it, Father," she said again with a wave of her hand, unused to hearing compliments from him.

"No," he said sharply, and his dark eyes flashed. "I will speak, and you will hear me. At least listen to me in the afterlife. I didn't believe in God when I decided to convert. I knew why I chose it and I felt that I was doing the right thing. I gave the Lord conditions. *'Give me victory and a son.'* It wasn't faith, it was a transaction. The moment I was baptized, though, and His light filled me, I was shaken to my core. And then the Almighty gave me everything I wanted, as if He knew that I was a child who needed rewards as incentives. But on the day of my confirmation—some time passed between the two sacraments, you know—I was different, more mature. I believed then, and I wanted to enter the next circle of knowledge. That day"—he moved his fingers in the air as if he were trying to catch a shadow—"your mother was pregnant . . . I saw the candlelight flicker on the chapel wall and I thought the lights soared toward me like some bright fiery sign. A crown of flames. I was confirmed and God touched me with the tip of His finger. Dobrawa went into labor and you were born." Her father sighed. "Bolesław was born on the day we defeated Wichman. You were born on the day of the sacrament. He won his crown with his sword. You . . ."

"Got the crown because of the marriage you arranged."

"We both know that your path might have ended with Eric's death," he pointed out. "But you kept going."

"I did what you told me to do. I kept pushing the horizon away."

"You achieved what I could only dream of. You are an anointed queen. The first. Not my firstborn, but you. Do you see what's on your temples?" he snorted. "The sacred oil. The crown of flames I saw on the day you were born."

She touched her temples. After a moment, she said thoughtfully:

"My son was my greatest challenge, too. I thought that I knew everything, could do everything, but when I stood on the shores of England, I realized how wrong I'd been."

"You never made my mistakes though, daughter."

"How do you know? Were you watching me?"

He didn't answer. He just looked at her and smiled sadly.

"Go. They're waiting for you."

Dusza led her to a castle that resembled the cathedral in Canterbury. Dust motes swirled in the light. Silver-white doves flitted between the columns. The marble under her feet gave way to sandstone, and a few steps later she saw the colorful tapestry with a golden dragon of Wessex.

"This is the nave of the kings of England," whispered Dusza.

They stepped forward to meet her. Alfred, known as the Great, though he was short and slender. He wore a cloak that looked like the one Cnut wore during his coronation. Edward the Elder. Ethelweard, Athelstan with beautiful gray eyes, Edred, Edwin, Ethelred. Their queens were there, too. Elgiva, Elfida, Eadla, Edith, Elfgifu. Some with light hair, some with red. Tall and pale. Glittering with brooches and rings.

"English silver is the most beautiful in the world." Elgiva smiled at her.

"The queen already knows that." Ethelred winked at her. "Has Santaslaue come for her danegeld? Which one? The one we paid her husband Sven? Or her beloved Olav? Or perhaps the one her son Cnut took?"

"Leave her alone." Alfred the Great smiled. "Silver doesn't matter in the afterlife. The soul does. Where are your manners, great-great-grandson?"

"Forgive me, my lady," Ethelred apologized.

"There is nothing to forgive," she replied. "I struggle with them, too."

She noticed Edmund Ironside with a scarf tied around his neck. He nodded to her, just as he had done years ago on the island. She looked around for his sons fearfully.

"Don't search for the living among the dead," he said sternly. "Cnut kept his word. He avenged my death."

"Santaslaue," said Alfred the Great, "will you rest with us, Queen Mother?"

She looked beyond them to the place that had been left for her and saw an empty throne.

One day, Cnut will sit there, she thought, and turned to Dusza.

"Should I stay here?"

"Don't you want to see what's next? Follow me."

They walked into a wooden cloister. Yggdrasil. Ash, the sacred tree of life. A cross was carved into its branches. The doors opened and she saw the nave of Danish kings. The father-in-law she'd never met sat on a stone throne. Harald Bluetooth.

Perfect nickname for him, she thought, smiling to the silver-haired old man.

There was a rock behind him, a rock she'd seen in Denmark. The runes scratched into its surface read: THE ONE WHO BAPTIZED.

"Świętosława," Harald said officially. "Queen of Denmark. Take your throne." He gestured for her to sit.

The pretty Tove appeared at her side, her hair as red as Sven's.

"I can finally embrace you! We Slavs need to stick together," she greeted her as warmly as a mother. "It's difficult being married to a Viking, isn't it?" She chuckled.

"I'll tell you what's worse." Świętosława held her close. "Two of them!"

They giggled like girls. Harald cleared his throat. Tove whispered to her quickly:

"He tried so hard, but I never knew whether he could distinguish the Holy Trinity from . . ."

"I know how to count!" Harald interrupted her. "Don't embarrass me in front of my daughter-in-law! My lady," he addressed her again, "if it wasn't for you, our blood would never have reached the nave of English kings. You were such a handful for Sven that he ended up going to conquer England!" Her father-in-law had a booming laugh.

"You overestimate me, Harald. Sven is a born predator."

"But Cnut is different." Tove smiled radiantly. "He's a true Christian ruler. We did well with that boy. Your son. I can't wait for him to die; I want to meet him!"

"Allow me to take my leave," said Świętosława. "I haven't seen everyone in the afterlife yet."

Wrzask, Zgrzyt, and the lynx Dusza all ran ahead. Dusza led her through another cloister. The first thing she felt was wet sea spray, and she tasted salt. Then she saw him.

He was the only one who looked the same as when she'd last seen him. He wasn't young and beautiful. He was lean and tall, his veins visible under the skin. His head was shaved and his face sunburned, covered by a fine web of wrinkles. Olav Tryggvason stood before her, wearing a monk's habit.

"How do I look to you?" she asked in a trembling voice. "Old and ugly?"

"Old." He nodded.

She sighed with relief.

"Where's Tyra?"

"In the room of suicides," he replied. "She starved herself to death."

"Someone told me that." The memory bounced around Świętosława's mind. "Did that not count as having worried herself to death?"

"The Lord is listening," Wilkomir reminded her.

I know, she thought. *You don't understand. I'm afraid.*

"The Bold One's husbands aren't here either," Great Ulf pointed out.

"Will you walk with me?" Olav asked, and she was almost certain his voice shook a little, too.

"We'll wait here." Ulf stopped Wilkomir and Dusza. "We'll wait."

Olav used a twisted cane to support himself. They walked upward and she could hear his heavy breathing. He stopped for a moment to wipe his forehead, then he continued. When she followed again, angelic voices reached her from inside the tower.

Without love, one loses everything, and remains among death's dark shadows.

"Paulin of Aquileia," Olav said, clearing his throat.

"I thought it was an angel," she replied with a blush.

He looked at her and nodded. They started to walk again. Eventually, they reached a wooden porch in front of carved doors. He touched them and said:

"I haven't finished yet."

A handful of wood shavings lay on the ground next to a few chisels.

"Did you do this yourself?" she asked, studying the carved lovers.

He nodded.

She touched the carvings. She moved her hand along the slender figure of the man, his arms stretched wide.

Olav leaned on the door and touched the woman he'd carved. He ran a finger along her arm. They both stopped their hands, like the lovers, just short of touching.

The voice was nearing the end of the song:

The love of those kept apart links them together, while disagreements can shatter ties of kin.

"I haven't finished yet," Olav repeated.

"What will be here, above them?" Her fingers grazed the untouched wood above the lovers.

He pushed the door open without replying.

A winter night waited for them on the other side. Endless fields of snow stretched out before them, and above the whiteness pulsed an unearthly green light. Emerald spirals glowed with a splendid radiance. The gleam of a cool rose hue. A white dog was racing toward them through the middle of the icy wilderness.

"The northern lights," Olav said. "I always wanted to show them to you."

"And you have," she said, awestruck. "God's cold breath."

"This is my 'other world.'"

"It was worth dying to meet you in the afterlife," she whispered, pressing her body to his.

"I don't regret anything." He held her close. "We'd never have survived together."

She had desired him in her thoughts so often. Called him to her. Lusted for him. Chased him. Fled from him. And now, all of those desires were gone. All that was left was him.

"I don't want anything more from the afterlife," she said, and the confessor's voice echoed in her mind again: *Souls like that only find each other once in a thousand years.*

The white dog ran onto the porch steps, shaking snow off his tail.

"This is Vigi," Olav introduced him.

"Can I touch him?" she asked softly.

"So people really do change in death!" He laughed.

Dusza appeared behind them.

"Świętosława, it's time."

"For what?" she asked with surprise.

"Your brother is coming. You should greet him."

"Mother and Father are both in the Piast house. Even Oda's there," Świętosława said, reluctant to leave Olav and his northern lights.

"Your brother deserves the nave of kings, and only you can welcome him there." Dusza smiled.

"Go," Olav told her. "I'll finish carving the doors."

She ran down the tower steps with Dusza. The place that had opened into Westminster Cathedral before now led to Poznań's cathedral.

"What happened to my funeral?" she asked with surprise. "Have they buried me already?"

"A few years have passed on earth," replied Dusza. "Don't worry, you'll get used to time passing differently here."

She saw a multicolored crowd in the church. Her brother's coffin was huge, but then he wouldn't have fit inside a smaller one. A straight-backed Kalmir stood at its head, holding the Holy Spear. Stojgniew stood beside him with Saint Peter's sword. The Piast eagle lay across the coffin lid in silks, as if it were trying to cover Bolesław with its feathers. A golden stallion stood by the bier. A riderless horse.

"Ecce Agnus Dei!" the priest exclaimed, and two rows of soldiers who stood on either side of the coffin in diagonal lines reaching out knelt in unison with a metallic crunch.

"The Eagle's Wing," said Wilkomir. "His personal guard."

They began to sing a song and it thundered around the cathedral. Somehow, she knew those were the words of Saint Gregory of Narek.

Make your mercy dawn with the breaking of day.
Make your righteous sun shine on the gloom of my heart with morning light.

Mieszko II stood at the foot of the coffin wearing a crown. He broke Bolesław's sword. The monk prince Bezprym stood beside him wearing a simple black caftan and tall riding boots. He banged his fist on Bolesław's shield. Golden-haired Otto, the youngest of her nephews, blew his father's horn.

"The king is dead!" the bishop announced.

"The king is dead! The king is dead!" the Eagle's Wing chanted, their fists at their chests.

Bjornar and Zarad, both old, stood up straight and blew the bone whistles for the last time. Bolesław's stallion shied away. He bucked, but Bezprym touched his neck and the horse settled.

Two women stood crying by the coffin, supporting one another.

"Did my brother have two wives?" she asked with surprise.

"He had more than that," Wilkomir reminded her.

"Yes, but not at the same time."

"One of them is his lover, Predsława, a Kiev princess. The other is Oda of Meissen, his wife."

Omold the bard stepped into the middle of the cathedral and began to speak:

Master of swords, lord of the battle, noble ruler of the fight.
He leaped over the silver ribbon of the Bug and plunged
his blade into the bellies of his foes.
He ripped out their purple intestines . . .

Predsława's lamenting grew louder.

"They went too far. 'Intestines'? That's hardly appropriate for the church." She heard a voice above her which made her flinch.

She looked up. Opposite her on the other side of the tower stood Archbishop Radim Gaudentius.

"You shouldn't complain in the afterlife," she hissed.

"You shouldn't get angry, either." He wagged a finger at her. "See, my queen? There are three sons standing by the coffin. You know what comes next. Where's the key?" he asked sharply. "Where's my key?"

She felt hot all over. She touched her chest. There it was, hanging from a silver chain.

"Lord, forgive me! I forgot! I let them bury me with the key to Adalbert's relic . . . Lord, forgive me."

"What have you done! Humiliation! Damnation!" Archbishop Gaudentius groaned, but he fell silent when he noticed Jordan, Unger, and Reinbern appear. Saint Bruno of Querfurt was above them, with Saint Adalbert himself. She bowed to the martyrs. Saint Adalbert waved away her self-reproach.

"Holiness is not found in bones, child," he whispered.

Gaudentius vanished.

Omold's voice reached them from Poznań's cathedral:

King of Poland, First of Kings,
Bolesław's fame is great.
Master of swords, lord of the battle, noble ruler of the fight.
The fearless Chrobry,
Who took the holy crown with iron,
Who bought it with blood and wore it with honor,
Leaves us all in mourning.
Cry! Sob! Lament!
This is a time of grief, sadness, and dark shadows.
Lonely wolves will whine, the nest is empty, and the fire has burned out.
Ash and smoke . . .

She saw the dead Emnilda and Duszan who came for Bolesław, unseen by the living who stood by his coffin. Maybe her brother's stallion saw them, for he pranced around fearfully, his hooves clicking loudly on the stone floor.

"Will he leave halfway through the liturgy?" she asked, surprised.

"Did you wait for the end of your funeral?" Wilkomir replied with a question. "You were gone before the communion."

She waited for him to bow to their parents in the Piast house. Mieszko walked him to the doorway with his hawk on his shoulder. Oda tactfully stayed inside.

"Go in peace!" their father said, raising his hand. "Go where I could not reach."

"Bolesław"—she reached out a hand—"welcome to the circle of the anointed."

He shook his head and his amber hair flew around his face. There was no crown on his head, but the bright mark of the sacred oil glistened on his temples like it did on hers. The fiery mark of rulers.

Brother and sister, holding hands, led by Duszan and Dusza, were the first to walk into the nave of Piast kings.

She saw the large stone palatium. Rugged and beautiful. She saw the dark red silk that decorated the wall. It looked as if the fabric was moving. She looked closer and realized that blood flowed inside the threads, pulsing like a living network of veins and arteries.

Two royal thrones waited for them. She heard the swish of large wings. A majestic white eagle landed on the thrones with one leg on each. Its wings were spread wide and it screamed, lifting its head high. It screeched loudly, like they had shouted at each other their whole lives. A predator welcoming two others, recognizing its nature in them. They saw more thrones shimmering behind theirs.

"There'll be more!" Bolesław smiled. "Look, I think this one's waiting for my Mieszko. But there's mist further on . . ." he said, surprised.

"You're the first in the Piast nave of kings," she said.

He squeezed her hand.

"What about you? Will you sit on four thrones?"

"I'd be running up and down the stairs." She laughed briefly. "No, brother. This is where I come from. I once came back to Poland as an exiled queen. Now, I am returning home. I choose the Piasts."

Bolesław looked as if he wanted to say something, but the words stuck in his throat.

"We won't have time to argue before the others get here, will we?" She nudged him lightly. "Olav said that people change after death."

"I don't know if they can change that much." He shook his head. "Choose then, Bold One. Which throne is yours?"

"I've sat on so many that I'll let you choose this one. You're older. Wait, I think I want that one."

Wrzask and Zgrzyt lay down at the throne's feet as soon as she sat down. Dusza the lynx shook her head, confused, and then graciously lay down between the other two.

"I saw Henry," he said.

"Who?"

"Emperor Henry. He died before I did."

"But after I did, right?" She thought about it. "Yes, it must have been after me."

"Some find grace in death."

"Did you see Otto III? He was one of the first that I saw."

"Liar!" She hit his arm. "I saw everything. Emnilda was the first you saw, not Otto."

"I wish she were here with us," he said gloomily. "I dreamed of eternity with her."

"At least you can spend time with her! I can see mine, but they can't see me. The power of baptism."

"Do you know what, Bold One? You got what you wanted even after death. Eric and Sven are in Valhalla, Tyra is with the others who took their lives, and you finally have Olav for yourself."

"Yes, and no," she said, wondering what Olav was going to add to his door. "You've made your mark on earth, you leave something behind. You stamped coins with your name. What about me? What will be left of me?"

"The bards' songs, sister," he said with a wink.

"Oh dear." She looked worried.

She switched topics to avoid remembering the rhymes.

"You did it, Bolz," she praised him. "You were crowned!"

"Are you telling me to remind me that you were first? Do you have to be better than me even after death?"

"Never!" She laughed, kissing his cheek.

He shone like golden dew.

The space before them opened up and she saw Poland from a bird's-eye view. She saw its gold beaches and the Baltic Sea's blue waves as well as the white mountain caps. A powerful kingdom.

From the Author

Świętosława's story kept me waiting for longer than any of my previous books. I had the idea before writing *Gra w kości* (*Game of Bones*), and it developed while I worked on the Północna Droga (The Northern Path) series. It is my favorite hunting ground, after all—the Piasts and the Vikings united in one narrative with a female protagonist to connect them. Those who know my earlier novels also know that I squeezed in references to Świętosława into almost every piece of work I wrote. The day I decided to write these books became a personal celebration of sorts.

Why now? And why didn't I write the ending to the Odrodzone Królestwo (A Kingdom Reborn) series instead, the one for which you keep asking? Well, I thought that Władzio* waited to receive his crown until he was seventy, so the rest of us can wait a little longer. Besides, this is a special year. This is the year we celebrate the 1050th anniversary of Poland's Christianization,† so I thought it would be worth adding my own fictionalized version to all the other voices speaking out. In *The Widow Queen* and *The Last Crown*, the baptisms are all so different: Mieszko, Olav Tryggvason and his missionary passion, Eric who refused to change his ways to accommodate the new faith, and Sven, who accepted it to achieve his own ends. Although politics may have influenced some choices, they were nevertheless all made by living, breathing people.

I had the idea for *The Widow Queen* a long time ago, initially written out in episodes. But when the day came when I could tell her tale, I realized that while my old idea was good, it could be better. Why? Because it had only one voice and didn't allow me to highlight the numerous points of view history has to offer. So, I rebuilt the construction I'd built in my head and decided to give a voice not only to Świętosława, but also to the men in her life, to examine their relationships from all possible angles. Then, it turned out that Astrid wanted to speak, and, since you know now that you've read the ending of *The Last Crown*, the sister's version had a right to be heard. And if her sister got a voice, how could her great brother Bolesław be kept silent? And Mieszko? Mieszko

---

* Władysław I Łokietek, also known as "Elbow-high" or Ladislaus the Short, King of Poland (1320–1333).
† The duology was published in Polish in 2016.

was there, after all, at the beginning. And so, the multiple voices made one book into two.

The Widow Queen begins around the year 980 and ends in around 997. *The Last Crown* ends after 1018, with its epilogue taking place after 1025. Forty years of Europe's incredible history! The beginning of Poland as a country, the beginning of the strong Kievan Rus, the empire and the Veleti both struggling to control Bohemia, the different conceptions people had of the empire. And the Viking invasions, where the Vikings change before our eyes from plunderers into "Christian rulers" (well, almost). The worlds of the pagans and the Christians seep into one another; rulers change faiths, but many of them remain convinced they have a choice. In these novels, I had the opportunity to travel from Poznań to Kiev, Merseburg, Rome, and to the Viking empires: Denmark, Sweden, Norway (I adopted the modern name for clarity's sake), and, finally, England. But this wild journey was possible only thanks to my heroine's fate.

Świętosława, Mieszko's daughter, embodies everything that is extraordinary. Let's begin with her name. Historians of Poland seem to have accepted her name to have been Świętosława, although none of the chroniclers ever actually name her. To them she is only ever "Mieszko's daughter and Bolesław's sister." So where did this holy name come from? The English *Liber vitae* from New Minster in Winchester (1031) identifies one of the church's benefactors as Santaslaue, King Cnut's sister. It was supposed that the daughter may have inherited her mother's name, and this was reconstructed as Świętosława (although it is possible her name was Stanisława or Sędzisława). I wondered what I should do when I thought of my heroine, and eventually decided to keep the name that has survived through generations.

The Norse sagas have immortalized Sigrid Storråda (the Haughty). She sometimes appears as Gunhild in the Danish tradition. Changing one's name after marriage was typical at the time. Her granddaughter Ingegerd became Irene after marrying Jarosław the Wise, and when she took her vows before death and became a nun, she was renamed Anne (Saint Anne of Novgorod). What is far more important is establishing whether the famous heroine of the sagas, Sigrid Storråda, is indeed our Świętosława. I assure you that she appears as quite a controversial figure. She burns her suitors, plots and is responsible for a great battle that rebuilt the entire political scene of Scandinavia. And, what is most surprising, she is a determined pagan. Rafał T. Prinke[*] has conducted a thorough investigation which concludes that Świętosława, Mieszko's daughter, and Sigrid the Haughty are two different women. I spent hours talking to Rafał

---

[*] R. T. Prinke, "Świętosława, Sygryda, Gunhilda. Tożsamość córki Mieszka I i jej skandynawskie związki," *Roczniki Historyczne* LXX, 2004.

and we have agreed to respectfully disagree on this matter, but I recommend his text to anyone who wishes to learn more about the Piast princess.

Why do I remain convinced that historical accounts and sagas speak of the same woman, though they use different names to describe her? Because Thietmar of Merseburg, the most informed chronicler of the period (he was almost Świętosława's peer) clearly states that Cnut and Harald, Sven's sons, were also the children of Mieszko's daughter and Bolesław's sister. And Adam of Bremen, based on information acquired from Sven's grandson, provides information on her earlier life, specifically that the Swedish king had conquered Denmark and forced Sven out, but Sven returned after Eric's death and married his widow, Olof's mother, and she subsequently gave birth to Cnut. He proceeds to call Cnut and Olof brothers. One might still speculate on the identity of Świętosława's mother, since she could be Mieszko's daughter by one of his "pagan wives," but I think that Theitmar of Merseburg dispels any doubts about her being Dobrawa's daughter when he refers to Świętosława as "Bolesław's sister." Thietmar's chronicle is the richest source of information on Chrobry's times because the chronicler admires Bolesław almost as much as he despises him. If Świętosława were not Dobrawa's daughter, he would have highlighted this to spite Bolesław ("half sister," "Mieszko's mistress's daughter," etc.).

This, then, is the image with which the chroniclers leave us: Mieszko's daughter and Bolesław's sister becomes the wife of Eric the Swede and gives him a son, Olof. After her husband's death, as queen dowager, she has a chance to go wild, as the sagas relate, and then she marries her late husband's main enemy, Sven Forkbeard, king of Denmark. She gives Sven two sons, Harald and Cnut, after which they have daughters. After the Battle of Svolder (1000), also known as the Battle at Øresund and the Battle of the Three Kings, her husband exiles her to her brother's country, but she's brought back from the "land of the Slavs"* after Sven's death by her sons Harald and Cnut in 1014. Did his mother accompany Cnut to England? If his sisters, or at least one of them, did, as the records of Westminster show, then why not his mother? I am not the only one who noticed the way in which Cnut took power in England, which strongly resembled the tactics of Sven Forkbeard when he sailed to Sweden after Eric's death. Cnut's biographer, Jakub Morawiec, points this out, too. Is this a clear indication that Cnut's mother accompanied him in the complicated operation that conquering England became? I think so. I was also inspired by the anonymous poem dedicated to some great lady (Świętosława?)

---

* A. Campbell (ed.), *Encomium Emmae Reginae*, London, 1949.

and quoted by Jakub Morawiec:* "Now that the difficult battles we have fought are ended, we can settle, my lady, in beautiful London."

I will return only for a moment to Queen Sigrid Storråda of the Norse sagas. I love sagas: I envy Scandinavia that tens of these incredible stories were recorded in Iceland in the twelfth and thirteenth centuries. I know the discourse concerning the historical accuracy of the sagas, and besides, anyone who reads them quickly becomes aware of how chaotic they are. One thing, however, is undisputable: it is better to have complex stories about one's ancestors than not to have them at all. Because even if it's evident that some of the rulers are presented as heroes and fight in wars and battles in which they never could have actually participated, the story still tells us much about the spirit of the epoch. It should be important for us Poles that "Burizleif, the powerful king of Wendland" is often described as "powerful." If that is how he was remembered in the twelfth and thirteenth centuries when the sagas were recorded, that suggests he was a figure of contemporary popular culture. Icelandic courts gossiped about Chrobry. They gossiped about Sigrid Storråda, too. In her case, and in the case of my other protagonists who appear in the sagas (Olav Tryggvason, Sven Forkbeard, Sigvald, Harald Bluetooth, Geira, Astrid, and even Vigi the dog), I used them as a source of inspiration more than as historical accounts.

Why did I write about Świętosława's sisters? Because of the sagas. It is worth noting that the Norse sagas blend Mieszko and Bolesław Chrobry into a single figure under the name "Burysław" or "Burizleif"—the powerful king of Wendland. That's where I found the story of his three daughters: Astrid, Geira, and Gunhild, as well as the tale of interesting marriage intrigue. I always wondered why our chroniclers mention Mieszko's seven pagan wives but then fall silent about their children when Mieszko marries Dobrawa. Were there no children? Did Mieszko only begin fathering children when he married Dobrawa? That's hard to believe. So, I used the legend and gave Świętosława two sisters who were mentioned in the sagas. The saga about Olav Tryggvason† claims that it was not his wife Geira who influenced the fates of the Norwegian kings so much as Jarl Sigvald's wife Astrid, and here is where I found my inspiration.

Another thing I would like to explain is my interpretation of Bezprym's fate. I didn't come up with it by myself, I was influenced by Prof. Błażej

---

* J. Morawiec, "Anonimowy poemat Lidsmannaflokkr i problem jego odbiorcy. Ślad pobytu córki Mieszka I, matki Knuta Wielkiego, w Anglii?", *Studia Źródłoznawcze* nr 47/2010.
† O. Snorrason, *The Saga of Olaf Tryggvason.*

Śliwiński's work,* which I recommend to anyone who wants to broaden their horizons.

It's also worth pointing out a detail that is important for us Poles. Bolesław Chrobry was crowned in 1025, making the dukedom into a kingdom. So, for the entirety of both these novels, Mieszko and Bolesław are dukes, while the three northern rulers who appear (Eric, Sven, and Olav) use the title of king, which is why Świętosława is also referred to as a queen. I have kept this dis-tinction, but it should be remembered that it does not signify the superiority of the Scandinavian kings, merely suggests different standards. The events described occur at a time in history when the kings in the north do not yet feel the need to become part of the Christian realms. This would have required following strict procedures to allow for a coronation to take place.

In both these novels, I have mixed the limited information provided by the chroniclers with fiction. It is often historical fiction as found in the Norse sagas. The story of Tore Stag and the magicians of the north may read like pure fantasy today, but those were the stories which provided the foundation for narratives about the Christianization of the north.

Historical heroes mix with fictional ones, depending on how much infor-mation I could find about them. And so, while the nobles who surrounded Cnut at the time of his invasion are real figures (including Eadric Streona!), we know nothing about Bolesław Chrobry's court, so his guards and friends are constructs of my imagination. The same may be said of Eric's, Sven's, and Olav's companions—although history has recorded the existence of Rogn-vald, Thorgils of Jelling and his sons, and the bishops: Sivrit and both Odd-inkarrs. The bards Skuli and Hallfred are also historical figures, but Omold is not.

We could spend eternity splitting the threads of reality and fiction apart, but I would prefer to show my readers paths they might follow to satisfy their own curiosity.

I included the history of Bodzia in *The Last Crown*. We know about it be-cause of the cemetery that was discovered near Włocławek by Prof. Andrzej Buko and the archaeologists from the Institute of Archaeology and Ethnology PAN. The novel's Golden Borough is heavily inspired by the artifacts recov-ered in Bodzia, but the story of how they got there is, of course, a product of my imagination.

The same may be said about the history of the extraordinary borough Moira, that is, Moraczew, into which I weaved the legend about Lesir/Lestek's golden ship, since scholars have been wondering for years where Mieszko's

* B. Śliwiński, *Bezprym. Pierworodny syn pierwszego króla Polski (986—zima/wiosna 1032)*, Kraków, 2014.

ancestors found the funds to build the great boroughs they constructed. The enormity of the Piast investment may be understood better when I say, following Tomasz Jasiński's example, that it was comparable to building the pyramids. And we cannot be certain that our ancestors raised enough capital from the slave trade, since there aren't enough coins uncovered from this period to suggest that, and there have been no Arabic coins found to confirm it.

The historians who have helped me (there will be more about them in the Acknowledgments) must have been horrified more than once, but in my attempts to respect my sources and history I have not forgotten that I am, after all, writing a novel, and thus serving two masters. Sometimes, the master of fiction took priority. In both these novels I often had to rely not on the sources (they say little about the rulers' private lives) but on my own imagination and vision. Besides, that's the most interesting part of writing—adding the elements that bring life to the skeleton of facts with which history provides us. I am fully aware that there is no one right way of visualizing Świętosława and that each of her fans will likely think of her differently. But for me, this is what she was like: a Bold Queen with two lynxes at her side.

I dedicated the books to all the anonymous, forgotten princesses, the nuns, wives, mothers, and rulers about whom history is silent, the girls marked in biographies of dynasties with a sad "N.N." If anyone can speak for them all, it's Świętosława.

CROWNS
HOUSES
KINGDOMS

Family Tree Key

Issue and/or the line of heirs
(in order of age, read left to right)

Marriages and cohabitations

siblings   Other relationships between characters

polygamy   and the descriptions of these relations

the crown goes
into the hands of Danes

The descriptions of historical figures follow the order of
appearance on the family trees, top to bottom and left to right

POLAND

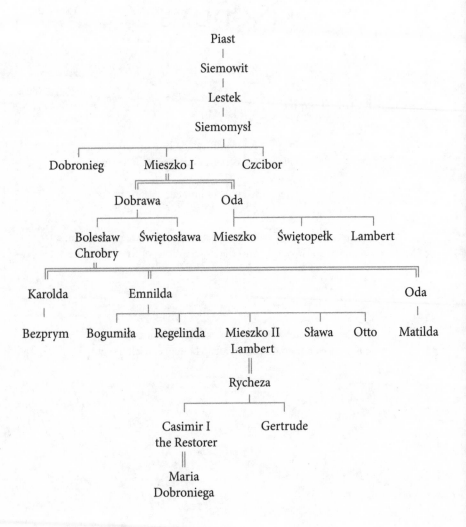

Piast
|
Siemowit
|
Lestek
|
Siemomysł

Dobronieg   Mieszko I   Czcibor

Dobrawa   Oda

Bolesław   Świętosława   Mieszko   Świętopełk   Lambert
Chrobry

Karolda   Emnilda   Oda

Bezprym   Bogumiła   Regelinda   Mieszko II   Sława   Otto   Matilda
Lambert

Rycheza

Casimir I   Gertrude
the Restorer

Maria
Dobroniega

POLAND

PIAST   the legendary founder of the Piast dynasty

SIEMOWIT   Piast duke (9th century)

LESTEK   Piast duke (9th century)

SIEMOMYSŁ   Piast duke (until approx. 950)

DOBRONIEG   older brother of Mieszko I, died in battle against Geron and Wichman

MIESZKO I   Duke of Poland (960–992), the first baptized Polish ruler

CZCIBOR   younger brother of Mieszko I, he fought at Mieszko's side near Cedynia and against Wichman

DOBRAWA   first wife of Mieszko I, a princess from the Přemyslid dynasty

ODA   second wife of Mieszko I, daughter of margrave Ditrich from the Northern March

BOLESŁAW CHROBRY   Duke of Poland (992–1025), first king of Poland (1025), Duke of Bohemia (1003–1004) (modern Czech Republic)

ŚWIĘTOSŁAWA   known in the north as Sigrid Storråda or Sigrid the Haughty (in Denmark she was sometimes also known as Gunhild), Queen of Sweden, Denmark, Norway, and England

MIESZKO   exiled from Poland by Bolesław Chrobry after his father's death

ŚWIĘTOPEŁK   died in childhood

LAMBERT   exiled from Poland by Bolesław Chrobry after his father's death

KAROLDA   second wife of Bolesław Chrobry, from Hungary (also known as Judith)

EMNILDA   third wife of Bolesław Chrobry; a Slavic princess

ODA   fourth wife of Bolesław Chrobry, a marchioness of Meissen

BEZPRYM   Duke of Poland (1031–1034)

BOGUMIŁA   a Polish princess (the name has been chosen by the author for one of Bolesław Chrobry's unnamed daughters)

REGELINDA   a marchioness of Meissen

MIESZKO II LAMBERT   King of Poland (1025–1031)

SŁAWA   a Polish princess (the name has been chosen by the author for one of Bolesław Chrobry's unnamed daughters)

OTTO   a regional duke

MATILDA   a Polish princess

RYCHEZA   wife of Mieszko II Lambert, daughter of a prince-elector of the Electoral Palatinate, granddaughter of Otto II, niece of Otto III

CASIMIR I THE RESTORER   Duke of Poland (1034–1058)

GERTRUDE   wife of Iziaslav I, Prince of Kiev

MARIA DOBRONIEGA   wife of Casimir I the Restorer, a Kiev princess and Duchess of Poland

SWEDEN

Björn Eriksson
├─────────────────────┬─────────────────────┤
Eric the Victorious   Olof Björnsson
‖   │
Świętosława   Styrbjörn the Strong
│
Olof Skötkonung

BJÖRN ERIKSSON   King of Sweden (882–932)

ERIC THE VICTORIOUS (SEGERSÄLL)   King of Sweden alongside his brother Olof (970–95), after Olof's death he won the battle for the throne against his nephew Styrbjörn

OLOF BJÖRNSSON   King of Sweden alongside his brother Eric (970–995)

ŚWIĘTOSŁAWA   known in the north as Sigrid Storråda or Sigrid the Haughty (in Denmark she was sometimes also known as Gunhild), Queen of Sweden, Denmark, Norway, and England

STYRBJÖRN THE STRONG   a contender for the Swedish throne following his father's death, defeated by Eric at Fyrisvellir

OLOF SKÖTKONUNG   King of Sweden (995–1022), the first baptized Swedish ruler

DENMARK

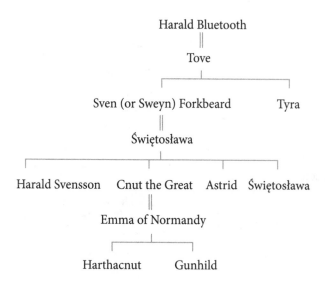

Harald Bluetooth
‖
Tove

Sven (or Sweyn) Forkbeard   Tyra
‖
Świętosława

Harald Svensson   Cnut the Great   Astrid   Świętosława
‖
Emma of Normandy

Harthacnut   Gunhild

HARALD BLUETOOTH   King of Denmark (958–987) and Norway (974–985), the first baptized Danish ruler

TOVE   a Slavic princess and Queen of Denmark, daughter of the Obotrite leader

SVEN (OR SWEYN) FORKBEARD   King of Denmark (987–1014), England (1013–1014), and Norway (987–995 and 1000–1014)

TYRA   Queen of Norway

ŚWIĘTOSŁAWA   known in the north as Sigrid Storråda or Sigrid the Haughty (in Denmark she was sometimes also known as Gunhild), Queen of Sweden, Denmark, Norway, and England

HARALD SVENSSON   regent of Denmark (1013), later King of Denmark (1014–1018)

CNUT THE GREAT   King of England (1016–1035), Denmark (1018–1035), and Norway (1028–1035)

ASTRID   a Danish princess

ŚWIĘTOSŁAWA   a Danish princess

EMMA OF NORMANDY   Queen of England, earlier wife of Ethelred the Unready

HARTHACNUT   King of Denmark (1035–1042) and England (1040–1042)

GUNHILD   Queen of Germany

NORWAY

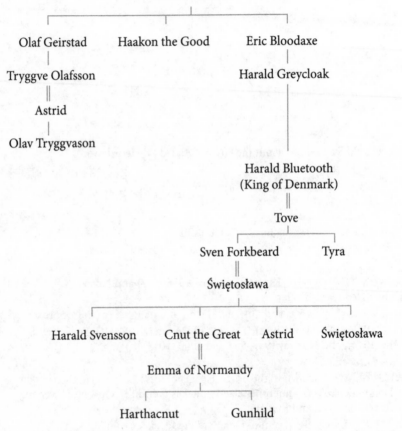

Harald Fairhair

Olaf Geirstad   Haakon the Good   Eric Bloodaxe

Tryggve Olafsson   Harald Greycloak

Astrid

Olav Tryggvason

Harald Bluetooth
(King of Denmark)

Tove

Sven Forkbeard   Tyra

Świętosława

Harald Svensson   Cnut the Great   Astrid   Świętosława

Emma of Normandy

Harthacnut   Gunhild

NORWAY

HARALD FAIRHAIR   King of Norway (872–930), he united the country and abdicated the throne to his son

OLAF GEIRSTAD   King of Vingulmark and Vestfold

Haakon the Good   King of Norway (934–960/961), son of Harald Fairhair out of wedlock, he grew up at English court and took the throne after Eric was overthrown

ERIC BLOODAXE   King of Norway (930–934) and Northumbria (947–954), his cruelty forced the nobility to bring back the son of Harald Fairhair, Haakon, from England to replace Eric

TRYGGVE OLAFSSON   King of Viken

HARALD GREYCLOAK   King of Norway (961–976)

ASTRID   Queen of Viken

OLAV TRYGGVASON   son of the King of Viken born after his father's death, King of Norway (995–1000)

HARALD BLUETOOTH   King of Denmark (958–987) and Norway (974–985), the first baptized Danish ruler. His vassal, jarl Haakon Sigurdsson, ruled Norway in his stead

TOVE   a Slavic princess and Queen of Denmark, daughter of the Obotrite leader

SVEN (OR SWEYN) FORKBEARD   King of Denmark (987–1014), England (1013–1014), and Norway (987–995 and 1000–1014)

TYRA   Queen of Norway

ŚWIĘTOSŁAWA   known in the north as Sigrid Storråda or Sigrid the Haughty (in Denmark she was sometimes also known as Gunhild), Queen of Sweden, Denmark, Norway, and England

HARALD SVENSSON   regent of Denmark (1013), later King of Denmark (1014–1018)

CNUT THE GREAT   King of England (1016–1035), Denmark (1018–1035), and Norway (1028–1035)

ASTRID   a Danish princess

ŚWIĘTOSŁAWA   a Danish princess

EMMA OF NORMANDY   Queen of England, earlier wife of Ethelred the Unready

HARTHACNUT   King of Denmark (1035–1042) and England (1040–1042)

GUNHILD   Queen of Germany

RUSSIA

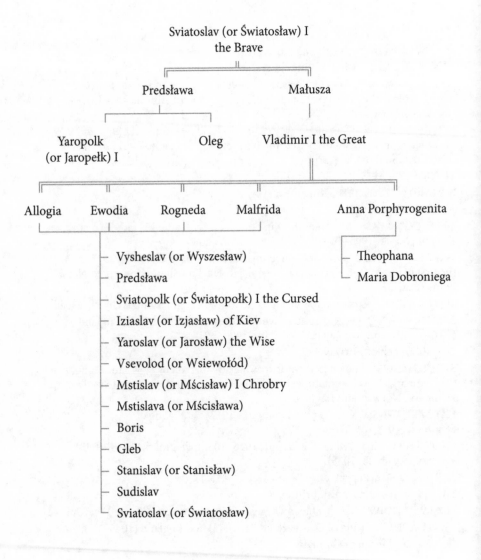

Sviatoslav (or Światosław) I
the Brave
║
Predsława   Małusza

Yaropolk   Oleg   Vladimir I the Great
(or Jaropełk) I   ║

Allogia   Ewodia   Rogneda   Malfrida   Anna Porphyrogenita

- Vysheslav (or Wyszesław)   — Theophana
- Predsława   — Maria Dobroniega
- Sviatopolk (or Światopołk) I the Cursed
- Iziaslav (or Izjasław) of Kiev
- Yaroslav (or Jarosław) the Wise
- Vsevolod (or Wsiewołód)
- Mstislav (or Mścisław) I Chrobry
- Mstislava (or Mścisława)
- Boris
- Gleb
- Stanislav (or Stanisław)
- Sudislav
- Sviatoslav (or Światosław)

RUSSIA

SVIATOSLAV (OR ŚWIATOSŁAW) I THE BRAVE   Grand Prince of Kiev (945–972)

PREDSŁAWA   wife of Sviatoslav I

MAŁUSZA   concubine of Sviatoslav I

YAROPOLK (OR JAROPEŁK) I   Grand Prince of Kiev (972–978)

Oleg   ruler of the Drevlyans (969–977)

VLADIMIR I THE GREAT   Prince of Novgorod (969–977 and 979–988), Grand Prince of Kiev (978–1015), younger brother of Yaropolk

ALLOGIA   wife of Vladimir I the Great

EWODIA   wife of Vladimir I the Great

ROGNEDA   wife of Vladimir I the Great, a princess of Polotsk

MALFRIDA   wife of Vladimir I the Great

ANNA PORPHYROGENITA   wife of Vladimir I the Great, daughter of Byzantine Emperor Romanos II

VYSHESLAV (OR WYSZESŁAW)   Prince of Novgorod (988–1010)

PREDSŁAWA   concubine of Bolesław Chrobry

SVIATOPOLK (OR ŚWIATOPOŁK) I THE CURSED   Prince of Turov, Grand Prince of Kiev

IZIASLAV (OR IZJASŁAW) OF KIEV   Prince of Polotsk (989–1001)

YAROSLAV (OR JAROSŁAW) THE WISE   Prince of Rostów, Grand Prince of Kiev (1016–1054, with breaks)

VSEVOLOD (OR WSIEWOŁÓD)   Prince of Volynskyi

MSTISLAV (OR MŚCISŁAW) I CHROBRY   Prince of Tmutarakan (988–1036) and Chernigov (1026–1036)

MSTISLAVA (OR MŚCISŁAWA)   Princess of Kiev, at Bolesław Chrobry's court from 1018

BORIS   the first saint of Kiev Rus' along with his brother Gleb

GLEB   the first saint of Kiev Rus' along with his brother Boris

STANISLAV (OR STANISŁAW)   Prince of Smoleńsk (988–1015)

SUDISLAV (OR SUDZISŁAW)   Prince of Pskov

SVIATOSLAV (OR ŚWIATOSŁAW)   Prince of Drevlians

THEOPHANA   wife of Novgorod posadnik Ostromir

MARIA DOBRONIEGA   wife of Casimir I the Restorer, a Kiev princess and Duchess of Poland

HOLY ROMAN EMPIRE

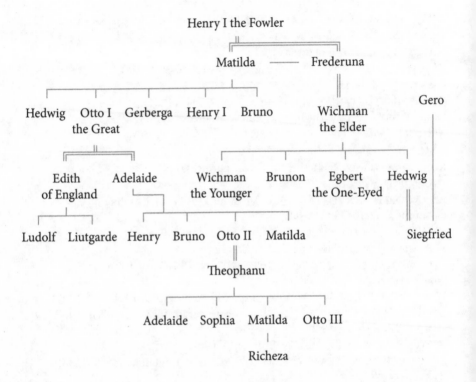

HOLY ROMAN EMPIRE

HENRY I THE FOWLER   Duke of Saxony (912–936), King of Germany (919–936)

MATILDA   second wife of Henry the Fowler, a saint

FREDERUNA   sister of Queen Mathilda

HEDWIG   Duchess consort of the Franks

OTTO I THE GREAT   Duke of Saxony (936–961), King of Germany (936–973) and Emperor (962–973)

GERBERGA   Duchess of Lorraine

HENRY I   Duke of Bavaria

BRUNO THE GREAT   Archbishop of Cologne, a saint

WICHMAN THE ELDER   a rebellious count from the Billung dynasty, married to Matilda

EDITH OF ENGLAND   wife of Otto I

ADELAIDE   a princess of Burgundy, second wife of Otto I

WICHMAN THE YOUNGER   a count of the Billung dynasty, he invaded the lands of Mieszko I on Geron's orders

BRUNON   bishop of Verden

EGBERT THE ONE-EYED   count of Hastfalagau

HEDWIG   wife of Siegfried, son of Margrave Geron

LUDOLF   Duke of Swabia

LIUTGARDE   Duchess of Lorraine

HENRY   died in childhood

BRUNO   died in childhood

OTTO II   King of Germany (973–983), Emperor (980–983)

MATILDA   Abbess of Quendlinburg

GERO   Margrave of the Eastern march (937–965)

THEOPHANU   a byzantine princess, regent for Otto III

SIEGFRIED   son of Margrave Geron, died in battle

ADELAIDE   Abbess in, among other places, Quendlinburg

SOPHIA   Abbes of Gandersheim and Essen

MATILDA   Countess Palatine of Lotharyngia

OTTO III   King of Germany (983–1002), Emperor (996–1002)

RICHEZA   mother of Casimir I the Restorer, daughter of Count Palatine of Lotharingia, granddaughter of Otto II, niece to Otto III

ENGLAND

Edmund I the Elder

Eadwig

Edgar the Peaceful

Elfgifu the Beautiful

Elfthryth

Edward the Martyr

Ethelred II the Unready

Elfgifu

Emma of Normandy

- Athelstan
- Egbert
- Edmund Ironside
- Eadred
- Eadwig
- Edgar
- Edith
- Elfgifu
- Wulfild

- Edward the Confessor
- Godgifu
- Alfred

ENGLAND

EDMUND I THE ELDER   King of England (939–946)

EADWIG   King of England (955–959)

Edgar the Peaceful   King of England (959–975), Eadwig's younger brother

ELFGIFU THE BEAUTIFUL   first wife of Edgar the Peaceful, known also as the Just

ELFTHRYTH   second wife of Edgar the Peaceful, first crowned Queen of England

EDWARD THE MARTYR   King of England (975–978), a martyr and a saint

ETHELRED II THE UNREADY   King of England (978–1013 and 1014–1016)

ELFGIFU   Queen of England, daughter of the Earl of Northumbria

EMMA OF NORMANDY   Queen of England, later wife of Cnut the Great

ATHELSTAN   prince of England

EDWARD THE CONFESSOR   King of England (1042–1066)

EGBERT   prince of England

GODGIFU   Countess of Vexin, later Boulogne

EDMUND IRONSIDE   King of England (1016)

ALFRED   prince of England

EADRED   prince of England

EADWIG   prince of England

EDGAR   prince of England

ELFGIFU   Countess of Northumberland

WULFILD   Countess of East Anglia

Acknowledgments

Writing the acknowledgments is the best part of writing a novel. They indicate that the hard work has ended, and I can go back to those who have helped me, not to plague them with more questions but to thank them for all their help. I'm lucky to have so many people who have supported my work, and they grow in number every year, which has led to my worrying that I might forget to name someone.

I will first mention the two people who have been telling me to write a novel about Świętosława for years. The first is Prof. Przemysław Urbańczyk with whom I worked on *Gra w kości* (*Game of Bones*), and the second is Dr. Jakub Morawiec, who has helped me navigate the meandering sagas when I wrote *Trzy Młode Pieśni* (*Three Young Songs*). I recommend Cnut's biography, Jakub Morawiec's *Knut Wielki. Król Anglii, Danii i Norwegii (ok. 995–1035)*, to anyone who may want to learn more about Świętosława's great son after having read *The Widow Queen* and *The Last Crown*. I will add that Jakub is an expert on Norse sagas, and I relied on his knowledge when writing my novels. Prof. Urbańczyk's numerous publications (from *Zdobywcy północnego Atlantyku* to *Trudne początki Polski, Władza i polityka we wczesnym średniowieczu*, and *Mieszko I Tajemniczy*) stand out from others thanks to their representation of early Poland not only through the lens of the east/west divide, but also through their consideration of the influence that the politics of the north had on our country. Przemek, Jakub, I thank you both most sincerely!

Professors Tomasz Jurek and Tomasz Jasiński have also helped me greatly. They are both exceptional medievalists and wonderful conversationalists. Thank you also to Anna Waśko for her translation of the saga about Olav Tryggvason, to Prof. Daniel Baga from the University of Pécs (though it is difficult to have any certainty about Hungarian influences in Chrobry's life) and to Prof. Andrzej Nowak and Rafał T. Prinke, because although we may differ in how we interpret Sigrid Storråda, I consider every one of our conversations to be truly enlightening.

I was also supported by people at the Adam Mickiewicz University in Poznań—Dr. Tomasz Ratajczak, an excellent expert on more than just medieval architecture, and Dr. Remigiusz T. Ciesielski, who is fascinated by Bruno of Querfurt and the Five Holy Martyrs. I was also inspired by Zdzisław

Cozac's fantastic films about the beginnings of Poland, from *Wyspa władców* and *Miasto zatopionych bogów* (about Wolin and Jomsborg) to *Ukryte gniazdo dynastii* and the newest which focuses on Poland's Christianization.

As always, I could count on my friends. The unfailing Michał Ostrowski (Ostry) helped me with wild animals. Piotr Wojcieszek (Wołodar) helped me with storms, Monika Zamachowska with herbs and healing, Przemysław Michalak with horses and riding, Pati Osińska with Moraczew. Thank you also to Agnieszka Książyńska, and the Czech Jaro Petrina, Vinga Sylvia Raichelt Rasmussen, Marta Petryk and Magda Mikulska.

Thank you to my publisher, Tadeusz Zysk, for finding various sources and patterns about which I knew nothing; for arranging wonderful meetings in Brzostek where I was inspired more than once while listening to the professors' stories; for an endless exchange of ideas and opinions; for challenging me; and for being at my side every time I tackled a new story in these last years. I love that we are both so interested in the Piasts and that they seem to matter as much (and perhaps more?) to both of us as the twenty-first century does. Oh, if only books "wrote themselves" as quickly as Tadeusz and I imagine them, we would have filled an entire library by now. But what I want to thank my publisher for most is his endless enthusiasm for our work together!

Thank you to the brothers Zysk: Tomek, for all his comments on and knowledge of English sources; Tobiasz for his patience with the covers; Andrzej for his great help in matters that were quite small; and Adam, because it's not easy to market an author who never wants to go anywhere.

Thank you to my editor, Boguś Jusiak, with whom I have met after a long break, even though we've already worked on books together before this. And thank you to the entire amazing team at Zysk i S-ka! I love writing, marketing, and selling books with you.

Finally, thank you to all my friends and readers who have waited for this book and who are (still) so patient with me. Thank you to my daughters: Julia, for being my first reader, and Kalina, who drew me pictures of Świętosława's lynxes so that I wouldn't mix up the colors of their eyes. And thank you to Dariusz for bringing the Vikings into our home. He has the aesthetic of the entire epoch in his head and every time I would complain that "I know I've seen it somewhere but I don't know where," he could always find the exact image I wanted. Besides, we've traveled together in the footsteps of Olav Tryggvason, Sven, Eric, Świętosława, and Otto III in the years I spent preparing to write their stories.